OTHER WORKS BY GARY YEAGLE

FICTION

Iron Fist Velvet Glove
Angels Footprints 1 - A Short Story Collection Vol. 1
Angels Footprints 2- A Short Story Collection Vol. 2
Lowcountry Burn — A Nick Falco Mystery
Delayed Exposure — A Nick Falco Mystery

With Marlene Mitchell
Seasons of Death — The Smoky Mountain Murders
Echoes of Death — The Smoky Mountain Murders
Shadows of Death — The Smoky Mountain Murders

NONFICTION

Little Big Men - The Road to Williamsport

HOUSE OF CARDS

GARY YEAGLE

House of Cards

Davis Studio Publishing

Louisville, Kentucky

DEDICATION

It has been said that if you want to know the heart of America, well then you better learn baseball. In every major city and small town across our nation you can find a ball field, whether it be a major league stadium, Little League field or sandlot where not only adults, but children gather to play the game of baseball. This book is dedicated to all the Moms and Dads who faithfully watch and support their young children at T-ball, Coach-Pitch and Little League games. Baseball is good!

INTRODUCTION

I was born and raised in the rolling hills and surrounding mountains of Williamsport, Pennsylvania in 1946. In 1939, Carl Stotz, a local insurance man in Williamsport, came up with the idea of Little League Baseball. After talking with a number of businesses he finally landed his first team sponsor: Lycoming Dairy who became the first named Little League team. I played a lot of sandlot ball with my friends down the street from where I lived. The field we played on was, at the time unknown to us as the field where Little League had started, so looking back to those days long since gone, we were playing on hallowed ground. We were just a bunch of ragtag kids who played baseball from sun-up until sundown. Those were the best days of my life. As young boys, too young to play Little League, we learned how to get along win or lose. We learned how to handle conflict and disagreements on that old field without any adult supervision. When I turned ten I was old enough to try out for an official Little League team. I made one of the teams and surprisingly found myself playing third base in 1959 for the *First named Little League team; Lycoming Dairy*. Our manager's name was Ollie Faucet and our team was often referred to as Ollie Faucet and his little drips.

The house I grew up in was not even one hundred yards from the field where the first Little League game was played and not fifty yards from the center field fence of Bowman Field, back in those days home of the Williamsport Grays, a member of the Philadelphia Phillies farm team system. Bowman Field still stands today and is the oldest minor league field in the country. I recall as a young boy, probably three or four years of age lying in bed at night, the towering lights from Bowman Field shining in my bedroom window. I remember listening to the names of the players as they were announced and soon had the Gray's lineup memorized. I would always sit with my father and watch the New York Yankees when they were televised. My father would explain

1

to me the various plays and goings on of baseball. I collected baseball cards and at one time had a number of Mickey Mantle rookie cards, which back then were not yet all that valuable. I had baseball cards from every player during that era of baseball. Years later when I moved out of my parents' house, I forgot all about my card collection and my mother eventually gave them away to some neighbor kid. If I had those cards in my possession today I'd be a millionaire many times over. Who could have known?

Many decades have passed since those days long ago and I find myself approaching seventy-one years of age and living in the St. Louis area. Over the years, I have remained a Yankee fan as well as a Pirates fan. That being said, while living here in St. Louis, the home of the St. Louis Cardinals, it's hard not to root for the Cards as they are called in this section of the nation. St. Louis, without a doubt is a baseball town. St. Louis has one of the strongest if not the strongest fan bases of any major league team. Baseball in St. Louis is a way of life for many who live here. From spring training until the last pitch of the World Series, St. Louis is a Mecca for baseball lovers.

House of Cards, although a work of fiction, is packed with baseball stats: quotes, dates, records and so on, many of these in regard to past St. Louis Cardinal teams. I went to great effort to get my facts straight but baseball statistics can be every complex. If I have misquoted any player, date, record or statistic it was purely by accident. I hope you enjoy reading this book as much as I did writing it. *Play ball!*

Gary Yeagle

CHAPTER ONE

RICH SIMS HAD ALWAYS CONSIDERED THE SEVENTH-inning stretch at Busch Memorial Stadium nothing more than an aggravating interruption to a pleasant evening at the ballpark. When the final out came into play at the end of the top of the seventh, thousands of spectators rose to their feet and made their way slowly through the throng of people to the restrooms and concession stands. Balancing a tray containing two large beers and a coke in one hand and four hotdogs, nachos and peanuts in the other, he dodged his way in and out of the massive cattle drive of human flesh traveling in the opposite direction. Weaving from side to side, he skillfully maneuvered his way into the oncoming mass.

Realizing his progress was painfully slow, he made his way against a wall on the right and watched the sea of avid fans adorned in Cardinal red: hats, jerseys, tee and polo shirts all displaying the St. Louis Cardinals logo. Sipping from one of the beers, he smiled and thought, *It's good to be a baseball fan...it's good to be a Cardinal fan!*

Suddenly, a man about Rich's age emerged from the crowd and stepped toward the wall and nodded while he took the final bite of a hotdog and washed it down with a long swig of soda. Gesturing toward the fans, he mentioned, "What a madhouse!" Opening the side flap of a trash container, he deposited the empty cup and asked, "You come to many games?"

Rich smiled and answered, "I'd say around twenty or so a year." Looking at the man's Pittsburgh hat and team jersey, Rich asked, "You from Pittsburgh?"

"Originally, yes. I was born there. I lived in the Steel City until I was thirty and then I moved to St. Louis."

"So, I take it from your Pirates attire you're still a Pittsburgh fan?"

"Well, you know how it is. When you grow up in or near a city that has a major league team, that becomes *your team!* But, to be honest, it's hard to live here in St. Louis and not be a Cards fan. I'll always root for my boyhood team, but if the Pirates are not in the playoffs or the World Series, I'll go with the Cardinals if they make it." Looking at the thinning crowd, the man tipped his hat and started up the walkway. "See ya around."

Rich placed his beer back into the tray and went in the opposite direction. A minute later, he walked through a short breezeway, seconds later, the massive, manicured grass of Busch Stadium spread out before him down below. Making a left he started up the steps to where his seat was located. Nine rows up, he began the process of the all too familiar side-to-side straddle step while he balanced the trays and made his way past numerous fans that smiled or nodded while he squeezed by.

Monica, Rich's wife, noticed her husband who was struggling past a rather rotund man. Getting up from her seat, she reached for the drink tray as Rich plopped down in his seat and positioned his tray in the empty seat next to him. Monica handed him a beer, took a long drink herself and commented, "I gather it was nuts as usual down there?"

Handing her one of the hotdogs, Rich responded, "Yeah, but that's just part of coming to the park. It's part of the baseball process: the smells, the fans, everyone in a good mood." Taking a bite out of a hotdog, he gazed in the direction of the distant Cardinal bullpen. "Harley not back yet? I thought you told him to be back here by the bottom of the seventh."

Wiping mustard from the side of her mouth, she nodded and remarked, "I'm not worried. It's his birthday." Raising the set of binoculars hanging around her neck she focused on the bullpen area where she noticed a long row of young boys and girls lined up next to a low retaining wall. "I can't see him. I'm sure he's on his way back."

Lowering the binoculars, she went on, "You know how persistent our son can be, especially when it comes to anything baseball related. He told me he wanted to get Jim Henke's autograph. He'll be back soon." Nodding at the tray on the seat, she added, "Besides that, when did you ever know Harley to turn down a hotdog at a ballgame?"

Rich took another bite and held up his beer in a toasting fashion. "You're right, there's nothing quite like a hotdog at a Cardinals game."

Monica looked out across the field and asked, "So, in the eleven years we've been hitched, how many games have we attended here at Busch?"

Proudly, Rich answered, "Probably around two hundred and fifty. It's our home away from home!"

Adjusting her sunglasses, she asked, "Do you remember your first Cardinals game?"

"Like it was yesterday. It was back in 1964, the seventh game of the World Series. Let's see; it's now 1995, so that would have been thirty-one years ago. I was five years old and my grandfather took me to the game. That was the first time I ever had a hotdog at a ballgame. It was the best thing I ever tasted. It was a great series. The Cards had a third baseman back then by the name of Ken Boyer. The Yankees third basemen was Clete Boyer, Ken's brother. It was really interesting to see two brothers competing against one another. It was the only time I ever got to see Mickey Mantle play ball. We won the series in seven games. That was back when the Cards played at Sportsman's park over on Grand Boulevard. Even back then, I knew the Cards were the team for me."

Handing the nachos to Monica, Rich continued after he took a swig of beer. "Look at all the fans here this evening. The Cards have the best fans in baseball. This team has given their fans, over the years, their money's worth. When you come to a Cards game you can rest assured they'd give you their best."

Pointing the half eaten hotdog at her husband, Monica elaborated, "The fan support for this team is superior. Take a look at this year and how horrible the team has performed. We'll be lucky to get seventy wins. The playoffs, let alone the World Series are not on the horizon for the Cardinals this year." Gesturing at the surrounding fans, she smiled and commented, "And yet, the fans still come. It's easy to root for your team when they're on top. But, to continue to support your team when they're near the cellar...now that's a fan!"

Looking around in agreement, Rich remarked, "And I might add that you and I are right at the top when it comes to being avid fans. I'm not saying we're in a category of our own, but you'd be hard pressed to find a couple more obsessed with the Cards than we are."

Raising her beer, Monica proudly announced, "Here, here!" Dipping a chip into the yellow cheese sauce, she continued, "My most memorable game was the night we met for the first time right here at the stadium down there in the third base line seats. That was what, twelve years ago? I'll never forget that particular night here at the park. I was so depressed. Nothing was going right for me. Two of my girlfriends convinced me to go to the game that night. We sat right next to you. You were so kind and patient with me as I poured out my pathetic life to you, with all the problems I was plagued with. I remember how you told me you'd give me a call later that week. You called me the next day and took me to another game. The rest is history. We started dating and my life turned around. If I wouldn't have gone to that game and met you, I don't know what would have happened to me. That night changed my life. That's why I always say baseball is not just a game, it's about life!"

Crunching into a nacho covered chip, Rich went on, "And let's not forget the fact that we got married right here at Busch Stadium prior to a game. I wore my tuxedo and you wore your wedding gown; both of us wore our Cardinal hats. How many Cardinal fans can say they've done that?"

"Not many," said Monica. "I guess maybe we are more obsessed than the average fan."

Looking toward the Cards bullpen, Rich laughed, "And let's not forget Harley; who has attended over two hundred ballgames here at the park. We brought him to his first game when he was six months old."

"And as the years passed," remarked Monica, "he took to the game like green on grass. I'd venture to say for a ten-year-old, he knows more about baseball than most adults. You mention baseball around Harley and you're in for a long conversation."

The Cardinals shortstop stretched and took two practice swings, then stepped up to the plate when the bottom of the seventh got underway. Pushing loose dirt to the right of home plate around with his spikes, the batter dug in and positioned himself for the first pitch.

Harley, realizing he needed to get back to his seat, took one last look into the bullpen. There sat Jim Henke and two other relievers along with the bullpen catcher. Despite the fact he and other numerous children were waving hats, baseballs and programs at the players in hopes of obtaining an autograph, the players continued to ignore, or at least not respond to the young fans. Harley knew the players were professionals and their focus was on the game. Turning to head toward a set of steps that would lead to the top of the first level, Harley glanced at the scoreboard. The game was still scoreless.

Walking slowly, Harley watched as the Pirates pitcher wound up and after a high leg kick delivered the first pitch of the bottom half of the inning. The batter swung and made contact resulting in a high pop up behind second base that the Pittsburgh second baseman caught with little difficulty. The next Cardinal at the plate was one of Harley's favorites: Danny Langford. As Harley continued down the aisle next to the right field fence his thought process, which was usually focused on baseball, took over as he reviewed Langford's stats in his mind: 314 batting average, twelve home runs; thirty-one RBI's. Harley stopped and watched when Langford took the first pitch. The scoreboard indicated a called strike.

Moving toward the steps once again, Harley heard the crack of the bat, followed by the familiar loud roar of the crowd. The fans seated next to the right field fence stood and pointed while looking toward the sky. Turning in the direction of the field, Harley noticed the Pirates right fielder back peddling toward the warning track. Looking up, Harley saw the ball at the last moment. Instinctively, he raised his left gloved hand and jumped as the ball slapped into the leather of the glove. At the same exact time Harley jumped, three fans seated in the first row also lunged at the ball, slamming into Harley, knocking him over the side of the waist high railing. Harley's legs caught on the top of the railing as he plummeted to the ground eight feet below. He heard the sickening, crunching sound, and then he passed out.

Pittsburgh's right fielder stared down at the unconscious boy at his feet while the ball Harley had caught slowly rolled from his glove. The thirty thousand plus fans fell to an eerie silence, everyone staring down at the field. The right fielder turned and signaled vigorously for help. Pittsburgh's center fielder ran over and the Cardinals bullpen emptied out, the players running to the young fan.

Monica, after witnessing the miraculous catch and immediate fall to the field focused the binoculars on the situation and then suddenly realized that the boy was Harley. Grabbing Rich by his shoulder she spoke in a panicked voice, "Oh...my God! It's Harley!" She pushed Rich toward the aisle. "We have to get down there!"

Rich, grabbed a nearby usher, "That was our son who fell over the fence. How do we get down there?"

The usher, with a look of astonishment on his face, thought for a moment, but then answered, "With this crowd it's about a ten minute walk. Follow me." Removing a two-way radio from his belt he started down the steps. "This is Lee out in right field. That boy who fell? I have his parents with me. We're on the way down." The usher turned back to Monica and Rich, spoke and pointed back down at the field. "The doctor is heading out to right field. If your son has to go to the hospital they'll probably take him out through Gate B."

Monica watched when a golf cart emerged from the Cardinal side of the field and raced across the grass. Stopping at a logjam of people near a small tunnel, Monica with tears in her eyes spoke to Rich. "If anything serious happens to Harley, I'll never forgive myself."

Dr. Jonathan Lucas, Cardinals team physician, stepped out of the cart as it came to a halt next to the fence. The players separated, allowing the doctor access to the fallen fan.

Pittsburgh's right fielder spoke to the doctor. "I was just going for the ball when this kid suddenly flies over the fence. I think his arm might be broken. I heard it snap when he hit the ground. Is he going to be all right?"

Gently turning Harley's head, the doctor quickly surmised. "He's breathing." Opening his medical bag he removed a small capsule and cracked it open. Running the smelling salts beneath Harley's nose, the boy was jerked back to consciousness.

Bleary eyed, Harley stared up into the faces looking down at him. Then he saw Jim Henke standing next to the kneeling doctor. Smiling weakly, he tried to rise up and spoke directly to Henke. "Today...is my...birthday. I just wanted...to get...your autograph,

Jim."

The doctor interrupted Harley and ordered softly, "Don't try to get up, son. Are you in any pain?"

It was then that Harley felt the massive pain shooting up and down his right side. With tears filling his eyes, he answered, "My arm...really hurts."

"Let's have a look. This might hurt a little, but I have to check your arm."

The doctor gently raised Harley's right arm and following a loud cry of pain, the doctor announced, "His arm is broken." Looking closely at Harley's eyes, he added, "He might have a concussion. We need to get this boy to the hospital. If you gentlemen will help me get him on the stretcher in the back of the cart, we'll get him off the field and then to the hospital."

Once in the front seat, the doctor ordered the driver. "Drive us over to gate B. The paramedics can take over from there."

The cart no sooner pulled out when Henke saw the ball Harley had caught and dropped lying next to the fence. Walking over, he picked up the ball and stood with the other players while they watched the cart pull away. Henke looked down at the ball in his hand when Paul Blumfield, Pittsburgh's right fielder joined him at the fence and asked, "You gonna be all right Jim?"

Jim tossed the ball into the air, caught it and took a deep breath to control his emotions. "All that kid wanted was my autograph and now look what's happened. I hope he's okay."

Just then, on the big screen, the cart was shown speeding across the field. Harley, like he had seen players do at many a game during injuries, raised his right arm and gave a thumbs up. The crowd instantly went into a roaring ovation. Blumfield pointed at the screen and remarked, "Would you look at that! That's some kid!"

Arriving at Gate B, Monica thanked the usher as she approached the golf cart and spoke to the doctor. "I'm Mrs. Sims, Harley's mother." Bending down, she ran her hand across Harley's forehead. "Are you okay, Son?"

Harley looked up at his mother and father who were now at his side. "They said my arm is broken." Still wearing the glove on his left hand, he looked for the ball. "The ball...where's the ball? I know I caught it! Where is it?"

Rich spoke up. "Right now, we can't be concerned about that. Just try and relax." Turning to the doctor, Rich asked, "Okay, what happens next?"

Dr. Lucas placed his hand on Rich's shoulder. "The paramedics are on their way. They should be here in a few minutes. They'll be taking your son to St. Louis Children's Hospital. It's about five miles from here. I would suggest one of you go along in the ambulance and the other follow in your vehicle. You'll need to sign papers when you get over there so the doctor at the hospital can set the boy's arm."

Harley let out a low groan when he tried to raise his arm. The doctor gently lowered the arm and spoke softly, "Harley, if you continue to move your arm the pain will get worse. Try and lay still. The paramedics will be here soon."

Seeing the tears in Harley's eyes, Monica asked in an irritated voice, "Isn't there some sort of pain reliever you can give him?"

"Yes, I have a number of pain medications with me, but if we drug him now when he gets to the hospital he may be too groggy to answer the attending physician's questions. As soon as they know what they're dealing with they'll give Harley a pain reliever."

Rich guided Monica off to the side. "I'm going to go get the car and drive over to the hospital. You wait here and go with Harley in the ambulance. Everything will be fine." Without waiting for her response, Rich went to Harley's side and patted him on his right arm. "I'll see you at the hospital, Son."

Rich, arriving at the hospital, ran into the emergency room, went to the front desk and explained, "My name is Rich Sims. My son had an accident over at Busch Stadium. Have they arrived with him yet?"

The woman at the desk smiled pleasantly and answered, "They just took him back." Looking to her right, she pointed, "Go through those automatic doors, then take a right and then a left. Your son is in Room 17."

"Thank you," said Rich as he walked quickly to the doors. The door to Room 17 was wide open, Monica seated in the corner, fumbling with something in her purse. Rich sat next to the bed, took a long, deep breath and asked, "Where's Harley?"

Popping a mint into her mouth, Monica answered calmly, "The

doctor was in to see him already. They asked him a few questions, gave him some pain medicine and took him to a room down the hall where they'll set his arm. They said it'd be about an hour. The doctor assured me everything would be fine. I already signed all the necessary paperwork." Reclining back into the chair, Monica stated, "Harley never ceases to amaze me. The last thing he asked when they were wheeling him out of here was if the Cards were still winning."

It was just after eleven o'clock when Rich returned to the room with two cans of soda. The doctor was talking to Monica while Harley, propped up in the hospital bed, sipped on an apple juice. "Ah, just in time," said the doctor. "Turns out the break was clean. It was a routine procedure. Harley was a trooper." Tapping the cast on Harley's right arm gently with an ink pen, the doctor explained, "This cast will have to remain on the arm for six to eight weeks. Considering Harley's age, I'm leaning toward six. Younger people tend to heal more rapidly. I'm going to write you a prescription for pain medicine. After about a week, a baby aspirin every day should do the trick. He needs to keep that sling on except at night when he's asleep. For the next few weeks Harley has to be careful not to run into anything or fall on the arm. If everything works out the way it should, Harley should be back to normal in about two months. We'll be keeping Harley here overnight so we can run some tests. When he hit, his head got quite a jolt. We want to make sure he doesn't have a concussion. Barring any other complications, he should be released tomorrow afternoon sometime. Any questions?"

Nodding in approval, Monica spoke, "No, I think we'll be able to get through the next six weeks or so." Smiling at Harley, she added, "It looks like a lot of watching TV for you for the next few weeks."

"If there's nothing else," said the doctor, "I've got another patient up the hall. Oh, and one other thing. You'll need to see your family doctor next week to see how Harley's getting along. Sometimes the first week in a cast can be the roughest."

After the doctor left the room, the nurse entered while reading Harley's chart. "I see this young man will be spending the night with us. Are your folks planning on staying for the night?"

Monica looked at Harley and commented, "I think you're in good hands. I don't see any reason for us to spend the night, that is, unless you want us to, Harley."

Harley finished his juice. "I'll be okay, Mom. Why don't you go on home? Somebody has to feed Ozzie." Looking at Rich and then Monica, Harley lowered his eyes and apologized, "I'm sorry I ruined my tenth birthday surprise." Holding up his injured arm, he explained, "This is probably the worst birthday I've ever had. When I caught that ball, I remember thinking how great the day was turning out to be even though I didn't get Jim Henke's autograph. Now look. I didn't get his autograph and I've gone and broken my arm. And on top of that…I won't be able to finish the season with my ball team. I won't be able to practice for the next couple of months. You always said Dad, that I needed to keep practicing everyday so I wouldn't lose my edge."

"None of this is your fault, Harley. Sometimes, things in life just get in the way of what we want to do, but in a couple of months you can get back to your daily practice and before you know it, next spring will roll around and you'll be trying out for a ten to twelve-year-old Little League team. Look at it this way: you're simply on the disabled list. How many times over the years watching Cardinal games have you seen players get injured? Sometimes they have to take a year off, or maybe months. But, they always come back, sometimes better than ever! You're only going to be laid up for about eight weeks. You'll have plenty of time to prepare yourself for the tryouts next spring."

The nurse, who had left the room returned with a broad smile plastered across her face. "Harley has two visitors waiting outside. They say they're ballplayers…major league ballplayers!"

Harley was at a loss for words, but Rich spoke up, "Well…show them in!"

Within seconds the nurse guided the two players into the room. Both men were dressed in casual slacks and dress shirts, one sporting a St. Louis Cardinals hat, the other the Pittsburgh Pirates. The man in the Cardinals hat was the first to speak, "Hello there, Harley…"

Before the man could finish speaking Harley broke in with a huge smile on his face. "I know who you are. Jim Henke, Cardinals relief pitcher: ERA 2.08, win-loss record so far this year at 4-0, twenty-seven strike outs, seven walks." Looking at the other player, Harley didn't even take a breath, "And you're Paul Blumfield, right fielder for the Pirates; batting average, 317, nine stolen bases, six home runs. You won the golden glove award two years ago."

Rich did his best to explain. "Harley here is a miniature version of a baseball encyclopedia. There isn't much about baseball he doesn't know."

Monica chimed in, "He not only understands the game, but he plays ball as well."

Moving closer to the bed, Jim asked, "So you play on a team then?"

Motioning at his arm, Harley smiled but then frowned, "Well, yes, I did. I play on the seven to nine-year-old team at our local Little League. Up until my fall at the park tonight I had a 3-0 record. Just last week, my coach told me if I kept pitching the way I was I had a shot at going undefeated."

Jim nodded in agreement. "Every pitcher's dream!"

Paul jumped in on the conversation and addressed Harley's parents. "Will your son be healed up so he can pitch at the end of the season?"

"No," answered Rich. "The doctor told us it would be six to eight weeks and even then Harley has to take it easy for a couple of weeks."

Harley, wanting to be involved in the conversation enthusiastically remarked, "My dad says I'm on the disabled list. Remember Paul, last year when you sprained your ankle and you were out for almost a month?" Changing the subject, Harley went right on talking, "I'm going to be a major league pitcher someday, just like you, Jim. I'm going to pitch for the Cardinals."

"After meeting and talking with you, young man," said Jim, "that sounds like a goal you could very well accomplish."

Snapping his fingers, Harley spoke again, "I almost forgot about the game. Did the Cards win?"

"Speaking of the game, we did win. The final score was 1-0 and you caught the winning ball."

Frowning, Harley answered, "Yeah, but I must have dropped it on the field when I hit."

"That's exactly what happened," explained Jim. "After they

carted you from the field I found the ball lying next to the fence. Didn't you tell me it was your tenth birthday and you were trying to get my autograph?"

"Yes, but that didn't work out."

From behind his back, Jim produced a baseball and held it up. "I've got that ball right here. I not only autographed it for you but I got the entire team to sign it."

"And that's not all," said Paul. "I also have a ball with me everyone on the Pirates team signed as well."

Harley reached out and took the signed ball from Jim, laid it on the bed next to him and took the ball that Paul offered. Looking at his parents, Harley couldn't believe what was happening. "The guys on my team will never believe this!"

Harley, holding both balls, smiled at the players and then addressed his parents. "You know when I said before this was the worst birthday I've ever had? I was wrong. This is the *best* birthday I've ever had!"

Jim reached out and shook Harley's hand. "Happy birthday." Turning to Rich and Monica, he tipped his hat and stated, "It's getting late. We best be on our way so Harley can get some rest. It was nice to meet you folks."

After the two players left the room, Monica spoke up, "It is getting late. The doctor told me you need to get some rest, Harley. They are going to run a few tests on you tomorrow and then we'll get you home. Are you sure you'll be all right without one of us being here with you?"

Clutching the signed ball from the Cardinals in his right hand as if he were preparing to throw a two-finger fastball, Harley smiled. "You and dad go on home. I'll be fine. I'm so excited I don't know if I'll be able to sleep."

The nurse, standing by the side of the bed, held two pills and a glass of water in her hands. "Harley, after you take these pills you'll be in La La land before you know it."

As Rich and Monica headed for the door, Harley stopped them just before he took his pills. "Don't forget…feed Ozzie!"

CHAPTER 2

SITTING ON THE SWING ATTACHED TO THE OAK TREE, Harley ate the last of the banana he had for breakfast. Laying the yellow peel on the arm of the wooden swing, he glanced around his backyard. Ever since he had been three year's old, he had spent countless hours behind his house in the yard practicing the game of baseball, preparing himself for his future of being a major league pitcher. His parents had gone to great lengths to transform the two acres behind their house on the outskirts of Arnold, Missouri into an ongoing baseball camp designed to give Harley every opportunity to practice daily. Their backyard was quite unusual. A pitcher's mound, complete with the rubber and a rosin bag; sixty feet away, home plate with a painted batter's box and welded wire backstop. Then there was the hanging tire on the tree near the corner of the lot where he would throw two hundred pitches a day, rain or shine. The pitching machine Rich and Monica had gotten him for his eighth birthday stood just inside the open garage door, next to the set of weights they got for him when he turned nine. Looking up at the bright morning sun, Harley shook his head in disgust. Everything he needed to become a better ballplayer was in that backyard, but at the moment and for the next couple of weeks all he could do was sit and think about when he could start practicing again.

His dismal thoughts were interrupted by his mother's voice from the open kitchen door, "Harley, I'm letting Ozzie out." Harley no sooner looked toward the house when Ozzie, a ninety-pound lab bounded down the deck steps and across the yard. The seven-year-old family pet raced across the yard, picked up a tattered tennis ball and brought it to Harley's feet where he dropped the ball, backed up a few feet and waited patiently. Picking up the ball, Harley laughed as he looked at the jet-black canine sitting in front of him. "You're crazy...you know that Ozzie!"

Gently tossing the ball underhanded toward the corner of the fenced-in yard with his good arm, he watched as Ozzie tore across the grass, scooped up the ball before it even stopped rolling and returned to the swing and dropped the ball at Harley's feet. Backing off, the dog looked down at the ball and then into Harley's face, the entire time, his tail wagging back and forth. Picking up the ball again, Harley threw it in the opposite direction. Following fifteen minutes of ball tossing, Harley stood and walked toward the garage, Ozzie following close behind, the soggy tennis ball in his mouth. Looking back at the dog, Harley exclaimed, "Ozzie…you have way too much energy!"

Putting the banana peel in a trashcan just inside the garage, Harley gazed around the two-car facility. The right side of the garage was where Rich always parked his old pickup truck and his motorcycle: a Cardinal red '69 Sportster Lowrider chopper. The back wall of the garage was covered in a large four-by-ten foot banner that stated boldly: STREET SMART – HIGHWAY BRED! The wall surrounding the banner was displayed with various Harley Davidson paraphernalia Rich had collected through the years. The two remaining walls on the right and left were crammed with banners, signs, T-shirts, hats and assorted St. Louis Cardinal memorabilia. Harley's father had three loves in his life: Monica, the St. Louis Cardinals, and Harley Davidson motorcycles, in that order.

Taking down an old ball glove from a shelf, Harley softly placed his right hand into the leather and smiled. He couldn't wait until he was back to practicing again. Ozzie laid his ball on the garage floor and curled up on an old frayed rug in the corner. Pounding the fist of his good hand into the old glove, Harley gazed up at the four by eight foot framed corkboard covered with old ticket stubs from Cardinal games. Reading one of the tickets in the lower left hand corner of the corkboard to himself, *Section 42, Row DD, Seat 12,* his thoughts were interrupted by his father's voice, "Quite a collection, isn't it? There's close to five hundred tickets on that board. I bet there isn't a better collection in the city." Tapping one of the tickets, Rich explained, "Like this one right here. It's my favorite ticket stub. This represents the game where I first met your mother." Moving his hand slightly upward, he touched a pair of tickets and went on, "And these two are special.

These are the tickets from the night your mom and I got married at the stadium. This one here is the first game we took you to when you were just a baby. Here's an interesting one you'll probably always remember. That night at the park just a little over a month ago where you made that great catch, fell over the fence and broke your arm. There are a lot of memories on this wall. There's tickets up here dating all the way back to the 1940s when my dad, your grandfather, started to go to Cardinal games."

Placing the glove on a workbench, Harley asked, "Did grandpa ever play Little League when he was a boy?"

Rich, grabbing a shop towel from the bench, started to wipe down his chopper. Running the rag over the metallic red fender he smiled. "No, he never had a chance to play Little League. When your grandfather turned ten years of age, the concept of Little League baseball was still in its infancy. Most of the teams were in Pennsylvania. When your grandpa was old enough to play, there were no leagues here in St. Louis or for that matter the state of Missouri."

"So, if gramps couldn't play baseball on an organized team then how did he play ball?"

"Like most folks in the 1940s, Gramp's parents didn't have a television. Back then, believe it or not radio was the main source of family entertainment. Your grandfather used to tell me about when he, his brother and two sisters along with their parents would sit around the large console radio they had in their living room and listen to Cardinal games. He just took a liking to listening to the Cardinals."

With a look of confusion on his face, Harley asked, "Gramps really never got a chance to actually play on a team?"

Picking up the glove, Rich pounded his fist into the pocket and answered, "Gramps played a lot of ball in the neighborhood where he grew up. He played sandlot ball with the other kids up the street. I remember him telling me about those games. During the summer months he'd be up at the crack of dawn, eat breakfast, and then it was off to a nearby ball field over near Forest Park. Gramps referred to it as a skin diamond. There wasn't a blade of grass in the infield…just dirt and cinders. He told me they had two benches there; one you could sit on, the other falling to pieces. The backstop was lopsided and there were numerous holes in the chicken wire fencing. According to your grandfather they never had enough kids for two full teams. They could play a full nine-inning game with as few as six kids. For bases they always used sections of newspaper weighted down with rocks. They never had enough gloves or bats. After your team was finished batting and you went out to the field, the opposing players would toss you their gloves."

Reaching up, Rich took an old battered baseball bat down from a top shelf and held it out to Harley. "This was your grandfather's bat he used back in the 40s. Back then, money was tight. As a kid you had to make things last a long time, maybe forever. As you can see this bat was taped and nailed together a number of times. Look at all the gouges and nicks in the wood. I bet this bat is over fifty years old."

Harley ran his fingers over the rough wood surface and asked his father, "So, by the time you were born, they did have Little League Baseball here in Missouri?"

"Yep. I remember when I turned ten I walked down Tenbrook Road to the local Little League, tried out and made a team. Gray's Market was the name of the team and they started me out on third base. We played eighteen games during the season and wound up with a record of two wins and sixteen losses. We came in last place. My second year playing for Gray's, the coach, Mr. Grimes, asked me if I wanted to take a shot at pitching. I had a pretty good arm so I said I'd take a stab at it. Turned out I could throw the ball about sixty miles an hour. Nobody could hit my fastball. But, I had control problems. I walked a lot of kids and beaned a few. We came in second place that year and I made the all-star team. We won the district playoffs, but lost in the state tournament to a team from Joplin."

Placing his arm around Harley's shoulder, Rich guided his son to the edge of the garage and pointed at the hanging tree tire. "Listen to me, Son. You've been throwing at that tire ever since you were five years old. And because of that and everything else you've done as far as practice goes I believe at ten years of age you're better than most kids your age. You already have a better fastball than I had when I was your age and you've got a great curve. This fall, after your arm is healed up we'll start working on developing a cutter and maybe a slider." Nodding at the weights in the corner, Rich explained, "And if you keep lifting, by next spring your fastball could be up around seventy."

Hanging the shop towel on a hook, Rich leaned against the side wall of the garage. "So, what are your plans for today?"

Harley frowned and answered, "Same ol' thing I've been doing for the past month: watching television, reading some of my old baseball books, organizing my baseball cards. I'd rather be out here in the yard practicing, but we both know that's not possible right now."

Placing his arm around Harley's shoulder, Rich guided him in the direction of the pickup. "Listen, I've got an idea. You do know that the Missouri State Little League Playoffs are being held right here in St. Louis this year."

"Yeah, but that's clean on the other side of town over by St. Charles."

Smiling, Rich corrected his son, "Well, that got changed at the last moment. Turns out they have some major problems at the Maryland Heights complex. A major sinkhole opened up just beyond second base and they are also having some serious electrical problems. They got the electrical problems fixed and filled in the sinkhole but Little League Inc., the powers to be in Williamsport, Pennsylvania are concerned about player safety so they decided to move the playoffs to our Little League field here in Arnold. Our field isn't quite as extravagant, but we do have enough playing fields to accommodate the different teams from around the state. The fields are in great shape, the lights all work, there's plenty of parking, so *we* get the state playoffs." Opening his wallet, Rich extracted a twenty and handed it to Harley. "There you go."

Harley, taking the money gave his father a strange look and asked, "What's this for?"

"Simple," said Rich. "You can't go to the Missouri State Little League Championship Playoffs without any money for dogs and sodas. It's just after eight o'clock in the morning. The first game is at nine. I have to drive right by the field on my way to the shop in Imperial. I'll drop you off. I'm only going to work until around two today. Your mom is working the second shift this week at the hospital so she won't be home for supper. You can catch the nine, eleven and one o'clock games. I'll drop by the field after work and we can see the afternoon games. So, if you're going to catch that first game we better get cracking."

Rich walked around and climbed in the pickup and continued to speak, "Your mom already knows all about this. C'mon, get in!"

Harley fastened his seatbelt as Rich pulled out of the garage and looked across the seat at Harley. "You can't tell me going to the state playoffs isn't more exciting than sitting in front of a television set?"

Harley folded the twenty and stuffed it into his front jeans pocket. "Well, if I can't practice or play baseball, I guess the next best thing would be to actually watch some games."

"And besides that," remarked Rich. "You'll be watching some of the best ten, eleven and twelve-year-olds in the state. You can get an idea of the caliber of players you'll be facing next year."

Turning out of their sub-division, Rich changed the subject. "Your mom was right when she mentioned earlier this year that the Cards might not have such a hot year. That game when you broke your arm wound up a four game series with the Pirates. We lost three out of four games played. This last week we split with the Mets and the Cubs. Right now, we're sitting at 19-27 as far as a win-loss record goes. The Cards are travelling today and tomorrow they start a three game series with the Phillies."

Merging onto Church Road in Arnold, Harley gazed out the passenger side window and asked, "Our all-star team didn't do too well in the district playoffs. I guess De Soto is representing our district."

Ten minutes later they came to Schneider Road and made a left into Arnold's Little League Complex. The parking lot was jammed with cars and buses from around the state. Stopping at the corner of the front lot, Rich smiled at Harley. "There ya go, Harley. Enjoy the games. I should be back around two thirty or so. See ya then."

Harley watched as the pickup left the lot in a cloud of dust. Crossing the lot to the main gate, he walked down the paved walkway that separated Field #3 from Field #6 and zigzagged his way through the crowd of parents, local fans, umpires and ballplayers from Missouri teams.

Cutting in between Field #3 and the concession stand, Harley decided on a cold drink. He could get something to eat later on. Standing in line, he spoke to a man in front of him, "Excuse me, could you tell me where the first game is going to be played?"

"Sure, sonny. The field right behind you. Webb City verses De Soto. Game starts in twenty minutes."

The bleachers on both sides of the field were packed, but Harley did manage to locate a seat at the very top on the end of the elevated metal seats. The Webb City team finished up with their infield practice, while the groundkeepers raked the infield dirt and fresh lime was laid down the foul lines and the batter's box. The coaches from both teams met with the umpires at home plate and presented their lineups. Harley looked around at the spectators he was sitting with. They were all wearing scarlet colored jerseys with the names of the Webb City players listed on the back. He overheard a small boy ask his mother, "When does Bucky play?" Harley smiled and took a drink of his soda and thought about how much he loved baseball as he watched a Webb City pitcher and catcher continue to warm up down the third base line.

A man sitting next to him talked with what appeared to be his wife while he read a schedule. "If we win this game then we get to play the winner of the five o'clock game between Joplin South and Jefferson City."

Suddenly, everyone's attention turned to the field when an eight-year-old girl standing in front of the pitcher's mound began to sing The Star Spangled Banner. It always amazed Harley how patriotic most people seemed to get, especially at a baseball game. Everyone stood, many placing their right hand over their heart or removing their hat, older men who were obviously veterans saluted the American flag flapping in the breeze in center field. The young girl's shrill voice made many of the fans wince, but they still applauded her effort when the National Anthem was over. The crowd no sooner settled back into their seats when the home plate umpire shouted, "Play ball!"

Webb City took the field as the manger gave his pitcher some last minute instructions. De Soto's first batter stood off to the side of the plate and took a few practice swings and the fans from De Soto yelled and shouted words of encouragement at their lead-off hitter:

"C'mon Brent…you can do it!"

"Start us off buddy!"

The young boy stepped into the batter's box and positioned

himself, his left foot right on the edge of the box, his right back a few inches. The Webb City pitcher looked in at his catcher and shook off the first sign, then nodded as he agreed with the requested pitch. He wound up and fired a fastball on the outside corner. The batter took the pitch as the umpire yelled, "Strike one!"

The batter backed out from the plate and looked down at the manager who was the third base coach. Going through the complicated process of giving his player a sign designating what he wanted him to do, the manager with his right index finger, tapped his nose twice, then his hat brim, then his left elbow and then the hat brim again. The player nodded and stepped back to the plate and waited for the next pitch. Another fastball, but this time right down the pike. The batter squared himself and slid his hand up the bat as he went into a bunting position. The ball bounced in front of the plate and rolled down the third base line. The third baseman, the pitcher and the catcher all attacked the ball, the pitcher scooping up the slow rolling ball and off-balance, fired it toward first base. The ball sailed over the first baseman's head, allowing the base runner to advance safely to second base. Harley shook his head in approval at having the batter bunt the ball early in the game. It had taken Webb City by surprise. Then, he shook his head again, but this time in disapproval of the way the pitcher had hurried the throw. He had plenty of time. Rich had always instructed him: *When you field the ball, take just a brief moment, even if it's only for a tenth of a second, think about what you're doing, then throw the ball.*

An hour and ten minutes later the game ended. The final score: De Soto 4, Webb City 3. As the two teams lined up for the customary end of game handshakes, Harley thought about the level of sportsmanship in Little League verses the big leagues. In a major league game, the opposing players from competing teams hardly ever congratulated the winning team. In the majors if a pitch hit a batter it was a rare occasion when the pitcher apologized to the batter. He thought about the Little League Pledge: *I trust in God. I love my country and will respect its laws. I will play fair and strive to win, but win or lose I will always do my best.*

The man sitting next to him who had been reading his schedule interrupted his thoughts. "Excuse me son. You must not be from the Webb City area. You're not wearing their team colors."

Harley confirmed the man's statement. "No, I'm not from Webb City."

"Then, you're from De Soto?"

"No, I live right here in Arnold."

"Well whether you know it or not, you're sitting with the Webb City fans. You should have sat on the other side of the field if you're rooting for De Soto."

"I'm not rooting for either team," pointed out Harley.

The man, confused, looked at his wife then back to Harley. "You have to be rooting for one of the teams. During the game I watched you when you nodded and shook your head in agreement or disapproval of different plays."

Harley smiled at the man. "If my dad were here he'd tell you I was analyzing the game."

The man seemed amazed. "Analyzing the game! What do you mean?"

"Well, since you asked. Earlier, before the game started you told your wife that after Webb City won the game they'd be playing the winner of Jefferson City or Joplin later in the day. Since your team lost to De Soto, you're one step closer to the loser's bracket and one game out of the winner's." Looking out at the field, Harley explained, "Because the manager of the Webb City team doesn't understand that baseball is a game of inches, you lost the game. The way I see it, Webb City could have *and* should have won the game."

The man, quite interested, asked, "And how's that?"

Harley turned, facing the man. "First of all, your catcher, number 7, doesn't frame the ball."

The man looked at his wife, then at Harley. "Frame the ball. What on earth does that mean?"

Pointing down at the field, Harley went on, "Any catcher worth their salt understands the importance of framing the ball. It's the catcher's job to pull the ball in toward the plate. You see, sometimes a ball might be just off the plate, inside or outside. A good catcher after catching a pitch that might be considered a ball moves his mitt slightly toward the plate pulling the ball in, causing the pitch to appear to be a strike. It doesn't always work, but when it does, it can change the outcome of a game. Your pitcher struck out seven batters and walked five. If the catcher would have framed the ball percentages dictate that those five walks could have been reduced to maybe only two or three. Those five walks resulted in De Soto scoring two runs. Two or three less walks means De Soto might have only scored one run rather than two based on walks."

The man sat silently as Harley continued, "And another thing; remember in the third inning when your second baseman, number 15 hit that ball to deep center field?" Without waiting for the man to respond, Harley explained, "The Webb City player ran right through first base. Then, when he was down the first base line, he decided to run to second, didn't have enough time and was cut down. It's obvious that the manager of the team did not instruct his players how to run the bases correctly. The player should have made the decision to go for second before he even got to first base. Rather than running through the base, he should have, a few feet from the bag, stepped to his right, then stepped on the inside corner of the base with his right foot and continued on to second. Because he didn't do this, he was thrown out. This is important because the next batter got a single which would have scored a run for Webb City if the previous player would have made it to second base. That's a run your team should have had but didn't get due to poor base running. The way I see it, Webb City, if they would have played a smart game should have won the game 4-1 rather than losing by a score of 4-3. That's why baseball is a game of inches."

Harley stood and finished his soda. "Listen, I've got to get something to eat before the next game. I hope your team does well for the remainder of the tournament."

As Harley walked down the bleachers and disappeared in the crowd, the man, still in amazement held up his hands and remarked, "What was that kid talking about…a game of inches?"

A young man in his late twenties seated behind the man spoke up. "I played Little League, high school and college ball. That kid is nothing short of a baseball genius. He knows exactly what he's talking about. Baseball is a game of inches."

CHAPTER 3

AFTER STANDING IN A LONG LINE AT THE CONCESSION stand, Harley walked over to a table where the condiments were located. Squirting a line of mustard and a forkful of pickle relish across his hotdog, he grabbed a napkin and his soda and turned to walk over to the T-ball field where he knew there wouldn't be a lot of people. He only took three steps when he was stopped by a voice, "Harley…Harley Sims!"

Looking to his right, Harley smiled when he saw Matt DeLoach, a local Little League umpire approaching. Dressed in the standard black umpire uniform, Matt tucked his facemask under his left armpit and wiped his sweating brow with a handkerchief and spoke again, "I was wondering if I'd see you at the state playoffs. How's your arm?"

Slightly raising his right arm cradled in the sling, Harley indicated, "Went to see the doctor last week. He said it looked like the cast might be coming off in two weeks. It'll probably be the end of August before I can get back to my daily practice." Nodding at Field #3, Harley frowned and remarked, "You don't know how much you miss playing baseball until something happens where you can't play for a while."

Placing the handkerchief back inside his pants pocket, Matt stated, "I guess you'll be trying out for the ten to twelve-year-old division next spring. Our league sure could use more players like you, Harley. The people here in Arnold who are in the know as far as Little League goes are saying you're the best ballplayer to come along in years; some say the best they've ever seen in this area."

Harley looked off into the passing crowd and nodded in the direction of three boys pushing their way through the crowd. "What about him? Aaron Buckman. I've heard people say he's the best from these parts."

Turning to watch the three boys pass by a few yards off, Matt shook his head in disapproval. "Aaron Buckman; now there's a sad situation. He just turned twelve years old earlier this year. He's more than a child, he's a man-child: six foot, two inches tall, two hundred eighteen pounds. I'm a thirty-three year old man and Aaron Buckman is taller than me and he outweighs me by a good thirty pounds. Next year will be his last year in Little League. This past year, he hit twenty homeruns in eighteen games. He can hit the ball a ton. I've seen many a pitcher try and pitch around the boy, but he's got so much power he can muscle the ball out of the park no matter where it is in relation to the plate. Defensively, he plays about the best first base I've ever seen. For his size he's quick as a cat and he makes a big target for the infielders."

Harley watched as Aaron disappeared in the crowd. "What about his pitching?"

"His pitching is not his strength. He has control problems and has a nasty habit of hitting batters. Why just this last year he injured two players; broke one kid's arm with an eighty mile an hour fastball. All he's got is a fastball. He'd never make it in the bigs as a starting pitcher, maybe a reliever, but not a starter. Personally, I think he should concentrate on playing first base. That and his hitting skills could get him to the majors, that is, if he keeps his nose clean. He'll be lucky to graduate from high school. In short, he's got an attitude problem and he won't listen to anyone. He's always in trouble. To tell you the truth, baseball might be the only thing that kid has going for him. Potentially, he has a great future playing baseball, but from the way things look he might just keep traveling the wrong road."

Tapping Harley on his right shoulder, Matt pointed at the umpire's trailer. "Look, I gotta go. I'm umpin' the next game behind the plate. I've got to grab a bite. Listen, tell your dad I said hey!"

Passing the concession stand, Harley made his way up the paved road toward the T-ball field and thought about Aaron Buckman. Aaron was two years ahead of him and he had never faced Buckman in a game. He had heard some of the kids talk about him and how intimidating he could be. He had a reputation as a bully; a rough kid who could back up what he said. His parents had warned him to give Aaron Buckman a wide berth, as he was a known troublemaker.

The T-Ball field parking area was packed with cars but the field itself was empty. Sitting on the bottom row of bleachers, Harley gazed out across the tiny version of a baseball field and thought back to when he was three years old. Thanks to his parents who were avid St. Louis Cardinal fans, he had been raised in an environment of baseball. If he and his parents were not attending a Cardinal game, they had the game on all three televisions in their home. Throughout their home the walls were decorated with photographs of present and past Cardinal players, pennants and famous moments in past Cardinal baseball history.

He thought back to his younger years; when at the age of three his parents had played hour after hour of catch with him in the backyard, until catching a baseball became second nature. By the time he was four, he could not only catch, but could bat, run the bases and in general knew how the game of baseball was played. He had become as obsessed with the Cardinals as his parents.

Finishing up his hotdog he got up and walked out to second base and recalled his days of T-ball. At first, his parents had decided to not enroll him in the T-ball program because they thought he was too advanced and would have too many questions; questions like why there were twelve to fifteen players on the field, why did every player on each team get to bat every inning, why did no one ever strike out, no one was ever tagged out and they never kept score. His parents were not too far off the mark as Harley had asked all those questions and quite a few more.

Finally, his mother and father explained to him that T-ball was the very first introduction to baseball or for that matter a team sport that four and five-year-old boys and girls were introduced to. It was more of a social event designed to socialize children into the concept of team sports. So, at five years of age, Harley was enrolled in the T-ball program. It was ridiculous. All of the other children were learning the game. Harley already understood baseball. Every time he stepped up to the T, he would hit the ball over everyone's head and race around the bases. Harley actually caught the ball and would tag runners out. Most of the other parents were upset at how well Harley played compared to their children and complained, saying that Harley was too advanced to play with their children.

Harley walked across the outfield grass to the center field fence and looked at the adjacent field where at the age of six he played one year in the coach-pitch league. His coach-pitch experience only lasted one year as the league decided to move Harley to the seven to nine-year-old division where he had played and excelled for the past two years. Looking down at the cast on his right arm he thought about how his year had been cut short. Turning, he started back across the field. There was nothing he could do about his current situation except wait until the cast came off and then he could get back to his daily practice for the upcoming tryouts for the coming springtime.

Walking around a cinderblock wall on the right side of the field, Harley came face to face with Aaron Buckman and his two fourteen year old henchmen. Lighting up a cigarette, Aaron stopped Harley from retreating around the other side of the wall. "Well, well, look who we have here! If it isn't little Harley Sims." Sarcastically, he thumped one of his companions on the shoulder, took a drag on his cigarette and blew three smoke rings off in to the air. "Boys, this is ol' Harley, the best ballplayer in Jefferson County."

Harley, sensing trouble, tried to back away, but was stopped as one of the older boys cut him off from going around the wall. "What's the hurry?"

Harley looked into the boy's face and answered, "I don't know you. I've never seen you around here before."

Aaron stepped closer, his hulking six foot, two-inch frame seemingly dwarfing Harley who stood under five foot. "That's 'cause he ain't from around here. These boys are my cousins from down in Imperial." Reaching out, Aaron quickly grabbed Harley's ball hat and held it out for the other two boys to see. "Looks like a brand new Cardinal hat." Removing his warn hat from his large head, he placed it on Harley's, the large hat coming down over his ears which caused Aaron and his cousins to break out in laughter when Aaron suggested, "I think we should trade. I need a new hat."

Harley quickly removed the oversized hat from his head and stated, "I'm not interested in trading."

Adjusting the band on the inside of Harley's hat so it would fit him, Aaron smirked, "Well, you don't have a choice. You think you're better than me or somethin'?"

Before Harley could respond, Aaron spoke to his cousins,

"Harley here thinks he's the best ballplayer around these parts. At least, that's what people tell him. The truth is...I'm the best and everybody knows it! I can hit better than Harley, I'm a better defensive player than Harley and I can pitch better than Harley." Grabbing the hat from Harley's hand he placed his old hat back on Harley's head. "The only person who doesn't know that I'm the best ballplayer in St. Louis is Harley here. Isn't that right, Harley?"

Realizing that he was in no position to argue with Aaron Buckman, Harley agreed, "Well, yeah I guess you can hit a lot better than me and I have to admit you do play a good first base." Harley hesitated for a moment and then continued, "I wouldn't say you're a better pitcher. The word around here is that you have control problems. I'll admit you can throw the ball a lot harder than me, but at least when I throw a baseball it goes where I want it to."

Aaron stubbed out his cigarette on the side of the block wall and looked at first Harley, and then his cousins in amazement. "You say I have control problems!" Pointing at Harley's cast, he laughed and pointed out, "I think you're the one who has no control. How much control does it take to go to a Cardinals game, fall onto the field during the game and break your arm? You're an idiot, Sims!"

One of the older boys suggested, "C'mon Aaron, we gotta go if we're goin' to meet those girls."

Looking at the boy, Aaron spoke, "Gimme another smoke!"

The boy removed a wrinkled pack of cigarettes from his shirt pocket, extracted one of the white cylinders and handed it to Aaron, who, removing a lighter from his pocket, lit up. Blowing a long stream of smoke toward the sky, Aaron smiled and stepped close to Harley. Thinking for a moment, he finally spoke, "Listen, you got any money on you, Sims?"

Harley removed the large hat from his head and tossed it to the ground and answered, "Look, I've got to go."

Aaron reached out and shoved him up against the block wall. "You didn't answer my question, Sims. Ike I said, do you have any money?"

Harley realizing that the situation was not improving, answered, "Yeah, I have a few dollars."

"Good," said Aaron. "I need to borrow five bucks from ya. I've got a hankerin' for a coke and I'm flat broke."

Harley looked at the cousins and then back to Aaron, who stepped nose to nose with Harley and ordered, "Let's see how much you have. Don't worry, I'll pay you back."

Harley frowned and said something he probably shouldn't have. "Look, Buckman, I've heard all about how you borrow money from other kids. They never get paid back. The fact is, you just plain take money from kids."

Aaron backed off slightly and held out his large hands, "Ya know, Sims...you're right. I guess I do take what I want. Now, are you going to give me that five bucks or do I take it?"

One of the cousins laughed and pointed out. "Look at it this way kid. You already have one broken arm. You don't need another one...right?"

Aaron reached out, touched the cast and remarked, "Yeah, it's be a shame if that happened."

Harley reluctantly reached into his pants pocket and withdrew his money. Aaron grabbed the five bills from his hand and counted them. "Looks like ol' Harley here has fourteen dollars. Tell ya what, Sims. "We'll take...I'm sorry...we'll borrow ten from ya. You can keep the four ones. Wouldn't want ya ta starve or die of thirst." Holding up the ten, Aaron laughed and commented, "Drinks are on me cousins!"

Turning to walk away, Aaron hesitated and walked back to Harley, picked up his old hat and placed it on Harley's head, took a drag on his smoke and with a stern look on his face spoke, "One more thing, Sims. You tell anybody about this hat business or about the money, I will break your other arm. See ya around."

Harley pitched the hat to the ground and stood as he watched the three boys disappear around the side of the wall. Walking over to the bleachers he took a seat and a deep breath. His parents were right about Aaron Buckman. *He was a troublemaker.* For a brief moment, Harley considered running down to the concession area and telling one of the two officers he had seen about his confrontation with the three boys, but then remembered what Aaron had said would happen to him if he said anything about what happened. No, he'd wait and talk with Rich. He'd know what to do.

Seated in the bleachers at Field #6 where the three o'clock game was to be played, he watched a groundskeeper operating a riding mower pulling a metal net designed to smooth out the infield dirt. The bleachers were starting to fill up when he saw his father approaching as he waved. Taking a seat next to his son, Rich asked, "So, how have the games been so far?"

Harley took a drink and responded, "All right, I guess."

Rich took a seat and gave Harley a strange look. "'All right, I guess,' is not an answer I would expect from a boy whose entire life is centered around baseball. What's up?"

Looking at his father, Harley answered, "I guess there are things more important than baseball. Listen, I hope you don't mind, but I'm really not interested in watching the other games. I need to talk to you about something that happened here at the park."

Rich sat back and gestured, "Okay, let's talk then."

Harley looked in the direction of the T-ball field, hesitated, and then spoke, "Not here."

Rich sat forward. "You're really serious about not watching the other games...aren't you? For my son to pass up a ballgame, it's got to be serious. How about this? I was going to grab a couple of dogs here at the park. I'm starving. What say we head on over to Imo's and grab a large extra cheese and pepperoni."

Harley nodded in approval. "That's sounds good, Dad."

Pulling out onto Tenbrook Road, Rich turned off the radio and flipped the air-conditioner on high, but remained silent.

They were no sooner down the road a hundred yards when Harley asked, "Aren't you going to ask me what this is all about?"

Rich looked across the seat and answered, "I figure you'll let me in on that when you're ready to tell me."

Harley looked out the passenger side window and answered, "Now is as good as any other time, I guess." Turning in the seat facing Rich, Harley began, "I had a run-in with Aaron Buckman and two older boys who were with him. He said they were his cousins. I was over at the T-ball field minding my own business when they confronted me..."

Ten minutes later they pulled into Imo's lot just as Harley was finishing up, "...and then they left."

Rich sat back in the seat and rubbed his hand across his chin. "So, let me get this straight. They took your hat and ten dollars from you and threatened to break your other arm if you said anything about what happened. That about sum things up?"

Harley answered, "Yep that's what happened."

Rich opened the truck door and suggested, "Let's go on in and order and we'll talk this through."

Taking a corner table, Rich ordered drinks and their pizza. After the waitress left, he placed the menu in between a napkin dispenser and salt and pepper shakers. "Harley, as your father, it's my job to be here whenever you have questions about life or some sort of problem. Your mother and I have tried to raise you in a fashion where, at times we allow you to make your own decisions. So, let's start this off by me asking you what you think should be done."

"That's easy, Dad. I think somebody should beat the crap out of Aaron Buckman!"

"Your mother and I are not what you would refer to as violent people, but in this case, I'm sure your mother would agree with me in saying that Aaron Buckman, as you say, should have the crap beat out of him. Unfortunately, you are not the one who is going to make that happen. If you were to go up against Buckman, he'd destroy you. I mean, he could really hurt you."

Fiddling with the salt shaker, Harley asked, "Can't we, or I guess I should say, you and Mom talk to Aaron's parents? I mean, he can't just be allowed to go around doing whatever he feels like."

"Talking with his parents is an option, but that is also something that is not only impossible but fruitless."

Harley stared across the table, not understanding what his father said.

Rich nodded and remarked, "I can tell from that look of confusion on your face that what I just said doesn't make much sense to you."

"You're right," said Harley. "It doesn't make any sense at all. You and Mom have always taught me the best way to deal with things is to talk things out and now you say that's impossible as far as Aaron's parents are concerned."

"Here's the thing," said Rich. "I know Aaron's father...Frank Buckman. We grew up together in the same neighborhood over off of Watson Road in the city. We went to the same elementary, middle and high school together. Frank Buckman, even as a little kid was always in trouble. He spent time in a juvenile detention center a number of times when he was in high school. I remember my parents telling me that Frank Buckman was headed for a life of crime and would no doubt wind up in prison, which is where he is today."

With a look of astonishment, Harley leaned forward and whispered, "Aaron's father is in prison?"

"That's right. He got six months in Bonne Terre for beating up three men at a bar down in Soulard. I think Frank has about two months to go before he's out. The point is, sure, I could drive down to Bonne Terre and request to see him in prison. I'm not so sure he'd agree to talk with me. And, if he did, I don't think he'd give a crap one way or the other. He doesn't care anything about his son, Aaron. He'd probably just laugh and say, 'It's just a hat and ten dollars!'"

The waitress arrived with their pizza, sat it on the table and asked if there was anything else. Rich told her everything looked fine. After she left, Rich took two slices, bit into one and commented, "Dig in!"

As Harley reached for the pizza, Rich continued their conversation, "Back to what I was saying. Frank Buckman always has and probably always will be a man of violence. He always wants to punch someone. That's the first thought that comes to his mind. He'd never consider talking things out and coming up with a peaceful solution to a problem. Aaron, his son appears to be just like his father. So, you see it's impossible to speak with Aaron's father and expect to get any positive result."

Taking another slice of pizza, Rich went on, "Now, let's talk about Aaron's mother and why it would be fruitless to speak with her. First of all, she is not the most reliable mother a boy could want. She's with a different man each month. She doesn't give a rat's you know what about her son. Besides that, she can't control the boy. He does what he wants, goes where he wants. There is absolutely no discipline in his life. Speaking with Mrs. Buckman would be a waste of time. If I thought it would do any good, sure your mother and I could go and speak with her, but it would result in the same attitude Aaron's father has. In short, his parents don't give a crap about the boy. He lives in a different world than you do, Harley."

With a look of hopelessness Harley looked at his father. "So, what do we do then?"

"I know this is not the answer you're looking for, but for the moment we do nothing. I'm going to say something that you will no doubt not agree with. Aaron Buckman does not have the luxury of being blessed with a set of good parents like you are. He's had a rough upbringing. A boy like that needs to be cut some slack…but only to a point. The only way you can defeat a kid like Aaron is to outsmart him. Look at it this way. You already know you cannot physically defeat him. You have to use your head. In life you have to pick your battles. Going up against Aaron Buckman in a hand-to-hand fight is not going to turn out in your favor. When you think about it, he really could break your other arm…or worse. Aaron, at this point in his life is a stupid young man. He may not always be that way, but right now…he is. You can't fix stupid! Baseball is the one thing in his life he's good at. It could be the one thing that saves him from a life like his father has experienced. So, rather than trying to bring him down, despite what he did to you, the next time you run into him, maybe you could suggest that since you and he are the best ballplayers around here, maybe you could practice together. A little humbleness can go a long way in life. Maybe you could ask him to help you with your fastball and you might be able to help him to develop a curve. Through baseball, maybe you could actually be a reason for him to turn his life around. Like your mother always says. Baseball is not just a game…it's about life."

Folding his hands, Rich emphasized, "Remember, in life, doing what's right is always the best decision. *And,* just because you do the right thing, that doesn't mean everyone is going to agree with you. Take this Aaron Buckman situation; I think it's safe to say that nine out of ten people would tend to agree that Aaron should be taken out behind the woodshed and get the beating of his life. Once again, you're not the person that is capable of handing out that beating. And here's the strangest part of dealing with a violent twelve-year-old. If he does break your arm…or worse, nothing if anything at all that will amount to much will be done to him, because he is only twelve year's old. I really don't think you want to get another broken arm because of ten dollars and a baseball hat. Do the right thing here and use your head. Think about this: is it more important to see Aaron Buckman go down or for you to be able to play ball next spring? If you're going to be a professional ballplayer, that and that fact alone should be your number one priority."

Biting into a slice of pizza, Harley smiled at his father. "Tell ya what, Dad. You and mom have never led me wrong. I'm not saying that I'm going take your advice, but I'll think about it." Taking a swig of soda, he went on, "Let's talk about something else."

Snapping his fingers, Rich pointed his drink at Harley. "The Phillies play the Cards tonight at seven fifteen. Something else," said Rich. "Do you know what they are televising before the game tonight?"

Making a strange face, Harley answered, "No, not really."

"Here's a clue. We watch this event every year. It's about the greatest players and managers in the game of baseball and it's not the all-star game."

Suddenly, it came to Harley. "The Baseball Hall of Fame inductee ceremonies are tonight. I wonder who's going to get in this year?"

"I already know the answer to that question," said Rich. "Five players have been voted in and it's kind of ironic that we are going to be watching the Phillies and the Cards play tonight because three of the five players are on those two teams. First of all, we have Richie Ashburn and Mike Schmidt of the Phils. The third member that you will be glad to hear about is Vil Gazaway Williams. His final game was with the Cardinals in 1910."

The waitress who was wearing a Cardinals jersey, approached their table, laid down their check and asked, "Will there be anything else?"

Rich finished his drink and answered, "No, I think we're fine, but we will need a to-go box for the rest of our pizza."

Minutes later, turning onto Rt. 141, Rich asked Harley a question. "Okay...time for some Cardinals history. You ready?"

Harley turned in the seat and answered enthusiastically, "Okay, give me your best shot!"

Rich thought for a moment and then spoke, "Speaking of the Hall of Fame. Who was the last St. Louis Cardinal to be inducted prior to tonight's event?"

Harley pursed his lips as he thought, "Well, let's see. It's either

Lou Brock, Enos Slaughter or Red Schoendienst. Let me think about this for a couple of seconds." Tapping his fingers on the padded dash, he continued to speak, "I'm pretty sure Lou was inducted back in 1982 and I think Slaughter went in '85. I'm going to go with Red in 1989. He played professional ball from 1945 up until '63. He played on the 1947 Cardinal team that won the Worlds Series, had a lifetime batting average of .289 and had 1,980 hits."

Rich laughed and commented, "You're right…it's was Schoendienst. I'm not sure about all the other stats you gave me, but then again, I haven't studied the history of the Cards like you have."

Turning off the highway, Rich entered the sub-division where they lived. Passing the third house on the right, he commented and pointed at the SOLD sign planted in the yard next to the paved driveway. "Looks like the Spears' place finally sold. They just put the sign in the front yard this morning. Mable, down the street informed your mother that a family from Texas bought the house. From what she said, apparently the company he works for transferred the husband up here to the St. Louis area. She also said they have two children, a boy about your age and a younger sister. I guess they are going to move in later this month."

Pulling in their driveway, they were greeted by Ozzie who ran back and forth on the other side of the fence. Getting out of the truck, Rich handed Harley the pizza box. "Take this inside and put it in the fridge. The game won't be on for another three hours. Maybe tonight will be the game where the Cards start to turn this year around."

Harley hesitated at the back door and gave his dad a thumbs up. "Go Cards!"

CHAPTER 4

HARLEY PULLED OUT A CHAIR AT THE KITCHEN TABLE and spoke to his mother, "Good mornin' Mom." Taking in a deep whiff of the smell of frying bacon, Harley added, "I wake up for bacon!"

Monica turned and greeted her son, "Mornin' Harley. How does pancakes and bacon sound for breakfast?"

Petting Ozzie on his head, Harley agreed, "Pancakes sound good. We have plenty of maple syrup? The last time we had pancakes we ran out of syrup and we had to use strawberry jam. I mean, it was all right but it wasn't the same as good ol' maple syrup."

Opening the pantry door, Monica removed a large bottle and placed it on the table. "Got plenty of syrup. Think I'll scramble up a few eggs to go with. I already fed Ozzie. Today is going to be a busy day. Both you and Ozzie have doctor appointments."

Rich walked into the kitchen, yawned, stretched and overheard the conversation, commenting, "That's right, Harley. Today you get that cast removed from your arm and Ozzie gets his yearly checkup."

Harley reached for the morning paper and remarked enthusiastically, "Yeah, and that means soon I'll be back to practicing." Pouring a glass of juice, he flipped to the sports page. "The Cards start a three game series with the Cubs tonight. Right now, we're twenty-seven games below 500. This has been a horrible home stand. The Marlins took three from us, and then we lost two out of three to Houston. After the series with the Cubs, we head out west for three games each with LA, the Padres and the Giants. At the rate we're heading, we're not even going to make the playoffs." Running his finger down over the National League Central standings, Harley folded the paper in half and shoved it across the table. "It's too depressing to read about." Sitting back in his chair he finished the juice and announced, "But like you're always saying Dad, '*That's baseball!*'"

Picking up the paper, Rich unfolded it and turned to the sports section. "There's an article in here about the Joplin South team who beat that team from Watkins Mill for the state title. They're 5-0 in the Great Lakes Regionals. They play a team from Indiana tomorrow for the Great Lakes Championship. If they win they are headed for Williamsport, Pennsylvania and the Little League World Series Playoffs. I can't remember the last time Missouri had a team go to Williamsport. Every kid who has ever played Little League baseball dreams of going there."

"Does that include you, Dad," probed Harley. "Back in the days when you played for Grey's Market, did you have a desire to go Williamsport and play in the World Series?"

Pouring a cup of coffee, Rich dumped in a packet of sweetener and smiled. "You bet I did! Especially the year I made the all-star team and we won the districts. And the further we got in the state championships the more excited I got. I can't imagine any youngster who plays ball not getting excited about the prospect of going to Pennsylvania and playing up there. Little League Baseball is the largest youth sports organization in the world. Every year, hundreds of thousands of teams, not only from this country, but also from over a hundred countries on six continents step on Little League fields around the world. I've heard it said that somewhere around two million children participate each year in Little League. In the back of their minds I suppose that every one of those kids dream of going to Williamsport."

Harley sat back in his chair. "Not me. I've got bigger fish to fry. I've got a much larger goal in mind and that's being a pitcher in the major leagues, hopefully for the Cardinals. Let me ask you this, Dad? How many of the kids that actually get to go to Williamsport wind up in the major leagues?"

Pointing his cup ay Harley, Rich responded, "You bring up a good point, Son. When you consider the number of kids that have gone to play in the Little League World Series there is no doubt only a handful that gets to the big leagues. Players like Boog Powell who went on to play for Baltimore and Lloyd McClendon who later on played for Pittsburgh. I really can't think of any others right now, but I know there are a few more who have made it to the major leagues."

That's my point," said Harley. "Going to the Little League World Series is not a qualification for becoming a major leaguer. Baseball is a number's game. I bet that not even one percent of the kids that make the journey to Pennsylvania wind up on a major league team."

Rich sipped at his coffee and looking out over the top of his cup, stated, "All right, Harley. I'll agree that baseball is all about the numbers. There are virtually stats for everything: batting average, RBI's, innings pitched, on base percentage and on and on. Here's some numbers, some mathematics that will blow your mind. I'm saying that it's harder for a Little League team to win the Little League World Series than it is for a major league team to win the World Series as we know it."

"Come on Dad, you can't possibly believe that."

Monica, poring pancake batter onto a cast iron skillet jumped in on the conversation. "I'm afraid I've got to go with Harley on that, Rich. How do you figure the Little League World Series is more difficult to win that the Major League World Series?"

"It's all about the math," said Rich. "Math is one of your favorite subjects, right Harley?"

"Yeah, it is, but what does that have to do with what we're talking about?"

With an air of confidence in his voice, Rich went on to explain, "If I have heard you say, 'You can't defeat a mathematical equation,' one time I've heard you quote that phrase a hundred times. And, you're right. A mathematical equation cannot be argued: two plus two equals four."

Monica placed two pancakes in front of Harley and pointed her spatula at her husband. "I can't even imagine where you're going with this."

Sliding the maple syrup across the table to Harley, Rich held up an index finger to make his point, "First of all, in the major leagues we presently have twenty eight teams with a roster of twenty-five players on each team, which equates to seven hundred major league ballplayers. Each year when spring training starts, would you both agree with me that every one of those teams and all of those players have the same goal in mind; winning the world series that year?"

Monica, back at the stove nodded in agreement, "Okay, I'll give you that."

Harley spoke up and disagreed, "Well, I don't. Sometimes there are major league teams that are in a rebuilding year and they know right up front that they don't stand much of a chance in even having a winning season, let alone go to the series. And then there are those players who may be coming back from an injury from the previous season. They may be interested in just getting back to playing ball, not winning or going to the World Series."

"I'll go with that," said Rich, "but you can't say that rebuilding teams or players that are coming back from injuries do not have an opportunity to go to the series. Anything is possible. Would you agree with that?"

Monica placed a plate of pancakes in front of Rich and answered as she addressed Harley, "I think we have to give your Dad that one. At the beginning of the major league season, despite the fact that certain teams may be favored to go to the series, each team starts out on an equal basis, and your father is right…anything can happen!"

Opening the syrup bottle, Rich continued with his math lesson, "Okay, we've established that there are twenty-eight major teams and seven hundred professional major leaguers at the start of the baseball season each year." After slathering his pancakes with maple syrup, he pointed the bottle at Harley. "Here's the next part to the equation. At the end of the regulation season we have the major league playoffs, which eventually leads to the World Series. You can figure somewhere in the vicinity of twenty-five to thirty-some playoff games depending if there are some sweeps or if a playoff series goes the full five games. Once the teams are established as American and National League Champions we then have a best of seven games to determine the World Series Champion."

Cutting into the stack of pancakes, Rich took a bite and continued speaking, "The figures that I have just given you cannot possibly equal what a Little League team has to go through to get to their world series."

Stopping for a moment to allow what he said to sink in as far as his son and wife were concerned, he looked at Harley and Monica who were staring at each other in wonder. Finally, Harley spoke to Monica, "You were right Mom, when you mentioned earlier that you didn't know where Dad was going with this. I don't know about you, but I'm confused."

Laying down his fork, Rich smiled. "I've only given you half of the numbers that will prove my point. Here's the other half that probably no one considers. We have already established that there are less than thirty major league teams who want to win the World Series at the beginning of each year. In Little League, there are hundreds of thousands of teams that want to win the prestigious world title and be crowned Little League Champions. We have also agreed that there are seven hundred professional ball players in the major leagues who have a desire to win the World Series. In Little League, there are around two million kids who want to win the Little League World Series. I also told you that there are approximately twenty-five to thirty-or-so playoff games to determine who goes to the World Series in the majors. In Little League, even though an individual team only has to play thirty some playoff games to get to Williamsport, considering the number of teams involved there are over thirty-seven thousand playoff games around the world that determines the eight teams that eventually go to Williamsport. And here's my final point. The two teams that play in the Little League World Series play one game to determine the champion. One wrong pitch, one wrong throw, one wrong decision...you lose the game! In the major leagues, you get to play the best of seven to determine the outcome...the eventual winner. A team could have one, two or even three bad games, but can still win the next four and win the title. You can't argue with the numbers. The Little League title is much more difficult to win."

Monica sat down at the table after placing a bowl of scrambled eggs and a plate of bacon next to the syrup. "Well, Harley, I don't think we can, after your father's rundown of the numbers disprove his theory. I think Little Leaguers have a much more difficult road to follow on the way to the championship."

Harley scooped out a spoonful of eggs and commented, "I'll admit that the numbers point in that direction, but you can't compare the level of competition of Little League to the major leagues. In the Major League World Series, every player involved is a professional at whatever position he plays. I'd say that they are pretty close to being fully developed at their baseball skills. Ten, eleven and twelve-year-old kids that play baseball even at the highest level in Williamsport are far from their potential. The competition cannot possibly be as tough."

Monica, with a mouthful of eggs spoke out of the side of her mouth, "I can see your point, Harley, but I can also see what your father's saying. After hearing both sides of this morning baseball debate, I'd say that everything is relevant."

Harley shot his mother an odd look and remarked in a frustrating manner, "There you go again, Mom. Using a word that a ten-year-old does not understand. What does relevant mean?"

"Relevant means pertaining to, or I guess maybe a better way to put it would be, all things being equal. Major league players face on a daily basis the best pitching, hitting and coaching in the world of baseball. Little Leaguers are faced with the same thing, but at a different level, especially when, and if they get to play in Williamsport. The ten, eleven and twelve-year-olds that go up there are faced with the best pitchers, hitters and coaching that major leaguers face; it's just a different level…but, nonetheless, still baseball."

"Well, if I have learned anything over the first ten years of my life it's this. When your mother and father agree on something that you don't; you wind up losing the argument. But, that still doesn't change my mind on what started this subject. I still don't have a dream of playing in the Little League World Series. My focus remains on becoming a major league pitcher."

Taking a bite of eggs and then a swallow of juice, Harley looked at both Rich and Monica. "When I was younger, let's say around three or four I had a dream of being in the major leagues. But, something my history teacher, Mrs. Simcox said last week made me realize that I don't have a dream, but a goal of being in the majors. She explained to us that everyone should have dreams or a dream in life, but it's more important to establish goals. Dreams are simply something we imagine happening to us sometime in the future and it's hard to work towards something that you just imagine. A goal, on the other hand, is something that you can actually work toward. Mrs. Simcox made me realize that I have been working toward a goal, rather than a dream for the past few years. She taught our class that by setting up a series of small goals that eventually you'll be able to reach the larger goal you are striving for. They are kind of like stepping-stones. Take me, for instance. T-ball, coach-pitch and the last two years spent in the seven to nine-year-old division were each a stepping-stone to the next level. When I start playing next year in the ten to twelve-year-old group, I'll be at yet another level, followed by pony league, high school ball, college, the minor leagues and then, my final goal: a pitcher in the big leagues."

Rich pushed his plate to the side. "Your teacher sounds like a pretty smart cookie. What she told you sounds like good advice. I think it's safe to say that most people don't even think about what they want to do with the rest of their life until they get to high school. What I'm saying is that it's unusual for a young man at the age of ten to have his life planned out. Both your mother and I admire you for over the past few years practicing daily to be a professional ballplayer. Most kids your age can't make their mind up from one day to the next as to what they want to do. I say these things because I don't want you to be disappointed if you don't wind up pitching for the Cardinals. There are twenty-seven other major league teams and each and every one of them is always on the lookout for new, upcoming talent. I have no doubt that with your attitude and work ethic, that you can become a major league pitcher, but claiming that you are going to pitch for the Cardinals might be something you may not be able to control."

"I agree with your father," said Monica. "To become a major league ballplayer is something many a young man has dreamed about, but few ever get to realize. At this point in your life you are far advanced when it comes to playing baseball. The farther up the baseball ladder you go the more difficult it will be to be the best. Next year when you are playing with the ten to twelve-year-olds, you'll find that every one of those kids knows how to play the game. At the high school level, you'll be competing with kids that have been playing ball probably as long as you, some believe it or not maybe, your equal or even better. *When* you go to college, no doubt on an athletic scholarship, you'll be playing with and against many players who will be drafted into the major leagues. I emphasized the word, *when* you go to college, because it's important that you have a career to fall back on later in life. There has been many a major leaguer, who after their ball career is over, despite the amount of money they made who winds up broke. An education is vitally important in today's world. Baseball will always be *baseball,* but the loyalty that teams have for their players and players for the team they are with has changed with the times. Owners of teams, those in the front office, even managers have to constantly search for players that will enhance their chances of having a winning team, not just now but in the future. If a team takes on twenty-five players and keeps all of those players until they retire, I guarantee you, that team will not fare well in the long run. My point is just this, there is no guarantee that when you get drafted that the Cardinals are the team that's going to pick you up. Why, you may wind up playing for the Cubs!"

"The Cubs!" blurted out Harley. "Don't say that! The Cubs are St. Louis's bitter rivals."

Rich laughed. "So, you're saying that you'd turn down an offer from the Cubs?"

"Of course not. I'd just rather play for the Cardinals…or any other team than the Cubs."

Finishing his eggs, Harley gave his last bite of bacon to Ozzie who sat patiently by his chair. "I understand why you're so set on me going to college, but don't you think if I was good enough to be picked up by a major league team right out of high school, that they'd pay me pretty well."

"I'm sure they would," said Rich, "but that's not the point. What happens if you get injured and your career is cut short? You could wind being another sad statistic of being another, so to speak, uneducated athlete according to the business world. You're going to college and there's no discussion or objection that you could possibly come up with that will change the minds of your mother or myself. I know that we on many an occasion have talked about how baseball is about life. The opposite of that is that life, to most people is not about baseball. Life can be a bumpy, rough road and those who prepare themselves find that the road of life is easier to follow."

"Listen," said Monica. "We need to get this day moving. Harley, you need to get changed and ready to leave. Your appointment is at eight. Your dad will be dropping Ozzie off at the vet's office for his checkup and then he will spend the day at the shop with your father."

Rinsing off his plate, Rich commented, "And tonight when

Ozzie and I get home we expect to see you Harley without that cast on your arm."

Snapping her fingers, Monica interjected, "One more thing I forgot to mention. When I was out early this morning watering the plants in the front yard Mable walked across the street and informed me that the Scotts are moving in later today."

Walking his dish to the sink, Harley repeated, "The Scotts?"

"Yes, the Scotts. Remember when your father told you that a new family had bought the Spears' place."

"Yeah, I do remember that conversation. I think Dad said they are from Texas."

Rich, looking at his watch, remarked, "Actually, Dallas."

"Anyway," said Monica. "I think that this afternoon I'm going to bake one of my famous pineapple upside down cakes and then we can walk it up the street and welcome them to the neighborhood."

Harley, standing in the kitchen doorway, asked, "I don't have to go, do I?"

"Of course, you have to come along. You're part of our family."

"But that seems like such an adult thing to do."

"Well, nonetheless, you're coming along. That's what neighbors do."

"I don't remember anyone coming to welcome us to the neighborhood when we moved in."

Rich laughed. "The reason you don't remember is because when we moved here you were not even two years old yet. Mable brought us an apple pie and the Bluffton's up the street stopped by to welcome us. Your mother is right. You are coming along tonight. They have two children that are about your age. How would you feel if we moved to another state and you had to leave all your friends behind? Wouldn't you appreciate meeting someone your own age, maybe make a new friend."

Comically, Harley threw his hands in the air. "Once again, when your parents agree on something, as a kid, you lose the argument. I guess I'll be going along to meet the Scotts." Smiling, he saluted his parents, turned and walked down the hall to his room, speaking back over his shoulder, "I'll be ready to go to the doctor's office in a few minutes."

Walking across a paved downtown parking lot, Harley looked at the Northwest corner of Busch Stadium two blocks up the street and remarked, "We haven't been to a Cards game since I broke my arm."

Stopping at a crossing, Monica smiled and placed her arm around Harley. "I didn't tell you this, but I think your father has tickets for the third game of the series, which is two days from now. He wanted it to be a surprise so don't say anything about how we talked about the game."

The light changed and they started across as Harley answered, "Don't worry, Mom; I'll act surprised. Maybe I'll go down to the bullpen and see if Jim is around."

"I think Jim would like that."

One block later they climbed a set of concrete steps and entered a downtown office complex housing a number of local physicians. Getting on the elevator they got off on the third floor and entered the second door on the left: *Dr. Raymond Skimmer.*

Approaching the front desk, a receptionist looked up, noticing Harley and his mother. "Good morning, Harley." Looking down at her appointment pad, she remarked, "Let's see, your appointment is for nine o'clock. You're a little early, which normally would be good, but the doctor is running about a half hour behind. I hope that won't be a problem."

Monica pulled out a chair and sat as she looked around the room at three other patients who were waiting to see Dr. Skimmer. Patting the seat next to her she silently offered Harley the seat.

Harley stuck a piece of gum inside his mouth and waved her offer off as he stated, "If it's all right I'm just going to walk down the hallway here and look at Dr. Skimmer's collection of Cardinal Championship Pennants and photographs. It's one of the best past Cardinal history collections in town."

Entering the mahogany paneled hallway that led back to three patients waiting rooms, Harley stopped and marveled at the two walls of pennants, photographs and plaques, many which were autographed by Cardinals players. On the left hand wall, he admired Cardinal players whose number had been retired: Stan Musial, #10, Ken Boyer, #14, Dizzy Dean, #17 and further down the wall there was Lou Brock, #20 and Bob Gibson, #45. At the end of the hall there were photographs of Cardinal Hall of Famers:

Steve Carlton, Johnny Mize, Hoyt Wilhelm and on and on.

Smiling, Harley backtracked up the opposite wall as he looked at the past Cardinal World Series Pennants. The first one back in 1926 and the most recent being in 1982. Next came the twelve National League Pennants the Cardinals had won. For the next half hour Harley stood in the hall and read statistics and memories of the famous names and dates. He was engrossed in reading about Miller Huggins, past Cardinal manager when he was interrupted by his mother's voice: "Harley...we're up!"

Following her down the hall to the last door on the left, they entered only to be confronted by Doctor Skimmer who was his old enthusiastic self. "Well, hello there Harley. I bet you've been waiting for this day for weeks. Just hop up there on the end of the table and we'll get that cast off and have a look see."

Climbing up on the table, Harley gazed around the walls that were tastefully decorated with framed photographs of American and National League ballparks. Looking at the pictures in awe, he named off all the stadiums; Camden Yards, Fenway Park, Yankee Stadium and right around the room without missing a beat until he came to the last picture, which he proudly identified, "Busch Stadium."

Doctor Skimmer smiled at Harley's mother and commented, "It's always a pleasure when you bring Harley by. I always learn something new about the Cardinals." Turning back to Harley the doctor stated, "My receptionist told me that you were waiting out in the hall, taking in my collection of Cardinal baseball plagues and pennants. So, tell me. Who is your favorite Cardinal player...ever?"

"That's easy," exclaimed Harley. "Stan, The Man Musial; the greatest and most popular Cardinal player in history. He played on three different World Series Championship teams: 1942, '44 and '46. He played in twenty-four All Star games. I also like Ken Boyer. He was the league MVP back in 1964 and the only Cardinal player to hit for the cycle twice..."

Monica, waiting patiently for her son to take a breath interrupted, "I'm sure Doctor Skimmer would like to talk baseball with you all afternoon but I know he has other patients waiting. Let's see about getting that cast off your arm."

"I agree," said the doctor. "Let me explain the process while we proceed. It's actually quite painless. First, we remove this sling." Removing the cloth sling, he laid it to the side as he examined the cast. Next, he reached for a handheld miniature saw that reminded Harley of a smaller version of the circular saw hanging on the wall of their garage. The doctor held up the tiny saw and pressed the ON switch, which was followed by an immediate low buzzing sound. It reminded Harley of being at the Dentist office. Turning the saw to the Off position, the doctor explained, "This tool is designed to cut just the surface of the cast. Don't worry, it cannot cut deep enough to reach the skin. After I run this the length of the cast, then I'll use a pair of surgical scissors to cut the cast loose. The only thing you'll feel will be a slight pressure. If you feel any pain whatsoever, just let me know and I'll stop the procedure. Are you ready?"

"Guess so," answered Harley.

Doc Skimmer turned on the saw and putting his young patient at ease asked a question as he began to cut. "I know you've read my walls of past Cardinal history, but tell me, did you learn anything new while you were out there waiting?"

Harley responded immediately, "Yes, I did. I never thought about it before but the last time the Cardinals played in the World Series and won was back in 1982. They played on two other National League playoffs, but lost both in '85 and then again in '87. The series in '85 was won by Kansas City in seven games. The interesting part I never knew before was that the series was known as the I-71 Showdown because both teams were from Missouri. The other thing I didn't know about the '87 series was that one of the games was the 500th World Series game that was played."

Before Harley realized it, the cast had been sawn and cut from his arm. Doctor Skimmer laid the severed cast on a nearby table and examined Harley's bare arm. "There, now that wasn't all that bad...right?"

Harley looked down at his arm and rather than answering the doctor, asked a serious question of his own. "My arm looks like it shrunk! It's smaller than my other arm. Please don't tell me that my arm will be that size for the rest of my life!"

The doctor laughed, "No, you're arm will return to its normal size. What you are witnessing is what we refer to as Atrophy. The type of Atrophy you have is caused from decreased activity, which leads to a lack of muscle tone. This can easily be resolved with exercise and nutrition. Let's try some movement." Guiding Harley's arm in a slow upward movement, then in a downward fashion, the doctor asked, "How'd that feel?"

Harley looked at his mother and answered, "Kind of weird."

"Did you feel any pain?"

"Just a little, but it's not anything I can't deal with."

"Your arm looks fine. I'm going to give you a pictured list of exercises that I want you to perform twice daily for the next two weeks." Addressing Monica, he went on to explain, "Make sure Harley gets plenty of protein and calcium in his diet. I want to see him back here in two weeks, In the meantime, maybe a week from now, he needs to start lifting some light weight, no more than two to three pounds to start out."

Harley perked up. "We have a set of weights out in our garage. Can I use those?"

"That would be perfect, but no more than three pounds until I say different. Depending on how things go you should be back to normal long before the tryouts for Little League next year. I'm going to expect to see you pitching on a team by then so it's important that you follow my recovery instructions to the letter. Understand?"

Harley nodded his head in agreement and hopped down for the table. "See you in two weeks, Doc!"

Outside, walking down the sidewalk, Monica asked Harley, "How's the arm feel?"

Moving his arm slowly up and down, he answered, "It feels kind of strange to move it, but I think it's going to be fine. I can't wait to get home and start lifting weights."

Monica reminded him, "Remember what the doctor said? I can understand that you're anxious to get started on the road to recovery, but I think you just need to take it easy for the rest of the week. We can get started on those weights next week."

CHAPTER 5

TOTING THE PINEAPPLE UPSIDE-DOWN CAKE, HARLEY followed Monica and Rich up the paved road and stopped at the Scotts' place. Wiping her feet on a brown WELCOME mat, Monica rang the doorbell and waited patiently. After a few seconds when no one answered, Harley suggested, "Looks like no one is home. I say we go back home and eat this cake ourselves."

Monica was about to respond to her son when the door suddenly opened and a tall woman with long black hair fashioned in a ponytail greeted the trio of neighbors. "Why, hello there. You must be our new neighbors. My name is Nancy Scott."

Monica smiled and answered, "We're the Sims. We live three houses up the street." Turning, she introduced the rest of the family, "This is my husband, Rich and our son, Harley. We thought we'd bring you a treat to welcome you to the neighborhood."

Mrs. Scott was apologetic as she glanced back inside the house. "Please come in. I'm afraid the house is a mess. We've got boxes stacked everywhere."

Rich and Harley followed Monica and stood humbly to the side while the two wives continued their conversation. "I'd offer you a place to sit but the couch and chairs are full of boxes." Snapping her fingers, Mrs. Scott remembered, "I have some folding chairs in the kitchen. Just let me grab them and we can be seated. I need a break anyway."

Monica took the cake from Harley and suggested, "Here, let Harley give you a hand." Harley, not the most sociable person, unless the subject of baseball was being discussed, rolled his eyes at his mother and reluctantly followed Mrs. Scott to the kitchen, where she handed him two grey, padded chairs. Carrying four chairs herself; she followed Harley back to the spacious living room. "My husband and two children are out on some errands right now. They should be back any minute."

Holding up the cake, Monica asked, "Where would you like me to put this?"

"Why don't we take it out to the kitchen? I'll put on a pot of coffee. When my husband gets back we can enjoy some cake with coffee and get acquainted."

Monica looked back over her shoulder at her family and winked, "Sounds like a plan."

Seating himself in one of the folding chairs, Harley looked around the cluttered room and asked his father, "I really didn't get much of a choice in coming along on this visit, but please tell me I don't have to drink coffee when we eat the cake?"

Rich laughed, reassuring his son. "I'm sure Mrs. Scott will have something other than coffee you can drink."

Monica and Nancy returned to the living room and took seats while Mrs. Scott spoke, "A lady by the name of Mable dropped by early this morning with an apple pie. She seemed nice."

"Mable is nice," said Monica, "but she can be a bit of a busy body."

Nancy laughed and responded, "Well, I suppose every neighborhood has a Mable." Hearing voices in the rear of the house, she held up her index finger. "That must be my husband and the kids." Raising her voice, she summoned the rest of her family, "Don, we have visitors from up the street."

Within seconds, a slender man who was even taller than his wife stood by two children when they entered the living room. The man immediately walked across the room and shook both Monica and Rich's hand and commented, "Nice to meet you folks."

Mrs. Scott stood and introduced her children, placing her hand on each child. "This is my oldest, Drew. He just turned ten. And this is his sister, Roxann, who is six." She then introduced the Sims and then gently suggested to her husband. "Don, we need one more chair from the kitchen brought in. Monica brought us a cake and I have some coffee brewing. I thought we could take a break and just relax for a bit."

After bringing in another chair, Don sat and laid a bag he was carrying on top of some boxes. Crossing his legs he asked, "So, tell me Rich, what do you do for a living?"

Rich gestured with a wave of his hand. "I own a small motorcycle repair shop over in Imperial. I've always had a passion for bikes so, after I graduated from high school, I started to repair bikes in an old garage I rented. It just kind of went from there. I've been there for close to fifteen years now."

Don continued the conversation as he asked Monica. "Do you ride motorcycles as well?"

"Only on the back of one of my husband's bikes. I've never gotten up the nerve to try and ride myself."

Pushing long locks of red hair from her daughter's face, Nancy asked, "Are you a stay at home Mom or do you work outside the house?"

"I'm a registered nurse at a hospital in Fenton, which is just up the road a few miles."

Rich jumped in on the conversation as he addressed Don. "The word around the neighborhood is that you got transferred to the St. Louis area by the company you work for."

Don smiled. "That's correct. I work for a company that I have no doubt you are familiar with; Anheuser Busch. I'm in data processing. They brought me up here to set up and run a new wing of our computer center." Nodding at Nancy, he further explained, "My wife is a homemaker; a full time job to say the least."

Looking at the St. Louis Cardinal jerseys Rich and Harley were wearing, he smiled and reached for the bag he had previously laid to the side. Opening the sack he removed a Cardinal hat and jersey. "I had to drop by my new office today and the staff there gave me these articles and told me if I was going to live and work in the St. Louis area it was imperative I become a Cardinals fan. Ya know, it's rather funny. When we lived in Dallas, it was and still is to this day a football town. It's all about the Dallas Cowboys. Down that way, it seems wherever you go in or around Dallas you see folks sporting Dallas football jerseys and hats. I had always heard St. Louis was a big baseball town. Growing up in Dallas as a kid you just kind of grow up rooting for the Cowboys. I guess it's the same here, but rather than football, it's seems that the St. Louis Cardinals have captured the interest of local sport fans."

"You hit the nail right on the head," remarked Rich. "Aside from the New York Yankees, I'd say St. Louis is the second most popular team in the nation."

Harley added, "The Yankees are not all that popular around here, Dad. This is pure Cardinal country. We have the St. Louis

Rams and also the Blues, but the Cardinals have the biggest fan base."

Mr. Scott placed the hat and jersey back in the sack and spoke to Harley. "I take it you're a big Cardinal fan?"

Monica answered the question. "Our son is far more than just a Cardinal fan. He is a baseball fan of great magnitude. He plays on a team; actually, he's been playing since he was three years old. Fair warning: don't get into a conversation with Harley about baseball. He'll talk your ears off with facts and figures."

"Well then, it must be your son's lucky day," announced Mr. Scott as he reached into his pocket and withdrew four St. Louis Cardinal tickets. "As a new middle management employee of Busch, I was informed I have access to season box seats. Seeing as how my family, at least for the moment are not big baseball fans, whenever there is a home game, Harley, you and your family are welcome to use these box seats."

Monica objected, "We couldn't do that. Those box seats were given to you and your family. We wouldn't feel right."

"Nonsense," said Mr. Scott. "We couldn't use these tickets this year if we wanted to. There are only a couple of months of the season left and they tell me I'm going to be really busy at work until Thanksgiving. If you do not use the tickets they may just go to waste. It would be my pleasure if you would at least go to a few games."

Looking at his mother in shock, Harley held out his hands almost in a pleading fashion. Monica relented and agreed. "Well, I guess we could go to a few games thanks to the generosity of Busch."

Mr. Scott stood, walked across the room and handed the four tickets to Harley. "These tickets are for a three game home stand with the Cubs starting tomorrow night. I hope you'll be able to go."

Harley turned to Rich and with great excitement, added, "Mom already told me at the doctor's office this morning about how you were going to surprise me by going to see the Cubs play the Cardinals. Now, we have free tickets...and box seats at that. Can we go Dad...please?"

Looking at Monica, Rich responded, "I don't see us having any other choice but to honor Don's request. So, tomorrow night we'll watch the Cards take on the Cubs."

Mrs. Scott got up, gesturing toward the kitchen. "That coffee should just about be ready."

Monica, commenting, got up and joined Nancy. "I'll cut the cake."

Don, rubbing his hands together looked at Drew. "How about some cake?"

Drew smiled. "Okay"

Roxann trailed the women into the kitchen, when Harley spoke up, "So, Mr. Scott, you said that Dallas was a football town. I don't know all that much about football. I have heard of the Dallas Cowboys and I'm not sure if there are any other professional football teams in Texas, but I do know there are two major league baseball teams in the Lone Star State: the Houston Astros in the National League and the Texas Rangers in the American. We've played the Astros twice so far this year." Pulling a rumpled Cardinals schedule from his pants pocket, he unfolded it and scanned the schedule. "Let's see, it looks like we play them again in August."

Smiling at Mr. Scott, Harley switched gears and started to talk about the American League. "The other Texas team; the Texas Rangers were, at one time, the Washington Senators from 1961 to 1971. Then in 1972 they moved down to Texas."

Monica, Mrs. Scott and Roxann entered the room carrying trays of coffee, plates, napkins and cut sections of cake. Rich tapped Harley on the shoulder. "I think Mr. Scott has had enough of a rundown on the history of Texas major league baseball. Let's eat!"

Don removed some boxes from a coffee table, while the girls placed the trays on the circular piece of furniture. Nancy motioned at the table and remarked, "Every man for himself. There's cream and sugar for the coffee and I've got some lemonade in the kitchen for the kids."

Drew walked to the table and grabbed a plate of cake and asked his mother. "Do you think it would be all right if Harley and I had our cake out on the back porch?"

"I don't see why not," came the answer, "That is, if it's okay with Harley's mother that he be allowed to go out back."

Pouring creamer into her coffee, Monica answered, "I'm sure the boys have a lot of things they can discuss. Harley, why don't you go with Drew?"

Sitting on the back steps leading down to the yard, Harley put his glass of lemonade on the top step and took a large bite of cake. Drew picked up his piece of cake and commented, "You sound like you know a lot about baseball."

"Well yeah, I guess I do," said Harley. "My Mom and Dad say I'm obsessed with the game. I practice every day out in my backyard. Someday I want to be a major league pitcher. I'd really like to pitch for the Cardinals. My folks keep telling me if I get to the majors as a pitcher that in itself would be quite an accomplishment. So, how about you, Drew? Did you play any ball down there in Dallas?"

"No, no baseball for me."

"That's right, your Dad said Dallas was a football town. So, I guess you play football then?"

"No, I don't play football either."

"Well then, what sport do you play? Soccer, Basketball, Ice hockey?"

"I don't play any sports at all."

Harley was just about to take a swig of lemonade when he hesitated and asked in amazement, "No sports at all! How can that be? Every kid plays some sort of sport."

"Not me," said Drew. "It's not that I don't want to play any sports; I just can't."

Harley took a drink and asked, "Why not?"

Drew smiled at his new friend and answered, "You see, I have a phobia."

Confused, Harley inquired, "Pho...bi...a. I don't know what that means."

"A phobia is a fear of doing something. There are all sorts of phobias. Some people have a fear of flying in an airplane; others, a fear of dogs or of even going outside of their house. I have a fear of any sort of ball or any type of hard, physical contact."

"I don't understand. How could you have a fear of any type of ball?"

"When I was three years old my parents and I were at a company picnic where my father worked. We were watching a softball game while sitting down the first base line. I got hit in the head with a line drive. I was in the hospital unconscious for three days. When I finally came around, the doctors discovered I had this phobia. So, that's why I can't play any sports. I'm really scared of getting hit with a ball or of getting hit by another player."

Trying his best to understand what he was being told, Harley responded, "So let me get this straight. You were not born with this phobia. It just kind of happened to you?"

"That's right. The doctors say as I grow older I may grow out of it or I may have to feel like this for the rest of my life."

Taking another bite of cake, Harley stated in disbelief, "I can't imagine not being able to play baseball. Baseball is such a part of my life. I live, eat and sleep baseball. To tell you the truth, I can't imagine life without baseball. I've been practicing every day of my life since I've been three. If I didn't have baseball in my life, why I don't know what I'd do."

"Now you sound like my parents. When I turned five they noticed how I was moping around and they told me since I couldn't play sports I needed to have a hobby. My grandfather had always been a stamp collector and I was always amazed at his collection, so I started to collect stamps. I've only been collecting stamps for five years but I have hundreds of different stamps. I have stamps of different cities and countries and of famous people. I even have three baseball stamps. I don't know much about baseball but I know what my three baseball stamps are about. I have a 1911 Miller Huggins stamp. He was a star second baseman for the Cardinals and then he was a manager for the New York Yankees. I also have a 1909 stamp of Rube Waddle who played for the St. Louis Browns. The other baseball stamp I have is Mordecai "Three fingers" Brown. It's a 1911 stamp. He played for the Chicago Cubs. I also took up playing the piano at the age of five. I've won a few musical contests. My folks say if I keep practicing I may be able to get a music scholarship to college. *And,* by the end of this year I should have my green belt in karate…"

Interrupting Drew, Harley held up his right hand, "Whoa…whoa…whoa! How can you possibly collect stamps, play the piano and take karate lessons all at the same time?"

"My mother says I'm well rounded. The stamp collecting was all my idea. She suggested I try a few piano lessons and I liked it, so I just kept playing. Now, the karate thing, well that was my father's idea. He felt I needed to learn how to protect myself. So, for the last four years I've been taking lessons…"

Harley interrupted Drew once again and asked, "This karate that you practice. Is it like those Kung Fu movies on TV?"

"No, it's nothing like that. That's all acting. This is the real thing."

"But I thought you said you were afraid of any physical contact."

"The karate I take is only close or light contact. We are trained very well. No one ever gets hurt. And, besides that it's not just about being able to defend yourself. The training they give you teaches you discipline, patience, self-control and a high level of confidence. There are ten different levels before I can get to the black belt level."

Harley, quite interested asked, "Black belt. What does that mean?"

"It's the highest level of karate there is. I already have my yellow belt and by the end of the year I'll probably have the green."

"So, when do you get to the level where you can beat the crap of out of someone?"

"You're never taught to beat the crap out of people. When you get to a certain level of black belt, your hands are referred to as lethal weapons, so if you start beating up on people you could really get in trouble."

"Then, what's the point?"

"I guess knowing that eventually I'll be able to defend myself if it ever comes down to it."

Harley laughed and shook his head. "A few weeks back I wish I would have known some karate."

"Why's that?"

"A local bully by the name of Aaron Buckman took my new Cardinal hat and ten dollars from me. At the time, my right arm was broken. He and two of his cousins threatened to break my other arm if I said anything. Maybe you could show me a few moves."

"This Aaron kid. He lives around here?"

"He lives on the other side of town and goes to a different school. All the kids around here are afraid of him. I don't run into him much. Well, that is until next spring when I try out for the ten to twelve-year-old Little League. He's two years older than me. I'll be playing against him, or I might wind up on the same team he's on. He's really a good ballplayer. A lot of people in the area think I'm the best baseball player in my age bracket. Aaron doesn't like that. He thinks he's the best."

"Is he better than you, I mean at playing baseball?"

"He's a better fielder than me and he can hit better, but when it comes to pitching, I have better control."

"Getting off the subject of Aaron Buckman, Drew asked, "How often do you practice baseball?"

"I practice every day, rain or shine. Well, I take that back. There have been a few days now and then when I was too sick, but other than that…every day." Holding up his right arm, Harley corrected himself. "I haven't been able to practice for the past two months. I broke my right arm at a Cardinals game. I just got the cast removed this morning. I'm really looking forward to getting back to my practice routine."

"I know what you mean. It's the same thing with the piano. I have to spend an hour every day at the keyboard if I want to keep getting better."

Finishing off the cake, Drew washed the last bite down with a swallow of lemonade then asked, "Is baseball the only hobby or interest you have?"

Harley chuckled. "I do have a hobby. I collect baseball cards. I have some really old cards from the forties my grandfather gave me. I have the complete sets from this year, 1995, all the way back to 1987. For Christmas every year, my parents always get me the set for the past year. Whenever I get birthday money, I save it up and go to a local baseball card shop and buy older player cards. Maybe you could come down to my house sometime and see my collection."

"That'd be great and I can bring along my stamp collection for you to see."

"That sounds neat. I could take a look at those baseball player stamps you told me about."

Mrs. Scott interrupted their conversation when both mothers walked onto the screened-in back porch, "Drew, you and your new friend have to wrap things up in the next couple of minutes.

Harley's mother said they have to get back down to their house. Harley's father asked if you would like to go along to the Cardinals game tomorrow night. Why don't you and Harley work that out?"

Harley was beaming as Monica and Nancy headed back inside the house. "It'd be great if you'd go along. Your first St. Louis Cardinals game. I was only six months old when my parents took me to my first game."

Drew seemed hesitant. "I don't know. I don't know anything about baseball. How any players there are, how the scoring works. I don't know if I would enjoy myself."

"Are you kidding me? Going to a Cardinal game is a blast. I'll teach you everything you need to know as the game goes along. You'll catch on in no time. Besides that, the Cards will be playing the Cubs; our enemy!"

Drew frowned and asked, "How can this Cubs team be your enemy. It's just a game...right?"

"Well," said Harley, "they're not an enemy like a soldier from some other country like in the movies. It's just a polite way of saying that we as Cardinal fans don't like the Cubs. Actually, there are two teams from Chicago: The Cubs and the White Sox."

"If these teams are both from Chicago then these White Sox must be an enemy also."

"No, the White Sox are okay. They play in the American League. The Cards play in the National League. It's pretty rare that we would ever get to play the White Sox. Normally, the only way that would happen is if we were both in the World Series at the end of the season."

"Have the Cardinals ever won the World Series?"

"Yes, they have. They won the World Series title nine different times. The Cubs and the White Sox are not even close to what the Cardinals have accomplished. The Cubs have won the title twice, way back in 1907 and 1908. It's been 87 years since they have won the series. The White sox are no better, also winning two titles: 1906 and 1917. They haven't won baseball's greatest title in 78 years. It's only been eight years since the Cards held the title."

Standing, Harley asked, "Well what do you think? Would you like to go with my family? Besides watching the game, we get to eat hotdogs and peanuts and drink sodas. It'll be a great night at the park."

Drew stood and answered, "I'm not really good at making decisions without thinking things over. I'll have to think about this. It might be a problem for me. It's hard for me to watch other people play sports because I know it's something I'll never be able to do. If I do decide to go what time will we leave for the game?"

Opening the screen door, Harley answered, "The night games normally start around seven fifteen to seven thirty, so if you're planning on going along you need to be at my house no later than six. We like to get there early so we can watch the players warm up. Tell you what. If you show up by six, then we'll head downtown. If you don't show up, then we'll go on by ourselves. Fair enough."

"Sounds fair," agreed Drew.

Walking down the front walk of the Scotts' house, Monica asked Harley, "How did you get along with your new friend?"

Harley, carrying the empty cake pan looked at his mother in amazement. "I wouldn't exactly call him my new friend. We just met and we didn't even talk for an hour."

"All right then. Let me rephrase my question. How did you get along with Drew?"

Stepping onto the paved road, Harley responded with an unusual answer, "He seemed nice, but more than that, he said he was well rounded; at least that's what he said his mother said about him. When he first walked into the room with his father I thought he appeared odd, like some of the kids I go to school with; you know, the nerd type. But, after talking with him I realized how talented he is. I've never met a kid with so many different interests, and he's good at all of them. Did you know he doesn't play any sports?"

"Yes, his mother explained to us about his phobia. She told us her son is very intelligent and picks things up quickly."

Shaking his head in wonder, Harley agreed, "I can't imagine doing all of the things he does. He collects stamps, plays the piano and holds a yellow belt in karate. He even knows a few things about baseball I don't! I feel kind of stupid. I don't know a thing about stamps aside from the fact that you need one to mail a letter. I don't know anything about the piano or even karate."

Rich broke in on the conversation. "Did he say he's going to the game with us tomorrow night?"

"He said he was going to think it over."

Approaching their house, Ozzie ran back and forth, barking next to the fence. Rich smiled. "I'm glad things are getting back to normal around here. Ol' Ozzie is healthy as an ox according to the vet and you no longer have your cast. I guess in a couple of weeks you can get back to some serious backyard practice. Spring is a few months off, but before you know it, it'll be time for the ten to twelve-year-old tryouts. I think you have some great years of pitching ahead of you in Little League."

CHAPTER 6

RUNNING DOWN THE STAIRS, WITH OZZIE CLOSE BEHIND, Harley heard the buzzing sound of the doorbell. Shouting to his mother, who was in the kitchen, he announced with certainty, "I bet you anything that's Drew." Yanking open the front door, it was no surprise when Harley saw Drew standing there in khaki shorts, brown deck shoes and a bright red T-shirt.

Looking down at his wristwatch, Drew stated, "Six o'clock on the nose." Picking up the edge of the shirt, he shrugged his shoulders. "I wanted to fit in so I thought maybe if I wore something red I might look like a real Cardinal fan."

Overhearing Drew's heartfelt comment, Harley's mother who was now in the front room, suggested, "Why don't you lend Drew one of your Cardinal shirts? It's not like you don't have enough."

Agreeing with his mother, Harley motioned toward the stairs. "C'mon up to my room and I'll get you that shirt." Both boys raced up the steps, Ozzie at their heels.

Entering Harley's room, Drew stood and looked around the ten-by-twelve foot decorated cubical in awe. "You really are a fan. There isn't a spot left on the walls for one more pennant or picture." Sitting on the edge of the bed, he ran his hand over the worn bedspread. "You even have a Cardinal bed cover."

Rummaging through one of his dresser drawers, Harley held up a Cardinals shirt that looked like it was brand new. "Here, try this on for size."

Drew quickly stripped off his T-shirt and slid the shirt over his head, then held out his hands, displaying himself. Nodding in approval, Harley smiled, "A little big, but it looks just fine."

Rich's voice sounded up the stairwell as he joked, "C'mon boys! We leave in two minutes!"

Ozzie who had positioned himself smack dab in the middle of the bed sat up and held out his right paw.

Amazed, Drew asked, "What's with him?"

"He knows when we leave the house he gets one of his treats." Opening a large glass jar on top of the dresser, Harley grabbed one of the large size Milkbones and handed it to Ozzie who immediately took the treat, went to the top of the bed and curled up next to the pillows."

As Ozzie crunched into the canine dog treat, Harley tapped Drew on his shoulder, "C'mon, we better get downstairs."

Monica stood by the front door. "Dad is out front with the car...let's go!"

Hopping in the backseat, Drew reached in his pocket and removed a twenty-dollar bill, which he handed to Monica. "I took this money out of an old cigar box I keep in my room. If we get something later on to eat you can use that to feed me."

Monica handed the money back and answered, "Keep your money, Drew. We're paying for everything tonight."

Folding up the bill, Drew quickly strapped himself in while asking Harley, "What kind of food do they have at the stadium?"

"You wouldn't believe it," said Harley. "You can get anything from a hotdog to a steak dinner. Hotdogs are my favorite. There's just something about the way they make them at the ballpark. I always get a bag of peanuts and a large drink. You can get nachos, or burgers or tacos."

Sitting back in the seat, Drew asked, "How long has the stadium been here in St. Louis?"

Monica looked across the seat at Rich and comically rolled her eyes as she smiled, realizing Drew was in for a long conversation.

Moving sideways so he was facing Drew, Harley began, "Well, the first ballpark the Cardinals played in was called Sportsman's Park. They played there from 1953 until 1966 when Busch Memorial Stadium was built..."

Twenty-five minutes later, Rich pulled into a downtown parking lot, two blocks from the stadium. "Okay gentlemen, we have arrived." Turning in the seat he handed the boys their tickets and addressed Drew. "From here it's about a five minute walk."

Getting out of the car, Drew looked at the surrounding tall buildings. "This reminds me of downtown Dallas."

Monica, stepping out of the car added, "I was in Dallas my senior year of high school. Our girl's fast pitch softball team had to travel down there for a tournament."

Starting up the sidewalk, Drew asked in a curious fashion, "Is softball different than baseball?"

Harley was quick to respond. "The basic rules are the same but the pitcher throws the ball underhanded rather than overhanded, plus a softball is larger than a regulation baseball."

"So, you play softball as well as baseball?"

"No, not really. Out in our backyard from time to time my mom gets her old glove out and pitches to my dad and me. She can still throw the ball up around ninety miles an hour."

Turning to Monica, Drew asked, "Do you still play on a team?"

"No, not anymore. I just like to get out in the backyard once in a while and show the boys here that I can still bring the heat."

"Bring the heat…what does that mean?"

Harley, once again was quick with an answer. "That's a baseball term that means my mom can really throw fast."

Drew thought for a moment, then asked, "If I remember right, when we were out on my back porch yesterday you said you wanted to pitch for the Cardinals. How fast can you throw a baseball?"

Proudly, Harley answered, "Well, right now I'm only up to about sixty miles an hour, but by the end of next year I hope to be up around seventy."

"Is that good for someone our age?"

Rich chimed in, "Better than average. If Harley keeps practicing he could be throwing in the high eighties by the time he gets to high school."

"How fast do you want to throw," probed Drew?

Harley tapped his right arm and answered, "If the old arm holds out I plan to throw close to one hundred miles an hour when I get to the major leagues."

Stopping for traffic at the street in front of the main entrance to the stadium, Drew looked around in amazement at all the people coming from every direction and filing into the main gates. Turning in a circle, he raised his hands and remarked, "This reminds of going to church back in Dallas."

Rich gave Monica a strange look as he asked, "What do you mean, Drew?"

"On Sunday mornings back home in Texas it was just like this. We went to a church on the other side of town. Folks came from every direction; women wearing their Sunday best, the men all dressed up in suits. This stadium reminds me of that church. We had over ten thousand members and every Sunday they would come to worship God. Just look at all these people, wearing Cardinal red. It's almost like they are coming to worship the Cardinals."

Rich laughed as they started across the street. "I've never heard Cardinal fans described in quite that fashion before, but when you think about it you might not be too far off the mark. We do hold them in high esteem."

On the other side of the street, Monica got her ticket out and spoke, "Get your tickets ready boys. We're getting ready to go in."

After passing through the turn style Rich guided Monica and the boys off to the side. "The first thing we need to do is locate our seats and get settled in. After that I'll get a couple of beers for Monica and myself. If you're interested, Drew, Harley can then give you the grand tour. We've got over an hour before the game gets started."

Looking around in total awe, Drew asked, "This place is so large. What if we get lost?"

Monica reassured Drew. "With Harley as your official guide, I guarantee, you won't get lost. He knows this stadium like the back of his hand. Let's get to our seats."

Walking down the concrete steps into the box seats area on the third base side, Rich pointed at the field and commented, "These are great seats. A lot of foul balls are hit down this way. Maybe we can snatch one tonight."

Following Monica and Rich down the steps, Drew asked, "What's a foul ball?"

Pointing at home plate, Harley supplied the answer. "See those white lines running down both sides of the field. If the ball is hit outside of those lines that's called a foul ball and sometimes the ball can go into the stands or roll close enough for a fan to grab it."

Looking at the field, Drew asked, "Did you ever get a foul ball?"

"No, but the last time I was here I caught a homerun ball and wound up breaking my arm. C'mon, let's head up to the top deck. Drew ran up the steps and followed Harley who stopped and leaned on the metal railing. Pointing out at the field, he explained,

"See that dirt area out there. That's what we call the infield. There are four bases; first, second, third and home plate. The team who is on the field has to supply four infielders, a pitcher and a catcher. The infielders are called the first baseman, the second baseman, the shortstop and the third baseman. I'll tell you how all that works when the game starts. It'll be easier to explain that way."

Dodging their way in and out of the growing crowd they made their way up to the next level. Walking down to the last row of seats, Harley pointed at the outfield grass and explained, "That large grass covered area is what they call the outfield. Over there, that's called left field, just below is center field and then on the other side is right field. From home plate to the left and right field fence is 330'. In center field it's 402'. There are three players who are positioned around the outfield. Once again, when the game starts, I'll tell you what they do." Holding his arms out, Harley went on, "This stadium can seat over fifty thousand fans. The average attendance is normally around thirty thousand or so but because we're going up against the Cubs tonight, it could be a packed house. Let's go up to the top level."

Minutes later, Harley and Drew were seated on the top level in two of the highest seats. Drew looked down over the stadium when a number of players emerged onto the field and started the routine of warming up: wind sprints, sit ups, stretching exercises. Drew, not understanding, spoke up. "It looks like the game has started."

Harley laughed. "No, the game hasn't started. The players are just getting warmed up. This is a good thing to do. It can prevent you from getting injured."

Gesturing down at the infield, Drew inquired, "Who are those men dressed in red and brown?"

"Oh, that's the grounds crew. They are responsible for keeping the field in good condition. You see, if the field isn't maintained properly when the ball is hit it can take an odd bounce and make it hard to field. The playing surface has to be as perfect as possible. That means the grass is mowed to a special height every week. Before every game the grounds crew has to rake the infield dirt, chalk down the foul lines and the batter's box and wet down the infield to cut down on dust. There's quite a bit that goes into preparing for a game. Like the actual baseballs. The home team, in this instance, the Cards have to supply about one hundred and twenty brand new balls for the game. When they first get the balls they have a sheen on the outside. This sheen makes it hard for the players, especially the pitcher, to grip the ball so before each game the head umpire has to rub down the balls with a baseball rubbing mud. They say the only place you can get this mud is on the New Jersey side of the banks of the Delaware River. In the old days before they discovered the rubbing mud they used to use tobacco juice, shoe polish or even soil from beneath the bleachers. But now, the baseball rubbing mud is very fine, almost like a thick chocolate pudding." Searching the box seats along the third base line, Harley pointed out, "Our seats are just past the home team's dugout. We better get back down there. They'll be throwing the first pitch before we know it."

Back down on the second level, they were confronted by a mob of people going in every direction. Leading Drew to the side of the wide aisle, Harley pointed at a row of trashcans. "C'mon, I know a short cut. With this crowd we'll never make it back to our seats in time."

Following Harley through the throng of fans they finally arrived at a door with a sign that stated: EMPLOYEES ONLY. Drew stopped Harley as he reached to push the door open. "That sign says we can't go in there. We're not employees."

"I know that. There are a bunch of doorways in the stadium where fans aren't allowed to go. In my years of snooping around this place I've discovered most of them. Behind this door there's a long corridor that cuts in behind the concession stands. We can get to the other side of the stadium quicker if we cut through here."

"But what if someone sees us?"

"Most of the employees back here are vendors. I've cut through here lots of times and no one has ever stopped me. C'mon, let's go."

Harley pushed open the door and Drew followed as they entered a narrow cinderblock aisle. No one paid them any attention as they walked swiftly down the long corridor. Harley turned and remarked, "We're almost at the end. Just up ahead we take a right then go through another door and we find ourselves headed for the opposite side of the stadium."

Turning the corner they came face to face with three other people. Harley stopped and remained frozen as he stared into the face of Aaron Buckman and his two cousins.

Aaron dropped a cigarette butt to the concrete floor and stomped it out with his untied boot. "Well, well, we meet again!" Looking at Drew, Aaron placed his hands on his hips and smirked, "Who's this you've got with ya, Sims?"

Harley, remained calm and answered, "This is Drew. He's my new friend. He just moved here from Texas."

"I thought everythin' in Texas was bigger!" Stepping close to Drew and looking down into his face, he looked the small boy over from head to toe. "If this is what they call big down in Texas I'd hate to see what small is!"

Harley started to reach for the door, but was prevented from doing so by one of the cousins. Rolling his eyes, Harley explained, "Look Aaron, we don't want any trouble. We just want to go back to our seats and watch the game."

"Sure, you can go back to your seats, but first we have some business."

Backing away from the two cousins, Harley asked, "What business?"

Looking at his cousins, Aaron laughed in a cocky fashion and removed a Cardinal hat he was wearing. "This hat should look familiar to ya. Remember when I traded hats with ya over at the Little League State Championship Tournament. I'm ready to get my old hat back, but I see you're not wearin' it. Looks like you've got another new hat. Where's my old hat?"

Trying to stay on the good side of Aaron, Harley answered, "I left it over at the field that day."

"So, what you're sayin' is my hat wasn't good enough for ya to wear?"

Stepping close to Harley, Aaron reached out and touched Harley's right arm. "I see the cast is gone." Looking at Drew, Aaron went on, "Did your new friend here tell you how stupid he is. Did he tell you he actually fell over the fence right here at the stadium in front of thirty thousand people and broke his arm?"

Surprisingly, Drew spoke up. "Is this the Aaron kid you told me about, Harley? The one who took your hat and ten dollars from you?"

Before Harley could answer, Aaron stepped closer to Drew. "Well, I'll say this for ya. For a sawed off little runt ya sure are cocky. I don't know how things work down in Texas, but around here, smartin' off like that could get ya in trouble. Tell ya what! Why don't ya just stand to the side and keep your trap shut while Harley and I trade hats." Turning back to Harley, Aaron braced himself in a show of power. "Well, Harley what's it gonna be? You gonna hand the hat over or do I just take it from ya?"

Harley remained silent and remembered what his father said about how dangerous a kid like Aaron Buckman could be.

"Just like I thought," said Aaron. "Ya don't have the guts to fight me and you're too stupid to just hand your hat over." Aaron reached for Harley's hat but then Drew stepped in front of him, knocking his arm away. Harley, along with Aaron and his two cousins stared at each other in disbelief.

Aaron looked down at Drew and gritting his teeth, spoke slowly, "You've got to be kiddin' me! Maybe you don't realize it kid, but I could pound ya into a fine powder. Now get out of my way. I want that hat!"

Aaron reached for the hat once again, but Drew knocked Aaron's arm to the side. Before Aaron could react, Drew swept Aaron's right leg with his left and Buckman went down like a sack of potatoes. Within seconds, Drew was on top of him, his left elbow just touching the tip of Aaron's nose. Drew's right hand hovered just above his clenched left fist. Aaron, in shock, tried to get to his feet, but Drew hit his fist, forcing his elbow down hard on Aaron's nose. Aaron froze for a second as Drew went on to explain, "You move again and I'll drive your nose through the back of your head...understand?"

Aaron looked at his two cousins and ordered sternly, "Don't just stand there...do somethin'!"

Drew withdrew his elbow and quickly reached down and with his thumb and index finger twisted Aaron's nose to the side while he spoke to the cousins. "You make one move toward me and I'll twist his nose right off!" Without looking up at Harley, Drew asked, "Do you want this hat he took from you back?"

"No, he can keep it. Let's just get out of here!"

"You told me he took ten dollars from you...right?"

"Yeah, that's right."

Twisting Aaron's nose again, Drew asked politely, "Aaron, do you have any money on you?"

Aaron, through a strange, nasally voice answered, "Five dollars…that's all I have on me."

"What about your friends here. They have any money?"

Aaron didn't respond quickly enough as Drew twisted the nose further. "Do your friends have any money?"

Carefully reaching into his pocket, Aaron withdrew a five and laid it on the concrete floor while ordering his cousins. "Give them another five…now!"

One of the boys removed a wallet from his jeans, took out a five and handed it to Harley.

"Okay, Harley," said Drew. "Pick up the other five, go over and hold the door open. I'm going to let go of Aaron's nose and we're out of here."

Watching Harley open the door, Drew gave one last twist, rose to his feet and ran through the door as he yelled to Harley, "Run for your life!"

The last thing Harley saw was Aaron getting slowly to his feet as the metal door closed. Turning to follow Drew, he ran smack dab into a man who was coming out of a men's room. Harley apologized and ran in the direction Drew was running. Drew stopped next to a trashcan and looked back at the crowd when he saw Aaron and his two cousins pushing their way through. Suddenly, Aaron spotted Drew and Harley as he yelled, "There they are!"

Realizing that Drew was clueless where they were in relation to their seats, Harley motioned down the aisle, "C'mon, we have to lose them before we get back to our seats."

Running down the aisle, moving in and out between hundreds of fans, they rounded a corner when Harley quickly pulled Drew inside the door of a gift shop. Moving in behind a row of Cardinal shirts hanging in a front display window Harley peered through the apparel display. When Aaron and his cousins ran by the shop, Harley grabbed Drew and said, "We're going the other way. It'll take longer, but it'll be safer."

Stepping out into the aisle, Harley checked to make sure their pursuers were gone and commented, "What you did…that was amazing! That stuff you did to Aaron…is that what they teach you at karate?"

Drew kept looking back as he answered, "The arm and leg

sweeps were but that nose business is something I read in a book."

"A book...what kind of book?"

"When I first started my karate lessons I decided to read up on self-defense. I discovered there are a lot of ways to defend yourself, especially if you're not all that strong...like me! The book I read about twisting an opponent's nose was called: Basic Survival for Nerds. There were all kinds of neat stuff in there that you can use to defend yourself."

Harley stopped and leaned up against a wall. "Let's stop for a breather."

Checking back down the aisle to make sure they were not being followed, Harley smiled. "Well, book or no book, you sure put the whammy on ol' Aaron. He just laid there...helpless."

"We were lucky," said Drew. "One of the things they teach us in karate is that it's all about perception. If your opponent is convinced he is at a disadvantage, then you hold the upper hand. If Aaron wasn't so intimidated and would have pushed my hand away from his nose, he and his two friends would have beaten the crap out of us." Looking back down the aisle again, Drew asked, "Do you think this is the end of this?"

"I doubt it! Aaron Buckman has a reputation around the Arnold area as a tough kid. He's known as a local bully, but he can back up what he says. That's what makes him so dangerous. Aaron won't want it to get around that some new kid from Texas got the best of him. He is not just going to move on and forget this. So, from here on out, we need to be careful."

"Does he know where we live?"

"No, but still, we need to look out for each other. Hopefully I won't have to see him until baseball tryouts this coming spring." Checking the aisle again, Harley started up the corridor, "C'mon, in ten minutes the game will be starting."

Five minutes later Drew and Harley emerged from the lower level when Harley suggested, "I think it would be better if we don't mention anything about what happened with Aaron and his two pals."

"You're right," said Drew. "If my parents found out I used karate on some kid here at the game, they might not let me come back."

Starting down the box seats Harley checked the surrounding area for Aaron and his cousins. The crowd of nearly forty-five thousand broke into a loud cheer just before the National Anthem came to an end. Taking their seats next to Harley's parents, Rich looked at his watch and commented, "I thought you boys were never going to make it back."

Blowing off his father's remark, Harley explained, "Well, there was a lot for Drew to see since this is his first time here."

Leaning forward, Rich looked over at Drew and asked, "So what do you think about our stadium?"

"I learned quite a bit," said Drew. "I think the most interesting thing was some of the crazy people we saw."

Monica stopped herself from taking a drink and asked, "What do you mean?"

"Nothing, except that there are all kinds of people here tonight." When Monica looked back toward the field, Drew gave Harley a wink, signifying that their secret was just between the two of them.

By the time the first inning came to a close Monica smiled at Rich. While watching the action they listened to Drew's questions and Harley's answers:

"What is a leadoff hitter?"

"What is a walk?"

"What is the strike zone?"

Harley responded to each and every question and never seemed to grow tired of answering:

"The leadoff hitter is very important. It is his job to get on base by any means possible: a base hit, a walk, being hit by a pitch."

"A walk is when the pitcher throws four balls outside of the strike zone. When this happens the umpire awards the batter a free trip to first base."

"The strike zone is the area where normally a batter can hit the ball. It goes from his knees to his shoulders and can be different depending on the player's size."

The question and answer marathon went on until the bottom of the seventh inning, the Cubs in the lead by a score or 2-0. Rich suggested a trip to the bathrooms and then another round of hotdogs and drinks.

Standing in a long line at the concession stand, while Rich

visited the men's room, Drew looked at all of the long lines and asked, "Why do they call this the seventh inning stretch and how did it get started?"

"Very interesting question," said Harley, "and I have the answer. No one can be sure of exactly how the seventh inning stretch got its start, but there are a number of different ideas where it came from. Back in the late 19th century a man by the name of Brother Jasper of Manhattan College, who was the coach of their baseball team, noticed that as the game went on his players began to get restless, so he decided to call a time out so the players and the spectators, as well, could stand up, stretch and move around. Another version, and the most popular reason for the seventh inning stretch is that a man by the name of Harry Wright of the Cincinnati Red Stockings back in 1869 noticed that fans, usually around the seventh inning, started to get up and move around. This may have been how it all got started. Your guess is as good as mine."

All the while Harley was giving his expert explanation, Drew kept looking for Aaron and his cousins. "Stop worrying about Buckman," said Harley. "He won't try anything with all these people around."

A roar of the crowd signaled something had happened. Drew looked toward the ramp that lead back to the seats and smiled. "Maybe the Cards got a run."

"Well, they better get something going, emphasized Harley. "It's getting late in the game."

By the time Rich and the boys returned to their seats, the fans were on their feet, clapping and yelling. Rich looked up at the scoreboard that read; St. Louis 2 - Chicago 2. Turning to the boys, he spoke with enthusiasm, "Looks like our boys tied the game up!"

Finally, in their seats, Rich handed Monica a beer and asked, "What happened!"

"You and the boys missed all the excitement. We started the inning off with a pop-up to the shortstop, followed by a walk. A homerun to left center field scored two runs and tied the game."

Looking out at the scoreboard, Drew took a long drink and remarked, "Does this mean our team, the Cardinals, could win the game?"

Harley took a bite of his second hotdog of the game and explained, "We'll just have to wait and see. Lee has always been a clutch hitter."

Lee worked the pitcher to a full count while every fan in the stadium was on their feet, repeating, "Lee, Lee, Lee!"

The Chicago pitcher gave a nod to his catcher and fired a fastball on the outside corner. Lee swung and connected solidly with the ball going to the left of Chicago's second baseman. Diving, he stabbed the ball, and on one knee threw the ball to the shortstop who, after catching the ball grazed second base with his left foot and fired a bullet to first, the ball slapping into the first baseman's glove just before Lee's foot stepped on the bag. The umpire signaled with an enthusiastic gesture of pumping his fist, the final out of the inning. The crowd let out a resounding sound of disappointment. Harley took another bite of his dog and spoke up, "Evers to Tinker to Chance!"

Drew sat and asked Harley, "What does that mean?"

Harley finished his dog and took a swig of his drink, then explained, "That's a baseball term that started a long time ago in Chicago. Back in the early 1900s the Chicago Cubs had one of the most famous infields ever. John Evers played second base, Joe Tinker was shortstop and then there was Frank Chance on first. They were one of, if not the smoothest double play combinations ever. What you just saw was a double play which means the team on the field gets two outs in a matter of seconds. The words, *Evers to Tinker to Chance* today, means a *sure thing* or a *well-oiled machine,* which is how smooth Chicago's infield was. To this day, Evers, Tinker and Chance are known as the greatest, most colorful and memorable double play combination of all time."

Sitting and listening in amazement, Drew finally asked, "How do you know all this stuff?"

Harley smiled, "It's baseball…it's what I do!"

Crossing Clark Street, Harley looked back at the stadium and commented, "I can't believe we took the lead 3-2, then wind up losing in the top of the ninth by a score of 5-3 to the Cubs, of all teams! This year is turning out to be a nightmare for the Cardinals and the fans."

Drew, who was more upbeat about the outcome of the game,

stated, "Well, didn't you say that this was a three-game series?" Without waiting for a response, he motioned back at Busch Stadium. "There's always tomorrow. Maybe the Cards will win the next two?"

Harley frowned and shook his head. "I sure hope so. The last thing we need is to get swept by the Cubs!"

Drew, in confusion, looked at Rich who answered the question. "If one team takes all the games of a series it's called a sweep. It's very exciting for Cardinal fans when we sweep a team, but to get swept yourself, well around these parts it's quite embarrassing. Tomorrow night the game could and no doubt will be completely different, *and* if you boys are interested, Drew's father called me just before we left the house tonight and told me if we wanted to go to the other two games he'd see to it that we get tickets…box seats again!"

Harley, stepping up on the curve gave Drew a high five. "You don't even have to ask me. I'm always up for a game. How about you, Drew?"

"If it's all right with your parents. I'd like to see the next two games." Pulling the twenty from his pocket he waved it in the air. "One thing I really want to do tomorrow night is buy my own Cardinals hat."

Monica laughed as they continued down the sidewalk. "Looks like St. Louis just got their newest fan!"

Lurking at the edge of a parking lot, next to a delivery truck, Aaron lit up a cigarette and pointed it toward Drew and Harley who were trailing the adults. "If it's the last thing I do, I'm going to get even with that little punk from Texas."

CHAPTER 7

HARLEY AND OZZIE STOOD BY THE BACK GATE AND watched while Monica and Rich left simultaneously for work. His parents felt he was responsible enough to be on his own. Besides that, they knew exactly where their son would be; in the backyard, going through his daily, regimented baseball practice.

But today was different and would continue to be so for the next couple of weeks. Sitting in the swing toward the back of the yard, he looked at the tire hanging from the tree, the same tire he had thrown hundreds of thousands of pitches through. He thought back to when his dad had first hung the tire and had demonstrated the art of throwing a baseball with control. He had started this routine when he was just three. He'd stand a few feet away and try his best to toss the ball at the tire. At first, the ball never even made it to the tire, but with daily practice, within a month the ball went through the tire more times than not. As the months and years passed, his parents kept increasing the distance he had to throw the ball until he reached the age of seven, when the official distance of Little League baseball was his goal. That was three years ago and now at the age of ten he could not only throw the ball through the center of the tire, but to the left, right, up or down, still remaining in the circular open area. He could hit the inside or the outside of the tire on either side, top and bottom. He was a control pitcher. His fastball was clocked at just over sixty and his curve at forty-five miles per hour. His changeup was one of his best pitches. Rich had worked with him for hours on end, explaining that in the majors the difference between a pitcher's fastball and changeup was normally about ten miles per hour at best. The difference in Harley's fastball and his changeup was closer to fifteen miles per hour.

Getting up, Harley walked to the backyard pitcher's mound, placed his right foot on the front edge of the rubber two inches from the right and thought about the distance. Going through the motions of a pitcher, he turned the invisible ball in his hand over and over and finally gripped it as he would for a two-finger fastball. Rocking forward, he pushed himself back, swinging his arms back, his left foot planted solidly. Bringing his arms back and to his chest, he pushed off with his left foot and turned his right foot so it was on the front edge of the rubber. Twisting slightly sideways, he extended his left arm and brought his right hand back and then finally following a waist high leg kick, he brought his right arm forward and released the invisible ball. He watched the imaginary ball cut through the center of the tire opening. Silently, he spoke to himself, "Strike one!"

His thoughts were interrupted by a voice at the front of the yard. "Hey Harley...what are you doing?"

Turning, Harley saw Drew when he opened the fence and entered the backyard. Ozzie, racing to welcome Drew, circled the young boy and ran back to Harley.

Gesturing at the tire hanging from the tree, Harley tried his best to explain what Drew had no doubt witnessed. "I'm just going through the motion of being a pitcher. I can't really start pitching for about two weeks."

Drew held up two leather bound albums and remarked, "I brought along part of my stamp collection. I know you said you wanted to see those three baseball stamps I told you about."

Laying the albums on the swing, Drew walked to the tire and commented, "So this is the tire you were telling me about." Walking to the pitcher's mound, Drew stated, "This distance looks smaller than what we saw at Busch Stadium."

"It is smaller," answered Harley. "It measures exactly forty-six feet, the distance from home plate to the pitcher's rubber, according to Little League standards."

Drew looked down at the rubber. "How far is it in the major leagues?"

"Exactly sixty feet six inches from the front edge of the rubber which measures all the way to the back of home plate. The rubber itself is eighteen inches behind the center of the mound."

"So, just like you told me down at Cardinal Stadium. Baseball is a game of inches."

"That's right. Think about some of the close calls we saw during the three games we went to this week. An inch or a fraction of a second can make a difference not only in the play but in the outcome of the game." Walking over and sitting down on the swing, Harley asked, "After watching three major league games, how do you feel about baseball?"

"I never thought I would say this," shrugged Drew, "but after seeing the games and starting to understand how the game is played, I think I like baseball. But, I will say this. As a new Cardinal fan, I am disappointed that we lost two out of three to those Cubs."

Harley reached down and gave Ozzie a pet on the head. "At this point I don't really think it makes much difference. This year is pretty well shot. The Cards are not even going to make the playoffs."

"How are the Cubs doing this year?"

"Actually, pretty good. Right now, they're sitting at 57-56, just above .500. At this time of the season that means more than likely they'll make the playoffs, but they won't win the World Series."

"What makes you so sure they won't win the whole thing?"

Harley held up an index finger. "Because of the curse...that's why!"

Drew, now seated on the swing, repeated, "The curse. What on earth are you talking about?"

"In 1945, a man who was an avid Cubs fan owned a business named the Billy Goat Tavern. William 'Billy Goat' Sianis, decided to take a live Billy Goat to a World Series game being played in Chicago against the Detroit Tigers. Sianis was allowed to bring the goat to the game, first of all because there were no signs stating that animals were not allowed and besides that, he paid for a ticket for the goat. Well, as the game went on fans that were seated near Sianis started to complain because the goat smelled. The owner of the Cubs; P.K. Wrigley ordered the police to put Sianis and his goat out of the park. Needless to say, Sianis was quite mad. When the police were escorting Sianis and his goat out of the stadium he turned and told the police to give Wrigley this message: 'The Cubs, they ain't gonna win no more. Until they allow a goat into the stadium they will never win a World Series game again!' And to this day, they never have."

"That's crazy!" said Drew. "You can't possibly believe the Cubs haven't won because of some stupid curse?"

"I don't believe they haven't won because of the curse. I think their teams just haven't been good enough."

"Have the Cubs fans tried to do anything to lift this curse?"

"You name it…they've tried it! They had Sam Sianis, William's son show up at a Cubs game with a goat, but it didn't make any difference. They've even had religious leaders come and pray over the ball field, but nothing seems to work. The curse is still going strong."

"If you don't believe in this curse," asked Drew, "then why have the Cubs gone for all those years since the curse without winning a World Series?"

"There are a lot of things that go into winning the World Series. Your best pitcher could get injured and if he normally wins fifteen to twenty games a year, and let's say it's halfway through the season, that's somewhere in the area of seven to ten games you may possibly lose. Every game is important. If one or two of your best hitters get injured that means less base runners which means less runs scored. Close calls that go against you could mean the difference in a game. But, despite these things and many I haven't even mentioned, the team with the best record at the end of the year wins the title. The Cubs over the past years just haven't had one of the better teams."

"Do the Cubs not have players that are as good as some of the Cardinal players?"

"Sure, they have good players. Each player is considered the best at what he does, or he wouldn't be in the majors to begin with. Now, if you're talking this year, overall, I'd say the Cubs have a better team which means they have for the most part, better players."

Drew looked off into the woods behind Harley's house and shook his head in wonder. "Ya know, when I was down in Texas, I was known as a pretty smart kid, at least in school. I knew the smart kids in school, but no one, I mean no one knew as much about a particular subject as you."

"I could say the same thing about you, Drew. I've never met a kid who is so good at so many things: the piano, stamp collecting and even karate. It still amazes me the way you handled ol' Aaron Buckman down at Busch Stadium."

"Like I said, we were lucky."

Suddenly, for no apparent reason Ozzie barked three times.

Drew looked at the black dog and asked, "What does he want?"

"He wants someone to throw his favorite tennis ball for him. It's lying right there by your feet. Why don't you give it a toss toward the back of the yard? If one of us doesn't throw it he'll just keep barking until we do."

Drew bent down, picked up the tattered ball and threw it toward the garage. It bounced off the cinderblock wall and rolled beneath a holly bush. Ozzie didn't hesitate to chase the ball and with his nose push the branches to the side and snatched the ball. He returned to the swing, dropped the ball at Drew's feet, backed off and waited. Looking at Ozzie, Drew asked, "What do I do now?"

"Throw it again! It'll take at least fifteen to twenty throws before he gets tired. When that happens, he'll take the ball into the garage and lay on his old blanket in the corner."

Picking up the ball, Drew tossed it way beyond the garage and Ozzie took off.

Harley smiled at his new friend and remarked in a surprised fashion, "You've got a pretty good arm for somebody that never played baseball. Let me ask you something? I'm not saying it could happen, but just suppose you didn't have a fear of being hit by a baseball, do you think you'd like to play the game?"

Drew watched while Ozzie raced back to the swing. "I don't know. I mean, even if I did want to play that doesn't mean I could. Like the doctor said, I may have to live with this phobia the rest of my life. To tell you the truth, I may have to just watch baseball from the stands."

"But what if you could play?"

Tossing the ball once again, Drew looked down at the ground. "That would take a miracle. Just because I have a good arm doesn't make a difference. It's a mental problem I have and that mental problem prevents me from playing sports."

Harley leaned forward. "Listen to me. I was right there when you confronted Aaron. You told me you also have a fear of bodily contact. You weren't afraid of Aaron and his cousins."

"That's where you're wrong. The whole time we were across from Aaron in that hallway, I was nervous as all get out. I just called his bluff."

"Yeah, but you still performed. You felt the fear and did it anyway!"

"What does that mean?"

"It's something my father is always saying. He read it in a book somewhere. According to the man who wrote the book, if you have a fear of something the best way to get over it is to go ahead and do it anyway, even if you are scared. Eventually, if you keep doing the thing you fear, it will become second nature and the fear will be gone."

"That's easy for someone like you who has no fear."

"You couldn't be further from the truth. I've had plenty of things I've been afraid of growing up. My greatest fear was when my parents decided I needed to start taking swimming lessons when I was three years old. They took me to the YMCA where they had a program where young children could learn how to swim. I was impossible. When they lowered me into the water I screamed and wouldn't stop. Finally, after four weeks the swimming instructor said I was just too afraid of the water and my parents should wait for a couple of years and then try again. Then, one Saturday my dad took me out on the Meramec in a rowboat to do some fishing. Well, we get out in the middle of the river, he stands and pushes me overboard and starts to row away. My dad shouted at me, 'Swim and feel the fear anyway!' I was so mad I couldn't see straight. I started to flop around in the water, moving my arms and legs. I struggled and followed my dad all the way to shore. Ya know, by the time I was standing on the riverbank, I wasn't mad anymore. That's when my dad explained to me how to feel the fear and do it anyway. Maybe we can do the same thing about your fear of getting hit with a baseball."

Throwing the ball again for Ozzie, Drew looked at Harley in confusion. "What does your father tossing you in the river have to do with me and my phobia?"

Harley got up and pointed at the garage. "I have something I want to show you."

Ozzie and Drew followed Harley, Ozzie curling up on his old frayed rug, the ball at his side. Inside the garage, Harley walked to the corner of the garage and pointed, "This is what I wanted you to see."

Leaning on a black metal machine, Harley explained, "This is called a pitching machine. What you do is set it up on the pitcher's mound. It is designed to hold eighty baseballs. There is a control board on the back of the machine. You can set the machine so it pitches a ball every seven or ten seconds. It's like having a professional pitcher in your backyard who never gets tired. You can set the speed of the pitches anywhere between forty to ninety miles an hour. For instance, I can set the machine to throw a ninety-mile an hour fastball, followed by a seventy mile an hour curve ball, followed by a changeup. If you stand in the batter's box you can experience eighty pitches in a row. The seven or ten second delay between pitches gives the hitter time, just like in a real game to try and guess what the next pitch will be. This machine has helped me to become a better hitter, but more than that, it has helped me to become a better pitcher. When I am waiting for the next pitch, I get to feel what a hitter feels, what he might be thinking. You see, in baseball when a hitter steps up to the plate a battle of wits begins. The hitter wants to get to first base or even beyond. The pitcher's job is to prevent the hitter from hitting the ball, or at least hitting it effectively. If the pitcher can get the hitter to swing at a ball out of the strike zone there is a possibility that it might be a routine grounder or a pop-up; easy outs. There's a lot more to the battle between hitters and pitchers, but the reason I wanted to show you this is because this machine might be the answer to your problem."

Drew walked to the machine and looked down into the empty black metal container and remarked, "I'm lost...I don't understand what you're saying."

Harley reached for a basket of baseballs and started to empty them into the container. "First, we fill up the machine."

Drew stood and watched in silence. While grabbing the second bucket, Harley flipped a ball softly to Drew who was standing just two feet away. "Here...catch!"

Drew instinctively opened his hands and caught the ball. Before he said a word, Harley dumped more balls into the machine. "There, now that wasn't too bad...was it? You just caught a baseball!"

"Yeah, but that was nothing. It was only a short distance and I bet it wasn't even going five miles an hour. It was harmless. Even if I wouldn't have caught it, it wouldn't have hurt me."

"Well, that's a start," smiled Harley as he dumped a third basket into the container. "I have an idea. What say after I get this thing loaded up, we play some simple catch?"

"I've never played catch before," objected Drew. "If I miss the ball and it hits me, I could get hurt *and* that's what I'm afraid of happening."

"Look, we'll start out just a few feet from one another. That way, even if you do miss the ball, it won't hurt." Dumping the last bucket of balls, Harley walked to a wall shelf that contained four ball gloves. Taking down one of the gloves he handed it to Drew. "From the way you were throwing the ball for Ozzie I can tell you're right handed. Try this on for size."

Sliding his hand inside the glove, Drew smiled, "It feels good on my hand."

Back up a few feet and we'll get started. Grabbing a glove himself, he pointed out, "Now, I'll have to throw underhanded because my right arm is not completely healed yet. You catch the ball and toss it back to me. You can throw it as hard as you want?"

"I guess so," said Drew nervously. "I can't believe I'm actually doing this!"

Harley flipped the ball to Drew who not opening the glove pocket, allowed the ball to fall to the ground. Harley assured his friend. "It's okay. You'll catch on in no time."

Following five minutes of tossing the ball back and forth, Drew smiled. "I've only dropped the ball twice. This doesn't seem so bad."

Motioning with his glove, Harley suggested, "Why don't you turn around and go back three or four steps. We'll try it at a little longer distance."

"Okay," said Drew as he turned and took two steps. Harley tossed the ball underhanded with as much force as he could muster, the ball hitting Drew squarely in his back. Instantly, Drew turned and yelled, "I wasn't ready!"

"I know, I just wanted you to experience getting hit by the baseball. Don't tell me that hurt?"

"No, it didn't hurt. I just wasn't ready!"

"Well, now you know that if you miss the ball at this new distance it won't hurt."

Drew picked up the ball and threw it with all his might at Harley, the ball slapping into the glove. "That's the stuff," shouted Harley. "Bring the heat!"

An hour passed when Harley, after catching a ball waved his hand. "I have to sit down. My arm is getting tired. I don't want to overdo it." Sitting on the swing, Harley pointed out to Drew, who sat on the ground at the base of a tree. "You really did good. You only dropped the ball four times. So, how does it feel to not be afraid of a baseball?"

"It feels pretty good. I was a little nervous when we started but after a while, it felt so natural to throw and catch the ball. Maybe if I keep practicing I could learn how to catch better than most kids my age."

"I don't think there's a maybe to it. After watching you manhandle Aaron Buckman and with the ease you've learned to play catch, I think you can do anything you set your mind to. Playing catch is just the start for what I have planned," said Harley. "C'mon, help me get that pitching machine out of the garage, then I'll explain what we're going to do next.

Minutes later, the machine was set up just behind the pitcher's rubber on the mound. Setting the machine pitch speed at forty miles an hour, Harley picked up his glove and informed Drew, "All right, when I give you the signal, turn the machine on. I'm going to stand on home plate and catch or attempt to catch all eighty balls that are thrown my way. Let's set the time at ten seconds."

"What do I do?" asked Drew

"You just go sit on the swing and watch because, when I get done then it will be your turn."

"Ah...I'm not too sure about that. How fast were you throwing the ball to me before?"

"Probably twenty...maybe less."

"So, you expect me to start catching baseballs that are traveling twice the speed I am now used to?"

"Yeah, but forty miles an hour is still pretty slow. Besides that, I have the cure for that. You just sit and watch."

Harley set the machine for random pitches, walked to home plate and positioned himself. "Now the distance is about forty-six feet. When I give you the signal hit the on switch."

Harley held up his glove as he nodded at Drew, "Turn it on!"

Drew flipped the switch and seconds later the first ball was ejected with a slight popping sound. The ball slapped into Harley's glove. Harley dropped the ball and waited for the next pitch, which was a little to the left. Making the slight adjustment, he snagged the ball and dropped it to the ground. Following thirteen straight minutes, Harley caught the last pitch and walked to the machine and turned it off. In amazement, Drew stood and joined him, "That was incredible! You only dropped one ball. You're really good at catching."

"All right, now it's your turn," said Harley, "but we're going to try just one ball first and then you can step away from home plate and tell me what you think. We won't try all eighty balls until you're comfortable. Before we get started I want to show you something else. Let's round these balls up and get the machine loaded."

Harley dropped the last three baseballs into the container and instructed Drew, "I'm going to go stand at home plate without a glove. I'm going to allow myself to be hit by a few pitches so you can see in case that happens you really won't get hurt."

Standing on the mound, Harley gave the signal and Drew flipped the switch. Harley waited and when the first pitch was ejected he turned sideways, protecting his right arm and shoulder. The ball bounced off of his lower left arm and fell to the ground. Ten seconds later the next pitch hit his left knee and rolled off to the side. The third pitch, hit him about waist high. Stepping away from the plate, he walked to the machine and turned it off. "There ya go, Drew. If you can stand up to Aaron Buckman you can handle a forty-mile an hour pitch. What do ya say?"

Hesitant, Drew finally relented, "Okay, but with one change. I get to take a glove with me. That way I'll have to catch the ball to keep from getting hit. Without the glove I don't think I could just stand there like you did."

"Fair enough. And another thing. You can step out whenever you feel uncomfortable or if you get nervous."

"I'm already nervous, but I'm willing to give it a try."

Drew walked to the plate, held the glove up in front of himself and took a deep breath, while bracing himself. "No, no, no," said Harley. "You need to try and relax. You look like you're standing on railroad tracks with a freight train bearing down on you. Take it easy. Okay, I'm going to turn the machine on. Remember, you have ten seconds before the first pitch and then ten in between each pitch after that."

Gritting his teeth, Drew spoke nervously, "Let it rip!"

Harley flipped the switch and Drew waited. Ten seconds seemed like an eternity, but then the first pitch was ejected. At the last second, Drew stepped out of the way and yelled at Harley. "Turn it off! That ball looked like it was coming at me at a hundred miles an hour!"

Turning off the machine, Harley walked to Drew and put his arm around him. "Look, I understand how difficult this must be for you. We don't have to do this. I just thought maybe it would help. We can quit right now and come back later or even tomorrow and try again or we can just forget the whole thing."

Frustrated, Drew threw the glove down to the ground and placed his hands on his hips, "I'm not a quitter. I just have a phobia…that's all!"

"Maybe we should call it quits for the day."

Drew picked the glove back up and stood on the plate. "No! If I can face down Aaron Buckman, no baseball ever made is going to scare me. Like you said; 'Feel the fear and do it anyway!'"

Harley waked back to the machine and said, "Ready?"

Drew stared directly at the machine and answered with a tone of anger, "Let's go, fire torpedo one!"

Harley silently counted down the seconds before the ball would be released. A pitch directly at Drew's chest followed the sound of the ejected ball. Drew, backed away as the ball slammed into the glove and dropped onto the plate. Drew looked down at the ball and with a look on his face as if he had escaped certain death, he took a deep breath, but was then reminded by Harley, "You've only got a few seconds to get ready for the next pitch!"

Bracing for the next pitch, he yelled, "Feel the fear!"

The next pitch came; it was low and just grazed the edge of the glove and rolled off to the side. Drew quickly prepared himself for the next pitch, which he stepped out of the way of and then the next pitch hit him on his right hip. He wasn't prepared for the fifth pitch that hit his right shoulder. Backing out the box, Harley could see Drew had enough for the time being. Turning off the machine, he ran to Drew who had walked over to the garage and collapsed on the ground. Worried, Harley asked, "Are you okay?"

"Yeah, I think I'm okay," muttered Drew. "Those two balls that hit me scared the living daylights out of me!"

"Are you injured?"

"No, it just scared me when they hit. I've never experienced that before." Putting the glove on top of his head he grinned, "Looks like I've got a long way to go before I can catch all eighty pitches…doesn't it?"

Seeing Drew was okay, Harley sat next to Drew and laughed. "I think you've had enough of my weird training for today. I say we go inside and grab some lunch."

Ozzie walked over and dropped his ball next to Drew. Drew laughed as he picked up the ball and tossed it out into the yard. "Apparently, Ozzie hasn't had enough."

Sitting at a picnic table on the screened-in back porch, Drew took a bite out of his sandwich and asked, "Well, how do you think I did out there?"

"I think you did great," said Harley, "when you consider you looked scared out of your gourd!"

"I'd like to try again tomorrow."

"Okay, but I think it would be best if this is another one of our secrets. I'm not so sure my parents would approve."

"My parents have always been very protective of me. They would flip out."

Taking a scoop of potato salad, Harley asked, "So what do you want to do for the rest of the afternoon?"

Drew reached for a jar of mustard. "We still have my stamp collection to look at and then we can take a look at your baseball card collection. By the way, who do the Cards play next?"

CHAPTER 8

THE BALL SLAMMED INTO DREW'S GLOVE AND NOT believing he had finally caught one of the machine pitched baseballs, he jumped up and down while running around the yard, Ozzie following close behind. Harley turned off the machine, laughing at the spectacle of Drew and Ozzie emerging from the left side of the garage. Drew held up the ball in victory and shouted, "I did it! I really did it! This is the first forty-mile an hour baseball I've ever caught. What's next?"

"Well, we could increase the speed of the pitches? Let's say maybe to fifty miles an hour, but before we do that I think you need to stand there and see how many of the eighty pitches at forty you can catch. After that, we can go to fifty."

Drew walked to the plate. "Load that thing up and let's get started then! Who knows, I might catch a couple dozen!"

Fifteen minutes later, Harley shut down the machine after Drew caught the last ejected ball. "That's it," yelled Harley. "According to what I counted you caught thirty-seven. Not bad for a piano playing, stamp collector! Do you want to turn it up to fifty or try and catch more at forty?"

"Neither, right now I need a break. That wore me out. I've got a long way to go before I could ever be as good as you. Remember yesterday week when you caught seventy-nine out of eighty?"

Walking to the back porch steps Harley grabbed a soda and handed it to Drew. "You'll get there. You just need to relax more. This is all new to you. I've been doing this for years. It's second nature to me." Sitting on the bottom step and rubbing his right arm, he stated, "Next week I should be able to start throwing with my right arm, and I'm not talking underhanded. It'll be good to get back to practicing."

"Listen," said Drew, "last night I had my mom run me up to the library here in Arnold. I decided to learn some things about baseball...maybe some things *you don't know!*" Reaching into his jeans pocket, he took out a piece of legal paper and unfolded it. "I'm not very good at memorizing stuff, so I wrote down what I discovered." Clearing his voice, he went on, "Do you know when the first ever double play was turned?"

Harley smiled confidently, "No, and if you have a date written down, it can't be true because they didn't start keeping track of double plays until the 1930s so no one actually knows when the first double play was."

Disappointed, Drew confirmed, "That's right. Once again, I'm amazed you know all this stuff."

"The stats about baseball are unending," said Harley. "As much as I know about baseball, there's that much more I don't know. What else did you learn at the library?"

"I learned that in the beginning years of baseball, back in the late 1800s, that there were not many double plays and when there was it was considered rare. Now days, there is hardly a major league game where at least one double play is not turned. It's considered a routine play these days. Now the triple play...that's different!"

"I agree. The triple play is considered a rare play and even more rare is the unassisted triple play where a single player makes all three outs."

"I know," said Drew. "I read about the unassisted triple play. There have only been ten completed to date. There has only been one unassisted triple play that involved a St. Louis team and that was back in 1925 when a shortstop by the name of Glenn Wright of the Pittsburgh Pirates snagged a line drive, stepped on second base and then tagged out a runner."

"Well, you're just full of surprises today," said Harley. "I didn't know that either." Standing up, he motioned at the pitching machine. "Let's load up the machine and see if you can catch at least fifty of the pitches."

Two hours later, Harley turned off the machine and walked to the plate where Drew stood. Holding up his glove, Drew asked, "How'd I do this last time?"

"We've gone through an eighty pitch cycle three times," said Harley. "The first time you improved by catching forty-three pitches. This last round equaled sixty-two. You're getting better…and fast. In a couple of days you might be catching all eighty."

Pointing at the machine, Drew stated confidently, "Tomorrow, I want to take the speed to fifty."

"Are you sure? Ten miles an hour can be a big difference. I know it doesn't sound that much faster…but it is."

"Let's see how you do at fifty," suggested Drew. "I want to see if you can catch all eighty pitches."

"Okay," said Harley. "Load the machine up!"

Drew shook his head in amazement as Harley caught the final pitch, threw the ball into the air and caught it behind his back. Turning the machine off, Drew spoke in admiration. "You caught all the pitches. Do you think I could ever be that good?"

"Sure, it just takes practice. Tomorrow we'll let you have a go at fifty miles an hour."

Gathering up the balls, Drew stopped and addressed Harley, "I want to thank you for being so patient with me. I'm not quite sure if I'm completely over the fear of getting hit, but I know I'm a lot better than when I first started." Holding up the glove, he admitted, "Having a glove in front of me is my safety net."

"I guess that's one way of looking at a baseball glove," said Harley, "but their purpose rather than protecting the player is to catch the ball. Back before the 1870s they didn't have gloves. They played barehanded. The first glove ever used was by a player by the name of Doug Allison who played for the Cincinnati Red Stockings. He had an injured left hand so he wore a glove to protect his hand and still allow him to play. Charlie Waitt, an outfielder for St. Louis back in 1875, wore the first confirmed glove. They were flesh colored. As time went on more and more players started using gloves. The gloves back then were nothing like the baseball gloves they use today. Back then, they were just leather gloves with the fingers cut out. They were not really designed to catch a ball, but rather to knock it down so the player could pick it up. Past baseball history is funny in a way. A long time ago players in the field would leave their gloves on the field when it was their turn at the plate, but this was banned by the major leagues in 1954."

"I'm glad I'm learning to catch a baseball today rather than back in the 1870s. I can't believe players would actually catch balls barehanded. That's insane!"

"Come in the garage," said Harley. "I want to show you something."

"The last time you wanted to show me something in the garage, it turned out to be that pitching machine. What is it this time?"

"I just want to show you all the different gloves my dad has." Ozzie followed and curled up on his rug.

Harley turned the dial on a lock on a metal cabinet and removed five different gloves. These gloves are professional, just like the ones used in the majors. By now, you've probably no doubt guessed that my family, when it comes to baseball, goes to the extreme. We practice a lot together and they insist on the best equipment."

Laying the gloves on a workbench, he picked up an odd looking glove and held it up. "This is a catcher's mitt. Notice I didn't say glove because it's called a mitt. Only a catcher uses it. It's heavily padded and has a much wider area to catch a ball than the other gloves. It is designed to catch balls that can be thrown as fast as one hundred miles per hour. A catcher in a normal game has to catch somewhere between one hundred and forty to one hundred and fifty pitches, game after game and this glove is made to do just that."

Picking up another glove, Harley placed it on his left hand and held it up. "This is a first baseman's glove. It's heavily padded just like the catcher's mitt but is longer in length which allows the first baseman to scoop up poorly thrown balls by other infielders."

Trying on yet another glove, Harley went on to explain, "This is an infielder's glove. It is the smallest of all the gloves with open webbing that allows infield dirt to fall through so when the infielder grabs the ball out of the glove, he's grabbing the ball and not dirt. The next glove is an outfielder's glove. It's pretty much the same as the infielder's glove except that it has a larger pocket and is longer which allows the player to snag fly balls or scoop up balls that get past the infield." Smiling, he put his hand into the final glove. "And this is my favorite, the pitcher's glove. It has a closed webbing that prevents the other team from seeing how the pitcher is grasping the ball which prevents them from guessing what the next pitch may be."

Drew picked up the catcher's mitt and slipped it on his hand. "This feels good." Pounding his fist into the padding, he stated with conviction. "This is what I want to do!"

Harley looked at his friend and asked, "What do you mean?"

"I want to be a catcher in Little League. You said yourself I was catching on quick when it comes to catching a baseball."

Doing some quick math in his head, Harley responded, "Little League tryouts are in eight months. You just can't expect to get on a team because you can catch a ball. There's a lot more to the game than just that. I mean, first of all you have to learn the game and all the rules and regulations. Then there is learning how to hit; knowing the difference between a ball and a strike, how to run the bases, how to steal a base, how to tag up following a deep fly ball, how to slide and a whole lot more. I don't know if you can learn all that in just eight months."

"Why not...you can teach me!"

"Look, I'm willing to teach you the game, I just don't know if there is enough time between now and next March, and besides that, being a catcher is one of the most difficult positions to learn. You not only have to be able to catch, you have to be smart. A good catcher knows every hitter that comes to the plate. He knows what kind of pitch they like and what they don't like. He has to know the pitcher like the back of his hand. He has to be able to know when the pitcher's curve ball is not breaking correctly or when his fastball has no pop or recognize when his pitcher is getting tired. The catcher gets hit more than any other player. He can get hit with a hundred mile an hour foul tip, or get clobbered by the bat from an over swing and then there are home plate collisions."

"Hey, I handled Aaron Buckman...didn't I?"

"Yes, but he wasn't in a position to hit back."

"Look," said Drew, "I know I can do this! As far as learning the game I can go to the library and read books on how the game is played. I pick things up fast. You just need to show me what to do and leave the rest to me. Maybe you're having a problem understanding why I want to play baseball. Up until we met I was convinced I would never play any sport...ever! Then, I met you and everything changed. You taught me how to 'Feel the fear!' I'm up for the challenge. I know I can do this. Do you think it was easy to learn how to play the piano or to learn karate? It wasn't, but I hung in there and made it. This is the same thing…just something new. Promise me, you'll teach me!"

Harley held up his hands. "All right already! I can see there is no talking you out of this. I guess, in a way you're no different than me. A lot of people have told me that it's next to impossible to become a major league pitcher, but I just keep on practicing like it's going to really happen. No one could ever talk me out of my goal, so I understand what you're saying."

Placing the pitcher's glove back on the workbench, he turned back to Drew and said, "I'll teach you how to play baseball, even how to be a catcher, but first you need to prove something to me…and to yourself."

Tossing the catcher's mitt on the bench, Drew hesitated, and then asked, "What's that?"

"You have to prove to me you're ready. You have to prove to me you're no longer afraid of being hit by a baseball. So far, you've stood at home plate with a glove in front of you…your safety net. You need to show me you're not afraid. We need to go out there and you need to get hit by ten machine pitched balls. You can't step away from the plate or avoid getting hit. You have to take ten hits in a row. If you can do that, I'll be convinced you're ready. If you can't do that, it's no big deal, I just won't be able to train you because you won't be ready."

Drew stared over at the pile of gloves and spoke softly, "No glove?"

Harley answered, "No glove! That's the deal."

Drew took a deep breath, turned and started to walk out of the garage, "Let's do it!"

Walking directly to home plate, Drew positioned himself and watched Harley walk to the pitching machine. "How long will this take?"

"That depends. Do you want it set at every seven or ten seconds?"

"Let's make it seven. That'll mean it'll be over in just over one minute."

Harley reached for the switch. "Let me know when you're ready."

Drew looked toward the sky and closed his eyes. "Okay,

God…this could be the most important moment of my life." Opening his eyes, he looked directly at Harley and ordered, "Let 'er rip!"

Harley reached for the ON switch and yelled, "Try and relax Drew!"

The first ball popped out of the ejector and hit Drew square in the stomach. Drew winced and gritted his teeth and bent slightly when Harley yelled, "Remember…seven seconds!"

The second ball just grazed his pant leg and seconds later the third pitch hit his upper right arm, followed by two consecutive hits on his lower left leg. The next pitch was a direct hit to the stomach and then a pitch hit his shoulder. Twenty-one seconds later, Harley turned the machine off and ran to Drew whose face was full of tears. Placing his arm around his friend, Harley asked, "Are you okay?"

Speaking through the tears, Drew managed to get out, "I only took nine hits. The seventh ball missed me. Turn the machine back on. I have to get hit one more time!"

Harley objected, "That won't be necessary. You've proved yourself!"

Drew stood up straight and faced the machine, "A deal's a deal! Turn the machine back on!"

Harley, seeing Drew was quite serious walked back to the machine and asked, "Are you sure?"

Drew braced himself and answered through the tears, "I've never been so sure of anything in my life!"

Harley flipped the switch and waited. The ball was ejected and hit Drew right in his gut. He bent over but then instantly stood back up and smiled. Harley immediately turned the machine off and noticed something he hadn't planned on. Walking to where Drew stood, he shook his hand, "Well, you did it. But, here's the thing. You did a lot more than what you think you did!"

Drew looked at Harley in confusion but remained silent.

Harley laughed and explained, "Remember when I stood and caught eighty pitches in a row at fifty miles an hour? Well, we forgot to set the machine back to forty. You took ten hits at fifty…not forty, but fifty!"

"You'll train me then?"

"You betcha I will! Let's take a break and then we'll get started unless you want to wait until tomorrow."

"We've only got eight months. Every day of training will be important. Let's rest up for a few, maybe get some water and then we can get started."

Sitting in the shade of a large tree at the corner of the yard near the chain link fence, Harley opened a bottle of water and asked Drew, "How do you feel? Are you sore from those hits you took?"

"Maybe a little," remarked Drew, "but it's not as bad as I thought it would be. My stomach hurts some and my right arm is still tingling."

Harley looked down at two bruises that had formed on his arm and asked, "How are you going to explain those bruises?"

"I'm going to tell my folks the truth! I'm learning how to play baseball."

"Do you really believe they'll think you just snapped out of your phobia?"

"No, they're not stupid. I'm going to tell them about the pitching machine and how getting hit with the balls helped me to get over my fear. Believe me, they'll be so amazed I'm over my phobia they might not ask that many questions."

"Do me a favor," said Harley. "When you tell them about the machine don't mention you stood in front of it without a glove. Parents have a different way of looking at things. It'll be our secret just like the Aaron Buckman thing; agreed?"

"Agreed," said Drew. Lying back in the warm sun, he placed his hands behind his head and closed his eyes.

Harley rose up on his elbows and changed the subject. "The Cards are still on a downward swing. Last night they finished up a west coast road trip against Los Angeles, San Diego and San Francisco. Los Angeles took two out of three and the Padres and the Giants swept us. In short, we lost eight out of nine games. That's what you call pathetic! We are now sitting with a win-loss record of 41-63. We've only got thirty-nine more games to play this year. We'd have to win out, which I'd say is impossible if we have any remote chance of getting into the playoffs."

Drew, sitting up, gave Ozzie a pat on his head. "How are those Cubs doing?"

"I'm pretty sure they're headed for the playoffs. Who knows?

This might be the year they break the curse."

Standing, Drew downed the last of his water. "So, besides what we have already done today, what are you going to teach me?"

"Since you have a desire to be a catcher let's go back into the garage so I can show you the equipment you have to wear. It's quite a getup! C'mon."

Opening a full-length wooden cabinet next to his set of weights he began to remove items as he explained each one. "First, we have the catcher's mask, which protects your face. It can easily be removed if you need to go after a foul ball behind the plate. Other than that, when on the field, it is always worn, except for close plays at the plate. We'll talk about that later." Hitting the edge of the workbench with the mask, he went on, "This mask is very important. A lot of foul tips can come off the bat and hit you right in the face or head area. This is a very important piece of equipment. Second, we have the chest protector, which once again, protects the catcher's chest area from foul tips. Third, the shin guards which are buckled on to protect your legs and knees. Next, we have knee guards which help to preserve your knees. Last, but not least we have the throat guard and a pair of protective inner gloves. Without these to help you catch balls that can travel up to one hundred miles an hour, your hands will get really soar."

"What about a glove, or as I recall you saying, the mitt?"

Reaching into the cabinet Harley pulled out a well-used catcher's mitt. "This is the mitt I use when I'm catching for my dad or mom. It's an official Little League approved size." Handing the glove to Drew, he pointed out, "This is the size glove you'll be using."

Sitting down on an old chair, Harley explained, "Watch carefully how I put the equipment on. You want to make sure everything fits snuggly, but still allows you to move around freely." Strapping on the shin guards, Harley explained, "A catcher has to be quick as a cat, ready to move to the left or right in a fraction of a second. You have to be ready to get up from your haunches and run to pick up a bunt and then throw to first. You touch the baseball more than any other player on the field other than the pitcher. You have the advantage of seeing the entire field and can direct players to shift one way or the other if needed. I know all this sounds like a lot, but you'll get the hang of it."

Putting on the chest protector, he continued, "The first thing we're going to do is load up the machine and I'll demonstrate the position the catcher must take and then I'll catch or attempt to catch all eighty balls. After that, you can put the equipment on and give it a try."

Completely dressed in the protective equipment, Harley stood, picked up the mitt and said, "Let's go. I need to walk around a little and get used to this outfit. I haven't had it on in quite some time."

Following Harley out into the yard, Drew asked, "Are you going to try and catch all eighty pitches?"

"Why not? That's what your goal is going to be. I want you to see how it's done before you try it."

Walking over to the machine he explained the control panel to Drew. "Right now the machine is set for fastballs at fifty miles an hour. What I want you to do is from time to time change the type of pitch. You can see here on the panel where it reads: fastball, curve, changeup, cutter, slider and so on. You can also make an adjustment where the ball will go to the inside or the outside of the plate with any one of these pitches. You can set the machine to pitch the ball high or low as well. You need to mix your selections up so I don't know what's coming. This way you'll be able to see how I react to different pitches. However, in an actual game you'll always know what the pitcher is going to throw. Now, I'm going to set up at the plate. Give me a few seconds to get myself in position and then let 'em come."

Drew waited for a few seconds and after Harley went down into the customary catcher's position, waited another few seconds then hit the switch. Seconds later a fastball slapped into the open catcher's mitt. Harley dropped the ball to the side and gave Drew a thumbs up. The next three pitches were all fastballs that Harley corralled with ease.

Drew changed the pitch selection to a curve and waited. The next pitch headed for the inside corner but then cut over the plate and bounced off the edge of the mitt. Harley shook his head and waited for the next pitch which was yet another curve. Anticipating the curve, he snagged the ball. Drew then switched the selection dial to a changeup and then a curve, followed by a fastball. Drew continued to change up the pitches and Harley continued to amaze him with the ease of moving to the right or left at the last moment.

The last ball slapped into the mitt and Drew signaled it was over. Turning off the machine, he walked to the plate and shouted, "You only missed three pitches! That was great!"

Getting up, Harley walked in a circle and commented, "I haven't done that in some time. I forgot how hard catching can be. Are you sure this is the position you want to play?"

"Yep, I think is it. I'll know better after I give it a whirl. Get out of that equipment and let me try it on for size."

Ten minutes later Drew was suited up. Standing, he commented, "This feels kind of awkward."

Gesturing at the yard, Harley suggested, "Why don't you walk around some, maybe even run a little to get loosened up."

Drew walked along the chain link fence with Ozzie while Harley gathered up the balls and filled the machine. He no sooner looked up when he saw Drew down in the catcher's position at home plate. Drew gave him a thumbs up and smiled through the mask.

Harley turned on the machine and waited for the first pitch, which was a curve. It bounced off the edge of the mitt. The next two pitches were curves that, like the first, bounced off the mitt to the ground. Harley switched to a fastball that slammed into the glove knocking Drew onto his backside. Turning off the machine, Harley walked to the plate and helped Drew to his feet. "Don't worry! It's just going to take some getting used to. You might want to place your right foot back a little further than your left. That will give you better balance. Are you ready to go again?"

"Yeah, let's go!" said Drew.

The next pitch was a fastball right down the pike that bounced off the mitt, followed by two more misses.

Harley yelled to Drew, "You're closing the mitt too soon. Keep the mitt open. When the ball gets into the pocket the glove will automatically close around the ball." Drew missed the next two pitches but then snagged two in a row. The last ball bounced in front of the plate and miraculously Drew scooped it up.

The machine off, Harley suggested, "Let's rest for a bit and then we'll try it again if you're up for it."

Drew laid the glove on the ground and stood as he stretched. "Rome wasn't built in a day. It took years!"

Harley patted him on the shoulder and commented, "We don't have years. We only have eight months!"

An hour later, Drew after catching the last three pitches, stood and walked over to the garage and sat down against the side of the cinderblock building. Harley joined him and handed him a cold bottle of water. "You did better that time: thirty-five caught pitches. The first time you only snagged twenty-three. You're just getting started and you're already improving. I think you've had enough catching activity for the day. Why don't you get this rig off and we'll rest up for about a half hour then I'm going to have you stand at home plate and I'm going to explain the strike zone to you. If we have enough time I might start to teach you how to run the bases.

Five o'clock rolled around when Rich pulled in and parked next to the garage. Drew, realizing he had to get home gave Ozzie a pat on the head and told Harley he had to go. Harley handed him the catcher's equipment and suggested, "Why don't you take this stuff along and wear it around the house. I know that sounds crazy but if you're going to become a catcher, that equipment must be as comfortable to you as an old pair of jeans."

"That sounds like a good idea. It'll be a good way for me to tell my parents I'm over my phobia and I've decided to play baseball. I'll surprise them by coming to the table with this getup on."

"How do you think they'll react? What do you think they'll say?"

"I'm not sure, but it's going to be interesting. I'll give you a call after supper and let you know how it all went down."

Rich watched as Drew walked through the front gate with their catching equipment. "Where's your friend going with our catcher's gear?"

"He's just borrowing it for the night. Drew and I had one of the most amazing afternoons I think I've ever had. I'll tell you and mom all about it at dinner tonight."

CHAPTER 9

PULLING INTO A PARKING SPACE AT THE FAR END OF Arnold Park, Rich pointed at the deserted ball field, "Just like I thought. No one else is using the field."

Monica climbed out of their car and looked up into the late morning sun. "February 16th. You've got to admit that sixty-three degrees for this time of year is unusual. We should be able to get some good practice in today."

Drew and Harley stood at the back of the car while Rich unloaded his truck, handing Drew his catcher's gear and Harley a professional heavy-duty bag that contained a number of baseball bats and two dozen balls. Rich grabbed another sack containing bases and gloves and looked around the park.

Drew walked onto the field and put his gear on a picnic table behind a large wood and welded wire backstop as Harley announced, "Next week on the twenty-fourth the Cardinals pitchers and catchers report for spring training and before you know it, it'll be opening day."

Strapping on the chest protector, Drew announced, "It's the same thing we're doing. We're getting ready for Little League season which is right around the corner."

Watching her husband walk to the pitcher's mound and dump the balls around the rough circular dirt area, Monica spoke up, "It really is amazing the way you've come along, Drew. Seven months ago, you were scared to death of a baseball and here we are today, months later and you're well on your way to becoming a potential Little League catcher. I admire you for your drive and courage in conquering your past phobia."

Drew smiled. "My parents took me to see our doctor. Surprisingly, he was not that amazed at the change in the way I felt. From the very beginning he said I might grow out of my phobia. After examining me and asking me a bunch of questions he said my thought process of being afraid of moving balls or physical contact had been reversed because of my interest in baseball. My parents support me one hundred percent on my wish to play baseball. They feel if baseball is the reason why my fear is gone, then I should concentrate on getting better at it."

Rich walked out toward second base and yelled, "Are we going to get started or what?"

Picking up his glove, Harley looked at his mother and whispered, "Sometimes Dad reminds me of a little kid."

Monica smiled and stood, picking up her own glove. "Your father is just so proud of you. He wants to see both of you do well. Come on, let's hit the field."

The bases all in place, Monica stood on first, Rich, second, Harley, third and Drew at home plate. Rich fired a ball at Harley on third and shouted, "Let's get warmed up by throwing the ball around the infield for a few minutes."

Harley stabbed the ball and threw it across the infield to Monica, who stepped on first base and fired the ball to Drew, who after catching the ball threw a bullet to second. Rich caught the ball and shouted, "Now, that's what I call a good start!"

Following five minutes of round robin throwing and catching, Rich signaled everyone to the pitcher's mound. "Okay, we've got a little over a month before Little League tryouts. Harley, your fastball is up to sixty-nine miles an hour and I'd say you're way past being your old self. Your arm is healed and growing stronger every day. I have no doubt whatsoever that you'll make a team. Now Drew is a different story."

Picking up a ball lying next to the pitcher's rubber, Rich went on, "Most of the ten-year-olds that will be trying out will be coming up from the seven to nine-year-old group from last year. The managers have already seen these kids play for a couple of years, some since they have been four years old. Not many kids at ten years of age are that good at the catcher position. Now, there will be a number of kids that are eleven and twelve years old, who have a year or two under their belt of playing in the ten to twelve-year-old league that have already established themselves as a catcher. You're going to be the new kid on the block. The kid from Texas. What we have to do is make you appear better than what you are. Here's the thing. The managers are looking for the best kids they can get. Most of the kids at ten can, at times, still seem awkward. What we have to do is make you look like a miniature major league player. You've seen and been to enough major league games since you moved here to know how a major league catcher functions. That's what you have to do. Now, let's get started on some catcher routines. Everyone, take your positions!"

Drew assumed the catcher's position behind home plate while Monica returned to first base and Rich over to third. For thirty minutes, Harley who stood behind and off to the side of Drew rolled one ball after another out in front of home plate simulating a bunt or a light hit. Drew would, just as if he were in an actual game, rise up quickly, run to the ball, field it and throw to either first base or third. Halfway through this process, Rich ran over to second and the practice continued with Drew firing the ball to second base. Following swigs of water, Rich and Monica took turns standing behind Drew and would toss the ball high into the air, sometimes down the first base or third base line, but mostly behind the plate. When they tossed the ball they would yell, "Now," signifying the sound of the bat. Drew would have to turn, remove his mask, search for the ball and then catch it, then toss the ball to Harley who was on first.

Monica looked at her watch; two o'clock. Walking toward the pitcher's mound she signaled, "That's it!" Gathering with the others at the mound, she wiped her brow and commented, "Listen! I'm going to run home and feed Ozzie then I'm going to pick up a bucket of chicken and the fixin's. I'll be back in about an hour with our lunch. You three are going on a three mile run down by the river." Leaving her husband and the two boys standing on the pitcher's mound, she tossed her glove in the backseat of the car, backed out and waved good-bye.

Walking to the picnic table, Drew removed his mask and asked, "This three mile run. Where does it start?"

Pointing at the tree line, Rich answered, "There's an old paved road that isn't used for public transportation any longer. It goes through the woods, swings around and comes out at the north end of the park. The last half-mile is through the park itself. We'll wind up right back here. Let's get these spikes off and get into some sneakers and head out. We'll pile our equipment in the front seat of the truck. Make sure you each grab a water. There won't be any areas where we can get a drink once we start."

The equipment in the truck, Rich pointed up the road and said, "Let's go!"

At the end of the paved park road, they came to a dirt intersection where they continued straight onto a rutted semi-paved road that appeared to have been unattended for years. Surrounded by trees on either side the trio started up the road at a slow jog.

Harley joked, "I'm sure looking forward to the Cardinals having a better year than last year. Mom was right when she said way back in June that we'd be lucky to win seventy games. I can't believe we wound up with a win-loss record of 62-81. We were next to last in the Central Division; the only team worse than the Cards was the Pirates. I was looking over our year-end stats last night. We had a horrible year: last in the league in runs per game, on base percentage, total hits and RBI's. We lost six of our last eight regular season games. We even got swept by the Cubs in late September."

"This coming season has to be better," said Rich. "One of the things that bothers me about this past season is that we had fifty, one run games of which we lost twenty-five. I bet you a dime to a dollar that if we could go back and look at every one of those games we lost, there could have possibly been a way to turn those into victories."

The road took a sharp right and ran next to a set of elevated railroad tracks on their left as Rich continued, "Well I for one am quite optimistic about our Cardinals this year. A lot of things are happening. A businessman by the name of William Dewitt Jr. purchased the Cardinals this past year. It's been my past experience that whenever there is a new owner things start to change. Tony La Russa will be our new manager this year. He's coming to us from the Oakland A's."

"And that's not all," interjected Harley. "During the off season we acquired some new players. We picked up outfielder Willie Magee from Oakland. We signed Todd Stottlemyre, a right handed pitcher also from Oakland."

Rich added, "We also signed Mike Gallego in the infield and got Dennis Eckersley, another right handed pitcher from Oakland."

Drew jumped in on the conversation, "This La Russa, the new manager. How often does a major league team get a new manager?"

"That depends," said Rich. "Remember, when you get to the major leagues it's more than just a game; it's a business...the business of winning. Players are paid high salaries to win games and the manager of the team has to always lead the team in that direction. If a team has a good year, the manager will get credit and if the team has a down year, the manager, more than likely, can and often does have to shoulder the blame. During the Cardinals history they have had sixty-two different managers. The first manager the St. Louis team had was way back in 1882. His name of Neth Cuthbert. Since then, the team has gone through over five dozen managers."

Making a left at the end of the straight road, Drew asked, "So it doesn't make any difference if the players and fans like the manager or not. It's just about winning? How do we know we're getting a good manager? Has he ever taken a team to the World Series?"

"Yes," answered Rich. "He had three really good seasons where he went to the series three years straight. In 1988, he lost in the series to Los Angeles and then in 1989 he won the series over San Francisco. He came back the next year in 1990 and lost to Cincinnati. He knows how to win. I think things are looking up for the Cards: new owner, new manager and some new additions to our pitching staff and lineup."

Rich brought up a new subject he knew would grab the interest of the boys, especially Harley. "There's been talk the Cardinals are thinking about building a new stadium."

Harley reacted just about the way Rich figured. Stopping in his tracks, he repeated, "A new stadium?"

Rich signaled to Harley, "C'mon, let's keep moving."

Harley, now running right next to Rich, asked, "Why would they want to put up a new stadium? What's wrong with the one we have now?"

"Like I said before. Baseball is a business. Sooner or later every stadium will get replaced with a newer, more updated facility. The Cards have been playing down at Busch since 1966. Baseball has changed over the years, especially from the viewpoint of the typical fan. Coming to the stadium is about a lot more than just attending a game. People want to experience the moment. They want more comfortable seating, better food selections and on and on. I don't think it's anything to get upset over. Besides that, it'll probably take a couple of years before they get everything ironed out."

Stopping at the intersecting dirt road that would lead back to the park, Rich signaled for them to stop. Taking a drink of water from his bottle, he asked, "Do you boys want to cut up here or continue to the end of the park. I'll leave it up to you."

Drew asked, "How far have we come so far?"

"Not quite two miles," said Rich. "If we take this dirt road, we'll be back at my truck in about five minutes."

Harley spoke up as he started up the dirt road, "I have to use the restroom, so I'm going to head on up."

Drew followed and agreed, "It's the restroom for me also."

Rich waved at them and continued up the paved road that ran adjacent to the river. "I'll see you when I get finished."

Heading up the dirt road, Drew asked, "How far to the restrooms?"

Harley picked up the pace. "About a quarter mile or so. We'll be there before you know it. It's on the other side of the ball field."

Drew caught up with Harley. "What do you think my chances are when we try out for Little League?"

"Don't worry…you'll be fine! Besides that, we still have a month to get you ready. One of the things you're better at than any of the catchers I've seen your age is your ability to get after a bunt. Most kids are slow to react and when they do get to the ball they hurry their throw. You're quick and you've got a strong arm."

"Speaking of the bunt," said Drew. "Do you know when it was first invented?"

Harley laughed. "I see you've been down at the library again studying up on baseball. I'm afraid this time I do have the answer to your question. No one can be sure when the first bunt actually happened, but we do know the name of the player that made it famous…and a part of baseball. His name is Dickey Pearce and he was a shortstop back in the 1860s. Back in those days if you hit a ball in the infield and then it went foul it was still considered a hit. Well, Dickey Pearce was really good at bunting the ball, or as they called it back then, 'The tricky hit'. Even after they changed the rules so that when the ball crossed the foul line, it was a strike and if it was on the third strike you were automatically called out,

Pearce continued to outsmart the opposing infield with his bunting abilities."

Running up the paved road near the ball field, Harley asked, "I don't suppose you read about the squeeze play as well, did you?"

"No, but I do know what a squeeze play is. Remember when we went to the Cards last home game and they attempted to pull one off. It failed. It wasn't even close."

Harley went on to explain, "The squeeze play was invented at Yale University by Dutch Carter and George B. Case. Today, the bunt is more commonly used than the squeeze play. Why, you could go an entire season and not see a squeeze play in the majors on most teams, but the bunt is an important part of the game. This is something you, as a catcher, should always be aware of, especially in a close game in the late innings."

Passing the picnic pavilion, Harley pointed at a small green cinderblock building located next to a sawdust-covered playground. "The men's room is on the opposite side. C'mon."

Finished, Harley waited for Drew outside of the building. As Drew exited, Harley pointed at a thick wooded area west of the ball field and noted, "It doesn't look like my dad has returned from his run yet. It could be about a half hour before my mother gets back with our lunch. There's a trail over there in the woods that is not used as much as the walkway around the lake. By the time we get around to the other side, our lunch should be here."

"Okay," said Drew. "That's fine with me."

Walking around the southern tip of the lake they made a right onto a paved path that led back into the tall trees and dense shrubs. Drew looked off into the thick trees and commented, "It's really peaceful. I would think people would like walking through here."

Leading the way, Harley pointed out, "People do come back here but not as much as the walkway around the lake."

Suddenly, the path was blocked as Aaron stepped out from behind a tree and stood in the middle of the pavement. "Hello there, boys! Out for a stroll…are we?"

Turning, Harley looked back the way they had come. Aaron's two older cousins blocked the path behind them. Seeing Harley's reaction, Aaron remarked smartly, "If you're thinkin' of runnin' that ain't gonna happen."

Aaron stepped toward Drew and smirked. "It's different now

than it was the first time we met down at Busch Stadium. I didn't know what to expect. That's been what…almost six months ago. I've been askin' around about you. Seems ya know some karate. I wasn't prepared for that the last time we met…but now, I am!"

Harley's mind was racing and he remembered what his father had told him about Aaron. How dangerous he could be? Hesitantly, he asked, "What do you want Buckman?"

Walking to Harley, Aaron placed his index finger right in Harley's face. "What I want is a little payback. The word got around that your new little friend over there got the best of me. I've got a reputation to live up to and I can't have it goin' around some little twerp from Texas took me down!"

Harley just couldn't stand there; he had to say something. "Why is it every time I run into you, you have your two cousins with you. It's like you can't do anything without them to back you up." Harley knew he was pushing his luck and the only thing he could think of was to talk their way out of what was rapidly appearing to be an unpleasant situation.

Aaron laughed. "My cousins could care less about you two idiots! I don't need them when it comes to you wimps!"

Harley looked at the cousins. One nodded and the other remained silent.

Aaron looked at Drew and then back to Harley. "Your friend here needs to be taught a lesson. He made me bleed, which is what I am going to make him do."

"You can't be serious," said Harley. "You can't expect him to fight you. You outweigh him by over a hundred pounds. That hardly seems fair."

"Fair ain't got nothin' to do with it," snapped Aaron. "Maybe he should have thought of that before he practically twisted my nose off my face!"

Surprisingly, Drew spoke up, "It's all right Harley. A bully like Aaron is going to do what he wants. I'm not afraid of you, Buckman!"

Before Drew could ready himself for an attack, Aaron bolted into Drew knocking him off his feet. Drew went down hard, his head slamming into the grass and dirt on the side of the path. Harley started to move toward Aaron, but then thought better of it as one of the cousins stepped forward and blocked his way. Glassy eyed, Drew slightly dazed, looked around as if he were not sure of his whereabouts. Aaron sat on top of him and reached down, grabbed his nose and twisted it until blood squirted out the nostrils. Drew yelled in pain as tears filled his eyes. Aaron slapped Drew across the face, stood and looked at his cousins. "Well, that set things straight for now."

Turning to face Harley, Aaron smiled in a cocky manner and asked, "You want to try and do anythin' about this Sims?"

Harley was so mad he couldn't see straight, but he knew he had to restrain himself. If he got another broken arm his parents would be upset beyond belief. Slowly, he shook his head, indicating no.

"Just like I thought. Little creeps like you always hang together." Looking down at Drew holding his nose and wiping his eyes, Aaron laughed and pointed at Drew. "One more thing. Earlier we were watchin' you practicin' over at the ball field. Little League tryouts are in a month. Ol' Harley here will make a team because he's everyone's golden boy. You, on the other hand Drew will never make a team if I have anythin' to do with it. What I'm sayin' is that it's a long time between now and the tryouts. It'd be a shame if little ol' Drew here got injured to the point where he couldn't play. Now, you just think about that. Somethin' could happen to ya and ya might not even see it comin'. It might be tomorrow, next week or the week after. Ya just never know." Turning to the cousins, Aaron ordered, "Let's git out of here!" Within seconds the trio disappeared in the woods.

By the time Harley crossed the path, Drew had sat up and was trying to wipe the blood from his shirt. Kneeling next to his friend, Harley, asked, "Are you okay?"

Drew smiled as he wiped his tear stained face. "It really hurts, but other than that, I'll survive."

Getting to his feet, he leaned on a nearby tree. "Well, what do you think about my great karate abilities now?"

"Look, there was nothing you could do. He's too big. Just like my father told me. He's a dangerous kid. My dad says he's stupid and you can't fix stupid. How does your nose feel? Do you think it's broken?"

"I've never had a broken nose so I don't know what that must feel like." Touching his nose gently, he moved it from side to side, up and down. "Aside from the throbbing sensation, I think I'm fine." Removing a handkerchief from his pants he wiped the blood from his face and looked down over his shirt. "What are we going to tell your folks about this blood?"

"My first thought is that we should tell them exactly what happened."

"If it's the same to you, I'd rather not tell them what happened. That would only lead to them asking us a lot of questions that eventually would lead to what happened last year down at the stadium and then they would be grilling us about why we didn't tell them about that. I need some time to think about this. If it's okay with you we just need to tell your parents when we get back to the field I tripped and hit my nose on a rock or something. Remember, we agreed to keep what happened down at Busch a secret. Now, there's just a little more to the secret."

"You didn't have a chance to fight. Aaron just flat out attacked you. What could you have possibly done? If you would have tried to fight back, I think you'd be in a lot worse shape than you are right now. C'mon, we better head back to the field. When we get there, the story is you fell while running and hit a rock. I'm sure they'll believe us. What reason would they have not to?"

Rounding a long curve in the path, Drew continued to wipe his face as he commented, "I think the bleeding has stopped and the pain is easing up. What do you think about what Buckman said about the possibility that I might get hurt sometime in the next month and wind up missing the tryouts?"

"I think that was just a bluff. I think he's trying to scare you into not going to the tryouts." Stopping next to an old bench, Harley placed his hand on Drew's shoulder. "But, here's the thing. If he attacks you again we have to agree right now that we'll go to our parents."

Drew started up the path, "Agreed!"

Emerging from the trees, Harley nodded toward the ball field where Rich was sitting on the picnic table drinking water and Monica was arranging their lunch. "Okay, here we go. It's no big deal. Remember, you tripped and hit your nose on a rock…that's it!"

Drew agreed as they walked across the road, passed the vehicles and onto the field. Monica looked up and instantly noticed Drew's bloodstained shirt. "What on earth happened?"

Flashing a stupid smile, Drew answered, "I was running along, tripped on a tree root, fell and hit my nose on a rock. It's nothing to worry about. It bled for a few minutes but then stopped."

Monica's motherly instinct clicked in as she got up from the table to inspect Drew's nose. "Are you sure you're okay? Maybe we should take you to the emergency room to make sure it's not broken."

"Drew gently objected, "There's no pain whatsoever. How could it be broken when I feel fine?"

Rich interjected, "Remember, Monica is a trained nurse."

"That's true," confirmed Monica. "Are you experiencing any dizziness? Is your vision clear?"

Drew sat at the table and looked at the bucket of chicken. "I'm fine. It was just a stupid accident."

Rich spoke up again, "If the boy says he fine, I say we eat our lunch and see how things go. I can't tell you how many times as a youngster I fell and got nosebleeds."

"All right," said Monica, "but if you start feeling odd let us know immediately."

Passing out paper plates, plastic spoons and forks, Monica removed the lid from the bucket, while Rich opened containers of mashed potatoes and green beans and commented, "After we're finished eating we can spend a couple of hours working on your hitting, Drew. Your catching skills are coming along pretty well, but we still need to do some work on your hitting. Remember, a well-rounded catcher has to be able to contribute hitting skills along with his ability to catch."

Placing a wing on his plate, Drew asked, "In your opinion, who is the greatest catcher of all time as it stands right now?"

Rich was about to answer, but Harlcy beat him to the punch. "According to the top ten best catchers as of right now, Yogi Berra is number one."

"Not necessarily," corrected Rich. "Yogi's ability behind the plate was not as good as the number two catcher, Johnny Bench, but what placed Yogi at the top is that besides being a great catcher, he was a pure hitter: three time MVP, fifteen time all-star, won ten World Series with the Yankees, hit three hundred and fifty-eight homeruns and led the Yankees in RBI's from 1949 until

1955."

Taking a bite of potatoes, Drew asked his next question, "Are there any St. Louis catchers in the current top ten?"

"No, I'm afraid not," said Rich. "There are some great catchers on the list: Mickey Cochran, Roy Campenella, Carlton Fisk and even Gabby Hartnett who played back in the early 1920s, but who knows? One of the greatest catchers ever may someday play for the Cardinals."

At three thirty, Monica began to clear off the picnic table. Tossing the bucket of chicken bones and empty containers in a trashcan, she took a long drink of soda and suggested, "I say we get in about an hour of hitting practice and then we run the bases."

Monica dropped the catcher's mitt to the ground and picked up the section of cardboard where by means of a black magic marker she had notated Drew's results. As Harley and Rich joined them at home plate, she announced the tally, "Twenty plate appearances, five hits, seven strike outs, two long fly balls that would have been more than likely caught, two infield pop-ups and four infield balls that would have been fielded. You made contact with the ball sixty-five percent of the time and your batting average came in at .250. That's pretty good and it's better than last time out where you only got four hits and you struck out nine times." Patting Drew on his shoulder, Monica congratulated him, "You're getting better. What say we sit down, grab a drink and rest for a few minutes, then we'll repeat the process but this time with Rich doing the pitching?"

As Harley and Drew walked back to the table where there was a cooler of cold waters, Rich and Monica picked up a few balls that were lying around the infield. Drew turned to Harley and looked back at the filed, "Do you really think your parents bought into that business about me falling and hitting my nose on a rock?"

"Sure," said Harley, "why wouldn't they believe us? Like I said before. They have no reason to not believe what we told them."

Taking a bottle out of the cooler, Drew frowned, "I just don't like lying to my parents...or yours."

"If you're talking about what happened down at Busch Stadium months ago, I don't think we lied to your parents or mine. We just didn't tell them what happened *and* we agreed why we shouldn't.

Now, this crap that happened today back there on the trail? I guess we did lie to my parents, but if we told them the truth that would only lead to the incident down at Busch."

Taking a drink, Drew looked off into the woods. "For all we know, Aaron and his cousins might be out there in those trees watching us right now. Remember what he said about what a shame it would be if I got injured and missed the tryouts. He said if he had anything to do with it, I was not going to make a team. He said I'd never see it coming. That bothers me."

"Well, there isn't a lot we can do about that except to be on the lookout and be careful; where we go…what we do."

Drew smiled and took another swallow. "I know what I'm going to do. I'm going to pray for Buckman!"

Confused, Harley responded, "Pray?"

"Yeah, tomorrow morning when I go to church with my family, "I'll lift Aaron Buckman up in prayer!" Snapping his fingers, Drew grinned, "Maybe you'd like to come to church with us tomorrow. We can both pray for Aaron."

Harley, not sure how to answer sputtered, "I don't…know…all that much…about praying. I'm not sure I'd know what to do at church."

"That's easy!" beamed Drew. "You just sit there and worship God."

Looking back at his parents, Harley admitted, "Maybe I have a phobia of sorts…of going to church. Like I told you before, we only go twice a year: Easter and Christmas and even then, I feel uncomfortable…out of place."

"Well," said Drew, 'I'm still inviting you to go along. I'll give you the same deal you gave me when you invited me to my first Cardinal game. You told me to be at your house at six o'clock. If I wasn't there, it wasn't any big deal. Church service is at nine o'clock. We leave the house at eight thirty. If you are at my house by then, you can go along, if not…it's no big deal!"

Rich yelled from the field, "You boys about ready to get started again?"

Harley threw his empty water bottle in the trashcan and started for the field as he spoke to Drew, "I'll think this church thing over!"

CHAPTER 10

"WELL, I'M SORRY HARLEY ISN'T GOING TO CHURCH with us this morning," said Mrs. Scott. "Maybe some other time."

Drew looked out the backseat window at the falling rain and answered, "I was really looking forward to him coming along but I guess it's not going to happen. He told me his parents only go twice a year. Stop the car!" shouted Drew as he pointed up the street. "It's Harley!"

Harley stopped at the end of the drive and waved. Rolling down the window, Mrs. Scott smiled and nodded toward the backseat. "Get in here before you get soaked!"

Hopping in the backseat, Harley wiped the rain from his face with the back of his hand. "I was planning on getting here on time, but things are nuts down at my house this morning. The hose on our washing machine broke about an hour ago and the kitchen is flooded."

Mrs. Scott turned in the seat and spoke to Harley. "I'm so sorry your parents are having problems this morning, but I'm glad that you can still go along with us."

Roxann looked across the seat at Harley and smiled sweetly. "I would like to meet your dog sometime."

"I'm sure Ozzie would like meeting you too," said Harley. "Maybe Drew could bring you by sometime and you can play with Ozzie."

Looking in the rearview mirror, Don asked, "Ozzie! That's an unusual name for a dog."

"Now you've done it, Dad," said Drew. "We'll be talking baseball all the way to church."

Before anyone could respond, Harley answered Don's question. "Our dog, Ozzie, is named after Ozzie Smith who is the current shortstop for the St. Louis Cardinals. He played for the San Diego Padres from 1978 until 1981 when he was traded to St. Louis. He has played for the Card's ever since. As a matter of fact, the first year he played for us we won the World Series. That was in '82. He's been to fifteen All-Star games, was the National League Most Valuable Player in '85 and has thirteen Golden Glove awards to his credit."

Parking at the far end of the church lot, Don commented, "Looks like it's going to be a full house today. We'll probably have to sit up front."

As they approached the structure Harley looked at the plain brown building; large glass double doors, no stain glass windows, and no steeple. He hadn't been to church that many times, but the Catholic Church he and his parents attended each Christmas and Easter was a beautiful old stone structure, with large oak, stained glass entry doors flanked with two large fig trees potted in what he always thought were golden planters. A huge, gleaming white steeple topped the church. The building he was about to enter was just a large, plain square cinderblock structure.

Drew's father had been right. The church was packed. An older baldheaded man approached and guided them down the aisle on the left to the very front row where they were seated in a row of regular looking chairs. Harley thought again to himself, *No pews, just regular chairs.* S*trange!*

He was ushered into the row of seats first and wound up sitting next to a woman who had to be in her eighties. The woman placed a wrinkled hand on his shoulder and welcomed him. "God bless you, young man!"

Harley looked at an elevated grey-carpeted stage. Once again, he was confused. The Catholic Church had bright red carpeting, gigantic statues of people who were no doubt famous religious people of the past, an ornate, golden looking table with a large white Bible. Drew tapped Harley on his leg and asked, "What do you think?"

Harley sat back in the chair, turned and looked back at the rows of people seated behind them. "It's different…very different than what I'm used to."

Drew was about to say something when his mother tapped him on his leg and placed her index finger to her lips, a signal for him to remain quiet. A woman stepped up on the stage and began to read a number of announcements.

Near the back of the stage stood three people. Two men were holding guitars, and the third, a woman who stepped up to a microphone. One of the guitar players started to strum the strings and announced the first song, inviting the congregation to sing along. The words to the uplifting tune were bought up on a large screen behind the stage and everyone seemed to join in. Noticing that Harley was not singing, the woman on his right leaned close and nodded at the screen and smiled. Harley began, "Shout, shout on high..."

The woman, pleased that he was participating clapped her hands and looked toward the ceiling. Looking around, he noticed other people who had raised their hands and held their heads up high. Drew was singing and Roxann was clapping her hands along with her mother and father.

The song no sooner ended when a man dressed in casual slacks and a blue shirt stepped onto the stage. He waited until the last note was played then walked to the microphone, cleared his throat and began to speak, "Welcome to City on the Hill, a church where all are welcome. If you are visiting us for the first time or a long-time member, we teach from the Bible." Holding up what looked like a well-used Bible, he went on, "Today, our message is yet another story about David. Today's story is one of the most popular Bible stories there are. It's the story of how a young shepherd boy goes out onto the battlefield and defeats the mighty Goliath, a giant in the Philistine army. Let us begin."

Harley was mesmerized as he sat and listened to the story of David and Goliath. Unlike the priest, who had seemed so regimented and businesslike, this pastor was just standing in front of the people and telling them a story, a very interesting story.

Forty minutes later, the story came to a close and the pastor went into some dialogue about receiving communion. A man on either side of the aisle passed a plate containing shredded bread and a metal container that held small plastic cups of what looked like grape juice. Each person, as the articles were passed down the aisle, took a piece of bread and a cup of the juice and simply held it. When the men came to his aisle, Harley leaned over and asked Drew, "Am I allowed to have some of the bread and juice?"

Drew smiled and gave his answer, "Yes, you may."

Ten minutes later, following the collection and some final

messages, the service ended when the pastor told everyone to "Go in peace!"

Exiting the main part of the church, the Scott's stopped to say a few words with the pastor. Introducing Harley to the man, Mr. Scott spoke, "Harley, this is Pastor Franks...Pastor, this is Harley Sims, Drew's close friend and neighbor."

The pastor reached and shook Harley's hand. "Why yes, I've heard quite a bit about this young man. According to Drew's parents you are the little miracle worker who lives up the street from them."

Harley, not sure how to respond, shrugged and sheepishly asked, "Miracle worker?"

"Yes. You're the young man who did what the doctors could not do. You single-handedly relieved Drew of his phobia."

Harley, not much on receiving compliments, held up his hands. "It was nothing that big. We just started to play some catch and it just sort of went from there."

Pastor Franks continued the conversation, "I understand that you have a dream of playing in the major leagues. A pitcher, I believe...is that right?"

Harley, politely corrected the pastor. "I don't have a dream of becoming a major league pitcher...it's more like a goal. I practice every day."

"You remind me of myself when I was your age. I grew up on the outskirts of Paramus, New Jersey. I practiced day and night. I was an infielder. I played three years of Little League, four years in high school and three years in college. Some major league scouts were interested in me but then, in my junior year; something happened that changed my life. I got the calling from God!"

Harley, not understanding what the man had said, slowly asked, "What do you mean by the calling?"

"God spoke to me and I knew I was supposed to go into ministry, so I up and quit baseball...just like that!"

Harley couldn't believe what he was hearing. "You had a chance to play in the majors and you gave it up? That's hard to believe. I can't imagine anything standing in the way of my goal of playing in the big leagues."

"Well, that was just me," said the pastor. "I'm not saying that anything will change your mind. Despite the fact I didn't get to go to the majors I still love baseball. Living in St. Louis, over the three years I've been here, the Cardinals have grown on me. That being said, my favorite part of baseball still remains Little League. I understand both you and Drew here will soon be trying out for a Little League team this spring."

Everyone was half-soaked running across the parking lot in the pouring rain before they hopped in the car. Don, sitting behind the steering wheel started the car and immediately turned on the wipers. Backing out of the parking space, he announced, "I'm starving. How about you Harley? Are you up for the buffet over at the Golden Corral?"

Harley immediately refused, "I'm afraid I didn't bring money along for lunch."

Mrs. Scott laughed. "Lunch is on us today, especially since you didn't get to have any breakfast."

Roxann spoke up, "I'm starving too! When we get there I'm going to have a fried chicken leg."

The restaurant was crammed with people, but Mrs. Scott managed to locate a table in the far corner next to the windows. Drew's father stood and spoke to Harley. "This is one of our favorite places to eat. Normally, we go up to the salad bar first and get our salads, and then later we hit the buffet. It's up to you, Harley."

Harley was agreeable and answered, "I think I'll just go up with you guys and start with a salad."

Back at the table, Don blessed their food and finished up by saying, "Let's eat!"

Mrs. Scott shook some salt onto her salad and spoke to Harley, "So what did you think of the service at church?"

"It was really different than what I've experienced the few times I've gone with my parents."

"In what way?" probed Don.

"Well, for one thing when we first went in it didn't remind me of a church, but I forgot all about that when the pastor started to speak to us. That story of David, and what was the giant's name?"

Roxann answered the question, "Goliath!"

"That's right," said Harley. "His name was Goliath. That story was amazing. The best part of the story for me," said Harley, "was when David killed Goliath by slinging a single stone at him with his slingshot and knocking him down, then he just walks up to him and cuts his head off with Goliath's own sword."

"The point of the story," said Mrs. Scott, "is that in our everyday lives we are going to be faced with giants; people or situations in our lives that seem insurmountable, but, just like David in the story. If we have faith in God there is nothing we cannot deal with."

Minutes passed, when Roxann pushed her small salad plate to the side and asked, "Can I get my chicken leg now?"

Mrs. Scott smiled at her daughter then spoke to Drew, "Why don't you walk your sister up to the buffet and help her get what she wants."

Drew stood instantly and remarked, "Fried chicken sounds good to me; maybe some mashed potatoes and some corn…"

Before Drew finished his sentence, Harley was on his feet. "Yeah, and how about some hot rolls too?"

Guiding Roxann next to the salad bar the trio approached the long stainless steel and wood buffet area. The line was long and Roxann frowned as she looked at the tray of chicken that was going down fast. "They are going to run out by the time we get there!"

Placing his arm around his sister's shoulder, Drew assured her, "Don't worry, they have lots of chicken."

Harley chimed in, "And I bet they have a leg just for you!"

By the time they got in line, the chicken had all been taken except for one single wing in the bottom of the pan. Roxann looked up at her brother and gave one of her pouting looks. "It's all gone!"

Just when they got in front of the pan, a woman emerged through a set of stainless steel doors as she carried a tray full of hot, steaming chicken. Drew smiled when the woman dumped the assorted pieces of chicken down into the pan. Roxann smiled when she saw a number of legs tumble and fall into the pan. "I'm gonna get two!"

Reaching for the tongs laying in the pan, Roxann's arm was brushed to the side as someone stepped in front of her. Aaron Buckman smiled brashly at both Drew and Harley. "Well I guess they let anybody in this place!"

Roxann spoke up, "Hey…no butting in!"

Looking at her, Aaron smirked, "Who's this little twerp?"

Drew looked back at the table where his parents were seated and answered, "She's my sister."

Looking down at the pan, Aaron grabbed the tongs. "Me and my dad, we really like chicken, especially legs."

Harley spoke up, "I thought your dad was in prison."

Motioning with the tongs at a table, Aaron explained, "He was, but he got out this weekend."

Looking in the direction Aaron had pointed Harley noticed a muscular man seated by himself, wearing a tan T-shirt. His arms were covered in tattoos and he had earrings in both ears. His unshaven face was topped with a bald head.

The man was just finishing gulping down a large plate of potatoes when he pushed the plate to the side and finished off a large drink. Aaron started to take one chicken leg after another. Piling seven legs on his plate, he held up the last leg with the tongs and displayed it to Roxann. "Would you like one of these?"

Roxann smiled, "Yes please."

Aaron laughed and took a bite out of the leg, "Sorry, they seem to be out of legs at the moment." Turning to Drew, he gave a cocky smile. "See you creeps around and remember what I said over at the park. You'll never see it comin'."

Before they realized what was happening Roxann ran back to their table. Harley, in a state of panic tugged on Drew's shirt. "C'mon we have to get back there before she blows everything for us."

"No…wait!" said Drew. "My sister doesn't know the whole story. All she can tell my parents is that some mean kid took all of the chicken. I know how my folks operate, especially when it comes to my sister. They'll wait and speak to me first before they do anything."

"But what if your dad comes over here and starts to ask questions?"

"He won't do that. Roxann didn't get injured in any way. She just got her feelings hurt. I say we go on and get our food. When we get back to the table if anyone says anything, we'll deal with it then. Let's wait and see what happens."

Grabbing a plate, Harley started around the corner of the buffet table after placing a wing on the plate. Drew, at his side was plopping a scoop of mashed potatoes on his plate as he looked over at the table where Aaron and his father were seated. Aaron noticed his stare and nonchalantly waved a chicken leg at him. Taking a large spoonful of corn, Drew commented, "What a jerk! I have half a mind to walk over there and tell his father what he did to my sister."

"Forget that!" warned Harley. "My dad told me all about Aaron's father. He said they went to high school together. According to my dad, Mr. Buckman was even worse than Aaron is. Talking to him about his son's behavior would be a waste of time. My dad's advice was simply to avoid Aaron and I think we should do the same with his father. Besides that, did you get a good look at Aaron's father? He reminds me of one of those professional wrestlers on television. When we get back to the table, we have to blow this thing off. The last thing we want is for your father to go over there and talk with them. When we get back to the table, let me do most of the talking."

Approaching the table, Harley spoke up before Drew's parents had an opportunity to speak. "You'll never guess what happened over there at the buffet!"

Sitting down at the table, Harley went on as if what had happened wasn't anything to be concerned over. "Some kid I know; he actually lives on the other side of Arnold, took all the chicken legs before we had a chance to get any."

Mrs. Scott spoke up. "Roxann said he butted right in line and that he was rude."

Cutting into a slice of meatloaf, Harley agreed, "That's just the way he is. His name is Aaron Buckman. He's nothing more than a local bully. He's two years older than Drew and I." Gesturing with his head out into the restaurant, he further explained, "Aaron is here with his father today, who by the way was just released from prison. My father says Aaron has had a rough life growing up so far and he hasn't had the luxury of having good parents. I've had a few run-ins with him and I always just ignore him." Noticing another tray of chicken being brought out, Harley spoke to Roxann. "C'mon, let's get those legs before they run out again!" Jumping up from the table, Roxann followed him across the room.

Mrs. Scott addressed her son. "Do you know this Buckman kid…this bully?"

"Not really. Harley told me about him right after we moved in. Believe me, this is not a problem. The kid just took some chicken for himself and his father. Roxann is now getting her chicken. I say we just forget this and enjoy our lunch."

Roxann smiled when Harley placed two fresh legs on her plate. Looking down the long table, she warned, "Here comes that mean boy again!"

Harley suggested, "Why don't you go back to the table. I'm going to grab a couple of things myself."

Aaron was carrying a plate piled high with desserts: blueberry pie, brownies, carrot cake and Jell-O. He walked up to Harley and watched Roxann walk off. "Well, well, well! Aren't you just the polite young man." Looking over at their table, Aaron asked, "Where's your pal? Too afraid to come back up here?"

Quickly, Harley reached down and scooped a ladleful of gravy onto Aaron's varied desserts and followed Roxann as he spoke to Aaron, "You'll never see it coming!"

It was then that Aaron stared down at his gravy-soaked desserts in disbelief. Not sure what to do, he laid the plate down and returned to the dessert area, all the while staring in Harley's direction.

Back at the table, Harley sat down as he bit into a roll. Mrs. Scott thanked him for assisting Roxann in getting her chicken and then asked, "I see you were talking to a boy over there. Was that this Aaron Buckman?"

"Yeah, that was him."

"Is everything okay? Did he give you any trouble?"

"No, everything's fine. He's enjoying his dessert."

Don gestured at Harley and took a drink. "Drew here tells me you and your parents are some of the biggest Cardinal fans in the city. I kind of gathered that the first time we met after we moved here. Over the past few months of working for Anheiser Busch, I'm beginning to realize that being an avid St. Louis Cardinal fan is quite common for people who live in this area. A lot of people at Busch are really upset right now, what with the Cardinals recently being sold. What do you think about that?"

Harley thought for a moment and then answered, "My dad was

just talking about that the other day with Drew and me when we were over at the park practicing. I don't think it's that big of a deal. The Cards are still the Cards! Last year we had a horrible year. The way I look at it, we can only go up from here. Who knows, this could wind up being a great baseball year for us."

Mrs. Scott changed the subject. "Drew has been keeping us posted about his daily practice. As you may know, he is determined to make one of the Little League teams this spring. He tells us both you and your father think he's got a good chance."

"I think he has more than just a good chance," said Harley. "He's only been at it now for around seven months. My dad says he has a lot of talent, but more important than that; he has heart! My dad has always taught me you can teach talent and skills, but heart is something you can't teach. You either have it or you don't. Drew has it!"

CHAPTER 11

TURNING OFF THE IGNITION, RICH SAT BACK AND SMILED at Drew and Harley who were seated next to him. "Well boys, this is it; Little League tryouts. I've heard that somewhere between seventy-five to eighty ten-year-olds have registered this year. Of the eight existing teams there are a lot of vacancies to be filled." Looking at his watch, he announced, "It's almost eight o'clock. Tryouts start at nine sharp. I'll be back this evening at five to pick you up. Good luck and I'll see you then."

Harley opened the door and hopped out. Drew followed and assisted Harley as he grabbed their equipment from the back. Drew picked up his catcher's gear and looked around the complex. "Do you think Aaron will be here today?"

"I doubt it," said Harley. "He's already on a team and won't report until practice begins next week. There's nothing he can do to prevent you and I from trying out for a team."

Sitting on the grass, Drew looked at a number of kids carrying equipment across the paved lot. "Eighty kids...that's a lot of ballplayers. Will there be enough open spots for kids and what happens to the ones who don't make it?"

Harley leaned on the chain link fence and watched a group of men who were busy preparing the infield on Field #3. "It's like this, Drew. The league has eight teams with a roster of fourteen players on each team. That means the league needs one hundred and twelve players to fill the league roster. Team managers usually try and draft players that can play multiple positions."

Drew checked the bottom of his rubber cleats and asked, "And you just happen to be one of those players who can play a number of positions."

"I can, but I prefer to pitch. I understand how to play other positions, but pitching will always be my strength. Now, your strength is catching. You also could play in the outfield. I mean, if a manager likes the way you hit and does not need a catcher, he may try you at another position. This happens a lot because there are kids that get chosen, just because a slot needs to be filled. The truth is every player that comes to the tryouts will wind up on a team…not necessarily a regular Little League team, but on what is called the morning league."

Drew looked up at Harley in confusion. "I don't understand."

Sitting down by the fence, Harley explained, "After this weekend of tryouts, there will be what they call a draft. All the players trying out for teams will have been seen by all eight managers. Everyone's name and their main playing position will be posted right here at the league office. A couple of days later the managers will begin to make their choices. The last place team from last year gets to make the first choice and so on until they get to the first place team and then it starts over again until each team has filled its roster. Any players left are placed on the morning league that plays on Saturday mornings. What's left are players that are not ready for the league. Kids who still do not completely understand the game or those who cannot hit or field very well. They play on the morning league until the following year when they have developed their skills better and then they will probably be chosen for a regular Little League team."

Drew thought for a moment and then stated, "So the first few kids chosen are the best players, but they go to the teams with the worst records from last year."

Throwing a ball into the air Harley caught it with his glove. "That's right. This way the teams will be more even and no one will have an advantage over the other teams."

Drew picked up his catcher's mitt and pounded his fist into the webbing. "You'll be the first one to be picked. How do you feel about getting to play on the worse team?"

"That's okay with me. Just because a team didn't do well last year, doesn't mean the same thing will happen this year."

Their conversation was interrupted by a voice, "Hello there boys! I was hoping I'd see you both here today."

Pastor Franks gave the boys a wide grin as they both stood and reached for his extended hand. "Why are you here?" asked Drew.

"Funny thing!" said the Pastor. "I just got a call two days ago from the league. Turns out the manager for the last place team, the Cougars, received a job opportunity out in Colorado. He had to transfer his family out there. His assistant manager from last year is not returning, so the league needs a coach for last year's team. One of the board members goes to our church and knew how much I liked baseball, especially Little League, so he asked me if I would be interested in coaching a team this year. I said yes and here I am!" Looking across the field, he excused himself. "Look boys, I've got to run. I've got to attend a quick meeting for the managers before practice starts. Good luck today!"

Watching Pastor Franks walk along the fence line, Drew commented, "Looks like you're going to be playing for the Cougars."

"Maybe…maybe not," said Harley. "We'll just have to wait and see." Lying on the grass Harley went into a hurdle's spread, turning his right leg and bending his torso toward his outstretched left foot. "C'mon, let's get our stretching in before we have to report to the field."

At precisely nine o'clock Drew and Harley stood amidst the mass of young boys huddled down the first base line of Field #5. A group of men, mostly league officials and managers stood in a circle in front of the visiting team dugout. Drew leaned toward Harley and whispered, "I'm glad my parents aren't here. That would make me nervous."

Harley looked at the parent-filled bleachers, and added, "I bet you a lot of the parents here today have very little knowledge of the rules or have played much ball in their lives. Just wait until the season starts. You'll be amazed at the way some parents yell at their kids, the umpires and the managers. If my parents did that at one of my games, I'd be embarrassed…"

Suddenly, a loud voice magnified by a microphone on the pitcher's mound, reverberated around the field, "Gentlemen, could I please have your attention?"

It took a few seconds but the group of young boys turned toward the pitcher's mound and became silent. Looking up into the bleachers and then back at the boys the man continued, "Good morning! My name is Dave Meddler and I'm the President of the Arnold Little League. The gentleman standing directly behind me is the Vice President, Sam Duncan. Standing over by the home team dugout are our current board members. The sixteen gentlemen lined up on my right are this year's team managers and assistants. We also have a number of parent volunteers standing out by second base who will assist us for the next two days during tryouts. I would like to welcome not only the youngsters who are here today but the parents as well. The tryouts for the 1996 Arnold Little League will begin in a few moments, but first I would like to cover our agenda for the next two days. Day one will consist of fielding, pitching, catching and throwing skills. Day two we will be focused on hitting, running, stealing bases and decision making on the field. We will break for water and snacks around one o'clock both days and then continue until five when all the players will be excused. The tryouts will end at five o'clock on Sunday. Decisions on player's chosen and what teams they will be playing on will be made on Tuesday and they will be posted here at the main office on Wednesday. Good luck to everyone. Now, let's get started. First of all, I need all the players to line up starting at home plate and stretching down the first base line and beyond, shortest to the tallest. Once that is established, we will count off starting with one until we get to the end of the line. It is extremely important you remember your number since that will be your number for the next two days."

With the aid of the volunteers it only took the boys a few minutes to get lined up. Satisfied, Dave gave the signal, "Count off!"

The boy standing next to home plate yelled out, "One!"

Down the line it went, "Two, Three, Four, Five…"

The count finally came to Drew as he shouted, "Fourteen!"

Harley waited patiently for his turn, listening as the count continued, "Forty-one, Forty-two, Forty-three…"

Harley belted out his number loudly, "Forty-four!"

The count finished, Dave spoke again, "Okay, the next thing you have to do is when I give the signal you need to run down to the tents set up in center field. There are five tents with large signs on the front: Pitchers, catchers, infielders, outfielders, and finally, multiple positions. You need in an orderly fashion to report to the tent representing the position you play. When you get there give the people at the table your full name and number. You will then receive a square green section of paper with your number written on it. This will be pinned to the back of your shirt. If you have other positions that you play then you must report to the multiple position tent where you will receive an orange tag that will be attached to your number. When this is completed you must gather at the rear of the tent that represents your main position. Gentlemen...to your tent!"

Harley stepped back and waited for Drew while a hoard of boys ran by. Signaling to Drew he joined him as they jogged down the first base line. "Listen," said Harley. "They'll probably split us up into groups so I'm not sure if we'll get to talk much. I might not get to see you until our snack break later on this afternoon. How do you feel? Are you nervous?"

"No, I'm not nervous. I thought I would be...but I'm not. I feel pretty good."

Arriving at the first two tents, Drew slapped Harley on his shoulder and winked, "I'll see you down at the multiple position tent."

Confused, Harley was about to respond but then a man behind the pitcher's table spoke to him, "Your name and number please."

Watching Drew walk into the catcher's tent, Harley answered, "Sims...forty-four."

Passing the catcher's tent, Harley saw Drew standing in line at the multiple position tent. Getting in line behind him, he asked, "What are you doing?"

Giving Harley a thumbs up, Drew smiled. "You said earlier it was an advantage to play more than one position. You said I might be chosen as an outfielder if they have too many catchers. I need every advantage I can get. Remember, I'm a stamp collecting, piano playing, karate kid, and now I'm a catcher. So, why can't I be an outfielder too?"

"You're right," joked Harley. "I forgot how well rounded you are!"

Receiving an orange tag on their number, they walked back to the pitcher's and catcher's tents and waited for the beginning of the tryouts. Looking around at some of the kids nearby, Drew asked, "Do you know any of these kids?"

"Yeah, I know quite a few of them, some since way back in T-ball. I played with and against most of them last year in the seven to nine-year-old group. See the tall kid over there leaning on the tent. That's Dickey Lambert. He's a pretty good pitcher. He's not much on throwing fast, but he has a good changeup and curve. See that kid in front of the infielder tent? Well, that's Kimbah…I can't really pronounce his last name. He's from Africa. He's the fastest kid I've ever seen. I've seen him score all the way from first on a double."

Dave Meddler's voice got everyone's attention. "Okay, before we split up into individual groups I need everyone to gather behind home plate. We're going to have you take three laps around the outfield. You will not begin until I blow a whistle. You are required to complete all three laps even if you can't run the distance. If you have to pull out and walk at some point, that's fine. This is not a race! It's simply part of warming up."

Grabbing Drew by his arm, Harley started toward home plate. "My dad told me they would do this. That's why we ran all those three-mile runs over the past few months. Here's the way I see this. Kimbah and a couple of other kids will take off and run like antelopes. No one will be able to keep up with them. When we get in the group we want to be toward the front. This is important because the managers don't know much about you. This is your chance to show them what you're made of. When we take off just stay with me. We need to pace ourselves until the last lap, and then we'll smoke most of these kids. They'll expect most of us to be grouped up in the middle. They are going to notice those who pull away from the pack at the end and they'll also notice those who are well behind the pack. C'mon, let's get a good position."

Moving to the front of the group, Harley tapped Kimbah on the shoulder. "This is my friend from Texas. His name is Drew. He's a catcher."

Kimbah gave Drew a wide tooth-filled grin and raised his right hand to receive a high five and said, "Aye!"

Drew no sooner slapped Kimbah's hand when the whistle sounded. Kimbah was up the first base line like a shot, three other players a few feet behind, the rest of the group all packed together like sardines. Rounding the corner of the right field fence, Harley and Drew found themselves bogged down near the front of the pack. As they approached center field, Harley bumped Drew on the shoulder, "C'mon, we have to get out of this group!" When they turned the corner at the right field fence of the second lap, six players blasted by them. Harley picked up the pace as he shouted at Drew, "We gotta keep up!"

In center field, Drew saw Kimbah already crossing home plate for the second time. Shaking his head in wonder he pulled up next to Harley. As they approached home plate, Harley pumped his right fist. "When we get to first base we need to really kick it in!"

By the time they were at the right field fence they were neck and neck with four boys that separated them from the leaders. Realizing Drew and Harley were trying to pass them, they ran as fast as their legs would carry them. Harley and Drew stayed right next to them as they made the turn at left field to head home. One of the boys gave up and slowed to a trot, another completely stopped and stepped to the side, gasping for air. The remaining two boys kept up their fast pace and did not allow themselves to be passed. Crossing the invisible finish line, Drew and Harley were directed by three volunteers to a table where there were bottles of cold water waiting. Drew stopped and placed his hands on his hips and looked back at players who were crossing home plate and those who were staggering behind. "Well how did we do?"

Harley forced a smile through his heavy breathing, "C'mon, let's grab some water. I think we came in sixth and seventh...excellent!"

Sitting next to the chain link fence Drew placed the cold bottle on his forehead and watched as the last few remnants of players staggered toward the finish line. Pastor Franks passed in front of where they were and winked, "Good run, boys!"

Harley held up his bottle in a toasting fashion. "I think you impressed the managers so far. I think you've got a leg up!"

Drew got a somber look on his face as he watched the last player cross home plate. Harley noticed the sad look and asked, "Why the sad face?"

"I don't know," answered Drew. "Maybe it's because in a few minutes we'll be split up. I won't be with you. You won't be at my side to tell me what to do or what I'm doing wrong. I mean, that's the way it's been for the past eight months. It's like I'm getting kicked out of the nest and now I have to fly on my own."

Putting his arm around Drew, Harley explained, "Well, I guess that's a pretty good way to explain it, but here's the thing. *You can fly!* You just ran faster than seventy other players. You have an orange tag on your number that makes you stand out as not only a potential catcher but as an outfielder as well. You'll do fine. Just remember to stick to the basics and hustle on every play. Don't forget. You have heart! Besides that, if you don't make a team you'll have to listen to ol' Aaron Buckman and his crap. The best way you can get back at him is to make one of the teams."

Their conversation was cut short when Dave Meddler's voice reverberated around the field. "Gentlemen...good job on running! Now, we need pitchers to report to Field #3, catchers Field #4, infielders to Field #2 and outfielders will remain on this field. It's now about nine thirty. We'll practice until one when we'll break. Let's have a great practice session!

Harley got up and pulled Drew to his feet. "I'll see you at one. Now, go play some ball!"

Harley stood with sixteen other pitchers while they received their instructions. "The first thing we're going to do this morning is to get your arms warmed up. We'll split up into two rows of eight and play some light catch for the next ten minutes. We have four pitching areas set up so after we get warmed up, you'll be splitting up into four groups of four and we'll see what you can do."

Throwing the ball back and forth with Dickey Lambert, Harley listened as he heard the constant slapping of the balls as they hit the gloves of sixteen pitchers. It was one of the sweetest sounds he thought he had ever heard. He thought about the long summer and how he had missed weeks of practice. Gripping the ball, he fired a two-finger fastball to Dickey and smiled to himself. *I'm back!*

Minutes later, he was standing on a pitching rubber down the third base line as one of the managers assumed the catcher's position forty-six feet away. Another manager stood behind him and gave direction. "You are going to throw twenty pitches: five fastballs, five curves, five changeups and the last five are your choice. Are you ready?"

Harley looked at the bright white, temporary home plate and smiled. "Yes sir!"

Another manager stood off to the side with a clipboard and a speed gun. The manager behind the mound spoke to Harley again, "Okay, let's see your fastball. I need the first two right down the middle, then the next two on the inside and outside corner of the plate. The last one is your choice." The manager flipped a ball to Harley and said, "Let 'er rip!"

Harley assumed his normal stance, took a deep breath, wound up and fired his first pitch. It passed over the center of the plate. The manager with the clipboard smiled and announced loudly. "Right down the pike…sixty-three miles an hour!"

During the next five minutes Harley quickly worked his way through the curve ball and changeup phase, his last changeup clocked at forty-seven. The manager wrote something on the clipboard and yelled out to Harley. "Okay, Sims…let's see what you have for us these last five pitches."

Time to shine, thought Harley. Gripping the ball slightly off-center, he placed his thumb beneath the ball and his index and middle finger slightly to the right side. He wound up and just as he released the ball he put a slight sidespin on it that caused the ball to move two inches to the right at the last second. The ball caught the inside corner and slapped into the catcher's mitt. Staring down at the glove the manager who was standing with the clipboard looked at his speed gun and then shouted to Harley. "I think you just threw a hard cutter at sixty-one miles an hour. Did you mean to throw a cutter?"

Proudly, Harley responded, "Yes sir. My dad and I have been working on throwing the cutter for the past month."

"Let me see that pitch again."

Harley repeated the process, the pitch cutting into the hitter at the last second on the corner.

The manager announced, "Excellent cutter…sixty-two! You've got three pitches left."

Harley finished up with a curve, a changeup and then a blazing fastball clocked at sixty-nine.

"Okay Sims. Grab some water and take a few, then head back out to the outfield for some casual catch while the second group goes through the routine."

On Field #4, Drew stood by home plate while he received instructions from one of the managers. "Have you ever used a pitching machine?"

Since he had learned to catch in Harley's backyard by using a pitching machine, Drew wasn't quite sure how to answer, so he responded, "Some."

"Okay then," said the manager. "What we are going to do is set the machine at fifty miles an hour. The machine will throw ten fastballs to you. Then we'll move on to ten curves followed by ten changeups at forty. We'll finish up by setting the machine to throw you twenty pitches at random. This will give us an opportunity to see your reaction time. Ready!"

Drew, put the mask on his face and went into the catcher's stance, his left foot slightly further back than the right. Pounding the mitt with his right hand, he spit and nodded for the machine to be switched on. Ten seconds passed when the first ball slapped into the glove. Just like in Harley's back yard he tossed the ball to the side and awaited the next pitch.

Minutes passed when the last changeup was caught. Steadying himself for the next ten random pitches, Drew requested, "I don't suppose we could turn the speed up some, say like to sixty or so?"

The manager smiled and responded, "No, that will be done later this afternoon."

The first pitch was an inside fastball that Drew caught and framed perfectly. The manager approved with a nod and made a notation on a clipboard and waited for the results of the next pitch.

The final pitch, a curve ball was caught easily by Drew, who tossed the ball up into the air, caught it behind his back, rose and removed his mask and asked, "What's next?"

"Break time!" announced the manager. "Everyone is to report to Field #5 for a snack and a forty-five minute rest. Report back to this field at two o'clock."

Harley located Drew sitting up against the fence, already eating his box lunch. Plopping down next to him, he asked, "What's for lunch?"

Taking a bite out of a sandwich, Drew spoke with a full mouth, "Looks like ham and cheese, bag of chips, a fruit cup and an oatmeal cookie." Not waiting for a response, Drew swallowed and asked, "How it'd go with the pitching?"

"I think I did all right. They were pretty impressed when I threw my cutter. How did it go with you?"

"I caught every ball. I tried to act as professional as I could, like you suggested. I really don't know what they think of me. No one indicated either way if they thought I did well or if I didn't."

Harley opened his box and removed the sandwich. "Well, I just happen to know that so far they're impressed with you."

Surprised, Drew gave Harley an odd look. "And how would you know this?"

"On the way over here for lunch I ran into the pastor...Mr. Franks. He told me he overheard two of the managers talking about that fireball catcher from Texas. Unless there is another player who catches here from Texas, they were talking about you."

Finishing his sandwich, Drew laid his head back and closed his eyes. "Think I'll take a short nap before the afternoon session."

Thumping Drew on the leg with his glove, Harley ordered, "On your feet. That's exactly what everyone will do. Not us! We're going to go to the opposite side of the fence and I'm going to pitch to you. You're going to catch for me. While everyone else is lounging around, you and I will be practicing. Who knows? If they see how well you and I are together we might end up on the same team."

Picking up his mitt, Drew looked at some of the other players sitting next to the fence. "Don't you think that's a little...bold?"

"Yeah, it probably is, but so what! Being bold and making a team is better than being shy and sitting around and not making one of the teams. I'll leave it up to you."

Smiling, Drew pounded his glove. "Let's walk over there and see if you can *bring the heat!*"

Harley casually walked off forty-six feet, stopped and turned. Drew had already assumed the catcher's position. Putting on the mask, Drew gave Harley the sign for a fastball. Harley nodded and delivered a direct hit over the center of the plate, a resounding slap causing the attention of those close by. By the time Harley threw his ninth pitch a crowd of players and parents had gathered next to the fence.

Drew got up and walked to Harley and whispered, "Okay, now what do we do?"

Not paying any attention to those watching, Harley grinned at Drew. "Just go back down there and keep calling the pitches. Don't pay any attention to our spectators!"

Sunday afternoon, the second and final day of tryouts, Drew

stood off to the side and took a few practice swings with a 29", 23 oz. Louisville Slugger bat. The batter in the box was instructed to take his final at bat; a bunt, and run the play out down to first base. The batter squared up, hit the ball in front of the plate and was easily thrown out. A manager standing next to home plate, glanced down at a clipboard and yelled, "Scott…you're next!"

Drew approached the plate and adjusted the batting helmet.

The manager looked Drew over and then looked back at the clipboard and spoke, "Drew Scott…catcher…right?"

Stepping into the batter's box, Drew answered politely, "Yes sir."

"Okay, Mr. Scott, here's the drill. You get twenty swings. Strikes count as an at bat. The manager catching will be calling balls and strikes. Good luck!"

Digging in his right foot next to the back of the box, Drew planted his left foot in closer toward the plate. Adjusting the batting glove on his right hand, he then touched the brim of his helmet, before taking a deep breath and swinging the bat twice; a routine he had gotten into.

Staring out at the pitcher, he waited patiently for the first pitch. The pitcher went into his windup and released the ball. Drew focused on the pitcher's right hand and picked up the ball the moment it left his fingers. It was a fastball. It looked like it was going to be inside. He held up and watched the ball slap into the catcher's mitt. The manager yelled, "Strike!"

Stepping out of the box, he took two swings then stepped back in going through his routine. The next pitch looked identical to the first. He swung and made solid contact sending the ball just to the right of first base.

For the next few minutes Drew took his swings, concentrating on the things Rich, Monica and Harley had taught him: *Wait for your pitch; take control; be patient; don't give the pitcher the advantage by swinging at a bad pitch.*

Hitting a line drive over second base, Drew smiled to himself. *That would have been a base hit!*

His time at the plate went quickly and before he knew it, the clipboard manager ordered, "This is your last pitch, Scott. You need to give us a bunt and then run the bases."

Drew positioned himself in the box and thought about the

conversation he and Harley had about the bunt; *the tricky hit!* Over the past few months one of the things he had excelled at was the bunt. The pitcher wound up and delivered a pitch just off the center of the plate. Drew, at the last fraction of a second, stepped into the pitch, the barrel of the bat making contact with the ball. The ball was placed perfectly between the pitcher and the first base line. Drew was already running toward first base when the pitcher reacted. Drew's right foot touched the bag just before the ball slapped into the first baseman's glove. Stopping a few feet down the line, Drew returned to first base and asked a manager, "Was I safe?"

The manager smiled and answered, "Yeah, you were safe. Nice hit. Go on and finish up running the bases."

Crossing home plate, Drew picked up his bat and approached the man with a clipboard. "That was a drag bunt. I was safe so make sure that gets marked down as a base hit." Walking over to the dugout he picked up his glove and ran to the outfield.

At four thirty Drew and the rest of the boys on Field #3 were told to head on over to Field #5 for the final announcements of the day. Drew managed to locate Harley in the crowd of talking youths. Throwing his catcher's mitt at him, Drew asked, "How'd you do today?"

"I did fine," said Harley. "The question is, how did you do?"

"Did all right," said Drew. "Got six hits, made good contact with the ball. Even pulled off a drag bunt. I don't think they were expecting that. Didn't strike out one time. So, what's next?"

"There is no next! That's it...the tryouts are over."

Dave Meddler walked up to the mic and addressed the players and those watching from the bleachers. "Tryouts for the 1996 Arnold Little League have come to a close. I would like to take this opportunity to thank all of the players who have attended over the last two days as well as the parents who have spent time with us. The draft will take place next Tuesday behind closed doors right here on the facility. The results will be posted Wednesday morning at the main office. Thank you and have a great day!"

"Well that's it!" said Harley. "Three days from now we'll know what teams we're on."

Surprised, Drew spoke up, "You talk like we've already made a team. That's easy for you to say. Everyone wants you on their team. I mean, you knew before we even came to the tryouts you'd make a team. For all I know, I might be playing on that morning league."

Spotting his dad's truck when it pulled into the lot, Harley pointed, "C'mon, my dad's here to pick us up. He told me this morning that tonight we're going out for dinner. Your folks know all about it. They're going to meet us at the restaurant after we go back to my house and get cleaned up."

Halfway across the parking lot, Harley stopped and looked at Drew. "Listen, I know you're concerned about if you made one of the teams, but here's the truth. I don't much care about what any of those managers think about you. All I know is that eight months ago you were scared to death of a baseball and now you can catch with the best of them. I consider you a hero and the best friend I've ever had!"

CHAPTER 12

DREW ADJUSTED THE RIGHT PANTLEG OF HIS TEAM uniform, making sure it was the same length as the left, picked up his glove and walked to the far end of the home team dugout. Looking at the square white roster sheet tacked to a small section of corkboard, he smiled as his eyes ran down over the list of player names where he thought he would never see his name; *Drew Scott,* batting in fifth position on a Little League baseball team. He focused on the penciled in letters directly following his name; RF.

Sitting down on the long bench, he re-tied his left shoelace, then moved both of his ankles up and down until he was satisfied his rubber cleats were tied correctly. Looking again at the roster sheet, he smiled to himself when he saw the team name at the top of the sheet titled *Cougars.* Thinking back to that Wednesday over two weeks ago, when after school, Rich had driven he and Harley to the Little League Complex, parked the truck and told them to go into the main office to see the results of the draft. Harley knew exactly where to look for his posted name, the last place team from the previous year, the Cougars. Big as life, there was his name, *Harley Sims,* first pick-pitcher.

Happy for his best friend, Drew smiled, but was looking at the other rosters where hopefully, his name would be posted. He scanned the various teams: Lions, Tigers, Leopards, Spartans, Rangers, Knights and finally, the Barons. His name was not posted. He had not been drafted for a team. Sadly, he moved down the hall to where the morning league players were listed, when all of a sudden Harley shouted at the top of his lungs, "I can't believe it. You made the Cougars!"

Drew was frozen. He couldn't believe what he had just heard. Pointing at the printed roster, Harley said. "There it is in black and white. Drew Scott, ninth pick, catcher-outfield. We're on the same team. Can you believe it?"

Staring in disbelief at the Cougars roster, Drew stood in silence when a voice from behind the boys got their attention: "Hello boys. I was wondering when you two were going to show up." Pastor Franks tapped the Cougars roster with a pencil and asked, "Well, what do you boys think about being on the same team?"

Harley shrugged his shoulders and answered, "I pretty much figured I would get chosen early in the draft, more than likely by the Cougars, but tell me, how did Drew wind up on the Cougars?"

Pastor Franks placed his arms around both boys and answered, "You boys need to refer to me as Joe. We're not in church. We're on a ball field"

Drew and Harley looked at each other and nodded in agreement as Joe went on, "Now, let me explain how you fellas wound up on the Cougars. I think every team manager expected me to take Harley in the first round, and *I did!* The Cougars only lost three players from last year's team and they all happen to be outfielders. We also have two players that are catchers from last year. Blake Reynolds is twelve and solid behind the plate, but the other catcher, who can also play the infield is not as good as Drew. I knew there were a number of players that would be chosen before Drew so I waited until the second round and drafted Drew as a catcher-outfielder."

Drew came out of his daydreaming when Pastor Franks stepped down into the dugout and walked to the roster. Removing a pencil from behind his ear he drew a line through a name and then wrote on the roster. Turning back to Drew, he sat next to him on the bench and explained, "I know I told you for this first game of the season I was going to start you in right field, but there has been a change. Blake has a touch of the flu, not that serious, but I'm not willing to take the chance of playing him. I'm putting you in as starting catcher. So, get your gear on and head on down the third base line. We've only got about twenty minutes before the game starts."

Reaching for his shin guards, Drew asked, "Does Harley know I'm catching?"

"Yeah, I told him. He's waiting down the line for you now. So, get moving!"

The shin guards in place, Drew slipped into his chest protector, grabbed his mitt, mask, throat guard and interior gloves and ran down the third base line where Harley stood waiting.

Signaling to Harley who stood forty-six feet up the line, Drew attached his throat guard, slipped on his gloves and facemask, went down into the catcher's position, and gave Harley a signal for a fastball.

Harley wound up and delivered a strike down the center of the bullpen home plate.

Drew fired the ball back and signaled for a curve, which Harley delivered on the outside corner.

Minutes passed when Pastor Franks approached and signaled for his starting pitcher and catcher. Kneeling down in front of the boys, he asked, "How do you feel, Harley?"

Harley slapped the ball into his glove and looked out at the field. "I feel great. I'm ready."

Looking up at Drew, Joe asked, "What about it Drew. How do you see things?"

Nodding his head, Drew responded, "His fastball has a lot of pop and his curve ball is breaking just like it should."

"All right then," confirmed Joe. "This is your first Little League game. We're going up against the Barons. Last year they were 17-1. A number of their players are returning. They are a very good hitting team. Last year they averaged eight runs a game. Most of their players have never faced you, Harley. I'm depending on you to keep runners off the base paths. We're going to play a smart game. If you can keep them from getting runners in scoring position, we can win this game by playing small ball…"

The conversation was interrupted when Aaron Buckman who was running around the outfield fence line, approached and boldly stated, "Well, if it isn't Frick and Frack!" Looking at Drew with an obvious look of disgust, Aaron spit and remarked roughly, "I guess the league must be pretty hard up this year. I guess they'll let just about anybody be on a team!"

Pastor Franks was about to intervene but was cut off by Aaron who pointed at Harley. "Remember what I said over at the park awhile back about how you'll never see it comin'? Well, today when I step up to the plate you'll definitely see it comin'! I'm gonna take both of you right out of the park, Sims. There's no way you can pitch around me! That is…unless you back down and decide to walk me. I dare you to pitch to me! See you turkeys on the field." Spitting once again, Aaron wiped his lips with the back of his hand, laughed and jogged away.

Joe looked at his young pitcher and catcher and asked, "What was that all about?"

"It's nothing," answered Harley. "That was Aaron Buckman. He's just a bully."

The pastor responded, "I know who Aaron Buckman is. I watched him play a few games last year. You don't have to observe that type of kid very long to figure out he's got problems." Joe placed his arm around both boys and walked them to the chain link fence. "I know how to deal with a kid like Aaron. You just go out there and give me the best game you can. Let me worry about Mr. Buckman."

The last few notes of The Star Spangled Banner echoed around the field as the parents in the stands gave out a loud resounding cheer. The home plate umpire stood just behind the plate and yelled, "Play Ball!"

Joe stood at the corner of the home team dugout and high-fived the nine Cougars who ran onto the field and assumed their positions. Harley stood just behind the pitcher's rubber and gazed at the crowd of spectators. One thing for sure. More parents seemed to attend the ten to twelve-year-old games. The previous year at the seven to nine-year-old level the most spectators he had witnessed was less than a hundred, but today, the bleachers were packed: mothers, fathers, brothers and sisters all cheering for a specific player. Then, he spotted his father who was seated on the home field side. His father made eye contact with him and gave him an enthusiastic thumbs-up. Harley gently nodded, turned and looked around the field at the infielders and the outfielders, as they proudly stood ready to back him up. He removed his team hat and looked at the bright orange C that significed his team, the Cougars. He looked down over his starched white uniform with the *Cougars* emblazoned across his chest. He looked at home plate where Drew was just putting on his facemask. *My first Little League game,* thought Harley. *It doesn't get any better than this!*

The umpire threw a brand new baseball to Harley. Looking down at the bright white sphere in his right hand he turned and looked at the center field scoreboard. *Someday,* he thought, *I'll be standing on the pitcher's mound at Busch Stadium getting ready to pitch to the Cubs, the Pirates or some other Central Division National League team, but at the moment, I have to deal with the hard hitting Barons...and Aaron Buckman.* Turning back to home plate he saw the batter who awaited his first pitch.

Digging his cleats into the dirt directly in front of the rubber, Harley assumed his stance and looked in at Drew who was flashing the sign: fastball. Taking a deep breath, he gripped the ball and thought, *I'm gonna give this kid the heat right down the center.* Winding up, he released the ball and followed through, ready to field the ball if it was hit in his direction. The batter didn't swing and the umpire shouted, "Strike one!" Drew fired the ball back to Harley and winked.

Two fastballs later, the umpire yelled, "Strike three. You're out!"

The ball was back in Harley's possession as the left-handed second batter dug in at the plate. Drew gave the sign for an inside curve. The batter was completely confused as he stepped back from the ball, but then it cut over the inside corner for a called strike. Following another fastball, Harley finished off the second position batter with a change-up that he missed by a wide margin.

The third batter of the inning swung at the first pitch; an outside curve and popped the ball up, resulting in an easy infield fly. Harley pumped his fist as he ran toward the dugout. *Three up...three down!*

Joe greeted each player when they approached the dugout. Once everyone was seated, he confronted his players. "Okay boys. We just held the Barons. I have a plan for our first at bat. Here's what we're going to attempt. Their starting pitcher is a three-year veteran. Last year he went undefeated 7-0. He throws a lot of off-speed stuff. He only uses his fastball until he gets ahead in the count, then he starts in with changeups and curve balls that are not in or near the strike zone. He's smart and knows that the batter, behind in the count has to protect the plate and more times than not, will take a swing at a bad pitch. Today, gentleman, in this first inning, he is going to be faced with a very different team. Here's our plan..."

Casey Daniels, a left handed hitter, stepped up to the plate and looked down the third base line where the pastor gave him the sign.

The Baron's pitcher stared in at his catcher, wound up and delivered the first pitch.

Just like Joe had predicted it was a fastball. Casey squared up at the last moment and bunted the ball down the first base line. As Casey sprinted for first base, the Baron's catcher, pitcher, third baseman and Aaron, who was the first baseman were all taken completely off-guard. The catcher, finally reacting, ran up the line after the slow rolling ball that hugged the inside of the foul line. The throw from the catcher was late and the runner was called safe.

Ten minutes later, Aaron, in disbelief threw his glove to the ground as he placed his hands on his hips and looked out at the scoreboard: Barons 0 – Cougars 2. Pastor Joe's plan of playing small ball worked. A combination of two bunts, smart base running, a double steal and a hard liner that bounced off Aaron's glove gave the Cougars an early lead.

Back in the dugout, after congratulating his team, Joe spoke to Harley and Drew. "The first batter you're going to face this inning is none other than your ol' pal, Buckman. Now, we could just walk him, but I'd rather not do that. We'd be putting the tying run at the plate. That's too risky with this team. They are capable of scoring three or four runs before you know what's hit you. You need to pitch to Buckman, but make sure you don't give him anything he can hit. Stay on the corners, switch up your speed and pitch selections. Normally, he never swings at the first pitch. He'll just let it go on by, even if it's a called strike. It's a confidence thing with him. He's a very aggressive hitter, but after what happened last inning, he'll be swinging for the fence. He doesn't like the inside part of the plate. Remember, he's just another hitter, a dangerous hitter, but just another hitter. Now, don't worry…just relax. He'll give you the first pitch. After that, it's up to you. Let's see what you guys can do!"

Harley took the rubber and turned the ball over and over in his right hand. Drew put on his mask and pounded his mitt. Aaron stepped out of the dugout and walked to the plate as if he owned the field. With his bat on his shoulder, he looked down at Drew and spoke in a cocky manner, "Get ready to see the ball go over the fence, Scott!"

Taking his position in the box, he glared out at Harley. Not wasting any time, Harley wound up and delivered a fastball right down the pike for a called strike. Aaron just stood there and left the ball sail by. Shrugging as if the pitch were no big deal, he readied himself for the next delivery. Drew moved to the far outside of the plate and gave the sign. Harley nodded and threw another fastball out of the strike zone; too far out for Aaron to reach the ball. Aaron held up and smiled back at Harley as if to say, *You don't have anything!*

The next two pitches were fastballs in the same spot and the count went to 3-1. Drew called time and walked out to the mound to speak with Harley. "He's not biting on that outside stuff. Do you just want to go ahead and walk him?"

"No!" said Harley. "He's seen my fastball four times now; the last three way outside. He knows I won't give him anything right over the plate. I think he'll be expecting another fastball. I'm going to give him an inside changeup. Between the pitch location and the change in speed we might mess up his timing."

Bumping Harley's glove with his mitt, Drew spoke with enthusiasm, "Well, in the next few seconds we'll know!"

Aaron stepped back in the box and crowded the plate in expectation of another outside pitch. Harley smiled to himself, *You guessed wrong, Aaron. The ball's gonna come in on you!* Taking a little extra time he stared in at Drew, wound up and released the ball. Aaron, realizing the pitch was going to be on the inside of the plate tried to readjust his stance but there wasn't enough time. He swung hard and hit the ball with the lower part of the bat. The ball sailed out over top of the infield and seemed to hang in the air. The left fielder backpedaled thinking it was going to be a long fly out, an easy catch. He felt the cinders of the warning track crunch beneath his feet and he knew the fence was just a few feet away. The ball had reached the top part of its upward momentum and was now descending rapidly. With his back against the fence he reached up, but the ball was a foot above his reach. The crowd went into a loud roar as Aaron touched first and jogged toward second. Harley couldn't bring himself to look at his adversary while he rounded the bases. He was sure Aaron was staring at him and he wasn't about to give him any more satisfaction than he already felt.

Drew walked out to the mound and shrugged. "He might be a

bully, but he sure can hit. That pitch was inside. I didn't think he'd be able to get enough bat on the ball to hit it out."

Pastor Joe joined them on the mound. "Okay, so he got the best of you Harley. We'll get him next time. We're still ahead 2-1. Let's concentrate on getting these next three outs. Let's not spend any more time worrying about Aaron Buckman. Every pitcher gives up a home run now and then. Great pitchers forget it and move on. How do you feel, Drew?"

Drew smiled as he looked out at the scoreboard. "Hey, we're still winning this game. We'll get that run back."

Five minutes later, following a strike out and two ground balls, the Cougars congregated in their dugout. Pastor Joe clapped his hands and smiled. "If they can't score another run, then they can't win this game."

The second and third innings went by quickly, neither team getting a man on base.

In the top of the fourth after striking out two batters in a row, Harley was once again faced with Aaron Buckman. The Pastor called a time out and walked to the mound where he signaled for the entire infield to gather. Looking directly at Harley and Drew, he explained, "We're going to give Aaron Buckman a pass…a walk, but not intentional. You still need to show him you are not afraid of his power. Throw him three outside pitches…all curves. Then, on the fourth pitch throw him deep inside; make him move back off the plate. Either way, if you hit him or it's a called ball four, he'll be standing on first. Don't give the next batter anything to hit for the first two pitches, then I want you Drew, on the third pitch to act like you drop the ball. When you get up to look for it I want you to kick it off to the side. Make sure you kick it far enough away from you so Aaron will steal second. Then here's what we'll do…"

Looking at the infielders, especially the second baseman, Joe asked, "Do we all understand the play?"

Everyone nodded or answered, "Yes sir!"

Looking at Drew one last time before he walked off the field, Joe remarked, "When you drop the pitch make it look good…convincing."

Aaron was already standing at the plate when Drew returned.

"Get ready…Mr. catcher! With one swing of the bat I'm tyin' this game up!"

Looking out toward the mound he gave Harley a smug grin, swung the bat twice and readied himself for the first pitch. It was an outside curve, followed by two more identical pitches. The count stood at 3-0. Drew gave Harley the sign for an inside fastball. Gripping the ball tightly, he placed his two fingers across the seams, wound up and threw hard. Aaron saw the ball moving inside and stepped back just like before, but his reaction time was too late as the ball smacked into his lower left side, sending him to the ground with a wince of pain."

The umpire checked to see if the batter was okay, while Aaron stood and glared out at Harley. Harley looked over at Joe, who nodded his approval as Aaron jogged down to first all the while glaring at Harley. The next batter stepped up and watched two fastballs on the outside corner go by. The next pitch was an outside slow curve that Drew could easily handle. After the ball went into the mitt, he dropped it to the ground, stood as if he didn't know where the ball had gone and kicked it to the side. Drew, still acting confused turned in a circle looking for the ball. Aaron, seizing the opportunity to get himself into scoring position took off like a shot for second. Just like they planned Drew picked up the ball and threw it to the second baseman too late. After sliding, Aaron stood up and proudly stared at Harley who was standing near the back of the mound. The second baseman joined Harley where they briefly spoke. Harley, still not on the mound looked at Aaron, who drifted off the bag, bouncing back and forth as if he were taunting Harley like he was going to steal third. Harley turned and started back to the mound when suddenly the second baseman reached out and touched Aaron on his back with his glove, then removing the ball from the glove held it up for the umpire to see. The ump looked immediately at Harley who was holding up both his hands, indicating he did not have the ball. The umpire pointed at Aaron and shouted, "You're out!"

Aaron couldn't believe what had just happened and he approached the umpire, "No way! I can't be out. The play was over!"

The umpire remained professional and stated, "You were off the bag, the ball was still in play and time had not been called. You're out!"

The Baron's manager raced onto the field and confronted the umpire. "What was that? He can't be called out. The play was over. It was a dead ball!"

Joe ran out on the field and joined in on the loud conversation. "What's the problem, Ump?"

Chet, the Baron's manager answered the question, "He called my man out and it was a dead ball... that's what!"

Joe remained calm and spoke to Chet, "You need to read up on the rulebook, Chet. Unless time was called or the pitcher has the ball in his possession on the rubber, the play is not over. Simply put, your man here got caught off the bag while the ball was still in play. I have a copy of the rulebook back in the dugout if you'd care to take a look."

Disgusted, Chet motioned to Aaron, "C'mon, Buckman...you're out, but this game is far from over!"

Walking right past Harley, Aaron gave him a dirty look, when Harley spoke low so only Aaron could here, "Like you said. You'll never see it comin'."

In the bottom of the fourth, the Cougars were unable to get a man on base due to a strike out and two pop-ups. In the top of the fifth, following a throwing error by the third baseman, Harley struck out the side. The bottom of the fifth was a repeat performance for the Cougars, the Baron's pitcher settling down and pitching well. Going into the top of the sixth the score remained the same: Cougars up by a score of 2-1. Before Harley walked out to the mound hopefully for the last time during his first game of the season, Pastor Joe took him off to the side. "If it's three up and three down, then you don't have to face Buckman again. These next three hitters are the top of their lineup. This is the third time these particular players have seen you. They've seen your fastball, curve and changeup. They know what to expect, they just don't know when it will come. You've got a two-hitter going: that single in the fifth and Buckman's homerun. How do you feel? How does your arm feel?"

Harley moved his right shoulder and responded, "I could pitch another game if I had to."

"All right then," said Joe. "Get out there and show 'em whose boss!"

Three fastballs later, the first batter of the inning walked back to the dugout. The second batter, after a 2-0 count, hit a long fly out to center field. The third batter of the inning swung at the first pitch hitting a hard ground ball to the right of Harley. Going down on one knee, the ball bounced off his chest. He picked it up and threw the runner out at first; game over!

Aaron who was standing on deck slammed his bat to the ground, realizing he was not going to get another crack at Harley. Walking toward home plate to join Drew in celebrating their first victory, Aaron casually approached and spoke with pride, "Just like I predicted, Sims. I took you out of the park and if you wouldn't have hit me I'd have done it again. This is just the beginnin' of the year and I'm ahead 1-0."

Drew jumped in on the conversation and added, "You just don't get it, Buckman. It's not about you. It's about your team. Your homerun doesn't mean squat to me. The fact is the Cougars, my team, beat your team, the Barons 2-1. You lost today and you always will with your loser attitude!"

Twenty minutes later, Drew and Harley met their families by the chain link gate that led from the field. Mrs. Scott was the first to speak. "Congratulations boys! I never imagined that baseball could be so exciting!"

Mr. Scott shook Drew's hand. "Good job, son. I can't tell you how proud I am of you."

Rich placed his arm around Harley and spoke with pride. "Your 1-0 so far this year...a two hitter."

Monica interrupted and suggested, "C'mon, we've got to get moving if we're going to make the Cardinals home opener with the Expos. The hot dogs are on me!"

CHAPTER 13

USING A SMALL PIECE OF WOOD, DREW CLEANED THE dirt from the metal cleats on the bottom of his shoes. Banging his cleats on the wooden bench, he remarked, "After two years of playing in Pony League in these metal cleats, at times I still can't get used to them. I will say this though, they do give a player better grip on the field. When we played Little League we always wore rubber cleats and I was never afraid of being cut by metal spikes, especially on close plays at home. But, now it's different. You could get cut in an instant."

"Welcome to high school baseball," said Harley. "We play our first game tomorrow."

"Well, myself," said Drew, "I can't really see that much difference from Pony League to high school ball. In Little League, we played six inning games and the field dimensions were cut down. In the Pony League we played seven inning games by major league rules and field dimensions. High school ball is pretty much the same as Pony League."

"Except for one thing," emphasized Harley. "The players. By the time most of these kids get to high school they've been playing ball for ten years, maybe longer. When we played Little League and even in the Pony League, the number of kids that were serious about becoming major leaguers were not that many. But, when you get to the high school level, the number increases. The amount of innings per game we play and the field dimensions may be the same, but the level of talent increases dramatically. We'll be facing some of the best hitters in the area. As a matter of fact, we'll be facing some kids we've never even seen."

"Speaking of the best hitters," said Drew, "have you heard anything lately about Aaron Buckman?"

"I haven't heard anything new. As far as I know he's still out in California. Like we heard, after the '96 Little League season, his dad met a woman who was quite religious. The next thing ya know, his dad up and decides to move out west to marry this woman. I guess he found religion."

"Do you think ol' Aaron is still playing baseball?"

"I don't know. Ya know, I think about him once in a while. He moved with his father, let's see, that was over five years ago. As much of a pain in the butt that he was you can't say he wasn't a good ballplayer. We only played the Baron's twice back in '96. He only got two hits off me, that one homerun and a single. He still hit eighteen homers for the year. He was a load at the plate."

Tying his spikes together, Drew asked, "Do you think Buckman will play in the majors?"

He's got the talent but I'm not sure about his attitude. I never really talked with Aaron about that. For all we know, he might wind up in prison. But, then again, we might face him years down the road when we play in the bigs."

Drew laughed. "*You* may play him in the *bigs*. You've already determined that's what you want to do with the rest of your life. Even though I enjoy playing ball, I haven't decided what I want to do with my life. You, will no doubt go to college on an athletic scholarship for baseball. I'm not sure that's in my future. I still play a mean piano. My mother is still convinced I'll go to school on a music scholarship. You can play baseball better than nine out of ten kids and I can play the piano better than most kids my age. We'll both go to college. You'll probably be drafted by a major league team, play a few years in the minors and then move up to the majors. My father wants me to major in business."

Walking to the end of the Fox High School home team dugout, Harley picked up a bat and his spikes. "You don't give yourself enough credit, Drew. You're as good as any catcher I've seen during our years together. Even if you don't get a scholarship for baseball, you can still play ball *and* the piano in college."

Drew stood. "I guess when you look at things, we do make a pretty good pitcher-catcher combination. In your three years of Little League you went 19-2. You never allowed more than three runs in a game. You had two no-hitters and a number of one and two hit games. You were one of the best hitting pitchers in the league. And let's not forget our years in Pony League where you went 24-3 over two seasons with another no hitter to your credit."

Walking out to the front of the dugout, Harley pointed out.

"But, let's not forget that you caught every one of the games I pitched except five. Think about it. The five games I lost over the past six years, I didn't have you catching for me. That says a lot about you."

Joining Harley outside of the dugout, Drew added, "I guess we did win a few games, didn't we!"

"Time sure does fly," said Harley. "It's hard to believe seven years have passed since we started to practice together in my backyard. You've come a long way, Drew. We've had a pretty good ball career together over the past few years and starting tomorrow when we play Seckman, we'll be turning a new page of our baseball careers."

Looking at the parking lot, Drew pointed. "Your mom is here. I've got to tell you. I'm a little nervous when I think about you driving us home."

Walking across the field, Harley shook his head. "Hey, I'm sixteen years old and I have a valid learner's permit for the state of Missouri. As long as an adult is in the car with me, I'm permitted to drive. Next month, you'll be getting your permit and before you know it we'll both be cruising the streets of Arnold."

Following Harley down the third base line, Drew joked, "Jefferson County motorists beware!"

Monica was leaning up against her car, dangling the keys at Harley when the boys approached. "Are you ready to drive us home?"

Throwing his bag, which contained his gear in the backseat, Harley grabbed the keys and answered, "I'm ready, but Drew has his doubts."

Drew, also tossing his catching gear in the back, climbed in, fastened himself in and sat back as if he were royalty and waved his hand in the air. "Home James!"

Shaking his head at Drew's humor, Harley got behind the wheel, turned the ignition key and waited for his mother to get in on the passenger side. "Listen, Mom. I've never driven with you in the car before. It's always been dad these past weeks while learning to drive. He's a maniac. He makes me so nervous: 'Look out for that stop sign! Watch your speed! Pay attention to the other drivers on the road!' It's hard enough learning to drive without having someone yelling in your ear all the time."

Monica smiled at her son. "I promise you. As long as it looks like you're not going to run over some old man with a walker or a woman with a baby stroller, I'll keep my tongue."

Looking in the rearview mirror, Harley backed out, turned to the right and headed out of the lot. Monica, changing the subject, sat back comfortably in the seat. "Speaking of your father. He told me he was going to get tickets for opening day of the 2002 season at Busch Stadium, which starts this weekend. Do you think you boys are up for the first Cardinals home game of the year? We open with a three game home stand with the Rockies."

From the backseat, Drew spoke up, "Count me in! I think this is going to be the year for the Cards to not only take the National League Championship, but the World Series."

Turning onto Jeffco Blvd., Harley checked the rearview mirror again and commented, "It's been twenty years since we won the World Series. We're due! It's not like the Cardinals haven't had their opportunities. Back in 1996 when we first started Little League it was a good year for the Cards. That was Larussa's first year as manager *and* unfortunately, Ozzie Smith's last. We ended up the regular season with a win-loss record of 88-74. We went on to beat San Diego in the best of five and then in the NLCS, we forged ahead of Atlanta three games to one. I was sure we had things wrapped up and we were heading for the World Series, but then the Braves won three straight games and eliminated us. The Yankees won the World Series beating Atlanta in six games. That was the 23rd time the Yanks won the title."

Monica jumped in on the conversation and added, "After the 96' season, despite the fact that we didn't get to go to the World Series we still had a good year and I thought that '97 would be our year. That year turned out to be disappointing for many a Cardinal fan. We all thought the Cards were on a roll, but things didn't turn out so well. We finished in fourth place in the division; eleven games back but there were still some wonderful moments I remember about that year. The thing that will always stand out to me about that year was when Mark McGwire came to the Cardinals at the end of July. He hit twenty-four homeruns for us that season, fifteen in September; a club record for a single player hitting homeruns in a month."

"I remember that year as well," said Harley. "The one thing that sticks out in my mind was that five hundred and seventeen foot shot McGwire hit out over the left field scoreboard. Remember, Drew, we were at the game. We couldn't believe how he clobbered that pitch."

Harley stopped for a red light at the intersection of Jeffco Blvd. and Hwy 141 when Monica spoke up, "The following year, 1998, wasn't much better than '97. We came in third place in the Central Division, nineteen games out of first place. Mark McGwire was a bright spot for the Cardinals, even though we didn't make the playoffs. That was an amazing year for baseball in general. Some folks, still today, say Mark McGwire and Chicago's Sammy Sosa saved baseball. It has always been thought that a great number of fans lost interest in the game following the baseball strike in '94. Sosa and McGwire went head to head during the '98 season in pursuit of Roger Maris' homerun record of hitting sixty-one homeruns in a single season in 1961."

The light turned green and Harley passed through the intersection as he announced, "Here's a stat probably almost no one knows. Mark McGwire, known as *Big Mac,* averaged a homerun every 10.61 times at bat while Babe Ruth averaged a homerun every 11.76 times at the plate. Therefore, McGwire was more consistence when it came to hitting the long ball."

Drew leaned up in between the seats. "How on earth would anyone know a remote statistic like that?"

Passing a slow moving truck, Harley responded, "It was just something I ran across while reading a baseball book a few years back. I thought it was amazing so I guess I just remembered it."

Keeping the conversation going, Monica commented, "McGwire hit five hundred homeruns faster than any player in history. Babe Ruth's record of hitting sixty homers stood for thirty-four years when Maris hit sixty-one. Maris's record stood for thirty-seven years."

Slowing down to make a right turn onto Hwy 141, Harley elaborated, "Roger Maris was an amazing hitter. He finished his career playing, believe it or not for the St. Louis Cardinals in 1967 and '68. We won the pennant both of those years and Maris played in the '68 World Series. He hit his final homerun in early September of '68. It was his two hundred and seventy-fifth homerun."

Crossing the overpass above Rt. 55, Harley went back to the Sosa-McGwire story. "In '98 McGwire started off the season by hitting a homerun in each of his first four games. In mid-April, he hit three in one day against the Diamondbacks and then in May he clobbered three in one day against the Phillies. By the time June rolled around, Mark had thirty homers and was almost halfway to passing Maris' record of sixty-one. Sosa at that time had logged twenty round trippers. By the end of the season, McGwire hit seventy and Sosa hit sixty-six. That was an incredible year for the home run."

Heading down Old Missouri Road, Harley smiled and held up an index finger to make a point. "The thing I'll always remember about last year was Bobby Bonds who broke McGwire's previous record of seventy homers by swatting seventy-three out of the park. It's hard to imagine anyone beating Bond's record."

"That's the same thing they said for years about Babe Ruth's record," said Drew. "When McGwire broke Maris' record everyone said it would stand forever and then, three years later, we now have a new home run record. It kind of makes you wonder what's going to happen in the next few years. Major league players are bigger, stronger. It wouldn't surprise me one bit, if within the next few years someone up and belts out seventy-five or maybe even eighty homeruns."

Harley made a left turn into the sub-division where they lived and remarked, "That wouldn't surprise me. Baseball has always been a game of surprises. In any game on any given day, something can happen that has never happened before or a record could be broken. There are so many aspects to the game."

As they pulled into the driveway, Monica spoke to Drew. "You're having dinner with us tonight. Actually, your folks and your sister will be here in about a half hour. We're having a cookout in the backyard; nothing fancy, just dogs, burgers and some chicken. So, you boys have just about enough time to get cleaned up."

Stepping out of the shower, Drew grabbed a towel and walked into the adjoining bedroom where he found Harley looking out the window. Drying his hair, Drew asked, "Anything interesting out there?"

Slipping on a fresh Cardinals T-shirt, Harley answered, "Your sister, mom and dad just showed up. Roxann looks like she's carrying something."

Joining Harley at the window, Drew nodded down at his younger sister. "That is no doubt my mom's potato salad. It's pretty good stuff."

Sitting on the edge of his bed, Harley opened the drawer to his nightstand and removed a small red eight-by-ten folder. "This is a paper I turned in for a school project back when I was eight years old. I did a lot of research on this. I think you'll really enjoy reading it, especially after what we talked about on the way home today."

Drew was about to ask what the paper was about, when they were interrupted by Monica's voice, "Boys! You need to get down here. We'll be eating in twenty minutes."

Taking the folder with him, Harley bounded for the doorway, "C'mon, we can go over this later in the backyard."

Following a number of small duties, like getting a bucket of ice from the house, bringing out the hamburger and hot dog rolls, mustard and ketchup bottles, Harley joined Drew on the swing. Holding up the folder, he explained, "I got an A on this paper when I was in fourth grade. We had this horrible teacher by the name of Mrs. Mitcheltree. She was a cranky ol' biddy that didn't give any of her students credit for anything."

"But you said you got an A on your paper," said Drew. "She must have liked something about what you wrote."

"Turned out she was a huge Cardinals fan. Had been for years. The paper wasn't about the Cardinals, but it was baseball related." Opening the folder Harley flipped to the third and final page where there was a handwritten note. "Look what she wrote!"

Taking the folder. Drew looked at the professional handwritten note: *Mr. Sims. Your research is impeccable!*

Handing the folder back to Harley, Drew inquired, "So, what did you write?"

"The history of the homerun! I wanted to write something about baseball but I couldn't make my mind up. There was so many things about baseball, things that are always changing. Then, I thought, what is the most exciting play in baseball? And then I realized it was the homerun. It can and often is a game changer. Like that game at Busch Stadium toward the end of the season last year where the Cards hit a walk off homerun to win the game. That doesn't happen often, but when it does the game ends with a bang! The homerun always has, is now and always will be the most exciting play in baseball."

"I see what you're saying," agreed Drew. "And players like Ruth, Maris and McGwire are some of the most famous because of their ability to hit the long ball." Nodding at the folder, Drew inquired, "And this is what the paper is about?"

"Yes, but things back in the early days of baseball were different than they are today. Back then fields had very large outfields and homeruns were normally inside the parkers. Homeruns over an outfield fence were rare and sometimes the fence was too far out for a ball to be hit over it. Hitters were discouraged from trying to swing for the fence, because it was thought they would fly out. Actually, back then if a ball was caught on one bounce it was an out and if the ball bounced over the fence it was considered a homerun. So, the general wisdom of baseball back then was to try and manufacture runs or play small ball, sort of like what we did back when we played Little League for Pastor Joe: bunting the ball, stealing bases and place hitting."

Laying the folder on the swing, Harley continued, "After World War I, baseball changed significantly when the live ball era started. The manufacturing process and the materials used to produce baseballs was changed making the balls livelier. In the 1920s, baseball put into effect a number of rule changes: they prohibited the use of the spitball and added the requirement that balls be replaced when worn or dirty.

"Power hitters like Babe Ruth took advantage of the changes because the balls were easier to see and hit. As baseball's popularity grew, outfield seating was built which reduced the size of outfields, which meant long fly balls could clear the fence for a homerun. The teams with sluggers on their roster won the championships until the other teams began to focus on the power game rather than the conservative inside game."

Monica's voice interrupted the conversation, "Boys...soup's on!"

Minutes later, back on the swing, each armed with a plateful of hotdogs, mac and cheese, coleslaw and potato salad, the boys continued the history of the homerun. Taking a huge bite from a dog, Harley pointed out, "In Babe Ruth's day it wasn't always easy to determine if a ball was in fact a homerun. The foul lines at the corners of the outfield fence were not very sophisticated. They were nothing but ropes running from the fence to the bleachers. Sometimes the only way to determine if a ball was a homerun was to see it physically land on the other side of the fence. Today, there is little doubt when a homerun occurs. In the old days they used a rule referred to as 'fair when last seen!' This leads me to believe that despite the fact Roger Maris and Mark McGwire both beat Ruth's record the Babe didn't get credit for a lot of homeruns he actually hit. I read an article in a book called *The Year Babe Ruth Hit 104 Home Runs.* According to the author, Ruth lost a number of homeruns, possibly as many as fifty to seventy due to the when last seen rule. If this is, in fact true, Babe Ruth's potential homerun record of 104 homers in a year would probably never be broken." Stuffing a forkful of mac and cheese in his mouth, Harley pointed the empty fork at Drew and added, "And here's something I discovered. Early in Ruth's career there was still a rule in force stating that an 'over the fence' homerun that would end the game would only count for as many bases as needed to force the winning run home. For instance, if a team was winning 2-0 and the opposing team hit a grand slam in the bottom of the last inning, when the man scoring from first stepped on the plate, the game was officially over and the hitter did not get credit for the homerun. It was very possible this rule may have robbed Ruth of a number of homers. This, added to the when last seen rule means Ruth could have had a year when he hit far more than sixty and his total for his career of 714 may have been greater. We'll never know."

Taking his last bite of coleslaw, Drew asked, "Is there anyone even close to going beyond Hank Aaron's current record?"

"At the time I wrote this paper, I really didn't think about that, but here it is eight years later. We'd have to do some more up to date research, but more than likely the only players I can think of that might have a shot at Aaron's record are probably Barry Bonds, McGwire and Sosa. I don't think any of them have hit 600 yet, but if they stay healthy and keep playing for the next few years one of them may bypass Aaron for the all-time homerun leader."

Getting up and tossing his empty paper plate into a trashcan next to the swing, Harley went on to explain, "There are some other interesting things I put in the paper. For instance: the longest homerun ever as far as we know was hit back on September 10th, 1960 by one of the all-time greats. Mickey Mantle blasted a homer estimated at a distance of six hundred and forty-three feet. This has always been controversial because they measured the distance the ball traveled after it stopped rolling."

"Speaking of home runs," said Drew. "Since I've been catching for you over the last six years you've hit what; five or six homers?"

"Five to be exact," confirmed Harley: "Three in Little League and two in pony ball. But that is about to end. In Little League, it's not uncommon for a pitcher to also be a good hitter. The same can be said about Pony League as well. My dad has already prepared me for when I go to play college ball. I will then be viewed the same as in the minor or major leagues for my ability to pitch...not hit. I will then spend almost no time practicing my hitting skills but will constantly hone my pitching skills. On the other hand, you will always have double duty with your catching skills as well as your ability at the plate as a hitter. That's why catchers are so valuable."

Standing, Drew also deposited his plate and cup into the trash container and commented, "I'm really looking forward to opening day at Busch. Wouldn't it be great if the Cards could start off the season by sweeping the Rockies?"

"That would be a great start, but for now all we can do is wait until we see how things pan out. We had a pretty good preseason, but when the actual season kicks off, it's hard to predict the outcome. Things change so rapidly in baseball."

Walking to the tree next to the swing, Drew picked up two gloves and a ball. "How about some catch?"

Harley caught one of the gloves Drew threw in his direction. Pounding the glove with his right hand, Harley responded, "Why not? It's what we do!"

CHAPTER 14

REMOVING HIS MASK, DREW SLOWLY WALKED TO THE pitcher's mound as he looked at the base runner standing on second base. The Fox High School team manager joined them around the rubber. Mr. Sanders wiped his brow with the back of his hand and commented, "It's the top of the seventh, we're ahead 3-2…one out. After that double they have the tying run standing over there at second. Their next three hitters are the top of their lineup. This is the third time you've faced these players this game, Harley. None of them has gotten on base so far, but I'm concerned that you might be getting tired. How do you feel? Do you have enough to finish out this inning?"

Harley rotated the ball held in his right hand and answered, "I feel all right…maybe a little tired. You need to ask Drew here how I'm doing. He knows me better than anyone. I'd be the last one to admit I can't finish up. But, if Drew says my stuff isn't working, then you can pull me and bring in a reliever."

Smiling, Drew reached for the ball. "Your fastball has lost some of its zip and your curve is hanging too long. We've been in jams like this before and you've always pitched your way out." Looking at the next batter who was standing in the on deck circle, Drew handed the ball back to Harley. "You've struck this next kid out twice this game; our ol' friend Kimbah. You just need to buckle down and bring the heat. The problem we really don't want to be faced with is to have Kimbah standing over there on first. I remember him from Little League; the fastest kid I've ever seen on the base paths. He stole on you four times in Little League. I can almost guarantee you that with only one out and the tying run on second, he might be laying down a bunt."

"I agree," said Sanders. "If he lays down a bunt there is a very good chance the tying run could reach third, but then if we throw the runner out then we've got two outs. But, here's the issue. If the current batter reaches first safely and is successful at getting the man on second down to third, then we'll be faced with not only the tying run on third but the go ahead run on first. We know Kimbah is like greased lightning. With only one out their manager will probably give him the green light to attempt to steal second. They may even try a double steal. What do you think, Harley?"

"I think we should pitch to Kimbah. He doesn't like the inside of the plate. I'll give him a steady diet of inside pitches. This should make it difficult for him to bunt."

"Okay," agreed Sanders. "Let's see what you guys are made of!"

Kimbah took the first two fastballs in tight and both were called balls. The next pitch in the same location was a called strike. Harley fired yet another fastball on the inside but it was too far away from the corner of the plate. "Ball three!"

Harley knew his next pitch had to be over the plate since he couldn't afford to walk Kimbah and put him on first.

Going into the stretch, he checked the man on second, then turned his head, focused on the center of the plate and threw an eighty-seven mile an hour fastball. Kimbah swung at the pitch, the ball bouncing in front of the plate and rolling down the first base line. Kimbah was out of the box like a shot. He was passed the ball by the time Drew reacted. Harley, recovering from his follow through, didn't have enough time to get to the ball. The first baseman ran to cover the bag while Drew ran the ball down. Looking at third, Drew could see the man who had been on second was going to reach third without any difficulty. Now, it was a race between Kimbah and Drew. Would Kimbah or Drew's throw arrive first? Drew scooped up the ball and fired it down the line, but Kimbah, at the last possible moment slid in head first below the tag. Both Drew and Harley heard the dreaded call from the umpire, "Safe!"

Mr. Sanders walked slowly out to the mound where he signaled for the entire infield to gather. "All right boys. Here's the situation. The tying run is at third, the lead run at first. With only one out I think it's a safe bet to figure the runner on first will attempt a steal. Even if we throw him out the runner on third will score and tie this game up. Here's what we're going to do. We're going to walk the next batter loading the bases. If the next batter after that hits a long outfield fly the runner from third will score on a tag up. But, if we can get him to hit to the infield we may have a shot at a force out at home, maybe even a possibility of ending the game with a double play. Harley, after you walk this next player, don't give the next batter anything good to swing out, but keep it around the plate."

After throwing four consecutive outside pitches, the umpire awarded first base to the next batter. Harley stood on the mound and slowly turned as he viewed a Seckman runner on each base. Turning, he faced the third man in their lineup; a kid he had struck out in the first inning and then forced into an infield pop-up in the fourth. After running the count up to 2-2 Drew signaled for a cutter. Harley agreed, wound up and released the ball. The ball sliced across the plate as the batter swung and missed. "Strike three!"

Walking the ball halfway out to the mound Drew shouted words of encouragement to Harley. "We don't need a double play now. Just concentrate on this next man."

The next batter had two of the four hits Harley had given up. Harley knew if he gave this kid anything over the plate he'd make contact. With the count 2-2, Harley stepped off the plate, forcing Kimbah who had taken a large lead off second back to the base. For the moment, Kimbah was the runner they had to be concerned with. If he managed to score, they'd be trailing by a run going into the bottom half of the last inning.

Harley intentionally threw the next pitch way outside making it a full count, realizing the runners, especially Kimbah, the go ahead run, would be off and running on the next pitch. Going into the stretch, Harley looked at the runner on first who was just coming off the bag. The runner on third was one step off the bag, but Kimbah was four steps off second, coiled like a spring ready to take off at the slightest opportunity. Harley stepped back off the mound, the three runners retreating back to their respective base. Harley went back into his stretch and looked in at Drew, then back at their second baseman, who was trying his best to keep Kimbah close on second. Going back toward the bag, Kimbah then ventured five steps off second, keeping his eye on both the second baseman and Harley. Suddenly, Harley spun around and fired the ball directly at the lower front corner of second base. The second baseman, cutting to the bag placed his glove at the corner of the bag. The ball slammed into the glove just before Kimbah, his outstretched hand reaching as he slid back to the base was tagged out. The umpire, very animated, signaled by pumping his fist, "You're out!"

Harley dropped his head in relief. *Game over!*

Drew threw his mask to the ground and ran out to the mound. Reaching out he shook Harley's hand. "Like you said yesterday. 'Welcome to high school baseball!' The season is just getting started and we're 1-0."

Walking back to the dugout, Drew looked at the bleachers. "I see your folks didn't make it to the game. That's got to be a first for you. I can't remember a game where at least one of them wasn't present."

My mom had to work late," said Harley, "and my dad has some mechanical problems with a bike he's been working on. Speaking of parents, I didn't see your folks here today either."

"My father, as usual, is working and my mother, even though supportive has never been much on watching baseball. She did say she'd be here right after the game. I have a dental appointment in Fenton, so I can't hang around. She should be here any minute. Are you driving home again today?"

"Yes, my mother said she'd be here about an hour after the game. I think I'll just spend some alone time sitting in the bleachers soaking up some late afternoon sun."

Seeing his mother standing next to the dugout, Drew slapped Harley on his shoulder. "My mom's here. I've got to go. See you tomorrow at school. Remember, this Saturday…opening day at Busch with the Cardinals!"

Ten minutes later both dugouts had cleared out, the players, students and parents had deserted the field. Harley stared out at the scoreboard where a student was removing the large plastic numbered cards. A man on a tractor pulled a metal grating around the infield. A number of students and parents were in the process of closing down the concession stand. Sitting back on the wooden bench of the dugout, he smiled and thought, *God, I love baseball!*

Tying his spikes together he picked up his equipment bag and started to walk by the bleachers when he was interrupted by a female voice, "Excuse me…Harley Sims?"

Harley stopped and looked at the far end of the bleachers, noticing a girl about his age dressed in a fashionable grey sweat suit seated on the bottom row of metal seats.

Never having seen the girl before, Harley hesitated in answering. The girl asked again, "Harley Sims?"

Harley, not that comfortable around members of the opposite sex, responded in a skeptical voice, "Yeah, I'm Harley Sims. And... you are?"

The girl pushed a metal walker at her side away as she slowly and awkwardly stood, extending her hand. "Elmira Madison...pleased to meet you."

Once again, not all that comfortable, Harley took her hand and answered, "Harley...Harley Sims." Thinking how idiotic he had reacted, he apologized, "I'm sorry, that was stupid. You already know who I am." Following a moment of awkward silence, Harley asked, "Do you attend school here at Fox?"

The girl sat back down, brushed long locks of auburn hair from her face and apologized, "I'm afraid I can't stand too long without my walker." Seated, she went on to answer Harley's question, "I just transferred here to Fox. My parents just moved here from New York State. My father's parents who are getting up in age, own a large farm out off Telegraph Road. They just got to the point where they couldn't keep the place up themselves, so they offered my parents a deal they couldn't refuse. If we agreed to move here and take care of them and the farm, they would sign over everything to my parents. My father, just the other day was joking that he had become a gentleman farmer. He has been an insurance agent for all of his working life. After we get settled in he might continue in the insurance field. He hasn't decided yet. My mom is a homemaker, so she'll be doing the same thing just like back home except that she'll be on a farm. This is quite a change for us, seeing how we've always lived in the city."

Harley, still nervous, tried to think of the next thing he should say. "Ah...and what city would that be?"

"Elmira, New York...just beyond the Northern Pennsylvania border."

Harley thought for a moment, and then gave the girl an odd look as he stated, "Elmira, New York. So, you're from Elmira and your first name is Elmira."

"That's right. My father loved Elmira. He hated to leave but he said it was he and my mother's responsibility to care for his parents. My mother's favorite song is Elvira, still today a popular Country and Western tune. The story has it that while my father was rushing my mother to the emergency room just before I came into this world, the last song he heard on the radio was Elvira. I guess he got to thinking...Elvira...Elmira...go figure."

Feeling a little more at ease, Harley remarked, "Elmira Madison. Kind of just rolls off your tongue."

Correcting Harley, she spoke up, "Actually, no one calls me Elmira. My friends call me Mira."

Smiling back, Harley emphasized, "Mira Madison. Still has a nice ring to it." Thinking again, he went on, "So, going back to the beginning of this conversation. How is it you know who I am?"

"When I first arrived here at school last week, I didn't know anyone. It's hard when you're new to get to know people, especially with my injury. I've found the best way to fit in when you're new is to listen to what others say. To be honest with you, the comments I heard about you were quite interesting. You see, I've always been a big baseball fan. Growing up in New York, I've always rooted for the Yankees."

"Fair warning," said Harley. "You don't want to get me talking about baseball. This could wind up being a very long conversation with me doing most of the talking and you listening."

"Well, it only makes sense you'd be a fan of the great American pastime living here in St. Louis. I've always heard St. Louis fans were somewhat fanatical."

"I wouldn't call us fanatical...we're just really behind our Cardinals. For many fans in this area baseball is more than something that rolls around every spring. It's a way of life. My father always says it hovers above everyone's level of ignorability. People get excited before the actual season even kicks in when pitchers and catchers report for spring training in February. Everywhere you go you'll see people from all walks of life walking around in Cardinal T-shirts and hats. You don't have to drive very far before you'll see someone with a Cardinals bumper sticker or a billboard along the highway about the Cardinals. What you said about hearing how fanatical we as Cardinal fans can be, we here in the St. Louis area have definitely heard about the New York Yankees. A lot of the fans in this area don't care much for the Yanks. They feel, over the years the only reason they have won the World Series more than any other team is because they always spend the most money, therefore attracting some of the best players. Myself, I've never bought into that theory. Baseball is a business when you think about it and it only makes sense if you want to win you're going to have to stack your team with the best possible players. I've met a lot of folks here in St. Louis who are Yankee haters."

Taking a seat next to Mira, Harley went on to explain, "Many fans here would never admit it, but the Yankees, if you go with year by year historical results have been and still are considered the most successful baseball franchise there has ever been. It might not always be that way, but for now, you can't argue with what the Yanks have accomplished: twenty-six World Series titles to date. Their first World Series Title came back in 1923 and the last time they took the title was in 2000."

Looking at Harley in amazement she waited until he was finished, then added her own knowledge of the World Series. "The Yanks may have the best overall winning record as far as the World Title is concerned, but still, St. Louis Cardinal fans have a lot to be proud of. If I'm not mistaken, St. Louis has taken the World Series nine times, the first being back in 1926, and their last title in '82. Currently they are second place amongst all other major league teams."

Harley, amazed at Mira's baseball knowledge, kept the conversation going as he stated, "And who is the third most winning team in World Series history?"

Mira didn't even hesitate as she answered immediately, "The Boston Red Sox…five titles."

Before Harley could agree, Mira asked a question of her own, "Do you know how many times the Cardinals have played the Yankees in the World Series?"

Proudly, Harley answered, "Yep…five times. Their first meeting was back in 1926 when the Cards beat the Yanks in a seven game series; the Cards coming out on top four games to three. Then, two years later in '28 they met up again in the series with the Yanks sweeping the Cards by winning four straight."

Mira spoke up as she finished the history of the two teams going head to head. "In 1942 and '43 they played in back to back World Series, the Cards winning the '42 series in five games and then the very next year the Yanks returned the favor winning in five. The final time they played was in 1964 where the Cards won in seven games. So, St. Louis fans can actually say that in five World Series matchups with the Yankees they have won three out of the five."

Harley sat forward as he looked into the green eyes of this, what he considered, a strange girl. "I can't believe how knowledgeable you are about baseball. I've haven't talked with all that many girls for any length of time in my short life, but I have to admit I'm really impressed. In fact, the only other female I've ever talked to about baseball has been my mother. Most females are not interested in baseball. I guess what I'm saying is you're a rare female…at least in my opinion."

"I've always been interested in baseball. While other little girls in my neighborhood were interested in dolls and that sort of stuff I was content to play catch with my dad or go to the batting cage. When I was seven, I pitched in a Minor League Softball League for seven to eleven-year-olds. I could play any position, but pitching is what I was best at, well, that is aside from hitting. I held a .450 batting average. After that I graduated up to the nine to twelve-year-old Little League Softball bracket where I played with older girls. That was the year the team I was on went all the way to the regionals and got eliminated in the championship game. After that I played Junior Little League Softball until I was fourteen, when I started Senior League Softball. I only got to play one year when I had my accident. The summer after my first year of Senior League ball, I was with my parents on a vacation down at the Gulf Shores. We were on our way home back to Elmira on a Sunday morning. The driver of a semi-truck lost control of his rig and crossed over onto our side of the highway, sideswiped our car, sending us off over the guardrail and into a field where we rolled four times. My parents escaped serious injury. I, on the other hand wasn't so lucky. My spine got twisted and both of my legs and my right arm were broken. I was in the hospital for months in rehab. They set my arm and my legs but my spine was injured to the point where I would always walk with a limp. That was two years ago and for the past year I've been getting around better with the help of my walker. I can walk, but not for long periods of time. The doctors tell me my softball career is all but over. I could learn to pitch again, but with the way my legs and spine are I could never get the leg power needed to be an effective pitcher. I could never stand at the plate and hit the ball, because even if I did manage to hit it, I couldn't run to first base. At first, I was pretty depressed, but after some counseling, I learned how to deal with the cards I had been dealt. So, now my interest in baseball and softball is confined to watching games, like the one you pitched today."

After hearing Mira's story, Harley apologized the best he could, "I'm sorry you can't play ball any longer. I've been playing ball since I was about three. If something happened to me and I could no longer play, why, I don't know what I'd do. When I was ten I broke my right arm trying to catch a homerun ball down at Busch Stadium. My arm was in a cast for six weeks. I couldn't practice and it just killed me, and that was just temporary. I knew eventually I'd get back to pitching. I admire you for your courage. I can't imagine myself ever being that strong and accepting the fact that my ball career is over. I have always had a goal of becoming a major league pitcher. It's been my life...at least so far."

"Well, Mr. Harley Sims, let me tell you what I've learned about life. You hear a lot of things about people...good and bad. Most of the good things you hear don't turn out to be all that good and the bad things you may hear are never as bad as they say. But you, and the way I saw you pitch today. It was really something! I heard you were a good pitcher and it turns out that after watching you, I am of the opinion you're better than they say. From where I sat today and watched you pitch...you're a natural. When you turned and picked that runner off second you surprised everyone here at the ballpark."

Harley stuck out his right hand and confirmed, "You said you were having a rough time getting to know people here at school. Well, you just made a friend. Listen, you have to meet my mother sometime. She was a fast pitch softball player just like you. She can still bring the heat with a ninety plus mile an hour fastball. I bet you two would have a lot to talk about."

Reaching for his hand, Mira responded with a broad smile. "Friends it is then, Harley! Maybe, later this summer you could come out to our farm. We have horses and about five hundred acres. Do you ride?"

"If you mean horses...no! The closest I've ever been to a horse was at the state fair two years ago. I wouldn't have the slightest idea of how to ride a horse."

"It's easy. My parents took me riding at least twice a month since I was a baby. When I was old enough they put me on a pony and eventually I was big enough to ride the big boys. It's very relaxing to just mount up and ride off into the surrounding countryside. Riding, for the past few months has been my savior. My mother is afraid I'll fall and reinjure myself, but my father claims it's good for me. I have to walk into the stable myself, saddle and bridle the horse, climb up and ride off. When I'm finished I have to unsaddle the horse, water the animal and put him out to pasture with the others. Actually, it's become my job to care for the four horses on the farm."

"So, you're not afraid of falling off?"

"If I fall... I fall. If there's one thing I've learned since my accident it's that you can't go through life playing the victim. I think you should come out to the farm sometime and ride with me. It's more relaxing than you can imagine."

"All right, maybe I will come out there later this summer and take you up on your offer."

Changing the subject, Mira motioned toward the empty ball field. "I guess we kind of got sidetracked from our baseball conversation. "Did you know the Yankees started out as the Baltimore Orioles back in 1901?"

Harley, learning something about baseball he didn't know, answered, "No, I didn't know that."

Following a shared solid hour of baseball talk, Mira looked at the parking lot and gestured, "My father's here to pick me up. I've got to go." Standing slowly, she reached for her walker and then Harley's hand. "It was nice to meet you Harley. You are my first real friend in Missouri. Let's see...we play a team called Kirkwood next...right?"

"That's right," answered Harley. "Next Wednesday, right here on our home field. Are you going to come to the game?"

Slowly shuffling away from the bleachers, Mira looked out at the ball field. "Wouldn't miss it for the world. Don't forget, you said you'd come out to the farm sometime. I have a baseball card collection that's pretty amazing. I think you might like to see it."

Harley shouted back at her as she slowly made her way down the third base fence line. "I collect cards myself. I have a vintage Mickey Mantle card."

She turned, stopped and gave Harley a thumbs up, then continued walking awkwardly down the fence line.

Harley stood and watched as she put her walker in the rear of the pickup, then slowly climbed in the truck. She waved one last time as they pulled away.

The truck no sooner left the lot when Monica pulled in. Getting out of her car she tossed the keys to Harley and asked, "Who ya waving to? Don't recognize the vehicle."

Catching the keys, Harley smiled. "Oh…just a new friend I met after the game. I'm going to tell you something but I don't want you going all nuts on me. It's a girl!"

Monica, surprised at her son's answer, climbed in the passenger side and responded, "Well you can tell me all about it on the way home."

Throwing his bag in the backseat, Harley got behind the wheel and started the car. "Her name is Elmira Madison, but her friends call her Mira. She just moved here from New York. She knows a lot about baseball, especially the Yankees. She understands pitching. Up until I guess about two years ago she was a fast pitch softball player…a pitcher…and pretty good from what she tells me. She had a serious accident a while back that has now prevented her from ever pitching again. She invited me over to a farm her grandparents own over off Telegraph Road sometime to ride horses. She has to use a walker. From what I can tell she seems really nice."

Monica removed a stick of gum from her purse and asked, "Why did you think I'd go, according to you, 'All nuts on you,' because you met a girl?"

"Look mom. For years now you've been informing me the day would come when something besides baseball would become important to me and more than likely it would be a member of the opposite sex. But, it's not like that. I was attracted to her because of her knowledge of baseball."

"So, this girl was not very attractive as far as looks are concerned?"

"I didn't say that. She was very attractive, but the things she knew about baseball just sort of consumed me."

"You say she was attractive. What did she look like?"

Rolling his eyes, Harley realized he was going to have to admit Mira was pretty. "Well, she had long dark hair, a nice face, and despite her physical disability she looked like she was in good shape. And, oh yeah, she had these green eyes."

"That's a problem," joked Monica as she tapped Harley on his shoulder. "When a man notices a women's eyes that means he is paying attention to her. It took your father months before he could tell me the color of my eyes. You spend, what, a few minutes with this girl and you already know what color her eyes are. I've got news for you. You may think your interest is centered on her baseball knowledge, but you may find out that it goes much deeper. We females can be rather powerful without trying very hard."

"C'mon Mom. You can't be serious. I just met her."

"That's the way it always starts. I *just met* your Dad at a Cardinals game years ago and look what happened to us. We got married."

Turning onto Jeffco Blvd. Harley looked in the rearview mirror and laughed. "I can guarantee you, this friendship is based on our common interest in baseball. Nothing more! Now, can we please change the subject because the way we're going you'll have me married off and raising a family before we get home."

CHAPTER 15

SEATED HIGH UP IN THE UPPER DECK OF BUSCH Stadium in the last row of seats, Harley and Drew looked down over the familiar scene below. The grounds crew were busy with last minute field preparations, a television crew made final adjustments to their sophisticated electronic equipment, a few lingering players from both the Cardinals and the Rockies went through their regular pre-game warm-up routines.

Drew, reclining comfortably in his seat squirted a wavy line of mustard on one of his two hotdogs as he gazed down over the numerous fans that were filtering into their assigned seats. "Looks like it's going to be a big crowd tonight."

Harley, opening a bag of peanuts, nodded in agreement. "It's always a great crowd on opening day. The Cards always pack in the fans no matter what the occasion is, but opening day is like a celebration. Fans have been chomping at the bit all winter for the beginning of the season and tonight; it's finally here once again. When you think about it, St. Louis fans, going back over a hundred and twenty years have been coming out to the ballpark to watch their team play. I was reading an article last week about how the Cards have improved their fan base over the decades. The article said that from 1882 until 1891 the Cards, which back then were named the St. Louis Brown Stockings averaged between fifteen hundred to just under five thousand fans per game. The first year; 1882, when they started playing at Sportsman's Park, they had a yearly attendance of around one hundred and thirty-five thousand and by 1891 the yearly total of fans attending games came in at two hundred and twenty thousand. Last year's National League average was 2.4 million fans. So, the Cards topped the league average last year by almost seven hundred thousand fans. So, what does that tell you about how loyal and supportive Cardinal fans are?"

Biting into his second dog, Drew as always was in amazement

of Harley's baseball knowledge, especially about the Cardinals. "It never ceases to amaze me how you remember all these facts. I've been coming with you to Cardinal games for six years now and we always sit up here in the upper deck before the game starts. It never fails. Every time we come up here you always have some sort of baseball fact you inform me of. Well, this year, not to be outdone, I have come supplied with my own remote baseball information. Do you know how many hotdogs are sold here at the stadium on a yearly basis?"

Harley laughed as he bit into his own hotdog. "No, but I think I'm about to find out."

Producing a folded paper from his pants, Drew unfolded the wrinkled document and started to read, "According to research that has been conducted, the average amount sold per year is over eight hundred thousand." Holding up his index finger, he went on, *"And...there's more!* Fans consume over one hundred and eighty-one thousand pounds of nacho chips and nearly thirty-two thousand gallons of nacho cheese. In a typical season, seven thousand feet of paper towels and fifteen thousand feet of toilet paper are used. Fifteen thousand gallons of beer are sold during an average game."

Pointing at the hot dog Harley was holding, Drew kept right on talking, "That hotdog you have in your hand has quite a history with baseball. It is thought that the hotdog was around in the 1870s and 1880s. However, the most famous legend about the hotdog took place in 1905 when a man named Harry M. Stevens brought some hot dogs to a game in New York. Stevens was an immigrant who settled in Columbus, Ohio where he was a combination minister and bookmaker. He moved to New York and started to supply scorecards to major league teams and was soon known as the 'Scorecard man.' On one occasion, while at a game, ice cream sales were slow because of the chilly weather so Harry sends someone out to get some sausages and Vienna rolls and sold them to fans. Back in those days they were called, 'Red Hots,' and the hot dog has been a part of baseball ever since."

Holding his unfinished dog on high, Harley acknowledged, "The almighty hotdog!" Taking another bite, he smiled and swallowed. "Over the years coming down here to the stadium I have definitely contributed to the hundreds of thousands of hot dogs sold."

Snapping open a peanut shell, Del inquired. "Tell me more about this girl you met after our game earlier this week. You mentioned something about her yesterday, but we really didn't have much time to talk at school."

Chewing the last bite of his dog, Harley waved his hand like it wasn't any big deal. "Her name is Mira Madison and she just moved here from some town by the name of Elmira. It's somewhere up in New York. She just happened to be at our game with Seckman. She talked with me after the game while I was waiting for my mother. Turns out, she knows a lot about baseball...and softball. She used to be a softball pitcher but she got injured in an automobile accident and can't pitch anymore. I gotta tell ya. Talking to her was like talking to you or one of the guys on our team. She was very interested in what I had to say and the things she talked about are things most girls in a million years would never know. She lives on a farm out off Telegraph Road. I might go out there later this summer and do some horseback riding with her."

Drew glanced toward the sky in wonder. "And this is how it all starts!"

"How all what starts?"

"You know. This boy-girl stuff. I'm sure your parents have had that talk with you."

"Yeah, they have discussed that with me, but meeting this girl has nothing to do with that. She's just a friend."

"I've got news for you pal," said Drew. "They are not called girlfriends for nothing. There's a big difference between a friend and a girlfriend."

Harley half laughed. "And you know this how? I mean you've never even been on a date with a female. What makes you an expert on male-female relationships?"

Drew placed his index finger to the side of his head. "Knowledge, my friend, knowledge! My mother went to great lengths to explain to me what can *and will* happen when I start to get interested in the opposite sex. I asked her the same thing you just asked me; what made her an expert. She gave me this funny look as she explained, that in case I didn't notice, she was in fact a woman. She told me she knew how the game is played. Before she met my dad, she dated a number of boys in both high school and college. When she met my dad, she knew he was the one for her. When they first met, it was just a matter of friendship, but that changed quickly into a serious relationship. In short, she reminded me that meeting someone in life you really care about can actually change your life and you can wind up going in a completely different direction than what you had planned on."

Harley drank some soda as he looked at Drew. "That will *never* happen to me. I've worked too hard to get where I am now as a pitcher. Every day of my life since I was old enough to understand the game, I have had a goal of becoming a major league pitcher and I'm not going to allow some girl, or for that matter, anyone stand in my way or interfere with what I consider to be my destiny. I'm well aware that someday, I'll meet the girl of my dreams, as my mother puts it, but that girl, whoever she may be is going to have to understand how important baseball is to me. I can't even imagine feeling stronger about anything in life than I do about pitching."

"I get what you're saying," said Drew, "but I don't think it's about not following a dream you have or stopping to work toward a lifelong goal just because you meet a girl, let's say, you fall in love with. It's just adding another thing to your life. My mother told me that life can be and often is a juggling act." Tossing two crumpled napkins in the air he began to juggle them, switching from one hand to the other. Successful, he then added a balled up paper hot dog holder and attempted to juggle all three items. Drew laughed as seconds later the three paper articles tumbled from his hands to his feet. "Did you see what just happened? When I added the third paper item everything got screwed up and I couldn't even handle the first two items, let alone the third. That third item, or something new, whatever it may be, can throw off your regular rhythm causing you to be unsuccessful at handling the other things you're already good at."

Sitting back in his seat Drew propped his feet up on the back of the seat in front of him. "Think about it? Baseball is the only thing you have concentrated on ever since you were a toddler. You've never been faced with juggling anything else. When we first met, I was juggling playing the piano and taking karate lessons, not to mention my fear of participating in sports. Then, as we well know, you convinced me to give baseball a try. I never said anything to you back them, but it was quite difficult to add baseball to my already crammed life of juggling activities. What I'm saying is that at some point in your life you're going to be faced with juggling something along with baseball. It may or may not be this girl you just met. I'm just saying."

Stuffing his hotdog holder down into his empty cup, Harley smirked. "I really don't like to think about that sort of stuff. I'm only sixteen years old. I've got my whole life ahead of me. Sure, I'll admit there have been times in the past when my mind had a tendency to wonder. I've had moments when I wonder what the girl I'll marry will look like. I've even spent time pondering how many children I'll have and what they'll look like. I've even wondered what kind of a house I'll live in and where it will be. To me, this is always kind of scary. It's like I'm looking into the future and those thoughts always interfere with what I really want to think about…and that's baseball. And you're right! Unlike you, I've never had to juggle anything other than baseball during my sixteen years of life so far. I've always admired you and your ability to be good at so many things while my talent is strictly centered on baseball. Getting back to this girl I just met. I don't see her as a threat to my goals in life. Like I said, she's just a friend. She told me she was coming to our next game. I'll introduce you to her."

Realizing Harley had just put an end to their boy-girl relationship topic, Drew changed the subject. "Who are the starting pitchers for the game today?"

Harley, as usual on top of game stats, answered with confidence, "Matt Morris is pitching for the Cards tonight and Dennie Neagle is on the mound for the Rockies. Last year was his first year with Colorado."

Standing, Harley motioned down at the field below. "We better get back to our seats. The game will be starting in less than a half hour."

Following Harley down the steep concrete steps of the upper deck, Drew commented, "I was talking with my dad the other day. He told me he was amazed at how I had adapted to baseball and that he was glad I had chosen baseball rather than basketball, football or ice hockey. As far as he's concerned baseball is the smart man's sport, at least as far as it goes for potential injuries. In the other three major sports, the physical contact can be brutal leading to season or even career ending injury. I got to thinking about what he said and the more I think about it the more sense he made. I've watched ice hockey and have witnessed some of the body checks and the, what seems like incessant fighting. Then, there's football. Aside from being a punter or place kicker there is no position on any given play where you might not get run over by some three hundred pound plus opponent who can knock your lights out. In basketball, especially under the rim in the paint, elbows are flying, players scrambling for the ball. I've seen basketball games where players get knocked unconscious. In baseball, the amount of times where players actually run into one another are minimal at best."

"I agree with you on that," said Harley. "On rare occasions two outfielders can collide or someone could get spiked in a close play on the base paths. The most dangerous play in baseball, and I might add, one of the most exciting as far as fans are concerned is the close play at home." Taking the escalator down to the next level, Harley continued with his rundown on potential baseball injuries. "To be honest, I think the pitcher and the catcher are the most susceptible to injury when on the field."

"You're right," said Drew. "The pitcher and the catcher are more mobile on every pitch than the rest of the players on the field. Pitchers are more likely to get arm injuries and catchers are prone to develop knee problems from constantly getting up and down."

Passing a long row of concession kiosks, Drew stopped and gestured toward a large sign advertising oversize drinks. "How about some drinks before the game gets started. I'm buying!"

Harley walked toward the sign above a crowded kiosk. "I'm in!"

Standing in a long row, Drew commented, "I'm not quite finished with the research I did on baseball facts you might not know of." Moving up slightly in the line of waiting customers, Drew went on to explain, "Seeing how today is opening day, do you have any idea of what the Cardinals win-loss record is for opening days?"

Looking at Drew with interest, Harley asked, "Okay, get your paper out. Normally when you spring something like this on me you always have it written down."

Drew laughed. "I guess over the past six years, you've rubbed off on me. There are times when I have to write past baseball facts I want to share with you down, but what I want to share with you now, I was able to memorize. Over the past one hundred and twenty years the Cards are 65-54-1 on opening day."

Gazing at his friend in wonder, Harley inquired, "When you say one, I can only assume you mean at some point the Cardinals played a game to a tie on a past opening day."

"That's correct. Back in 1891 on opening day the St. Louis Browns and the Cincinnati Porkers played to a 7-7 tie."

Looking at Drew in disbelief, Harley exclaimed, "The Cincinnati Porkers! Where did you come up with that name?"

"They were actually a team who played in the majors. Before the early 1900s there were a lot of teams with odd names. The first opening day the Cardinals ever played in 1882 was against a team call the Louisville Eclipse. Back in those days there were teams by the names of the Cleveland Spiders, The Chicago Colts, the Chicago Orphans, the Indianapolis Blues, Pittsburgh Alleghenys, Louisville Colonels and the Toledo Maumees." Stepping even closer to the drink counter, Drew continued with his newly acquired baseball knowledge, "The longest opening day win streak by St Louis is seven years in a row from 1947 to 1953. The longest losing streak of opening day games sits at five from 1938 to 1942."

Finally, at the counter, Harley slapped Drew on his shoulder. "I don't know what's more amazing; the stats you gave me or the fact that you even know them!"

Drinks finally in hand, the boys bumped and fought their way through the shoulder-to-shoulder crowd. Ten minutes later they were seated as the National Anthem came to an end. Leaning forward, Monica addressed the boys, "We were wondering if you two were going to show up for the first pitch of the Cardinals season."

Gesturing at the seats behind him, Harley explained, "It's nuts up there at the concession stands. There must be forty thousand fans here tonight."

Following a few more pre-game festivities, the umpire yelled, "Play ball," and the 2002 baseball season in St. Louis kicked off as the leadoff batter for the Rockies stepped up to the plate.

Following two strikeouts and a long fly ball, the top of the first inning came to a close. The Cards fared no better in the bottom half of the inning as they stranded a runner on second.

By the time the fourth inning rolled around, the Cards had taken a 3-1 lead. Harley looked out at the surrounding seats in every direction there was a sea of red. He wondered what it was like to stand on the mound in front of forty thousand people. The most people he had pitched in front of was when his team had gone to the regional championship game in Little League. If he remembered correctly there had only been about three thousand in attendance. He recalled how nerve racking the noise had been and how hard it had been to concentrate. Looking back now, it was a learning experience. He figured by the time he got to the majors, he'd be used to larger crowds.

Tapping Drew on his shoulder, who was flipping through a program, Harley brought up something they had discussed earlier. "Remember when you told me about the Cincinnati Porkers and all of those other teams with strange names?"

Looking up, Drew responded, "Yeah…what of it?"

"Well speaking of strange names, did I ever tell you my all-time strange names Cardinal line-up?"

Drew sipped at his drink. "What are you talking about?"

"A couple of year ago, I was looking over all the names of past and present Cardinal players and I came up with a starting line-up of players with strange names. You'll never believe the names I came up with. Now, mind you, these are actual people who played for St. Louis. Pitching, we have Vinegar Bend Mizell and catching him is Pickles Dillhoefer. Dillhoefer played back around 1919 and Mizell pitched for the Cards from 1952 to 1960. On first base we have Moose Baxter, second base, Creepy Crespi, at shortstop, Rabbit Maranville and finishing up the infield at third, Jap Barbeua. The three outfielders are Boots Day, Steamboat Fisher and Possum Whitten. How's that for a weird name line-up?"

Drew gave Harley an odd look. "And you say the names you just rattled off are the actual names on these players?"

"Actual names…probably not. I can't imagine parents naming their son Vinegar Bend or Pickles. More than likely they were their nicknames, but that's how they were listed on the all-time players list. There were a lot of other players with nicknames as well, especially back in the late 1880s and the early 1900s. I guess nicknames were more commonly used back then."

The crowd roared as St Louis' center fielder caught a long fly ball at the warning track to end the fifth. Standing, Drew announced, "I don't know what's gotten into me tonight. I've already had two dogs, peanuts, two large drinks and a candy bar and I'm still hungry. I'm gonna go grab another dog. Care for anything?"

Harley, raising his hands, commented and patted his stomach, "If I eat another bite I'll burst!"

"Back in a few," said Drew as he made his way past Monica and Rich.

Bounding up the concrete steps, he walked down a wide semi-crowded aisle. A minute later he arrived at the long lines of fans standing in line at the closest concession stand. He always marveled at the variety of sizes and shapes of those who came to a Cardinal game. People from all walks of life: many who came to numerous games throughout the year, some who probably couldn't afford to be here, but yet they still somehow paid the admission price of a ticket to see their beloved Cards on opening day. Men in five hundred dollar suits stood next to others in ragged jeans and torn sweatshirts. Mothers holding young babies, fathers explaining to their sons and daughters what the menu board behind the counter advertised. *Harley was right,* thought Drew. *Baseball is not just about the game…it's about life. A hot dog tastes the same to the rich man as well as the poor. When we sit in the stands and root for our team we are all equal. We are St. Louis Cardinal fans.* A warm, fuzzy feeling swept over his body and at least for the moment he was proud to be a Cardinal fan.

The line next to him began to move up, revealing fans standing in a third line: an extremely rotund man wearing a triple X size Cardinal shirt, three business people talking with each other, a woman wearing a pink Cardinal sweat shirt, a young boy clutching a few dollars in his hand. Then, Drew's eyes fell on someone he never thought he would see at the game. The line in front of him moved and he remained still, not believing who he was staring at. The man standing behind him tapped him on his shoulder, indicating that Drew should move forward. Stepping out of line, Drew had suddenly lost his appetite. Backing away from the line he continued to stare at the person in the third row. He just couldn't believe it. Turning, he ran back to the section where he had been seated. At the end of the long row where Harley and his parents were seated, Drew got Harley's attention and motioned for him to come out to the aisle. A base hit got though the infield, which caused the crowd to roar. Harley couldn't hear a word Drew was saying, so he stood up and walked by his parents out into the aisle. Before Harley could say anything, Drew pulled him up toward the main aisle above them. Pulling him off to the side, Drew looked toward the concession stand where he had just been. Harley, noticing the look on his friend's face, asked, "What's wrong? You looked like you've seen a ghost!"

Taking a deep breath, Drew stepped back out away from the oncoming crowd. "It's worse than that. I saw Aaron Buckman over there at the concession stand."

Giving Drew a look as if he were nuts, Harley responded, "That's impossible. He's in California with his dad."

Drew objected, "I know what I saw, Harley. I've been close enough in the past to Aaron Buckman to know what he looks like. He's grown taller...*and bigger!* I know it was him!"

"How can that be?" argued Harley. "He's in California!"

"Not today he isn't. He's right here at Busch Stadium. He was no more than a few feet from where I was standing."

"Now, just on hold on for a second. Let's suppose the person you saw standing in line was, in fact, Aaron Buckman. Just because he moved out of state doesn't mean he doesn't have the right to come back to Missouri and watch a Cardinals game."

"I know that! But what if he's come back for more than just a game. God forbid! What if he moved back here? I remember that day six years ago when I heard he had moved out west. That was a good day...no more Aaron Buckman in my life. If it turns out he has moved back, that's just one more thing in my life I have to juggle!"

"Calm down," pointed out Harley. "For all we know he might be back here visiting his mother. So, what if he was standing in line at the concession stand. If it was him that might be the last time you ever see him again in your life. He was nothing more than a bag of wind anyways. He didn't keep you from playing Little League and if he has moved back here there is nothing he can do to prevent you or I from playing high school baseball. Besides that, it's been six years since he moved. Maybe he's changed. Tell ya what. Let's walk over to the concession area and see if he's still there. If he is, maybe we'll just walk up to him and say, 'Hello!' He can't do anything to us here at the game. Don't forget…you're a black belt. You could probably take out ninety percent of the people here at the game. Come on. Let's walk over there and have a look see."

After standing off to the side for a few minutes and observing the fans walking back and forth from the stand, Drew finally admitted, "I'm sure it was Buckman. But, then again, it has been six years. Maybe I was mistaken."

"Well then, since we're here at the stand are you going to get anything?"

"Yeah, I guess so. Are you sure you don't want anything?"

Looking out toward the field, Harley thought and then answered, "It's the bottom of the fifth. We've got four more innings of opening day baseball to watch. I think I'll take you up on your offer and grab a large drink." The crowd roared as another Cardinal run crossed the plate, the score now 4-1. St. Louis was well on its way to logging yet another opening day victory.

CHAPTER 16

MONDAY MORNING, HARLEY SLOWLY ENTERED THE kitchen, Ozzie at his heels. The eager family dog with much excitement in his step walked over to the cabinets in the corner where his food and water bowls were located. Monica dumped a healthy portion of chunked dog food into the bowl, which Ozzie went about devouring. Harley seated himself at the table, grabbed a banana and began to unpeel the yellow fruit. Rich, seated on the other side of the table lowered the newspaper he was reading and announced, "After taking the Rockies down on opening day 10-2, we lost the next two games. So, after our first three game series of the new season we're 1-2. The Cubs fared no better. Cincinnati took two out of three from them as well. The Pirates took two out of three from the Mets. I think it's going to be a tight race this year."

Pouring a glass of juice, Harley laughed. "You crack me up, Dad. You and everyone else who tries to predict how the upcoming season will turn out. Don't get me wrong. As a baseball fan living here in the St. Louis area I'm just as excited about this year as any Cardinal fan there is. But, when you think about it, trying to forecast how the season will end up is nothing more than a shot in the dark. There are just too many variables to consider: unforeseen injuries, player slumps, even the weather in some cases. What happens if two out of our five starting pitchers get injured or if the team falls into a slump? When and if these things occur, it could mean we lose games we might normally win. Every game during the season is important. One game at a time, I say. At the end of the regular season it really doesn't make any difference if we win the pennant by one game or ten. It's always nice to run away from the other teams during the year, but we both know that's pretty rare. Look at last year. Out of the six divisions in the American and National Leagues only two teams ran away during the year. The Yankees at the end of the season held a fourteen game lead over

Boston. Seattle finished up fourteen games in front of Oakland. The other four divisions were pretty close. Cleveland beat out Minnesota by just five games and the other three races were decided in the last week of the season. Atlanta nudged out the Phillies by a game and a half and Arizona nipped San Francisco by a narrow margin of two games. The Central Division turned out to be the most exciting with down to the wire results. We wound up in a tie with Houston. They had a better head to head record than we did so we wound up in the wild card position. What I'm saying is that one game can make a difference in relation to who wins the pennant. Great ballplayers play every game like it's the final game in the World Series. The fact that we came in first place the last two years does not guarantee we'll repeat with a first place finish this year or even second or third."

Cutting into a thick slice of French toast, Rich took a bite, wiped maple syrup from the side of his mouth and stated, "That may be true but past stats prove for the most part a year end first place finish is almost always followed up with a first or second place finish the following year. Back in 1926, '27 and '28 we came in first, second and then first again during that three year run. In 1930 and '31 we had back-to-back first place finishes. From 1942 through 1947 we experienced six years of being in first or second place. I could go on and on. A great year is normally always followed by if not another great year, at least one that is considered a good year."

Harley poured syrup over his breakfast and answered with confidence, "Let's go back to the years of 1926, '27 and '28. You forgot to mention that in 1929 the Cards fell to a fourth place finish when the previous year they came in first. Fourth is not what I would call a good year. You mentioned 1930 and '31 first place finishes. But, in 1932 they came in sixth place dropping five positions from the previous year. You didn't mention 1964 when they came in first and then the next year dropped to seventh place. So, your theory of a first place finish always being followed by a great or good year doesn't always pan out. It'd be nice if we could take the National League pennant again this year, but we still have one hundred and fifty-nine games left to play. It's a long season."

Sitting at the table, Monica sipped at her morning coffee. "I don't know what I'd do without listening to you two go on and on over your breakfast baseball debates." Snapping her fingers, she remembered. "When I was at the grocery store last evening, I ran into Pastor Joe, your former Little League coach. He told me you and Drew are going to have a new ballplayer on your high school team."

Harley gave his dad an odd look, then stared at his mother. "What are you talking about...a new ballplayer? The season is already underway. Everyone who tried out wound up on the varsity or the junior varsity team. There are no new players available in the school."

"That's where you're wrong, Son," said Monica. "There's a new kid who just moved here to Arnold." She stared at Harley and waited for the question she knew would come.

Finally, Harley asked, "And does this new kid have a name?"

Getting up, Monica went to the stove and took two slices of French toast as she answered, "The kid's name is Aaron Buckman!"

Both Harley and Rich looked in Monica's direction in disbelief, Harley the first to speak, "Aaron Buckman! Drew was right!"

Turning from the stove, Monica remarked, "Then you and Drew already know all about this?"

"No, we don't know anything about him moving back here. It's just that when Drew went to the concession stand late in the game on opening day he told me he thought he saw Aaron standing in line. I told him that was not possible because he's still out in California. I tried to convince him he was seeing things but he swore up and down it was Buckman. I guess he was right. He wasn't seeing things!"

Rich joined in on the conversation. "So, how does Pastor Joe know all about this?"

"Simple...Aaron is living with him."

Harley just about choked on a mouthful of food as he cleared his throat. "What? Why on earth would he be living with Pastor Joe?"

Seated back at the table, Monica calmly explained, "According to the pastor, Aaron's father's religious transformation with the woman he met ended after a few short months. They split up and Aaron's father returned to his old ways of drinking, fighting and in general just plain raising cane. Apparently, they had an apartment in Los Angeles. His dad was working construction and I guess made pretty good money but he was constantly in and out of jail, so Aaron, as usual was on his own. He played Pony League ball and one year in high school. The pastor said that Aaron can still the ball a ton. His father, just a few months ago finally got sent back to prison. Aaron figured he couldn't make it on his own so he gathered up what little money he had and grabbed a bus back here to St. Louis. He contacted his mother, but she wouldn't give him the time of day. Pastor Joe was out jogging last week over by the Arnold Little League Complex and discovers a man sleeping in the dugout of Field #5. When he approached the man and asked him if he was okay he recognized the man, in fact, was a seventeen year old youth: Aaron Buckman. The pastor couldn't believe it. Aaron was visibly upset. He remembered Joe from Little League. After he calmed down Aaron told Joe he didn't want to wind up like his father. He figured if he moved back here he could finish his high school years and live with his mother but she didn't want anything to do with him. He said the only thing good he had in life was baseball and that's why he went to the Little League complex. He didn't know where else to go. The long and short of this whole situation is Aaron is living with Pastor Joe, and as long as he keeps his nose clean Pastor Joe said he could stay with him for as long as he wanted. He starts school tomorrow at Fox High. The Pastor has already contacted your coach, who remembered Aaron from his Little League days. So, life has come full circle as they say. Aaron Buckman, a kid who has always been a thorn in your side, will now be playing on your team."

Sitting back in his chair Harley held out his hands. "Hold on a minute. How can Aaron go to school without the permission of his parents or at least one of them?"

Monica answered as best she could, "I'm not sure, but I think Pastor Joe has worked that out."

Rich looked across the table at Harley and inquired, "How do you feel about Buckman being on your team?"

"I can't believe it. I'm sitting here listening to you guys tell me all this, but to tell you the truth, I won't be convinced it's true until I see Aaron in a Fox High School baseball uniform. And, even then, it's hard for me to imagine he's changed. He's never liked me and just because we might be teammates doesn't mean he'll change his stripes. Does Drew know any of this?"

"I doubt it," said Monica. "You can make his day and tell him on the way to school later this morning. By the way, we'll be leaving in ten minutes, so if you're going to eat you better get a move on."

Finished eating, Harley placed his dirty dishes in the sink, ran upstairs, threw on one of his favorite Cardinal T-shirts, gave Ozzie a pat on the head, grabbed his books, ran down the stairs and out the back door to the garage. Starting the car, he pulled around the side of the house and drove up the street stopping in front of Drew's house where he honked the horn three times. Within seconds, Drew ran out of the house and hopped in the back of the car, smiled and greeted Harley and his mother, "Good morning. Looks like it's going to be a great day."

Driving up the street, Harley looked in the rearview mirror and sadly remarked, "Well you better enjoy it while you can because I'm about to burst your bubble!"

Fastening his seatbelt, Drew joked with great enthusiasm, "Fire away my friend. There is nothing you could drop on me this morning that would squash my zest for life!"

"How's this for squashing your zest? Remember when you told me at the game last weekend you saw Aaron Buckman and I didn't believe you? You did see him there. He's moved back here and that's not the half of it. He's going to be on the Fox High School baseball team."

Drew sat in silence as he stared out the backseat window at the passing trees.

Harley repeated himself, "He's going to be on our team! Did you not hear what I just said?"

"Yeah, I heard what you said. Why did he come back? Why didn't he stay out there on the west coast?"

Turning onto Highway 141, Harley spoke to his mother sarcastically, "Why don't you explain what happened. I don't think I can drive and talk about Aaron Buckman at the same time."

Turning in the seat so she was facing Drew, Monica began, "I found out about all this yesterday when I was at the store..."

Harley no sooner pulled up in front of the main doors of the high school, when Monica finished, "...so it looks like Aaron will be staying with Pastor Joe, at least for the time being. He really has no place else to go."

Getting out of the car, Drew joined Harley who tossed the car keys to Monica, who walked around to the driver's side and spoke, "I'll be back to pick you boys up later this evening around seven after ball practice. See you then."

As Drew watched her drive off he spoke to Harley, "Do you think he'll be at school today?"

Walking toward the double doors, Harley answered, "I have no idea. I can tell you this. I'm not going to worry about it. I mean, think about it? Maybe we should be excited. There isn't a high school in the state that wouldn't welcome the talent he brings. Let's just get through the day and see what happens." The bell sounded for the first class of the day and they entered as Harley slapped Drew on his back. "I'll see you at lunch. Keep an eye out for Buckman."

At eleven thirty, Harley walked out the door of his mathematics class when the lunch bell sounded. Just as he was about to enter the cafeteria, he was stopped by a familiar voice, "Harley...hold on!"

Mira, stabilizing her body with her walker leaned up against a row of lockers. "Heading for lunch?"

Smiling, Harley responded, "Sure am. Why don't you join me? I'm planning on meeting my friend Drew. I told him all about you. I'll introduce you. I think you'll like him. He's quite the character."

"I'd love to have lunch with you but I have a doctor's appointment downtown. It's with a specialist. I'm only scheduled for a half day here at school. We're going to discuss the possibility of yet another option. If it succeeds, I might be able to walk without this stupid metal contraption. Listen, I really have to go. If I don't see you in school the next couple of days I'll be at the game this Wednesday." Reaching into her pocket she produced a plastic protected baseball card. "Here, I want you to have this. You can add this to your collection. If you already have this card, I'll try to come up with one you don't."

Staring down at the card, Harley answered in amazement, "This is a very old and valuable Red Schoendienst card. It must be worth quite a bit. I couldn't take this."

"Not to worry. I know you're a huge Cardinals fan. I'm a Yankee fan so therefore that card is more valuable to you than it is to me. Believe me, if Red played for the Yankees I wouldn't be giving his card to you. It's not Schoendienst's rookie year. His rookie card is very rare. That card is a 1945 M114 Baseball Magazine Supplement series. Then, in '46 they released a card on Red that is extremely rare. The Sears St. Louis Cardinals Postcard set. That card in your hand is a 1949 Bowman Card. Red is probably in the eyes of most Cardinal fans the most well-known second baseman to ever wear a Cardinal uniform. Albert was his real first name but as we all know he went by Red. The Cards picked him up in 1945 as a left fielder. Then, in '46 they put him on second base where he helped them to win their third World Series in five years."

Harley looked down at the card, then at Monica with awe. "First of all, it's amazing that you would even give me this card. Secondly, I can't believe you know so much about Red Schoendienst."

"Before yesterday I didn't know much about him. But, when I decided to give you this card, I boned up on some of his past history. Look, I have to go."

Harley stood and watched as she slowly hobbled down the hallway, weaving in and out of the many students making their way to lunch. For the most part no one paid her any attention. Turning to enter the cafeteria, Harley thought, *She sure got my attention!*

Interrupted again by a familiar voice, Harley stopped and turned back as Drew approached. "That girl with the walker. Is that Mira…the girl you were telling me about?"

"Yeah, that was her and she gave me this baseball card. It's a '49 Bowman. They're pretty valuable."

Taking the card, Drew examined the photo and asked, "It's looks very old. How valuable is it?"

"I don't know. I'll have to look it up in my newest edition of Baseball Cards Digest when I get home tonight." Taking the card back he carefully placed it in his shirt pocket. Scanning the numerous long tables scattered around the large room, Harley spoke, "Do you see Buckman anywhere?"

"No, but as big as he is he should stick out like a sore thumb."

Approaching the cafeteria line Harley glanced up at the menu board. "Today I'm going with the spaghetti."

Grabbing a dented metal tray, Drew added, "I think I'll go down that road too."

Placing a garlic bread stick on his tray, Harley continued to look around the large area. "I don't think he's here. Like you said. He won't be hard to miss."

"Uh...oh! I think that's him over there in the corner," expressed Drew. "I can't really see the face, but I'm pretty sure it's him!"

Harley looked in the direction Drew had indicated where he spotted a large male student seated at a corner table by himself. Receiving a large glob of spaghetti on his plate he grabbed a set of utensils and confirmed, "Yep, that's ol' Aaron. He looks exactly the same as he did six years ago when he left, except for the fact that he's even bigger than he was back then."

Grabbing Harley by his shirtsleeve, Drew asked nervously, "What if he sees us and comes over to our table? What if he causes trouble?"

"I really don't think that's going to happen. Remember what my mom said about how Aaron is living with Pastor Joe and has to toe the line? He'd be stupid to pull some crap his first day of school." Grabbing a salad, Harley went on, "C'mon, I'm feeling adventurous. Let's go join him at his table."

Drew followed Harley across the cafeteria as he whispered, "Are you crazy! Do you not recall that we are not exactly some of his favorite people?"

"It'll be okay," reassured Harley. "Look at him just sitting there by himself. He probably doesn't know anyone. It's been six years since he left. We'll just walk over there and say hello. The worse thing he can do is tell us is to mind our own business."

Looking around Harley in Aaron's direction, Drew awkwardly agreed, "Okay, I'm right behind you!"

Aaron was taking his last bite of spaghetti when Harley walked up to the table. "Aaron...Aaron Buckman! We heard you moved back here to Arnold. Mind if we have a seat?"

Pulling out a chair without being invited to do so, Harley seated himself. Drew, reluctantly followed suit and sat directly across from Aaron. Aaron pushed his sauce-stained plate to the side and then smiled, speaking in his normally deep voice, "Harley Sims and Drew Scott. I heard you two were attending school at Fox." Looking around the crowded room he shrugged his large shoulders. "It's nice to finally run into someone I know."

Harley bit into his garlic bread and continued the conversation, "We heard you moved back to Arnold. My mother talked with Pastor Franks and he filled her in on what happened; how things didn't work out for you on the coast and that you had decided to move here with your mother."

"My mother," sneered Aaron. "Now there's a loser for you if you've ever seen one. When I lived here before she didn't want anything to do with me. Why on earth I thought she would now is beyond me, but I didn't have much of a choice."

Drew jumped in on the conversation. "During your six years out there did you still play ball?"

"Sure did! That's about the only thing that saved me. I played pony ball for a man by the name of Coach Dilford. He convinced me that if I was to have a future as a professional ballplayer it was not going to be pitching." Looking directly at Harley, Aaron emphasized, "Even though I can heave the ball at around a hundred miles an hour I have no control. He taught me to concentrate on my abilities as a first baseman and a hitter. Then, I played one year of high school ball, before I decided to move back here."

Harley dumped a packet of ranch dressing over his salad and asked, "Did you attend any Dodger games when you were out there?"

"Yeah, I did, but only when the Cardinals were in town. I'd wear my Cardinal hat everywhere I went. Folks out there didn't appreciate it much. It didn't take me long to figure out that being a St. Louis fan in Los Angeles wasn't a good idea. After my father was sent back to prison I decided to work for a couple of weeks and save up enough cash for a bus ticket back here to Arnold. Well, when I got here you know the rest of the story. If it wouldn't have been for Pastor Joe I don't know what I would have done."

Drew swallowed a large bite of the pasta and then asked, "So, now that you're here...what's your plan?"

"Things couldn't have worked out better. The Pastor is offering me three hots and a cot. He even took me to the Cards opening day last weekend."

Drew spoke up, "We know, we saw you at the game."

"Why didn't you come and speak with me?"

"Well," said Harley, "first of all we only saw you from a distance. We weren't exactly sure it was you."

"And secondly," remarked Drew, "We figure we still weren't on the best terms with you."

Finishing up his milk, Aaron stood. "That crap is all in the past. Right now, other than Pastor Joe you guys are the only friends I've got. Listen…I've got to get to my next class. I'm still trying to figure out where everything is around this place." Walking off, he turned and smiled, "See you guys at ball practice tonight. Put a good word in for me with the coach. I'm going to need all the help I can get."

Harley and Drew sat in silence for a number of seconds while they watched Aaron walk through the cafeteria and out the doors. Finally, Drew spoke up, "Well, I'll be dipped! Who would have thought that Aaron Buckman of all people could change? Just from talking with him, why he's almost likeable!"

"Yeah, it seems like he has changed, but he still has a tough row to hoe; father in prison, mother who doesn't give a crap about him. For the moment, the only thing he really does have is baseball. It makes me think about what my mother is always saying and this is one of the moments when I have no doubt that its true. *Baseball is just not a game…it's about life!*"

CHAPTER 17

HARLEY GLANCED UP AT THE OVERCAST, GREY SKY AS he slowly walked across the paved lot to the ball field. He switched his worn equipment bag from his right to his left shoulder. Thinking back, he remembered when watching the late news the previous night before turning in for bed the weatherman said there was a slight chance of afternoon showers.

Sitting on the bottom row of metal seats in the bleachers on the third base side of the field, Harley removed the '49 Bowman Schoendienst card from his pocket and examined it closely. The top right hand corner was ever so slightly bent which meant that this defect would decrease the value of the card. Thinking about it, he didn't value the card because of its monetary worth, but rather the value that the card represented because Mira had given it to him. He didn't know why he felt this way. Aside from baseball and the fact that he was a pitcher and she used to be, they held nothing else in common.

Placing his bag on the bleachers he leaned back and looked up at the rapidly moving clouds, his thoughts once again returning to Mira. *It must really be hard for her,* he imagined. According to her, not that long ago, she had been a very talented fast pitch softball pitcher. *Life is so fragile,* he thought. In a matter of seconds during the accident, her life took a dramatic turn. The thought that she could no longer pitch was sad enough; let alone the fact that she couldn't walk without the aid of a walker. It must be horrible to realize you'll never walk normally or even run again. He couldn't imagine himself ever having that much courage. If he couldn't pitch, well he didn't know what he'd do. Baseball, especially pitching, had been the main focus of his life for the past thirteen years. He couldn't even fathom all that coming to an abrupt end. Mira appeared to be a much stronger person than he could ever be.

Looking out at the empty field, his thoughts drifted away from

Mira and honed in on what he viewed as the new and improved Aaron Buckman. His size was still intimidating, but now he seemed to have a more pleasant disposition about himself. The fact that Aaron was going to be a member of the Fox High School baseball team might just be what his father always called a "Game changer!" Last year Fox had finished dead last in the district, but this year with the addition of not only he and Drew, but now the long ball hitting Aaron Buckman, they might just be a force to be reckoned with.

Coach Sanders appeared at the end of the dugout and commented, "Looks like it could be a wet practice today. If it rains too hard we'll have to cancel. The forecast for tomorrow is clear, so if today turns out to be a bust we can get some work in tomorrow."

Looking out at the sky, Harley responded, "I think this is going to blow over, besides that we need the practice. I hear Kirkwood beat us both times we played last year."

Sitting down on the bench, Coach Sanders went on to agree, "That they did." Changing the subject, the coach stated, "I guess you heard about Aaron Buckman moving back to Arnold. He'll be added to our roster. I remember him vaguely when he played Little League ball. You pitched against him…right? What can you tell me about him?"

Harley shook his head in amazement. "He's a pure hitter. Every single time he steps up to the plate he's a threat. He can change the outcome of a game with a single swing. He really doesn't have a weakness at the plate. I guarantee you. He'll win some games for us."

Interested, Sanders asked his next question. "How about defensively? How would you rate him as a first baseman?"

"For his size, he can really move. I've witnessed him get to balls I thought for sure were going to get by him. He makes a large target for infielders and has an exceptionally long stretch allowing him to grab bad throws."

"I'm going to have a short meeting before our practice today and introduce him. If Buckman is as good as you say, he'll probably be our starting first baseman. Of course, that depends on how our newest player performs."

Stomping his feet to make sure his spikes were comfortable,

Harley grabbed his glove and started out of the dugout. "I'm going to head out to center field and do some stretching."

Positioning himself on the grass that was still dry despite the now and again rain drops, Harley went into the hurdlers spread position and stretched forward allowing his fingertips to touch the tip of his right spike. He repeated the exercise twenty-five times and then switched legs.

Ten minutes into his stretching he saw Drew running across the field in his direction. Drew flopped down on the ground, crossed his legs and asked, "Did you run into Buckman after lunch?"

"No, how about you?"

"I passed him in the hall after my two o'clock class. He smiled and nodded at me but that was about it. That reminds me. Right after lunch I called my dad at work and asked him to look up that Red Schoendienst card Mira gave you. My father is nothing short of a genius when it comes to computers. Within two minutes he called me back with the info. That particular '49 Bowman card is #111 in the series that year. He said the card is valued between two hundred and fifteen dollars to two hundred and thirty dollars depending on whom you purchase it from. I think it's unusual for a girl you hardly even know to fork over a card worth two hundred dollars."

Harley did a few deep bends and responded, "Well, I guess it is a little odd, but I figure she's just nice. She told me she's coming to our game Wednesday. You'll get to meet her then." Glancing toward the infield, he picked up his glove. "Come on, I think the coach is getting everyone together."

Drew stood, and following Harley across the outfield grass, he pointed, "There's Buckman now...down the third base line. At first glance you'd never even imagine he's just a high school ballplayer. He looks like a major leaguer."

"You're right on that," said Harley. "I'm glad I don't have to pitch to him this year."

By the time they reached the infield all the other players were gathered around the bleachers, Aaron on the very end. The coach and his two managers waited until everyone was seated. Holding his hands out to his sides he looked up into the sky. "It looks like we're going to get our practice in. We may get a few sprinkles but I think that's going to be about it." Signaling to Aaron, he smiled.

"At this time, I want to introduce you to the newest member of our ball team."

Aaron got up, walked over and stood next to the coach who seemed to be dwarfed by his size. Looking up into Aaron's face, Sanders continued, "Boys, this is Aaron Buckman. Some of you may remember him from your Little League days. I feel he is going to be quite an asset to our team. Now, let's get to work!"

Harley, along with three other pitchers jogged down the foul line to an open fenced-in area just outside the right field line where there were two pitching lanes. This was Fox High School's bullpen. Harley smiled as he stepped on the rubber of Lane #1. Brian Deats, a kid he knew from Little League, stood on the makeshift home plate and waited for Harley's first pitch. Harley took a deep breath and delivered a fastball. Deats nodded in approval after he caught the ball and threw it back. Harley smiled when he thought about the Fox High School bullpen. It was nothing more than a slightly enhanced version of what they called a bullpen back in Little League. Firing a curve to Deats, his mind wandered and he thought about where the term bullpen originated. There were a number of theories as to where the term came from but the most common origin is thought to have come to life back around 1909. In those days, Bull Durham Tobacco was a big sponsor of baseball and in almost every park they were advertised on large outfield signs that were forty feet high and twenty-five feet wide. As a promotion, The Bull Durham Company stated that if a batter could hit the sign they would be paid fifty dollars and they would receive a carton of tobacco. In 1909, there were nearly fifty Bull Durham signs in the league and fourteen players won. The next year, 1910 the signs increased to one hundred and fifty and eighty-five players hit those signs. That year over forty-five hundred dollars and ten thousand pounds of tobacco were given away. This, to most baseball experts is where the term bullpen derived. Harley was brought out of his daydreaming when Deats yelled, "Let's switch up!"

Coach Sanders stood next to home plate, a bat and a used baseball clutched in his hands. Waiting until all the infielders were in position, he looked around at the players, ending up with Aaron standing a few feet to the right of first base. "Okay," yelled

Sanders, "we're going to start with some routine grounders. Field the ball and throw to first." With that he tossed the ball in the air and hit a slow roller to third. The third baseman charged the ball, scooped it up, hesitated for a brief second then fired the ball to first where Aaron snagged it, turned and threw the ball quickly back to Drew. The next ball was hit to the left of the shortstop. He backhanded the ball, fumbled it, recovered, picked it up with his bare hand and rifled it to first. The throw was low, but Aaron scooped it up on a short hop and once again fired the ball home. Nodding in approval, Sanders hit the ball to the second baseman who fielded the ball cleanly and made a good throw to first. Next, the coach hit the ball to the right of Aaron, who quickly took three steps to his right, snagged the ball and ran to the bag. "Good job," yelled the coach. "Let's go around the infield three more times and then we'll try some double plays."

A half hour passed and the threat of rain as well. The sun began to peak out from behind the clouds when Coach Sanders signaled everyone to the pitcher's mound where he addressed the team. "We've got about an hour and a half left before we call it a day. We're going to spend the remainder of practice focusing on our hitting. It doesn't make any difference how good we are defensively if we cannot produce runs. Wednesday we'll be going up against one of the best pitchers in the league. He is basically a fastball pitcher. He'll throw a curve once in a great while but speed is where he lives. He can throw close to ninety. We'll be setting the pitching machine at that speed. Everyone gets twenty-five cuts at the ball. Remember, wait for your pitch. Now, let's see what we can do."

Drew remained behind the plate while the infielders assumed their positions; the remainder of the team went to the outfield to shag fly balls. Harley positioned himself in center field where he caught a number of long fly outs. Drew was the fifth player to step to the plate. He smiled after hitting a line drive base hit down the third base line on the very first pitch. Twenty-four swings later he walked away from the plate having logged seven hits.

Harley was next and for some reason kept popping the ball up in the infield, only logging three hits during his time at the plate. For the next hour player after player stepped to the plate and challenged the machine. The only player on the team who had not taken his swings was Aaron. Sanders signaled, "Buckman…you're up!"

Aaron walked to the dugout and put on his batting gloves and selected the heaviest bat allowed by high school baseball rules and walked to the plate. The coach stopped him before he stepped into the box. "Buckman! So far I've been quite impressed with your hustle, your arm and your fielding ability. I know you're known for your power hitting. You need to show me that what I've heard about your ability at the plate is true. Any questions before we begin?"

Aaron humbly smiled, stepped into the box and held up his bat. "No sir. I'll let my bat do my talking." Digging in at the plate, he adjusted his batting gloves, touched the brim of his hat took one swing and waited. The manager switched on the machine and seconds later a ninety mile an hour fastball blew by Aaron and slapped into Drew's mitt. Drew, in wonder looked up at Buckman and softly asked, "What was wrong with that pitch?"

"Nothing," said Aaron calmly. "Don't you remember that I always take the first pitch?"

Thinking, Drew responded, "That's right, I do remember that."

Going through his routine of adjusting his gloves and touching his hat brim, Aaron swung the bat and waited as he commented. "If the next pitch is in the same location it's out of here!"

Drew watched as the ball exited the tube of the machine. Reaching up to catch the blazing fastball, he heard the crack of the bat, stood and watched the ball sail over the shortstop's head, steadily rising until it passed over the chain link outfield fence, continued over the grass area, bounced on the edge of the parking lot and hit the side of a parked school bus. Turning back to Drew, Aaron remarked, "That felt good but I didn't quite get all of it."

Stepping away from the plate Aaron allowed the next pitch to cross the plate then he stepped back in and waited for the machine to release the next ball. The pitch was outside. Aaron moved toward the plate slightly and clobbered the ball over the right field fence in foul territory. Preparing himself for the next pitch, he took one swing and waited patiently. Seconds later the ball cleared the left field fence by forty feet, flew over the parked buses and landed on the roof of the school. Harley, Coach Sanders, Drew and everyone else stood frozen as they watched the ball bounce off the tar-covered roof. The manager standing next to the coach was about to say something when Aaron hit the next ball over the fence in the same location, the ball smashing through a classroom window. Aaron backed away from the plate as Drew stood and commented jokingly, "Guess we should have evacuated the school before we let you take your swings!"

The manager next to Sanders put his hands on his hips and stared at the school in amazement. "Those last two homers had to be near to what...close to four hundred fifty feet. How old is this kid?"

Sanders smiled and answered, "Seventeen...eighteen. He sure can hit!"

The next five pitches resulted in two more homeruns, two long fly outs and a ground ball the third baseman caught but the force of the ball knocked him to the ground. Aaron, ten minutes later finished up hitting a total of nine homeruns and two potential base hits.

The coach smiled and commented to the manager, "Looks like we have a new first baseman. Call everyone in for a short meeting then cut 'em loose."

One by one the boys exited the field, Aaron the first to walk off. Drew and Harley remained until everyone else had left. Harley pounded his fist into the pocket of his old glove. "Well I'd say that was quite a performance. Kirkwood is going to have their hands full."

Looking toward the roof of the school, Drew added, "To say the least. Come on. I think I saw your mom over by the parking lot."

Monica was seated in the front passenger seat when the two boys approached. Harley hopped in behind the wheel and Drew climbed in the back. Before either one of the boys could say anything, Monica remarked, "I got here just at the end of hitting practice. Buckman can still hit."

"That's an understatement if there ever was one," said Harley. "Did you see him hit one of the school buses, put another on the roof of the school and break out one of the classroom windows?"

"No, that must have happened before I drove up. I just caught his last five swings, two of which were over the fence. Is Coach Sanders happy with Aaron's performance?"

"I don't see how he couldn't be. Aaron is a one man wrecking crew at the plate. I'm sure he's going to be our starting first baseman."

Drew leaned up in between the seats. "One of the team managers said the ball that hit the roof was close to a five hundred footer. That's unbelievable!"

As Harley backed the car out, his mother mentioned casually, "By the way, I met your little friend."

Harley gave her an odd look. "My little friend. What and who are you talking about?"

"Elmira Madison. She was sitting over there in the grass watching batting practice. When she got up to leave I noticed she had a walker. From the way you described her, I figured it was her. When she started to walk by the car, I stepped out and introduced myself as your mother. She knew who I was as soon as I told her my name. She told me she had met you twice. Said that you had told her I was a former fast pitch softball pitcher. She also told me she used to pitch. We must have talked for nearly ten minutes."

Drew laughed and sat back in the seat. "It's over for you Harley. I told you the other day this is how this sort of stuff gets started. Now, this new girl is even friends with your mother. It won't be long before you're toast!"

The rain started to fall and Harley turned on the windshield wipers as he backed the car out. "So, she met my mother. That doesn't mean a thing."

"I hate to tell you this, Son," said Monica, "but meeting me does mean something. I was quite impressed with her. Neither one of you boys know this, but Rich and I are planning a barbeque in our backyard this coming Saturday."

"Okay, so we don't know about this barbeque you're throwing," remarked Harley. "What's any of that have to do with you meeting Elmira Madison?"

"I invited her and her family over for the afternoon…to the barbeque."

Harley looked across the seat at his mother in total disbelief. "How could you do such a thing without getting with me first?"

Monica gave her son an equal look of disbelief. "In case you haven't noticed your father and I make all the decisions about our family. We really don't have to get your permission as to who we invite to our home."

"But Mom...I just met this girl. I hardly even know her. This could be awkward! Drew here hasn't even met her yet."

Drew laughed, "Don't go putting this off on me just because I've never met this girl. When and if I do get to meet her it's not going to be awkward for me. I'm kind of excited about coming down to your house this Saturday: barbequed chicken, maybe some dogs and burgers, baked beans and potato salad. I don't know what you're worried about. Sounds like a wonderful afternoon."

Harley, seeing that he was not getting his point across, turned the wipers on high as the rain started to fall heavily. "Let's just drop this barbeque business. Let's talk about something else." Monica turned and looked at Drew who shrugged his shoulders in wonder.

Harley read the last page of War and Peace, closed what he considered to be a very boring book and looked at Ozzie who was curled up at the bottom of the bed. "You're lucky to be a dog, Ozzie. You don't need an education to survive. Being a teenager is not all it's cracked up to be: reading assignments and studying subjects that will absolutely have no effect on one's future." Looking at the Cardinals clock on his bedroom wall he tossed the book on a chair and stood. "It's almost ten o'clock. I'm tired. What say we hit the hay?"

Ozzie, for some strange reason always knew what his master meant when he mentioned hitting the hay. The black dog got up went to the head of the bed and snuggled in between two large Cardinal pillows. Harley laughed and started for the small attached bath, when a knock sounded on his door, followed by his mother's voice, "Harley...can I come in?"

Speaking to his unseen mother, Harley responded, "Come on in!"

Monica entered and closed the door behind her. Sitting on the edge of the double bed she reached out to pet Ozzie on his head. "Looks like you two are just about to turn in."

"Yeah, I was just about to brush the ol' ivories then hit the sack. What's up?"

"I was just about to ask you the same question. Tonight at dinner you didn't have much to say about Mira except for the fact she gave you that valuable baseball card. Ninety-nine percent of our conversation was centered on Aaron Buckman and how impressive he was at ball practice. When your father mentioned the upcoming barbeque and that he was anxious to meet the Madison's, you clammed up tighter than a drum. It was shortly after he asked if Mira was coming along that you excused yourself from the table. I know on the way home you mentioned it was going to be awkward for you if she came over to the house. Now, that being said, I know there are a lot of things in life that can make people feel awkward. Generally, when it comes to other people's awkward moments I try to mind my own business, but you're my son, so I just can't let something you may be uncomfortable about just slip by and not find out what the problem actually is."

Harley slumped in a chair next to his cluttered desk and let out a long sigh. "It's kind of hard to explain. It just seems like every time I make friends with someone or someone comes into my life, they always have some sort of problem. I'm not talking about just a regular ol' friend, but someone who you get close to or who always seems to be in your life."

Shifting in his chair to get more comfortable, Harley tried to explain as best he could. "Take Drew for instance. You have to admit when he first moved here from Texas and we met him he was a strange little kid...not what I would consider *normal!* Think about it? A ten-year-old who had never played a single sport and had no desire to do so. Rather than sports, he collected stamps, played the piano and was involved in karate. You can't sit there and tell me that Drew Scott didn't strike you as abnormal! Remember, he had a phobia about getting hit by a baseball or any type of ball or of having any physical sports contact. Then, there's Aaron Buckman, who I've known since grade school. Now there's a boy with a problem. A bully if there ever was one. He has always pushed me around, stole my hat and took money from me, threatened me and always badmouthed me to other kids always claiming he was a better ballplayer than me. Now, this Elmira Madison comes along, a girl who like me was a pitcher, but due to some freak accident will never be able to walk in a normal fashion let alone run. Then, on top of that she up and gives me a baseball card worth over two hundred dollars. Who does that? She can't be normal."

Monica pursed her lips and thought for a moment, finally speaking up, "Let me ask you a question. Do you consider yourself *normal?*"

Giving his mother a strange look, Harley responded without even hesitating, "Yes, I consider myself a very normal sixteen year old high school kid."

"If that's true then you're the only one who looks at you and sees a normal young man."

In amazement, Harley sat up and asked, "How could anyone say I'm not normal?"

"Everyone you know or that your father and I know...that's who!"

Harley stood, walked to the bedroom window and looked out into the darkness. "I can't believe you'd say something like that. No one has ever accused me of being abnormal!"

Monica smiled. "Being abnormal doesn't label a person as some sort of freak. It just means that you do things or function in a manner that most people don't...therefore you're not normal."

Turning back to face his mother, Harley demanded, "What is it I do that labels me as abnormal?"

"Where do you want me to start? Your entire life has been somewhat abnormal. Think about this? If it happens to be raining most children would be content to remain inside and watch television or play games, but not you. I can't recall the number of times your father and I have stood at the kitchen window and observed you standing out in the backyard in the pouring rain as you went through your daily pitching routine. I've seen you out there in the snow, sleet...even hail. No other child I know of would endure those types of conditions to complete their goal in life. All of our friends and neighbors think you're abnormal. They have never put it in those exact words. They use terms like focused and determined, but what they really mean is you're not normal. Guess what...you're not a normal young man and I for one am glad you're not. It takes a great deal of self-motivation to do what you do every day."

Crossing her legs, Monica pointed out, "Let's talk about your three so-called abnormal friends: Drew, Aaron and now this Mira. "I'll admit that Drew was a weird kid when we first met him, a young boy with a problem...a phobia. Look at him today. You have said a number of times he's the best high school catcher in St. Louis...far better than anyone else. So, even though he has conquered his phobia problem, if he is, in fact the best catcher in this city, that makes him unusual, a cut above all the other catchers. Aaron, so it seems, is trying to turn over a new leaf. Does he hit like a normal high school ball player? That question answers itself. Aaron Buckman is not a normal ballplayer. This girl, Mira, is faced with a number of physical problems, but yet she is playing the game of life with the hand she has been dealt. Everyone has some sort of problem or at least something in their life that others view as not normal."

Getting up Monica walked to a globe of the world attached to a wooden stand. Spinning the globe, she commented, "The world is full of color. It's more than just black and white. There are countless shades of color: red, orange, green, blue, and on and on. Look at it this way. The world may just very well be a large coloring book and we, each one of us are the crayons." Sitting back on the bed, she continued with her strange analogy, "Have you ever looked inside of a coloring book that has not been marked up or colored in?"

Harley thought and then answered, "I suppose I have."

"And what do you see on the pages of the untouched coloring book?"

"A bunch of plain old black and white images of pictures...unfinished pictures."

"That's exactly right...unfinished. If we were to give that book to twenty or thirty different kids from ages of two up to maybe ten years of age and allow them to color what would the end result be?" Without waiting for her son to respond, she explained, "The pages would all be marked up or colored in, and no matter what the choice or variation of the colors the children choose to use or whether they color within the lines or not, each page, actually the entire book comes to life, each picture representing an individual idea or concept. In short, we, all of us are the crayons that leave our mark on the world. Some of us are not used all that much so we're full size while others who are more popular are used quite often, meaning that we are short or dull while some are sharp and pretty. Others yet are looked upon as ugly colors. Some are broken in half. We all have different color names and sometime our labels have been ripped or worn off. Despite all these differences we all do the same thing; we color the world in our own unique way. We are all different colors but yet still exist in the same box of crayons." Getting up, Monica ruffled her son's hair. Hesitating at the door, she turned and remarked, "I'm very proud of you, Harley. You're one unusual young man, not normal by any means. Good night."

After sitting for a few moments in silence, Harley addressed Ozzie who was now at his feet. "Mom's a pretty smart ol' gal…isn't she?"

CHAPTER 18

EXITING THE FRONT DOORS OF FOX HIGH, HARLEY spotted his mother standing next to her parked car on the school lot. Dangling the car keys from her right hand, she asked when he approached, "How was school today?"

Catching the keys when she tossed them to him, Harley answered and walked around to the driver's side. "I was kind of nervous all day. I couldn't concentrate on my schoolwork. I was so worried about passing my state driving test. I just hope I don't freeze up."

Monica reassured her son, "I'm sure you'll do just fine. You've been driving on your learner's permit for months. Using baseball terminology, it's about time for you to step up to the plate and take the test so you can get your restricted license so your father and I will no longer have to be with you whenever you drive."

As Harley turned right on Jeffco Blvd., she kept on talking. "This is a busy day for you. After you pass the driver's test, you get to drive me home, grab a quick bite and then it's back here to the high school for your game against Kirkwood. How do you feel about your chances tonight?"

"I think we're ready for Kirkwood. The talk around school is that a lot of students and parents are going to be at the game; the main reason...Aaron. The dynamic hitting display he put on at practice Monday afternoon has stirred quite a bit of interest."

"I agree," said Monica. "When you think about it, high school baseball doesn't get the crowds like high school football and basketball. Aaron Buckman seems to be singlehandedly changing that mindset, at least here in Arnold."

The mother-son conversation changed from the upcoming game to what they had to do to get ready for their weekend barbeque. Pulling off the ramp from Rt. 55 South at the Imperial exit, Harley made a right and then a quick left into the parking lot of a Jefferson County Driver's Test Station. Getting out of the car, Monica handed him the required papers needed for his test and nodded at a nearby fast food restaurant and stated, "I'm going to walk over there and grab a cup of coffee. You can pick me up there when you're finished. Good luck."

Harley was a little surprised that his mother was not coming along, but in a strange sort of a way was glad she was giving him some space. His parents had always been there for him. But now, he was in high school, no longer a boy, but according to his father a young man, capable of making his own decisions. Entering the glass door, he took a number and seated himself.

There were only two other people seated and one person at the counter. Fidgeting with the papers his mother had given him he thought about the conversation he recently had with his mother about Aaron Buckman. He had stirred quite a bit of interest amongst not only the students at Fox High but the teachers as well. He had overheard talk in the hallways in regard to the fact that many students who knew Aaron from the past were not that excited about him attending their school. He refused to be a part of that. If Aaron was willing to try and change that was good enough for him. Aaron Buckman was not only a fellow student, but also a member of the ball team he played on. What was it that Coach Sanders said: *We as a team must support and be there for each other.*

His daydreaming was interrupted when his number was called. Walking to the counter, he made his reason for being there known. "My name is Harley Sims and I'm here for my restricted driver's test. Here are my papers."

The girl took the documents and without saying a word scanned the various paperwork, then pointed to another row of chairs in the corner. "Please have a seat. An instructor will be with you in a few minutes." *So far, so good,* he thought as he sat down.

He wasn't even seated for a minute when a man exited a door on the left of the counter, looked down at a clipboard he was carrying and announced, "Harley Sims!"

Harley raised his hand and before he could utter a word, the man motioned toward the front door. "Let's get to your vehicle."

Forty-five minutes later, Harley pulled into the office lot, turned off the car and sat back. Holding up his hands, he asked, "Well, what's the verdict?"

The instructor smiled pleasantly. "You passed as they say, with flying colors. Here are your papers back and your temporary restricted driver's license. Your actual license will be mailed to you in about a week. Remember, the only time you can't drive is between 1 am and 5 am. In six months if you have a clean driving record you can then apply for a full Missouri Driver's license. Drive safely."

Harley looked down the wooden bench in the home team dugout to where some of his teammates were seated. The fourth Kirkwood runner had just crossed home plate as Harley shook his head in wonder and thought, *Top of the first inning and we're already losing 4-0.* Kirkwood was clobbering Deats. It was early in the game and the prospect of the Fox Warriors losing their first game of the year looked like it was not only a possibility, but also rapidly becoming a reality.

Spitting on the dusty concrete at his feet, he looked up when the crowd reacted with a loud cheer as Kirkwood's ninth batter of the inning hit a long fly ball that was corralled by the center fielder. Drew ran to the dugout, threw his mitt on the bench and sat next to Harley while the other players returned. "I can't believe it. We haven't even had our first swings and we're down by four."

Harley looked out at the Kirkwood team who was taking the field. "What do you think went wrong?"

"I'll tell you what's wrong. They're killing Deats. They're jumping all over his fastball and his curve as well. This could be a long night."

Coach Sanders stood in the center of the dugout and got everyone's attention. "Listen up! They got the jump on us but this game is far from over. We have to dig ourselves out of this hole we find ourselves in. We have just as many opportunities to score runs as they do. What we can't do is panic! Don't go out there and try to get all four runs back in our half of the first. We just need to chip away at the lead they now have. Remember, their pitcher is going to throw a lot of fast stuff. Now, let's try to get a couple of runs back before we have to take the field again."

Walking to the edge of the dugout, Drew watched as their leadoff batter selected a bat and approached the plate. Turning, he addressed Harley, "I don't like losing. I never have, but at times there just doesn't seem to be anything you can do about it. Deats keeps mixing up his pitches and the other team has him figured out. It's hard to be behind the plate, trying to call for the right pitch for a particular batter at a particular time. Every time one of the Kirkwood players scored I asked myself. What could I have done to prevent that run from scoring, because the truth is every play starts with me giving the pitcher the signal."

"What's with you today?" asked Harley. "We've lost games before. You're acting like this game is already over. We haven't even had our first licks at the plate yet. In a baseball game, runs cure everything. Things look a lot different when you're winning. Right now, that's not us." Suddenly the crowd roared as the leadoff batter hit a long fly ball that was caught by the right fielder. "That's just the first out of the bottom half of the first inning. They have to get a lot more outs before this contest is over. Now, go on. You're on deck."

Standing at the edge of the dugout, Harley looked out at the surrounding fans on either side of the infield. He knew his parents were out there seated somewhere, but what about Mira. He hadn't seen her for the last two days in school. He hoped she was all right. Earlier in the week, she said she was going to be at the game. Sitting back down he wondered how her visit to the specialist had gone.

Aaron walked past Harley to the large orange water cooler at the end of the dugout. Filling up one of the paper cups, he gulped down the water and refilled the cup as he watched their second batter take a called strike three. Yelling at Drew who was walking toward the batter's box, Aaron encouraged the young catcher, "C'mon Drew…get us a base hit!"

Drew took the first two pitches, which were outside. With the count 2-0, he waited patiently guessing that the next pitch would be a fastball just like the first two. The delivery came; he swung and lined the ball to the left of the pitcher who lunged at the ball but missed it by two feet. Kirkwood's shortstop leaped at the ball that was just out of his extended reach. The ball slammed into the glove but bounced out and hit the ground. The shortstop recovered quickly, picked up the ball, got to his feet and fired the ball to the first baseman. The umpire signaled *out* as he pumped his right fist and pointed at the bag with his left hand. The throw had just beat Drew's effort to get to the base. The first inning was over and still Kirkwood held the lead, 4-0.

Aaron, who had been waiting in the batter's box for his chance at the plate with a runner on, was disappointed. Disgusted, he returned to the dugout, grabbed his first baseman's mitt and jogged out to the infield. When Drew ran back to the dugout, Harley was waiting. "That was a good hit. Their shortstop made an excellent play to get you out. It was close, it could have gone either way."

Coach Sanders walked down to where Harley stood and asked, "How do you feel today?"

Harley, having an idea why the coach had popped this particular question, answered, "Great coach! Are you thinking about putting me in?"

"Not just yet. If Deats settles down and can hold them from getting any more runs, I'll leave him in. But, if they score again before we do, I might have to send you to the mound. Are you sure you're rested enough?"

"I feel fine. I've had almost a week's rest…six days. If you need me…I'm ready to go."

Looking out at the field, Sanders with a look of concern, stated, "Let's just wait and see how this next inning pans out."

The coach shook his head in doubt as Deats walked Kirkwood's first batter on four pitches. The next batter bunted for a single, placing men on first and second. The third hitter hit into a routine double play, leaving a man on third. Deats walked the next batter who stole second, now placing two more potential runs in scoring position. Sanders signaled for time and walked slowly to the mound. Placing his hand on Deats' shoulder, he explained very calmly, "Look, you need to get this next guy out. If they score another run, I'm going to pull you."

Deats remained silent but nodded his understanding of the situation. When the coach returned to the dugout he motioned to Harley. "Start warming up. We may need you." Harley was no sooner out of the dugout when Kirkwood's next batter popped up to first. The top of the second ended, Kirkwood still in the lead.

Sanders, clapping his hands encouraged his team, "All right…we held them. Now let's get some runs and get back in this game!"

Aaron, their cleanup hitter, slowly walked to the plate, went through his routine and waited for the first pitch, which as always he let go right on by, normally for a called strike. Confidently, he smiled back out at Kirkwood's pitcher and readied himself for the next delivery. The pitch was low, but Aaron got the thick part of his bat on the ball sending it to deep center field. The crowd stood and cheered as the ball looked like it was going to clear the fence. The jubilation of the crowd quickly turned to a moan of dissatisfaction as Kirkwood's center fielder caught the ball right at the edge of the warning track.

Back in the dugout, Aaron apologized to Coach Sanders, "Sorry coach, I just didn't get enough on the ball to get it out of here."

Slapping him on his back the coach responded, "That's okay Aaron. I think you gave them something to think about. Maybe next time. Don't worry about it."

The next hitter, after running the count up to 3-2, swung and missed a curve ball for the third strike. The next batter, Deats struck out; the second inning ended.

Harley continued to warm up out in the bullpen as he watched Deats get through another inning without allowing any more runs. In the bottom of the third the Fox High school bats were silent, the inning ended with the score still at 4-0.

Deats, once again kept Kirkwood at bay in the top half of the fourth. With two outs in the bottom of the inning, Drew got a base hit just over the second baseman's head. Aaron stepped to the plate and glared out at Kirkwood's pitcher. After letting the first pitch go by he stood ready for the next: a fastball right down the pike. Drew was off and running when Aaron hit a line shot down the third base line. The ball ricocheted off the corner of the wooden foul line fence and made it past the running right fielder, allowing Drew to make it safely to third. Popping up from a routine slide, Drew broke for the plate when he saw the cutoff man bobble the throw from the outfield. The play at home was close, but Drew slid beneath the tag. *"Safe!"* yelled the home plate ump. Aaron reached second, tried to get down to third but was thrown out easily. The fourth inning ended with Kirkwood still in the lead 4-1.

The fifth and six innings passed by quickly without either team getting a man in scoring position. Fox managed to get the leadoff batter on first both innings but failed to bring the runner around to score. In the top of the seventh, Deats walked the first two runners, which caused Sanders to turn to Harley. "Sims! You're going in."

On the way out to the mound Harley fist bumped Deats who was on the way in. "Good job."

Drew, crouching at the back of the plate smiled to himself. He always enjoyed catching Harley's pitching. Three batters and seven minutes later, Harley had pitched his team out of a jam and prevented Kirkwood from getting any insurance runs as he struck out two batters and got the last one to ground out to Aaron on first.

In the bottom half of the seventh, Kirkwood's pitcher walked the leadoff hitter and then gave up another base hit to Drew, putting men on first and third. Kirkwood's manager watched as Aaron walked to the plate. Calling time, he walked to the mound, talked with his pitcher for a brief second and then decided to bring in a reliever. Aaron stood silently to the side as Kirkwood's relief pitcher took a few warm up throws. The umpire signaled for Aaron to step to the plate.

Harley, from the dugout, watched as the imaginary chess game that baseball presented at times of trying to outguess your opponent had begun. Kirkwood's manager had to realize how dangerous Aaron was at the plate and with one swing could tie the score. Sure, they could consider walking Aaron, but that would bring the go ahead run to the plate. If he was in the position Kirkwood's pitcher was in, he'd pitch to Aaron, carefully, but he'd still pitch to him.

The catcher returned to home plate, took his accustomed position and gave the sign. The pitcher checked the runners, went into his stretch and delivered a pitch directly over the plate. As usual, Aaron didn't even attempt to hit the ball as he let the pitch go by. *"Strike one!"*

So far everything was going just like Harley had imagined. Walking the length of the dugout, he thought, *This next pitch could be very interesting. What would I do if I were in the Kirkwood pitcher's shoes? I'd throw something off the plate and try to get the batter to swing at a bad pitch, and then the count would be even, 1-1.* The pitcher did exactly what Harley had anticipated, throwing the ball way outside. Aaron coiled as if he were going to swing but then held up. *"Ball one!"*

Harley knew the pitcher could afford to waste another pitch, which he did, the ball way outside. *"Ball two!"*

The pitcher, on the next pitch had to bring it in closer. He knew it and so did Aaron. The pitch came and was outside, but still off the plate. Aaron swung and connected, the ball sailing for the right field fence. The crowd roared, but then the ball went foul, missing fair by three feet. Kirkwood's pitcher let out a long sigh of relief as he turned to face Aaron again. Checking both runners, he took the sign, hesitated then delivered a fastball on the lower part of the strike zone. Aaron swung smoothly and sent the ball on a line drive toward the left field fence. Kirkwood's left fielder raced toward the line but the ball hit just in front of the fence, bounced up and fell in the warning track. The runner on third scored easily and Drew slid safely into third. Aaron stopped between first and second which caused the cut-off man to throw the ball to the second baseman, who in turn, looked Drew back to third and tossed the ball to the first baseman. Aaron stopped and starting to run back to first, stopped, and moved toward second. Drew was off third base threatening to score. The first baseman looked him back and faked a throw over to third. It was just enough of a distraction to allow Aaron to take off for second. The first baseman decided he could throw Aaron out as he flipped the ball to the shortstop who was covering second. The throw was low and Aaron, sliding, collided with the smaller shortstop who was blocking the bag. The shortstop caught the ball but it was knocked loose and rolled out toward center field, allowing Drew to score. Lying in the dirt of the infield Aaron smiled as he watched Drew cross the plate. The score now 4-3.

Fox's next batter stepped to the plate as Aaron and his team members yelled words of encouragement:

Be patient!

Just a base hit…that's all we need!

The shouts and words of confidence ended quickly as the batter swung at the first pitch; a long fly ball to the right field corner in foul territory. Aaron looked down at the third base coach and got the signal for him to run if the catch was made. The ball slapped into the right fielder's glove and Aaron took off for third. There was not enough time to hit the cut-off man so the ball was thrown directly to third. It bounced once, but arrived to the left of the bag as Aaron slid in, *"Safe!"*

Harley, standing in the on deck circle pumped his fist when the call was made. Walking slowly to the plate, he thought, *Bottom of the last inning, tying run on third, two outs. It's up to me. I've got to get a hit!* Stepping into the box he looked at the dirt at his feet. The bright white lines of lime had long since been erased that designated the boundaries of the batter's box. Looking out at the opposing pitcher, his mind was racing: even though he had practiced for years in his backyard to be an excellent hitter, over the years as he had progressed as a pitcher his mind was more accustomed to think as a pitcher rather than a hitter. He had been in the position the Kirkwood pitcher was facing a number of times in the past. He knew with the tying run standing just ninety feet away he wasn't going to get much to swing at, but then again, they couldn't afford to walk him, thus placing the go ahead runner on first. He decided he was going to make the pitcher wait for the first two pitches unless they were right down the center of the plate. The longer he made the pitcher stand out there on the mound, the better his chances were of getting to first base.

The first pitch, a fastball on the inside, came across the plate. Realizing the pitch was going to be called a ball, Harley backed off as he listened for the umpire's voice. "Ball one!"

The next pitch was in the same area as he let the pitch go on by. "Ball two!"

Preparing himself, he knew the pitcher was going to have to come with a strike on the next pitch. Receiving the sign, the pitcher went into the stretch, looked over at Aaron, then delivered the ball, a little high but still in the strike zone. In a split fraction of a second Harley deduced that if he held up it would be a called strike. The ball began to dip slightly and his instinct told him to swing. A line shot above the third baseman's head. He wasn't even two steps out of the box when he witnessed the third baseman leap high into the air, his right arm completely extended. Miraculously, he snow coned the ball at the very edge of this glove, three-quarters of the ball exposed. Coming down with the ball, the third baseman displayed the ball to the infield umpire who signaled the third out. The game ended abruptly, the final tally, Kirkwood 4 - Fox 3.

Harley almost had to laugh at how close the ball had been to being a base hit, which would have tied the game. Returning to the home team dugout, he remembered what his parents had always told him: *Baseball is a game of inches.* The game was over and they had lost. There was nothing he or anyone else could do to change the outcome. His baseball mentality was already preparing him for the next game in two days against Parkway South.

Joining his teammates in the dugout, Harley untied his spikes as he listened to the coach address the team. "Boys…we almost came back to tie the game, but we fell just short. There is no sense in dwelling on this game. It's in the past. We need to look forward to Friday's game. Good game…I'll see you all at practice tomorrow after school."

Drew was slow to remove his catcher's gear as he stared out at the now empty field. Harley bumped him on his arm. "Forget this game! Like the coach said we need to concentrate on our next outing."

Drew frowned, "I guess so. If that last ball you hit would have just been a tad bit higher, the game would be tied and we'd still be out there on the field with the possibility of winning."

Knocking Drew's hat off his head, Harley laughed, "Well, get over it. Things for the rest of the evening are looking up."

"What are you talking about?"

"I got my restricted license this afternoon. That means I can drive us up to Steak and Shake for burgers and a shake…without one of my parents along. Freedom…at last!"

Minutes later, the dugout was empty as Drew was just taking off his protective vest. Harley was in the process of placing his glove and spikes in his equipment bag when Mira stepped around the corner. "Hey guys…good game. Of course, it would have been better if you'd won, but even the best teams lose a game now and then."

Harley's face lit up as he introduced Mira to Drew, "Drew, this is Mira, the girl I've been telling you about. Mira, this is Drew, the best catcher in these parts."

Drew, not the least bit shy got up, walked over and offered his hand which Mira shook firmly, "Nice to finally meet you, Drew. Harley thinks quite a bit of you."

Before Drew could respond to her compliment, Aaron walked in the opposite side of the dugout. Embarrassed, he apologized, "I'm sorry…didn't mean to interrupt. I forgot my water bottle."

Harley objected, "You're not interrupting a thing. I was just introducing Drew here to my new friend, Mira. She just transferred here to Fox from New York."

Noticing her walker, Aaron politely crossed the dugout and extended his hand. "Good to meet you."

Getting an idea, Harley blurted out, "I just got my driving license today. Drew and I are headed up the street for a bite. Would you two care to tag along?"

Aaron smiled, but declined, "Sounds good, but Pastor Joe is going to be picking me up. He's taking me out for dinner. Maybe next time."

Mira jumped in on the conversation, "I'm afraid I'll have to take a rain check as well. My folks will be coming for me in about a half hour."

Harley led the way as the foursome made their way down the third base fence line toward the parking lot. Aaron was especially careful to not get too far ahead of Mira whose progress was slow via her walker.

Mira complimented him on his previous, after school hitting display. "I saw you at practice Monday. That was some hitting clinic you put on. I can't believe the one you hit on the roof of the school."

Drew chimed in, "And let's not forget hitting one of the school buses and taking out a classroom window!"

Aaron shrugged humbly. "Just doing what comes natural."

CHAPTER 19

DREW SAT ON THE EDGE OF HARLEY'S BED AS HE
flipped through one of many baseball card albums Harley had lined
up on a five-shelf bookcase. Ozzie, as usual, was curled up at the
top of the bed nestled down in the pillows. Ozzie sprang from the
bed when the doorbell rang and dashed down the stairs. Drew
smiled and laughed, "Boy, Ozzie is quite the watchdog, isn't he!"

"Are you kidding me," joked Harley! "If any robbers ever broke
into this house ol' Ozzie would probably lick them to death."
Looking at a Cardinals clock on his dresser, he tucked in the T-
shirt he was wearing and looked out his upstairs bedroom window.
"There's a strange car in the driveway. I bet you anything that's
Mira and her folks."

Placing the album back on the shelf, Drew asked, "Nervous?"

Harley shot him a look of confusion. "Why would I be
nervous?"

"Well, I was just thinking. You get to meet her parents, she gets
to meet yours. It seems to me things are moving right along.
Before you know it, you'll be walking down the aisle."

"Very funny. I've got news for you pal. I don't plan on getting
married until after I'm pitching in the majors. That's over eight
years from now. I might even wait until I'm in my thirties."

Heading for the stairwell, Drew looked back at his friend. "If
society has learned anything about male-female relationships over
the years, history proves that many a young man has stated they
were going to hold off on getting hitched. The truth be known,
nowadays it seems like a lot of fellas get married right after
graduating from high school. Some may make it through college,
but shortly after, they find themselves setting up household with
their new little lady. It's just a matter of time my friend."

Scooting Drew down the steps, Harley grinned. "You talk too
much!"

By the time the two boys reached the living room, Monica had just finished up with the introductions as she gestured at the boys to step forward. "Harley, Drew, you've already met Mira and these are her parents, Alex and Marcie. Alex, Marcie, this is Harley my son and his friend Drew. Drew is Roxann's brother."

Harley looked directly at Mira and noticed she was leaning on a cane, not the customary walker he was accustomed to seeing her with. He thought about saying something but refrained from doing so as mentioning the walker might be inappropriate. Mira's mother stepped forward and offered a tinfoil covered dish. "These are brownies that Mira and I made early this morning," Gesturing at her husband who was holding a covered dish she went on to explain, "We also brought some mac and cheese. It's still warm. Where would you like us to put the food?"

Reaching for the mac and cheese, Monica suggested, "If you'll just follow me into the kitchen if you'd like you can give Nancy and me a hand with the baked beans and the potato salad we're preparing."

Monica gave Harley instructions, "Why don't you and Drew take Mira and her dad out to the backyard." Speaking to Mr. Madison, she pointed out, "The men are out back firing up the grill. Harley, make sure you introduce your father and Drew's dad to our guests."

Minutes later, following some quick introductions, Alex joined Rich and Don at the grill while Harley, Drew and Mira trailed by Ozzie walked to a small picnic table by the ball field. Passing the garage, Harley asked the question he wanted to ask inside the house. "Mira...what's with the cane? The last time we talked you told me you were going to see a specialist and you might not have to use the walker any longer."

Stopping and holding up the cane, Mira smiled. "The doctor put me on a new type of steroid that strengthens my leg muscles. It's only experimental right now. The doctor said I need to start lifting weights and has put me on a protein diet. He said if everything works out I might be able to get around with the cane and eliminate the walker."

Harley grinned. "That's great news."

Drew joined in on the conversation and asked, "Do you think at some point in the future you'll be able to pitch again."

"I asked the doctor the same question and he said that was

probably not in my near future. I'll probably never get back to where I was before the accident and to be honest if I can get to the point where I can just walk like a normal person, I won't be dissatisfied if I can't pitch."

Looking out at the practice field out behind the garage, Mira raised the cane and stated, "Enough about me. So that must be the field you practiced on all those years?"

Harley sat on the bench of the table. "Yep, that's the one. I don't use it much these days because it's set up to Little League measurements." Gesturing at the suspended tree tire, Harley pointed out, "I still throw about a hundred pitches a day at the tire. It keeps me sharp, especially on my off days when I'm not scheduled to pitch."

Spotting two gloves and an old baseball lying at the end of the table, Mira picked up the ball and tossed it to Harley. "Let's see what you can do."

Harley laughed and answered, "You've already seen what I can do on the field."

"I know, but I find this tire business quite interesting. I'm only asking for a short demonstration."

Drew grabbed the catcher's mitt and walked off toward the hanging tire and announced, "I'll catch!"

Harley, realizing he had been outvoted picked up the remaining glove, placed the ball in the webbing and shrugged, "Okay, but just a few pitches."

Getting up. Mira made her way to a nearby tree and pointed at the tire with her cane. "I want to see a fastball right down the middle then maybe one each on the right and left inside of the tire."

Harley positioned himself on a pitcher's rubber, which was the exact distance for the majors, and spoke with a comical confidence, "Prepare to be amazed!"

Drew stood directly behind the tire and went down into the catcher's stance and yelled, "Okay!"

Harley gripped the ball, looked at the tire, and then following his standard windup released the ball. Mira stared in amazement when the ball passed through the opening and slapped into Drew's mitt. Throwing the ball back to Harley, Drew yelled, "Now the right inside of the tire."

Seconds later the ball nipped the right inside edge of the tire and Harley waited for Drew to return the pitch while Drew yelled, "Now the left."

The next pitch was a repeat performance, the ball clipping the left inside edge of the tire. Walking back to the picnic table, Harley tossed the glove on the table and winked at Mira. "I better not throw any more. I already had my workout early this morning. I need to rest up for this coming Tuesday which is our next game."

Mira picked up the glove and slammed her fist into the worn leather. "You have great control for someone your age. If you keep throwing like that, you're headed for a major league career."

Drew took a seat at the end of the table and added, "That's been Harley's plan before we even met. I agree, he'll wind up in the major leagues. He's got the skill, the discipline and the desire."

"What about you, Drew," asked Mira. "You're no slouch yourself. Can you see yourself playing in the bigs?"

"Probably not. There are a lot of kids who play ball who are better than me. My plans are to go to college on a music scholarship playing the piano, but if by some chance I'm offered an athletic scholarship for playing ball, I won't turn the opportunity down. I'll graduate from college with a musical degree, but as far as playing in the major leagues that seems like a world away for me."

Changing the subject, Mira held up her right hand to get the boys' attention. "I was doing some reading last night and I ran across some very interesting information. Do you know how many major league baseball players have come from Missouri?"

Mira paused for an answer while Drew and Harley looked at each other and shrugged. Harley finally answered, "That's something I've never thought of. I don't have a clue."

"Well, this probably is not exact but it turns out there is somewhere in the area of five hundred and seventy-five and just under three hundred that hail from the St. Louis area. I came across some very interesting names. Did you guys know that Yogi Berra and Joe Garagiola grew up together in an area of St. Louis called the hill?"

Looking at Harley, Drew asked, "Is that true?"

Harley nodded. "Yes, it's true. They were both catchers in the major leagues. As it stands right now Yogi might go down in history as the best catcher there ever was, but that remains to be seen. There's a lot of baseball left to be played before this old world stops spinning. Yogi was an odd sort of ballplayer. I never got to see him play. He retired long before I was even born. It's been said of Yogi that he wasn't much to look at and it always appeared like he was doing everything wrong, but the guy could really hit. I think he played for the Yankees his entire career. I'm not sure. Mira here is a big Yankee fan. What do you know about Yogi?"

"I know quite a bit about ol' Yogi. He played nineteen years in the majors from 1946 to 1965. The first eighteen years he was a catcher for the Yanks then his last year he played for the Mets. His number was retired in 1973 and that was the same year he became a hall of famer."

Laying her cane on the table, Mira held up her hand to make a point. "I could tell you a lot about Yogi Berra or for that matter anyone who ever played for the Yankees, but I want to hear more about this hill area of St. Louis where Yogi and Joe Garagiola lived."

"The hill," said Harley, "is a middle class working Italian section of St. Louis. As a matter of fact, if you like great Italian food the hill is the place to go. Now, let's get back to this Berra - Garagiola childhood relationship. As young boys Yogi and Joe, so it's said, lived on Elizabeth Street. They both grew up playing baseball and eventually were both drafted by the major leagues. Later on, after their careers ended, they were both inducted into the hall of fame. Yogi was a hall of famer because of his skills on the playing field, but Joe, after retiring became a play by play KMOX announcer for the Cardinals and went on to an after baseball life as a very popular baseball announcer. He was inducted into the hall in 1991 for Outstanding Broadcasting Accomplishments. The street where Berra and Garagiola grew up on the hill became known as the hall of fame place. Years after they both retired Garagiola made a comical statement saying that when it came to catching in the majors he was not only not the best catcher in the league but not even on his own street when he was growing up."

Drew, finding the topic of past players from St. Louis interesting, asked, "Was there anyone else on the list you found interesting?"

"Yes, there was," chimed in Mira. "I read about the Boyer boys. They were from Alba, Missouri and came from a family of fourteen children, seven boys and seven girls. All of the boys wound up playing professional ball but only three; Cloyd, Ken and Clete made it to the majors. Cloyd seems to be the least famous of the three. He played from 1949 through 1958. He started out with the Cardinals for four years and then finished up his career with the Athletics."

Leaning forward, Mira continued, "Now, Ken and his brother Clete are a different story. When people talk about the Boyer brothers they always refer to Clete and Ken. Ken played in the majors from '55 to '71 and Clete started as well in the big leagues in '55 but got out in '69. They were both infielders."

Drew was about to ask a question when they were interrupted by Monica, "Soup's on. Come and get it. Everything is set up on the back porch. If you want, you can eat out here on the table."

Harley was the first to get up. "I'm starving. I didn't have much for breakfast this morning."

With the aid of her cane, Mira got to her feet, "Burgers and dogs. Doesn't get any better than that!"

Minutes later, the three were back at the old table, their plates full of chips, potato salad, baked beans, mac and cheese and deviled eggs."

Mira squirted some ketchup on her burger and stated, "It never ceases to amaze me what seems like the unending statistics there are in the game of baseball. There are stats for everything. Baseball is such an amazing sport. You could attend any number of games in a row and see something you may have never seen before. Let me ask you boys this: what is the most amazing or unusual thing you've ever seen or heard of that happened at a game?"

Drew answered immediately, "It's so strange you would ask us that because just last night I was watching a college baseball game on television and there was a triple play."

Harley gave Drew an odd look and commented, "A triple play! I'll be the first to admit the triple play is a rarity in the game, but with the skill of todays' players and the way the speed of the game has increased, even though the triple play is a rare occurrence there are many more strange things that can and have happened."

"That may be," pointed out Drew, "but this was an unusual type of rare play. Let me explain. It just wasn't a triple play; it was an amazing triple play. It was accomplished without the ball even being hit!"

Both Harley and Mira looked at Drew as if he were nuts. Setting the play up for them Drew went on to explain, "There were runners on first and third with no outs. The batter is out on a called strike three. The runner on first was going on the pitch and was thrown out at second while the runner on third broke for home and was thrown out as well. Hence; a triple play…an odd triple play!"

Mira bit into her burger and remarked, "How about you, Harley. What have you seen or heard about that seemed amazing to you?"

"Well, there are so many things I've seen or heard over the years." Snapping his fingers as if he suddenly remembered something, he continued, "The twenty-four inch homerun is one of the oddest things I've ever heard of."

Drew almost chocked on a fork full of baked beans. "The twenty-four inch homerun. That's sounds…no, that's impossible! How could that possibly be?"

"I know it sounds impossible," said Harley, "but according to past history it did happen. There was a player by the name of Andy 'Pepper' Oyler who played for Baltimore back in 1902. During a game when Oyler was at bat he ducked away from a high inside pitch that actually hits the bat and ricochets down in the mud in fair territory. Oyler saw the ball buried in the mud and took off running. The opposing catcher, pitcher and the infielders looked everywhere for the ball but it went unnoticed while ol' Pepper rounded the bases for an inside the park home run."

Mira gave Harley a sideways look. "Is that story really true? It sounds unbelievable."

"I know it sounds unrealistic, but think about it? The ump couldn't call a foul ball because he didn't see where the ball went. The ball made contact with the bat and landed in fair territory. Of course, a play like that would never happen today because the fields are in much better condition."

Mira scooped up some potato salad and looked at Drew commenting, "Well, I think we can agree that the story of the shortest homerun tops your rare triple play."

Drew agreed, "No doubt!"

Harley spoke up as he finished the last bite of his hotdog.

"Here's another interesting story. It's the story about the girl who struck out Babe Ruth."

"As a Yankee fan, I thought I knew everything there was to know about the Babe. I never heard anything about a girl striking him out. Was this during a regular game?"

"No, it was an exhibition game held in Chattanooga, Tennessee. The story goes like this. There was a girl by the name of Jackie Mitchell who was born around 1912. She grew up enjoying baseball and by the time she was six she began to show real potential as a future pitcher. She played ball in and around the Chattanooga area and when she turned seventeen in 1931 she was offered a contract with the Chattanooga Lookouts. It so happened that the Yankees had scheduled an exhibition game with the Lookouts. She wasn't scheduled to pitch that day but after their starting pitcher gave up a double and a single in the first inning the manager pulled the pitcher and called on Jackie to pitch. The first batter she was to face was Babe Ruth. Her first pitch was a ball that went over Ruth's head. She then proceeded to strike the Babe out on three pitches, the last one a called strike. What's even more amazing is that the next batter was Lou Gehrig, who she also sent down with just three pitches. After that she became famous as the girl who struck out Babe Ruth. She died in 1987."

"Well, I've got to tell you that being the only female here involved in this baseball conversation the story of this Jackie Mitchell ranks right up there with the twenty-four inch home run story."

"Okay, okay," said Drew. "As a catcher, I have to get a catcher's stat in here. Did you guys know that Johnny Bench, who caught for the Cincinnati Reds for seventeen years could hold seven baseballs in one hand?"

"Here's something I bet you guys don't know," said Harley. "During World War II, the United States government decided to make hand grenades the size and weight of a baseball because they felt the average young man who entered the service would be able to toss one with relatively good accuracy."

Thinking that he had topped everyone else's unbelievable stories, Harley continued, "Here's another little known fact that most people who follow baseball are not aware of. John Dillinger played professional baseball."

Giving Harley an incredulous look, Mira held up her hand for him to stop talking. "Hold on here a minute. Are you referring to John Dillinger, the ruthless killer and bank robber?"

"One and the same," stated Harley.

Mira pushed her empty plate to the side. "I can't wait to hear this story!"

Petting Ozzie on his head, Harley gave the remainder of his hot dog to his canine friend and explained, "John Dillinger grew up in Indiana and like most red-blooded American boys followed baseball. Actually, he was an avid Cubs fan. He played the infield, mostly shortstop and second base and around the neighborhood he was known for his speed and was nicknamed the *Jackrabbit.* As a young boy, in between playing baseball with his friends he was constantly getting into trouble. This went on for years until, after too many run-ins with the police he decided to join the Navy. This was short-lived as he deserted and went back to Martinsville to live with his father. He tried his hand at different jobs but always seemed to fail so he turned to the only thing he was good at and that was his skills on a baseball field. He played for a number of teams who were willing to pay him and the regular team he played for was the Martinsville Athletics. In 1924 Johnny Dillinger had the highest team batting average and led Martinsville to the league championship. During the off-season, it turned out that the very game he loved led to his eventual life of crime. There was an umpire and small-time crook by the name of Edgar Singleton who got Dillinger involved in his first robbery. It was a grocery store and things fell apart as the owner of the store beat the snot out of Dillinger. During the scuffle, Dillinger's gun went off and the storeowner was wounded which netted ol' Johnny ten to twenty years in a state reformatory. Those who ran the institution soon realized Dillinger's baseball skills and soon he found himself playing for the reformatory team. After serving nine years, he was transferred to a much harsher prison where he turned down an offer to play ball for the prison and decided to hone his criminal skills. In 1933, he was released from prison an educated criminal and he embarked on a crime spree that left him a national hero in the eyes of the average citizen. He always returned to Chicago where on a regular basis he would attend Cubs games. The day he was shot at the Biograph Theater by the Feds, the Cubs were not in town and who knows? If Dillinger had been a White Sox fan he may have lived a little longer as the White Sox played a double header with the Yankees that afternoon."

Drew stood, walked around the table and high-fived Harley. "That was, without a doubt, the best story of the afternoon. I don't know about you guys but I'm ready for some dessert."

Harley got up and suggested, "Let's go!"

Minutes later the threesome was back at the picnic table, with a plate of brownies and large bowls of vanilla ice cream.

Harley placed a small bowl of ice cream on the ground, which Ozzie devoured quickly. Smiling at the dog, Harley joked, "Ozzie always loves it when we barbeque out back. Like today; he got a hot dog *and* ice cream."

Snapping her fingers, Mira spoke up, "I almost forgot the main thing I wanted to tell you after I got here. I got so wrapped up in our baseball stories that it slipped my mind. It's not good news for the Fox baseball team."

Confused, Drew took the last bite of a brownie, "What on earth are you talking about?"

Mira hesitated but then answered, "Aaron Buckman is moving again."

Harley couldn't believe what he was hearing. "What do you mean…moving? Please don't tell me he's moving back out to the coast with his father?"

"No, he's moving to a small community outside of Chicago."

Drew, still confused held out his hands. "The only other place he could go is with his mother and she lives here. Did his mother move to Chicago?"

"It has nothing to do with his mother. He's going with Pastor Joe."

"That doesn't make any sense," said Harley. "Pastor Joe has a church here. Why would he leave?"

"He didn't have a choice. He is being transferred to a church near Chicago. It's a much bigger church than the one he pastors here. Since, Aaron's mother agreed to give parental custody to the pastor, Aaron is going along."

"How did you find this out?"

"My parents have been looking for a church to attend since we moved here. We heard some good things about Pastor Joe's church so my parents dropped by to talk over the possibility of attending there. Pastor Joe said he would be more than glad to tell us all about the church but that he was moving…and soon."

"How soon?"

"He said he and Aaron were driving up to Chicago in two days. That means tomorrow they'll be gone."

"I can't believe this," said Harley. "I was really looking forward to playing with him on the same team."

Drew seemed sad as he added, "I wonder if he'll play ball up there in Chicago?"

Harley smiled. "I think Aaron Buckman will play baseball wherever he goes. He's that good!"

Mira reached down to pet Ozzie on his head. "I really didn't get to know Aaron that well, but he seemed nice."

Harley laid in bed in his dark room and stroked Ozzie's head. Looking at the glowing face of the Cardinals clock on his dresser, he noted the time, one ten in the morning. He smiled and thought about all the stories he, Drew and Mira had shared out in the backyard. It had been a good day. He wondered if he'd ever see Aaron again. He had been looking so forward to having him as a teammate. Closing his eyes, he smiled to himself and put his right arm around his bedfellow and yawned, "Good night Ozzie."

CHAPTER 20

HARLEY MADE THE LEFTHAND TURN OFF JEFFCO BLVD onto Telegraph Road. According to the written instructions Mira had given him at school, it was just over three miles to Becker Road, where he was to go right with their farm located a half mile on the left.

It was the last day of October and the bright color of the fall leaves were at their peak. Placing the folded instructions back up behind the visor, he thought about the fact that baseball season had come to an end once again. The 2002 World Series had come to a close as Anaheim defeated San Francisco four games to one ending the fall classic.

Coming out at the bottom of a long hill, he noticed a field of trees on the right, the crimson red and golden yellow leaves a reminder that winter was just around the corner, with all its cold days, snow and ice. A prelude to the saddest time of the year; *no baseball!* Most folks, even the most avid Cardinal fans would file away the past year as history and move on with their lives until the next season rolled around.

Not me! thought Harley. To him, baseball was a way of life: twenty-four hours a day three hundred and sixty-five days a year. Despite the fact he had played the last game of the 2002 Fox High School baseball schedule at the end of May, he continued his regimented daily practice of throwing at the tire in his backyard, lifting weights and running. Coming up on Becker Road on the right, he turned and thought, *Every day of practice is one day closer to getting to the major leagues.*

Travelling down Becker road, he took note of the thick woods that flanked both sides of the pavement. Mira told him to look for the long white fence on the left that marked the beginning of her family's property. Rounding a small curve, there it was, a three-rail white fence that looked like it had recently been painted. The next thing he was to look for was the entrance to the farm, a ten-foot-wide white trellised entryway topped with a sign that read: Wooded Acres.

It wasn't more than a few seconds when the entranceway came into view. Turning left he drove slowly down a gravel road also fenced on either side. Tall maple trees stood on the opposite sides of the fencing like armed guards, the wind blowing the bright red leaves down on the road and the surrounding grass. Just like Mira said, it was only a short drive, where the three story stone house stood at the end of a circular drive. A concrete fountain, that at the moment, was not working was home to three birds that frolicked in the still water. On the left side of the house the gravel road continued on around the side and on the right there was an overgrown garden. Pulling up in front of the house, Harley no sooner stepped out than a large white dog raced out of the woods on the left and greeted him as she sat and raised her large right paw. From the porch he heard Mira's voice, "Don't mind Gracie…she's our ambassador and greets everyone who comes up the drive. Come on inside and meet my grandparents. My parents are in town running some errands."

Gracie followed them across the porch and in the front door where she went to the kitchen, where according to Mira her water bowl was located. Making a right at the bottom of a staircase, they walked into a sitting room and then an attached living room where an older couple sat. Mira made the introductions, "Gram, Gramps…this is Harley Sims the young man I've told you about. Harley, these are my grandparents on my father's side; Floyd and Erma."

Floyd tried to get up but had difficulty. Harley went to the chair and spoke, "Please, you don't have to get up because I'm here." Shaking Floyd's hand, he then crossed the room to where Erma was seated in a rocker. Reaching out, touching her on the shoulder, Harley complimented the woman, "I like the way your home sets back in the woods."

Erma smiled graciously and responded, "That's why Floyd and I named this place Wooded Acres when we purchased it a few years after we married."

Floyd added, "That was what…fifty-three years ago. Back in those days we were both full of you know what. We started out with a few hogs and then got some cattle and chickens. Before long we planted corn and some barley. After all these years, time just sort of caught up with us. About the only thing the wife and I do now is tend the garden, which at the moment is a mess. The only animals we have on the farm now are four horses, and of course…Gracie."

Floyd changed the subject and offered Harley a seat on the couch. "Mira tells me you're quite the baseball fan…a Cardinals fan I believe."

Sitting on the couch next to Mira, Harley answered, "Been a fan since I guess the day I was born. Try to get to as many home games as I can."

"Mira says you're a pitcher, and according to her, a pretty dang good one. She claims you want to be a major league pitcher."

"That's the plan. But, then again, that's down the road quite a few years."

Winking at his wife, Floyd went on to explain, "Me and Erma, well, we've been rooting for the Cards since we got hitched. We didn't have much money when we were first married so we moved in with her folks, then we rented an apartment for three years, saved our money and wound up buying this farm when it went up for auction. We never thought we'd get the place, but it turned out by God…we did! It took everything we had to get the place up and running. We really couldn't afford to go anywhere or do much of anything. We had a small radio that we would listen to Cardinal games on. Those were the good ol' days. We'd pop a couple of beers and make us up a bowl of popcorn. I remember the first game we listened to. It was back in 1949. The announcers on the radio were Harry Carey and Gabby Street. The Cardinals came in second place by one game that year, the Brooklyn Dodgers beating us out. Anyways, the Dodgers went on to the World Series and got beat in five games to those dang ol' Yankees who I have never cared for."

Joking, Mira spoke up, "Hey, be careful…now you're talking about my team. Besides that, we can't stand here and talk about baseball all day. Harley came by to do some riding."

Erma spoke up, "So, you're not only a ballplayer but a horseman as well."

Harley corrected the woman. "If you're trying to ask if I ride horses, the answer is definitely no! I've never been on the back of a horse before. This will be my first time. Mira has been after to me for months to come over and ride with her."

Floyd nodded at his granddaughter. "Harley, you couldn't ask for a better teacher. Mira has been riding since she was knee high to a grasshopper." Joking, he slapped his knee. "Why, a couple of riding lessons from her and you'll be riding in the Kentucky Derby!"

"All right, all right, it's getting pretty deep in here," said Mira. Turning to Harley she pointed with her cane. "Let's head out back to the stables and get this day underway."

Following Mira, Harley smiled at Mira's grandparents. "It was really nice to meet you folks."

Following Mira through a large country kitchen where Gracie fell in line behind them, they crossed a large screened-in back porch, then it was a short walk when they arrived at the four stall stable where the heads of four horses stared out at the new arrivals through individual open windows. Approaching the small barn, Mira pointed at the first horse. "The first thing we need to do is introduce you to our four legged friends." Reaching up, she patted the side of the first horse's face. "This is Molly. She's the only female we have. She's the gentlest of the four. You'll be riding her since this is your first time out. Next, in line we have Henry. He's the tallest and the oldest horse we own. Next, we have Rubin. He's what's called a bay. And finally, we have Mickey. We just purchased him a few months ago from a farmer up the road who was selling out. I couldn't believe it when my dad brought him home seeing how his name is the same as my favorite ballplayer of all time, Mickey Mantle."

Entering the barn, Harley stopped and took in a deep breath of air. "That smell reminds me of when my parents and I go to the state fair and we're in the horse barns. The hay just smells so wonderful."

Mira joked. "Yeah, the smell of hay and horse manure does tend to grow on you." Taking an apple from a small bucket, she handed it to Harley. "When we get in Molly's stall give her this. It will be a sign of friendship and help her to get to know you. Just hold out your hand flat and she'll take the apple."

Opening the stall door, Mira entered and motioned Harley to follow. "Just stand over there in the corner while I get her turned around." Talking gently to the horse Mira stroked the side of the horse's long face, "Molly, you've got a visitor today. Let's turn around and say hello."

Mira guided the large animal around so she was facing Harley. The horse's large round eyes fell on the stranger standing at the front of her stall. She whinnied and stomped her foot once.

Harley backed up slightly. "Okay, what did that mean?"

"She's just saying hello…that's all. Now, step forward slowly and extend your right hand so she can smell your scent, then with the other hand give her the apple."

Harley gingerly took four small, slow steps and held out his hand. He could feel the warm breath caress his fingers when the large head nudged his hand.

"Okay," said Mira, "give her the treat."

Molly leaned her head down and took the apple followed by a loud crunching sound. Leading the horse through the stall door Mira led Molly to the far end of the barn and positioned her against a back wall. "Let's get her saddled up."

Pointing, Mira asked, "Would you hand me one of those blankets on that shelf."

Selecting a multi-colored rectangular blanket, Harley handed it to Mira and asked, "I suppose this makes riding easier?"

"It's not for you…it's for the comfort of the horse." Throwing the blanket over Molly's back she went on to explain, "The blanket helps to keep the horse's back from chaffing from the constant movement of the saddle."

Gesturing at a row of saddles, Mira instructed Harley. "Pick up that third saddle. It's not as heavy as it looks. Walk over here and place the saddle over the blanket then we'll get her cinched up."

Hoisting the saddle, Harley carefully placed the saddle across Molly's back and stepped back. "Now, what?"

"Like I said, we get the saddle cinched." Hooking the various cinches together like she'd done a thousand times before, she stood, placed her left foot in the stirrup, reached up and grabbed the saddle horn and hoisted herself up and in the saddle with what appeared to be little effort. Pointing down at the stirrup, then the horn and then the saddle itself, she pointed out, "That is for your feet, this is where you sit and this is what you hold on to if you start to get nervous or think you may fall. Now, let's go out to the small corral behind the barn and I'll let you climb on board."

Outside in a fenced-in area, Mira told Harley to sit on the fence and watch while she led Molly around the circular path twice. Stopping and dismounting she gestured, "Up you go!"

"Okay, here's goes nothing," said Harley as he placed his foot in the stirrup, grabbed the saddle horn and in one smooth motion found himself seated upright. Looking down at Mira, he smiled, "That was pretty easy. Now what?"

Walking to the front of the horse, she gave Harley the rundown: Molly is so gentle you really don't have to concern yourself with guiding her that much. When we head out in a few minutes I'll take the lead and she'll simply follow. All you have to do is sit up there and enjoy the ride. Now, give her a gentle nudge with your feet and she'll start walking. When you want her to stop just pull back on the reins, not too hard but just enough so she knows you want her to stop. Go on."

Harley gently tapped Molly's sides and surprisingly she moved off. Smiling, Harley commented, "This stuff really works."

Completing the circle, he pulled back on the reins and the horse stopped. "This is great!"

"All right, why don't you and Molly go around a few more times while I go back in and saddle up Henry then we'll head down toward the river."

Harley was on his fourth time around when Mira pulled up next to the fence atop Henry. Opening the gate, she gestured, "Walk Molly out here and stop next to Henry. Then we'll head up the trail."

Seconds later, Harley found himself next to Mira and Henry. Smiling in approval, Mira urged Henry forward and Molly followed without a signal from Harley. Side by side they started up the path that led into the surrounding woods. "So," inquired Mira, "What do you think of my grandparents?"

Holding the reins with one hand and the saddle horn with the other, Harley responded, "They seem really nice. Floyd seems like quite the Cardinal fan."

"That he is, and don't let Erma fool you. If you ever have the opportunity to watch a Cardinals game with her, you'd be amazed. She knows all the rules and how the game is played. She always points out the mistakes the players make. She has three pet peeves when it comes to professional baseball. She feels the players are way overpaid and because of the vast amount of money they are paid they shouldn't make a lot of the mistakes that take place on the field. She hates it when a hitter takes a called third strike and totally disagrees with the way most players run down the first base line. She feels players should be fined for not hustling."

Interested, Harley ducked under a low hanging tree branch and asked, "How so?"

"All right," said Mira. "Let's start with running to first base after the batter hits the ball to the infield. Most players, and you know this is true, if they hit the ball to the third baseman or the shortstop, even the second baseman in some instances, automatically figure they are going to be thrown out so they don't give it their all to make it to the bag. Now, I'll be the first to admit that the infielders of today's baseball are going to throw the runner out ninety-nine percent of the time, so why try to beat a throw you are not going to. But here's the thing. Once the ball is hit you never know what's going to happen. I saw the perfect example of this at the end of last season. I forget who the Cards were playing, but one of the players on the opposing team hit a sharp ground ball to third. The third baseman had to dive for the ball, which he managed to knock down, then had to get to his feet, take three steps, grab the ball and fire it to first where he still beat the runner by a good three steps. It wasn't even close. The runner was easily called out. If the runner would have been blasting down the line there is a good chance he would have been called safe. Getting to first base could make the difference in a game. My grandmother thinks most ballplayers should be injected with a dose of Pete Rose. I don't have to tell you that Pete was nicknamed Charley Hustle. It's a known fact when Pete played everyone on the opposing team knew when he hit the ball they were not going to be able to lollygag. Pete made the other team do things faster than they normally did which always made him a threat."

Leaving go of the saddle horn for just a second, Harley pointed at Mira then grabbed the horn again as he explained, "When I played Little League every player hustled on every play because that's what we were told to do. We didn't know any different. We weren't playing for money…we were playing and hustling because we loved to play and we desired to win so we ran hard, we threw hard, we swung hard."

Mira guided Henry around a slight curve in the dense trees and remarked, "I would never argue with this philosophy of hustling in baseball but there is a fine line most baseball fans do not consider and that's just this: baseball is more than just a game. It's a business. Sure, the average fan who attends a baseball game sits in the stands and munches on nachos and a hot dog and has a beer or two and doesn't even realize what a big business baseball really is. When owners are paying players big salaries, the players actually become a commodity...a valuable commodity. Each player on a team is a part of that particular franchise's puzzle for that year. If a player gets injured a part of the puzzle becomes missing. How many times have you been watching a game when a runner is sprinting down the first base line and they sprain a hamstring and down they go? When this, and other types of injuries occur a player could be out for days, weeks, months or for the rest of the season. So, let's get back to running full out to first base. I think most managers would agree it's not worth losing a player to injury trying to beat out a play where they are routinely going to be thrown out. It's all about the mathematics of baseball. That being said, I think most professional ballplayers are capable of making a decision on when and when not to hustle in todays' game of baseball."

Smiling, Harley shook his head in amazement. "I've never looked at it that way before but you're right. I've never viewed myself as a valuable commodity, just one of the players on a team."

"That's because you're not being paid. Fox High School has made no investment in you. If you get injured and have to sit out for the season, the high school fans, as limited as they are still come to the games. High school ball is a sport...not a business. In the major leagues fans fill the seats not just to see their team play, but also to see their favorite players in action on the field. The fans are the reason why clubs make money. Without the players, there would be no fans and without the fans there would be no baseball."

Bringing Henry to a halt, Mira pointed at a large grass covered area that could be seen through the trees. "That's Bee Tree Park over there. We take a left here and that'll lead us down to the Mississippi. There's a large area next to the river where our horses enjoy the sweet grass that grows there. It's only about a five minute ride from here."

Following Mira down the dirt path, Harley continued their baseball conversation. "You said your grandmother had three pet peeves about professional ballplayers: being paid way too much and the fact that many of them don't hustle down to first base. What was the third one?"

"The third one is the one she's most adamant about. Taking a called third strike. She says it's the cardinal sin to just stand there and get called out. She claims that if the batter doesn't swing at the ball then nothing happens, except the hitter walking back to the dugout and possibly leaving a runner or runners stranded on base."

"Well from a pitcher's standpoint I am always relieved when the batter takes a called third strike. As a pitcher that's a gift for me, especially if there is a runner in scoring position. In Little League, they taught us that if you've got two strikes on you then you must protect the plate. If the ball is close enough to be called a strike then you could have possibly hit it. Our manager never yelled at us for striking out, because we at least tried to hit the ball, but he would get upset with us if we went down without swinging at the ball. He explained to us that nothing happens until you hit the ball. Why just stand there when you could have possibly made contact. Whenever the ball is hit there is always a possibility that an opposing player will make an error or make a bad throw. Who knows, why you might even get a base hit...but you have to swing at the baseball! Players always try to outguess the pitcher. As a pitcher, I always try to fool the batter. If the count is 0-2, 1-2 or 2-2, the next pitch or maybe the next two pitches are going to be off the plate. And, because they are protecting the plate then maybe I can get them to go for a bad pitch. I've even seen some of the best hitters in baseball take a called third strike, even if the ball is right down the pike. Myself, I always swing at the ball if I have two strikes on me. If I strike out, well then so be it. But, I'm not just going to stand there and hand the other team an out."

Falling back so she was abreast of Harley, Mira asked, "Now that you've finished your freshman year at Fox as a starting pitcher how do you think the team did...*and* how do you feel about the year you had?"

"As far as our team goes we went 12-10. We didn't make the playoffs. Myself, I feel I had an okay year. I pitched six games and went 5-1. I only walked three players and one of those was intentional. I averaged nine strike outs per outing which means I fanned fifty-five hitters. My ERA came in just a tad over 2.50. I only gave up seven hits for the year, threw three shut outs. Had a batting average of .324. So, all in all I can't complain."

"During the off-season what area do you plan to improve on?"

"That's easy. I'd like to get my fastball up to the high eighties and I need to improve my move to first to keep runners on the bag. I had six bases stolen on me this past season, three in one game. As a matter of fact, those three stolen bags were the reason I lost the one game I did. I've been working with my mom and dad out in our backyard. My dad says runners can read me and that I'm too predictable. He reminded me that, as a pitcher, it's my job to keep the runners on base close to the bag. He told me when I throw over to first, that I don't put much on the throw. In other words, I just lob it over there and the runner always gets back to the base safe. I have to add another dimension to my move toward first. It's okay to try and keep the man close, but I have to have the attitude that I can pick him off. What I've been working on is, after I throw one or two lobs over to first, then the next time I'm going to fire the ball to first like a fastball. I have practiced this in the backyard and I have actually picked my dad off a few times. He told me once I establish that I can pick someone off, then opposing players will become leery of stealing on me."

An hour passed when Mira stood and suggested, "Why don't we head back to the farm. Looks like it's starting to cloud up. Henry could care less about the rain, but Molly will freak out especially if there is any thunder."

Walking across the grassy meadow, Harley continued their afternoon baseball conversation. "Do you know who stole the first recorded stolen base?"

Placing her foot in the stirrup, Mira hoisted herself up and replied, "No, but I think I'm about to find out."

Harley, now seated atop Molly grinned and explained. "Back in 1865 a player by the name of Ned Cuthbert who played for the

Philadelphia Keystones stole the first recorded stolen base. Later on, in his career he went on to be the first St. Louis Cardinals manager. The Cardinals have had their share of stolen base champions over the years. Back in 1888, St. Louis had a player by the name of Arlie Latham who stole one hundred and nine bases that year. Then in 1890 another St. Louis player; Tommy McCarthy captured the stolen base championship by stealing eighty-three. Then, over the next fifty years or so the Cardinals had a number of base stealing champions: Patsy Donovan, Frankie Frisch, Pepper Martin and Red Schoendienst. None of these players even came close to matching ol' Arlie's one hundred and nine stolen bases. In the late 1960s and the early 70s, the Cards dominated the stolen base category with eight all time base stealing champion Lou Brock. His best year he stole one hundred and eighteen bases. About ten years passed when the Cardinals had yet another superstar on the base paths and that was Vince Colman who won six consecutive base stealing awards. His best year was '85 when he nabbed one hundred and ten stolen bases."

Mira, impressed with Harley's baseball knowledge joked when they made the right hand turn at the park. "If your future playing skills on the ball field ever get to the point where they match your knowledge of the game you'll wind up being a superstar of great magnitude!"

Snapping her fingers, she continued the base stealing conversation as she remembered something, "Do you remember earlier this year when we had that cookout at your house?"

"Yeah, I do remember that," said Harley. "What made you suddenly think about that?"

"All this talk about baseball stats reminds me of some of the things we talked about that day. You know, all the crazy plays and things we heard about baseball, like the twenty-four inch homerun." Before Harley could respond, Mira smiled and went on, "This talk about stolen bases reminds me of yet another weird baseball story from the past. It seems back in 1908 there was a player for Detroit by the name of Germany Schaefer who stole second base twice in the same inning and he only came to the plate once."

Harley gave Mira a strange look and commented, "Now, that's hard to believe. How could that even be possible?"

"Story has it," pointed out Mira, "that Germany was quite the prankster when on the field. He would do odd things like wear a raincoat over his uniform letting the umpires know it was raining too hard to play or he would carry a lantern onto the field letting them know it was too dark for a game. Davy Jones, one of his teammates tells this story. They were playing a game against Cleveland and Detroit had two men on base. Jones himself was standing on third and Germany on first. Germany, realizing they had to get Jones home breaks for second base trying to set up the double steal. Cleveland's catcher doesn't bite and does not throw down to second. Germany slides in safe and now Detroit has runners on second and third. On the next pitch Germany takes off back to first base. Everyone on both teams can't believe what they are seeing as Germany slides back to first…safe. Since, at that time in baseball there was no rule about stealing a base you had already been on, the play stood. The next pitch, ol' Germany yells, 'Let's try this again,' as he takes off for second. This time, the catcher had had it with Germany's shenanigans and fires the ball to second. Germany slides in safe and Davy Jones scores from third as well, so Herman Germany Schaefer stole second base twice in the same inning and was safe both times."

Harley pulled Molly up next to Henry and remarked, "That's unbelievable!"

Mira looked over at Harley and asked, "After we get back and get the horses settled in you are planning on staying for supper…right?"

"Yep, that's the plan. What's on the griddle tonight?"

"I have no idea but whatever it is it'll be good. My mother is quite the cook."

Bringing Henry to a halt, Mira looked off into the trees. "I really enjoy the fall. The leaves are especially bright this year."

Harley nodded in agreement and then spoke, "You look so normal sitting on a horse."

Mira gave him an odd sort of look and replied, "What do you mean?"

"What I mean is that ever since we met earlier this year you have always had a walker or your cane. But, up there sitting on Henry no one would ever know you had at one time required a walker or that you now use a cane. You look so normal…so natural."

"I do feel normal when I'm on one of our horses. When I'm in the saddle, I'm just like everyone else."

Nodding at the cane stuck in the side of the saddle, Harley asked, "Was that slot made for your cane?"

Touching the end of the cane, Mira laughed, "No, this is an actual western saddle and this slot is for a rifle which here on the farm we have no use for so I just stick my cane in there when I'm riding." Pulling the cane out she twirled it above her head and then lowered it, aiming the cane directly at Harley as if she were holding a rifle. In what she thought was a western drawl, she ordered, "This here town ain't big enough for you and me, partner, so move out!"

Harley laughed so hard he had to hold on to the saddle horn to stop from falling. Mira reached out and hooked his left arm with the cane. "Don't you go falling off Molly and getting injured. Remember, next year you're going to be Fox High School's star pitcher!"

CHAPTER 21

MIRA SAT BACK IN HER SEAT AND TOOK IN THE spectacle of Busch Stadium. The manicured grass, the perfectly marked foul lines, the raked infield and the large American flag fluttering in the gentle breeze. Taking a drink from a large soda, she remarked. "So, this is where the Cards play. This is the first time I've been to the stadium. I've been to Fenway Park, Camden Yards and of course, Yankee Stadium, but this just seems so different. Fenway, where the Red Sox play has been around since 1912 and is known as major league's oldest ballpark. It's famous for the Green Monster, the huge left field fence. Camden Yards, the home of the Orioles, has two orange seats that mark where Cal Ripkin Jr. hit his two hundred and seventy-eighth homerun and Eddie Murray hit his five hundredth. And then there's Yankee stadium where my father has taken me once a year since I was six. What is the seating capacity here at Busch?"

Harley was quick with an answer as he sat down next to Drew. "Busch Stadium can seat just over forty-six thousand. There is hardly a game during the season where the attendance is less than thirty thousand. The fans in St. Louis are the best in baseball. They always support the Cards no matter how well they are playing. Take this year, 2005. The Cards didn't start out so hot, but right now we're seven games up with over the second half of the season to go. I really feel good about our chances this year."

"And that's not all," added Drew. "This will be the last season the Cards will play on this field. Next year we'll be playing at the New Busch Stadium."

Harley looked down at the field and commented, "I know, it makes me sad to think I'll never sit up here in my favorite seat after this season ends. I've been coming to Cardinal games ever since I was six months old. That's sixteen years of coming down to this park. I bet I've attended over four hundred games here at Busch. I've got a lot of great memories here, like the time when I was ten and I fell over the fence and broke my arm in front of thirty thousand fans. I always walk down to the section where I took my nosedive and think about that moment. At the time it happened I wasn't so happy, but it's something I'll always cherish and never forget. It's going to feel strange to sit in a brand new ballpark."

"It seems like such a gigantic undertaking," said Mira. "To demolish this stadium and have a new one up by the beginning of next season seems impossible. Next April is only ten months away."

Harley held out his hands and gestured at the surrounding seats. "It'll go pretty fast once they get started."

Drew got in his two cents and agreed. "They've already started construction on parts of the new stadium…haven't they?"

"Yes, they have. Last June they started Phase 1, which is the construction of the outer walls of the new stadium and come this November Phase 2 will kick in where they'll begin the demolition of this stadium. I read an article in the paper about how and when they plan to go about the transition. Later on this year during construction of Phase 3 they'll put in the playing field and then after the 2006 season opens Phase 4 will finish up with the construction of the left field mezzanine. They estimate the cost of construction at three hundred and sixty-five million."

Drew cracked open a peanut and laughed, "That's a lot of bags of peanuts!"

"This article I was reading went on to say they estimate the square footage at around a million and a half square feet covering twenty-eight acres. Amazing!"

"I'll tell you what's amazing," said Mira. "Is that you know all this stuff. How is it that you can memorize all these facts, figures and numbers?"

"That's what my parents are always asking me. When it comes to my schoolwork, I'm horrible in history but when it comes to the history of baseball I remember everything I read. My mother says when it comes to baseball I'm abnormal for my age."

"I'll second that," said Drew. "Ever since I met Harley I've had to put up with his constant baseball facts whether they're current or in the past. I've been dealing with this obsessive baseball knowledge for close to eight years. It's become contagious. I constantly find myself looking up statistics I think Harley may not know so I can combat his ever-present knowledge of the game. So, I too have become sort of abnormal."

"Well that makes three of us then," said Mira.

Drew and Harley gave each other an odd look and then stared at Mira in silence.

Mira took a handful of peanuts from the bag Drew was holding and explained, "I'm saying we're all abnormal because we're here at a Cardinals game *and that* is abnormal when you consider we just graduated from high school earlier today. I don't know how you two feel but for the last twelve years I have been waiting for the day I'd graduate from high school and today is that day. I am now a high school graduate. Most of the kids we know are off on a summer vacation before they go to college in the fall. Many of them will be celebrating at parties tonight, but here we sit at the first game of a three game series with the Pirates. I guarantee you, there are not many Fox High School students other than the three of us here today. I'd say that's makes us abnormal. Despite the fact that I'm a die-hard Yankee fan living here in St. Louis, well it's hard not to root for the Cards. Speaking of the Cards, what do you think their chances are of going all the way to the World Series this year?"

Harley was confident as he answered, "It's a long season and we're almost three months in. The Cards are in first place, not a commanding lead, but still a substantial lead for this time of year. Personally, I think this could be a year when the Cardinals wind up being a great team."

Drew swallowed a peanut and held up his right hand. "I would like to see the Cards go all the way this year, but that doesn't mean they'll wind up being great. I think baseball fans misuse the word *great*. For years now I've gotten into the habit of trying to learn a new word or the actual meaning of a word every day. I open the dictionary and randomly place my finger on a page and whatever word comes up I read its meaning. On one of these occasions the word *great* became the word of the day. If I remember, the dictionary defines the word great as, *Large in size or number; larger than usual.* How does this definition equal a team as great? Maybe a better way to put it would be to say that a certain team is better than other teams. If a team wins the World Series in the eyes of baseball fans they are considered great! Does this mean that particular team is larger than the other teams? No, it means they played better. So, what causes fans or experts in baseball to say a team is great?"

Harley stared at Drew in wonder, and then answered, "I never thought about greatness like that. I think using the word *great* is our way of saying a certain team is the best, be it that year or back through history. I can tell you this, baseball has been around for a long time. Major league baseball started back around 1869 and the game was played even before that. Thousands upon thousands of games have been played since 1869 but the number of teams considered great is limited. I've read about the top fifty greatest baseball teams of all time and the Cardinals are only on that list three times. The 1934, '42 and '67 teams. In 1934, the Cardinals went 95-58 and won the World Series over Detroit in seven games. They were known as the Gashouse Gang. They were a scrappy team and only took over first place in the last three games of the year. Then in '42 the Cardinals had Stan Musial and Enos Slaughter who both wound up being hall of famers. That team edged out Brooklyn by just two games to win the National League pennant. That year we beat your Yankees, Mira, 4-1 in the World Series and that was the beginning of a three-out-of-five year run of winning the fall classic for the Cards."

Drew shelled another peanut and looked at Mira shaking his head in amazement while Harley continued with his rundown of great Cardinal teams. "Finally, in 1967, the Cards fielded yet another great team! We went 101-60 that year and beat the Red Sox in the World Series. The '67 Cardinals were a great team. Tim McCarver was the starting catcher and as far as pitching is concerned we had Bob Gibson and Steve Carlton. That was an incredible team!"

Finished, Harley sat back and took a drink of his soda and commented, "Looks like the fans are starting to pour in for tonight's game."

Mira sat forward and spoke, "Wait a minute! That can't be the end of this conversation about great teams. We haven't answered Drew's question about why fans say certain teams are great." Without hesitating she went on, "I think I have a reasonable answer to the question. Now, I haven't studied the game like

Harley has and I haven't been to as many major league games as either of you, but I have been to a few plus I've watched hundreds of games on television. This is just my opinion, but here's what I think. I feel it's more difficult for a team in baseball today to become great than it used to be years ago. Teams today are more equal. I say this because at one time in baseball there were only a handful of teams that had what we call a superstar on their team. Teams that had one, two or maybe three outstanding players could over the course of a season win more games. Today, it's different. Every team in the majors has a number of superstars. The field of teams is more balanced. Every team has a forty-man team roster. Many teams have players that can play at a number of different positions. Players in today's game are faster, stronger and more intelligent when it comes to the ins and outs of the game. Every player on a team is very good at what they do or they wouldn't be in the majors. That being said, I am of the opinion that all players, regardless of their talent level, experience four different skill levels on the field. There are times when players make things happen, times when they wait for things to happen, times when they allow things to happen and even moments when they don't know what's happening."

Drew stood and stretched while he finished his drink. "This sounds confusing. We are talking about baseball…right?"

"Yes, we are talking about baseball. Let me break down the four skill levels I mentioned. First of all, players that make things happen. A third baseman can attempt to catch a foul ball and seeing that the ball is going into the first couple of rows in the stands dives without any hesitation into concrete steps, wooden chairs and a number of spectators without any regard for his own safety. The player could back off but makes the play happen by diving into the stands and often catching the ball. Another example is the outfielder that runs into the outfield fence running full speed to catch a fly ball. The player who reaches down and hits a low outside pitch that is not in the strike zone for a base hit and drives in the winning run. Players who do these sort of things don't have to, but they choose to make things happen! Now, let's look at players who wait for things to happen. A player at the plate might wait for *their pitch.* He waits, trying to get walked, but winds up striking out, many times on a called third strike. Or how about the base runner that hesitates and waits a tad bit too long before running to the next base and gets thrown out. Then, there are players who allow things to happen. A pitcher allows a base runner to get a large lead off first rather than holding him on. This results in a stolen base. Or how about the infielder that tries to throw the ball before it's caught. And yes, there are even moments when players, no matter how talented they may be, might not know what's going on. Like a play where the first baseman forgets about the man standing on third and rather than throwing to the plate makes a throw to second and the man from third scores. All of these plays, and many I haven't mentioned, often make the difference in winning or losing the game. Players can experience a game when they are constantly making things happen. A player can go four for four, drive in five RBI's and make a number of spectacular plays all in the same game and then a week later they can strike out four times and make two costly errors in a game costing the team a loss."

Crushing his now empty soda cup, Drew placed it in the seat next to him and stated, "So, what you're saying is that a team can only become great if their players are making things happen?"

"Well, yeah, I guess I am. But I'm still not sold on this great team business. Look at it this way. At the end of the regulation season a team could be thirty games out in dead last and they could wind up playing a final three game series with the first place team in their division, the first place team being touted as great and the last place team as not so hot! We know that anything can happen in baseball and in this case, let's just say the last place team sweeps the division leader. In this case, would the last place team be called great because they beat the division leader three straight games? No, they wouldn't. The first place team would still be referred to as great and the last place team would still be just that…in last place. What I'm saying is teams that generally win the division title or the playoffs and even the World Series do so because they have players that make things happen on a more regular basis than other teams. The best teams don't wait on or allow as many things to happen over the course of the season. Sometimes a great team can be just a little better than the other teams. How about when a team wins their division by a half game after the entire season is played? You could very easily go back and review games where someone on the division winning team made something happen that changed the outcome of a game. If there ever was a team that made things happen all the time there is a possibility they would never lose a game. But, we'll never see that type of a team for a number of reasons. Players get tired, players go into a slump, weather conditions, personal matters in their lives. It's all about emotions. In a fraction of a second a player can decide to make a play happen or not. These split second decisions can and often alter a game…and the season. But that's baseball!"

Changing the subject Mira announced, "I need another drink. What say we head down to the concession stands and get some refills?"

Walking down the elevated concrete steps to the lower level, Drew asked Mira, "So, it's off to Kentucky University for you this fall."

"That's right. I'm going to the best veterinarian school there is. I'm going to study to become an equine vet. I'll be able to work with horses the rest of my life. I think my love for horses equals my love for the game of baseball. My father's brother lives in a small town outside of Lexington called Versailles. He has a small horse farm there. My first year at school I have to live on campus but my sophomore, junior and senior years I'll be able to live with my uncle and his wife on their farm. They told me they know most of the large horse farm owners in the area and I can probably get a job at one of the larger farms while I'm at school. Who knows, I may wind up living in Kentucky, in or around Lexington. There are lot of horses down that way and a big demand for qualified vets."

Harley smiled. "Sounds to me like you have your life pretty well planned out."

Hopping on an escalator to the lower level, Mira tossed her cup into a trash container. "I think all three of us have our potential futures lined up. You and Drew are off to the University of Missouri on baseball scholarships. You'll both play college ball for four years then no doubt get drafted in the minor leagues and eventually wind up in the majors as professionals."

"Back up a minute," said Drew. "Harley and I both get to play ball for Missouri, but only Harley received an athletic scholarship. Harley got the last baseball scholarship the school offered so I had to go on a music scholarship for my musical talents. Missouri's baseball coach was instrumental in making that happen. When he discovered I had been catching for Harley for the past eight years he talked with the school's music department because he didn't want to break us up. So, I get to play in the school orchestra *and* play baseball."

Rounding a corner on the lower level, the lines at the concession stands were starting to grow as fans stocked up on all their favorite baseball snacks. Getting in line, Mira asked Harley, "How do you feel about pitching in college next spring?"

"I think it's really going to be different. My parents sat down and explained to me that it was going to be a whole new world for me. My father told me college ball is a lot different than high school baseball. He said in college when it comes to sports it gets down to the nitty gritty. For instance, there are about five million kids in the United States who play Little League or a form of Little League each year. Only about four hundred thousand play ball in high school and somewhere between five to six percent of high school ballplayers play in college. That equals somewhere in the vicinity of twenty-two thousand college ballplayers each year. Out of that group around fifteen hundred are drafted into the minor leagues and after the first two years about five hundred remain. Out of those five hundred maybe a hundred make it to the majors."

Moving up in line, Drew frowned. "You make it sound almost impossible to get to the major leagues, from five million to a hundred. I wonder what percentage that works out to be?"

"Let's see," said Mira as she whipped out her cell phone and went to the calculator mode. Following some quick finger work, she announced, "Looks like it works out to around 0.002 percent. Sounds impossible...doesn't it?"

"It doesn't sound impossible to me," said Harley. "I've been working and practicing my entire life to achieve my goal of being a major league pitcher. If, for some reason I don't make it, I'm not sure what I'll do. I've never even considered not making it. I figured if I kept at it that it was just a matter of time."

Paying for their drinks, Harley handed Mira hers and stated, "I think I've come a long way in the past few years. I started out as one of five million Little Leaguers and I'm now one of the twenty-two thousand ballplayers in college. My parents have kept records of each year I have played since Little League. I think I have a past record that's okay."

Grabbing his drink from the counter, Drew bumped Mira on her shoulder and shook his head. "Harley is being way too modest. The career he has had, not only as a pitcher but also as a baseball player, is way more than *just okay!* He is what I consider to be a great player. He's a player who makes things happen on a more regular basis. He rarely allows things to happen or waits for things to happen and he is *always aware* of what's going on during a game. I should know! I've been his catcher for the majority of the games he's pitched. I know Harley when he's on the mound. I know how he thinks and what he's going to do on every pitch."

Following Harley and Mira out into the increasing number of Cardinal fans entering the stadium, Drew went on, "I was with him in Little League when he was throwing his fastball in the mid-sixties and now he can bring it in the low nineties. I betcha by the time he's through with college he'll be close to a hundred. He's got a nasty four-seamer and a split finger fastball, to go along with a curve, slider and cutter. His best pitch, from my viewpoint as a catcher, is his changeup. It's a good fifteen miles an hour slower than his fastball. Then there's his knuckle curve, which just drives hitters nuts. Harley is a control pitcher. He can paint the corners, brush a batter back. He always puts the ball exactly where he wants it. Over the years, he's only thrown me four wild pitches. In short, Harley Sims is destined to be a major league pitcher."

"Enough already!" said Harley. "What about you, Drew? You're no slouch yourself! Don't you remember right after we first met and you explained to me about your phobia of being afraid of playing any sport? I remember the first time I convinced you to play catch with me. You've come a long way from back then. You're better than any catcher I've ever seen for your age. And here's the thing. You can hit. There have been many catchers down through the history of the game that have been strictly used for their defensive skills and their catching abilities. But you, cannot only do those things well, you can really hit. I think when it's all said and done you'll find yourself someday playing in the majors."

Mira broke in on the conversation. "I think it would be great if you both wound up on the same major league team."

"The chances of that happening are slim," said Harley.

"Remember only about fifteen hundred college players are drafted yearly into the minor leagues. As a future prospect, you really don't get a choice who will draft you. Each year on June 5th and 6th the draft takes place and there are fifty different rounds of the draft and normally what happens is the best players in the college world of baseball get chosen in the first few rounds. So, what could happen is a player can be drafted for a team they may not necessarily care for. Over the years my father has always kidded me about the possibility of being drafted by the Cubs, who we all know are not well liked by Cardinal fans. The way the draft works is that the team with the worst win-loss record of that year gets the first draft pick and it goes from there. I always said I wanted to pitch for the Cards, but my parents keep reminding me that whatever major league team drafts me that I should feel a great sense of accomplishment by getting to the minors and then the major leagues. For all we know Drew and I could wind up in different leagues or playing against one another in the same league."

Walking up a flight of stairs, Drew commented, "Well I'm not concerned about that right now. That's fours year down the road. There's a lot of baseball to be played over the next four seasons."

Mira, right behind Drew, spoke up, "I heard some kids talking right before our graduation ceremony. Apparently ol' Aaron Buckman is playing Double A ball for the Cubs."

Harley stopped at the top of the steps. "Really, what else did they say?"

"I just overheard the end of the conversation. One of the kids said they heard after he graduated he went to a walk-on tryout the Cubs had. Between his ability to play first and the way he clobbered the ball out of the park they were impressed. Last year he played Single A and this year had moved up to Double A. Who knows, you two might wind up playing against each other and Aaron in the future."

Following Harley and Mira through a short passage that led back out to field seating on the lower level, Harley pointed down at the first row of seats next to the outfield fence. "Right down there is where I went over the fence years ago. Come on, let's walk down."

Seconds later the trio of young ball fans stood next to the fence and looked down over the side to the warning track, Mira inquiring, "How far of a drop is it from up here?"

Harley gestured with his drink. "They told me it was around eight feet. When I was in the hospital later that night I thought about what happened and it seemed like eighty feet. It happened so fast. I didn't even have time to brace myself. I was just going for the ball."

Mira thumped Harley on his right shoulder. "And if I remember when you first told me this story you said you caught the ball?"

"I did, but it fell out of my glove when I collided with the field. Later that evening, Jim Henke of the Cardinals and Paul Blumfield of the Pirates came to visit me. Jim brought the ball autographed by the entire team and Paul brought me a ball signed by the Pirates. That is by far the best birthday I've ever had."

The conversation was interrupted by a voice from down below next to the fence. "Harley Sims…is that you?"

Looking down at the warning track Harley noticed his ol' friend Paul Blumfield. "Paul, I was hoping you were in the lineup tonight. It's been a long time since we talked."

"That it has," said Paul. "It's been what…five, six years since you toppled over this fence?"

Harley smiled. "Closer to eight years. That was some night wasn't it?"

"Yep, it sure was." Looking up at Mira and Drew, Paul asked, "Friends of yours?"

"Yes," exclaimed Harley. "This is Mira Madison and Drew Scott. We all go to high school together. Well let me correct that. We did! We just graduated earlier today and this fall we'll all be off to college." Without skipping a beat, Harley went on with the introductions, "Mira, Drew, this is Paul Blumfield, one of the best outfielders in the game."

Paul laughed. "Used to be one of the best. I'll be thirty-nine this year. Next year will probably be my last. I'm really starting to slow down. My legs are not what they used to be and my arms ache quite a bit."

Harley, quick with his knowledge of baseball stats remarked, "I've been following you over the past few years since we met. Last year you had a batting average of .257 and hit nineteen homeruns. I think that's still respectable."

"That was last year. Right now, I'm holding at .230 and have only knocked three out of the park."

"Yeah, but it's still early in the season. There's a lot of ball left to play this year."

"True…very true, but still, next year is it for me. I'm looking forward to a life of fishing and I might take up golf. Over the years, I've grown tired of all the travelling and eating out all the time. I've got a son who is playing ball in his second year of college down in South Carolina. He's an outfielder like me."

"And I'm sure if you have anything to do with it, he'll wind up in the majors."

Dropping his glove to the ground, Paul moved closer to the fence and explained, "When I was a youngster growing up I dreamed of playing in the major leagues *and* my dream came true. For the past seventeen years I've had the privilege of being a major leaguer. As a major league ballplayer and a father, it would give me great pride if my son played professional ball. But, here's the thing. My son has a mind of his own. He wants to be a medical surgeon; wants to save people's lives. If it turns out that's what he does with the rest of his life, then I'm okay with that."

Looking directly at Harley, Paul inquired, "That day when Jim and I paid you a visit at the hospital, I recall you saying you wanted to pitch in the majors. Did you ever make that Little League team you were going to try out for?"

"I sure did," said Harley. Motioning toward Drew, he went on, "And Drew here has been catching me ever since. This fall we'll both be playing ball for Missouri. I can't imagine anyone else other than Drew behind the plate when I'm on the mound."

"I know what you mean. The only team I've played for all these years has been the Pirates. I gotta tell ya. To me, there's nothing better than baseball friends." Turning, Paul gestured toward a group of fellow Pirate players doing stretching exercises in center field. "I've made some great friends over the years playing professional ball and not just on the Pirates. I've made friends with players from every team we play. I've met some great Cardinal players over the years. I think that's the one thing I'll miss the most, the common bond players share."

Laughing, Paul reached out and leaned up against the outfield fence. "My wife tapes a lot of the games I play. The other night when I was home in Pittsburgh she asked me what on earth I'm always talking to the first baseman about after I make it to first base. Over the years you get to know players from other teams quite well."

Looking up at Mira, Paul asked, "So, what made you hook up with these two young ballplayers?"

Holding up her cane, Mira answered, "I used to be a ballplayer myself...fast pitch softball, but then I got injured and could no longer play." Waving the cane in the direction of the field she continued, "I still love the game of baseball. I've been a long time Yankee fan, but I'm starting to root for the Cards."

Interested, Paul asked, "Are you off to college as well this fall?"

"Yep...University of Kentucky. I'm going to study to be a veterinarian specializing in horses."

Pointing up at Mira, Paul laughed. "Now there's something I've never done...ride a horse!"

Harley jumped back in on the topic. "You should give it a try sometime. I rode my first horse this past summer. It was very relaxing."

Paul was distracted as one of the players yelled across the outfield to him. "C'mon, let's throw a few!"

Paul picked up his glove and smiled up at the three high school grads. "Good luck this summer when you're away at school." He started to jog away but then stopped turned and walked back and tossed a ball he had in his glove up to Mira. "There ya go young lady. Keep these two young ballplayers in line!"

CHAPTER 22

DREW PLOPPED DOWN IN A FOLDING CHAIR WHILE Harley unfolded one of his own. Taking his seat, Harley looked around the parking lot and commented sadly, "I would have thought there would be more here today. I bet there isn't even thirty people here."

Drew surveyed the lot and remarked, "Maybe it's just too sad for most Cardinal fans. Busch Stadium has been here since, well I can't remember what you told me."

Harley opened a bottle of water, sat back and stared across the street at the stadium. "Busch opened back in 1966 and has proudly served St. Louis for close to forty years as the home of the Cardinals. I, along with many baseball fans here in the area, will really miss this ol' ball field. I'll never forget this day, November 7th, 2005, the day they started the demolition of Busch Stadium."

An older woman carrying an oversize bag stopped and looked down at the two boys and then at the stadium. "Are you boys Cardinal fans?"

"Yes ma'am," Harley proudly announced. "I've been coming to games since I was a toddler. Are you a fan?"

The woman stood as straight as she could and stated. "A lifetime fan, I am! My name is Evelyn Gottshall. I just turned eighty-two last week. I've been attending Cardinal games for the past seventy-two years. When I was ten years old my family lived just down Grand Avenue from Sportsman's Park. Me and my two older brothers and a kid up the street used to sneak in the field and watch the Cardinals play whenever they were in town. I got married right out of high school and my husband and I continued to go to Cardinal games. We didn't have a lot of money but we always scraped up enough to go to a game and enjoy a hot dog and a beer. Then in 1953 when the Cards moved to Busch Stadium we continued to be Cardinal fans. By then, Ralph, that was my husband, had a pretty good job with the railroad so we could afford to attend a game now and then. Ralph and I were at the seventh game of the 1964 World Series when the Cardinals beat the Yankees in the final game 7-5. My memory isn't as good as it used to be but I think it was the year after that the Cards started to play at Busch Stadium II, which was referred to as Stadium Plaza. Ralph and I would drive downtown on occasion whenever we could to catch a game. Then in 1980, just a few years away from retirement my husband got killed in a railroad accident. After that I didn't attend any Cardinal games for about three years. It was just too hard to go to the games by myself. Our son, who lived down in Texas at the time, knew of my love for the Cardinals and bought me season tickets. He said Ralph would have wanted me to go to the games. I haven't missed a home game since 1983." Looking across the street she muttered, "It's sad they're tearing down the stadium where I've been coming for so long. I was hoping to get one of the bricks from the stadium but the police told me I couldn't go near the demolition site. It's too dangerous. That's why I came down here today. To get one of those bricks and say good bye to my ol' friend...Busch Stadium."

"Do you live close by...how do you get to the games?" asked Harley.

Pointing up the street the woman answered, "I live three blocks north of here at a senior citizen facility. I've been there now for almost ten years. I can still get around so whenever there is a home game I just walk down here to the stadium. When the game is over I walk back to the Missouri Gardens...that's the name of the place where I'm living. Of course, I watch all of the away games as well on the television in my room."

"Well I wouldn't feel too bad about not getting one of those bricks," said Drew. "Harley and I have been sitting here in this parking lot and watching the demolition for the past hour. We've seen the police turn away hundreds of people wanting to get a brick or some other type of the destruction as a souvenir."

"And another thing," added Harley. "Even though the current stadium is being destroyed, next spring there'll be a brand new stadium for the Cards to play in. So, you'll still be able to walk down here for home games."

"No, I'm afraid my days of sitting in the stadium and watching the Cards play has come to an end. I got a call from my son last month. He's having some problems with his business and it looks like he might go belly-up. He informed me that it looks like he will no longer be able to get me season tickets. Now, I guess I'll be watching all the Cardinal games, home and away, at the senior center. I'll really miss coming to the games. It's been such a part of my life." Wiping a tear from her eye, she bent down and took Harley's hand and then Drew's. "Didn't mean to go and get all emotional on you two lads." A tremendous noise caused her to turn and look at the stadium as a large piece of heavy equipment knocked down a large section of the stadium wall; bricks, metal posts and dust flying in every direction. "Sad...so sad," she muttered as she turned and started slowly up the street.

Harley and Drew were both at a loss for words when Harley stated in defiance, "We're going to steal two of those stupid bricks before we go home!"

Drew hesitated in his response but then whispered as if someone nearby might hear. "What do you mean...steal two bricks?"

Harley got up and walked to the curb of the street and gestured at yet another section of wall tumbled to the ground with a large crash followed by a rush of dust floating across the street. "What I mean is we are going to walk up the street and grab some lunch while I explain to you how we are going to grab two of those bricks over there when we come back." Folding his chair, Harley motioned up the street. "Let's pitch these chairs in the car and go to lunch. I'll give you the lowdown on the way."

Getting up, Drew still confused, asked, "Before you fill me in on *how* we are going to steal two bricks, I need to know *why* we are stealing bricks?"

"We're going to get one for Evelyn Gottshaw, have it engraved and then take it to her at the senior center. You saw how upset she was. If anyone deserves one of those bricks it's her. You heard what a fan she is. It sounded to me like Cardinal baseball is the only thing she has left in her life."

"Okay," said Drew, "I get that. But why two bricks? One is for the old woman. Who is the other brick for?"

"Well, I just thought while you're over there stealing one brick you might as well grab another for my parents. I know they would enjoy having an engraved brick from the stadium to add to their collection of Cardinal memorabilia."

Following Harley to the car, Drew stopped dead in his tracks. "Whoa…just hold on a sec! You did say while *I'm stealing* one of the bricks. Why are we not *both going?*"

"Because one of us has to drive the getaway vehicle. You know I'm a better driver than you. You always get so nervous, especially in traffic. Besides that, you're a faster runner than me."

Opening the car door, Drew agreed, "I am faster than you, but that happens to be when I'm running the base paths during a game, not sprinting down the street carrying two bricks with the police on my tail!"

"The police are not going to run after you. Do you think for a moment they'll leave their assigned duty to chase some fan with two bricks down the street?"

"Well, if I was a cop I sure wouldn't."

Throwing his chair in the backseat Harley started across the lot. "C'mon, let's get lunch and lay this job out."

As they crossed the street, another huge section of wall crumbled to the ground in a cloud of dust and debris.

Parking the car at the corner of Walnut and S. 8th Street, Harley turned in the seat and spoke to Drew. "Okay, let's go over one more time what we talked about back there at the restaurant. You walk down 8th to Clark. The closest pile of bricks along Clark Street is approximately twenty yards from where the police on Clark are stationed. You walk down Clark, casually cross the street and before they realize what's happening you grab two bricks and take off back up Clark to 8th and then to Walnut where I'll be right here waiting with the car running. When you get here I'll have the back window open. Toss the bricks in then get in yourself. Before you know it we'll be on Market which we'll take us to Jefferson and then to 64…simple!"

Reluctantly, Drew stepped out of the car and leaned in the open window. "You do realize if we get caught we're nineteen years old and that makes us adults in the eyes of the law."

Harley reassured Drew, "We're not going to get caught. It's just a couple of bricks. Now, get out of here. You should be back here with the bricks in fifteen to twenty minutes."

Harley watched as Drew walked across Walnut and then down

8th. Sitting back in the seat he took a drink of water from a bottle and thought about what Drew had said about them being nineteen. As freshmen at Mizzou, they had experienced college life now for just over two months. They were rooming together in the same dorm and kept to themselves. Every evening out on the lawn adjacent to their dorm Harley would pitch to Drew, following their routine of stretching exercises.

Looking up the street he noticed Drew was no longer in sight and would soon be on Clark Street. Thinking back again to the late afternoon practice sessions outside of their dorm he remembered when last week a girl stopped by and watched them for a full five minutes and then approached. She introduced herself as a freshman reporter on the school newspaper. She had been assigned to write a story about someone from the freshman class who was unusual. When she found out Harley and Drew were both going to be playing on Mizzou's baseball team and that they had been a team themselves for the past nine years, she said she might write an article on them. After asking a number of questions and taking some notes, she left saying she couldn't promise them anything but she was going to work on the article and turn it in.

His line of thought was interrupted when a police cruiser slowly passed while the officer looked over at him. Harley simply nodded and then looked away. Within the next few minutes Drew would come running up the street with the heisted bricks.

Drew turned the corner of 8th, and there just up the street was the pile of debris which, with any luck would be minus two bricks in the next minute or so. Two police officers stood some twenty yards away while they talked and drank cups of coffee. He crossed the street immediately. There wasn't anything to think about. It was a simple task, walk across the street to the pile of bricks grab two and walk off, or depending on the reaction of the police, if he was even noticed he might have to run.

The police were not even looking in his direction when he approached the brick pile. He checked one more time on the officers then walked up to the pile, selecting a brick that appeared to be undamaged, then searched for another brick that would be acceptable as a gift. Tossing a broken brick to the side he was just reaching for another when he heard a voice that carried authority,

"Hey you…get away from those bricks!" Grabbing a second brick he turned without looking at the police and ran up the street as he checked traffic. There was a line of cars at the intersection of Clark and 8th, so he was going to have to run farther up Clark before crossing. A number of people stared at him as he sprinted up the street with the two bricks tightly clutched in his hands."

Harley checked the street once again. Still no sign of Drew with his cargo. Taking another drink of water, he thought about the Cardinals and the last time they had won the World Series…1982! *That was a long dry spell,* he thought. *Maybe 2006 will be our year what with the new stadium and all.*

It was just starting to spit snow when Harley's chain of thought was interrupted by Drew's out of breath voice as he chucked the two bricks into the open back window. "I don't think they followed me but we still need to get out of here!"

Running around the car, Drew hopped in and Harley checked the street and pulled out. Drew looked out the back window when they came to a red light. "They saw me just before I took off. The police know what I look like. God, I hope this doesn't make the news tonight."

Blowing off what Drew said, Harley asked, "Did you get two nice ones?"

"I really didn't have much time to pick out the best bricks that were probably in the pile but I did grab two that were not broken." Wiping brick dust from his hands, Drew continued, "You did say you were going to get these bricks engraved?"

"That's right…one for Mrs. Gottshaw and the other for my parents. When we get back to my house I'll hide the bricks outside somewhere in the bushes at the edge of the property until I have time to go to an engraver." Making a left hand turn onto Jefferson, Harley noticed Drew staring out the rear window. "I think you can stop looking for the police. The second after you grabbed those bricks they probably forgot all about you."

Turning and looking at the falling snow Drew announced, "Ya know, that's the first time in my life I have even stolen anything…anything!"

Heading up the ramp to Rt. 64, Harley motioned his head toward the backseat. "Let's take a look at the bricks."

Reaching into the backseat Drew held up one of the rectangular objects and inspected it closely, "I tried to pick out two where the edges were not chipped and the surface was relatively smooth for engraving. Like I said I really didn't have that much time."

Harley approved and stated, "If the other brick looks like that one, then I say you did an excellent job!"

Placing the brick in the backseat, Drew looked up into the grey dreary sky. "Looks like wintertime is finally here. It's hard to imagine that in a few months we'll be getting ready for baseball season at Mizzou."

Getting off the exit at Rt. 141 in Arnold, Harley looked at a restaurant at the corner of the first red light. "My folks have informed me they're taking me out to eat tonight before I go back to school tomorrow. My mother is concerned since I've been in college that I'm not getting nutritional meals."

"It's just as well I get back home anyways," said Drew. "I'm playing the piano at church service tomorrow morning and I've got to practice."

Sitting at a corner window of the Pasta House Harley searched the menu of Italian selections while Monica rummaged through her purse. "I know I put a coupon in here I cut out of the paper for the Pasta House."

Rich picked up a menu and started to look over what was offered. "I might go with lasagna tonight." Looking across the table he asked Harley, "How about you son. What suits your fancy?"

Putting down the menu, Harley announced, "I don't even have to look. I'm going with the spaghetti and meatballs with an extra meatball for Ozzie. You know how he loves Pasta House meatballs."

Monica laughed. "There isn't too much Ozzie doesn't like."

The waitress delivered a basket of hot, fresh rolls and then asked if they were ready to order.

She no sooner left the table when Rich buttered a roll and spoke to Harley. "I was reading an article the other day about a pitcher from Japan. I forget his name but the article said within the next year he may be playing over here in the major leagues. The article stated he had an unusual style of pitching. He has what they call a *short stride delivery!"*

Harley, taking a bite out of a roll himself, asked, "Short stride delivery? I've never heard that before."

"I can't recall everything that was written but it was pointed out that most pitchers extend their lead leg during their delivery. In this split second of time the batter normally picks up the ball as it leaves the pitcher's hand. This is an advantage to the experienced hitter. But, *not so* with this Japanese pitcher's short stride. Because of his short stride the ball leaves his hand before his leg is completely extended which makes, according to the article, the ball almost seems invisible. What they are saying is that the ball is much more difficult to pick up out of the pitcher's hand which gives the pitcher an added advantage. If you're interested, I thought maybe next weekend when you're home we could go out back and experiment with this short stride business."

Harley gave his mother and then Rich an odd stare. "You can't be suggesting that I change the way I pitch after all these years."

"Off course not," stated Rich. "I'm just saying maybe you could, with a few months of practice, develop a short stride pitch to go along with your regular style of pitching. It's just something to think about. Look at it this way. If you mix in an occasional short stride pitch, I think it would really throw off the hitters you face. Look at it in this fashion. In just four short years of college ball you'll no doubt be drafted into the minors by a major league team. If you are going to add another pitch or style of pitching to your portfolio you need to get it done within the next couple of years. In the major leagues they pay you well for your pitching abilities. They expect you to deliver the goods, so if you're going to get better or try something new...now is the time."

Taking another bite out of his roll, Harley smiled, "Tell you what...I'll think it over next week while I'm back at school."

Rich smiled as well. "Fair enough!"

Reaching for her beer, Monica chimed in, "Speaking of college, we've talked about this college baseball business with you a number of times while you were in high school. Every player on every college team is the cream of the crop from high school. Many of the kids you will face on opposing teams in college may be future major leaguers. College kids are stronger, faster and they can hit and throw better. There will also be more competition at the pitching level for the future draft spots that will become available when you graduate college four years down the road. You will not be able to rest on your past laurels. If you expect to be one of the fifteen hundred out of the twenty-two thousand college players that get drafted, you have to outshine ninety percent of those you play with and against."

"As long as we're talking about the minor leagues four years down the road," said Rich, "I've done some research on the Cardinals farm system. If you get drafted and go right to Triple A ball you'd be playing for Memphis, which is in the Pacific Coast League. However, the chances of going from college right into Triple A are slim. You might start out in Double A, which means that if you're drafted by the Cards you'd be a member of the Springfield team which is in the Texas League. I think there's a good chance you could go to a Single A team, which the Cardinals have three different levels of play. There's the Advanced A team in Palm Beach of the Florida State League, then there's Class A from the Quad Cities, which is part of the Midwest League, and finally the Short Season A Division in New Jersey, which is in the New-Penn League. Of course, there's always a chance they could place you in the Rookie Class that plays in Johnson City, Tennessee, which is in the Appalachian League. What I'm saying is there is no way to tell what team will draft you or where you could wind up playing for the first couple of years. That's why it's so important to hone your pitching skills now. Remember what we talked about? How that out of the fifteen hundred drafted each year, that after two years only five hundred remain."

"I know," said Harley. "I've heard all the so-called horror stories of being in the minor leagues for any extended period of time. The long bus rides from one city to the next, many times out of state, eating at greasy spoon restaurants, playing in front of crowds that are not what you would call sell-outs. It's all about paying your dues, about earning your way to the top. On top of all that, you are not going to make all that much money as a minor league player, especially in the lower ranks of the farm system. When I get drafted I hope to go in the first few rounds and start out in at least Single A. I've worked too hard all my life so far to fall down at the finish line."

By the time they pulled in the driveway it was dark and snow was gently falling. Inside the house, Harley climbed the stairs to his bedroom with Ozzie right on his heels. Changing into a heavy grey sweat suit with the Cardinals logo emblazoned across the front, he pulled one of ten different Cardinals ball hats down from the tall dresser and placed it on his head. Ozzie, who was curled up on the bed perked up when Harley announced, "Come on boy...we brought you something special home for a snack!" Side by side they ran down the stairs, across the living room and into the kitchen where he found his mother and father sitting at the kitchen table with hot cups of coffee. Scooping up the to-go container from the counter, Harley headed for the door that would lead to the backyard and smiled. "Me and Ozzie are going out back. I'm going to throw a few pitches at the tire and Ozzie will get his meatball!"

After Harley exited the kitchen, Monica smiled at her husband. "That's our boy! He is surely destined to become a major league ballplayer. Who else his age would venture out into a snowy evening to practice his pitching with the temperature below freezing?"

Rich sipped at his coffee. "Not many, that's for sure. If for some unforeseen reason he doesn't make it, it won't be from a lack of trying!"

Ozzie, focused on the container in Harley's hand raced to the garage then returned and circled Harley twice, then went into a sitting position and raised his right paw. Opening the container, Harley laughed, "There's no foolin' you...is there?"

An hour later, following a succession of pitches at the hanging tire, Harley walked to the bench next to the large oak tree by the fence and sat while Ozzie joined him. The snow had become heavier and had started to cover the low grass. Pitching Ozzie's tattered tennis ball off toward the back of the yard, he watched as his faithful companion raced after the ball and then returned, dropping the ball in the snow and waiting for the next toss.

Minutes later, Ozzie took a much needed rest while Harley stroked the canine on his wet head. "You're the best friend I've got, Ozzie. You just want to love and be loved. When you look at all the crap that goes on in this world we just can't seem to grasp this love concept. But you...you get it!"

CHAPTER 23

HARLEY TOSSED HIS GLOVE TOWARD THE THIRD BASE bleachers by Missouri's practice field and joined Drew as they sat on the metal seating. Drew began the process of removing his marred shin guards while he looked up at the overcast sky. "Looks like we finished practice just in time. There's a storm brewing."

Harley untied his spikes and surveyed the grey sky. "It does look like a storm."

"Any significant snowfall we're going to get this winter has already fallen over the past few months," said Drew. "According to the weather channel it's clear sailing as far as any snowfall from here until spring. That reminds me. Aren't major league pitchers and catchers supposed to report to spring training this month sometime?"

Tying his spikes together, Harley slipped his socked feet into a pair of deck shoes. "Let's see, it's February 17th right now. In the Grapefruit League teams have to report somewhere between February 18th and the 22nd. The Cardinals will be reporting, as usual, to Roger Dean Stadium down in Juniper, Florida on the 18th. It looks like we're going to have a strong pitching rotation this year, plus we also have some good relief pitchers. We lost a starting pitcher, a second baseman, left fielder and a relief pitcher as free agents. We traded a pitcher and acquired a second baseman and a relief pitcher. It's way too early to tell for sure, but I've looked over what we have this year and I think the starting potential line up looks good. I personally think the Cards are primed for this year; our first year in the new stadium."

Inspecting some loose lacing on his catcher's mitt, Drew noticed Coach Meadows and his assistant, Coach Craig, as they approached. Meadows stopped short of the bleachers, spit and looked at the foreboding black clouds and then at his two junior varsity players. "Boys, I've got something I want to talk to you about. As you are well aware the regulation season starts in two weeks. In most cases the junior varsity travels with the varsity team and as a general rule plays the junior varsity team of whatever school we happen to be playing. Freshmen, and normally sophomores, are not generally involved with varsity squad games, but this year with the season right around the corner I find myself *and the team* in a bit of a pickle."

Placing his right foot on the bottom of the bleachers he went on to explain, "I've currently got four starters in our varsity pitching rotation. Our best pitcher, Stark, has come up with a pulled muscle in his right shoulder and Brockman, my third best, has a serious case of the flu. Our starting catcher has got some problems with his grades that temporarily disqualify him from playing with the team. I've been watching you two since we began spring practice and I am of the opinion that you're better than the pitchers and catchers I've got left on the varsity. So, next Wednesday, when we leave for South Arkansas State, you'll be my starting battery for our first scheduled game this year. So, between now and when we leave don't do anything stupid. The fact is we need you two fellas."

Tipping his ball cap, he and the assistant walked off. Drew gave Harley a look of astonishment and stated, "I guess we're moving right up the ol' ladder."

Picking up his glove and spikes, Harley dug his watch out of his pocket and checked the time. "It's almost five o'clock. What say we hit the shower, get cleaned up and go uptown for a bite?"

An hour later Drew hopped in the front seat of Harley's car and inquired, "What local eating establishment are we going to bless with our presence tonight?"

Leaving the main road of the campus Harley made a right turn on Rt. 163 and headed south. "There's a place I heard about this morning. It's about two miles outside of town. I guess a lot of students go there. They're supposed to have pretty good grub from what I hear."

"I hope so," stated Drew as he patted his stomach. "I'm starved! I missed breakfast and only had a candy bar for lunch. I'm in the mood for a good burger and a pile of fries on the side."

"Now that you mention it, that does sound good."

Rain was just starting to spit when they pulled into a dirt

parking lot that fronted a long, one-story, faded, clap siding structure. A flashing red neon sign advertised: *Great Food – Ice Cold Beer.*

Drew pointed at four large windows where there were various hanging beer signs and asked, "Are you sure we can get in this place. They serve alcohol here and we're only nineteen."

"We're not coming here for the alcohol, we just want something to eat," said Harley. "I've heard it's the place to hang out. You can get a beer here or you can have dinner, play pool, shoot darts, watch sports on one of their large screen televisions and even dance on Friday and Saturday nights when they have a live band. Like I said, a lot of college kids come here."

Getting out of the car, Drew nodded at a number of motorcycles and pick-up trucks parked at the far end of the lot. "Looks on the rough side if you ask me. Not many students drive pick-up trucks and ride choppers."

Starting for the door, Harley laughed, "You worry too much. C'mon, let's get those burgers."

Just inside the entrance doors a rather huge, muscular individual who was perched on a tall stool confronted them. The man gave Drew and Harley the onceover but remained quiet while they passed and were greeted by a passing waitress. "What'll it be tonight gentlemen…the bar area or the dining section?"

Harley was quick to respond, "We're just here for dinner so I guess the dining section."

Grabbing two menus from a stack on a small side table she motioned, "Follow me please."

Passing through a large crowded room, there were a number of people seated at the bar and standing around holding beer bottles as they talked and watched two suspended televisions above the bar, while they viewed a St. Louis Blues hockey game and a Basketball game. A group of bikers and locals were gathered around three pool tables while another group was playing a game of darts in the opposite corner of the large room. As they were passing the pool tables, a rather large baldheaded individual with diamond earrings in both ears backed up to make a shot and bumped directly into Harley. Turning in frustration the man sneered at Harley and spoke roughly, "Watch where you're goin' pal!"

Harley instantly apologized, mainly because the man presented himself as rather ominous, well over six-feet in height, muscular tattooed arms, leather vest advertising the group he rode with, *The Demons,* and a face only a mother could love. Running his large hand across his untrimmed light beard, the man looked Harley up and down, gave him a look of disgust and then went back to his pool game.

Seated at their table, Drew gazed back toward the pool area and commented, "Now, that was one rough person you bumped into."

"Excuse me!" said Harley, "but I believe *he* bumped into me."

"Well either way, I think we dodged a bullet out there."

Picking up a ketchup-stained menu Harley waved off Drew's concern. "Like I said, you worry too much. Let's order."

"I don't need to look at the menu. I've already decided. Cheeseburger, medium rare with extra bacon, fries on the side."

Harley chimed in. "Sounds good. I'm going with the same, minus bacon."

Five minutes later after they ordered, Harley sipped at his soda and looked around at the room. There were a dozen dining tables, of which only three were occupied with what looked like college students. Gesturing back out at the attached bar, Drew surmised, "It's almost like there's an invisible line that divides this section from the bar. It seems rather peaceful in here while over there it's like another world."

"Will you stop worrying," said Harley. "There is nothing to be concerned about. Tell you what. If you want we'll leave right after we eat."

A young college girl seated with two of her female friends gave Drew a casual smile that automatically changed his opinion of where they were. "Maybe we should hang around for a while after we eat."

Looking in the direction of the table where the girls were seated, Harley turned back to Drew. "Nothing like a smile from a pretty girl to change the way you think about things."

"Look who's talking. Ever since you met Mira you've changed."

Not understanding, Harley asked, "In what way?"

"Look, I'm not saying you've moved away from your love of baseball. It's just that a statement I made to you years ago has come true."

Harley, still confused, asked again, "What are you talking about?"

"It was shortly after you first met Mira. You and I were at a Cards game. We were sitting in your favorite pre-game seats in the upper level and we got to talking about her. I mentioned how my mother told me how a girl could change your life and you said that would never happen to you and that baseball would always be your main focus. We talked about how I was so multi-talented and had to juggle my time between stamp collecting, playing the piano and my karate lessons. You have only had to deal with your obsession with becoming a major league ballplayer. But now, you have Mira in your life and you have to juggle that along with your discipline of playing ball."

Reaching for his drink, Harley shrugged off Drew's suggestion that Mira was a distraction. "I've never considered Mira another plate in my life as you have suggested that I have to juggle. Mira has been nothing but pleasant to be around. She's just so different from all the other girls we knew in high school. It was her love of baseball that first attracted me to her. Why, there doesn't seem to be more than a few minutes that pass when we're talking that she doesn't bring baseball into the conversation. During the time I have known her she has been anything but a distraction from my goal of becoming a major league pitcher. If anything, she's been a help with her support. I haven't altered my regimented daily practice and I haven't allowed our relationship to interfere with the way I feel about baseball."

Drew, realizing that his best friend was becoming a bit defensive changed the subject. "Did you ever get those two bricks I stole from the construction site engraved?"

Now that the conversation was going in another direction, Harley seemed more at ease as he answered, "Ya know, I forgot to mention to you that I did take care of that. I guess I owe you an apology for not including you, seeing as how you did all the dirty work when it came to collecting those bricks. I went to an engraver in South City and told him I needed the bricks engraved for Christmas presents. Two days before Christmas he gave me a call informing me he had them ready. On Christmas Eve I went down to the Missouri Gardens where Mrs. Gottshall said she was living.

I went to the head desk, asked where her room was and found her sitting there reading a letter from her son. Surprisingly, she remembered me and asked where you were. She went on to tell me her son was doing better and that he had started another company and it looked like she was going to have season tickets for the coming Cardinals games after all. I could hardly get a word in as she sat there on her bed in a Cardinals hat and jersey. The walls of her room were covered with Cardinal pennants and programs. When I presented her with the brick and told her it was from you and I she broke down in tears."

Interested, Drew asked, "What did the inscription say?"

"I really tried to think about what to put on that brick and I decided on: *Emily Gottshall – St. Louis Cardinals Biggest Fan!* By the time I left her room she had invited a number of nurses and other residents who were passing by in the hallway to see her brick. I finally left and told her that maybe we'd see her at a game later on this summer. She laughed and said she'd buy us a beer."

"What about the other brick…the one we got for your parents?"

"I gave it to them for a Christmas present. When my dad picked it up he looked at the wrapping and joked that it felt like a brick. When he opened it, my mom laughed and said, 'It is a brick!' They asked me where I got it and I jokingly said you and I got it down at the demolition site at Busch Stadium."

Suddenly, their waitress was standing next to their table asking, "Who gets the bacon?"

Drew spoke up and reached for one of the two plates she held in her hands. "That'd be me."

Salting his fries, Harley reached for a ketchup bottle. "I was talking with my dad last weekend when I was home. He asked me if I was ready to pitch college ball. I told him I thought I was ready. Of course, at that time he was not aware that you and I would be moved up to the varsity team, at least for our first scheduled game. I can't wait to call him later tonight and give him the news."

Drew took a large bite out of his burger and stated, "I'm sure he and your mom won't be all that surprised. Ever since Little League you've always played above your age level. You have always excelled at the game."

"That's the very thing my father talked with me about. He told me I have to prepare myself for a different level of baseball. The game and the rules for the most part will be played just like it was in high school but at a higher, more intense level. Some of these kids that we'll be up against are the best players from high schools all over the country. Their mechanics will be well developed and they'll be on their game. They will have more confidence than high school players and I have no doubt they will be able to execute at the plate."

Pointing his burger at Harley, Drew added, "But let's not forget these great high school players who are now playing college ball have to face pitchers like you. Pitchers who are more aggressive, who can really spin the ball, who have more heat than maybe they've ever experienced. Ever since I started to catch for you, we agreed we would take it one game at a time. We should approach our first college game like we always have. With each player a new cat and mouse game begins. Some of these kids will be dangerous hitters but it's our job to evaluate each one and learn their strengths and weaknesses. If we gain a better feel for what they can and cannot hit over their ability to figure you out as a pitcher we can gain the upper hand."

"You make it sound so easy," said Harley.

"We've always approached the game that way. You've won about ninety-percent of the games you've pitched with me as your catcher. In this upcoming game with Arkansas, if we play our cards right, this will be another notch in your pitching belt."

Harley checked his watch and the time was just after seven o'clock in the evening. "Well, we've been sitting here for an hour talking baseball. I can't see any reason to hang around here any longer."

"I can," said Drew, "Come on...let's play some pool. All three tables are open."

Harley objected, "I've never played pool in my life."

Drew was on his feet and heading for the main room of the bar, "Come on, it'll be fun. I'll teach you." Not waiting for an answer from Harley, Drew walked to the first table, grabbed a pool cue from a rack attached to the wall and began to chalk up. Pointing his cue stick at the others on the wall. Drew suggested, "Pick one out and don't be choosy. These are bar cue sticks. They're probably warped." Running his cue over top of the green felt that covered the table, he remarked, "Just like I thought. Crooked as a dog's hind leg."

Taking down a stick, Harley looked over at the bar where the large man who had collided with him earlier that evening was giving him a look. Gesturing at the bikers standing at the bar, Harley leaned toward Drew and whispered, "I don't think this is one of your better ideas. We're getting some strange looks."

Drew looked at the group of men and blew off Harley's concern. "When we first got here I thought coming in here was a bad idea but you told me I worry too much. Now it's you who's doing all the worrying. It's just a game of pool."

Rolling his cue across the table like Drew had done, he asked, "Where did you learn how to play pool?"

"My grandfather lives down in the Dallas area and has a professional pool table in his basement. He played all the time and taught me the game." Racking up the fifteen balls with a wooden rack he went on, "Now, the game we're going to play is called eight ball."

Placing the cue ball in the center of the table a few inches from the near rail, he lined the cue up with the ball, all the while explaining. "You don't want to rush your shots. Take your time and hit the ball smoothly with a good follow through."

Harley smiled and repeated, "A good follow through...just like after I throw a pitch."

Drew smiled. "I never thought of that, but yes. The object is to try and get at least one ball or a number of balls in the pockets on the break. Here goes!"

Hitting the cue ball with a smooth motion it slammed into the racked balls and they scattered in every direction one of the stripped balls going into a corner pocket. "Okay, that means I have the stripped balls and you have the solids. You'll notice there are fifteen balls: seven solid and seven striped and the eight ball. Now, I get to go again because I sank a ball. I keep shooting until I miss a shot and then you go." After knocking in two more balls he finally missed a shot. "Your shot," said Drew. "If I was you I'd try to hit the two ball in the side pocket. It's a straight shot. Just take your time and hit the ball in the center, but not too hard."

Harley lined up the stick, looked at the two ball, drew back the cue and struck the side of the cue ball, the ball moving about an inch.

Drew placed the ball back where it had been and remarked, "That's what we call a miscue. Try it again. Take your time and concentrate. Look at the ball as if it were that tire in your backyard."

"Okay, here goes!"

Just as Harley was about to shoot, a large hand reached down and knocked the two ball in the side pocket. Both Drew and Harley looked up into the unfriendly face of the earring wearing man that had bumped into Harley. Giving them a cavity-ridden smirk, the man remarked sarcastically, "That's about the only way you'll ever knock a ball in a pocket."

Harley remained silent and looked back at Drew when the man spoke again, "You're pretty pathetic...aren't you."

Harley freely admitted, "Yeah, I guess you're right. I've never played before. I need a lot more practice."

Reaching for another ball, the man shoved it roughly across the table smashing into the others. "Well, practice is not somethin' you're gonna be able to do in here. We have these tables. If you remember when ya first came in here we were on these tables." Looking directly at Harley, the man emphasized, "You do remember how you rudely bumped into me when I was tryin' to play? We took a break and now we're ready to start playin' again, so why don't ya just move on."

Harley picked up his stick, walked over and placed it back in the rack as he agreed, "I think that's sounds like a good idea." Turning back to the man and the five bikers standing around him, he added, "I don't have a problem with leaving."

Drew had another idea, "Not so fast, Harley. We don't have to leave. When I lived down in Texas my grandfather took me to a number of pool halls and there was always an atmosphere of courtesy. Things like being polite to the players and waiting your turn at a table. What these fellas are suggesting doesn't seem right to me."

Directing his hard stare now in Drew's direction, the man stepped forward and leaned on the table. "Look, we come in this place all the time. We determine what's right and what's not right." Before Drew could respond he pointed at their matching yellow and black Mizzou baseball jerseys. "I see you boys play baseball for Missouri. Take a good look around this place. It's a sports bar. The one sport you don't see advertised in here is baseball. There isn't any St. Louis Cardinal or Missouri Tigers baseball crap on any of the walls. This is a football, hockey and basketball place. We don't cotton to baseball players or their fans around here." Walking around the table he stopped right in front of Harley and stated boldly, "I think baseball players are wimps. Real men play hockey and football. I was the startin' tackle on my high school football team. We were state champs. Most of my buddies here played football and we chew up baseball players."

Harley wanted to back up but had nowhere to go. Drew picked up the cue ball and walked to the head of the table and spoke, "Harley there is a pitcher and he can throw a baseball nearly one hundred miles an hour."

One of the other bikers laughed and commented, "So what. He's still a wimp."

Drew turned to Harley and motioned to him. "Come on over here."

Before the man standing in front of Harley could react Harley ducked under his huge right arm, joined Drew and whispered, "What's wrong with you. You're going to get us killed!"

Drew handed the cue ball to Harley and suggested, "I think a little demonstration is in order." Pointing down a long hallway past the restrooms, Drew nodded at a hanging beer sign flanked by two hanging lights. "It's about seventy feet down to the end of the hall. I'm saying that my friend here can throw this cue ball close to a hundred miles an hour and break that beer sign."

Another biker laughed and skeptically spoke up, "I'd like to see that." All the others laughed except for their large leader who signaled for silence as he stepped closely to Harley. "What's that gonna prove?"

Drew smiled and explained, "This demonstration will be in two parts. The first part will be Harley here breaking that beer sign. We'll talk about part two after that happens." Stepping back, he gestured down the hallway. "Harley...remember the tire in your backyard. If you break that light then we walk out of here, if you don't, well let's not talk about that."

Harley held up the cue ball and looked at the bartender. "I really don't want to damage anything in here."

The bartender smiled and answered, "Don't worry about it. First of all, I don't think you can actually break that light and secondly if you do, I'll cover the cost. This should be interesting."

Drew shrugged, "You heard the man. He just gave you the green light. It's a full count, bottom on the ninth, tying run on third. You need to throw some heat right down the middle."

Harley hesitated when Drew spoke again, "Harley, you really need to do this...and now!"

Harley looked at the man and then the other bikers and the bartender as other customers started to gather for the demonstration. Tossing the cue ball in the air he caught it and smiled back at Drew. "I hope you know what you're doing."

Drew held up his hands as if things were out of his control. "It's all up to you now."

Assuming the position, Harley went into his stretch, relaxed his shoulders, stared at the light down the hall, spun the ball in his right hand and then placed his index and middle fingers over the invisible seam on the cue ball and fired the pitch. In less than two seconds the light shattered and fell to the floor in pieces. The bar was filled with applause.

One of the bikers addressed their leader. "Come on, Luke, you have to admit that was pretty impressive."

Luke took another step toward Harley and said, "So, that doesn't mean a thing to me."

Drew picked up another ball and remarked, "That's because you haven't heard what part two of the demonstration is. As a catcher, I can throw the ball pretty hard and accurate myself." Turning, he fired the ball down the hall where it smashed one of the lights on the wall. He picked up another ball and tossed it to Harley and then picked up another himself. "Here's part two, Luke. Imagine that light being one of your legs or arms or even your head. Not a pretty thought."

Before Harley realized what was happening Luke stepped forward, grabbed him by his neck and rammed him hard against the wall with the pool sticks falling from their rack to the floor like pickup sticks. Getting in Harley's face he snarled, "Well ya ain't gonna have no opportunity to throw no balls at me!"

With a gargling attempt, Harley tried his best to speak,

"Drew...do...something!"

Drew stepped next to Luke and ordered him, "That's enough, let him down!"

Luke spit in Drew's face and yelled, "Back off!"

"That's enough!" said Drew. In one swift motion, he swept Luke's legs out from under him, causing him to not only release his grip on Harley, but tumble awkwardly to the floor. Drew waited for Luke to stand and then he drove his right shoulder into the large man's stomach, picked him up and flipped him over his back. Luke landed loudly on a nearby table that crumbled beneath his weight. Drew grabbed one of the broken wooden table legs and placed it across Luke's throat. The rest of the bikers began to move forward but were warned by Drew, "One more step and your leader will never utter another word."

Luke raised his hand for the group to stop advancing. He struggled slightly and Drew applied more pressure, which caused him to lie perfectly still. "Now here's the way things are going to go," explained Drew. "Harley, grab two balls and be ready to take some of these boys out. I'm going to let you up Luke, and then Harley and myself are going to walk out of this place." Looking over at the bartender, Drew asked, "What do we owe you for the broken sign and the light?"

The bartender, sensing trouble, held an old baseball bat in his left hand and a .45 caliber pistol in his right, smiled and answered, "Not a thing boys. Enjoyed the demo. Now you need to get out of here. I don't imagine I'll ever see you in here again. This kind of stuff is not good for business."

Drew let up the pressure on Luke's neck and motioned for Harley to start for the door. Following Harley, Drew spoke to the bartender, "You have great burgers here but I can't say much for your choice of clientele!"

Harley dropped the two pool balls by the front door and exited with Drew right on his tail. Harley ran to the car, jumped in and turned the ignition key. Drew walked backwards all the way across the lot in case Luke and his crew followed them. Safely inside the car, Drew motioned at the highway, "Let's get out of here!"

A few hundred yards up the road Harley turned to Drew and remarked, "Boy that was really a stupid move on our part. Do you remember the last thing the coach said to us after he told us we were going to be on the varsity?"

Drew, out of breath, responded, "No...what?"

"He told us not to do anything stupid over the next two weeks because he needed us."

"I guess that was pretty stupid, but what choice did we have? By the way, nice pitch down that hallway. If you had missed we'd be up you know what creek without a paddle. I could sure use a vanilla milkshake right about now. What say we hit Dairy Queen?"

CHAPTER 24

CROSSING THE ARKANSAS–MISSOURI BORDER, HARLEY gazed out the window of the bus and waved at the large, green WELCOME TO ARKANSAS sign on the side of the scenic highway. Unwrapping a candy bar, he stated with confidence, "Next stop...Magnolia, Arkansas, and our first win this season playing college ball."

Drew looked out at the passing countryside. "How long before we get to South Arkansas University?"

"I think we've got another two hours. The school campus is less than twenty miles north of the Louisiana Border."

"How would you know that?" asked Drew. "Have you ever been there before?"

"Nope, never have been. I looked it up last night on the Internet. I also found out that they only have about thirty-two hundred students attending and their school's tag name is the Muleskinners. Pretty amazing when you think about it. Missouri has around thirty-two thousand students which means our school is ten times larger than Southern Arkansas."

"That may be," pointed out Drew, "but that doesn't mean we're ten times better than their ball team!"

Harley agreed. "True. Last year they were tied in their conference but lost in a one game playoff for the title. We shouldn't take this team lightly. Remember, in baseball any given team can beat another team on any given day."

"Coach Meadows said their manager would probably start one of the returning varsity pitchers from last year. Their entire infield is returning, but two of their outfielders graduated last year. They averaged about 4 runs per game last year, so they are not what I would call a great hitting team. Defensively they're solid as a rock."

Harley placed the now empty candy wrapper in a trash slot in the seat in front of where they were seated and asked, "You ever been to Arkansas before?"

"Just like you," stated Drew. "I've never been before."

Pushing a button on the arm of the cushioned chair, the chair slowly reclined to a relaxing position as Harley noted, "Compared to all the trips we took in school buses during our baseball careers in high school, this charter bus is much more comfortable. Do you remember how uncomfortable the seats were and how the bus always seemed to smell like it had never been cleaned. Now, in college, we get to ride to our games in air-conditioned comfort. I just might try to grab a short nap. Wake me up in an hour."

Harley no sooner closed his eyes when the rear end of the bus suddenly jerked slightly to the right following a loud thud that summoned everyone to attention. Looking out the window, Drew with a look of concern plastered across his face spoke nervously, "What in the world was that?"

Harley gazed out the window and added, "I don't know but I don't think it was normal."

Within seconds the driver guided the bus to the side of the road and came to a complete stop. Getting up out of his seat, he opened the door and spoke to Coach Meadows who was seated in the first seat on the right. "Sounds like we just got a blowout on one of our rear tires. I'll just have a quick look."

The coach stood and asked, "Mind if I tag along?"

"No, but the team has to remain on the bus."

Understanding, Coach Meadows turned and addressed his team. "Boys, you need to stay in your seats. The driver thinks we may have experienced a flat. We should know something in a minute. Just sit tight."

Walking down the right side of the charter bus, the driver pointed at one of the rear tires that was shredded and smoking, the nauseating smell of burnt rubber wafting into the still morning air. Kneeling next to the destroyed tire the driver reached out and carefully touched the side of the tire. "Yep, just like I thought. This is the worst one I've ever seen. Probably ran over something. The bus company always keeps the tires in great condition. It's a safety measure they take quite seriously."

Coach Meadows backed away from the nasty smell and asked, "Do we have a spare?"

"No, we don't and even if we did we don't have the needed equipment to change a bus tire. This is much different than blowing a tire on a car. It requires some heavy-duty tools and an expert, and we have neither."

"So, what do we do now? Call for another bus."

"We could do that but by the time they'd get here it could be hours. I've been down this way on regular runs quite often over the years. There just happens to be a truck stop up the road. It's about three miles from here. We could make it there. It'll be slow going but it might be faster than waiting for another bus. I guess it's up to you. Since your game is in what…five hours from now, the decision is yours, wait for another bus or try and make it to the truck stop."

"How long would it take us to get to this truck stop?"

"If we leave right now, it could be about fifteen…maybe twenty minutes. That would put us there at eleven. They'll have bus tires in stock there, but we might have to wait in line depending on what other repairs are being made to trucks that have broken down. Normally they're pretty busy what with all the truck traffic down this way. We'll just have to wait and see."

Coach Meadows walked to the side of the road and stared off into the thick forest. Thinking, he turned back and gestured up the road. "I'm not interested in waiting on another bus. I say we leave and head to the truck stop and take our chances there."

"So be it!" said the driver. "I'll fire up the bus and you can take care of explaining to the team what's going on."

It wasn't even a minute when the bus pulled slowly back to the very edge of the highway and started its slow journey down the road. Coach Meadows stood at the front of the bus and spoke to the team. "Okay, boys…here's the deal. We've got a rather serious flat tire. We're going to drive slowly to a truck stop a few miles down the road where we can get the tire replaced. We're still two hours out from the university. I was planning on arriving there about twelve thirty at which point we were going to grab a light lunch, followed by a short pep talk and then some light practice at two o'clock. Our game is scheduled for four o'clock. This flat tire has thrown a monkey wrench into our plans since we don't know how long it will take to be on the road again. The driver informed me that they have a restaurant at this truck stop so I say while we're waiting for the repairs to be made that we eat now rather than waiting until we get into Magnolia. After we eat try and get some rest. Don't worry about anything. This will all work out."

Drew rolled his eyes at Harley and stated, "Well, so much for that nap you wanted to get."

Harley smiled and looked out at the slowly passing trees that lined the side of the highway. "One of those foul smelling school buses with the uncomfortable seats sounds good right about now. In all the years in high school we never broke down...not one time!"

Lying back in the seat, Harley took a long deep breath and remarked sarcastically, "Well, it looks like your starvation is about to come to an end. In about a half hour or so you'll be dining on some good ol' stick to your ribs truck driver food."

After crawling along at five miles per hour, the driver pulled the crippled bus into a large dirt and cinder parking lot next to a filthy corrugated building surrounding by old rusted truck parts and used tires."

Coach Meadows stood and spoke, "Boys, the driver has informed me that the restaurant is located next to the highway. He said it's a buffet and the food here is pretty good. I would suggest we eat now. I'll be along shortly after we find out how long this is going to take."

Drew stood and looked out the window again. "Ever dined at a truck stop before?"

"No," answered Harley, "but there's a first time for everything."

The restaurant wasn't anything to write home about. A one story cinderblock structure with dirty windows and a faded sign that simply read, GOOD FOOD – PHONES – SHOWERS – GIFT SHOP. Harley reached for the doorknob and entered, Drew followed close behind.

The inside of the building was simplistic. Tables, chairs and a long counter for hungry truckers, swinging doors that led to the kitchen, an old jukebox stood in the corner and a lengthy buffet table with trays of steaming food. On the left, there was a large doorway that led to the restrooms and a gift shop. Entering the restaurant portion of the building they were immediately confronted by an older women whose thin body was wrapped in a food-stained apron. She smiled broadly, displaying a mouth that was missing a number of teeth. Holding up a handful of menus she inquired, "Here ta eat boys?"

Harley looked at the buffet table and answered, "Yep and there's fifty-two more heading this way. We'll just have a table for two if that's all right."

Moving to a table next to one of four windows, she gestured, "Jus' foller me. Gotta winder table right ovah here fer ya."

Pulling out a chair, Harley sat and looked at one of the menus the woman placed on the table. "I won't be needing a menu. I'm going with the buffet."

Drew slid into a chair and spoke up, "Make that two. I'll have iced tea."

"Sounds good," added Harley.

The waitress scooped up the menus and gave them a wide grin and pointed at the buffet, "Well, ya jus' help yerselves to some vittles then. Be right back with those drinks."

Looking at a far wall that was decorated with a number of signs, Drew commented, "That's funny!"

Harley fiddled with a napkin dispenser and asked, "What's that?"

"Those signs over there on the wall. There is not one sign about the Cardinals. Down this way they seem to be focused on the Kansas City Chiefs or the Royals. Not one sign for the Cards. We're only a few hours from St. Louis. You would think there would be a lot of folks down here who root for the Cardinals."

Harley turned and looked at the Kansas City baseball and football signage, turned back and responded, "I don't think it's that odd. I'm not exactly sure where we are right now in Arkansas but we might be closer to Kansas City than we are St. Louis. In states where there are no major league baseball teams, baseball fans from those areas tend to root for or support the team that is closest to them."

The waitress returned with their drinks and spoke with an Arkansas draw, "Well, y'all best git to it. That food ain't gonna jus' walk ovah here. Grab a plate and git yerself a mess o' grub."

Minutes later, Harley set his plate of food on the table as he stared at Drew's selections of meatloaf, fried chicken, sliced country ham, sweet potato casserole, stewed tomatoes, mashed potatoes, green beans, baby carrots, a large salad and three hot rolls. "Good Lord," stated Harley. "The way you piled it on your plate you'd think this was your last meal."

Folding his hands Drew motioned for silence as he blessed the food then stabbed a small bite of meatloaf. "I told you I was starving." Swallowing his first bite, he followed with a forkful of mashed potatoes, then spoke again, "Getting back to what we were talking about before…about how folks who don't live in or near a city with a major league team root for the closest team to them. I guess major league baseball really is our national pastime."

"I don't agree," said Harley. "I don't think major league baseball is our national pastime, but baseball itself…*is!* Baseball is more than the thirty major league teams that make up the American and National Leagues. While there are only seventeen states that have a major league team there is not a major city or even a small community across this country that does not have a baseball field, be it Little League, high school or college ball. There are a great number of towns in this country that have constructed ball fields even if the town does not have a ball team. It's just there for local kids to play baseball. Why there must be hundreds of thousands of ball fields scattered across this country."

Biting into a slice of ham, he went on, "I was watching one of those sports shows they have on television last week and the host and his two guests were talking about the fact that the National Football League has or is in the process of taking over as our nation's national sports pastime. That's hogwash as far as I'm concerned. Apparently, they haven't done their homework. How many communities have a football field aside from high school and college towns where kids can go and play football? In comparison to baseball fields I'd say football is in a distant second place, maybe even third. Most towns have an outdoor basketball court at their local park where kids and even adults can play a game of hoops. The popularity of baseball goes much farther than playing fields. There are hats you can purchase for every major MLB, NBA, NFL and NHL team in existence." Taking a drink of tea, Harley made his point. "They are not called football, basketball or hockey hats…but baseball hats! Have you even heard of a football card convention or about anyone collecting football cards? Collecting baseball cards has a huge following and kids from as young as nine or ten years of age all the way up to adulthood collect them. The baseball hall of fame seems to be a vacation destination for a lot more sports fans than the football hall of fame. I could go on and on but I think you get what I'm saying. Baseball has always been, is now, and always will be our national pastime."

Drew cut into a slab of meatloaf and shook his head in amazement. "You don't have to try and convince me. I never looked at it that way, but you're right."

Suddenly, Coach Meadows was standing next to their table, interrupting their conversation. "I just got the word. We won't be pulling out of here until two o'clock. We've got about a two-hour drive before we get to the university, which means we will have no time for any practice when we arrive. We'll be going right from the bus to the ball field. So, keep yourself as loose as you can between now and when we get in. You might want to grab your gloves and throw a few pitches before we leave here. It may be the only chance you have to warm up."

Standing next to the bus inside the repair shop, Harley pounded the web of his glove and tossed a slightly used ball to Drew. "Let's go find us some grass and toss a few. That way we can do some stretching exercises."

Walking out of the oversized shed Harley led the way. They passed a number of old buildings when they arrived at the edge of the dirt lot. Down a slight hill, they spotted what appeared to be an old ball field. "Well, I be dipped," said Drew. "You were right when you said earlier that every town has a ball field. Here we are out in the middle of nowhere and there it is…a baseball field."

Walking down the grass-covered hill, Harley noted, "Doesn't look like its been used in years."

After the short downhill walk, they walked out to the pitcher's mound and surveyed the field. The backstop was constructed of old four by fours with a chicken wire backing most of which had holes here and there or was just hanging off. The outfield fence was rotten and falling down in a number of places. The pitcher's rubber was deeply imbedded in the dirt and half of home plate was missing. There were no bases to speak of other than flat rocks that had been placed in their proper place. An old dilapidated broken piece of plywood had been nailed on the top of the backstop with sloppily painted wording, Dunbaugh Stadium.

Drew walked to where home plate was and commented, "About

the only thing you can say is that someone keeps the grass mowed. Bet this field hasn't been used in quite some time."

Harley walked over to first base and stepped on a two-foot oblong stone and looked down at the surrounding dirt where it had been disturbed. "Well somebody has been on this field. There are footprints all over the place. I wonder who that someone is?"

Drew, looking off into a tree line on the southern edge of the old field, responded, "I can't say for sure but I think we're about to meet them."

Harley noticed the group of young boys as they emerged from the trees. Eight young boys, carrying bats and gloves slowly approached. As they came closer Drew thought that they looked like a motley crew, probably ranging in age from maybe seven to up to ten. Drew joined Harley at first base when the boys stopped just short of an invisible foul line. The group looked like a gang of kids that had stepped out of an old movie: tattered or ripped jeans, worn sneakers, old T-shirts and sweatshirts, five of the boys sporting ragged baseball hats. In their hands they held frayed leather gloves and the three bats they had between them looked like they had seen better days. The tallest of the group stepped forward and looked Harley and Drew up and down, then spoke, "Who might ya be an' what are ya doin' on our field?"

Harley grinned at Drew, then answered, "My name's Harley and my friend here is Drew. We're ballplayers and we're on our way down to play a game against Southern Arkansas University."

The boy standing next to the tall boy, smiled and stated, "You guys are gonna play the Muleskinners?"

"That's right," said Drew. "I'm a catcher and Harley here is going to be today's starting pitcher."

A short, overweight boy at the end of the group spoke up, "What team are ya on?"

Harley answered the question. "The University of Missouri. We're called the Missouri Tigers."

The fat kid laughed again. "That don't hardly seem right. There ain't no mule alive that can lick a Tiger."

The group joined in on the laughter and then the tall boy inquired, "Do ya live in Missouri?"

"Yes, we do," said Drew. "We're from St. Louis."

A boy standing in the middle of the group removed an old

battered St. Louis Cardinals hat from his head and smiled. "Then yer Cardinals fans…right?"

"Yeah, we're both big Cards fans."

Pointing at the hat in the boy's hand, Drew asked, "You boys all root for St. Louis?"

A boy standing next to the tall boy removed a Kansas City Royals hat from his head and waved it high. "We ain't all St. Louis fans. Some of us are fer Kansas City."

"'Tween the ten o' us," remarked the tall boy, "we're split right down the middle. Five o' us is fer the Cards an' the other five is fer the Royals."

Taking a quick count of the boys, Drew questioned them, "You said that there are ten of you. I only count eight."

"That's 'cause Richie's Ma wouldn't let him come along. She says he's got a bad cold. Zack couldn't come taday either, 'cause he had ta go ta his grandmother's funeral. So, it looks like we're gonna be a man short on both teams."

Harley jumped back in on the conversation. "Where do you boys live?"

"Just down the hill in a trailer court behind those trees in a holler. We come up here ta play ball ev'ry chance we git. We keep records. So far this year, the Cardinals are ahead 52 games ta 47 fer the Royals."

Another boy spoke up, "Yeah well that's gonna change taday. Richie's their best hitter and he ain't playin' taday. We plan on sweepin' the Cards."

Harley looked at Drew and stated to the group, "Shouldn't you boys be in school?"

The tall lad answered with a wide grin, "Nope…not taday. It's teacher's appreciation day or somethin' like that. They got the day off so we do too."

Understanding, Harley addressed the group of boys, "Looks like you boys have a problem what with both teams being a man short. How about this? Maybe Drew and I could play but we wouldn't be for either team. I can pitch and Drew can catch for both teams."

The tall lad rubbed his chin as if he were in deep thought then slowly answered, "Well that might be an idea."

The boy on the end objected and stated, "Nah, that'd never work. They's both Cardinal fans. It wouldn't be fair."

"How about this," said Drew. "Suppose Harley and I forget about being Cardinal fans. We'll just be independent…kind of in between. We won't root for the Cards or the Royals. We'll just pitch and catch and we'll act like the umpires. The winner of the game will depend on your teams."

The tall boy turned and spoke to the group. "That sounds fair ta me. Whadda the rest o' ya think?"

The rest of the boys nodded or spoke up in agreement. It was settled, Harley and Drew would be pitching and catching, but not batting. They would also act as umpires, Drew calling balls and strikes and Harley making the calls on the field.

The tall boy stuck out his hand and spoke, "Agreed. My name is Tommy Dunbaugh." Pointing at the boy standing next to him, he explained, "This is my younger brother, Timmy." Turing to Timmy, he ordered, "Give 'im the ball."

Timmy removed an old ragged, dirty baseball from his glove and tossed it to Harley. Harley held the dirty, frayed ball in his right hand, examined it closely then asked, "This the only ball you boys have?"

"Right now, it is," said Tommy. "We had another newer ball that Joey down there on the end got last Christmas but Richie hit it all the way out ta the outfield where it rolled under the fence, down the hill an' then inta the water o' the quarry. We were goin' ta dive in an' see iffin' we could find it but my Ma tol' us ta stay away from down there. One o' our friends drown there two years back. So, we lost our good ball."

Drew held up the ball from the bus. "Why don't we use our ball? It's practically brand new."

Tommy looked at the ball and nodded his head in approval. "That'll work. Since ya've never played here before at Dunbaugh Stadium lemme go ov'r the ground rules. Each team will have two infielders an' two outfielders. We'll play a nine inning game jus' like they do in the big leagues. During the seventh innin' stretch we always walk up ta the diner an' go in the back door. My Ma works up there in the kitchen. She always lets us have free cokes. Now, before we git started each team lines up on either side o' home plate fer the national anthem. One o' you will have ta line up on the Royal's side so things are ev'n fer the anthem. This week the Royals are the home team so one o' them has ta start the day by singin' the anthem. If yer wearin' a hat ya've got ta take it off. Ev'ryone has ta put their hand ovah their heart until the song's ovah."

Harley volunteered. "I'll stand with the Royals. Drew why don't you stand with the Cards."

Once everyone was in position Tommy nodded at the Royals and announced. "Okay. Somebody start ta singin'."

Everyone stood in silence, hats off and their hands over their hearts while one of the boys on the Royal's team took one step forward and began, "Oh say can ya see…"

Seconds later, the youth finished up off tune, "…an' the home o' the brave!"

The anthem complete, Harley yelled, "Play ball!"

One of the Royals players assumed his position between first and second and another stood dead center between third and short. The two other Royals players jogged out to the outfield.

Harley stood on the pitcher's mound, which was no longer a mound but rather a circular spot of dirt surrounded by low cut grass and weeds. Looking around the field to make sure all the players were ready he turned back and looked at the first batter, which happened to be Timmy Dunbaugh. Timmy stepped into the invisible batter's box and took two practice swings, then stepped back out of the box and asked Drew, "How fast can yer friend pitch?"

Drew, down on one knee answered honestly, "Close to a hundred miles an hour."

Timmy with a look of astonishment, signaled for his brother to approach the plate.

Tommy slowly walked to the plate where he met his younger brother who explained his feelings. "Drew says Harley can throw a hundred miles an hour. I can't hit no ball goin' that fast. None o' us can. I don't want ta be leadoff hitter. I ain't nev'r seen a hundred mile an hour pitch."

Tommy looked at Drew and called for time and then walked out to the mound. Harley looked at the boy and asked, "Is there a problem?"

"Yep…there is. Yer friend told Timmy ya can throw a hundred miles an hour. We can't hit no ball that fast. Do ya think ya could slow it up…a lot?"

Harley smiled. "I think I can handle that."

Walking back to the plate, Tommy put his arm around his brother and whispered, "I talked things ov'r with the pitcher and it's gonna be okay. You jus' git back in the box and git us a hit!"

Wiping away the dirt that covered the pitcher's rubber with his foot Harley looked in at Timmy Dunbaugh, an eight-year-old backwoods kid who couldn't have been more than four feet in height and not even seventy pounds. Timmy adjusted the ragged Cardinals hat on his shock of blond hair and hitched up his baggy, tattered jeans. Harley looked at the worn, unlaced sneakers on the young boy's feet and smiled to himself. Winding up, Harley tossed the ball with less velocity than he had in years, the ball on the outside of the plate. "Ball one!" yelled Drew as he tossed the ball back to Harley.

The next pitch was in the same place and Drew yelled again, "Ball two!"

The third pitch was over the plate and Timmy swung and missed, followed by Drew's voice, "Strike one!"

From the Cardinal side of the field Tommy and the other three Cards team members shouted words of encouragement:

Come on Timmy...git us a hit!

Don't swing at nothin' bad!

Wait fer yer pitch!

The Royals players shouted at Harley too.

Strike this guy out!

Give 'em the heat!

The next pitch was right over the plate. Timmy swung and hit a slow roller down the third base line. The Royals infielder on the left side of the infield charged the ball, picked it up and threw it to the player on first but the throw was late as Timmy stepped on the first base rock. The Cards players were jumping up and down and giving each other high fives as Tommy walked to the plate.

Setting himself up in the box, Tommy looked down at his brother on first, touched the brim of his ball hat twice, then his elbow and then the hat again. Harley smiled as he realized that Tommy was giving his little brother a sign of some sort. Maybe a hit and run play or a steal. *If nothing else,* thought Harley, *these kids know baseball.*

On the very next pitch, Timmy took off running toward second.

Drew, catching the ball, stood and had to wait for a boy to cover the base. By the time the ball arrived at second, Timmy had slid into the rock, the ball bouncing off the Royals player's glove and dribbled out to center field. Little Timmy took a quick look at the rolling ball and sprinted toward third when the outfielder raced to the ball and threw it to Drew at home plate. Timmy, standing on third gave his brother a thumbs up and yelled, "One duck on the pond. Bring me in!"

Tommy flashed another conglomeration of hat, shoulder and elbow touching secret messages down to Timmy. Harley smiled and thought, *Now what are they up to? Maybe a squeeze play.*

Tommy dug in at the plate and awaited the next pitch. Harley went into his windup when Timmy was down the line like a shot. The pitch was on the outside corner and Tommy laid down the perfect bunt, the ball going up the first base line. At first Harley decided to let the first baseman field the ball but when he saw he was making no move for the bunt he ran over and picked up the ball, but Timmy had already started his slide. Crossing the plate he jumped up and pumped his fist, Tommy running all the way to second. Standing on the second base rock, Tommy yelled, "Cardinals 1...Royals 0!"

When the fifth inning came to an end, the Cardinals were leading the Royals by a score of 5-3. Looking at his watch, Harley summoned both teams to the pitcher's mound where Drew joined the group. Tapping the watch, Harley sadly explained, "Fellas, it's one thirty and Drew and I have to be on our bus in fifteen minutes. I'm sorry, but we won't be able to finish the game."

"Really," said one of the boys. "The game is jus' about half ov'r an' we're only two runs behind. Can't ya stay fer jus' one more at bat?"

"Afraid not," said Drew. "If we did that we'd miss our bus and you boys wouldn't want us to miss out on beating those Muleskinners now would ya?"

Tommy stepped forward and handed the ball to Harley. "Guess not. It sure was nice ta meet you fellas. Iffin yer evah down this way agin, yer always welcome here at Dunbaugh Stadium."

Harley flipped the ball back to Tommy. "Why don't you boys keep this ball? We've got plenty in the bus."

Catching the ball, Tommy threw it into the air and caught it in his glove. "Thanks, we'll try not ta lose it down in that dang quarry."

Turning to walk away, Harley thumped Drew on his arm. "Got any extra money on ya."

Reaching into his pocket he pulled out his wallet and inspected the contents. "I've got a ten dollar bill...that's it."

Opening his own wallet, Harley pulled out a twenty and reached for the ten held in Drew's hand. "That makes thirty dollars. That ought to do it."

Turning, he handed the money to Timmy and grinned. "Here, take this money and get yourself a couple of new balls or maybe even a bat."

Tommy interrupted, "We couldn't do that. Our Ma said we wasn't supposed ta take no handouts from folks."

Thinking quickly, Harley corrected the young boy. "Oh, this isn't a handout. Let's call it our contribution to Dunbaugh Stadium. Surely, your Ma wouldn't have any objections to that...now would she?"

Taking the money, Tommy gave it to Timmy and smiled, "I guess not...thanks!"

Walking across the infield, Harley and Drew waved one last time. "See you boys around and good luck with your season."

Tommy yelled when they reached the edge of the grass. "Yer always welcome here at Dunbaugh Stadium. Drop by anytime. We're always here."

Harley looked out the bus window at the darkness of the night, an occasional light from a distant farm or home peeking through the tree lined Arkansas highway. Drew stretched and asked, "What time is it?"

Looking at the glowing face of his wristwatch, Harley yawned and answered, "Just after eleven. We probably won't get back until two or three in the morning. It's been a long day."

"But a prosperous day," said Harley. "We won our first game of the year knocking off the Muleskinners 5-1."

"That we did," emphasized Drew, "but the game got off to a rough start. Getting into Magnolia twenty minutes prior to the start of the game was definitely an event that was not to our advantage.

When you walked their first two batters on eight straight pitches, I knew you were not warmed up properly. Then, on top of that, their third batter got the base hit that scored what turned out to be their only run and we found ourselves down 1-0. I was sure Meadows was going to pull you, but then in the second inning you got things together and your control was much better. All in all, I'd say you pitched a great game. Walked three, struck out nine and gave up only one run on three hits. Your curve ball was off the charts. You caught their cleanup hitter looking twice. You really had command of the inside of the plate."

"When I took the mound in the top half of the fourth and we were only up 2-1, I felt like I had to be careful of my pitches. One wrong pitch, a hanging fastball that a batter clobbers out of the park and the game is tied or you find yourself on the losing end and it's in the late innings. But then in the bottom of the fourth when you sent that curve ball over the right field fence, giving us the lead 5-1 I was able to relax more. It's always nice to have a cushion to fall back on."

Drew yawned. "Well, nonetheless the year is just under way and we're 1-0. It was a long day, but it turned out to be a good one."

Sipping at a cup of coffee that had grown cold, Harley made a face and laughed, "Any day you get to play baseball is a good day. And *we,* the lucky ones, got to play two games. That game we won back down there in Magnolia was important because we got the season off to a good start but the game we played on that old field with the Dunbaugh brothers and their friends was the best game I've been involved in for years. It reminded me of when I was just a kid and how I spent hours in my backyard practicing. Those young boys, Timmy, Tommy and the others? They didn't have a pot to you know what in and yet they were happy, didn't have a worry in the world. And ya know why. Because they have baseball. They may not realize it now, but someday when they're older and faced with all the problems there are in this world, they'll be able to look back and know that the days they spent playing ball on that old field were the best days of their lives."

Drew smiled in agreement while Harley pulled his ball hat down over his eyes and spoke softly, "I'm gonna get me that nap now."

CHAPTER 25

DREW AND HARLEY WERE SIDE BY SIDE AS THEY walked across the practice field of Missouri State. Tossing a ball into the air, Drew caught it in his leather mitt and turned his attention to Harley. "Your fastball really had some zip to it this afternoon at practice. The ball is coming out of your hand perfectly. Your release point is going to be very difficult for batters to pick up. Your curve was especially good today. It's catching the outside corner and riding back over the plate. Very hard to read. I think later this week when we go down to Western Kentucky, the Hilltoppers are going to have their hands full."

"I hope so," said Harley. "We've lost two straight games since we were down in Magnolia. Right now, we're sitting at 1-2, but if we can win this weekend that'll put us back at .500 which is more respectable."

Approaching the first base line, Harley noticed a familiar sight. A Cardinal red sportster lowrider, it's distinct sound reverberating across the vast field. Pointing his glove in the direction of the paved road that ran next to the field, Harley smiled as he thumped Drew on his shoulder. "That's my dad. I wonder what he's doing here on campus."

Rich was just dismounting when he placed the shiny chrome kickstand in position when Drew and Harley approached. Harley waved, smiled and asked, "Hey Dad...what's up? What brings you up this way?"

Rich gave the two boys a forced smile and addressed Drew rather than Harley. "Drew, I was wondering if Harley and I could have a moment."

Drew tucked his mitt under his right arm and responded, "Of course. Look, I'm just going to go back to the dorm and grab a quick shower. I'll see ya later, Harley. Maybe we can grab a bite."

Pointing at a set of metal bleachers, Rich suggested. "Let's sit down. There's something I want to discuss with you."

Harley could tell by his father's tone something was wrong. Seating himself on the bottom row of seats Harley asked, "Is everything all right at home?"

Rich hesitated in his answer and slowly responded, "No, everything is not okay..."

Before Rich could finish his answer, Harley interrupted, "Is Mom okay?"

"Your mother is fine...it's Ozzie."

"Is he sick...what?"

A tear ran down Rich's cheek. "I'm so sorry son, but Ozzie died last night..."

Interrupting again, Harley with a tone of doubt denied what his father had said. "No, that can't be. I just saw him last weekend when I was home. He was fine. We were out in the backyard and just like always he chased that old tennis ball of his back and forth across the yard. He laid next to the pitcher's mound like he always does while I practiced throwing at the tire. He was perfectly fine. He can't be gone...he just can't be!"

Wiping the tears away from his face with a white handkerchief, Rich tried his best to explain, "He died from a heart attack...at least that's what the vet said. Your Mother left Ozzie out late afternoon like she always does, even threw the ball for him a few times. Later in the evening she called him in to eat but he didn't come running. So, she went out to fetch him and she found him curled up on that old rug he liked to lay on out in the garage. She thought he was sleeping, but it turned out he was gone. When the Doc arrived, following a quick examination he told us that more than likely Ozzie died in his sleep which is a good thing because he didn't have to suffer. Your mother said he passed away doing what he always liked to do...chasing his ball. I know that none of this makes things any easier, but we just thought that you might feel better knowing he didn't suffer, but died in peace."

Harley laid down his glove and wiped his eyes, got up and walked to a chain link fence that bordered the field. Leaning on the fence he looked out across the ball field. From behind he heard his father's concerned voice, "Are you going to be all right, Son?"

Turning, Harley faced his father and shook his head in sadness. "I knew this day would come sometime. I just didn't expect it so soon."

"Your mother and I talked about that. Do you know how old Ozzie was?"

"No, I guess I never thought about it."

"Sixteen…he was sixteen years old. That's pretty old for a dog. The doctor said that in dog years that equals about one hundred and twelve human years give or take. In short, Ozzie lived a very long life."

Sitting down again, Harley formed a sad smile on his face. "I know you're right about that, Dad, but it's just hard to accept. We've had him ever since I was three-years-old. He was just a pup when I was first learning how to throw a baseball. He's been with me out there in our backyard every day of my dream of becoming a major league pitcher. I can't even begin to tell you how many tennis balls he ran down over the years. He was the best friend any kid could have ever wanted. Rain, snow, sleet, hail, hot or cold, he was always by my side while I practiced. He was a good dog, wasn't he, Dad?"

Wiping his eyes again, Rich responded with a chocked voice, "Yeah, he was. Listen, your mother and I talked at great lengths about waiting until after you pitch this coming Saturday before telling you about Ozzie, but the more we talked it out the more we realized how upset you would have been if we didn't tell you right off. That's why I rode over here today. We thought it would be better to tell you face to face rather than over the phone."

"Thanks for coming today, Dad. Where is Ozzie now? Did the doctor take him away?"

"No, we decided that he should be buried out in the backyard. He loved it out there so much. We thought, that if you're up to it and if you can get some time off from school that you'd like to be involved in his burial."

"I would like to be involved. Actually, if it's okay with you and Mom, I'd like to bury him myself. Am I being too selfish?"

"No, not at all, Son. We figured that you might want to spend some alone time with him before you put him in the ground."

"Well, I better get moving then. I'll have to get permission to leave school, but I don't see that as a problem. If it turns out that I can't get back here by Saturday when the bus leaves for Kentucky, then so be it. Right now, I'm not concerned or focused on our next game. You always told me Dad, that whatever I focused on would reflect my feelings. There haven't been all that many moments in my life so far where I haven't focused on baseball, but Ozzie's death is one of them. I'm just going to go talk with whoever I need to about leaving school for the next day or so, then I'll drive home. I guess I'll see you and Mom later tonight. Thanks for coming, Dad."

"All right then, we'll see you tonight. Are you sure you're okay?"

"I've had better days, that's for sure. Ya know, I've driven from campus back to Arnold a lot, but the drive home today is going to be very hard."

"Be careful on the way home, Son."

Harley stood and watched as Rich mounted the chopper, waved good-bye and headed up the road. As Harley watched his father disappear in a clump of trees his thoughts were interrupted by the familiar voice of Coach Meadows. "I see you had a visitor."

Turning, Harley wiped at his eyes and gave a tearful answer. "Yeah, that was my father. He rode all the way up here from our home back in Arnold to tell me my dog passed away last night. His name was Ozzie and I had him for sixteen years. Coach, I've got to go home and bury my best friend. Who do you suppose I can talk to about getting some time off from school?"

Placing his large hand on Harley's shoulder, Meadows responded with a compassionate smile. "I can handle that for you, Harley. You just go on home and do what you have do. I'll speak to someone at the dean's office and explain that you had a death in the family, because that's exactly what it is. My wife and I lost our Collie last year. It was like losing a child. He was part of our family. So, you just go on and I'll take care of things. If you make it back by Saturday morning and still feel you're able to pitch, all right. But, on the other hand if you feel you're not up to it, we'll get by just fine."

Twenty minutes later, Harley was on the road headed for Arnold. Normally, when he journeyed back home he always tuned into one of his favorite radio stations, one of which happened to be a local sports talk show. Rather than turning on the radio he just drove along in silence. He couldn't get his mind off Ozzie's passing. The more he thought about it the more he realized the pain he was now feeling was greater than anything he had ever felt in the past. It was like a part of his life had been taken away from him, a part that could never be replaced. When he had returned to his dorm room Drew had been in the shower. Rather than telling him about Ozzie he just simply left him a note saying he had to head home for a personal manner. He knew he should have been more specific, as Drew would no doubt call Rich and Monica to find out what happened.

He recalled a conversation he had with his parents one night over dinner years ago. The topic had been that he would face problems in his life from time to time and anyone who expected to live a problem-free life was not very realistic. Problems could arrive on one's doorstep at any moment and without any previous warning. Problems have no feelings and they can and often do alter your life. It's not so much that problems occur in one's life, but how the individual deals with them.

He didn't look at Ozzie's passing as a problem but more of a serious letdown in his life. Ozzie had been such an important part of his childhood, being right there at his side through his Little League years right through high school. Ozzie had travelled the road of regimented routine of daily practice all those years, but now he was gone and Harley felt like he had to travel the rest of the journey by himself. Since he had gone away to college he didn't get to spend time every day with Ozzie and when he did come home on the weekends he always looked forward to seeing the black dog run up to the fence the moment he pulled into their driveway. In less than an hour he'd be pulling into the same driveway, but Ozzie would not be there to welcome him. He had tried his best to hold back the tears but suddenly he broke down and sobbed deeply. He couldn't imagine feeling any worse than he did at the moment. It almost seemed as if he were in a daze, the familiar sights of cars and trucks passing by on the other side of the highway, power lines, trees and buildings here and there suddenly had no meaning.

Soon, he found himself on the outskirts of Arnold and in just a few minutes he'd be home, the same house he had lived in for the first nineteen years of his life. Making a left hand turn onto the road that led to his home, he knew that soon his feelings of grief would increase. He wished that it was Saturday and that he was on his way down to Kentucky, but that seemed far away at the moment. He had to complete his final act as far as Ozzie was concerned. He had to lay his dear friend and companion in his final resting place. Pulling into the driveway he stopped the car and stared out into the backyard. He saw the tire hanging from the tree, his father's garage, the grape vine that ran along the fence at the end of their property. All these things and many others in that backyard he had grown up with, but now they meant nothing to him. Ozzie was gone.

Stepping out of the car, he hesitated and looked out at the backyard again. Normally when he came home for a day or the weekend from college he always met Ozzie out back and then they went in through the backdoor. He just couldn't bring himself to go out there. Walking to the front door he stopped and thought, *Here goes.*

As soon as he entered the house he saw his mother standing in front of the fireplace while she dusted off the mantle. Hearing the door open, she turned, gave him a gentle, caring smile, then went to him and hugged him and spoke softly, "I'm so sorry about Ozzie. Are you all right?"

Harley stared back at her and replied, "I'd like to say yes, but that wouldn't be the truth. I feel horrible, like my world has been ripped out from beneath me. When Dad came to see me he was quite upset. How are you, Mom?"

"We all feel bad about Ozzie, but we'll get through this and our lives will go on."

"I know this, but right now I find that hard to believe."

Holding him at arm's length, she smiled, "Drew called about an hour ago. He told us he got your note and was wondering if we were all okay. I told him about Ozzie. He said he was sorry and wanted to know if there was anything he could do."

"I feel horrible. I'm not doing so well. Where is Ozzie?"

"Your father placed him on the bed in the spare room. He just looks like he's asleep. Rich told me that you wanted to bury him by yourself. We're both okay with that. The doctor said we needed to get him buried today. Your father made a casket out of some plywood and he lined it with felt. He's out in the garage finishing it up as we speak. Why don't you go in and spend some time with Ozzie and then you can put him to rest?"

Wiping a tear from his eyes, Harley started across the living room, walked down the hall, hesitated and slowly opened the door. There was ol' Ozzie curled up in what appeared to be a sleeping position. Walking to the edge of the bed he sat and stroked the dog's head. How many times had he done that very thing over the past sixteen years? He recalled moments in the past when Ozzie had come to him for some attention and Harley had ignored him because he was too busy doing something else. Breaking down in tears he bent over and hugged his best friend and sobbed, "I'm so sorry, Ozzie. I'd give anything right now if I could only have you for one more day when you came to me. I'm going to miss you so much."

Running his hand over the black fur he felt the wetness from his tears. Getting up he went to the spare bath and returned with a towel and gently wiped Ozzie's back. Wrapping his pet in the towel he cradled him in his arms, walked out to the hallway then to the kitchen where his mother sat at the table peeling potatoes. Monica sadly asked, "Harley, are you sure that you want to do this all by yourself?"

Harley made his way to the back door of the house as he silently nodded yes.

Standing on the back steps that led down to the yard, he looked up at the sky, which had become cloudy. The wind had picked up and in the distance the sky was dark. His father walked from the garage carrying a pine box, pick and shovel. Seeing Harley on the steps he asked, "Where are you going to bury Ozzie?"

Slowly descending the four wooden steps, Harley walked to the rear of the pitcher's mound, stopped and gestured at the dirt at the rear of the circular area. "I think right here at the back of the mound. This is where Ozzie always laid while I was practicing my pitching."

Laying the box and digging tools on the grass, Rich looked at the distant foreboding sky and remarked, "Are you sure you don't want to wait until the storm passes?"

"No, that could last for hours and I want to put Ozzie to rest. Dad, I've never had to bury anyone before. I know that over the years we have attended funerals occasionally and I know they bury people at least six foot deep. How deep should I go for Ozzie?"

"I think about three feet should do. I'm just going to go on in the house and let you and Ozzie have some time together."

Laying Ozzie on the grass, Harley looked down into the casket. His father had done a good job; three-quarter inch plywood lined with beige colored felt. At the bottom of the homemade casket there was Ozzie's old frayed rug from the garage, two tennis balls and three large milk bones. Harley moved his head in agreement at the things his father was suggesting being placed in with Ozzie. Harley looked over at Ozzie, sadly smiled for a moment and then grabbed the pick and took his first bite of dirt from the back of the mound when a long roll of thunder sounded to the west.

It only took Harley a few minutes to shovel out the first foot of loose dirt, but then he began to hit rocks and hard clay. Laying the shovel to the side, he began to work at the rocks and clay when the first few raindrops starting to fall. Ten minutes passed when he figured he had gone down deep enough, a small mountain of small rocks, dirt and clay surrounded the open grave.

Removing the old rug, tennis balls and milk bones from the casket, he bent down and unwrapped Ozzie from the towel and then wrapped him in the rug, He couldn't bring himself to cover the dog's head. It seemed so final. Kissing Ozzie gently on his head, he gently lowered his friend down into the bottom of the casket, and then laid the tennis balls and the milk bones next to Ozzie. He smiled and lowered his head thinking about how peaceful Ozzie looked. Removing his Cardinals hat, he laid it on the dog's back then looked toward heaven and whispered. "When you get to heaven boy, I want them to know you're a Cardinals fan." Now, came the most difficult part; covering Ozzie with dirt. He reached down one last time and touched Ozzie's head almost expecting him to wake up, but he knew he was only fooling himself. He placed the lid on the casket and wept. Ozzie was truly gone.

A continuous roil of thunder peeled across the clouds somewhere above him and then a loud clap of lighting struck a few miles to the west. The sky opened up and the sparse raindrops turned into a pouring rain. A minute passed when Harley scraped the last few small piles of dirt in place and then tamped down the surface. Stepping back, he looked at the small mound where his friend laid buried. Throwing the shovel to the side he dropped to his knees in the wet dirt and raised his tear-stained face to heaven and awkwardly prayed, "God...it's me Harley. In the nineteen years of my life I've never come to you in prayer before. I believe my Mom and Dad are good people and I know in their own way believe in you and I guess I do too. That being said, I've never given you much thought one way or the other. I never found it necessary to call on you, but today...this moment is different. I don't know where else to turn."

Lowering his head, he wiped the combination of tears and raindrops from his face, raised his head toward the sky and continued, "I can't imagine why after all these years of only going to church a couple times a year that you would even consider listening to me now. Well this prayer isn't about me. You see...it's about Ozzie, my dog. If anyone deserves heaven surely it's our pets. It's said there's a place in heaven called the rainbow bridge, where humans cross and meet their pets and they live together forever in peace."

Harley grabbed a handful of wet dirt and held it up high. "I pray this is true because I have sent my dog to you. Please throw his tennis balls for him until the time that I arrive."

Placing the dirt back onto the top of the grave, he heard his mother's voice behind him, "Harley, you best come inside before you catch your death in this rain. Ozzie is in good hands now. Besides that, you've got a phone call. It's Mira. She knows about Ozzie and I told her you were out back burying him. She said that if you didn't want to speak to her right now that would be all right."

Harley slowly stood and soaked to the skin, his hair matted to his sad face, he answered, "I'll speak to her. Just let me get dried off."

After his mother entered the house, he bent down and patted the earth one last time and whispered, "You're okay now Ozzie. I'll see you someday on that bridge." Getting up he walked slowly up the steps and into the house where his mother waited with three large towels and a cup of hot chocolate."

Drying off Harley's head she stood back and inspected her son. "There now, at least you're dry. Are you sure you want to talk with Mira?"

"Yes, I'll just go in the living room and speak with her for a minute or so, and then I think I'd like to go to my room and lay down. It's been a rough day."

Sitting on the couch he picked up the receiver, took a deep breath and then spoke, "Mira...its Harley."

Mira's voice immediately had a calming effect on him. "I won't keep you long, Harley. When Drew found out about Ozzie from your mother he phoned me and asked if I knew what happened. That's when I found out about Ozzie. I'm so sorry he's gone. How are you doing?"

"Not all that well. I just buried him out in the backyard."

"Look, if it's too difficult for you to talk right now, we can talk later when you're up to it."

"Surprisingly, hearing your voice makes me feel better."

There was silence on the other end and then Mira asked, "Harley...do you need me?"

Harley thought and then responded, "Yes I do, but there's no sense in your driving all the way from Kentucky when I'm going to be coming down in two days with the team to play Western Kentucky."

"I was planning on driving down to watch you pitch on Saturday. I'll be there for you. Listen, I'm going to let you go. You're probably tired. I'll see you Saturday."

Harley listened as the phone went dead. Hanging up the phone he wished he was with her right now, but she was a few hundred miles away. Walking into the kitchen, he stood and watched his mother stir a steaming pot on the stove. "I think I'm going to go lay down. I'm not really hungry, so for now I'm going to skip dinner. Thank you for always being there for me, Mom."

Smiling across the kitchen she gestured with a large spoon. "You just go on and get some rest. I'll check on you later."

Harley sat on the edge of his bed and noticed the Cardinals pillows Ozzie loved to cuddle up in it. He looked around the room. You would have thought it was the room of a ten-year-old boy, a boy obsessed with baseball. He wasn't ten any more, but yet the room reflected his past years of deep interest in the Cards and his goal of becoming a major leaguer. There were Cardinal pennants for every year since he was one year old. There were team pictures of every team he had ever played on from T-ball through high school. His team hats from every team he had played on hung from hooks beneath a long shelf. There were assorted autographed pictures of players and memorabilia he had collected over the years. His room was a museum of his nineteen years of baseball. He teared up again when he saw the photo of himself with Ozzie when he was just a puppy. There in the framed photo stood a three-year-old boy holding a baseball in one hand and this small black puppy in the other. He lay back on the bed and placed his head where Ozzie used to curl up. *Things will never be the same ever again,* he thought.

He was awakened by a soft knocking on his door followed by his mother's voice, "Harley, is it all right if I come in?"

Looking at the Cardinals alarm clock on the nightstand, Harley sat up and answered, "Sure, come on in."

Sitting on the edge of the bed he stretched. He had slept for four hours. His mother entered with a tray of hot food and placed it on his desk. "That was some nap you had. I thought you might be getting hungry so I brought you up a plate."

Harley nodded a silent thank you but remained silent.

Monica sat on the bed next to him and asked, "Feeling any better?"

Getting up Harley walked to the window and looked out at the pouring rain, "Has it been raining this whole time?"

"Yes, it has."

Sitting on a chair at his desk he smiled at his mother. "Can I ask you something?"

"You know you can always ask me anything."

"Well, it's just that I'm a little confused. I understand and accept the fact that Ozzie has passed on. I guess I've got that figured out but there is something Mira said to me during our short phone conversation that's got my head whirling."

He stared at this mother as if he were waiting for an answer. Monica took a sip of coffee she had brought along and looked at her son. "You're going to have to be a little more specific than that if you're searching for some advice."

Scooting forward on the chair, Harley began, "During my phone call with Mira she asked me if I needed her."

"Okay," said Monica, "and what is so confusing about that?"

"I don't know what she meant."

"Let me ask you this. Did you answer her question?"

"Yes, I did. At the moment, I was feeling pretty alone so I said yes. Was that what I was supposed to say?"

"Well I'm not exactly sure. I wasn't involved in the conversation but I will say this. When you answered yes was it because she is a good friend or *your girlfriend?* There's a big difference in the two. You've been seeing each other now for going on five years. Where do you think your relationship with Mira is?"

Harley shot his mother an odd look. "You're kind of putting me on the spot with a question like that."

"It's not that hard of a question to answer, Son. You answered her question with a yes because you like her or *you really like her!*"

"Whoa, whoa, hold up there a sec." Harley looked out at the rain and then back to his mother. "I'm glad I decided to have this conversation with you rather than Dad, because this is getting a little awkward. By saying *really like her,* are you suggesting that I love Mira?"

Monica gave Harley a smile indicating that she understood his meaning. "Only you can make that type of a personal observation. That's between you and Mira. If I was her age and was seeing the same boy for almost five years I'd know what I meant. It seems to me she's reaching out to you with far more than just plain ol' friendship. Let me ask you something. Do you have feelings for Mira?"

Getting up Harley walked across the room. "This conversation is getting way out of hand. I can't believe I'm discussing the way I may feel about another female with my mother. In short, I take it you're saying she has feelings for me that go much deeper than just friendship."

"I guess maybe I am, but that's for you and Mira to work out."

Seeing that Harley was uncomfortable with the way his initial question had been answered, Monica changed the subject. "So, what are your plans for Saturday? Are you still going to pitch?"

Harley picked up the photo where he was holding Ozzie when he was a puppy and smiled. "Yeah, I'm going to stay the night then head back to Mizzou in the morning. That'll give me a day to relax and throw a few pitches. This may sound weird, but I think if Ozzie was here and he could talk he'd want me to pitch. I'm going to pitch the game on Saturday down in Kentucky in his honor."

Snapping her fingers, Monica reached into her shirt pocket. "Here, your Dad thought you might like this. When we first found Ozzie, we clipped a small portion of his fur off for you." Handing him a small plastic bag that contained a wad of black hair, she remarked, "Maybe this will bring you good luck."

Taking the bag, Hartley opened it and ran his fingers through the hair. "I'm going to hide this in my glove. Come Saturday those Hilltoppers will be lucky to get a single hit."

CHAPTER 26

HARLEY TAPPED DREW ON THE SHOULDER, BRINGING him out of a short nap as the bus pulled into the parking lot of L.T. Smith Stadium at Western Kentucky University. "Drew...we're here."

Drew grabbed a small knapsack from beneath the seat and looked out the window.

Coach Meadows met each player when they stepped from the bus and gave them instructions. "The locker rooms are through that door on the left of the building next to the playing field. Let's get in there and get suited up. I'll see you all on the field in a half hour."

Sitting on a wooden bench in front of a long row of lockers, Drew slipped on his spikes and addressed Harley who was buttoning up his Mizzou Jersey. "With any luck, three hours from now we'll be logging our second victory of the year and you'll be 2-0 for the season."

"That's the plan," said Harley. "Western is off to a great start. They're 4-0 and their best starter is on the mound today. It's our job to make sure after the game that they are 4-1, not 5-0. Let's get out there and toss a few. I want to work on my cutter a little bit. Coach Meadows told us this team thrives on the fastball, so if we expect to win we're going to have to mix things up some...keep them off balance."

"Drew pounded his fist into his mitt and stood. "All right then...let's do this!"

They no sooner stepped out of the building when their attention was caught by Mira's voice, "Hey guys! I just got here a few minutes ago. Are you guys ready to kick some Western Kentucky butt?"

Drew, realizing Harley would appreciate a moment alone with Mira, walked up a concrete walkway that led to the stadium and commented, "I'll just leave you two to say your hellos. I'll see you out at the bullpen."

Drew disappeared around a corner, at which point Mira gave Harley a kiss followed by a hug. "It's so good to see you. How are you feeling?"

"Well, I don't know if I'm a hundred percent," said Harley, "but I'm in the high nineties. I've got three things going for me today. I've got you in the stands, Drew behind the plate and this." Holding up the tiny plastic bag that contained Ozzie's hair, Harley explained, "I've got Ozzie right here with me. Three better friends a pitcher could not ask for. Listen, I can't talk long. I've got to get down to the field. I hope you understand?"

"If it was any other girl than me, they probably wouldn't understand. You just go on and get ready for your game. We've got all the time in the world, but right now you've got a game to pitch."

Giving her a quick peck on her cheek, Harley backed up the walkway and held up his glove. "See you after the game. Have a hotdog for me."

By the time Harley arrived at the bullpen, there was Drew already in his crouch position at the plate as he moved his shoulders back and forth and rotated his neck. Seeing Harley approaching he tossed him a ball and shouted, "Let's start off with a few easy tosses then we'll get into your fastball."

After lobbing the ball back and forth for a couple of minutes Harley waved his glove indicating that a fastball was next. He gripped the ball by placing his index and middle fingers perpendicular to the seams, his thumb, ring and little fingers on either side of the ball. Following a routine bullpen windup, he released the ball. After it slapped into the catcher's mitt Drew fired the ball back and yelled, "Nice movement. Now give me one up and in."

Following three more fastballs, Harley gripped the ball in preparation of delivering a floating curve. After releasing the ball, he watched it trim the outside front corner of the plate and then tail back. Jumping up after making the catch, drew fired the ball back and yelled with confidence, "That pitch right there will give these hitters the fits!"

Meadows gathered the team in the visitor's dugout for a short meeting and addressed the young men sitting in front of him. "Boys, this game is important. We are currently on a two game losing streak, which we need to snap today with a victory. We've got Harley on the mound for us. He got us our first win and I am confident that he can repeat his performance from Magnolia. Let's get him some runs early on in the game so there is not so much pressure on him. If we can jump on this team right out of the starting block, I think Harley can shut them down. Now, let's go win this game."

Fifteen minutes later, Harley stood on the mound with an early lead of two runs. In the top half of the first inning Missouri's leadoff hitter hit a line drive to the shortstop that bounced off his glove. He recovered but hurried the throw, which sailed over the first baseman's head permitting the base runner to advance to second with ease. Two deep sacrifice flyouts in a row enabled the runner to score. A double and a single created their second run of the inning and the final out came from a strike out.

Westerns' first batter stepped up to the plate and took Harley's first pitch, which was a slow curve on the outside corner for a called first strike. The next pitch was another curve in the same identical spot but with a little more mustard on it. Another called strike. Harley watched the batter move closer to the plate as he anticipated another pitch just off the plate. Harley knew the batter had to protect the plate and more than likely would not let another pitch that was close go by for a called third strike. Drew called for the next pitch, which Harley agreed with. Gripping the ball, Harley whispered softly to himself, "You're toast, pal!"

His third curve in a row started on the outside but quickly moved to the inside crowding the batter. Moving his arms away from the plate, he heard the ump yell, "Strike three...you're out!"

The next batter went down on five pitches and the final out of the inning was recorded as Drew caught a lazy pop-up behind the plate. The first inning was concluded. Missouri 2 - Western 0. As the Mizzou team ran from the field Mira jumped up waving her cane and yelling, "Give 'em the what for, Harley." It was then she noticed a group of five students who were giving her the evil eye.

She smiled back at them realizing she was probably the only spectator who was rooting for Missouri.

In the bottom of the third, Harley stood on the mound with a 3-0 lead thanks to an opposite field home run by his right fielder. In the second inning, he had fanned the first two batters and the third batter grounded out with a lazy grounder to the third baseman. Two innings were under his belt and so far, not a hit. He was now facing the bottom third of Western's lineup. He recalled what he had been told. This was a hitting team and they were good all up and down their lineup. He hadn't thrown a fastball yet and as long as they were willing to back off of his curve, he'd continue to use it. The first batter struck out, taking a low curve for a third strike. The second and third batters both grounded out to his second baseman. Three innings down and Harley found himself up with a three run lead.

Sitting in the dugout Drew took a seat next to him and explained. "All right, we've been completely through their lineup. They've all see you once and you've got their number…so far. Their manager, if he's any good is going to instruct his team to start going after your curve. Knowing this, we have to go in another direction. They may still be waiting to see your heat, but I think we should give them a steady diet of cutters, sliders and changeups. They are going to come out hard their second time around. What we need to do is change where their eyes are focused. They'll be out to attack your curve. We'll counter this by throwing the ball farther off the plate. I'm guessing that they'll go after some bad pitches. If we can get through the next inning or so with junk pitches, we can always go to your fastball later in the game if we need to. One inning at a time, Harley. How do you feel?"

"I'm feeling pretty good. I've got a three run cushion and I feel my curveball command has been effective. I've also picked up on the fact that these hitters like the top half of the strike zone. I agree that they will be looking for the curve but if I keep the ball breaking down maybe we can carve them up their second time around."

The leadoff batter took three practice swings, stepped in the box and looked out at Harley who was twirling the ball in his hand. Harley reviewed his first encounter with this batter. *I made him look foolish his first time at the plate. He'll be looking for some payback.* Drew called for the curve on the inside. Harley nodded and wound up. The ball was too far inside and the ump called, "Ball one!"

The next pitch was again too far inside. "Ball two!"

The next two pitches were on the outside corner but were fouled off bringing the count to 2-2. Drew signaled for a fastball down the center. Harley knew it was a good call. The batter would be looking for yet another curve. The ninety-seven mph fastball crossed the plate as the batter stepped back, fooled again. "Strike three!"

The batter turned to walk back to the dugout and flashed a quick smile out to Harley, indicating that that would never happen again. Harley smiled to himself. The next batter attempted a bunt but Drew fielded the ball cleanly and threw the runner out with room to spare. The third batter of the inning nonchalantly stepped into an inside curve and was awarded first base. The next batter hit a hard grounder to the second baseman who flipped the ball to the shortstop covering second base. The fourth inning ended with Mizzou still up 3-0 and Western still hitless.

At the bottom of the seventh inning Drew placed his arm around Harley just before they stepped across the third base line. "In case you haven't noticed the way this game is going you've got a no-hitter going into the seventh. You've faced their entire lineup twice now and they still haven't figured you out."

Harley slapped drew on his shoulder with his glove and answered with confidence. "I know we've got a no-no going on here but to tell you the truth I just want to win the game. We fooled all their hitters twice. It's going to take some real creative pitching if we expect to get through these last three innings keeping them hitless."

Drew smiled and started to walk backwards toward the plate. "One batter at a time, Harley. One batter at a time!"

The leadoff batter stared out at Harley for the third time during the game. So far, Harley had thrown one fastball and it had been to the hitter he was now facing. He had completely fooled this hitter in two plate appearances. Harley shook off Drew's signs for a curve and then a slider. Drew shot him the signal for a fastball and

Harley agreed. The ninety-eight mph pitch was right down the pike. The batter was ready, swung and missed for the first strike. Smiling back at Harley the batter dared Harley to throw another fastball. Harley was not going to play his game, he was in control. He decided to offer up another fastball but keep it way outside. Maybe the batter would bite. The batter swung at the pitch and fouled it down the first base line. *Again,* smiled the batter. This was raw power against power pitching. Harley nodded back at the hitter but then delivered a changeup which the batter swung through for the first out."

Harley was now confident that his fastball would work on occasion with this team. The next pitch, as soon as it left Harley's hand let him know that it was going to hang too long over the plate and the second batter of the inning slammed a liner down the third base line, which the third baseman stabbed at the last fraction of a second recording the second out of the inning. Harley received the ball in his glove and took a deep breath realizing that the great fielding effort of his third baseman had saved a sure hit. Harley tipped his hat to his infielder and then turned his attention to the third batter in their line-up. It was a pinch hitter; a player Harley had not faced yet. Harley decided to go back to the curve. The batter fouled off the first two pitches and then hit a towering fly ball that cleared the fence in foul territory. Drew looked back out at Harley and gave him a look indicating that that was a close one. Harley switched his grip for a cutter. The pitch was exactly where Drew called for it but the batter got the barrelhead of the bat on the pitch and it sailed toward the center field fence. Grady Kinzer, Missouri's center fielder back peddled, slammed into the fence and snagged the ball, but the collision with the fence knocked the ball loose and it popped out of the fielder's glove into the air. Miraculously, Grady recovered, reached out and gloved the ball before it hit the ground. Harley looked toward the sky and thought, *Seventh Inning over!*

In the top of the eighth Mizzou picked up another run on a walk, a stolen base and a sacrifice fly to score their fourth run of the game. On the way out of the dugout for the bottom half of the inning, Drew reassured his pitcher, "Harley, we got you an insurance run. Don't worry about the ninth. Just get the three outs this inning. We'll worry about the ninth when it gets here."

Harley walked the first batter of the inning after feeding him six curves in a row, four that the batter didn't bite at. Drew walked out to the plate and removed his mask. "Okay so you walked a man. It's not a big deal. Let's keep the ball in the lower part of the strike zone. If he does manage to hit the ball maybe we can force a double play or at least get a force out at second."

Harley's first pitch was in the dirt, which Drew scooped up and came up ready to throw to second but the runner made no attempt to advance. The next two pitches were low, a ball and a strike. Drew signaled for Harley to keep his pitches down and on the next pitch, the batter got over the ball and hit a roller toward Harley, who fielded the ball, turned and fired to second. The second baseman caught the ball stepped on the base and completed the double play with a bullet to first. The next batter hit a high pop up which the first baseman caught with ease. Harley walked off the mound and pointed his glove at Drew and thought, *Just one more inning, just three more outs!*

Drew sat down in the dugout and started to remove his shin guards, as he was the first batter in the top of the ninth. It wasn't even five minutes later when he walked back to the dugout and placed his bat in the rack, sat and shrugged his shoulders at Harley. "Everybody strikes out now and then." The next two batters struck out and while Drew was getting his gear back on he commented, "That's the worst inning we've had this year at the plate. But, here's the thing. We're still up four runs. They've got to be frustrated. They haven't even gotten a hit let alone a run. As far as I'm concerned, we've got this game in the bag. Now the only question is whether you can pull off a no-hitter. How's your arm?"

"A little tired but I think I can go another inning."

Coach Meadows broke in on their conversation. "If you weren't on the verge of tossing a no-hitter I'd pull you and bring in a reliever. The season is just getting started and I don't want my star freshman pitcher to get injured. Are you sure you can go another inning without stressing your arm?"

"No problem, coach. I've got a couple of tricks up my sleeve for this last inning."

"Well, I'm not so sure you need any tricks. You just keep pitching like you have for the first eight innings of this game and we'll walk away with the victory. You'll be facing the bottom third of their order. We've got a four run lead and mathematically we should win this game. If you get in any trouble out there…any type of trouble, I'm going to pull you."

Harley grinned confidently. "Coach, they're not even going to get a hit. I guarantee it!"

"All right Harley. Let's see what you've got left in the tank."

After the coach returned to the dugout, Harley winked at Drew and explained. "The surprise I have in store for Western is really pretty simple. I just don't want you to be caught off guard. I'm going to switch to my short stride delivery and mix in some knuckle curves."

Drew raised his mitt and started for home plate. "If that doesn't sound like a combination of confusion for a hitter then I don't know what is. You just give me the ball where you want it. You're in control."

Harley assumed his position out on the mound, dug his cleats into the dirt in front of the rubber and watched the first batter for the bottom of the ninth. The batter stepped into the box and looked out at Harley who gripped the ball for the knuckle curve. Thumb running along the lower seam, index finger bent down pressing hard on the ball, middle finger on the upper seam and ring and little fingers on the opposite side of the ball from the thumb. Looking down at his hand in the glove he thought about the knuckle curve and how he had used it sparingly over the few years he had thrown it. Overuse of the knuckle curve, or the spike curve as it was commonly referred to, could create blisters that would affect his pitching performance. The knuckle curve was a combination of three different pitches, a curveball, a breaking ball and a fastball. This triple-threat pitch was hard to pick up by the batter. His knuckle curve had a lot of topspin and broke late.

Placing his right foot on the edge of the rubber he let the ball relax in his hand but then tightened his grip as he nodded at Drew. The ninety-three mph combo pitch broke toward the batter who swung and missed, the ball passing over the plate. *Strike one!*

Drew fired the ball back and went down into his catcher's position ready to receive the next pitch. Harley positioned his fingers for a four seam fastball, as this particular batter hadn't seen his heat yet. The ninety-eight mph pitch painted the outside edge of the plate as the batter took a big cut, missing the ball a second time. *Strike two!*

Harley, receiving the ball again turned away from the batter and faced the outfield fence and pondered the next pitch. *Knuckle curve,* he decided, *but with a short stride delivery.* Turning back, he faced the batter, who was already in the box. Harley wound up but the batter stepped out, trying to throw Harley's timing off. Harley stepped off the rubber and composed himself. The batter stepped back in and waited. Gripping the ball, Harley decided to take a little extra time before his windup, making the batter wait for him. Nothing was going to happen until he delivered the pitch. He was in command. The knuckle curve came out of his hand earlier because of the short strive, giving the batter less time to read the pitch. The ball broke downward toward the lower part on the bottom of the strike zone. The batter decided that the pitch was low, tried to hold up, but swung through the pitch for a called strike three. Drew fired the ball back to Harley and shouted confidently, "That's one down. Two more to go!"

The second batter of the bottom of the ninth walked to the plate, knocked some loose dirt from his spikes with his bat, stepped in and prepared himself for Harley's first pitch. Harley decided on the short stride fastball. This batter had struck out once and hit a pop-up. The ball creased the inside corner at ninety-five mph. The batter held up for a called strike one. Receiving the ball from Drew, Harley thought, *Mix it up...keep them guessing! Time for the knuckle curve.*

Gripping the ball, Harley looked in at Drew and pictured the tire in his backyard and thought about Ozzie. Stepping off the rubber, he turned and looked at the back of the mound where Ozzie always laid while he was practicing. He whispered to himself, *Here goes...Ozzie!* Turning back, he faced the batter once again. Winding up he delivered the pitch, the knuckle curve heading for the center of the plate but then fell out of the strike zone. The batter, completely confused swung and missed. Strike two.

For the next pitch, Harley decided on a high fastball, which the batter fouled off, the ball bouncing off the screen behind the plate. Harley followed up with another high heater. The batter caught a piece of the ball, which slammed into Drew's glove. Second out of the inning. The batter slammed his bat down on the ground and walked back to the dugout. "One more," yelled Drew. "One more!"

Harley slapped the ball down deep into the webbing of his glove. His forefinger brushed the plastic that held Ozzie's hair and he smiled to himself. *Thanks for being here with me today, boy.*

Western's ninth man in the order stepped up to the plate, another pinch hitter. Coach Meadows walked out to the mound. As he approached Harley frowned and asked, "Don't tell me you're taking me, coach?"

"No…it's not that. You're doing fine. I just wanted to inform you that this kid at the plate can really hit. He rarely strikes out and has a good eye for the ball. He's actually their starting catcher. He's on the DL list right now, but he can still hit. I'd hate to see him ruin your no-hitter. Maybe we should give him a free pass and pitch to their lead-off man who you have struck out three times. It's up to you, Harley. We've got this game in the bag. It's just you and this batter now. You've got a great defense to back you up."

Harley smiled back at Meadows. "Don't worry coach. I've got this guy. I'm not going to give him anything good to hit."

"Okay then. Let's get this man out and then celebrate."

At Harley's side, Drew took in the conversation and after Meadows left the mound he looked in at the 6'2" 220 pound catcher who stood in the batter's circle swinging his bat. "This guy could pose a problem for us," said Drew. "He's their best hitter plus he's a catcher which means he used to seeing all sorts of pitches. You're going to have to be careful with this hitter. I'm sure he'd like nothing better than to put the kibosh on this no-hitter you've got going. How do you want to pitch this guy?"

"We're going to quick pitch him. He just came in the game. He's probably a little tight from sitting on the bench. If we don't give him a lot of time to think in between pitches we might screw up his timing. I'm going to start him off with a curve way off the outside of the plate then I'll come back with a knuckle curve, then fastball in and then a cutter and then another curve. If he makes it through that series then we'll talk. I'm going to short stride the first curve and the fastball. As soon as you throw me the ball back I'm not going to wait long before the next pitch. He's probably looking to do damage and we need to keep him off his game."

"All right, I'll get the ball back to you immediately after each pitch."

The batter prepared himself for the first pitch, adjusting his batting gloves and hat. He looked comfortable, relaxed. He had no sooner swung the bat the when Harley quick pitched him with a short stride curve outside of the strike zone. The batter was taken by surprise but held up, the ball too far out. *Ball one!*

As planned, Drew threw the ball back to Harley instantly. The batter stepped out of the box, but then back in and hadn't even taken a practice swing when Harley released the next pitch, a knuckle curve. Not ready for the pitch, the batter signaled for time out and backed off the plate. Before the umpire could react, the ball grazed the inside corner. S*trike one!*

The batter complained claiming that he had called time, but the ump said he had waited too late. The batter further complained that the pitcher was not giving him time to set up. The umpire told him to get back into the box and that the pitcher could throw the ball whenever he desired before time is called. The batter cursed under his breath, spit and stepped back into the box and glared out at Harley.

Harley wasted no time in the delivery of the next pitch as he went to the fastball, the ball on the outside of the plate but moving in. The batter gritted his teeth and hammered a line drive down the first base line, the bat shattering in a number of pieces. The ball was just foul and Harley breathed with relief. A few inches to the left and he was looking at a base hit. The count was now 1-2, pitcher's advantage. The batter stayed out of the box, not allowing Harley time to deliver another quick pitch. Finally, he stepped in and Harley quickly wound up and threw his next planned pitch, a cutter that was moving down on the plate. The batter timed the pitch perfectly and swung, the upper part of the bat connecting with the ball. It was a screaming shot directly back at Harley. Harley didn't even have time to think as he raised his glove to protect his head and the ball slammed into the leather knocking him back to the mound. The next thing he knew Drew was running toward the mound, tossing his mitt into the air and yelling, "No-hitter, no-hitter!"

Before Harley could get to his feet he was mobbed by the infielders while they threw their gloves and hats in every direction. Beneath the pile of squirming ballplayers Harley looked at the ball in his glove and whispered, "Thanks for being here Ozzie!"

Harley was the last one to get up from the pile as he looked over at the Hilltoppers dugout. The last of the opposing players were walking off the field. So much for any congratulations from the losing team. Then he saw Mira standing next to the railing on the visitor's side of the field. Getting up, he told Drew that he'd be along soon. He just wanted to say goodbye to Mira. Walking toward the fence, he crossed the first base line and was just about to say something to Mira when he was interrupted by a strange voice, "Congratulations there, young man." Turning he saw the Hilltoppers' manager approaching while he extended his hand. "That was quite a game you pitched this afternoon. I've been coaching ball here at Western for nine years and that's the first time we've ever been on the losing end of a no-hitter. I have to apologize for my team not coming over and shaking your hand. I guess they're a little embarrassed. We're slated to take our conference this year. This was the first loss of the season. Was that a knuckle curve you were throwing the last inning?"

Harley, always polite, answered, "Yes sir…that's right…a knuckle curve."

"Your name is Sims…that right?"

"That's correct, sir."

"And you're just a freshman?"

"Again, that's right."

"Well, Mr. Sims, it was a pleasure to watch you work out there today. I look forward to seeing you next year when we play again. If we have to face you next year, I'll be ready! Good luck with the rest of your season."

Harley watched as the manager walked off then turned back to speak with Mira, but was interrupted a second time by yet another stranger.

"Excuse me, young man."

Harley turned and found himself confronted by a burly looking older man with balding hair and a wide smile. The man offered his large hand and spoke in a deep voice, "Name's Buck Tillman…head scout for the Cleveland Indians. And you'd be…?"

Harley reached out and grasped the man's hand and answered, "Harley…Harley Sims."

"Am I to understand you're just a freshman up there at Mizzou?" Before Harley could respond the man continued, "When

I drove down here today I didn't expect to see a no-hitter. No one ever does because they're so rare. I really came down here to scout Western's lead-off man, Felix Martin. He's a senior. We've had our eye on him since he was in high school. He's got game when it comes to hitting the ol' baseball. So far, well except for today, he's batting just over .400. As a pitcher, I have to say you handled him quite well. Struck him out three times. You had their entire team fooled. I like the way you handle yourself. The way you quick pitched their last batter was amazing, not to mention throwing in a short stride combined with a knuckle curve. Let me ask you? Are you interested in a major league career or are you just playing ball while going to college?"

"I am interested in being in the majors and I'm not just playing ball while in college. It's the opposite. I'm going to college while I'm playing ball. I've had a goal of becoming a major league pitcher ever since I was five."

"Well if you keep on pitching like you did today you're going to have every team in the American and National League knocking on your door. Do you have an agent?"

"No, I have to finish up with my education before I'd even consider signing with a major league team. It's an agreement I have with my folks. Along with becoming a pitcher in the bigs I also must complete college."

The man smiled and handed Harley a card. "The only thing better than a ballplayer is a smart ballplayer. Here's one of my cards. I'm going to be keeping tabs on you for the next four years. I hope you'll remember this conversation when you're ready for the big stage." Tipping his hat, he backed away, "See ya around Harley Sims."

Harley watched Tillman walk away and then approached the fence where Mira was waiting. He apologized, "Finally, we get to talk. I'm sorry we were interrupted...twice!"

Mira grinned and held out her hands, "It must be your lucky day. A no-hitter, a congrats from the manager of the opposing team and then to top things off, a major league scout. The limelight is on you this afternoon."

Leaning on the fence, Harley hung his glove over the edge. "It is my lucky day, but it has nothing to do with any of the things you mentioned. It's my lucky day because you're here. I meant what I said earlier in the week when we talked. I do need you."

"Well if you aren't the nicest young man I've ever met. You always know the right thing to say."

The voice of Coach Meadows rang out from the other side of the field. "Sims, come on. Our bus leaves within the hour."

Turning back to Mira, Harley apologized again, "I'm sorry, but I've got to go. I know we didn't get much of a chance to speak before the game and it looks like we're not going to get any time now either."

"Harley...I know that and I understand. Look, I have an idea. If you're not busy next weekend, maybe you could drive down to my uncle's farm outside of Lexington and spend the weekend. He has hundreds of acres and over forty horses. We could do some riding, ya know, just have a relaxing couple of days."

"Right now, that sounds like a great idea to me. We're got two home games this week. One on Tuesday and then another on Thursday. I'm not pitching either game. Friday I have two classes, the second one ends at one o'clock. I can be on the road by one thirty. How long of a drive is it?"

"About six hours. I'll call you later in the week to give you directions. Listen, when you get there I've got a surprise for you."

"A surprise...what is it?"

"Now, if I told you that it wouldn't be a surprise, now would it?"

Coach Meadow shouted again, "Sims...now! Hit the shower and get dressed."

Mira reached across the fence and touched Harley's face and gave him a long kiss, backed away and said, "Now shoo. The sooner you get on that bus home the sooner we get to spend the weekend."

CHAPTER 27

HARLEY PULLED OUT OF MIZZOU AT EXACTLY ONE thirty-five Friday afternoon. He was looking forward to the upcoming weekend with Mira. He tuned into a local sports station as he cruised down the highway. The Cards had gotten off to a rough start in May losing four straight games. Two in Cincinnati and two in Houston. Four hours passed by quickly and he found himself crossing the bridge spanning the Ohio River into Louisville, Kentucky. Just a couple more hours and he'd be arriving in Versailles.

His thoughts returned to his current situation of just hurling a no-hitter. When he returned to the campus he had called his folks and gave them the rundown of the game, the fact that he had thrown a no-hitter the highlight of the call.

On the Southside of Louisville, he picked up Route 264, and then took 64 South toward Frankfort, Kentucky. He passed a billboard advertising the Cincinnati Reds. He thought about it and realized that in this part of the country the Reds were the closest major league team there was.

His daydreaming about how the Cards had done early in the season almost caused him to miss the turnoff from Route 64. Exiting at the last second onto Route 60, Versailles, according to Mira, was just up the road about sixteen miles where he was to take the by-pass around the town onto Lexington Road. Down the highway four miles on the right he'd see nearly a half mile of black fencing and eventually two stone pillars topped with a fancy wrought iron sign that read, Bluegrass Breeze Farm.

Traveling down Route 60 he passed a number of horse farms, each one displaying what seemed like an endless maze of black fences with small groups of horses grazing in the late afternoon sunshine. Mira had told him that the area around Versailles was known for horse breeding and training, not to mention Thoroughbred and Standard bred horses. There were also a number of farms that dealt with Saddlebred Pleasure horses. Mira said that there were eighteen well-known horse farms around the Versailles area, many of which he was now passing.

On the outskirts of Versailles on Lexington Road he passed two farms, Three Chimneys and Rock Hill, and finally pulled over at the Bluegrass Breeze entrance. Like most of the farms he passed on the way in there was a long paved road flanked on either side with more black fencing. He noticed while passing the previous farms that all of the buildings, probably horse barns and stables, were a pristine white topped with gray roofing and fancy looking cupolas. The Bluegrass Breeze barns and stables were also bright white but sported a deep blue color to their roofs. *Strange,* he thought.

Passing beneath the wrought iron sign he noticed a small lake on the left, surrounded by more fencing. On the right, he saw what appeared to be open, endlessly rolling green pastures. On the opposite side of the lake there were a number of barns and stables, all sporting a blue roof. The paved road took a sweeping right turn and there seated on top of a gently rising hill stood the main house of Bluegrass Breeze. Pulling up in front of the two story, stone pillared home, he came to a stop at the top of the circular drive. Stepping out of the car he saw Mira sitting on a porch swing on the right of the long front porch. Getting up, she raised a glass and yelled, "Welcome to Bluegrass Breeze!"

Grabbing his small single suitcase from the backseat he waited while she, with the aid of her cane, made her way across the porch to the front steps. Climbing the stone steps, he met her at the top where she placed her cane on a white wicker chair, gave him a hug and smiled into his face. "How was the trip down?"

"Very pleasant, your directions couldn't have been better." Placing his suitcase next to his feet he gestured at the surrounding landscape and went on, "You were right about all of the horse farms on the way in. Are they all as nice as this farm seems to be?"

"Most of them are nicer...more extravagant that Bluegrass Breeze. My uncle owns one of the smallest farms in the area. By most standards two hundred acres would be considered a large farm, but some of the farms down here cover well over a thousand acres. We have just over forty horses here at Bluegrass whereas many of the farms house hundreds." Taking him by his arm she suggested, "Grab you bag, and we'll head on into the house. My Aunt Bessie has prepared a late evening feast in honor of your arrival. I told her you'd be arriving around seven and it's just ten after now. My Uncle Ray is out in the back forty cutting down some dead trees. He said he'd be in around seven thirty. You're going to just love Bessie and Ray. They are so down to earth."

Standing in a large foyer topped with a modest crystal chandelier, Harley admired a huge walnut, carpeted staircase that led to the second floor. To the right a large liquor cabinet and on the left he could make out what appeared to be a den. Stepping into a large living room they were greeted by a tall, big boned woman with short grey hair and a broad smile. "Welcome...welcome to our home." Wiping her hands on an apron surrounding her waist, she extended her right hand.

Harley took the woman's hand while Mira made the introductions, "Bessie, this is Harley, the boy I've been telling you about. Harley, this is my Aunt Bessie."

Shaking the woman's hand, Harley spoke graciously, "It's nice to make your acquaintance. You have a beautiful home."

"Thank you, Harley." Turning to Mira, Bessie suggested, "Why don't you show Harley up to the room where he'll be staying. Dinner will be served in the dining room at eight. Ray should be here soon. We are so looking forward to getting to know you, Harley."

Leading Harley up the stairs, Mira explained, "I think you'll really like my uncle. He's a big sports fan. I think you'll have a lot to talk about."

At the top of the stairs they made a left and entered a long hallway and stopped at the first door on the left. Opening the door, Mira stepped back and held out her hand. "This is the room you'll be staying in. You can wash up if you want and unwind before dinner. I'll see you downstairs after you get freshened up." Kissing him on the cheek, she turned and started for the stairs. "I'm so glad you're here. It's going to be a great weekend."

Harley entered the country-style bedroom, laid his suitcase on the bed and walked to a large window that overlooked a maze of fencing that stretched to the north. He watched while three horses walked slowly down the fence line, stopped and then started to graze. Walking into the washroom, he turned on the spigot and splashed cold water across his face. He was glad he was going to get to spend some quality time with Mira.

Twenty minutes later, Harley descended the stairs where he stopped, not sure if he should venture into the dining room or just take a seat in the living room. From out of the den walked a tall, lanky man with a shock of blondish-red hair. Seeing Harley standing next to the stairs the man offered his hand. "You must be Mira's friend, Harley."

Harley shook the man's hand and responded, "Yep, that'd be me! You must be Uncle Ray!"

Pumping Harley's hand, the man laughed, "Like you said…yep, that'd be me! The girls just informed me dinner would be in about fifteen minutes. Why don't we sit down and get to know one another?"

Harley followed Ray across the room and took a seat in a comfortable recliner. Ray sat on a couch across from him and gestured toward a large picture window and asked, "So tell me Harley, what do you think of Kentucky horse country?"

"Well," said Harley, "I'd have to say it's quite beautiful. I do have a question maybe you could answer for me."

Ray sat back and crossed his right leg over his left. "Fire away."

"I was wondering about all the barns and stables at the various farms I passed. All of the buildings are a bright white with grey roofing, but your place is different. The buildings are white but topped with a deep blue. Why so different from all the other farms?"

"This is wildcat country. Ever since I've been knee high to a grasshopper I've been a University of Kentucky Wildcat basketball fan. Always will, I suppose. That blue color on the roofs represents their school color. Around these parts that deep blue is as important to some folks as the red, white and blue of our nation's flag. Down here you're deep in college basketball country. Woodford County, which is where you currently are and the surrounding counties are known for three main things; Kentucky Bourbon, horses and basketball, but not necessarily in that order depending on who you talk to. Basketball down this way is a way of life for a lot of folks young and old."

Mira entered the room and announced, "Soup's on! Bessie says it's time to be seated."

Ray stood and spoke to Harley, "After you, my friend."

Harley trailed Mira into the dining room where there was a long maple table. Ray sat at the head of the table, Bessie on his left, Mira on the right and then Harley. Harley took in the feast that was spread across the end of the table. Country fried pork chops, baked beans, mashed potatoes, glazed carrots, a huge bowl of salad, a pitcher of iced tea and a bottle of red wine. Ray held out his hands, signifying they join hands and then he proceeded to bless the meal. The blessing complete, Ray stood, clapped his hands once, picked up the plate of chops and handed it to Harley. "Why don't you get things rolling, Harley."

Harley stabbed a large chop and then followed with a scoop of potatoes and one helping of everything else passed his way.

Pouring himself a glass of wine, Ray offered to fill Harley's glass, but Harley politely declined. "No thank you...tea will be fine for me."

Cutting into his chop, Ray directed his next remark to everyone at the table. "Just before dinner I was telling Harley about the obsession people here in Kentucky have with Wildcat basketball."

"Yes, and that's not all," said Bessie. "Up in Louisville where my sister lives the state has the Louisville Cardinals, our in-state rival. This is definitely college basketball country. I see it everywhere I go, be it a city or small town. You don't see young kids tossing a football or baseball around. There is always a basketball hoop attached to a garage or a barn where you see kids constantly at practice. Speaking of Louisville, ya know it's funny. There are quite a few people up there who have either graduated from The University of Kentucky or who support the Wildcats along with Louisville alumni and supporters. I'd say it's about 60-40 in favor of Louisville over Kentucky. You see folks up there wherever you go either wearing Cardinal red or Kentucky blue. Now, down here it's different. I think it's safe to say that probably ninety-five percent of basketball fans side with Kentucky, while the remaining five go for Louisville. It's rare, to say the least, to see anyone in these parts wearing Cardinal red."

Swallowing a bite of potatoes, Harley confirmed, "What you have described to me sounds about the same way baseball fans feel in St. Louis. We have a professional football team and a hockey team as well. All of the high schools and colleges have basketball and football but baseball reigns supreme. Up my way, if you travel down any street or out to the country you see kids tossing a baseball around, rather than a football or basketball. You can see people everywhere you go, the grocery store or the mall or downtown wearing St. Louis Cardinal sweatshirts or hats. The people up there wouldn't even consider supporting any other major league team. And, just like your Wildcats have their rival, the Louisville Cardinals, we have our own rival, that being the Chicago Cubs. You'd be hard pressed to find anyone in the St. Louis area walking around with a Cubs hat or jersey on. I guess every part of the country has its own special team they root for."

Ray sipped at his wine and spoke, "Mira here tells me and Bessie you're quite the ballplayer. Said you pitched a no-hitter last week over in Bowling Green against the Hilltoppers."

Harley laid his fork down and stated, "Yes, I did. I didn't grow up much different than kids down here in Kentucky who spend hour after hour of their youth tossing a basketball at a hoop in hopes of one day playing in the NBA. There hasn't been a single day since I've been five years old that I haven't spent practicing my craft...which is pitching. When I finish up my college days three and a half years down the road, my goal is to be signed by a major league team."

Bessie was impressed. "You say you've never missed a day of practice. Mira told us you were nineteen, almost twenty years of age. That means you've been practicing daily for nearly two decades. That's quite admirable."

Holding up his index finger, Harley corrected Mira's Aunt. "Almost every day. I really didn't start practicing until I was three and then there was an eight week period back when I was ten where I broke my arm and I couldn't practice, at least very effectively."

Ray laughed. "Well I think we can give you a pass on that."

Everyone laughed and Mira smiled across the table at Harley, glad that he was getting along so well with her Aunt and Uncle.

The late evening dinner continued, mixed with varied conversation about Mira's schooling and how well she was doing, how busy the horse farm was this time of year and Bessie's three-acre garden at the edge of their farm that kept her hopping.

Finally, pushing a small plate to the side that had contained a slice of homemade apple pie, Ray stood and stretched. Checking his watch, he apologized, "You'll have to excuse me. I'm going to retire to the den. I always get an hour of Bible reading in before I turn in for the night."

Bessie stood as well. "And I've got to get these dishes washed and the leftovers put up."

Mira took her last swallow of pie and arranged her dirty plates and silverware in a neat pile. "Let me give you a hand."

"No...no!" objected Bessie. "You have a guest to entertain. It's such a nice evening out. Why don't you show Harley around the farm? I'll take care of everything in the kitchen. You two young folks just go on."

Mira refilled her glass of iced tea and offered to fill Harley's as she agreed. "All right, we'll just head out to the front porch and go from there."

Harley picked up his drink and followed Mira across the dining room and complimented Bessie. "The meal tonight was wonderful."

Leaning her cane against the side of the house Mira set her tea on a wicker end table and sat on an oversized hanging swing and patted the seat next to her. "Have a sit!"

Harley plopped down and looked out across the circular drive, the large water fountain and the manicured grass, then off into the distance. "Is all of Kentucky this beautiful?"

Mira curled one leg beneath the other and made herself more comfortable. "Some areas of the state are even more beautiful. Myself, I'd be happy someday when I'm settled down to live right around here."

Harley, interested, asked, "Explain settled down? I've never thought about that much myself. It seems like I've got a lot to do before I ever reach that point in life."

Mira looked Harley directly in his eyes and responded, "Ya know, get married, have a nice house and some kids. That's what most people do eventually. Your folks, my folks and millions of other people. I guess that's what makes the world go 'round."

Giving Mira and odd look, Harley emphasized, "I understand that. I'm just saying that someday, who knows, maybe we'll travel that road together."

Mira was about to take a drink but then set her glass back down and stared at Harley in amazement. "Why Harley Sims, if I didn't know you better I think you may have just asked me to marry you. Surely, that was not your meaning!"

Embarrassed, Harley sat forward on the swing and looking in the front window of the house as if they were being overheard, whispered, "No, that was not my meaning, but since that particular subject has suddenly been brought up there's something I want to get off my chest. And I say this in a positive way. I need to clear up what was on my mind just before I pulled in earlier this evening."

Mira didn't respond so Harley continued, "It's just that ever since Ozzie died I've kind of been on an emotional roller coaster. Then, on top of that I go and somehow manage to throw a no-hitter, and that's more emotion that I'm still trying to figure out, especially after talking with that major league scout. Anyway, when you called the house last week right after I buried Ozzie we talked on the phone and you asked me if I needed you."

Mira, deciding to speak, smiled broadly, "And you answered...yes! That made me feel good."

"Well, I'm glad that one of us seems to understand what's going on because after I hung up talking with you I was confused."

"Confused...about what?"

Harley pointed at himself and then Mira. "About you and me and where we are. After we hung up the other day I had about a half hour talk with my mother about this boy-girl business."

"You mean the birds and the bees' discussion every parent has with their children?"

"No, it was not that intense. I told her I was confused about what you meant by needing you. She explained to me that you might have become more than just a friend. After she talked with me I've been rolling this relationship stuff around in my head for over a week and I've come to the conclusion that I really do need you. I mean, I really like you, if you get what I'm saying."

"I know exactly what you're saying, Harley. We've been seeing each other now for going on five years. In all that time, I never even considered seeing another boy."

"I feel the same way about you."

Moving closer to Harley, Mira took his hand in hers and looked into his eyes. "Let's clear this confusion up. If you were to ask me right here and now or anytime in the next couple of years to marry you, I would not answer with a yes. But I wouldn't say no either. It's just not the right time yet. We both have over three years of college left and then I have my career as a vet and you're going to be in the majors, so talking about marriage right now, just doesn't fit. I say we take a rain check, which means that more than likely based on what we both just said that you'll ask me sometime in the future and I'll say yes. So, if you're okay with what I just said we'll just put this on hold for now. How's that sound?"

Sitting back, Harley let out a long breath and squeezed her hand. "That sounds great. It's like we know that it's probably going to happen and right now we don't need to worry about it."

Squeezing his hand back, Mira agreed, "I guess that does sum things up."

Leaving go of his hand she took a drink and winked. "Let's talk about something you're more comfortable with...baseball!"

Harley grabbed his tea. "That's right down my alley!"

"When I was at the game against Western we didn't have much of an opportunity to speak. I've been thinking about what I saw you do against the Hilltoppers and it was nothing short of amazing."

"That's what everyone keeps saying to me, but in all actuality, it was just another game."

"I don't think you give yourself enough credit for how well you pitch. I'll admit that a no-hitter is rare, but this is not a first for you. It may be your first no-hitter in college, but if I recall when you, Drew and I attended a Cardinals game right after we graduated, you told us that at that time you had thrown four no-hitters. I know that two were when you were in pony ball. When were the others?"

"They were both in Little League which I can hardly take credit for. A good Little League pitcher can overwhelm most Little League hitters."

"But still," emphasized Mira, "now you have five no hit notches in your baseball career belt. The percentage of pitchers at any level of baseball that have thrown one no-hitter let alone five has to be extremely low. There have been, are now, and always will be great pitchers in the majors who will never throw a no-hitter. To tell you the truth, Harley I don't believe the world has seen your last no hitter."

"There will be more no-hitters to come," said Harley, "but I don't know if I'll be throwing them." Throwing his hands in the air in a comical fashion Harley joked, "You're supposed to be showing me around the farm and so far we haven't got off this porch."

Grabbing her cane, Mira stood and pointed toward one of three stables. "Let's walk down there so you can meet some of my uncle's horses."

Walking across freshly cut grass, they passed through a gate and onto a paved one-lane road. Harley took in a deep breath of the evening air.

Opening the door of the first stable, Mira spoke proudly, "You are about to meet some of my Uncle Ray's best Kentucky Saddlebred stock."

Closing the door, Mira explained, "A true Saddlebred horse is American bred. They can be trained for numerous duties like barrel racing, competitive jumping, trail driving, carriage horses or just for pleasure riding. If you want to purchase a quality Saddlebred horse, Uncle Ray here at Bluegrass Breeze is the man to see."

Turning, she displayed the stable. "This is stable number one and the horses kept here are our breeding stock. As you can see they are taken care of quite well. These horses are worth quite a bit."

Trailing Mira past twelve stalls, six on either side, Harley looked into one stall after another and commented in a joking fashion, "These horses are cleaner than most people and their stalls are spotless."

Stopping at the last two stalls, Mira reached out and ran her hand across the nose of a tall brown and white mare. "This is Bernice. Tomorrow when we go out riding you'll be on her." Turning, she gestured at the opposite stall. "That's Sam over there. I'll be riding him. By the way, you did bring your ball glove and a baseball along…correct?"

"I did," said Harley. "You said that when we went riding we were going on a picnic and that we were going to toss the ball around a little. That reminds me. You said you had a surprise for me. What is it?"

Walking through another door at the end of the stable Mira laughed, "You'll find out about the surprise tomorrow." Looking at her watch she started toward the next stable. "It's almost ten o'clock. Let's say we see the other stables, then hit the hay. You're probably tired from the long drive following a day at school. We both need to get some rest. Tomorrow is going to be a busy day for us."

Harley felt a hand on his shoulder and then a soft voice, "Harley...time to get up. We've got a lot to do today."

Staring out the upstairs bedroom window at the early morning sunrise, he yawned and turned his head only to see Mira hovering above him at the edge of the bed, a wide grin plastered on her face. "Time to get up, sunshine! You've got ten minutes to shower and be downstairs for a big country breakfast, then it's off to the stables where Bernice and Sam await. Uncle Ray has already eaten and said he'd have the horses all saddled up for us at eight. That gives us about twenty minutes to eat. Bessie has packed a large picnic lunch for us to take along." Retreating out of the room, Mira reminded him, "And don't forget your glove and ball."

Standing on the porch next to Mira, Harley patted his stomach. "That was some breakfast. I don't know if I'll be able to eat our picnic lunch later on."

Starting down the front steps, Mira gestured for him to follow. "Don't worry, by the time lunch rolls around you'll be plenty hungry. Between riding and something else I have planned you'll work off that breakfast."

"Work off? I wasn't planning on doing any work this weekend. I thought we were going to relax. I hope your plans for the day do not involve herding cows and pulling weeds from a garden."

"No, nothing like that. C'mon, let's head down to the stable and get this adventure underway."

Approaching the stable they saw Ray standing next to two horses while he inspected the cinch on the taller horse. Seeing Mira and Harley he waved and confirmed, "Everything's ready to go, Mira." Petting Sam on his head and stroking his mane, Ray continued, "Got a lunch your Aunt made for you two right here in the saddlebags and your glove and a softball are also in there.

Where're ya headed?"

Mira, opening the gate to a small corral nodded to the east. "I thought we'd ride back to the edge of our property and then ride over to Rock Hill."

Mira mounted Sam. Harley, who had ridden with Mira no less than twelve times over the past few years, followed by stepping into the stirrup and hoisting himself up onto Bernice. Hanging his ball glove over the saddle horn, he opened the saddlebag and dropped in the ball he had brought along. Mira guided Sam through the gate and after Harley took Bernice out of the corral Mira kicked the gate shut and pointed east. "We'll follow the fence line of Uncle Ray's place all the way to the back edge of the farm, then we'll cut over into Rock Hill. There's a special place I want you to see over there. Rock Hill is much larger than Uncle Ray's place. I met Horace, that's the owner, when I first moved down here. He told me I was welcome to ride on his property any time I wanted. He's got hundreds of wooded acres. It'll take us about an hour of casual riding to get to the place I want to show you."

Guessing, Harley asked, "And that's the surprise…this special place?"

"No, that's not the surprise, but that's where it will take place."

Arriving at the fence that separated the two farms, Mira turned north and asked, "Didn't you say your next game is with Kent State?"

Following the fence line, Harley answered, "Yep. Drew and I will be going for our third win this year."

"So, what did your folks think about that scout from Cleveland talking with you after the Western game?"

"My Mom said she was pleased the man noticed my talent and that all my hard work over the years was starting to pay off. My Dad reminded me there would probably be many scouts during my college days that would approach me and that I had to keep my focus on graduating. He also reminded me many college ballplayers have gone on to the majors without graduating from school. Then when their ball careers were over, be it the minors or the majors, they wound up just another broke ballplayer with no education to speak of."

"How do you feel about that?"

"I think it's the right thing to do. I mean…let's face it. Twenty years in the majors is pretty rare. Most players only last for ten to fifteen years at best. Take my case. I'll be twenty-two when I graduate. I'll play minor league ball for at least a year or two before they call me up. That'll put me at twenty-four, so that means if I last twenty years I'll still be pitching at forty-four which is highly unlikely. Most players stop playing in their mid to late-thirties. That means that I've got to invest the money I make pitching in the bigs so I'll have enough when I retire from baseball. At that point, depending on how much I've salted away I may never have to work again, but I'll still have my business degree to fall back on."

"Sounds to me like you've got everything figured out."

"Everything has always fallen right in place for me, especially when it comes to playing baseball. I know I'm a lot closer to my goal of pitching in the majors than I was years ago. I've really worked hard to get to where I am now. If anything ever happened that would prevent me from being a major league pitcher, why I don't know what I'd do. It's like running a race and I'm approaching the finish line. I just don't want to fall down now that I'm getting so close."

Pulling up on the reins, Mira dismounted and opened a rusted cattle gate. Motioning Harley through, she handed him Sam's reins and then closed the gate. Remounting, she pointed at an old dirt road that disappeared in the trees. "We take that road for about a half hour and then we'll be at our destination."

Moving Bernice forward, Harley inquired, "So, what's it like to go to the University of Kentucky?"

"So far? I'm really enjoying myself. My instructors are great and I get to work with some great students who share my love for horses. I'm enjoying my time here in Versailles. They tell me when I get my degree from Kentucky as an equine vet, I can write my own ticket."

Fifteen minutes passed as they rode along taking in the beauty of the Kentucky countryside and talking about whatever came to mind. Finally, the road ended at a small clearing next to a crystal clear creek that ran next to a grassy meadow surrounded by tall cedar trees. Stopping next to the creek, Mira dismounted and held out here hands. "We're here...this is the spot."

Climbing down, Harley watched while Bernice joined Sam who

was lapping at the cool water from the creek. "You come here often? It seems so peaceful here."

"I usually ride down here two to three times a week. It is peaceful. I usually sit over there by that big cedar and just relax." Grabbing her glove and a softball from her saddlebag, she nodded at the creek. "Step down and bring your glove and the ball you brought along. The horses can stay here by the water. They'll be fine."

Stopping next to the large cedar, she dropped her softball on the ground and pounded her glove. "Let's play some catch so we can get warmed up."

Harley gripped the ball in his hand and asked, "Warmed up for what?"

"That's the surprise. After we toss the ball back and forth for a few minutes, then you'll find out what the surprise is. Give me some off speed stuff and then I'd like to see that knuckle curve you're so good at throwing. If you'll stand on that tree root over there, it's about the same distance from the pitcher's mound to the plate."

Locating a protruding tree root a few feet to his right, Harley ran his right foot through the dirt and grass in front of the root. Positioning himself in the customary pitcher's stance, he nodded at Mira and announced, "Here goes!"

A sixty-mile per hour curve ball slapped into Mira's glove, which she caught and threw back with little effort. Next, Harley threw a slider, followed by three more curves. Throwing the ball back to Harley, Mira stepped forward and pointed her glove at him. "I'm ready for that knuckle curve now."

Harley waved his glove at Mira. "Have you ever caught a knuckle curve before?"

"No...this will be a first for me."

"Well get ready then, because it approaches the plate differently than most pitches. Ready?"

Mira smiled and slapped her glove. "Bring it!"

Harley gripped the ball, relaxed, and then released it from his right hand with less velocity than he would normally throw the pitch. Mira caught the ball as she exclaimed, "Wow, you're right. The ball moves up and down and sideways all at the same time. I can see how this pitch could be very hard to hit. Let's see it a few more times."

Minutes passed when Mira picked up her softball and walked to the tree root. "My turn."

Confused, Harley asked, "What do you mean? Don't tell me you intend to pitch?"

"Exactly! This is the surprise. I've been working out at the university gym. My doctor said that if I can improve my leg and especially my arm strength then I could pitch again. I've been working on this for months and now I'm ready to show you."

Harley stepped off the tree root. "Are you sure about this? You don't have to prove anything to me."

Mira placed her hands on her hips and looked Harley square in his eyes. "Now listen to me, Harley. I've worked hard to get to the point where I am now so you just go over there by that flat rock out in front of the tree and getting ready to catch!"

Harley walked to the rock and stepped on it. "This one?"

"Yep, that's the one. I put it there a few weeks ago. It's about seventeen feet out from the tree which means it's almost forty-three feet from this root; the distance for fast pitch softball. All you need to do is assume the catcher's position and I'll pitch."

Harley squatted down and held his glove up. "Ready when you are."

Mira placed her right foot on the tree root and then her left. Holding her glove and the ball directly in front of her waist, she stepped back with her left, then in one smooth motion she pushed off with her right while moving her right hand in a windmill motion. The ball left her hand at precisely the same moment as her left foot made contact with the grass. The ball, with just a slight arch, slapped into Harley's glove.

Harley threw the ball back to Mira, stood and smiled. "That was amazing. How fast was that?"

Catching the ball, Mira stepped back on the root. "Just over forty. That's the best I've been able to manage so far. I can't put too much pressure on my leg, which is where a lot of the power in fast pitch comes from. I have to depend mainly on my arm strength. The doctor told me I'll never be able to play competitively, but just to be able to simply pitch makes me feel good about myself. That's the surprise. I can pitch again!"

Going down on one knee, Harley asked, "Do you want to throw

more?"

"Sure, but right now I'm only good for maybe ten to fifteen pitches, then I'm worn out."

Minutes later, Mira and Harley sat by the big cedar and drank from bottles of water. Leaning against the tree, Mira became serious. "Harley there's something I want to share with you, that is, if you're up for some advice."

Harley crossed his legs Indian style and responded, "Advice is always good…but advice on what?"

"Look, I don't want to stir up any bad memories and if I manage to do that I'm sorry. I know that deep inside you're hurting because of Ozzie's death. You had him in your life for sixteen years and now he's gone. I know you loved him. It's hard in life when we lose someone or something we love. When I had my accident and thought I'd lost my ability to ever pitch again I felt I lost something I loved dearly. Prior to the accident, I was well on my way to being a superstar in women's fast pitch softball. But that was taken away from me. I was bitter for almost two years when the minister at our church said something one Sunday that's stuck with me ever since. He said that in life there would be times when God takes something from us…something or even someone we may love. He stated that we must be prepared to let go of some of the things we love…but we must never let go of God's hand. I never forgot that and despite the fact I was bitter I never turned my back on God. I kept my faith and kept hold of His hand. Today, pitching to you is proof that God will reward us if we keep hold of Him. So, my advice is that even though inside you may be hurting, keep a tight hold on God. He can get you through anything."

Standing, Mira pounded her fist into her glove. "I feel like throwing a few more."

Harley grabbed his glove and laughed, "You were right about being hungry by the time we lay that picnic out. Between the ride out here, playing catch and your surprise pitching demonstration, I have a feeling I'm going to be hungry!"

CHAPTER 28

HARLEY STOOD ON THE PITCHER'S MOUND OF TAYLOR Stadium, often referred to as Simmons Field on Mizzou's Campus. The stadium was capable of seating just over three thousand and yet the crowd watching was no bigger than a typical Little League game. Maybe he had been wrong when he told Uncle Ray and Aunt Bessie that where he came from it was baseball that reigned supreme. *No, he hadn't been wrong!* Baseball, as a major sport, was top dog in the St. Louis area, but here in Columbia he found himself two hours away from St. Louis.

Drew slowly walked from home plate out to the mound, his mitt in his left hand, his protective mask in the other. Spitting on the ground, he nodded out toward center field and asked, "Have you taken a look at the scoreboard lately?"

Harley turned and gazed out toward the green, elevated scoreboard while Drew related to him the game stats. "We've got a six run lead. Kent State, in case you haven't noticed, has no runs and no hits. You've pitched seven innings of no hit ball. I didn't want to say anything because you seem so zoned in. Some of the guys in the dugout asked me just before we came out here for the top half of the eighth, if you realized you had a no-hitter going. I don't want to throw you off your game, but we're six outs away from your second no-hitter this year. I just thought you might want to know that."

"Thanks for the concern," said Harley. "You've been calling a great game behind the plate. To be honest, I'm more nervous than when we were down at Western. That seems odd because this Kent State team has shown minimal power at the plate, and that's the worst thing that can happen. There has been many a no-hitter screwed up by a batter that seems like an easy out."

"That's right. You'll be facing the bottom two-thirds of their lineup. These, what we hope, will be the last six batters have faced you twice. This line up is left handed heavy and five of the last six we have to face are lefties. So far in the first seven innings you've struck out fifteen. These last six batters have contributed for nine strike outs. Out of those six their cleanup hitter is by far the most dangerous. He hit two sharp line drives to the right side of the infield. A few inches either way and they could have both been hits. We need to be careful with this guy. He likes the fastball so I say we feed him a steady diet of off the plate braking stuff. Then in the ninth, once we get by him the only other threat is their eighth place hitter. He popped up once and hit a screamer that our third baseman snagged. Now, let's go to work."

Walking back to home plate Drew put his mask on, stood and waited for the first batter of the eighth. Kent State's cleanup man looked like a hitter with broad shoulders and muscular arms. Stepping into the box he stared out at Harley with confidence. Harley knew he would be looking for the heat. Drew signaled for the knuckle curve which he had not thrown so far in the game. Harley nodded in agreement, gripped the ball, took a deep breath, hesitated and let it go. Expecting a fastball, the batter swung early and was way out in front of the ball for strike one. With the ball once again in his hand, Harley waited for Drew's next signal, an inside changeup. The ball started for the center of the plate but then tailed off, crowding the batter. Thinking the pitch was too far inside, he pulled back his hands but the ball bounced off the bat handle and fouled off for strike two. Harley smiled when Drew signaled for the short stride fastball. The pitch was a blazing ninety-eight mile an hour fastball right down the tunnel. The batter swung for the fence, missed and fell to the ground when he lost his balance. The umpire pumped his arm and hollered, "Strike three!"

Harley started the next batter off with a curve that was too far out, then came back with another curve closer in that was called a strike. The count 1-1, Drew called for the next delivery, a heater up and away. *Excellent pitch!* thought Harley. The pitch crossed the plate outside the strike zone just above the batter's shoulders. The man swung but got under the ball hitting a lazy pop up to the infield."

Harley held the ball and looked out at his three outfielders, then around the infield. He could hear the chatter of his teammates:

Come on, Harley...get this last out!
Nobody reaches base...nobody!

Give 'em the heat!

The sixth man in Kent State's order came to the plate and Harley hesitated. Drew called time and walked out to the mound. Facing away from the batter, Drew asked, "Are you okay. You seem to be overthinking this next batter. You struck him out twice before. How is your arm?"

Facing center field as well, Harley answered, "My arm is fine. This guy has a good eye for the plate. He took me to a full count twice. He's not going to swing at anything that's not close."

"Look," said Drew, "Let's keep the ball down on him. C'mon, let's get this last out, go sit in the dugout and get ready for the ninth."

Back at the plate, Drew bent down and signaled for a low two-seamer. Winding up, Harley let the pitch rip. It was headed for the dirt but the batter swung and golf balled it to the right of the shortstop who fielded the ball on one hop and fired to first base for the out.

As Harley crossed the first base line a stiff blast of wind swept across the infield creating a small dust storm that blew a napkin and a paper cup past his feet. Shielding his eyes from the infield dust with the aid of his hat, he jogged to the safety of the dugout, sat and poured a cup of water from the large orange circular cooler at the end of the bench. Drew joined him and looked out at the field as the dust picked up again. Grabbing a cup of water himself, he stated, "Good news, bad news!"

Harley handed his cup to Drew indicating that he wanted a refill and asked, "What are you saying?"

Seating himself next to Harley, Drew handed him back his cup and explained, "The good news is that if this wind keeps up it's going to be even more difficult for the hitters to pick up your pitches. The bad news is your control could be altered by the wind. We may have to go with mostly fastballs, which are far less likely to be affected by the wind. We're going to need all the speed you can muster to counter this wind. Maybe it'll die down before we go back out there, but if it doesn't we need to have a plan. Fastballs, Harley…fastballs!"

The first batter for Mizzou went down swinging and when he returned to the dugout, Drew signaled him down to the end where he and Harley were seated. "Okay Marty, how's the wind out there?"

"The first two pitches were not that bad, but then the wind picked up and the ball was all over the place. That last pitch that I struck out on was a curve way outside. I held up and the wind moved it right over the plate before I had time to react. It's a real crapshoot in the box." The next two hitters went down as well, the second batter striking out and the third hitting a slow roller to the first baseman.

Grabbing his catcher's mitt, Drew stepped out into the wind and held up his hands. "Let's go see what Mother Nature has in store for us…*and Kent State!*"

Harley walked slowly out to the mound and watched while small clouds of dust blew here and there between first and second base. The sky was getting darker while the flag in center field flapped wildly as the wind picked up even more. Turning, he faced Kent State's first batter of the ninth. Drew called for a curve and waited. Harley didn't hesitate, wound up and let loose, but the ball was right at the knees of the batter for a called ball one. Four pitches later, the batter had worked his way to a full count. Harley turned and faced the outfield. *Heat down the middle,* he thought, *heat!*

The wind picked up and Harley stepped back off the plate waiting for the wind to back off. He stepped back on the rubber and concentrated on the center of the plate. The wind was still strong but weaker than what it had been. Harley wrapped his fingers abound the ball and prepared to throw a four seamer. *No sense waiting any longer. Throw the ball!*

The ball left his hand just when an untimely gust of wind blasted across the infield. Harley could feel his arm move ever so slightly to the right. He knew instantly that the ball was going to move to the inside of the plate. The batter watched the ball as it approached the plate, started to swing but then pulled back. "Ball four!" signaled the ump.

The batter threw his bat to the side and trotted down the first base line while Drew called time and walked to the mound. Removing his mask, he looked over at the man standing on first. "Okay, so we walked a man. Don't worry about him. We're six runs up. Keep the fastballs coming."

Harley looked around the stands. Most of the sporadic fans that had been watching had left because of the wind. *Crazy!* he thought. Here he was in the midst of tossing a no-hitter and there was no one watching, at least at far as it went for fans or students. Nonetheless, he had to get this next man out. Five fastballs later, the batter had struck out after fouling off two pitches. "That's one," yelled Drew. "Two more outs."

Harley's first pitch to the next batter was low and bounced in front of the plate, the ball glancing off Drew's mitt and rolling to the backstop. The runner on first advanced to second standing up.

The next batter. On the first pitch, hit an outside curve deep to center field. The center fielder caught the ball while the runner on second ran down to third. "Two outs," signaled Drew. "Let's get this last batter."

Harley, ball in hand, stared over at third at the runner, who was taking a large lead. On the first pitch to what Harley hoped was the final out of the game he noticed the runner was coming pretty far off the bag. Standing on the mound he watched as the runner took his lead. The runner took another step and then another, then took a step back and then a larger step toward home. Before the runner realized what was happening Harley stepped off the rubber and fired the ball to the third baseman, who applied the tag to the runner who had been caught too far from the bag. Game over!

A loud clap of thunder sounded and then the rain started to fall. Kent State's team quickly vacated the field while Harley's teammates gathered at the mound to celebrate not only the win but also their second no-hitter of the year. All of the players eventually headed for the dugout and the locker room while Drew stayed behind with Harley. Watching their teammates run from the field, Drew looked up at the sky and commented, "Bring it on, Mother Nature. It doesn't make any difference now." Looking at his best friend he noticed tears in Harley's eyes. Concerned, he asked, "You okay, Harley?"

Wiping his eyes with the back of his hand, Harley sniffled, "I'll be all right. I was just thinking about my ol' pal, Ozzie. You go on with the other guys. I just need a moment alone. I'll be along soon."

Slapping Harley on his backside with his mitt, Drew understood. "See ya in a few."

Harley watched Drew disappear down onto the confines of the dugout then raised his face to the sky allowing the rain to mix with his tears. It was only a few seconds when he was interrupted by a voice, "Harley Sims!"

Turning, Harley saw a man holding a folded newspaper over his head to prevent him from getting too wet. Sticking out his right hand, the man spoke again, "Buck Tillman. Surely, you remember me from that no-hitter you tossed down at Western two weeks back."

Wiping the mixture of tears and rain from his face Harley answered, "Yeah, I do remember you. You're the head scout for the Cleveland Indians. What brings you all the way out here to Mizzou?"

"I wanted to see you pitch again *and* you didn't disappoint me. Right after the game down in Western I flew back to Cleveland and told those who I answer to all about you. You would think that a freshman in college throwing a no-hitter would make people sit up and pay attention, but that's not the case. I mean, let's face it. You're not the only college kid to ever toss a no-hitter. You have to understand how major league baseball works when it comes to locating new blood. There are always new prospects on the horizon; players who look really good, that have the potential to play at the major league level. There is always some kid somewhere that scouts really like. I really wasn't able to convince them that you are as good as I think you are, so I decided to come over here to Mizzou and watch you pitch again. I expected to see some good pitching, but not another no-hitter! You've really got what it takes to make it to the majors. And another thing while I'm thinking about it. The way you picked that runner off at third was nothing short of amazing. When I go back to Cleveland and tell them that you threw another no-hitter it's going to cause people to sit up and take notice. I have no doubt, that you, Harley Sims, are major league material."

"I don't want to sound like I'm ungrateful for your interest in my future," said Harley, "but I think you're giving me way too much credit. I'm not trying to tell you how to do your job but I think that pitchers get way too much credit when a team wins a game. Take these two no-hitters I threw. If it wouldn't have been for some downright fancy glove work and speed from my infielders and outfielders I wouldn't have those no-hitters to my credit. And then there's the catcher, Drew. Without his baseball genius I wouldn't have been capable of getting through the lineups we confronted. Listen, I've got to get out of this rain. I'm sure I'll see you again. I can't promise you another no-hitter, but I'll give it my best. Nice to see you again, Mr. Tillman!"

Harley joined Drew in the showers and grabbing a bar of soap stepped under the hot water. "Just after you left that scout from Cleveland, ya know, the one who talked with me down at Western approached me before I got off the field."

Drew smiled, "So he came back to have another gander at you…that's good. I mean, two no-hitters in less than two weeks. Back to back games in your case. That has to be some kind of record in college or maybe even in the majors. You keep pitching like you have the last two games and you're going to capture the interest of many a major league scout." Drew allowed the water to wash away the soap from his body as he remarked in amazement, "The way you picked that man off over there on third was nothing short of incredible. No one saw it coming…especially the runner. I couldn't believe it!" Changing the subject, Drew commented, "I think we deserve steak dinners tonight. Dinner is on me."

Stepping out of the rear exit door of the stadium locker rooms, Drew and Harley were confronted by the rain that was now coming down in torrents. Standing beneath an overhang, Drew pointed across the wide expanse of open ground they had to cover in order to get back to the dorm. "Looks like we're in for a wet journey."

A female voice got their attention, "Excuse me, boys. I've been waiting for you to come out." Sitting on an old pile of tires sat a girl in a bright yellow rain slicker.

Drew looked at the girl closely and asked, "Do we know you? Why would you be waiting for us?"

The girl held up a legal pad and an ink pen. "You don't remember me from earlier in the year…do you?" She removed the hood on the rain slicker and Drew instantly recognized the girl.

"Yeah, I remember you. You're that girl we met on the side of our dorm one afternoon when we were practicing. You told us that you were on the school newspaper and that you were going to write an article on us. How'd that work out for you? I don't recall reading your article, but then again I really don't read the school paper, so I may have missed it."

"No, you didn't miss the article because my editor said it wasn't a topic that students would be interested in."

Harley tapped Drew on his shoulder and joked, "Did you hear that, Drew. We're not interesting enough to read about."

The girl corrected Harley. "That isn't what I meant. My editor told me that baseball here at Mizzou or any other college campus is not a sports topic that holds student interest. He said students would much rather read about the quarterback of Mizzou throwing the winning touchdown pass or one of our basketball players sinking a three pointer to end a close game. He said that's just the way it is and as a reporter I had to give the student body what they wanted…what they would actually read."

Harley sat on a pile of skids next to the girl and asked, "So why are you here now? Especially since Drew and I seem to hold no interest of our fellow students?"

"Because I understand baseball. You two have teamed up for two no-hitters in less than two weeks. That's news! I was wondering if I could spend maybe a half hour or so interviewing you two for my next article."

Harley looked at Drew then answered, "Sure…why not? When did you want to conduct this interview?"

"As soon as possible. A good reporter always strikes while the iron is hot. If we wait too long this may no longer be on people's minds. We could do it right here but this is not the most ideal place for an interview."

Snapping his fingers, Drew suggested, "Why don't you join us for dinner tonight. We're celebrating our no-hitter with steak and all the fixin's. We can talk while we eat. Whaddya say?"

"That sounds nice but steak is not on my budget."

"Not to worry," said Drew. "I told Harley I was buying tonight. You just come along and let me worry about the check."

"Well, since you put it that way, then I'll accept."

Drew smiled. "Good then. We'll pick you up at six at the fountain at the main entrance of campus."

Flipping her hood up, she placed her pen in her coat pocket and grinned, "See ya later." With that she was off running across the grass in the pouring rain.

Harley turned to Drew. "Why so generous with buying everyone dinner?"

Drew started walking out into the rain. "You deserve a steak, and in case you didn't notice that girl was pretty good looking!"

Joining Drew, Harley looked up into the rainy sky. "So, what you're saying is that you are no longer just a baseball playing, stamp collecting, piano playing, karate expert, but now you've added another topic of interest...a girl!"

Drew stated jogging, "Why not?"

Drew pulled out a chair for Melanie who had introduced herself on the drive into town. Seating himself, Drew remarked, "The Longhorn has pretty good steaks."

Harley looked out the window at the rain and picked up a menu. "I might go with the T-bone tonight. It isn't very often that I get to dine on genuine grade A steak. A baked potato and a salad and I'll be a happy camper."

Moments later they all had a drink in front of them and had ordered. Melanie produced her ink pen and legal pad and laid it to the side. "So, I understand both of you are from Arnold, which is south of St. Louis."

"That's correct," said Harley. "I was born and raised in Arnold and Drew moved there from Dallas, Texas when he was ten. That's when we met. A few months later we started practicing together and he became my catcher."

Drew, more interested in Melanie than talking about how he met Harley, asked, "And where are you from, Melanie?"

Unwrapping her utensils, she spread a cloth napkin on her lap and answered, "A mid-size town in New York. You've probably never heard of it; Elmira."

Both Drew and Harley were at a loss for words when Harley finally spoke up, "Elmira, New York? We know a girl from Elmira whose name actually is *Elmira!*"

Now it was Melanie who was temporarily speechless. Staring back at her two dinner partners, she exclaimed, "You know Mira Madison?"

Harley held out his hands. "I guess what they say about it being a small world is true. We met Mira our freshman year in high school. How do you know Mira?"

"Back in Elmira we played softball together in junior high on the same team. Now that girl could throw a softball. She was the best softball pitcher in the state. Then she was involved in an automobile accident that left her paralyzed and confined to a wheelchair. The next thing we all knew she and her family moved and we never heard from her again. Our team was never the same after she left. So, she went to school with you in this Arnold?"

"Yes, all four years," stated Harley.

"It sounds like you were good friends."

Drew laughed and added, "Harley and Mira are more than just friends. They've been seeing each other now for five years."

"Interesting! How is she getting along? I mean with her disability."

"When we first met," explained Harley, "she had to use a wheelchair but could get around in a walker. Over the years she has gradually improved and today walks with the aid of a cane. She rides horses like nobody's business. As a matter of fact, I just spent last weekend with her down in Kentucky. She is attending the University of Kentucky and has her sights set on becoming an equine veterinarian. You'll be surprise to hear that she can pitch again. She has been doing weight training and special exercises. She can only throw the ball about forty miles an hour and will probably never play competitively, but she is so excited about being able to throw again."

Grabbing her pen, Melanie asked, "Could I have her number. I'd love to speak with her."

"I've got an even better idea," said Drew. "She is going to be in Arnold this coming weekend. She, Harley and I have great seats for the Cardinals game this Saturday. Maybe you'd like to tag along. You could talk over old times and get reacquainted. It'd be just the four of us."

Melanie was beside herself. "If you think I wouldn't be imposing, I'd love to come along. A major league baseball game, hot dogs, popcorn, drinks and good friends. What could be better?"

CHAPTER 29

STANDING IN THE LONG LINE AT A SECOND LEVEL
concession stand, Drew opened his wallet and removed a twenty
and looked out at the throng of Cardinal fans. "The fans have
really taken to the new stadium. I bet there'll be over forty
thousand here tonight."

Harley gazed out at the passing crowd and moved to the side
allowing a man carrying drinks and nachos to pass by. "They say
since opening day the attendance has been better than anticipated.
The Cards are on a roll, sitting at 27-15. Since we were down at
Western the Cardinals have taken two out of three from the
Diamondbacks and the Mets. Last night we took out the Royals 9-
6. Carpenter got the win and Wainwright the save. We've got
Reyes on the mound tonight."

Moving up in line, Drew commented, "The girls really seem to
be getting along."

"Boy, you can say that again," added Harley. "From the
moment we picked Mira up at her place, she and Melanie haven't
stopped talking."

Looking over at an escalator jammed with fans, Drew asked,
"So what do you think of our new stadium?"

"I like it," said Harley. "The old stadium was the standard
cookie cutter version of Riverfront, Veterans, Three Rivers and
Atlanta's Fulton County Stadium. This new stadium is more of the
retro-classic look with the view of the St. Louis skyline. I
especially like the new integrated LED video and scoring system
and the digital ribbon board technology."

"I'll tell you what I think," said Drew. "They can update the
stadium with all the technology in the world but it's still baseball.
And that's what brings the fans out. Baseball will always
be...baseball. There are base hits, strike outs, walks and stolen
bases." Thumping Harley on his arm, he added, "And yes, there
will still be the occasional no-hitter!"

"Don't remind me. Over the past two days at school I've had three professors in class and a number of classmates tell me they are expecting a third no-hitter the next time I pitch, which is in seven days. It almost seems if I don't throw a no-hitter everyone will be disappointed."

"Yeah, it's sort of like Cardinal fans. We've been spoiled over the years with how well the Cards always play. The fans come to the game expecting them to win every time…"

"Next please!" The voice of the concession stand employee interrupted Drew's comment.

Entering section 242, Harley handed Mira a tray of hot dogs, peanuts and small condiment packages. Drew followed behind while he balanced a tray of drinks and two orders of nachos which Melanie took from him. Sitting, Harley arranged two hot dogs, a large soda and bag of peanuts on a small food tray next to his seat. Melanie scanned the field and remarked, "This new stadium is really nice. I've never been at the old stadium, so I can only assume this is better."

"Well, I don't know if it's that much better," said Harley, "just different. We are now sitting in a corporate box that is used by Anheuser Busch. Drew's dad works for Busch and from time to time we can get seats up here."

Melanie suddenly dropped some cheese sauce on her pant leg and Drew reacted instantly by offering her a napkin. Noticing how attentive Drew was toward Melanie, Mira gave Harley a friendly nudge and whispered softly, "It's nice they're getting along so well."

Not wanting to be that obvious, Drew asked Melanie, "You told us earlier in the week during our interview that you understood baseball. I know you said you grew up playing softball with Mira. Harley and I know all too well of Mira's love for the Yankees. Can we assume that living in Elmira, New York that you are a Yankee fan as well?"

"No, I'm not a Yankee fan or for that matter even the Mets. My parents are big Chicago baseball fans. They both were born and raised in Chicago, met in high school and got married after they graduated from college at which point my father secured a job position in Elmira. My mother still today is a White Sox fan and my father goes for the Cubs. During baseball season, they are always dinging on each other about how their team is the best in Chicago. Last year we went to Chicago when the Cardinals were in town. My dad was so adamant about winning the game and said he'd rather see the Cubs beat St. Louis more than any other team."

"The Cubs and the Cardinals have always been bitter rivals," said Harley. "Here are some interesting stats. I'm going way back now to when the Cubs were called the White Stockings and the Cardinals were called the Browns. They have played each other approximately twenty-three hundred times and in that span of time the Cubs have won somewhere in the area of fifty to fifty-five more games than the Cards. When you consider all the games they have played over the decades they have been pretty evenly matched."

Harley's explanation of Cardinals and Cubs past history was interrupted when the crowd of forty thousand plus fans cheered when the first inning came to an end with no score. Melanie cracked open a peanut and asked Harley, "How is it that you know so much about the Cubs and the Cardinals?"

Mira placed her arm around Melanie and explained, "If you spend any amount of time around these two you'll soon discover that baseball stats, current or not, are always a topic of conversation."

"It goes much farther than that," stated Drew. "For the last ten years that we've known each other, Harley has always been quick to surprise me with his baseball knowledge. Well, I try to come up with something now and then that I think he may not know."

"And," added Harley, "from time to time he succeeds."

The second inning came to an end when Mira spoke up, "I for one would like to hear more about the ongoing rivalry between the Cubs and the Cardinals."

Harley sat back in his seat and resumed, "The rivalry between these two clubs has two names that are not used much anymore. The Route 66 Rivalry and the Downstate Illinois Rivalry. It's been going on for a long time and no one can really say for sure what sparked the dislike for one another. It's more than likely a combination of things or events. For instance, back in 1928, the Cubs had a player by the name of Hack Wilson. He played in the majors for twelve years, six of which were with the Cubbies. He could really hammer the ball, but his skills at the plate were often overshadowed by his combative style of play, which often resulted in Hack starting fights with opposing players and sometimes even fans; hence, the Hack Wilson incident as it is known. During a game with St. Louis, Wilson gets upset with a heckling fan and charges up into the stands after the fan. A riot nearly broke out when five thousand fans ran onto the field. The fan sued Wilson for twenty thousand dollars but ol' Hack walked away from the incident without paying a dime. Another reason that could have contributed to the rivalry is known as one of the worse trades in baseball. As a matter of fact, when a bad trade is made in the majors you always hear players, managers or club owners say that it's Brock for Broglio, which in hindsight means that a trade turns out to be extremely lopsided. In 1964 Chicago decided to trade twenty-four year old Lou Brock for Ernie Broglio in a six player deal. The Cubs, early on, felt they had gotten the better end of the deal as Brock had not performed well in Chicago while Broglio, the previous year had won eighteen games as a pitcher and had a string of successful years in St. Louis. It seemed that Chicago had got the better deal. Not so! Brock was no sooner traded when he took off, hitting .348 that year and leading the Cardinals to a World Series Championship. Brock was also instrumental in leading the Cards to another world title in 1967 and a pennant in '68. Brock continued to play for the Cards up though 1979 and amassed three thousand twenty three hits and nine hundred and thirty-eight stolen bases. Eventually he was inducted into the hall of fame. On the other side of the coin, Broglio turned out to be a total disaster. His first year in Chicago he went 4 - 7 and held an ERA of 4.04. The worst part of the trade is what no one apparently seemed to know. It turned out that Broglio injured his arm halfway through the '63 season while still with St. Louis, but not much was said about the injury. Then, in 1964 he had Ulnar Nerve Surgery and by '66 he was no longer in baseball. This trade between the Cubs and the Cardinals in some baseball circles is known as the worse trade ever made. Even though that particular trade was made forty-two years ago, there are many Cub fans who still shake their heads in wonder about that trade. There is actually a group of Cub fans in Washington, D.C., mostly politicians and journalists who have come up with a Brock for Broglio Judgement Award for bad

344

decision making."

Drew stood up, stretched and looked out at the scoreboard. "Two innings gone and no score." Turning, he addressed his three companions. "I think I know of yet another, more recent reason why Cub fans and St. Louis fans are at odds. Back in 1998, which was just eight years ago, we have the Sosa-McGwire home run race. People say that year, the constant back and forth of slamming home run after home run between Sosa and McGwire was the resurgence of the popularity of baseball. The Cubs haven't won a World Series since way back in 1908, which was their second title, while the Cards have won nine since then. The Cubs have sixteen pennants to their credit and the Cardinals are currently setting at nineteen. So, the Cubs have had their opportunities over the years, but as it stands the Cardinals turned more pennant wins into World Series titles. You hear it all over town when Cardinal fans start talking about the Cubs, about how they always seem to choke. Well I think that in '98 Cubs fans were hoping that Sosa would come out on top in the home run race. This would at least give then some sort of bragging rights, but as we all know McGwire hit seventy that year beating out Sosa who slammed sixty-six."

Harley finished his drink and commented, "No doubt there are numerous reasons for the rivalry, even hatred or dislike that many Cub and Cardinal fans display for one another each and every year. My parents have always been diehard Cardinal fans, but always respected the Cubs as a great rival. Back in 2002 I remember a conversation my parents had one evening while we were having dinner. My Dad had been invited by one of his customers along to a Cubs game in Chicago against the Cards. They drove up there and had a nice dinner and then went to the game. The stands were packed just like they are here when the Cubs are in town. Suddenly, the catcher for the Cubs comes out and stands on home plate and announces that the commissioner of baseball has cancelled the game due to a tragic situation in the Cardinals family, meaning our organization. He asked the crowd to be patient and understanding but some of the Cubs fans booed. Shortly after the game my Dad, along with everyone else who had been present prior to the game, found out that Darryl Kile, one of the Cardinal pitchers had been discovered dead in his Chicago hotel room. My Dad said that after that he always had a bad taste in his mouth for people from Chicago. He realized it was wrong to lump all people from Chicago into what was probably a small group who had booed at that game, but he just found it hard to forgive the people of Chicago for the way they had reacted because the game was cancelled. Ya know, it's strange. He never attended another game in Chicago after that."

Mira crumpled an empty bag of peanuts and threw the bag in a nearby trash bin. "All this talk about the rivalry between the Cubs and the Cardinals reminds me of the east coast rivalry between the Red Sox and the Yankees. It's basically the same thing. If you happen to be from New York City or even nearby, and you travel to Boston for pleasure or on a business trip when you meet or are introduced to people there, one of the first questions you are going to be asked is are you a Yankee fan? If you're from Boston and you travel to New York it's the same thing. People want to know if you're a Red Sox fan. I'm sure it's the same way here in St. Louis and up in Chicago. And the display or dislike for a rival seems to be the most prevalent in baseball. I know that when the Boston Celtics or the Boston Bruins play the New York 76ers or the New York Islanders, there is that sense of rivalry but you don't see that deep resentment for your opponent."

Melanie jumped in on the conversation and added, "I really don't think this dislike is all that prevalent when it comes to the players themselves. I think Cub and Cardinal players, if the truth be told, respect one another and here's why. All major league baseball players no doubt hold a level of respect for fellow players on other teams, even if it is a rival team because they know what it takes to make it to the majors. The effort, the discipline, the days, weeks, months and years of dedicated practice. I think this dislike between the Cubs and the Cardinals, despite that there may be a few players who may not care for a player on the other team, has been sparked by the fans, the media, and at times maybe even from some people in the front office of these organizations."

Walking over, Drew placed his right hand on Melanie's shoulder and announced, "I think what Melanie just said is the most profound statement of the evening!"

Mira raised her cup. "Here, here!" Noticing her drink cup was empty she stood and motioned to Melanie. "C'mon, what say we girls walk down and get us some refills?" Grabbing Harley and

Drew's cups Mira started out into the aisle, Melanie following.

Drew sat down and propped his feet up, and tossed a peanut into his mouth. "Tell me this, Harley. Do you ever think this rivalry or feud between the Cubs and the Cards will ever come to an end?"

"I don't think the rivalry will ever end, but I do think there is a chance to put a serious dent in the bitterness between the two cities. If the Cubs could ever somehow win a World Series, then they would have something powerful in their corner to speak about. If they do win a World Series it would also take away some of the ammunition that Cardinals now possess." Changing the subject, Harley grinned at his friend. "It would seem that you and Melanie are getting along like two peas in a pod!"

Drew, jokingly objected, "Oh, come on. We just met. I hardly know the girl!"

Pointing at Drew, Harley shook his head, "Do you recall when I first met Mira and you told me that I was toast? Welcome to the loaf of bread, my friend! It couldn't be more obvious you two are no more than a few days or possibly weeks away from a serious date."

Drew, realizing Harley might just be right, waved off the thought. "Can we please talk about something else? Whatever happens…happens!" Looking down at the field, he watched while the Cardinals took the field for the bottom half of the third inning.

The girls didn't return until the fourth inning, and Mira, while handing a drink to Harley looked at the scoreboard and asked, "How did we score a run? We heard the crowd cheering and figured something happened."

Drew quickly updated the girls. "St Louis got a single up the middle to center field and then the runner stole second and advanced to third on the throw. The next batter slammed a double to center field, scoring the man on third."

Melanie handed a drink to Drew and asked, "How is our rival, the Cubs doing so far this year?"

Drew, who normally did not keep up with league standings, looked at Harley for the answer. Harley took a swig of his drink and responded, "I was just checking the standings in the paper last night. Right now, they are sitting at 17-25, ten and a half games back. Even though we're just two months into the season that's a lot of ground to make up. Out of the six games we've played against them so far this year, they took four from us."

Suddenly there was a very distinct crack of the bat followed by a hush that set in over the fans as they watched a ball hit by a Royal's player sail out into left field. The Cardinals left fielder back pedaled, looked at the rapidly approaching fence then back up at the ball. Just two feet from the fence he caught the ball easily and tossed it back to the shortstop who had ventured out into the outfield.

Getting everyone's attention Harley spoke up, "I've got something I want to share with our little group tonight. I wasn't going to say anything about it but sooner or later you'll find out anyways. I received three phone calls yesterday from not only Buck Tillman, head scout for the Indians, but two calls from other scouts. One from the White Sox and the other from your beloved Yankees, Mira."

Mira was the first to react, as she, with an air of excitement asked, "How did the conversations go?"

"The first call was from Tillman and really wasn't a surprise. It wasn't like he called me out of the blue. I'd already talked with him twice in the last two weeks. The second time I talked with him was right after the Kent State game. When he saw me throw the second no-hitter in less than two weeks he was impressed. He told me Cleveland was very interested in signing me, and the sooner the better. I would probably, depending on how things panned out, spend a year or two in the minors and then eventually be called up. He told me he hadn't forgotten the promise I made to my folks about finishing college before I went pro, but he said I could actually finish my college education in the off season or over the internet. We didn't talk money, but he said I could make okay money in the minors, and then in the majors, the sky was the limit. That is, if I remained healthy. He pointed out that's why I might want to consider making a move when I become eligible."

Melanie looked at Mira then remarked, "But you're not even twenty years old yet. Do they or can they sign someone that young?"

"Sure, and the reason why is because baseball has evolved into a young man's game. The days of forty year olds being able to play is an aberration, rather than the norm. In this modern era of baseball, especially these days, major league teams see the value of young, talented players as the future of their club."

Melanie opened her large purse and removed a small notepad and an ink pen. "Would it be all right if I jotted down a few notes for my upcoming article?" Wiggling her pen in the air, she smiled. "A good reporter has to be prepared at all times for a good story. So, let me ask you, Harley. What did these other two major league scouts who called you have to say?"

"The second call, from the White Sox scout was pretty short and to the point. After introducing himself their scout said the club got wind of this freshman from Mizzou who threw back to back no-hitters. He went on to say that they were in the process of rebuilding their pitching staff and were interested in some new talent they could build on. He informed me that he was coming to my next outing which is against Indiana State at Mizzou. He said he was looking forward to seeing me work. The third call was from a Yankees' scout. He didn't pull any punches; he was all business. He wanted to know if I had talked with any other clubs, what my plans for the immediate future were, was I ready to play in the Yankees' farm system and eventually for the Yankees. He went on to say that the Yankees had a strong farm system and depending on my abilities, they may start me out in AA, and if I panned out I could probably move up to AAA within a year. He also told me he was going to be attending the game with Indiana. That game will be quite interesting because Buck Tillman of the Indians said he was going to be there as well. Three major league scouts coming to see me pitch. To tell you the truth things are going way too fast for me. Last year I was a high school pitcher and here it is not even a year later and I've got three major league clubs knocking on my door."

Mira chuckled. "My dad has always told me to be careful what you wish for in life because you may just get it. Harley, you've been working toward a major league career since you've been five years old. From what you have told me in the five years I have known you, it was just a matter of time before you would reach your goal of becoming a major leaguer. It's like you've been training for and running a race of sorts for fifteen years and now the finish line is in sight. It seems to me that some of the decisions you felt you were going to have to make four years from now, may have to be made sooner than you planned. What do your parents think about all of this sudden interest?"

"After the last phone call, I sat down with them and we discussed the phone calls from these three major league scouts. My Dad said he knew this day would come and there would be many more before it was all said and done. My mother, along with my Dad said they were very proud of me and the fact that I had been contacted by major league scouts was something that 99.999% of people will never get to experience. They told me they were also proud of the way I stuck to my guns in telling all three scouts that I intended to complete all four years of college. Then, my mother said something that nearly knocked me out of my chair. She said she and my father had been talking recently, since after Buck Tillman first approached me at Western. They informed me that I was no longer a little boy or even a high school student, but a mature young man capable of making my own decisions. They thought over what I had told them about Tillman suggesting that I could play minor league and even major league ball and still get my college degree in the off season. They said it was my decision and mine alone and they would support me either way…"

Mira held up her hand and politely interrupted, "Are you suggesting that you might consider going pro before you finish your four years at Mizzou?"

"I really can't answer that right now," said Harley, "but I can tell you the way I might be leaning. It all has to do with major league baseball draft rules. I'm pretty sure the only way you can sign with a major league team without going through the draft is if you're an unrestricted free agent, which means that if I have graduated from high school and have not attended a four year college, or even a junior college I can walk on to any major league tryout that is available and I could actually get signed, that is if I'm good enough. But since I'm enrolled and currently attending a four year college I will not be considered eligible for the draft until I'm a junior, senior or twenty-one years of age, whichever comes first. I won't be twenty until later this summer, so that means I'd have to wait until next year about this time before I could become eligible. If I elect to drop out of school I still have to sit out for a full year before I can be considered for the draft. Either way, it looks like I have to wait until I'm twenty-one to be eligible. Right now, my plan is this. Continue to not only play ball for Mizzou but complete my freshman year. Then, I'll return next year as a starting pitcher for Mizzou and complete my sophomore year. Now, here's the thing. I'll turn twenty-one during my second year at school *and, at that point,* I become eligible for the draft. If it turns out that I go to a minor or major league team with only two years of school under my belt I can still get my degree in the off-season. So, for now I'm just a good ol' college kid like the rest of you. Right now, I'm not going to worry about the future draft, but I'm going to concentrate on being the best pitcher I can be and to continue to hone my pitching skills."

Drew, who had been sitting off to the side and listening held up his drink and remarked, "Here's to my best friend, Harley Sims; future major league pitcher."

Both girls stood and joined in on the mini celebration, when Harley raised his cup as well and added, "And here's to my best friend, Drew Scott, who whether he knows it or not is a great ballplayer himself. Ten years ago he stood in my backyard and told me was scared to death of catching a baseball, *and now,* he can hit better than me, run faster than me, can analyze players better than me. In short, I know in my heart that Drew will be a catcher in the major leagues."

The toast was suddenly interrupted as the crowd roared when Albert Pujols hit a towering homerun, following a walk and a single, adding three more runs to their side of the scorecard. The Cards were up 4-0 in the eighth. As Pujols crossed home plate, Harley looked out at the current box scores for both leagues. He thought about the three teams that were presently scouting him as he scanned the scores. The White Sox were beating the Cubs 7-0, Cleveland was losing to Pittsburgh 9-6 and the Yankees were ahead over the Mets 5-4 in extra innings. Sitting back, he gazed out at the lights of downtown St. Louis and wondered. *In three years I could be playing in the major leagues. But, for who?*

CHAPTER 30

"DOESN'T GET ANY BETTER THAN THIS," SAID DREW. Standing, he held up the hotdog in his right hand and the drink in his left and toasted all the St. Louis Cardinal fans that were rapidly filing into New Busch Stadium. "Friday night in late October, fifth game of the 2006 World Series, first season in the new stadium. We're up three games to one over the Tigers and could close this series out tonight! Do you realize that within three hours from now we could be witnessing St. Louis's tenth World Series Title?"

Harley raised his cup and joined in on the toast, adding, "It's been twenty-four years since our last title. That was back in 1982 when we defeated Milwaukee in seven games. It's been almost two and a half decades since we won the whole thing. That's the longest drought we've had between World Series wins since back in 1926. I think we're due."

Plopping down in his seat, Drew took a bite out of his dog. "It was an odd season this year. We finished up with a win-loss record of 83-78, just five games above .500 and a game and a half lead over the Astros. That's cutting it pretty close."

"What's really strange about baseball," said Harley, "is the reason why many a game over the course of a season are won and not stated or recorded in stats. The third base coach signals a man to go home when he should have held up and the runner is thrown out, or someone fouls off a two strike bunt attempt and ends an inning with men in scoring position. I could go on and on. The stats don't always tell the story of a winning season. For instance, at the plate this year there is not one category where the Cards came in first. In base hits, we came in seventh place in the division, fourteenth in doubles, eleventh in triples, fifth in homeruns and ninth in walks. Despite these stats, we still managed to win the Central Division Championship and Pennant." Snapping his fingers, Harley remembered, "Mira said she wanted me to pick up two new Cards hats at the game tonight for her grandparents."

"Come to think of it," said Drew. "Why aren't your folks here at the game tonight? They've got to be some of the most loyal fans in the city."

"They decided to go to a World Series party one of my Dad's customers is throwing in Ladue. Listen, I'm going to run down to the gift shop and pick up those hats while I can. If we win this thing tonight, later on it's going to be nuts around here. You coming along?"

"No, I think I'll just sit here and watch the crowd. People are amazing to watch. Like that guy down there coming up the steps. He's wearing a Pittsburgh Pirates shirt and a Phillies hat. I wonder who he's going to be pulling for? There's a woman four rows down holding twin babies that appear to be just a few months old and another older woman wearing a Cardinals tank top displaying one of those fake tans that makes you almost look orange. It's almost as entertaining as watching the game. If you don't mind I could use another drink."

Harley saluted and said, "I'll be back before the first pitch."

Drew settled back in his seat and watched the grounds crew put the final touches on the infield. He looked at his watch: seven-fourteen. The game was scheduled to start just after seven thirty. He noticed a young father who sat with two young boys wearing oversize Cardinal hats. They were probably brothers. Dad was explaining something about the field or the upcoming all important game while he pointed here and there. Bringing the set of binoculars his parents had got for him for his birthday to his eyes, he scanned the packed crowd. It seemed like there wasn't an empty seat. It was a sea of Cardinal red. Then he spotted a man wearing a Detroit Tigers hat in the midst of what seemed like endless Cardinal fans. Even though he was for the opposing team, the man was welcome here at Busch. Sitting in his seat the man held a beer while he talked back and forth with two Cardinal fans seated on either side of him. Even though they would be rooting for their own team they shared something in common; their love for the game of baseball.

Next, he turned the binoculars on the Cardinals dugout where he could see players standing or sitting, adjusting their spikes, putting on hats, picking up gloves, all the while talking with one another. Moving the binoculars to the visitors' dugout the Tigers were busy at the same pre-game tasks. He noticed one of the players who sat alone at the end of the long bench, his hands folded, his head lowered. Maybe the player was praying. He often wondered what the Good Lord thought about baseball. Over the years he had witnessed players of opposing teams praying as well. *It must be difficult being God,* he thought. Two different players from two different teams, both praying for the victory, but in the end only one would walk away the winner. Someone always had to lose.

His daydreaming was interrupted when Harley handed him his drink and hung his bag with the new Cardinal hats on the back of the seat in front of where they were, as he asked, "See anything out there interesting?"

Drew lowered the long distance glasses and answered, "Just people...happy people! I can't imagine anyone being here tonight that is not in a good mood."

Harley agreed as the players lined up on the field for the introduction ceremony. "I guess you're right. Coming here tonight, or for that matter any game in any city during the season is a method for a lot of people to escape a bad day at work or to forget about a problem they're having in their life." Hesitating he looked at the downtown skyline and then remarked with confidence, "Baseball is good!"

Following team introductions, the ceremonial first pitch and then the singing of the Star Spangled Banner, the crowd roared loudly when the Cardinals took the field.

Drew, clapping his hands, asked, "Who's on the mound tonight?"

Nodding toward the field, Harley answered, "Jeff Weaver. I hope he's on tonight. He was the losing pitcher in game two in Detroit. Detroit has Justin Verlander going for them. Detroit is down three games to one and their back is against the wall. That being said, they couldn't ask for a better pitcher than Verlander." Removing a scorecard and a pencil from his shirt pocket, Harley began to fill in both rosters.

"How's come you're keeping score tonight. Isn't it just as easy to look at the gigantic scoreboard the Cardinals have so conveniently constructed for the enjoyment of the fans?"

"I'm doing this for my parents. If the Cards win tonight then a scorecard of the final game of the 2006 World Series will be valuable. I'll think it will make a great stocking stuffer this Christmas."

Weaver stood on the mound and awaited Detroit's first batter, the St. Louis fans, chanting, "Cards, Cards, Cards!" Ten minutes later the top half of the first ended, Weaver striking out Detroit's first two batters, followed by a fly out to left field. Harley filled out the card and stated, "No runs, no hits, no errors!"

Detroit took the field as Verlander walked to the mound. The Cardinals lead-off man stepped up to the plate. The bottom half of the first took longer than the top half, but ended with the Cards unable to score. Completing the first inning of the scorecard, Harley reviewed what he had penciled in and commented, "Verlander is having control problems but even with the bases loaded he pitched his way out of trouble."

Drew smiled and tapped Harley on the shoulder. "In all the years and games I've caught for you, you have never…not ever, thrown two wild pitches and walked three men in the same inning." Joking, he bowed before Harley three times and laughed, "I might just be sitting with a future Cy Young winner!"

The top half of the second inning was a repeat performance for Weaver. He struck out the first two batters and the next man grounded out to the shortstop. Filling out the card, Harley remarked, "Weaver is on. He's struck out four of Detroit's first six men."

In the bottom of the second, the Cards started off with a line drive single to center field. The runner advanced to second on a sacrifice bunt and then to third on a hard hit ground ball. With two outs, the next man at the plate singled, driving in the go ahead run. The inning ended with a strike out. Waving the card in the air, Harley spoke with confidence, "We're up by one run! We're on our way to the World Series Title!"

Seeing a fan dressed in a Chicago Cubs jersey and hat who was returning to his seat, Drew asked, "So, how did our rivals to the north fare this year?"

"If you mean the Cubs," answered Harley, "not so good. They came in dead last this year. We played the Cubs in seventeen games this year and they swept us twice. One of these days in the future, Cubs fans will see their team win the World Series…mark my word!"

In the top of the third the Tigers finally came to life hitting a double and a single but unable to score. In the Cardinals half of the inning they started off the inning with a single, but then a double play and a pop fly ended the inning. The score remained 1-0, the Cards still holding on to a slim lead.

Removing two candy bars from his pocket he had purchased earlier, Harley tossed one to Drew and explained, "As the season drew to a close these two teams were not given much of a chance to be in the World Series. For lack of a better phrase they both sort of limped into the playoffs. They both struggled the second half of the season. The Tigers at one time held a ten game lead in their division but as the second half ended their lead evaporated and on the last day of regular season play Detroit loses to the Twins, but still had an opportunity as a wildcard team. The Cardinals didn't fare much better as the season came to a close. The Cards looked like a shoe-in. With just two weeks left in regular season play they were up seven games on the Reds and eight and a half on Houston. It appeared that they would walk away with the division title. But then the bottom fell out as we lost seven games in a row combined with the Astros taking eight consecutive games to crawl within a half game of the Cards. Thanks to the Atlanta Braves who defeated the Astros on the last day of play, the Cards barely, and I mean *barely,* took the division title. Both Detroit and St. Louis were considered underdogs going into the playoffs, and yet, here we sit."

Weaver took the mound for the fourth inning and the fans were still chanting, "Cards, Cards, Cards!" Detroit got on the board with a two run round tripper which put the Tigers up 2-1.

Updating the scorecard, Harley shook his head and looked at the surrounding fans who had grown less enthusiastic as their team no longer held the lead. "Things can change quickly in baseball. I'm sure that down there in the Tigers dugout they feel better with the lead, and in bars, restaurants and countless homes in the Detroit area fans are more confident than they were in the first three innings of this game."

In the bottom of the fourth the Cardinals didn't waste any time. Two singles, a throwing error and a sacrifice ground ball put the Cardinals back in the lead 3-2. The fans, with their team once again in the lead, were going nuts. An older lady sitting next to

Harley jumped up and down as she shouted, "We're gonna win...we're gonna win!"

Harley held the scorecard up and took a deep breath. "This card sure looks better than it did ten minutes ago."

Drew stood and motioned for Harley to stand. "I've got to hit the head. Want anything while I'm gone?"

"Come to think of it, I could use another dog. If we win tonight I might not have another chance to have a hotdog here at the stadium until next year."

"Another dog it is then. I'll buy. Make sure those Tigers don't grab the lead back while I'm gone!"

It wasn't until the bottom of the sixth when Drew slowly made his way up to their section and across to their seats. Handing Harley a fresh drink and a hot dog, he sat down and looked at the scoreboard. "It's crazy down there. The lines for the concessions and the bathrooms are jammed up. I see we're still in the lead 3-2. Did I miss anything?"

Unwrapping his dog, Harley sat back, took a large bite, swallowed and answered, "Not really. Neither team did anything in the fifth."

On the next pitch, Weaver grounded out to second base and the inning ended. Opening a bag of peanuts, Drew watched as the Tigers ran from the field. "Three innings to go. If the score remains as it is we walk out of here World Series Champions."

Harley pointed out, "There's a lot of baseball left to play in this game. Weaver still has to get through their order one more time...nine more outs. So far, he's pitched a great game." Checking his scorecard he went on, "He's struck out seven, only walked one man and has only allowed four hits and two runs. With the score being as close as it is, La Russa will probably bring in a reliever. He might let Weaver pitch in the seventh, but I think he'll make a pitching change in the eighth."

Drew agreed and commented, "Verlander has pitched a pretty good game himself. How's he look on the card?"

Scanning the card, Harley hesitated in his answer, then responded with, "Let's see here." A few seconds passed when he gave Drew the rundown on Detroit's pitcher. "Struck out three, walked three, three wild pitches, allowed five hits and three runs. It's still anyone's game. He's only down by a run."

The seventh inning for Detroit was uneventful as Weaver got the first two batters to ground out and then struck out a pinch hitter for Verlander.

"Smart move," said Harley. "Jim Leyland, Detroit's manager, can't afford to let the Cards score any more runs. His new pitcher, whoever it turns out to be, has to shut us down for the remainder of the game and hope that their offense can come up with some runs. Leyland has to decide what pitcher he's going to bring in and La Russa has to decide if he's going to keep Weaver on the mound."

Standing for the seventh inning stretch, Drew gestured down at the field as Detroit's new pitcher took the mound. Looking at the huge message board, the pitcher's picture and name flashed across the screen. Fernando Rodney. Grabbing a handful of peanuts from the bag, Drew asked, "Know anything about this pitcher?"

Harley thought for a moment and then answered, "He's one of the few pitchers in either league that can throw the ball over a hundred miles an hour. With his speed he can really shut a team down which is exactly what Leyland has in mind."

Harley stood and watched what seemed like thousands of people not only stand, but leave their seats for the restroom facilities or a late game snack and drink. "This could be the last baseball we see this year, that is if the Cards can hold on."

In the Cards half of the seventh, following a walk and two singles they put another run on the board and now led 4-2. As the Tigers ran from the field, Drew pointed at the scoreboard and stated, "Leyland may have made the wrong choice."

"That's baseball," said Harley. "Now that we have another run it'll be interesting to see what La Russa will do. If it were me, I'd bring Weaver out for the eighth. He's been throwing the ball well. Why fix something if it isn't broken. If he does get in trouble La Russa can always bring in a reliever."

Suddenly a loud cheer from the fans rang out and echoed around the stadium when Jeff Weaver stepped out of the dugout and crossed the first base foul line on his way to the mound. Drew joined in on the applauding and looked at Harley. "You guessed right. La Russa is leaving Weaver in. All he needs is six more outs and this year will be in the history books as another world title for the Cards."

Detroit's first batter in the eighth resulted in a fly out to center field. "Five more to go," said Drew excitedly. The next two men went down swinging. Watching Harley fill out his scorecard, Drew shook his head in amazement. "Weaver looks as strong as he did in the first. With a two run lead maybe he'll come back out for the ninth."

The tigers took the field while the confident crowd watched another Detroit reliever step to the mound. Checking the big screen, Harley confirmed, "Joel Zumaya. Leyland's rolling the dice again."

Harley checked the scorecard and commented, "I bet you a dime to a donut that La Russa will pull Weaver and send a pinch hitter to the plate."

Zumaya went to work and retired the first two Cardinal batters. Just like Harley figured, Weaver did not come out of the dugout for his next time at bat. "Good decision," said Harley. "Now La Russa will probably bring in Wainwright." The Cardinals pinch hitter struck out to end the inning.

"This is it," exclaimed Drew. "Three up and three down and we claim baseball's most coveted championship. My first World Series could be just minutes away!"

The surrounding fans were cheering and yelling, realizing that the moment they had been waiting for was just three outs away. The woman standing next to Harley, plopped down in her seat, took a long swig of beer and then wiped her forehead as if she were going to faint. Concerned, Harley bent down and asked the woman, "Are you okay, Ma'am?"

The woman, fanning herself with a program smiled back and answered, "Yes, I'm fine. This is the first Cardinals game I've ever attended. Normally I just watch the games on television. This is so exciting! I just have to sit for a moment."

Wainwright made the long walk from the bullpen to the mound accompanied by the approval of over forty-six thousand exuberant fans.

Drew looked down toward Detroit's dugout and commented, "Leyland's running out of time. Who's he got coming to the plate?"

Scanning his card, Harley answered, "Ordonez, Casey and Rodriguez. If we have to go further in their lineup then we've got Polanco and Inge."

Interrupting Harley, Drew raised the binoculars to his eyes. "Ordonez is at the plate. Here we go!"

The normal overtone of fan noise at a Cardinal game paled in comparison to the noise level that filled the ballpark. Every single person in the stadium was on their feet for what they hoped was the last three outs. The first out of the inning came easily when Ordonez grounded out to the second baseman.

A minute later Casey silenced the crowd when he hit his second double of the game to center field. Recording what had happened on his scorecard, Harley bumped Drew on his arm. "Doesn't it strike you as odd how one man, one player, in a matter of seconds can change how the crowd reacts. The crowd is still loud, but now that the tying run is coming to the plate the noise level seems to have dropped some."

Pointing at the screen, Drew related what was happening. "Leyland is bringing in a pinch runner for Casey. Ramon Santiago. He's probably one of those speedsters."

"That's a no brainer," said Harley. "A fast runner on second may be able to score easier than the typical base runner."

The next sequence unfolded when Rodriquez grounded out to the first baseman, who looked Santiago back and then tagged the bag. Clapping along with all the nearby fans, Drew had to shout to be heard. "That's the second out. We're one out away from the title!"

"Don't count your chickens before they're hatched," warned Harley. "Santiago is still standing out there on second and the tying run is at the plate. One swing of the bat and this game is tied. This could unravel quick or it could end quickly."

Harley's prediction of what *could happen* began to take form when Wainwright threw a wild pitch, Santiago sprinting over to third. There was a hush that fell over the crowd but then it picked back up again as Wainwright threw his next pitch that was called a ball. The crowd was stunned as they watched Polanco who drew a walk make the slow trot down to first base.

"Crap!" shouted Drew. "It's happening just the way you said it might! Two men on base with two outs and the go ahead run at the plate."

The crowd noise had returned with the anticipation of Inge, who now stepped into the batter's box as the last out of the inning, the last out of the game, the last out of the season.

Inge quickly fell behind in the count 0-2 and the crowd was jumping up and down, yelling and screaming. Wainwright wound up and delivered a slider that Inge swung at and missed. The game was over, the series was over, the season was over and the St. Louis Cardinals were World Champions in the world of baseball for the tenth time. The woman standing next to Harley grabbed him and gave him a full kiss on his lips. Drew laughed as he watched the fans celebrating in joy. Hats were flying, people were dumping drinks on top of one another while the Cardinal team members gathered behind home plate, jumping up and down and hugging one another as if they were little kids. Harley reached out and shook Drew's hand. "We did it. We're World Champions again!" Leaning forward he spoke directly into Drew's ear, as it was hard to hear with all the noise. "Let's sit and wait for things to calm down."

Drew and Harley sat in silence for the next ten minutes while fans slowly started to exit the stadium. Harley, reviewing his scorecard, placed it in his shirt pocket and sadly remarked, "Baseball is over for this year, but only for the fans and the players. It will be almost three and a half months before pitchers and catchers report for next season's training and then six weeks after that and we're into next April and the 2007 season. Most major league players will spend valuable time with their families, which during the regular season they cannot do because of all the travelling involved. Many of them will go on vacation, hunting or fishing trips or sitting on a beach somewhere down in Florida. Not so for a major league front office. Take the Cardinals front office for instance. I'm not really sure what all they do, but I imagine that starting within a few days or even weeks they'll start to prepare for next season. There'll be talk of who they may bring up from the minors or if they need to make some trades, depending on what their needs are. Scouts will be scrambling, like they always do in search of new talent."

Drew smiled and looked at Harley. "You mean…like you? It's been months since our season at Mizzou ended and yet, there is not all that many days that pass where you're not contacted by a major league scout. If it's not a phone call it's a letter or even a visit. After that second no-hitter you tossed this last season there was not a single game, home or away where there was not at least one major league scout in attendance. You will be the topic of many conversations between scouts and their front office over this winter. You had an unbelievable season."

Harley grinned, "Yeah I guess it was pretty good."

"Pretty good! I'd say it was excellent. Even though we came in third in the conference, we finished up 30-27, just three games above .500. You, on the other hand went undefeated, 12-0. Coach Meadows says you're the best freshman pitcher he's ever seen in all his years of coaching. He claims that if you pitch next year like you did this past season, you'll never see your junior year. You'll be signed by a major league team."

Drew stood and waved around the stadium. "It looks like the place is starting to empty out. Let's get out of here and hit White Castle on the way home and celebrate with some sliders!"

CHAPTER 31

SEATED AT THE LONG, ANTIQUE OAK TABLE, HARLEY looked around the large country dining room: matching oak buffet table, wainscot paneled walls sectioned off with a green and brown flowered wallpaper and an old fashioned chandelier suspended from the twelve-foot ceiling. It was a comfortable room, the logs in the stone fireplace snapping and crackling, the wonderful smell of pine and hickory filling the room. Large white flakes of snow gently drifted past the great picture window.

Grandpa Madison stood at the far end of the table and raised his hands and looked at all those seated at his table. At the opposite end sat Mira's father and mother. On her father's right, came Mira who sat next to Harley, then Harley's parents. On the opposite side of the long table sat Drew and Melanie, then Drew's parents and his sister, Roxann. Last but not least, Grandma Madison sat next to her husband. Reaching for his wife's hand, Grandpa humbly requested, "If everyone would stand and join hands, we will then bless the meal."

Mira stood with everyone else and held hands with Harley. Looking around the table at all the guests, she felt blessed. Directly across from her sat her best friend, Melanie, who took Drew's hand and nodded back at Mira.

Satisfied everyone was prepared for the blessing, Grandpa Madison began, "Dear Lord. We thank you for those who have come to our humble farm this day, the first day of the New Year. We thank you for our health and the roof above our heads. We thank you for the freedom that the men and women in our military provide. We thank you for this bountiful meal that has been set before us and we ask that you bless the hands of those who have prepared it. Amen!"

Hoisting his glass of wine, he smiled and continued to speak, "Here's to the first day of the New Year; January 1st, 2007. May each and every one who sits at this table prosper in the coming year."

Following the clinking of glasses and handshaking, Grandpa suggested, "Let's eat!"

Harley leaned sideways and spoke to Mira. "Everything looks so good. I've never had pork and sauerkraut before. I've had pork by itself...but never sauerkraut."

Passing a bowl of black-eyed peas to Harley, she explained, "Back east pork and sauerkraut is a New Year's day tradition. The combination of pork and sauerkraut and black-eyed peas is considered good luck and a great way to start the New Year off."

Buttering a hot roll, Grandpa Madison addressed Harley. "I understand you and Drew attended the final game of last year's World Series."

Smiling across the table at Drew, Harley stabbed a thick slice of pork and answered, "Yes, we did. It's the first World Series we've ever been to. It's something I'll never forget."

Grandma spoke up, "How do you think the Cardinals will do this year?"

Taking a scoop of sauerkraut, Harley responded, "Our starting pitching rotation is going to look different. I think our bullpen will be strong again. All of our position players are returning except for Ronnie Belliard who signed with the Nationals."

Harley's dad spoke up, "I think the Cardinals are in a great position to take the Central Division this year. I think our infield and outfield is as solid as it was last year."

"That's true," added Harley's mother. "But we can't forget how the Cardinals fell apart at the end of the regular season losing seven games in a row. We blew a seven game lead in our division."

Drew held up his hand. "But we still managed to take the World Series and in the end that's all that matters."

Grandma Madison took a bite of pork and with a mouthful spoke, "In the end it doesn't make any difference how a team wins the title. The record book will show in future history; St Louis Cardinals – 2006 World Series Champions!"

Grandpa looked down the table and asked Harley, "Speaking of the 2007 baseball season, I guess you and Drew will be returning for your sophomore year at Mizzou. Mira here has told the wife and I that you had a pretty good season this last year. She tells us you have had a number of major league scouts talking with you about your future."

"A number of scouts have shown interest in me," said Harley, "but I really can't consider any team until I'm twenty-one which means I'll have to complete my second year at Mizzou." Looking across the table at Drew, Harley went on, "It is not only me who scouts have been interested in, but Drew as well. The success I have experienced this past season has a lot more to do with than just my pitching abilities. As my catcher, Drew called each one of those games from behind the plate. The truth be told, Drew has had a number of scouts talk to him about a major league future in the big leagues. But, all that's down the road. Neither one of us may make it to the bigs."

Mira jumped in on the dinner conversation. "I don't think you boys give yourselves enough credit. What other college across this country could boast a pitcher-catcher combo that went 12-0 last year with back to back no-hitters."

Now, it was Melanie who spoke up. "There may be other schools that had a pitcher and catcher go 12-0, but back to back no-hitters by the same pitcher may be a first at the college level, but not at the professional level. I have been doing some research for an article I'm going to be writing for the school newspaper this coming March. From what I have been able to discover consecutive no-hitters by a pitcher has only happened one time in major league history and the pitcher was Johnny Vander Meer of Cincinnati. In 1938, he threw a 1-0 no-hitter against the Boston Bees. The very next day Vander Meer threw another no-hitter at Ebbets Field against Brooklyn beating them 2-0. What Vander Meer did back in 1938 still stands today in the eyes of baseball historians as the most unbeatable, unbelievable pitching feat in baseball history.

Harley's mother smiled at Melanie and remarked, "I think you've been spending far too much time around Harley, Drew and Mira. When they get together it's always baseball this and baseball that. I'd say they have rubbed off on you."

Melanie sank down in her seat and spoke humbly, "Perhaps I have said too much during our meal."

"Nonsense," said Drew's mother. "I find your comments and research very interesting."

"I agree," added Drew's father. "I'd be the first one to admit that my knowledge of baseball is quite limited but I do know the no-hitter is a rare event in the game."

"Well, seeing as how we are in the presence of a young man who has not only thrown two no-hitters, but back to back," said Melanie, "I feel it's important to mention he is standing in some pretty talented company when you consider the number of no-hitters thrown in baseball history. I'm not sure, but what he has accomplished in pitching those two consecutive no-hit games may be a first, at least in college. What Harley did is simply amazing!"

Harley sat back in his chair and held up his hands. "Look, I appreciate all the compliments, but like I said before, it was not just my effort that won those two games. Drew is just as responsible for those two victories as I am."

Grandma Madison reached for the potatoes and asked Harley, "With the 2007 college baseball season rapidly approaching when do you and Drew start training for this year?"

"Actually, we were supposed to start today, but I'd much rather be here enjoying this wonderful meal." Gesturing toward the large window, he pointed out, "Besides that, it's snowing. Drew and I have decided to wait until we return to campus in two days. Then we'll get started."

Drew's father asked, "And what does this training involve? I mean being at the college level one would think it would be more intense, than let's say high school."

"Normally, Drew and I would be training the same as last year, but my father discovered an off-season training regimen used by many major league pitchers. Coach Meadows, as it turned out, is familiar with the program and said it was not designed for young players under the age of eighteen, but since I am going to turn twenty-one this year, he would okay the training. The program involves an eight week program that includes various workouts for a pitcher and a catcher."

"Eight weeks," said Melanie. "That seems like a long time."

"It's really pretty normal. A lot of pitchers take time off in the off-season, but also realize that they need two months of throwing in order to get ready for spring training."

Curious, Melanie asked, "And what does the eight weeks include?"

"Well, there is a different program for pitchers and for catchers. Drew and I will be assisting each other during this training time. I will be glad to explain the pitcher's training but Drew will have to tell you about his training. It's rather complicated and doesn't make for very interesting conversation. I'd hate to bore everyone this afternoon."

Grandpa spoke up, "No, go right ahead. I find this very interesting. I'd like to hear about this training program if it's all right with everyone else."

Harley looked around the table and seeing no objections, he said, "Okay then...here goes! The first four weeks will take place in January. It's more about conditioning than it is training. The first part of the program is based on a flat ground, long toss system where, as the weeks go by, the number of throws and the distance increases. We throw every other day and on the days when we don't throw we will do some light weight lifting and get plenty of rest."

Drew's mother spoke up, "But what if the weather is bad...like today?"

"As long as it's not bitter cold out, we can still throw. Or, we can go to the gymnasium. Each week changes, not only in the amount of pitches and the distance but in the way the distance is handled."

Drew's father ran his fingers across his chin and commented, "This system sounds, well almost scientific. I guess I never realized all the preparation involved in the off-season."

Harley pushed his plate to the side. "If you think the first four weeks were scientific you're going to love the second four week program. Starting in February, Drew and I will start working on throwing bullpens. Bullpens are a series of blocks of pitches designed to simulate pitches at the exact distance of major league pitching which is just over sixty feet. They are also made from an elevated mound. It becomes a form of target practice. During this time we can work on the mechanics; follow through, where my lead foot lands, how I come off the mound. Coach Meadows informed me that if I stick to the eight-week program I would be more than ready for spring training."

Mira's grandfather seemed amazed as he poured himself a cup of coffee. "I've been watching the St. Louis Cardinals play for nearly sixty-five years. I've seen many a pitcher come and go. Some were average and some were just plain great, but I never knew until this moment, after listening to what Harley just told us, what a pitcher has to go through before spring training. I always thought spring training was the beginning, but as it turns out there is two months of regimented this and that before spring training even starts. Amazing!"

Grandma stood and walked to the buffet table. "Who's ready for dessert? We've got three kinds of pie; apple, cherry crumb and pecan and thanks to Drew's mother we also have a delicious looking chocolate cake."

Everyone waved off dessert for the moment, claiming they were too full, that is except for Roxann who said she would like a piece of cake. Cutting into the cake, Grandma spoke to Drew, "After hearing Harley's rundown on his training I think we're ready to hear about the program you will be using in the off-season."

"Well it's not all that exciting," said Drew. "It's a lot of repetition of various exercises."

Grandpa sipped at his coffee and then remarked, "I'd like to hear about these exercises. We've heard from Harley about what he will be doing, but that's only half of facing a hitter at the plate. As the pitcher he delivers the pitch, but we all know there has to be someone on the other end to catch the ball. So, what will you be doing for the next eight weeks?"

"First of all," answered Drew, "I will be on the catching end of all those long toss days and the bullpens Harley explained. That in itself is a form of conditioning. In addition to that my program consists of not only conditioning but stamina as well. Leg strength is a must for a catcher. I have to be at the top of my game when it comes to my feet, leg movement and explosiveness. I have to be in mid-season form on the very first day. This may seem unrealistic because pitchers, position players and hitters' speed and timing will improve as they get deeper into the season. As a catcher, I have to be able to catch a complete game or even be capable of catching a doubleheader on the first day. There are three things my program will focus on; receiving, blocking and catching. There are eleven different exercises in my program that will get me to where I need to be by opening day. These drills will enable me to gain the two most important physical tools a catcher needs, which are being able to block a ninety-mile an hour fastball in the dirt then throw the ball down to second base in a little less than two seconds."

Grandpa, deciding on dessert got up and walked to the buffet where he took a slice of apple pie that his wife had cut into eight sections. Using a can of Ready Whip, he covered the baked treat and returned to the table all the while talking, "This training and conditioning sounds almost militaristic. It sounds to me that being a catcher may be the most difficult position in baseball."

Harley, eyeing the luscious piece of cake his sister was eating, got up and walked to the buffet. "I just have to have a piece of that cake." Walking back to his seat he agreed with Grandpa. "You are precisely correct. Catching is without a doubt the most difficult position on a baseball team. Nothing saps your strength, causes more sustainable injuries and cuts a player's career short than putting on the tools of ignorance, which is what some players refer to the catcher's gear as. Catching requires more concentration and wears on a player's physical abilities more than any other position. That's why I respect Drew so much. He is involved in ninety-five percent of all the plays made during a nine inning game. He has to be prepared when I deliver a pitch to catch the ball. The outfielders and those in the infield always get ready *if* the ball is hit in their direction. Drew *knows* the ball is coming at him. I have the utmost respect for my catcher."

It was Melanie who spoke next as she stood, "I might as well join the crowd. I'm going for a slice of cherry with some of that whipped cream."

Grandma waved her cutting knife at Melanie. "You just stay seated child. I'll bring you a slice."

Laying down his fork, Grandpa asked Harley, "How do you think Mizzou's ball team will do this coming season?"

"That's the sixty-four thousand dollar question," said Harley as he looked around the table. "Drew and I have been told we will be returning as varsity players. We lost five seniors this year. Two starting pitchers, our second baseman and two outfielders. That means Coach Meadows will be bringing up at least five players from the junior varsity. We played some good ball last year but there were too many teams in our conference that were better."

Grandpa probed farther, "Do you think you have a shot at going undefeated again this year?"

"I doubt it. I was a new face last year. Many of the players I faced last season will be returning. If they do not know who I am yet, believe me, their coaches will inform them. They'll be ready for me. The teams I no-hit or shut out will be looking for some justified revenge on the ball field. The players I struck out a number of times last year will be harder to strike out this season. They've seen me on the mound. They'll know what to expect to a point. If nothing else, it's going to be interesting."

"Out of all the scouts that have been in contact with you last year," said Grandpa, "did anyone from the St. Louis organization talk with you."

"There have only been five teams that have not been in contact with me, one of them being the Cardinals."

"I find that to be very sad," said Grandma as she cut into the pecan pie. "You would think they would be interested in a hometown boy playing on the team. I cannot for the life of me imagine why they would not want to talk with you."

Harley tried his best to explain. "I'm afraid it doesn't work quite that way. Baseball is a business and part of that business is acquiring the best possible ballplayers that a team can get for their farm system. Some of these players down the line, and by down the line I mean months or more than likely a few years, will be able to advance to their major league team. Major league teams recruit and sign players for their skills, not where they come from. I'm sure Cardinal fans would love to see a hometown boy on their team, but those who make the decisions are going to base their choices on what they need to succeed as a team. I would like nothing better than to be signed by the Cardinals, but with all the teams that have looked my way, the chances of that happening are slim."

It was Drew's father who spoke next. "Let me ask you this. If you, and or Drew, make it to the majors will you be the first, or have other Mizzou ballplayers in the past played in the major leagues?"

As always, Harley had the answer. "I wondered the same thing, so right after Drew and I became freshmen we did some research on our own and found out that currently there have been around thirty-six Mizzou players who have gone on to play in the majors.

It all boils down to this. Drew and I, if we do wind up getting drafted in the majors will only have around a twenty to twenty-five percent chance of playing for the Cardinals."

Drew jumped in and added, "It's one of those glass half full, half empty deals. We have a twenty-five percent chance to play for the Cards, but we also have a seventy-five percent chance of not being a Cardinal player. Either way, it really doesn't make a difference to me." Both Grandpa and Grandma Madison gave Drew an odd look as if they didn't understand his comment.

Drew's mother spoke up in an effort to clear up any confusion. "Drew and Harley are the best of friends. My husband and I couldn't have asked for a better friend for our son. Over the past years that we have lived here we have grown to know Harley as a young man who is strongly determined to be a major league pitcher and from what has happened this past year with the major league scouts who have shown interest in him, I have no doubt he'll get there. Drew, on the hand is different. He has always been a young lad, who when he finds an interest goes after it with all he's got. He can play a piano like nobody's business and has become a second degree black belt in karate. I think it's the same with baseball with Drew. Even though his goal in life is not to be a major league player, he very well may wind up…just that. Drew can do anything he sets out to do. If he winds up playing the piano for a living or catching a baseball, we will always be proud of him."

Harley's father stood and walked over to the buffet and picked up a slice of Pecan pie and announced with a wide grin on his face. "Might as well jump on the dessert band wagon." Returning to his seat he went right on talking. "Since the majority of conversation has been about baseball during our meal, I have an interesting story to share with everyone. It happened at my shop yesterday about an hour before we closed. In walks this older man who looked to be in his eighties. He was looking to purchase a bike for his grandson. While we were standing at the service counter he takes notice of all the St. Louis Pennants and framed photos of Cardinal players I had hanging around the place. The old man asked me if I was a Cardinal fan and I said, 'Avid!' He told me he was a Cards fan and I get to talking about Harley and about his two-no hitters and about all the scouts who had been talking with him. He proceeds to tell me that he had been a major league umpire from 1956 until 1971. It was amazing to sit there and listen to some of the stories he shared. Like in 1961 when he watched as Mantle and Maris had their famous home run chase. He told me he had the pleasure of umping games where players like Ernie Banks, Willie Mays, Jackie Robinson, Hank Aaron and many other famous ballplayers had played in. Sitting there listening to this man was like stepping back in time. He told me he was there in 1966 when the first black umpire in the American League stepped on a major league field and then in 1970 when the first ever baseball strike ended after just one day. He was quite the character."

Monica thumped her husband on is arm. "That was an amazing story."

Grandma turned from the buffet and raised her cutting knife in the air and requested, "Anyone else for cake or pie?"

Following a number of no thanks and headshaking she took a piece of apple and returned to her seat at the table. "What does everyone think about our new stadium?"

Mira's father spoke up. "My wife and I have never been to a Cardinal game at the new stadium or for that matter the old one."

Rich chimed in. "Well, Monica and I went to, I guess it's around twelve games last year. We really like the new ballpark."

Harley commented, "Yeah, I think it's very nice. Mira and I went to a few games last year. Drew and I caught a couple as well."

Grandma looked at Grampa and sadly stated, "Well, the ol' man and I haven't been to a Cardinals game in years. I'd love to go sometime, but it's grown hard over the years for us to get around."

Drew's father snapped his fingers. "Tell you what, I've got a great idea. I can always get box seats from my boss at work. I'm sure I can get enough tickets for everyone here at the table, for let's say sometime in May. We can all go to the game together. Whaddya say?"

Everyone around the table nodded in agreement.

"That's it then," said Drew's father. "When I go back to work tomorrow I'll get to work on getting those tickets. I think it will be a fun time for all of us to go down to the stadium to root for the Cards!"

Harley reached under the table and squeezed Mira's hand,

leaned over and whispered. "The year is off to a good start!"

CHAPTER 32

HARLEY THREW A FASTBALL AND SIGNALLED TO DREW that he was warmed up. Walking over to the chain link fence ten feet on the other side of the left field foul line, he hung his glove on the fence and looked out at the parking lot of Taylor Stadium. Drew joined him and asked, "What's so interesting out there?"

Nodding toward the paved lot, Harley then looked back at the stands. "Is it just me or does there seem to be more fans here than usual?"

Leaning on the fence, Drew popped a stick of gum in his mouth and answered, "There are more spectators here than I've ever seen. This is our what...seventh home game this year and I think this is the largest crowd we've had."

"I was thinking the same thing. What's gotten into folks lately?"

"I'll tell you what's gotten into them...you! As a team, we're sitting at 9-5. This is the fourth game of the season you're going to appear in. So far, you're 3-0 this year with two shutouts and the last game you tossed which we happened to win 4-1. You've given up one run in three games allowing just nine hits. They're here to see you pitch. They're waiting for another no-hitter. The limelight is on you tonight, my dear friend. Your parents are here, my folks are here. Melanie has brought a bunch of her friends along. The local newspaper is here, not to mention our old friend, Buck Tillman and at least three other major league scouts I was told about. They're expecting more than just a baseball game tonight. They came to see the show and you just happen to be the star."

"I've got to tell you, Drew. It was a lot easier in Little League and even in high school. I never felt any pressure when I was pitching. Since those two no-hitters last year and going 12-0, it's like everyone expects me to win every time out. I try not to let it bother me, but it seems to me people have placed me up on a pedestal. In the back of my mind I almost wish I'd lose a game. I think maybe after that I'd feel more relaxed when I'm out there."

"Well you better get used to it, because this is just the beginning. Your goal of becoming a major league pitcher is becoming a reality. The goal you've been working toward your entire life is just around the corner. Later this year you'll be turning twenty-one and you'll be eligible for the draft. Next year at this time, I have a feeling you're going to be pitching in the minor leagues. The big stage awaits you. The year after that I think you'll be in the bigs. The expectations of the club you play for and the fans who watch you will be greater. The hitters will be tougher; you'll be a rookie. The pressure you may be feeling today is nothing compared to what in the near future you are about to walk into. I feel the pressure as well. I know people expect you to win. During these past two seasons, behind the plate I get nervous every time you throw a pitch. I can't afford to relax. If I make the wrong call for a pitch or lose one in the dirt, I could be the one who screws the game up for you. I agree with you on the fact that if we could lose a game the pressure would be far less. But, I don't think the day we lose a game is going to be today. Everyone here this evening is going to be pulling for you, well, that is except for those boys in those Western uniforms."

Wanting to get Harley's mind off the upcoming game, Drew changed the topic. "Opening day down at Busch last night didn't pan out. Good ol' April 1st, 2007. The Mets took the Cards out 6-1. Our pitching gave up six runs on twelve hits. We didn't score until the last inning."

Taking his glove from the fence, Harley thumped Drew on his shoulder. "Come on, we better head back to the dugout. The game will be under way in less than ten minutes."

A few feet from first base, a familiar voice got Harley's attention. "Hey there, boy!"

Looking at the end of the stands, there stood Mira, that great smile she always had plastered across her face. Walking over to the fence Harley smiled back. "I thought you said you weren't going to make the game."

"Turns out I was able to skip my last class of the day. My professor is a big baseball fan, so here I am. Your father told me about all the scouts that are here. Now, get out there and win this game and then you can take me out to dinner later."

Harley reached out and took her hand. "See ya after the game."

Joining Drew in the dugout, he listened while Drew went over Western's lineup. "It looks like they've got five returning players from last year. Their lead-off man and the second man in their lineup are the same as last year. Then their fifth, sixth and eighth hitters are the same. That being said, half of this lineup has faced you before. You've struck out every one of these players at least once. Not one of them was able to get a hit off you. You killed them last year with your off-speed, off the plate pitches. They'll be looking for the same thing again and probably lay off pitches that are not near the plate. If I was their manager I'd try to get your pitch count up early. You need to keep the ball over or near the plate. That way, they'll either get caught looking or have to swing. Don't let them control the tempo of the game. That is something we have to do. How do you feel?"

"I feel good," said Harley. "As always, I feel confident with you behind the plate."

Meadows gathered the team in the center of the dugout and gave them a rapid pep talk. "Okay boys! Last year we no-hit this team. I know Harley will give us a good game. Let's back him up not only with solid defense but let's put some early runs up on the board." Joining hands the team members gave a loud shout and then the starters took the field.

Harley walked to the mound and worked the dirt in front of the rubber with his right foot. Taking a deep knee bend he watched as Western's lead-off man walked to the plate, swung the bat twice, adjusted his hat and batting gloves and stepped into the box. Drew, in his crouch, looked up at the batter and welcomed him to the game. "How ya doin'."

The batter looked down at Drew, didn't offer a word or even a smile. Realizing that the hitter was totally focused on Harley, Drew gave his first hand signal. A fastball, high.

Harley agreed, wound up and let loose with a ninety-seven mph two seamer. Drew reached up, caught the ball smoothly and framed it, but the call was still, "Ball one!"

Drew thought the pitch should have been called a strike, but just like always it would take a few batters before he as the catcher could determine this particular umpire's version of the strike zone. He threw the ball back to the mound, crouched and gave the same signal. A high fastball. This next pitch may be an indicator of how the game was going to be called. Another ninety-seven mph fastball passed the plate just at the top of the batter's shoulders. The ump made the call. "Ball two!"

This time Harley did not agree with the call. Standing, he gave the ump a stern look and tossed the ball back to Harley. The count 2-0, Drew signaled for a changeup. Harley, realizing the umpire's concept of at least the top of the strike zone was tight, agreed with the call. Winding up, he threw a seventy-nine mph changeup that floated over the middle of the plate. The batter held for a called, "Strike one!" With the count 2-1, Drew called for a fastball just off the outside of the plate. Harley delivered the pitch, which the batter laid off of for a called, "Strike two!" The count was now 2-2 and this batter hadn't even attempted to swing at any pitch Harley offered. Drew was right. Their plan was to run up his pitch count. His next pitch was going to be fastball, down and away. If it was close the batter had to swing or be called out on a third strike.

He started his windup when the batter stepped out. They not only wanted to run up the pitch count but wanted to screw with his timing. The batter stepped back in ready for the pitch. The ninety-eight mph fastball sank toward the bottom edge of the strike zone. The batter swung and connected, hitting a line shot to the left of second base. The shortstop leaped, his glove extended high above his head. The ball tipped the top of the webbing and rolled out into center field. The center fielder who had been playing deep ran to the ball while the runner rounded first and thinking he could get an extra base sprinted for second. The center fielder fielded the ball cleanly and fired the ball to the second baseman who was covering. The second baseman one-hopped the ball and turned to apply the tag but the runner at the last second, realizing he wasn't going to make it applied the brakes and started back for first. The second baseman gunned the ball to the first baseman who put the tag on the sliding runner. The umpire pointed his arm at the prostrate runner and shouted, "You're out!"

Harley looked out at the scoreboard wondering if the line shot would be called an error or a hit. Within seconds he got his answer; base hit. The shortstop ran over to the mound and shook his head and apologized to Harley. "Sorry I didn't snag that one. If I'd of been an inch taller I'd have gloved it."

Slapping his shortstop on his shoulder with his glove, Harley reassured him, "It's all right. That was a clean hit. I'm surprised you even got your glove on it. Not to worry. It was for nothing. We gunned him down at first. No harm done."

Drew walked out to the mound and asked, "Well, we don't have to worry about any no-hitter. Are you all right?"

"I'm fine," said Harley. "Get back in there and get ready for a lot of heat."

The next batter struck out swinging and the third out was a pop up to the shortstop.

In the dugout, Drew grabbed a cup of water and sat next to Harley. "Okay, so the guy got a hit. It's not the end of the world or even of this game. We've got a long way to go before this ones in the books. We can still win this game, which, when all said and done is what really matters. Now, let's talk about who were going to face next inning."

The bottom half of the first went quickly as Mizzou went three up and three down. As Harley took the mound for the top of the second, Rich leaned over and spoke to Monica, "I hope all these people are not disappointed because Harley chances of throwing a no-hitter have gone out the window."

"It's just as well," stated Monica. "Now my son can simply relax and just win the game." The top of the second went even quicker as Harley got the three batters to ground out to the infield with a series of fastballs and a few sliders mixed in.

In the bottom of the second, following Mizzou's first man at the plate striking out, Drew singled to left field, but was doubled up when the next man at the plate hit a sharp ground ball to second base. The second inning ended with no score.

Harley waited at the back of the mound for Western's seventh man in the order to come out of the dugout in thc third. Thc young man who strolled up to the plate was short, but looked like a miniature tank, with legs that looked like small tree trunks and arms that were well developed. He crowded the plate, placing his left foot right on the edge of the lime marking, his right awkwardly placed back in the box as far as possible. He took one swing and then rested the bat on his shoulder. Harley wasted the first pitch throwing it way outside to see how the hitter would adjust his odd stance after the release of the ball. The kid didn't move and inch. Harley took the next signal, which was for a high and tight fastball which made sense since the hitter was crowding the plate. An inside pitch would tie him up, causing him to either swing and miss, foul off the pitch or hit a weak grounder to the infield. Just after Harley released the ball, in a fraction of a second the batter transformed his stance, moving his front foot back and coiling his body, the bat now off his shoulder. Following the crack of the bat, the ball sailed two feet above the third baseman's outstretched glove and kept rising, clearing the left field fence by a good four feet. The runner rounded the bases with little emotion and finally joined his teammates at home plate for a brief celebration as Western had taken a 1-0 lead.

Drew walked to the mound and stated quietly, "That kid really fooled us. The pitch you made was perfect. He just nailed it! It's not the first homerun you've ever given up and it won't be the last. Now, let's get these next three batters so we can get to work ourselves getting some runs. Keep the heat coming." Following a strike out and two outfield fly balls, the top of the third ended with Western in the lead.

As Mizzou ran from the field, a man sitting next to Monica, who just happened to be wearing a Western Kentucky University hat sat with two other men wearing Western jerseys. The man gently bumped Monica on her left shoulder and proudly announced, "That was my son that hit that home run. That pitcher out there on the mound isn't superman after all. He might have no-hit us last year but my son wasn't on that team. If he would have been, why, we may have even have won that game. Yep, Mizzou's wonder boy isn't going to win this one. I guess superman met his kryptonite in the form of *my son!*"

Monica looked at Rich and rolled her eyes toward this Western fan who was going about bashing her son. Rich touched her hand and shook his head slightly indicating to just let it go.

The man stood and waved his hat as he yelled toward Mizzou's dugout. "Take that wonder boy! Ya ain't gonna throw a no-hitter today! Ya ain't even gonna win the game! I wouldn't want to be in your shoes 'cause ya've got to face *my son, that's right, my son* at least two more times at the plate, that is unless they pull ya!"

The man sat back down and placed his hat back on his head. Monica had enough and thumped the man on his shoulder. "Look, you have every right as a fan to root for your team and even your son. Actually, I'm glad you're here supporting your son. That pitcher for Mizzou, that wonder boy as you have dubbed him, is my son!"

The man was about to say something but Monica leaned forward inches from the man's face and pointed at four men who were sitting directly behind home plate. "Do you see those four gentlemen seated behind home plate? They are major league scouts. Did they come here today to see *your son!* No, they did not. They came here to watch *my son!* My son is not a wonder boy or even superman. What he is, is an ordinary young man with extraordinary talent. You can say whatever you like about the opposing team and *so can I!* Unlike you, I will not sit here and bash your son as you have chosen to do mine. My husband and I have been lifelong baseball fans and *you,* my dear friend, give baseball fans everywhere a bad name. Now, you can sit here for the remainder of the game if you like and say whatever you want, but if you continue to ridicule my son, I'm going to make sure you have a very unpleasant afternoon."

The man, completely taken off-guard looked at his two friends in amazement and then stood. "Well, if you think I'm going to sit here and listen to you, then you are sadly mistaken." Turning to his friends he strongly suggested, "Come on, we're changing seats!"

Watching the three men walk down the stands, Rich looked at the surrounding fans and whispered to his wife, "Remind me to never get on the wrong side of you!"

Drew's mother remarked, "The nerve of that man."

Mira smiled and commented to Melanie. "It would seem at times in baseball when it comes to the fans that there is more action in the stands than there is on the field."

The bottom of the third started off with a ground out to third and then Mizzou's right fielder hit a single, but just like the previous inning, he got doubled up to end the inning.

For the next four innings the two teams went back and forth, Harley not allowing another hit. Mizzou got a double in the fourth and singles in the fifth, sixth and seventh but were unable to score. At the end of seven Western still led 1-0.

In the top of the eight, following an error by the first baseman and then a single with men on first and second and no outs, coach Meadows walked out to the mound. Holding his hand out for the ball, he calmly spoke, "Harley, I've got to take you out. We can't afford to give them an insurance run or two. We're only one run down and we're still in this game. You did a great job today."

Harley handed the ball to Meadows and made the slow walk to the dugout. He didn't look in the direction of his friends and family. There wasn't any reason. He knew they would understand why he had been pulled, especially his parents and Mira who understood how baseball worked in these types of situations in the late innings.

Sitting on the bench, the players on either side of him shook his hand and congratulated him on a game well pitched. He laid his glove at his feet and then untied his spikes. He watched as their reliever took the mound and threw a few pitches, when the umpire motioned for Western's next batter to approach the plate. Their reliever, a tall lanky lad who hailed from Kansas City made quick work of the scoring threat getting the next two men out, the first hitting a high foul ball behind the plate that Drew snagged and then a double play that ended the inning.

The bottom of the eight started off with a strike out, then a single to center field. On the next play the runner was forced out at second, still leaving a man on first with two outs. The next batter on a 3-2 count hit a high fly that looked like it was going out of the park. Harley and all the other Mizzou players stood and walked to the edge of the dugout in anticipation of the ball clearing the fence. All the Mizzou fans were on their feet. Western's right fielder back pedaled, leaped and caught the ball just as it was about to clear the top of the fence. A disappointing hush fell over the crowd as Western ran from the field.

Disappointed, Mira sat down and spoke to Melanie. "I was sure that one was out of here. That would have given us a one run lead going into the last inning. We have to keep Western from scoring in the ninth, and then we get one last chance to win this thing, or at least tie the game which would send it into extra innings."

In the top of the ninth, Meadows brought in yet another reliever. He was going to be facing the middle of Western's lineup. The first two batters went down on routine grounders. The next man stepped to the plate, the home run hitting kid who was responsible for the only run of the game. After allowing the home run in the third Harley had faced him in the fifth when he was called out on a short stride 3-2 fastball on the outside corner. The first pitch delivered by Mizzou's new reliever was a fastball right down the pike. The batter swung for the fence, lost his balance and fell to the ground. It was obvious that he was looking for another round tripper; an insurance run. Drew walked out to the mound and advised his reliever. "Keep the ball on the inside of the plate. That's where this guy is the weakest. Don't give him anything fat because he can knock it out of here."

The next two pitches were way inside, brushing the batter back from the plate. Drew signaled for another inside fastball. The pitcher came off the mound a little awkward and the fastball drifted toward the batter, who tried to get out of the way, but was nailed on his shoulder, sending him to the ground in pain. The umpire awarded first base to the runner, then walked toward the mound and gave a warning to the pitcher. Meadows instantly called time and stormed out of the dugout. Inches from the umpire's face, he demanded, "What was that for? He didn't hit the batter on purpose. He came off the mound incorrectly, causing him to lose control. That warning was completely uncalled for!"

The umpire wasn't in the mood to be disagreed with and strongly advised Meadows, "Coach, you need to go sit down. I've made my call and that's it. Now if you want to persist I can toss you out of the game. Your choice!"

Meadows spit on the ground and looked at the kid who was standing on first base. He had such a smug look on his face as he jumped back and forth as if he were going to steal the first chance he got. Turning, the coach returned to the dugout. Calling Drew over to the dugout, he informed him. "That kid on first base is cocky to say the least. I know he's going to attempt a steal on us. Tell the pitcher to keep an eye on him, maybe throw over to first a couple of times. Then, I want you to call for a pitch out. If we get lucky maybe we can nail this guy at second. Got it?"

"Don't worry," said Drew. "If he goes I'll get him!"

Walking out to the mound Drew quickly related the coach's plan. The pitcher looked over at the runner who was in a takeoff position, his right foot on the bag. Facing the next batter the reliever went into his stretch as the runner ventured from the bag. The pitcher looked in at Drew than back to the bag where the runner had taken another step. Stepping off the rubber he made a nonchalant toss over to the first baseman, the runner getting back to first easily. Giving the pitcher a sarcastic grim, he eased off the bag again. Drew had been right as rain about this cocky kid on first. He was responsible for the one run lead and no doubt upset because he had been hit. He was going to make his point by stealing second. Going into his stretch, the runner went further out than his first lead. Tossing the ball over to first base again, the runner dove back safely.

The ball, once again in his glove, the pitcher took the pitchout sign from Drew and thought, *Here goes!* Drew called for a fastball which would enable the ball to reach his glove quicker giving him the advantage of a couple of tenths of a second which could make all the difference. The runner was off with the pitch. He had gotten a good jump but the pitchout was perfect; chest high on the outside of the plate, too far out for the batter to swing. Drew stood, gloved the ball and made the smooth transfer to his throwing hand. The throw was a little high and the second baseman had to reach for the ball. Catching it, he swung the glove down in a hard motion smacking the runner on the side of his head. The umpire signaled, "You're out!" The runner, upset because he had been hit twice in the same inning, jumped up and shoved the second baseman hard in his chest. The second baseman threw down his glove and body slammed the runner. Within seconds both benches were emptied, players on both teams colliding like two opposing armies just behind the pitcher's mound. Players were pushing and taking potshots at one another. Harley had witnessed many a melee watching major league games on television and had seen a few over the years at Cardinal games but had never been involved in one himself. He remembered what his father always told him. *Avoid any fighting that takes place on the field. It's not worth it. You could get injured. Don't let your emotions overrule common sense!* Rather than piling on the mass of bodies that were piling up on top of each other on the field, he walked just to the fair side of the first base line and watched. It took nearly five minutes to restore peace as the players returned to their dugouts. The base runner was ejected from the game and the umpire had a brief conversation with both coaches.

The runner's father, who previously had been bashing Harley, was right down at the fence near home plate as he screamed at the umpire. "Come on, ump! The pitcher hit my son *on purpose*. Then, on top of that, their second baseman tagged him out on his head, again *on purpose*. How about fairness. Their pitcher and their second baseman should be ejected!" Everyone, all the fans and both teams watched as the spectacle continued to unfold. "If this game were umped down in Kentucky those two players would have be ejected. You must be from Missouri! I think you should be thrown out of the game!"

Rich looked over where the man and his two friends returned to their seats. "That guy was really giving it to the ump."

Monica gestured down at the field as Mizzou's first batter of the ninth walked to the plate. "This is our last chance to pull this game out."

Surprisingly Western's pitcher walked the batter on four straight pitches. Mira clapped her hands and spoke to Melanie. "Now, if we can just get that runner over to second in scoring position then we'll have a shot of tying the game."

On the very first pitch the second batter of the inning squared up for a bunt. Western's catcher came out from behind the plate, looked to see if he could get the force play at second, realized he didn't have the time, turned and threw the ball to first. The throw was wide, pulling the first baseman off the bag. He was called safe and Mizzou had men on first and second with no outs. Mira jumped up and clapped her hands again. "Things are looking up!"

The next batter stepped to the plate and took the first two pitches, a ball and a strike. The next pitch was in the dirt and the catcher had trouble finding the ball which had rolled beneath him. The man on second scooted down to third but the runner on first did not advance. Melanie grabbed Mira's shoulder and with a tone of excitement pointed out, "The tying run is just ninety feet away. A sacrifice fly or a hard grounder could score the run easily."

Western's manager walked to the mound, had a short conversation with the pitcher and the entire infield and returned to the dugout.

Western's catcher stood up and signaled by extending his arm for the intentional walk. Rich shook his head. "I can't believe it! A walk does set up the double play, but would allow the tying run to score."

The next batter ran the count to 2-2 and waited for the next delivery. A low fastball that the batter hit sharply to third. The third baseman backhanded the ball and forced the runner from third out at home. Everyone was safe, the bases still loaded but now with one out.

"This is what I love about baseball," said Rich. "You never know what's going to happen next."

The next Mizzou player stepped in the box. After three pitches Western's pitcher found himself ahead in the count 1-2. The catcher signaled for a fastball high and tight. The batter swung at the ball and hit a towering infield fly between second and first. Western's second baseman waved off the first baseman, caught the ball and looked the runner on third back.

Monica frowned. "That was an important out. Our chances of tying this thing up just went down dramatically." Turning to Drew's mother she pointed as Drew approached the plate. "It's all up to Drew now."

Drew stood next to the batter's box and surveyed the game situation. The bases were loaded, two outs, bottom of the ninth, down one run, tying run on third, winning run on second. What he wound up doing at the plate would determine who won and who lost. Western's outfield was playing slightly in to prevent the runner on second from going home in case of a routine single. The infield was playing back. They only needed one out. Drew thought to himself, *This would be the perfect time for a bunt.* The thought quickly left his mind as he recalled what Meadows told him just before he grabbed his bat and stepped out of the dugout. *The situation is simple, we need a hit!*

Drew stepped into the box and looked out at the opposing pitcher, swung his bat twice and readied himself for the first pitch. The pitcher didn't waste any time. He checked the runner on third, then focused his attention on Drew who stood poised at the plate. The pitch came. A fastball, low and outside. Drew simulated the bunt but pulled back and the call was for ball one. The infield reacted just like Meadows planned. Drew watched as the infielders took a few steps deeper toward the plate. Drew stepped away from the box and spit out his gum.

Back in the box, he prepared himself for the second pitch. It was another fastball but closer in. He showed bunt but held for a called strike, the count now 1-1.

Drew's mother stood along with everyone else but held her hands over her eyes as she spoke to Drew's father, "I can't look!"

Monica yelled toward the field, "Come on, Drew, you can do this!"

Melanie joined in on the cheering, "We need a hit Drew. We need it now!"

The third pitch was high for ball two. The pitcher took an extended amount of time before he stepped on the rubber. *He's nervous,* thought Drew. *He's overthinking this next pitch.* Finally, the pitcher took a deep breath, wound up and delivered a fastball right down the pike. Drew knew this was his pitch. Swinging at the ball he connected, the ball scalded down the first base line. The first baseman leaped to his right, his glove extended. The ball slammed into the glove as he fell to the ground. Staring at his glove, he reached over and held up the ball. The game was over. Drew ran through first base and down the line where he bent over thinking, *Just another inch or so and this game would have been ours.*

Monica grabbed her purse and looked at Rich, "That's that…we lose!" Turning to Drew's parents she suggested, "Why don't we grab a bite on the way home."

Mira overheard and made a suggestion of her own. "Harley and I are going out for dinner as soon as he showers up. Why don't you join us?"

Monica politely refused, "No, you kids go ahead without us. You don't get to see that much of one another. Enjoy your dinner."

Mira turned to Melanie and asked, "You and Drew have plans for tonight?"

Melanie started down the stands, turned and replied. "Just some fast food burgers and a movie. Drive safe on your way back to school."

Harley was interrupted from picking up his glove by Buck Tillman who stood at the end of the dugout. "You pitched a good game, Harley, two hits, one run." Winking at Harley, he held out his hand. "We'll stay in touch."

Harley shook the scout's hand and replied. "Will do!"

Next it was Mira's voice he heard who had been standing just behind Tillman. "Why don't you go on and get that shower. Don't dillydally too long. I'm starving!"

Seated at a window table at Longhorn Steakhouse, Mira poured a small portion of Thousand Island dressing over her salad as she stated with pride, "That was one whale of a game you pitched today."

"That's the same thing Tillman told me," said Harley. "We came so close to pulling the game out in the last inning."

"You did everything you could to win that game. Unfortunately, one of the hits you gave up happened to be a solo home run that turned out to be the winning run. That's baseball! So, you lost a game."

Popping a small cherry tomato into his mouth, Harley added, "It's strange that I lost today. Drew and I were just talking about that very thing prior to the game. We both agreed it might be better if we lost a game. Since we've been here at Mizzou we haven't lost, and now that we lost I think some of the pressure that comes from fan expectation is gone, if nothing else less expected."

Mira took a drink of water, inquiring, "We haven't talked all that much about the upcoming draft. In a couple of months you'll be turning twenty-one and you'll be eligible. June is just around the corner. Have you given the draft anymore thought?"

"I have given the prospects of entering the draft some serious consideration. Buck Tillman had lunch with my father last week and gave him some advice about the draft. He told my father if I was going to be involved in the draft I was going to need an agent."

"Have you considered anyone yet?"

"Yes, we have. Tillman told us about a young agent out of Florida. He's young and he hasn't been around as long as most agents, but Buck told my father he's really a good negotiator and only wants the best for the players he represents."

"How much do these agents or advisors charge for their services?"

"Good agents normally charge somewhere around three to six percent of what you're offered. Tillman told my father that we should look for an agent who'll charge us between three to five percent."

As their steaks were delivered to the table, Mira asked, "What about Drew? I know some scouts have looked at him as well. Do you think he'll enter the draft with you or will he decide to finish all four years of college?"

"We've had this conversation a few times. Drew's parents are not as obsessed with baseball like my parents are. Drew is not as dead set as I am on being a major league player. He is still leaning toward a career in music. I hate to think about it, but I may have to move on without him."

Cutting into her steak, Mira checked to see if it had been prepared correctly, then spoke, "You and Drew have been together for just over a decade as pitcher and catcher, but more importantly than that...great friends. You may lose him as your catcher but you will never lose his friendship. If Drew were here with us right now I'm sure he wouldn't have a problem with you moving on to the draft without him. Once again, remember that even though you may lose something in your life that you love, you must be prepared to let that thing go, but never let go of the hand of God. He's the best catcher there ever was. You can throw him any pitch there is in life and he'll be there to catch it. There is not a curve ball in life that the Good Lord cannot catch!"

CHAPTER 33

PULLING TO THE CURB, THE DRIVER ANGLED HIS THUMB toward the luxurious building and announced, "Here we are…the Tampa Bay Breeze Hotel, known for its elegant accommodations and exquisite dining." Rich handed the driver a twenty while Harley took in the lavish exterior of the building. White stucco walls with black hurricane shutters, and a four-tier fountain surrounded by tall palm trees.

As the driver pulled away, Rich gestured toward the enclosed glass turnstile doors. "What say we head on in and get this show on the road."

Passing through the rotating doors, Harley looked at the circular marble staircase on either side of the huge lobby. Walking past a large wall of mirrors, he stopped and admired he and his father. "When's the last time we went anywhere where we both had to wear a coat and tie?"

Thinking, Rich answered, "I believe the last time we got decked out this nice was three years ago when we attended your Uncle Jim's funeral."

Adjusting his tie, Harley followed his father to a large marble topped check-in counter where a uniformed employee stood. "How do we know where to meet this man or what he looks like?"

"He told me on the phone last night he'd be at a window table in the dining room and that he'd be wearing a red blazer and white pants."

Stopping just short of the reception counter, Rich asked a clerk, "Could you direct us to the dining area."

"Of course," said the man politely. "Go past the staircase on the right, then make a left. You can't miss it."

Passing the staircase, they saw an arched doorway up ahead. Rich pointed at a sculptured neon blue sign that read, *The Breeze.* "That must be it. Let's go on in and see if we can find this fella."

Just inside the entrance they came to a hostess desk where a young lady stood. Smiling, she inquired, "Just the two of you?"

Rich looked into the large room and responded, "Yes, just the two. We're supposed to meet a gentlemen here. He's wearing a red blazer."

The girl smiled again and confirmed, "You must be referring to Derron Wilks. If you go past the bar and into our back room you'll see him at one of our window tables."

There were a number of scattered couples and individuals seated at tables and a short line at a buffet with steaming trays of breakfast foods. Waiters in powder blue tuxedos scurried here and there. Stopping just past the bar, Rich scanned the tables near the windows where he saw a tall man with a neat crew cut stand and wave at them. "That must be our Mr. Wilks over there."

Wilks walked around the table and extended his hand to Rich and welcomed his two guests, "You must be Mr. Sims and this must be your son, Harley."

Shaking the man's hand. Rich responded, "That'd be correct and I take it you are Mr. Wilks."

Reaching for Harley's hand, Wilks addressed Harley, "Nice to meet you. Please have a seat. This will be a very informal meeting so you can just refer to me as Derron." Gesturing at two chairs, he asked, "How was your flight down this morning?"

Rich pulled out a padded chair and answered, "It was dark and raining when we left St. Louis, but by the time we landed here in Tampa, the sun was out and the temperature feels warmer."

Signaling a waiter over to the table, Derron asked Rich and Harley, "How about something to drink?"

Rich looked at Harley and suggested, "How about some iced tea?"

Harley agreed with a nod of his head.

Derron held up three fingers and addressed the waiter. "A pitcher of iced tea and three glasses please."

The waiter wrote down the request on an order pad. "Right away, sir."

Sitting back in his chair Derron crossed his legs and folded his hands on the table. "Why don't we get started with you, Harley, telling me a little bit about yourself? I already know a few things about you from talking with Buck Tillman."

Harley took a short breath, looked at his father and then began,

"Well. You already know we're from the St. Louis area." Gesturing at Rich he went on to explain. "My parents have always been huge baseball fans and like a lot of people in St. Louis are somewhat obsessed with the Cardinals. So, when I came into the world I was introduced to baseball at an early age. I was taken to many Cardinal games, not only as a baby but also as a young boy growing up. By the time I was five, I was already throwing a baseball and could hit better than other kids my age. I played T-ball, coach-pitch and Little League where I pretty much dominated as a pitcher. Then, I played a couple of years of pony ball, then pitched in high school. Up until I graduated from high school there wasn't a day that passed since I was five that I did not follow a regimented practice session in our backyard, well, that is except for a few weeks when I broke my arm. I have always had a goal of becoming a major league pitcher. I have never doubted for one second that I wouldn't make it. I know there are a ton of kids that grow up with a desire to be in the major leagues and I am also aware the chances of that happening for most of them will never come true." Handing a manila folder to Derron, Harley continued, "Here, in this folder are my stats going all the way back from my Little League days up until the game I pitched two days ago in college. In there you will find my win-loss record, my overall ERA by year, the number of strikeouts and walks I have accumulated and other interesting stats."

Derron opened the folder and scanned the first typewritten page, then closed the folder and laid it to the side. "I'll go over your stats later tonight, but to be honest with you, major league scouts are only going to be interested in what you've done as a pitcher in college. They may possibly look at your high school record, but what you have accomplished more recently at Mizzou will be more in line with what they'll look at. Speaking of that, Buck, knowing that you were meeting with me today, called me last night with your college stats. Last year as a freshman you were 12-0 with two no-hitters. This year so far, your 7-1. That equates to a college career record so far of 19-1 with an ERA of 2.94. If you keep pitching that way, there will not be a team in the American or the National Leagues who will not give you a long look. Buck told me the Indians are extremely interested in you, Harley. Buck knows a lot of scouts from different teams. You've got their attention and more than likely they'll all come knocking. That's why it's important for you to have a good agent."

Rich spoke up, "That's why we flew down here to see you, Derron. Buck highly recommended you. How is it that you know him?"

"I met Buck, I guess it's been about ten years ago. I played ball with his son for Florida State. He was a shortstop, I played second. I guess growing up I was a lot like you, Harley. Practiced every day, hoping and dreaming that someday I'd play in the majors. Everybody said over the years I was the best to come along in Arkansas. I piled up the stats in high school, but in college it was different. I found out I just wasn't good enough to make it to the majors. So, after I graduated, I decided I could still have a baseball career but it wasn't going to be playing ball but helping other young men to realize their dream of making it to the big leagues. I've been at this agent business now for six years. The first two years were slow but then things started to pick up and to date I have represented ten young men who were signed in the minors and currently I have two of my past clients playing in the majors."

"If I could ask," said Harley, "who are they?"

Derron smiled. "David Williamson who plays third base for the Nationals. This is his second season and then there's Clay Summers who is an outfielder for the Reds. This is his first year. They spent three years in the minors before they were called up."

Harley looked at Rich and then to Derron. "Then I guess we can only assume the other eight are still in the minor leagues."

Derron held up two fingers. "Only two."

Harley leaned forward and asked, "What about the remaining six? What happened to them?"

"They didn't make it. The truth is…most don't. I want to be up front with both of you. Only one percent of ballplayers in high school get signed in the minors whether they go to college or not. For those who do get signed in the minors the percentage goes down ever further…less than one percent. Harley, you're about to enter the final phrase of meeting your goal, but let me make myself clear. You have to be all in…one hundred percent. You can have all the talent in the world and a great attitude and still not make it all the way. That's why it's of the utmost importance you have an agent to walk you through and prepare you for when you enter the draft. You have the credentials, the heart and the attitude to go all the way. But you need more than that if you want to cross the finish line. You have to have persistence because the life of a minor league player is not all peaches and cream. There are a lot of misconceptions about the minors. Playing in the minor leagues can be, and often is, a tough row to hoe. Let's walk through the process so you know what you're getting into. First of all, if a major league club wants to sign you, when and if you sign you will not actually sign a contract with a major league club but with a minor league team in their farm system. This contract could be for as long as seven years. That does not mean you will play for that minor league team for the full contract because you may get bumped up to the next minor league level. Let's talk about those different levels."

"When you are officially signed, you will be sent to a mini-camp which is at a club's spring training facility. How you are evaluated there will determine what level of minor league ball you go to. The lowest end of the system is Rookie Ball. If drafted, I can't see you going to Rookie Ball because that's mainly for high school players who have been drafted. Next, comes the Short Season level which is made up of newly drafted college ballplayers and players from the previous year's Rookie Ball. The next level is Class A Ball. At this level teams play a hundred and forty game schedule in order to give them their first real taste of the demands of major league baseball. Class A is usually made up of players that have moved up from Short Season. However, at times, a club may decide to slot a newly acquired college player into this level."

Clearing his throat, excusing himself and then taking a drink of tea, Derron went on, "There is another level of Class A which is called Advanced Class A or High A. All players at this level are in their mid-twenties." Pointing his glass at Harley, he inquired, "You'll be turning twenty-one later this year…correct?"

"June 2nd," confirmed Harley.

"Excellent!" stated Derron, "because if you make it to Advanced A at twenty-one years of age, I have no doubt that you will be considered a big league prospect. There are two more levels in the minors we haven't discussed. Double A and Triple A. In Double A, you have a combination of the best of the best of Class A and Advanced A. If a player shines in Double A, they could be moved up to the majors, skipping Triple A. Double A is good because you get to play with a lot of players that are on the same level. Triple A, on the other hand is the parent major league club's taxi squad, as it is referred to. Those who play at this level are no longer prospects and can be called up to replace a player that is injured or being sent down. Most of the players in Triple A are in their mid to late twenties or early thirties."

Rich fiddled with a folded cloth napkin as he asked, "Based on what you've been told about my son, do you have an opinion of where, if signed, he may start out in the minors?"

"Yes, I do have an opinion. My opinion does not mean that's where Harley will go, but my opinion may not be too far off the mark. With your talent I'll think you'll bypass Rookie Ball and Short Season. They could start you off in Double A, but that's pretty rare. If I had to guess I'd say they'll probably slot you in A or Advanced A. Despite the fact they already know of your abilities they'll want to see how you perform in the minor league environment. If they start you in A you'll be playing either in the South Atlantic or the Midwest League where players are between twenty-one and twenty-two years of age. Now, this may take some time. How much time? Well, that depends on the needs of the parent club. I'd say as long as you perform on the level that you are now, you're probably looking at two to three years before you'll be wearing a major league uniform."

Harley agreed as he spoke, "My parents and I over the years have discussed this very thing. I have been preparing myself for the time I'll have to spend in the minors."

"I'm glad to hear that," said Derron, "because a lot of young men who get signed in the minors are not prepared for what lies ahead. Let's talk about money...the amount of money you can expect to make while playing in the minor leagues. The truth is, you'll make more money flipping burgers than you will playing in the minors. For example, in Rookie Ball you will be paid around eleven hundred and fifty dollars per month. The opposite end of the minor league pay scale is Double A and Triple A where in the first year you will be paid somewhere around fifteen hundred for Two A and seventeen hundred in Three A. If you equate this to a full year that means that in Rookie Ball a player can make around thirteen thousand a year, while in Triple A the player would bring in just under twenty-one thousand dollars. But you cannot calculate the money in that fashion because you will not be paid for the twelve months of the year, but only for the months you are in training and actually playing which comes in at around seven months. So, the Rookie ballplayer actually makes about eight thousand and the Triple A ballplayer brings in a little under twelve thousand. The average ballplayer in the minors makes less than fast food workers and in some cases is below the poverty level. You may ask yourself. Why would anyone play baseball for what seems like peanuts? The answer is simple. Everyone who is signed hopes that at some point in the future they will get the call to the majors where you can make better than an average living. I think right now the lowest amount paid to a major league player is around five hundred thousand. That's a big difference and why players try to gut it out. Most players don't make it. So, now that you have the monetary facts, Harley, how do you feel about this?"

Raising his glass Harley toasted his father. "Once again, my folks have always been supportive of my desire to play professional baseball. We have had many conversations around our kitchen table back home about this very moment, or what in the next few months could happen. The amount of money I'll earn in the minors is just yet another stepping stone on my journey to the big leagues. I am a single man and do not plan or getting married until after I'm in the majors. My folks have offered to allow me to stay at home while in the minors, so the truth is my expenses will be next to nothing. In the off-season, I plan on continuing my efforts to get my college degree in business and getting ready for the next season."

"It's a good thing to have the support of your parents," said Derron. "There is another aspect we have not discussed about the money you will make in the minors. And that's the signing bonus. That's where your agent comes into play. When a team makes an offer to sign you, your agent will negotiate a signing bonus. Now, there are currently fifty rounds in the draft. With your talent, I feel there is a good chance you will be taken in the top ten rounds, which means that you will be in the top twenty-five percent of players chosen. If you get chosen in the first round, signing bonuses can range anywhere from one million to as high as five million. I have also seen signing bonuses as low as seven hundred and fifty thousand in the first round. If you get chosen in the second round the bonuses can come in somewhere between four to five hundred thousand. The third round normally brings two to three hundred thousand. Even in the eighth, ninth and tenth rounds you can still get thirty to fifty thousand. I've seen bonuses as low as eight thousand and as high as a million in the tenth round. We could sit here all day and talk about the draft because it can be quite complicated. When we talk about signing bonus money in the draft it's all speculation. We have to wait and see what a team offers and then we negotiate. A sign on bonus is important because it can help to offset the low salary you will get in the minors."

Smiling, Rich raised his glass. "Well then, here's to the good ol' signing bonus!"

Derron raised his glass as well and then went on to explain, "The money issue in the minors is the least of the problems one can face. I don't know if you've thought about it Harley, but you will not have the security of having the same catcher behind the plate like you have over the past few years. Buck told me about your friend, I believe his name is Drew. He told me you two have been a pitching battery since back in your Little League days. Those days are about to end *and*, I might add, you will never feel the comradery that the pitcher-catcher relationship offers until you are established on a major league team. There will always be new catchers at the different levels of minor league ball. Just about the time you get used to a catcher he or you may get moved up and you find yourself with a new man behind the plate. It takes time to get used to a new catcher. My point is this. Are you ready to move on without Drew behind the plate?"

"Yes, I am. Drew and I have talked about this. I was hoping that he would enter this year's draft, but he has elected to finish up his four years at Mizzou. He has had a number of scouts give him a look, but this has not swayed him. I realize that I may have to move on without him as my catcher."

"I'm glad you feel that way because when you get to the minors you'll find it much different. You may meet some players along the way that you will face or play with in the majors. I can guarantee you you'll meet more players that will eventually fall by the wayside. It's like this, the minor leagues are like a giant hopper that all the minor league players are thrown into. The hopper is always shaking and out of the bottom emerges just a select few who will move on to a major league team."

Refilling his glass with tea, Harley looked squarely at Derron and stated, "I realize that I'll have to pay my dues in order to get through the minors to the majors, but this is nothing new for me. I've been paying my dues for years, standing out there in my backyard in the hot sun, in the rain, snow, sleet, whatever the weather, even on days when I was sick practicing my skills. I've invested a lot of time in my life to become a major league pitcher. There's no turning back now."

"The more we talk," said Derron, "the more impressed I am with your attitude, Harley."

For the next three hours Harley and his father asked question after question as Derron went on to the explain the complexity of the draft. Covering topics like the order of selection, free agents, the draft pool, the supplemental first round, drug testing, compensatory picks, negotiating rights, signing rules, registering with the commissioner's office and on and on."

Over lunch, which Derron ordered, he asked Harley, "How does all this sound to you?"

Taking a bite of roasted chicken, Harley responded, "Quite complicated. Sitting here listening to the whole process it's a wonder anyone ever gets chosen."

"It is a complex system but it works," pointed out Derron. "*And*, I might add again, that's why you need an agent. If you go into the draft without an agent you can still get signed but if you don't know how to negotiate with the powers to be you could wind up with a much lower signing bonus that you may have been awarded through an agent. Actually, I think going into the draft without an agent is like sailing into uncharted waters or venturing into the dark without a flashlight. It's like anything else in life. You can't expect to be an expert at everything you do, but you can surround yourself with experts who can guide you along your path to success."

Swallowing a bite of potatoes, Harley looked at his father, then to Derron. "Buck said you were not only a good agent but a good man. After sitting here talking with you for the past few hours I believe he steered us in the right direction. On the way down here this morning on the plane my father told me that it would have to be my decision if I went with an agent. I've made my decision, Mr. Wilks. I would like you to represent me in the upcoming draft."

Derron smiled, "I was hoping you'd give me the opportunity to represent you. I think you'll go pretty high in the draft. I've represented some talented players in the past but you are by far the most talented I've talked with. It would be my pleasure to be your agent."

Rick spoke up, "So what is our next move? Do we need to sign any papers or a contract with you?"

"Yes, but not now. What I'm about to say may sound underhanded or shady but believe me it's not. It's just the way things work in this business. I will only be an advisor to you until just before you enter the draft. I will not be paid anything until I am your actual agent. Therefore, you don't want to advertise to every Tom, Dick and Harry that we had a meeting. If major league teams find out you have an agent it may be more difficult to get you signed because clubs are aware that an agent will get a player a higher signing bonus. Scouts are always interested in your signing ability and will ask you if you have an agent or if you have talked with one. I am not advising you to lie. If you are asked this question you can answer by simply saying that you have talked with an agent but do not have one at this point which is the truth. It's the politics of baseball. The scouts know how agents work, and we, the agents know how the scouts and their clubs operate. In short, you deserve the largest signing bonus that I can negotiate for you."

Glancing at his wristwatch, Derron stood and announced, "Gentlemen, I'm afraid I've got to run. My daughter is having a dance recital in an hour. If I don't show up for this event my wife will have me tarred and feathered. Don't worry about anything we discussed. This will all work out. All you have to do, Harley, is go back to St. Louis and finish out the season. Keep piling up the good stats. Performance is everything in this business. I'll be in touch. If you have any questions about anything, don't hesitate to call me." Handing Harley one of his business cards, he shook both Harley and Rich's hand and smiled, "Have a good flight home."

Two hours later, Harley looked out the window seat of the plane as it sped down the runway. As the huge aircraft lifted off the tarmac, Harley turned to his father. "I think I made the right decision today in going with Derron. If everything works out the way he says, then next year at this time I could be pitching for a minor league team somewhere."

"At this point I think that's a given," said Rich. "You've got what...maybe four more games to pitch before Mizzou's season ends. It would be fantastic if you could pull out four more wins. That would put you at 11-1 this year with a two year stat of 23-1. In the majors that's Cy Young territory."

Harley thumped Rich on his arm. "Let's not put the cart before the horse, Dad. There is now, and there always will be pitchers that are my equal, some better. Let's just get me in the minors first." Looking out the window as the plane started to level off, Harley admired the passing clouds. "Ya know, Dad, I wish Drew was going into the draft this year."

"I know, Son. But, even if he did there's no guarantee he'd be drafted by the same minor league team. Like Derron said. You have to prepare to move on without Drew. He'll be fine. He'll decide what's best for him, just like you have to."

CHAPTER 34

HARLEY YAWNED AND STRETCHED AS HE ENTERED THE kitchen where he saw his mother busy at the table while she stirred a bowl of some sort on concoction. Rich opened the refrigerator and asked, "We only have a half gallon of milk. Will that be enough?"

"Lord, no!" said Monica. "We'll need at least two gallons. I'll need milk for the mashed potatoes and for the desserts I plan on making, plus some of our guests will probably want milk with their meal. There's a list over there on the counter of some other items I need. It's quite long." Pointing a large mixing spoon at Harley, she ordered, "You need to get dressed and go with your father. It's a lot of stuff to carry. I need you boys to go now. Our guests will start showing up around four o'clock which is only six hours from now. There's a lot that has to be done." Joking, she waved the spoon at them in a scolding gesture. "Get out of my kitchen and don't come back until you have everything on the list."

Rich snapped to attention and saluted his wife, "Yes Ma'am!" Grabbing the list from the counter he looked at Harley. "What are you waiting for, Son? You heard the queen. Chop, chop...move it. Meet me in the truck in five minutes."

Backing out of the driveway Rich smiled at Harley. "Today is a big day...a day we've been waiting for nearly two decades. Today all your hard work is about to pay off. I had trouble sleeping last night thinking about what might happen today."

Harley took a bite out of a cereal bar he had brought along and commented, "I slept like a baby. I'm not worried because it may not happen today. The draft is three days long. I may not get picked in the first few rounds, so we may have to wait until tomorrow or even the last day to find out who the team is who will select me."

"I really hope that doesn't happen, because your mother has put so much effort into this party she's throwing. It's going to be a full house today at the Sims place. We've got Drew, his sister and his parents, Melanie, Mira, her folks and her grandparents. She has also invited Father Joe, who was your Little League coach and your high school coach, Mr. Sanders and Coach Meadows as well. If you don't get selected today, not only your mother but a lot of other folks are going to be disappointed. Now, based on what Derron told you on the phone yesterday, I think you'll be taken in the first or second round. By the way, what was that all about when he told you there would be a surprise you were not expecting?"

"I don't know. He just said there was going to be a special surprise. I guess we'll just have to wait and see."

Stopping for a red light, Rich explained, "One of the reasons I didn't get much sleep last night was that I was up on the computer trying to learn more about the draft. The draft has always been the one facet of baseball I have always looked at as boring. It seems so complex. I guess I never had much interest in watching the draft because I didn't have a dog in the fight. Well, now I do! Sometime, maybe later on today you'll become a professional ballplayer. I wanted to learn as much as I could about the draft so I would understand what was going on. I learned that professional baseball has had a draft since back in 1921, but in the 1950s the legality of drafting players was questioned. The more successful teams in baseball claimed that the draft was anti-competitive and some folks even referred to the draft as a slave market."

The light changed and Rich continued with what he had learned. "Prior to the draft as we know it today, players were free to sign a contract with any team that offered them one. The wealthier teams offered much better contracts and could stockpile the better players while the teams that were not as financially sound had to settle for less talented ballplayers. Around 1947, baseball adopted the *Bonus Rule,* which restricted player salaries and reduced some teams from monopolizing the players market."

Pulling into the parking lot of Deirbergs, Rich hopped out and continued with his newly acquired draft info. "That Bonus Rule I told you about? It turned out to be rather ineffective. Teams would abide by the lower salaries but would at times pay players additional money under the table. It got to the point where in certain situations it became a bidding war for players. In 1964, just a year prior to our current draft being put into place, there was a winter meeting where major league teams could vote on the new and improved draft. The Yankees, the Dodgers, the Mets, and yes, our own St. Louis Cardinals were not in favor of the new laws governing how players were to be drafted. These teams tried to convince other teams to side with them, but in the end the only team to vote against the draft was the Cards."

Grabbing a shopping cart just inside the main entrance Rich continued to speak, "The MLB draft is a strange animal compared to the draft in professional hockey, basketball and football. In the NHL, NBA and the NFL players that are drafted normally within a year or two are expected to have an immediate impact on the team who drafted them. Not so, in baseball. A player who is drafted, at times even in the first round, can get lost in the minor leagues for years trying to hone their skills. The truth is the vast majority of first round picks never make it to the majors." Suddenly, Rich realized he was speaking negatively. "I'm sorry, Son. I know this is a big day for you and here I am spouting off about the down side of the draft."

"No need for an apology," said Harley. "I know I'll get signed. The reason I'll get signed is because of all the hard work and dedication I've put in all these past years. If I never see the mound in a major league game, it'll all be on me. Rather than focusing on all the players who don't make it, I'm going to do everything I can to get to the majors. If that means working harder than I have thus far, so be it. I intend to be one of the few who make it all the way to the top."

Rich, reading the list grabbed two cartons of large eggs and a package of grated cheese. Harley opened a large cooler and took two gallons of milk and stated, "Baseball has a long history behind it. There have been hundreds of thousands of players who have made it to the majors; some with long careers and some short-lived. There have also been hundreds of thousands of players who have played the game but never got to the majors. Players like Ben Taylor who played in the Negro League. One of the teams he played for was the St. Louis Giants in the early 1900s. Still today, he is considered the slickest fielding first baseman who ever played the game. He never played in the majors and yet he was inducted into the Hall of Fame. Then, there was Cool Papa Bell who is still known today as the fastest player to ever play the game. It was said by many that he was so fast he could turn off the lights and be under the covers before the room got dark. He was inducted into the Hall of Fame but never played major league ball. These men were great players but never made it to the top. Myself, I don't need to be great. I just want to pitch in the major leagues."

Outside, in the parking lot, Harley handed the last bag to Rich who stacked the bag next to the rest of the groceries and turned to Harley. "Listen, when we get back to the house, what with everything we need to do to get ready for this wingding and all the guests we're expecting, I may not get much of a chance to say this. I just want you to know how proud I am of you. Today, I get to see my son get drafted into professional baseball. That's something most fathers will never get to experience. Now, let's say we get these groceries home to Mom before she has a hissy!"

The groceries were no more on the kitchen table when Monica started to sort through the bags, placing items strategically around the oblong table. Using a container of mayonnaise as a pointer, she began to assign tasks. "The clock is ticking and I've got a lot of cooking to do, so I'm going to need your help. Rich, you need to vacuum the front and living rooms and then mop the kitchen floor along with some dusting. Harley, I need you to sweep the front porch, mow the front and back yards and set up the three large coolers in the mud room. They need to be stocked with beer and sodas and then iced down. I also need you to bring in those folding chairs we got at that yard sale last year. I have to make devilled eggs, bake a cake and two pies and get the ham in the oven. Now, let's get to work."

Sweeping the front porch, Harley was confronted by the mailman who was coming up the walk. Holding out a handful of assorted mail, Joe, the mailman, as everyone knew him smiled broadly. "Heard the news. Everybody in the neighborhood is talking about it. Our own Harley Sims is going to be playing professional baseball. All the neighbors are going to watch the draft this afternoon. Hope you get signed by the Cards. They could use a good kid like you."

Finished with the porch, Harley walked around the side of the house to get the mower. Opening the shed at the very back of their yard, he pulled out their old push mower and checked the gas level. It was only half full. Grabbing the five gallon plastic can that sat in the corner he unscrewed the gas cap and filled the tank to the brim. Starting up the side of the fence that bordered their property from the next door neighbor's house, he passed Ozzie's simplistic gravesite and smiled as he thought about his ol' pal who would always walk alongside him carrying one of his tennis balls while he cut the grass.

Putting the mower back in the shed Harley looked at his watch, 3:35. In twenty-five minutes their guests would start showing up. Walking across the yard he took the back porch steps in two strides, crossed the mud room and entered the kitchen where his mother was glazing a ham. Looking up she saw Harley and remarked, "You look like something the cat dragged in. You need to get upstairs, grab a shower and get dressed. People are going to be here soon and you're the star of this party!"

Following a hot shower and a quick once-over shave, Harley ran his fingers through his hair, splashed on some aftershave, slipped into a pair of casual slacks and a Cardinal polo shirt, along with a new pair of socks and loafers and raced down the stairs to the kitchen that was buzzing with activity. Drew's mother was busy putting the final touches on a chocolate cake while Roxann and Melanie sat on opposite ends of the table chopping and slicing cheese and vegetables. Melanie looked up with a greeting, "Good afternoon. This must be very exciting for you."

Harley agreed, "It is...it's very exciting!"

Just then, from the back porch, Drew and his father followed Rich as they carted a number of folding chairs to the front of the house.

Monica turned and addressed Harley. "You need to go into the living room. Father Joe, Coach Sanders and Coach Meadows are already here. Why don't you keep them entertained? The only ones that have not arrived yet are Mira and her clan."

Entering the front room, Harley saw the three men, who aside from his father, he considered the most important and influential men in his young life. As Harley approached, Father Joe who had been talking to the others stopped and extended his right hand. "And here we have the man of the day. Harley, how long has it been since we last talked?"

Shaking Father Joe's hand, Harley thought and then answered, "I guess it's been a few years."

Coach Sanders reached for Harley's hand as he explained, "Father Joe was just telling us about what a great player you were in your Little League days."

Harley shrugged. "That time of my life seems a world away right now. I remember those days and how excited I was to throw a seventy-mile an hour fastball."

Sanders added, "And by the time I got to coach you in high school you were throwing in the low nineties."

Coach Meadows placed his arm around Harley's shoulder. "This is a happy day and then at the same time, a sad day for me. Harley pitched his last game for me last week. I got to watch this young man pitch twenty games for Mizzou, nineteen of which he won. It has been a pleasure coaching him, but unlike you two fellas I only had him for two seasons." Laughing, he threw up his hands. "I think I may have got short-changed!"

Turning his attention to Father Joe, Harley asked, "How is ol' Aaron doing these days?"

"It's funny you should ask," said Joe. "I just had dinner with Aaron yesterday. When I informed him that you were going to be in the draft this year, he lit up from ear to ear. He said he would have liked to come along and celebrate, but he's got a game later this evening."

"Is he still in the Cubs organization?"

"That he is, and I might add doing rather well. As you know he started out in Single A ball, but just after a couple of months moved up to Advanced A. Right now he's playing Double A in the Sox's farm system. I really think a major league contract is in his future. It may not be next year, but maybe a year or two after that."

Just then the doorbell rang and in walked Mira with her parents and grandparents. Mira walked over and gave Harley a hug while Harley introduced the three coaches to Mira and her family.

Holding up a covered dish, Mira's mother asked, "Where do you want this mac and cheese? I just took it out of the oven before we left."

Mira's grandmother gestured at her husband who was carrying a cardboard box. "And we've got two pies here also."

Harley looked toward the kitchen and asked Mira, "Why don't you show your folks where the kitchen is. My mother can tell you what she wants done with the food." Mira and her elders no sooner left the living room when in walked Rich, Drew and Mr. Scott.

Walking to a large wide screen television mounted above the fireplace, Rich spoke to the entire group. "What say we get this set fired up? In a half hour, the pre-show for the draft will start."

Mira, entering the front room, interrupted. "Harley, you have a long distance call in the kitchen."

With a look of confusion Harley asked, "Who would be calling me?"

Following Mira into the kitchen Monica handed Harley the phone and went back to slicing the ham.

Walking out into the mudroom, Harley spoke into the receiver, "Hello, this is Harley."

A familiar voice on the other end responded, "Harley...its Derron. I'm just down the hall from where they hold the draft. This place is hopping. Every team has a representative in house. At six o'clock sharp the draft will kick off. I've been looking over all the prospects. There are a lot of pitchers in the draft this year, but I think you'll hold your own. After doing this for a few years you kind of get a feeling for the way things may go. I don't know if you'll go in the first round or not, but I think we can bank on someone taking you in the second. That being said we might not get an offer until later in the day. How are you feeling?"

"I'm feeling good. We have a lot of people here at the house to watch the draft."

"Look, when a team selects you, you'll be able to hear and see what happens. I'll give you a call right after you're picked and then we can get to work. And, one other thing, don't forget, you've got a big surprise coming soon. I'll call you later today. Good luck!"

Harley walked back to the kitchen and hung the receiver back on the hanging wall phone. He noticed Drew standing by the refrigerator with a strange look on his face. Taking a drink of the soda, Drew asked, "Who was that on the phone?"

Harley thought it was an odd question, but answered, "My

agent; Derron Wilks."

With that, Drew addressed all the females standing around the kitchen. "If everyone could grab a drink and come into the front room I have an announcement I'd like to make."

Everyone seemed to be frozen except for Drew's mother who picked up her glass of wine and proceeded to the front of the house. Looking at the others still in the kitchen, Drew emphasized, "I was serious. I have something I want to say everyone needs to hear."

Harley looked at his mother and shrugged. "You heard the man!"

A minute later Drew asked Rich to turn off the TV while he positioned himself by the front door facing everyone. Raising his drink, he proudly announced. "I'd like to make a toast to my best friend, Harley. When I first moved here to Arnold, I was a scared little kid who had a phobia about any type of ball thrown in my direction, so the world of most sports was not in my wheelhouse. But then Harley, through his patience and I must add, an awkward training program got me interested in baseball, and soon I found myself no longer afraid. He taught me everything about the game and I became a catcher. As a matter of fact I've been Harley's catcher for the past eleven years. Harley has been relentless in his pursuit of becoming a professional ballplayer and today that dream will come true. So, here's to you Harley. A better friend I cannot imagine having." Following Drew's example everyone in the room raised their drink.

Harley was about to say something when Drew spoke up. "I have one more thing to say. The phone call that Harley just received in the kitchen was from his agent, Derron Wilks. It was more than just a courtesy call from Mr. Wilks. It was the signal for me to announce a surprise Harley is not aware of." Drew hesitated and looked around the room.

The suspense was killing Harley who finally blurted out, "What surprise?"

Giving his best friend a wide grin, Drew proclaimed, "I, too, am registered in this year's baseball draft!"

Harley, not believing what he had just heard looked around the room and then said, "What? How can that be?"

"It's really not that complicated," pointed out Drew. "After you met with Derron, despite the fact that a few scouts talked with me I told you I was not going for the draft until I finished my next two years at Mizzou. You said you understood and that you were all right with that. You also indicated it was going to be hard to move on without me. I got to thinking and decided to go on this new adventure with you. A few days after you met with Derron I gave him a call, flew down to Tampa and told him I wanted him to represent me in the draft but that he couldn't say a word to you about it. So, here we are. There may be two local ballplayers that may get drafted over the next three days."

Crossing the room Harley extended his hand and stated in amazement, "Congratulations! I'm still a little confused here. You've been telling me ever since we started playing together that you were focusing your future on music. What about getting your degree in music from Mizzou?"

"I'm putting that on the back burner for now. I was playing the piano before you introduced me to baseball and if I do get signed in the minors, I'll be playing the piano long after I am no longer able or interested in playing ball. The window for playing the piano is much longer than being a professional ballplayer. So, why not try and make some money at this baseball business. If I don't at least give this a try then I'll never know."

Father Joe approached both boys and shook their hands. "This is absolutely amazing. Two young boys that I coached in Little League are going to be playing professional baseball!"

Turning, Harley addressed everyone in the room. "Am I the only one who didn't know about Drew being in the draft?"

Drew's mother answered, "The only three people here that knew prior to just a few moments ago are Melanie, Drew's father and myself. It was the big surprise."

Still, in amazement, Harley chimed in, "And what a surprise it was!"

Monica got everyone's attention and announced that in ten minutes all the food would be laid out on the dining room and kitchen tables. "Plates and utensils will be on the counter. There is plenty of ice cold beer and sodas out in the mud room in the coolers. There is also wine and champagne next to the refrigerator. Feel free to eat wherever you like."

Rich waited until she was finished and added as he turned the

TV back on. "The pre-draft show will be starting in fifteen minutes. Let's have a great time tonight."

Minutes later, Drew and Harley sat side by side in folding chairs next to the fireplace. Balancing a plate of food on his lap, Harley leaned over and whispered to Drew, "I can't believe that you decided on the draft. How do your parents feel about this?"

Shoving a devilled egg in the side of his mouth, Drew answered, "They agreed with me that professional baseball is something I should at least give a try. Just like you, in the off season I can continue my education."

Rich banged his fork on the side of his bottle of beer and got everyone's attention. "The pre-draft show is starting."

Everyone crammed into the front room while they watched a four-man team of announcers who sat at a table while they took turns explaining the draft and how the three-day process was going to be conducted. They mentioned a few of the top players and who they thought would be the first few picks.

At precisely six o'clock, the camera focused in on individual team tables where representatives made their picks. The fact that Harley or Drew's name was not mentioned as of yet was frustrating, but Harley had told everyone his agent had forecast that he was not going to be picked until the second round. Drew reassured the group, Derron Wilks had said he would be taken in the later rounds, probably meaning the next day.

At six thirty, the draft took a short break before the second round was to begin. Everyone in the front room stood, some getting refills on their drinks, others going for seconds or even dessert. Drew and Harley were still seated next to the fireplace, but this time armed with slices of pie. Taking a bite of cherry pie, Drew asked, "What do you think so far?"

"Well," said Harley, "I really never paid that much attention to the draft before unless it was to find out who the Cardinals picked each year."

"And this year with the Cardinals getting the thirteenth pick," said Drew, "they chose a third baseman from Arizona State."

"And that was just one of only two third baseman that were taken in the first round. I think it's amazing how the first round went. It was fascinating to see what different teams needed. The entire process is really interesting."

At seven o'clock the Supplementary first round picks were made which involved a lot of free agent players and then at eight o'clock the second round started. The second round picks process seemed to be moving along quicker than the first round as the Rays picked the forty-seventh pick, a left handed pitcher. Forty-eighth went to the Pirates, a right handed pitcher. The forty-ninth, a second baseman, went to the Royals. One name was called after another as teams made their selections. When the sixty-seventh selection was made, another right handed pitcher, Harley tapped Drew on his shoulder and whispered, "I'm starting to get the feeling that Derron Wilks may have miscalculated where I'll be picked."

Drew waved off Harley's concern and reassured him, "Look, there's still ten more picks before the second round is over. And besides that, if you don't go in the second, you'll be picked up tomorrow, maybe in the third. Don't worry about it. Have some faith. Somebody is going to pick you up."

Just then the sixty-eighth pick was announced, followed by the sixty-ninth from the Mets, an outfielder, and then the Padres, a third baseman. Harley finished the last swallow of his drink and looked at the large screen television and then at everyone who was in the room. "Ya know, Drew, you may be right. I may not go in the second round."

Five more players' names were selected and when the Yankees made the seventy-fifth pick, a right handed pitcher, Harley stood and looked down at Drew. "There are only two picks left in this round. You're right. I might as well just relax and wait until tomorrow. It's not going to happen today. I'm going to make myself a ham sandwich."

Seconds later, slapping a thick slice of ham on a piece of bread Harley reached for the bottle of mustard when he heard his name announced loud and clear. *The Cleveland Indians pick the seventy-sixth player in the second round. Harley Sims...University of Missouri!*

The first person he saw was his mother who was standing in the kitchen eating a piece of pie. She had a smile of approval on her face that only a mother could display as she wiped a tear from her eye. The shouting and hollering from the front room was followed by everyone coming to the table, shaking his hand and slapping him on the back. Mira stood off to the side and waited until the small crowd moved off. Walking to Harley's side, she softly reached out and held his hand. "Looks like ya made it there, Harley."

Joining Harley at the table, Drew reached for two slices of bread. "Suddenly, I'm feeling like a ham sandwich myself! Just like Derron said, the second round. Looks like ol' Buck Tillman convinced the Indians you're worth it. I'll expect to see you in a Cleveland uniform in the next couple of years."

The phone in the kitchen rang and Monica gestured at Harley. "I bet that call is for you. Why don't you answer it?"

Trying to contain his excitement, Harley picked up the receiver and answered, "Hello."

"Harley...its Derron. By now I'm sure you're aware that Cleveland has picked you up. Seventy-sixth pick in the second. I was starting to get a little concerned. I was sure you'd get picked a little higher in the round, but nonetheless we've got an offer on the table. Now, you don't have to decide immediately to sign with Cleveland right away. The Indians will have until July 15th to sign you. If you do not sign with them then you become a free agent but cannot sign with another team until next year's draft. As far as a signing bonus is concerned the recommended slot amount is seven hundred and forty-five thousand. I just talked with Buck Tillman. He said the Indians have big plans for you. Now, it's decision time for you. You can tell me right now if you want to accept their offer or wait and see if I can negotiate a higher signing bonus. This is just an estimate but I think I might be able to squeeze out maybe another hundred thousand, which wouldn't be too bad. You don't have to make a decision tonight. So, what do you think?"

Harley turned and faced the mudroom and gave his answer. "This is so amazing. I think I'd like to talk this over with my folks. Can I call you back later tonight?"

"Sure, most of us will be hanging around here most of the night. There is a lot of wheeling and dealing that will take place in the next few hours."

"Okay," confirmed Harley. "I'll call you back tonight. Does it make any difference how late?"

"No, you can call me at three in the morning if you like. Enjoy the evening and I'll talk with you soon."

Hanging up the phone, Harley walked over to his mother and whispered, "After everyone leaves later tonight you, Dad and I need to sit down and talk."

Concerned, Monica walked him back to the mudroom and asked, "Is there anything wrong?"

"No, there's nothing wrong. That was Derron on the phone. He just called to verify that I've been chosen by Cleveland. The reason why I need to talk with you and Dad is because they are offering me a lot of money and I want to make sure I handle this correctly. Listen, when we go back in there I don't want to discuss the money they've offered me. I'd feel like I was bragging. Come on, let's go back in. We'll talk later."

The grandfather clock in the corner of the living room chimed the time at eleven o'clock. Monica closed the door of the dishwasher and pressed the ON button. Wiping her hands on her apron she surveyed the dining room table. Taking a drink of coffee she sat down at the kitchen table where Harley and Rich were busy preparing their coffee. Popping a small sugar cookie into her mouth, Monica sighed, "The dishes are being washed and the leftovers are all put up. I'll worry about the rest of the house tomorrow."

Harley sipped at the hot coffee. "Mom, I want to thank you for all the work you put into the party tonight. Like I told you earlier I need to discuss what Derron talked with me about on the phone earlier. Aside from confirming the Indians had picked me up he told they had a signing bonus offer on the table for seven hundred forty-five thousand dollars." Not waiting for a reaction from his parents, he went right on, "Derron said that I can accept the offer as is and agree to sign or I can wait and see if he can negotiate a higher bonus. He thinks he may be able get an additional hundred thousand dollars. I told him I wanted to discuss my options with you and that I would call him back tonight with an answer. What do you guys think?"

Rich dumped a packet of sweetener into his cup, stirred the coffee with a spoon and then took a drink. Satisfied at the way it tasted, he sat back and looked around the kitchen and then back to Harley and Monica. "Over the years, how many times have we sat around this table and talked baseball? If we were not discussing how the Cardinals were doing we were talking about how you were coming along with your practice, Harley. This table holds a lot of precious memories. The day when your cast was removed, the night after you pitched your first Little League game, the time when you finally mastered throwing a slider, the time when we lost Ozzie, when you threw those two no-hitters back to back last year, and now you're about to be signed by the Cleveland Indians. I don't think it would be fair for myself or your mother to tell you what we think. Rather than doing that I'd rather tell you what we know. And that's just this. Your mother and I never for one moment doubted that you would make it to the majors. Today, you have taken what we both consider the final step to making that happen. It really doesn't make any difference whether it's seven hundred forty-five thousand or eight hundred and forty-five thousand dollars that Cleveland is willing to sign you for. My point is this. No matter how you stack it, that's a lot of money. It would take your mother and myself around eight years to make that amount of money. This decision is yours, Harley, and I think it would be foolish, considering all the work you've put in over the years to allow this opportunity to pass. Now, if you don't mind eventually pitching for Cleveland I believe you should sign with them."

Monica spoke up, "I agree with everything your father said. As far as the signing bonus is concerned that's up to you. If you're happy with what's on the table...fine. On the other hand, if you want Derron to go to bat for you and see if he can sweeten the pot...that's also fine. It's your decision. Either way, we want you to know how proud we are of you."

Harley smiled and stood. "That's it then. I'm going to give Derron a call and tell him to go ahead with the negotiating. I've decided that I'm going to sign with Cleveland even if their initial offer stands."

Rich finished his coffee. "Good decision, Son."

Walking into the front room, Harley sat on the couch and reached for the phone on an end table.

Ten minutes later, the call complete, he went back to the kitchen where he found Monica rinsing out her cup. "I made the call. Derron said he might not have an answer until tomorrow sometime. Where's Dad?"

Monica placed her cup on the counter. "He said he was heading up to bed. He's got to get up early tomorrow for work. I think I'm going to head up myself. I've got the early shift tomorrow at the hospital. Are you going to spend the day at Drew's for the draft tomorrow?"

"Yeah, that's the plan. The draft starts at one o'clock. I'm afraid when he is finally picked he won't have all the folks there that I had here today. His dad has to work tomorrow, Father Joe is driving back to Chicago. I guess the only ones that will be at Drew's house aside from Drew and myself will be his mother, Mira and Melanie. I sure hope he gets picked."

Monica yawned and placed her hand over her mouth. "Are you turning in?"

"Not just yet," said Harley, "I think I'm going to go out back and spend some time with Ozzie. I think he would like that."

Understanding, Monica kissed her son on his cheek and headed for the stairs. "Good night, Harley."

Sitting on the grass next to Ozzie's marker, Harley placed a Milk-Bone on the gravesite. A sad smile came across his face when he placed his right hand on the ground where Ozzie was buried. Wiping a lone tear from his eye, he whispered, "Well, Ozzie, we made it. All those days out here in this backyard when we practiced together and now it's paying off. I had a pretty good day, ol' boy. If you could have only been here…it would have been better." Raising his eyes to the star dotted black sky, he spoke again, "Dear Lord…it's me Harley. Please take care of my dog. I sure do miss him. If you could see to it, I would sure appreciate it if you would give him a big hug for me."

CHAPTER 35

EXITING ROUTE 75 SOUTH, HARLEY PULLED INTO A REST stop, got out and stretched. He had been driving for seventeen hours and had only stopped for gas and food. After visiting the restroom, he purchased a cold drink from a vending machine and then sat at a picnic table in a grassy area next to the visitor's center. Unfolding a map of Florida, he noted that he was an hour and a half north of Tampa. At Tampa, he would then get on Route 4 heading east and after an hour drive would take Route 27 South which would take him to Winter Haven, where Cleveland's spring training facility was located. It was February 12th, two days prior to when he was required to report, but with the long drive down from St. Louis, he wanted to get a good day's rest before he reported for spring training.

Opening an envelope he had received from the Indians organization he reviewed the schedule for the next few days. As a pitcher, he was required to report on February 14th. On the 28th Cleveland would begin a thirty-two exhibition game schedule playing the Astros. The exhibition season would end on March 28th and 30th with a two game series with Atlanta. Getting up, he walked back to his car. Pulling out of the rest stop, he looked at his watch, just after nine in the morning. Depending on traffic he should be arriving in Winter Haven in about three hours.

Cruising down the highway, Harley changed stations on the radio and thought about Drew. He had been the second pick in the fifth round of the draft. The Philadelphia Phillies had picked him up, and tomorrow, Drew would be making the long drive from Arnold down to Clearwater to Spectrum Stadium where the Phillies held spring training. They had agreed that even though Winter Haven and Clearwater were separated by a two hour drive, that during spring training they would try to hook up.

Rolling down the driver's side window, it seemed to Harley like it was just yesterday when back in October of last year the major league baseball season had finally come to a halt with Boston sweeping the Rockies four games straight in the World Series. The Cards finished up in third place in the Central Division, finishing up the season seven games behind the Cubs and two games below the Brewers. The thing he really liked about being a Cardinals fan was that despite the fact that the Cards were never really in the running this past season, the fans still came in support of their team. But, just like any other typical St. Louis Cardinals baseball fan, the past season was just that, last year. The new season was approaching rapidly and baseball fans across the nation were anxious for the wonderful sound of *Play ball!*

His daydreaming about the Cardinals had made the time speed by quickly and he found himself on the Tampa bypass that would take him to Route 4. His thoughts moved on to what Derron had called six weeks of intense training; a constant series of drills, chart pitches and scrimmages all of which would be documented and oftentimes filmed. These would be sent to Cleveland's front office where they would be carefully scrutinized. Derron had forewarned him. *Someone will always be watching you!*

Seeing the road sign for Route 27, Harley made a right and drove south toward Winter Haven. Passing a roadside fruit stand, Harley wondered if he'd ever get to play in the World Series, or if he'd ever get to the Hall of Fame. Suddenly, he realized this line of thinking was ridiculous. But, was it ridiculous? He had just been signed, thanks to Derron's negotiating skills, for eight hundred and fifty thousand dollars. He had always been a kid who was always thinking ahead to the next level. When he played Little League, he was thinking ahead to high school. While in college, he thought about the minor leagues and now that he was in minor league spring training, he was already thinking ahead to the day when he'd be in the major leagues.

Before he knew it, he was entering the town limits of Winter Haven. Pulling out the written instructions he had received from Derron he went three blocks, made a right and then a left, where he found himself on Cletus Allen Drive. Within minutes the stadium loomed into sight. Parking in the large parking area where there were just a few cars, he got out and decided to take a tour of the facility. A large sign hung above what he thought was the main entrance. Chain of Lakes Ballpark-Spring Training Field of the

Cleveland Indians. Walking across the lot Harley spoke to himself, "This is the place!"

Surprisingly, the front gate was open. Not seeing anyone around he walked by a concession stand and through a breezeway that led to the field itself. The field was empty accept for a man on a tractor who was mowing the outfield grass and another man who was doing some repair work to the infield just off of third base. Sitting down in a box seat section directly behind home plate he surmised that they were putting the final touches on the field. He no sooner got comfortable when his moment of relaxation was interrupted by a voice. "Howdy there!"

Turning to see who had spoken to him, Harley saw an older man dressed in coveralls as he slowly walked down to the box seats. The man, wearing and an old Cleveland Indians hat, was carrying a broom and a dust pan attached to an extension pole. Removing a rag from his pocket he wiped his forehead and inquired, "You look like a ballplayer."

Harley stood up and introduced himself, "I am a ballplayer. Name's Harley Sims. I'm from St Louis."

The man shook Harley's hand and plopped down in the seat next to him. "Don't get up on my part, sonny. I'm Seth Conway. I'm from right here in Winter Haven. As you can plainly see I'm way too old to be a ballplayer. I was a ballplayer at one time, but that was in my days of youth. I was pretty good but never made it to the minor leagues or even college. I was an outfielder."

Examining the man's broom and dustpan, Harley stated, "I assume you must work here at the park?"

"That'd be correct. I'm originally from Cleveland. Born and raised there. I've always been a big baseball fan...an Indians fan to be exact. When the wife and I decided to retire, we made the decision to move here to Winter Haven where the Indians always have their spring training." Looking Harley up and down, Seth asked, "What position do you play?"

"I'm a pitcher. Got drafted by the Indians last June and now I'm down here for spring training."

Looking out at the field, Seth sat back in his seat. "I've been working here at this ballpark during spring training for seven years now. Seen a lot of good kids go through this place. I try not to get too close to any of them because most of them don't make it to the majors." Apologizing, he went on, "Sorry, it's just that I've seen a lot of young men come here with hopes of going all the way and for many this place turns out to be the end of the line."

Harley held up his hand. "No need for an apology. The reason I say this is because I've already been informed about how difficult it is to get to the top and I'm prepared to beat the odds."

Leaning the broom against the seat in front of where he was seated, Seth smiled. "Harley Sims...I like your attitude!" Removing a circular tin from his coveralls he unscrewed the top and placed a small wad of chewing tobacco in the side of his right cheek. Presenting the can to Harley, Seth asked politely, "Don't suppose you chew, son?"

Harley held up his hand, "No thank you. I've always believed that alcohol and tobacco would affect my performance."

Placing the can back in the coveralls, Seth grinned, "Looks like you've had some good supervision in your life so far." Pointing the short handled broom down at the field, Seth asked, "Have you taken a tour of the complex yet?"

"No," said Harley. "I haven't been here for more than a few minutes."

"Well then, let me fill you in. The main stadium, where you are now seated, holds around seven thousand spectators. The complex will not be open to the public until the 28th. You ever played in front of that many fans before?"

"No, I haven't."

Seth slapped Harley on his shoulder. "While you're down here you won't have to worry about playing in front of that many fans because the main stadium is where the Indians themselves will practice and play exhibition games. You'll be over there to the right where there are four minor league practice fields. This complex offers everything any major league stadium in the country offers except it's a more cut down version. We have three concession stands, and three clubhouses, one for the major leaguers and two for the minors. There are nine batting cages, four outdoor and five indoor. We have fourteen bullpen mounds, and an Olympic size pool, weight room and training facility." Looking directly at Harley, Seth probed, "Do you have an agent?"

"Yes, I do have an agent. As a matter of fact he lives in Tampa, which I drove through earlier today."

"Has this agent of yours given you a rundown on what will take place over the next six weeks?"

"For the most part…yes."

"Well just let me say this. No matter how an agent prepares you for spring training, you really have to take it one day at a time down here. If you're interested I can tell you how the process works."

Interested, Harley smiled, "I think that sounds like a good idea."

"All right then," said Seth. "Two days from now pitchers and catchers report to club house number one. You'll receive a packet with information about the six week agenda and then you'll get a tour of the complex. The next day all players who have reported will get a physical to ensure they are in good health for spring training. The next day there will be a full workout for pitchers and catchers and the coaches and instructors here will get their first look at you. After that you get two days off. You can report here and go through your own routine or just take some time to relax. On the 19th, all of the other remaining position players will report and the following day they receive their physicals and then the next day there is a full workout with the entire group. From there on out its five days a week of drills and practice. Where will you be staying while here at Winter Haven?"

"I really lucked out on that part of spring training. My agent informed me that while here I will be responsible for my own lodging and expenses. Turns out he has a brother who lives in a place called Avon Park, which I understand is just down the road a piece. His brother has an available apartment over top of his garage where I can stay for free."

"You're fortunate to have such great support. Most of the new players who come here for spring training normally team up in groups of three or four and rent a place to cut down on their expenses. It's good that you're living alone. You see, many of these boys that will arrive here will be away from home for an extended amount of time for the first time in their life. Aside from when they are here at the park, they are essentially on their own. This can, at times, lead to drinking and partying which can cause players to be late for practice or perform poorly on the field. You're wise to stay away from these types of entertainment. The training program here is pretty regimented and if you veer too far from what is expected it may not go well for you."

"How regimented is the program?"

"Very, and that's why you need to be sharp from the moment you arrive each day until the day is finished. From seven to seven thirty in the morning you eat breakfast in the clubhouse. From seven thirty to seven forty-five you report to the field for stretching which is monitored closely because stretching is vitally important to your performance. From seven forty-five to eight forty-five there are a number of specialized training sessions and drills. Eight forty-five to nine o'clock there is a group warm-up. From nine to ten thirty there will be defensive drills; hitting and throwing and so on. At ten thirty there will be a number of inter-squad games. Normally by two o'clock in the afternoon your day is over."

Excusing himself, Seth stood and walked to the fence separating the box seats from the field. Bending over the fence he spit tobacco juice down onto the grass, then returned, picked up his broom and dustpan and stated firmly. "There's one other thing you need to be aware of Harley, and that's just this. For the next six weeks it's all about the numbers. There will be around one hundred and fifty players who will be vying for about one hundred minor league positions in the Indians minor league farm system. This means that you have somewhere around a sixty-six percent chance of moving on. On the flip side of the card it also means that you have a thirty-three percent chance of not making it. Now, out of these one hundred and fifty ballplayers there will be a mixture of new draft picks like you and also players from last year's Rookie Ball and Short Season divisions. At the end of spring training, which will be in the last week of March, the decision makers in Cleveland, based upon what they have seen or been told will make their choices. At that time players who have made the cut will be assigned to one of four minor league teams ranging from Single A to Triple A that represents the Cleveland Indians. The last week of March the Indians will head back to Cleveland to get ready for this year's major league season and the selected minor league players will head out to begin their minor league careers."

Harley thought for a moment and then asked, "And what happens to the fifty or so players who are not selected for the minors?"

"Glad you asked," said Seth. "That goes back to what I said

about how this could be the end of the line for some players. Those players will remain here in Winter Haven for what we call Extended Spring Training. For the next two and a half months they remain here and get specialized training on things they need to work on. It's a bleak place around here when official spring training ends. All the activity that exists during spring training is gone. There are only a few coaches that are still here, the concession stands are closed, there are no fans to speak of, and the media is not here. It's like being left behind. When extended spring training ends, those who are left may be called up to replace a position in the minors, but most of them will play in the Short Season League and will have an opportunity to return next year and give it another shot." Turning, Seth started back up to the main aisle. "I best get back to work. I'll be seeing you around the complex, Harley. Have a blessed day!"

Harley returned the good bye. "You too!"

Standing, Harley decided against taking a self-guided tour since Seth had given him the lowdown on the complex. Walking back to the car, he figured he'd drive on down Route 60 to Avon Park which was less than an hour away.

Pulling out of the lot he thought about all the information Seth had shared with him. He seemed like an honest man and was up front with Harley about the ins and outs of spring training. Taking down a slip of paper from the sun visor, he read the name and address of Derron's brother, Dillon Wilks, at 743 Lakeview Drive.

Driving past a series of small Lakes, he thought about Mira who would be starting her junior year at Kentucky this coming fall. It was going to be an odd summer for him. For the past two years, even though he and Mira had attended different colleges, they were still able to see each other on occasion. She was only a six hour drive from Mizzou. Now, she would be nearly fourteen hours away. He was truly on his own. His father had given him some good advice in their driveway back home just before he started the long drive down to Winter Haven. He needed to concentrate on being the best he could be. Listen to what the instructors tell you, do what they say, and most important of all conduct yourself in a proper manner. Of all the things he had said there was one thing that kept coming back to him. *Make yourself indispensable...absolutely essential!*

Passing a large grove of orange trees, Harley thought about that very thing, *being absolutely essential!* He had always considered every member of a baseball team as essential. Was there a difference between essential and absolutely essential? It was a fine line but he knew there was a difference. All players were essential but only a few were absolutely essential. Those who were absolute were what was referred to as five tool players and they were rare to say the least. A five tool player can hit for power, is an excellent base runner, possesses speed, and above average throwing and fielding skills. If a player was better than average at four of these five skills, they were considered good, but not a five tool player. When Harley played Little League, he was a five tool player. He could play every position. He could hit, run, field and throw better than anyone on the team. But, over the years his role on a team had changed as he drifted away from playing multiple positions to that of a pitcher. In high school and college he was not required to be a great hitter or even runner. His skills on the field were centered on his pitching skills. He was a good pitcher and as far as he knew there were no modern day five tool pitchers in the majors.

His thoughts about this five tool business caused him to think about Drew. The Phillies had made a wise choice in drafting him. He was most definitely a five tool player and for a catcher this was rare. He could definitely hit for power. On the base paths he was always a threat to steal. He had an arm that was second to none. His fielding ability was nothing short of amazing. Harley figured that with his above average skills Drew would probably start out in Double A. Smiling to himself he realized that there was a very distinct possibility that Drew would get to the majors before he did.

Entering the city limits of Avon Park, he pulled off at the first exit he came to and reviewed the instructions to Derron's brother's house. Once he got on Main Street and came to the town square, he was to go three more blocks and take a right on Valencia Court. The house would be on the left.

Pulling out, he looked for a street sign and soon found that he was already on Main Street. Three blocks later he came to the town square; a circular affair surrounded by quaint shops and small restaurants. On the other side of the square he continued on until he saw the street sign for Valencia Court. Making a right, he drove past a number of ranch style homes and after crossing a small bridge that led over a lake he came to 743. Pulling into the circular drive he stopped in front of the light green stucco home and stepped out. Staring at the spectacular view of the lake across the street, he stretched and took a deep knee bend, only to be interrupted by a voice, "Hello there!"

Turning to face the house, Harley saw none other than Derron Wilks walking down a series of red stepping stones from the house. Smiling, the man who appeared to be Derron offered his hand and continued, "You must be Harley Sims?"

Confused, Harley remained quiet.

Smiling widely, the man spoke, "It's always the same. Folks constantly get Derron and myself mixed up." Reaching for Harley's hand, the man went on, "Dillon Wilks, Derron's identical twin brother."

Harley apologized, "I'm so sorry…it's just that you're a dead ringer for your brother with a crew cut, glasses, and the same build. He never mentioned to me that you were his twin. When you came out of the house I thought you were Derron. Wonder why he didn't say anything about it?"

"He probably didn't even give it a thought. Ever since we've been knee high to a grasshopper people have had problems telling us apart. Listen, come on in the house and I'll introduce you to my wife. She has prepared some sandwiches for us and has baked one of her neighborhood favorites; Key Lime pie. Later on, we'll get you settled in over the garage."

Following Dillon inside the house, they were met in the front room by a striking woman with long blond hair, blue eyes and a smile that only a model was capable of flashing. Dillon made the introductions, "Harley, this is my wife, Greta…Greta this is one of the young men my brother is excited about representing."

Touching Harley on his shoulder, Greta spoke sweetly, "It's such a pleasure to meet you, Harley. Why don't we go out into our screened-in Florida room where we can enjoy some refreshments? Dillon, why don't you and Harley go on out back and I'll bring the sandwiches and drinks." With that she moved off into a hallway that led to the kitchen.

Leading Harley through the house, Dillon spoke, "My brother and his wife were just in town last evening and we had dinner together. He told us that you and Drew are the most promising young players he has ever represented."

Entering the Florida room Harley couldn't help but notice that the house butted up against a golf course. Walking to the screening he admired the manicured grass and watched when two golf carts passed by.

Joining him at the back of the room, Dillon spoke, "Golf is my passion." Motioning up the fairway, he explained. "That's the sixteenth hole just about two hundred yards from here. I play whenever I can." Gesturing at a wrought iron table and chairs, he suggested, "Please…have a seat."

Harley pulled out a chair. "I really like your home. I noticed when driving in that a lot of homes here in the area are ranch style."

"I suppose that's because there are so many retirees who live here. This will probably be the last home Greta and I will ever own and we realize that as we get older we probably won't want to run up and down stairs so we decided to get everything on just the one floor. That is…except for the garage where we have an apartment over top where you'll be staying for the next six weeks. I think you'll really like it. We have a television up there and a small kitchen and you'll have your own private entrance."

Dillon finished off his second glass of iced tea and looked at his watch. "Where does the time go? It's almost three o'clock. Why don't we grab your gear and show you where you'll be bunking."

"Sounds good," said Harley. "I would like to lay down for a couple of hours if that's all right?"

Greta spoke up. "Of course, it's all right. You're free to come and go as you please. When do you have to report for training?"

"I get tomorrow off and then I have to report back to Winter Haven. I'm scheduled to eat breakfast with the other players at seven each morning which means I'll be pulling out of here around six a.m. We finish up each day around two o'clock. So, I should be back here most days before four."

Greta stood and began to clear the table. "It just so happens that we are having a small barbeque here at the house tonight. There are seven couples who always have a get together on this particular week. This has been planned for a year and this year it's our turn to host our little gathering. It'll be kicking off around six thirty. You're more than welcome if you'd like to join us. Dillon here cooks up a mighty good steak. You're welcome to join…it's up to you."

Harley looked at Dillon. "You say steaks?"

"Yep and that's not all. We're going to have corn on the cob, fresh sliced tomatoes plus whatever everyone else decides to bring along."

"Count me in then. I'll just lay down for a bit and then I'd love to join you and your neighbors."

Harley turned on a window air conditioner and then laid back on a comfortable bed. Placing his hands behind his head, he suddenly realized how tired he was. Setting an alarm clock to go off at 5:50 he smiled and thought, *So far everything seems to be working out just fine. The day after tomorrow I'll be reporting back at Winter Haven and the next step of my journey will begin.*

CHAPTER 36

PARKING IN THE LOT AT THE CHAIN OF LAKES BALL Park, Harley looked at his watch. Six forty-five in the morning. It was February 20th and the last day of his first full week of spring training in Winter Haven was about to begin. Removing his watch, he placed it and his wallet in the consul, grabbed his glove, spikes and sunglasses, stepped out of the car, locked it and started across the paved lot. His destination Clubhouse #2, where he and the pitchers and catchers had shared breakfast together for the last few days. Just as he was about to enter the gate that led to the clubhouse he heard a friendly voice, "Hey Harley...wait up!"

One of Harley's newly acquired friends, Bobby Campbell, or Chic as he preferred to be called, followed Harley through the gate and slapped him on the back. "I'm starving. I wonder what they'll feed us this morning. Those pancakes we had yesterday were pretty good. The scrambled eggs and sausage isn't too bad either. Now, the biscuits and gravy we had on Tuesday left a lot to be desired. I'm used to eating a lot more for breakfast than they serve here at training camp." Grinning at Harley, Chic held up his glove. "You know what they say about Texas? Everything there is bigger!"

Harley poked fun at his new friend, "Well you're not down at Texas A & M and I'm not at Mizzou so I guess we'll eat what they put in front of us."

Entering a large section of the clubhouse that had been set up as a dining area, Harley and Chic sat at the same table they had for the past week. The other six players who sat at their table were already present. Jim Lassiter from Ohio State, Nelson Little from UNLV, Charley Wentz from Michigan and Fernando Sanchez of Minnesota. Then there was Lucky Verdon from Arizona and finally Chet Smith from upstate New York. Harley sat and nodded at the group of young pitching prospects.

Pouring himself a glass of orange juice, Nelson started off the morning conversation. "So, how do you guys think training has gone so far?"

Taking the glass pitcher of juice from Jim, Chet was the first to answer, "I think the first week has gone pretty well. It's a little bit different than what I thought we'd be faced with."

Charley placed a large scoop of scrambled eggs on his plate and responded, "How's that?"

Chet waved his fork at the group and explained, "I spent my first two years of high school at an exclusive military academy in New York. I dropped out after my second year. My folks were upset, but I told them I was set on being a major league pitcher and no amount of military training was going to make my curve ball more effective. The training we've been receiving here this past week is similar but with far less rules and regulations. Here we all sit dressed in our black jerseys with a Cleveland Indians logo on the front. Everyone for the most part is wearing shorts. One of the big differences here is that the instructors are here to help you, not to belittle you constantly. Here, if you make a mistake, no one orders you to run laps or drop and give them fifty pushups. What I'm saying is that so far I've got no complaints."

Changing the topic, Fernando, at the end of the table, asked Harley. "Hey Sims. How are the Cardinals going to do this year? What's the word on the street up there in St. Louis?"

Harley stabbed a strip of bacon and answered without hesitation, "I think we're going to have another down year. The experts feel the Cards pitching rotation is going to be getting off to a rough start. The team also made quite a few trades and acquisitions that should make for an interesting season."

"Speaking of interesting," said Charley. "Isn't today when all the position players report?"

Chic took a bite of eggs and answered the question with a full mouthful, "Yep, and tomorrow they'll be joining us for a full workout. It's gonna get crowded around here. Right now, we have nineteen pitchers and twelve catchers in house. That means that around one hundred and thirty more ballplayers will be filing in here today."

"The way I see it," said Jim, "as pitchers we face less competition than the position players are up against. Think about how many outfielders and infielders there are going to be here."

Nodding at the two tables where the catchers were seated, Chet spoke up, "And there are even fewer catchers here than pitchers."

A voice came in over the P.A. system instructing the group that they had five minutes left to eat and that catchers were to report to room number two and pitchers to room number three. Chic pushed his plate to the side and stood, "Well boys, what say we get this day underway!"

At exactly seven thirty two instructors entered the room where the young pitchers were seated in three rows of folded chairs. One of the instructors went about setting up a chalkboard that represented a ball field while the other spoke to the group. "Good morning gentlemen! Starting today and for the next two days we're going to be changing things up some. Today you are going to be watching films combined with some chalkboard diagrams for the next two hours. That will take us until nine thirty when we'll do our stretching and warm up. Around ten thirty we'll practice the things we have reviewed on film, then we'll break for lunch. There will be no inter-squad game today. After lunch, we'll go back to the field and continue defensive skills. There is coffee, juice and water over there on the table. We'll be starting in five minutes."

Walking to the table, Harley grabbed a bottle of water as Chic opted for coffee. Pouring a packet of sweetener into his cup Chic commented, "Well, this should be interesting. Just when I was getting used to our daily routine they up and throw us a curve."

Harley sat in the first row with Chic and laid his glove at his feet as one of the instructors got everyone's attention. "Let's get started. You, gentlemen, are professional ballplayers. You already know how to pitch and many of you have been doing so for a number of years. Over the next few days we're going to be talking about what, as a pitcher you see, hear and feel when on the mound. We are also going to talk about how you react to what you see, hear and feel, because the truth is your job as a pitcher is far more than just delivering a number of pitches and this is regardless of whether you're a starter or a reliever. The second the ball leaves your hand you must be prepared for any number of things that can happen. As a pitcher, you must be aware at all times to what is going on. How many outs are there, what about the runners on base, what inning is it, what's the score, who are you going to be facing not only during the current inning but the next inning as well. What you do on any number of different plays can influence the outcome of not only a particular play or inning but the game itself. So, my advice to you is to pay close attention to what you see and what we say these next few days because the difference between a good pitcher and a great pitcher is based on your game intelligence. The first thing we are going to talk about this morning is the first thing you do after the ball leaves your hand. Can anyone here tell me what that might be?"

Jim, in the back row spoke up instantly, "Get ready to field the ball."

The instructor smiled. "That is exactly right!" Holding up a new ball, he tossed it in the air and caught it on the way down. "This game that we play is called baseball gets its name from this little critter right here. A major league baseball weighs between five to five and a quarter ounces. Its circumference is between nine and nine and a quarter inches. It has a cushioned cork center that is wrapped in close to a mile of yarn and has a cowhide cover. This gentlemen…is a baseball!"

He tossed the ball toward the front row, which Harley quickly caught with his right hand. "Throwing a baseball, and at times fielding a baseball, is hopefully what you will be doing for the next ten, fifteen or if you remain healthy…twenty years. That ball that Mr. Sims caught can be a dangerous projectile! Baseball, in general, is considered a passive sport compared to its three main competitors. Those being football, basketball and hockey. That being said, you must, while on the field always be aware of the possibility of being hit by the ball. It can happen on any given play with little warning. You can get hit by a pitch while batting or you can get nailed by a ball hit back to you."

Looking at Harley, the instructor gestured to throw the ball back and then asked, "Mr. Sims. How fast can you throw?"

Harley shrugged and answered, "In the mid-nineties. I have at times reached around a hundred miles an hour."

"I think it's safe to say that everyone in this room can bring the heat…some faster than others, but still, even in the high eighties this ball can injure a person. It is estimated that the average speed of a hit baseball is around seventy-three miles an hour. This depends on the speed of the pitcher, the type of pitch and its position in or around the strike zone combined with how much of the bat the hitter gets on the ball. But, if a pitcher is throwing in the high nineties the ball can, when hit, travel somewhere between one hundred and twenty to one hundred and thirty miles an hour. As a pitcher, you are the closest player in fair territory in relation to the batter. Now, the ball is not always going to be hit directly at you or even near you, but you must always be ready to react if it does come in your direction. From the time the ball leaves your hand it can come back toward you at over a hundred miles an hour in just over two seconds. My point is…you don't have a lot of time to decide what you're going to do. Your reaction must be instinctive! How you come off the mound is essential, not only for how you are going to field the ball, but for your own protection."

Motioning for the other instructor to hit the lights, he continued, "We are now going to see some film that will give us examples of how to come off the mound after the delivery and immediately position yourself to field the ball if necessary. The first example is a pitcher who, after his delivery, falls off center of the mound." Stopping the film, the instructor explained. "Notice how the pitcher after landing with his lead foot falls to the right. He is off balance and if a ball is slammed in his direction there is a good change that he may not field the ball correctly. If a pitcher falls off to the left the same thing can happen. This also makes it difficult to field a ball on the opposite side of where you land. This is something an opposing team will pick up on quickly. In the case of a bunt they will try to bunt to your weak side. This could lead to a man reaching base, or even a run scoring, maybe even the reason why a game is lost. Now, let's take a look at a pitcher who comes off the mound properly prepared to charge the bunt straight on or to the left or right. This brings us to the next thing that may happen."

Forwarding the film, Harley and the others watched as a pitcher took a stab at a line drive grounded to the right of the mound. The instructor stopped the film when the pitcher knocked the ball down and it dribbled off toward third base. Looking out over the group he asked, "What just happened here?"

Harley hesitated but when no one else answered, he spoke up. "The pitcher, by trying to field a difficult grounder, screwed up the play by not allowing his shortstop to field the ball. When this happens, the hitter reaches first base safe. As a pitcher, you have to depend on your infielders to do what they are good at. This could have been a routine grounder by the shortstop, but because of the pitcher's interference this runner may have made it to first safely."

The instructor smiled and remarked, "Let's roll the film and see what happens." The group watched as the third basemen ran to the ball, gloved it but held up from throwing because the runner reached first base easily. Reversing the film the instructor, pointed out, "Notice the shortstop getting into position to field the ball. Mr. Sims was correct. A routine play opportunity is missed because the pitcher tried to do too much. As a pitcher, you have to know what your comfort zone is on either side of the mound. Depending on the pitcher this could be anywhere from two feet to as far as four. If you venture beyond that point, you're making things difficult for your infield. Does everyone understand what we're saying?"

Following nineteen head nods, the instructor nodded at his assistant to dim the lights and the film started running once again. They watched as a high popup was hit above the infield. The catcher, third baseman, first baseman all started to position themselves to make the catch, but the pitcher, despite the fact that the third baseman was waving everyone else off, tried to catch the ball and collided with his third baseman and the ball fell to the ground. The runner was safe on first. Looking out over the group, the instructor asked, "I need someone to explain to the group what happened here."

From the second row, Fernando spoke up instantly, "What we just saw happened to me during my last game in college, only the collision was with the first baseman. He waved me off and rather than allowing him to make a routine snag, I thought I had a better shot at catching the ball. I smacked right into him and neither one of us made the catch. The runner was safe on first. On the next play, he bunted over to second and then following a base hit he scored the winning run."

"Excellent answer Sanchez!" said the instructor. "Now, let's see an example of what a pitcher should do when an infield pop-up occurs."

The film started up and after a second or so there was another example of an infield pop-up. The shortstop and the second baseman both started for the ball. The pitcher moved to the side away from the area where the ball might land and pointed to the sky indicating where the ball was. The shortstop waved off the second baseman and made the catch easily. Stopping the film, the assistant hit the lights. The instructor smiled at Sanchez and then the rest of the group. "The hard truth is that if our Mr. Sanchez would have done what the pitcher we just witnessed did, then his team may have won that game. The simplest mistake during a game can turn out to be the factor as to why your team loses a game. Any questions?"

The group remained silent and the instructor rubbed his hands together. "Let's move on to another pitcher related situation that often can occur during a game. Roll the film, Joe."

The group sat and watched as the next segment came across the screen. A ball was hit sharply to the right of the first baseman who moved to his right and gloved the ball, but was too far away from the bag to arrive there before the runner. The pitcher broke for first while the first baseman flipped the ball to the pitcher just before he arrived at the bag. He fumbled the ball and the runner was not only safe but knocked the pitcher on his backside. The runner who had been on second advanced to third and then ran home on the missed play at first. "Can anyone in the room explain to me what transpired during this play?"

This time it was Lucky Verdon who answered, "I'll take a shot at it! The pitcher broke for first base because the first baseman had been pulled too far to make the play at first. He simply missed the ball when it was flipped toward him and on top of that gets run over by the runner."

The instructor walked over to the chalkboard and replied, "That was a good answer but not a *complete answer!* There were a number of mistakes that were made during this play. The first mistake was made by the first baseman who has a responsibility, if he has the time, to get the ball to the pitcher before he gets to the bag. I'm going to go back and roll this play again and you'll notice that the pitcher doesn't even glance toward the runner, so he is not aware of where he is or how close the play might be. After he drops the ball, he is in no position to look back at the runner at third or even have a shot at throwing him out at the plate. Now, let's look at the same situation but with a different first baseman and pitcher."

The film was running again. The ball was hit to the right of the first baseman who fielded the ball and flipped it to the pitcher before he got to the bag. Before he received the ball, the pitcher took a quick look at the runner to determine where he was up the base line. He caught the ball cleanly, stepped on the bag then turned and looked the runner back to third. The instructor walked over to the table and poured himself a cup of coffee and commented, "And that gentlemen is the proper way to cover first base and to prevent the runner on third from scoring. Let's take a short ten minute break."

After a long day of training, Harley followed Drew's direction to Clearwater but somehow had taken a wrong turn and found himself downtown. Pulling into a service station he gassed up and asked the clerk inside if he could tell him how to get to Spectrum Stadium. He found that he wasn't as lost as he thought. Two right hand turns and he found himself on Old Coachman Road. The stadium, according to Drew was located at 601. Passing a number of homes on his right he noticed that he was in the 1700 block.

It was only a few minutes when he saw the stadium on the left. When he had called Drew last evening they had agreed to meet at the stadium between three thirty and four. Getting out of his car he walked to an area where there were a number of picnic tables set up off to the right of the main gate. He watched as a number of young men, obviously ballplayers, exited the stadium. Finally, Drew appeared as he walked with two other young men. Seeing Harley, Drew walked over and introduced the two ball players with him. "Harley, I'd like you to meet Dan. He's from up around Milwaukee. He plays second base and this other chap here is Luke. He's from Ohio. He's an outfielder."

Dan nodded at Harley and then thumped Luke on the shoulder. "We need to go on if we're going to meet those two gals we met during practice today. It would seem that Luke and I have been invited to go dancing tonight. What are you guys up to?"

Drew answered the question. "I'm going to take Harley out to the Seaside Café for some good seafood, then I thought I'd whip him at some miniature golf. You'll see him later tonight. He's going to bunk in with us and then head back on Wednesday for Winter Haven."

Watching Drew's two friends walk off, Harley patted his stomach. "When do we eat? I'm famished."

Drew slung a small gym bag over his shoulder. "We can go right now. I've already had a shower. Leave your car here. I'll drive. It's only about twenty minutes from here."

Driving down Old Coachman, Drew asked, "Have you talked with Mira since you've been down here?"

"Yes," said Harley. "I just talked with her before I headed over here today. As it stands right now I think everyone is planning on coming down in two weeks. That will be about the halfway point of spring training. Speaking of that, how was your first week here with the Phillies organization?"

"To be honest, it's been difficult to adapt to. In a day's time I might catch, even if it's just for ten minutes at a time, a series of different pitchers. It's kind of unsettling. I guess I've grown used to your style of pitching. I know you like a book. I've read every page, every chapter over the years. I know what to expect and how you think, how your curve breaks. Every time I look out at the mound or in the bullpen there stands a stranger sixty feet away. Listen, I thought tomorrow we could go to this great beach I heard about. It's called Indian Rocks. It's about a forty minute drive from where I'm staying. I thought we could jog a few miles and soak up some Florida sunshine, maybe grab some lunch along the coast somewhere. You did bring your glove along like I asked...didn't you?"

"Sure did. It's in the trunk of my car."

"Good, because one of the things I'd really like to do when we hit the beach tomorrow is to have you throw me a few. I really miss catching you."

It was Friday, the last day of the third week of spring training and Harley, along with everyone else, ended their days of training by participating in inter-squad games. After three weeks of daily practice games, it had become mundane. Eight teams that consisted of nineteen to twenty players each participated in two games daily. Most players did not participate in both games but did have an opportunity to get in at least five to six innings of ball, five days a week. As a pitcher, Harley found it difficult to only stay in a game for no more than two, maybe three innings. He realized that this had to be done so every pitcher could be seen on a daily basis. Out of the five days he did get one day off from pitching, but he still had to do his daily stretching and specialized training. He still had to attend the daily group warm-up and be involved in defensive skills training.

Standing on the mound, he took the sign from the catcher, agreed with a nod and then let loose with a ninety-eight mile an hour fastball. The batter swung through the ball for strike three. The fourth inning ended with the team Harley was on currently winning by a score of 2-0. Running from the field, he got a cup of cold water and sat in the dugout. His team instructor sat next to Harley and slapped him on his leg. "Good job, Sims. You just threw four innings and only gave up one hit. Looking at this past week in the four games you been involved in you've pitched ten innings. You only gave up three hits and only walked two men. I like the way you covered first base in the first inning today. You come off the mound well and your pitching instincts are some of the best I've seen for someone your age. However, there are a couple of things I want to talk to you about. That knuckle curve and the short stride delivery that you use on occasion. Even though they are unique, that type of pitching is not going to impress any instructor on the field. Decisions on whether you move on to the majors as a pitcher will be based on your fastball, curve and changeup. You also have a nice cutter and a great slider which is good to have in your arsenal. Stick to the basics because that's what we're looking at. Now, that's it for you today. Like I said, nice pitching. Get some rest because you're going to go three or four again tomorrow."

Standing beneath the hot water coming from the showerhead, Harley thought about the upcoming evening. Mira and Melanie had driven down to Clearwater in a separate car while both his parents and Drew's had driven together. The plan was that Melanie and Drew's parents were going to spend a week in Clearwater and Rich and Monica would bring Mira along with them. They were to meet at the Hampton Inn in Winter Haven at five, then it was off to a great dinner at the Harbor Side Restaurant. He was looking forward to seeing his family.

He arrived at the Hampton at four and after checking at the front desk, discovered that Mira and his parents had not arrived yet. Relaxing on a comfortable chair in the spacious lobby, he nursed a cold drink and thought about how great it was going to be to see Mira every day for a solid week. Thinking ahead, he figured that as March ended in three weeks and spring training ended he would be assigned to one of Cleveland's minor league teams. With the season kicking in the first week of April, he'd have to report immediately to wherever he was headed. Mira was busy at school and now had a part-time job in Versailles at a horse farm down the road from her uncle's place. Once the minor league season started on April 6th, he wasn't going to have much time to spend with her. He might not get to spend any amount of serious time with her until after the season ended the first week of September. It didn't seem to him that being a professional ballplayer left much time for a relationship. This was just part of being a professional ballplayer. Half of the season you were on the road, and when you were playing at home, unless your wife or girlfriend lived where you played, the only real time you got to spend together was in the off-season. He was lucky to have a girl like Mira who was supportive and had an understanding how the world of baseball worked.

Thinking about Mira caused him to smile, when suddenly she walked through Hampton's large entrance doors. Seeing Harley seated by a large banana plant, she dropped her bag and ran as best she could across the room. Harley was hardly out of the chair when she gave him a long and large hug followed by a kiss. Holding her out at arm's length, Harley looked her up and down and commented, "You look great!"

Just then, in walked Rich and Monica, dressed in St. Louis Cardinal jerseys and Cleveland Indians hats. Noticing her son and Mira embracing, she tapped Rich on his shoulder. "Our son is growing up."

Joining the happy couple, Monica, followed by Rich gave Harley a hug and made a remark about the weather. "I can't believe how warm it is down here. Is it like this every day?"

"It is," said Harley. "We've had some great baseball weather down here." Looking over his parents he asked in amazement. "You two do realize that we are not in Jupiter where the Cardinals train."

Monica touched the edge of her Cardinals jersey. "Your father and I will always be die hard Cardinal fans." Reaching up she touched the brim of her new Indians hat. "It's just that now my son plays for the Indians organization...hence, the hat!"

Rich shook Harley's hand and then looked toward the check-in desk. "I'm going to get us checked in and then I'd like to grab a quick shower before we go out to eat. It's been a long drive."

Mira agreed. "A shower does sound good." Looking at Harley, she asked, "Do you mind?"

Harley waved off the suggestion that it was an inconvenience for his visitors to take showers. "Listen, why don't you guys go on up to your rooms, freshen up and I'll just wait down here in the lobby. But, don't be too long because I skipped lunch today."

Rich looked at his wife and Mira. "Can we be back down here in...let's say a half hour?"

"Thirty minutes it is then," said Mira as she headed for the elevator.

Harley looked out across the lake and thought about the last three weeks of spring training. It seemed like weeks four, five and six had passed quickly. It had been three weeks now since he had last seen his parents or Mira. He and Drew had continued to meet whenever they could. As the weeks sped by both he and Drew were confident they would move on and tomorrow was the day when those going to minor league teams would be posted not only in Winter Haven and Clearwater but all across the Grapefruit League. Pulling out his cell phone he hit Drew's number and waited.

Two rings passed when Drew answered, "Hello!"

Harley smiled and asked, "Where are you and what are you doing?"

"Right now, I'm sitting over here at Indian Rocks Beach looking out at the Gulf. How about you?"

"I'm sitting around just like you. There's a lake across the street from the Wilks' house. I'm thinking about tomorrow. We're not required to report until nine in the morning. They told us the clubhouse would be open at that time and that all players selected would be posted along with a list of those slated to remain for extended spring training."

Drew confirmed. "It's the same deal over here in Clearwater. Tomorrow, we'll know where we're headed."

Ten minutes later, Drew ended the call. "Look, it's going to get dark in the next half hour. I'm going to take another dip in the ocean and then I'm going to turn in for the night. Call me tomorrow when you hear something. I'll let you know as soon as I find out anything over here. Talk to you tomorrow."

Laying his phone on the bench where he was sitting, he watched as the sun was just a few minutes from setting in the west. Getting up, he too was going to hit the hay. Tomorrow was going to be a big day.

Friday morning, Harley was up early, dressed and out the door. He arrived in Winter Haven just prior to seven o'clock just like he had done five days a week for the past six weeks. Driving to the stadium he discovered that there were only a few cars parked there; probably stadium employees or some of the instructors. Recalling what they had said about the gates not opening until nine he drove a few blocks down the street to an all-night cafe and ordered bacon and eggs along with orange juice. Eating his breakfast slowly he thought he would have been more excited. *He knew* he was going to be one of the players that would move on to the minors, he just didn't know what level it would be. This was a day he had planned on years ago, even before he had played Little League. It was simply another step on his way to his goal of pitching in the major leagues.

Finally, at eight thirty, he paid his bill, hopped in his car and drove back to the stadium where he found the lot filled with vehicles. Parking near the back of the lot he stepped out and scanned the scene before him. Players from every corner of the nation: north, south, east and west leaned against their cars or stood around in groups talking, no doubt about their futures as professional ballplayers. For some, the morning would bring great news, while others, at least for the moment, not so great.

At exactly nine o'clock an announcement was made over the stadium P.A. system that the main gate was going to be open and that the players should report to the main clubhouse where the selections were posted. Harley waited until the large group filed through the gates and then walked slowly across the lot.

Entering the clubhouse doors, he stayed near the back wall as he heard yelling and loud voices, players standing off to one side while they made phone calls to their families or loved ones back home. The main hallway was jammed with players. Then he saw one of the young men he had grown close to over the weeks. Charley Wentz gave Harley a thumbs up and asked, "Where ya headed?"

Harley smiled back at the boy from Michigan and replied, "Haven't checked yet...how about you?"

Charley gave Harley a wide grin. "Can you believe it! They're sending me to Advanced A. I gotta run. I've got to call my folks."

Suddenly, one of his pitching buddies bumped into him. Chet reached out and shook Harley's hand. "They're sending me to Advanced A! I was hoping for A ball. Where did they place you?"

Harley smiled back at the boy. "Don't know yet, I was just waiting until things clear out some."

Seeing another one of his friends approach, Chet slapped Harley on his shoulder. "I've got to go talk with Henry." Walking backwards, he congratulated Harley, "Don't worry, Sims. You were the best pitcher they had down here this year. See ya at the top?"

Harley could see five large white posters on either side of the hallway, a few scattered players searching for their name. He stopped at the first poster on his right. *Extended Training.*

Moving on to the next poster entitled: *Class A,* Harley was convinced that at least he would be sent to Advanced A. He stepped to the next poster: *Advanced A.* He quickly ran his finger down to the S section. There was a Smith and then he saw Sanchez's name; another pitcher he had become friends with. That was it. He was not listed. Moving back to Class A, he was certain he would locate his name there. He found no last names starting with S. The only two charts left were Double and Triple A. He looked past the Double A poster to Triple A where he saw just two names, neither one his. He walked back to the Extended Training. *Surely,* he thought, *I'm not being left behind!*

A voice behind him spoke up, "Mr. Sims. You won't find your name on that poster."

Turning around Harley saw Max Miller, one of the pitching

instructors standing there, his large arms folded across his chest.

Harley, not sure what to say, gestured at the other posters. "I seem to be having trouble finding my name. I was sure I'd be in Advanced or at least A ball, but I wasn't listed. There were only two names on Triple A."

Placing his arm around Harley, Max led him down to the Double A poster, and ran his finger down over eight names, stopping at the last. There it was, written in black magic marker on that gleaming white poster. Harley Sims: Double A - Akron Aeros -Eastern League.

Harley stared at his name. "I can't believe it...Double A!"

Max laughed and shook Harley's hand. "You underestimate yourself, Harley. You're the best new pitcher we had down here this year. You just keep pitching like you did the last six weeks and I have a feeling that in time you'll be playing under the big lights. And, one other thing. That knuckle curve and that sort stride delivery you have. Just because I told you they were not that important here you might just want to throw that at those Eastern League hitters on occasion. Good luck, son!"

Practically everyone had left the building and Harley decided to walk back to his car and call his parents and then Mira with the good news. Halfway across the lot his phone buzzed. He no sooner answered when he heard Drew's excited voice: "Harley...they selected me for Advanced A. I'm going to be catching for a team called the Clearwater Threshers right here in the Florida State League. Have you heard where you're going yet?"

Harley was excited for Drew as he answered, "Yep, in a few days I'll be driving to Akron, Ohio to play for a team called the Aeros in the Eastern League."

There was a slight hesitation on Drew's end and then he blurted, "Wait a sec! Isn't that Double A Ball?"

"Yes...it is and it's more than I was hoping for. We both made it, Drew. We're both going to be playing in the minor leagues in just over a week from now. Are you going to stay in Clearwater or are you going home for a few days?"

"I'm driving home today. Listen I've got to hang up. I've got a call coming in. Probably Melanie or my folks. I'll see you back home in Arnold!"

Harley had to make two calls himself. Pulling up his parents' number, Monica answered just after the first ring. "This better be my son with good news! Mira is here with me. We knew you'd be calling this morning. Where's my boy headed?"

"Double A, Mom. I'm starting for home as soon as I hang up."

"Well don't hang up just yet. There's a young lady here who would like to speak with you. One other thing before I go. Make sure you call your father at work. It's all he could talk about this morning. We love you, Son and we're so proud of you. See you soon. Here's Mira."

A second later, Mira's voice sounded, "Looks like in the next few years I'm going to be married to a major league pitcher!"

CHAPTER 37

GUIDING HIS CAR INTO A TRUCKSTOP NORTH OF Columbus, Ohio Harley sat back and took a relaxing breath. He had left Arnold just after midnight and here it was six hours later. Driving across Illinois, Indiana and now part of Ohio he estimated that he was still ahead of schedule. He was required to report to Canal Park, home of the Akron Aeros at two o'clock. Turning on the car light he unfolded a map of Ohio. He only had a three-hour drive until he arrived in Akron. That meant even if he stopped for breakfast he'd still be there with time to spare. Throwing the wrinkled map on the passenger seat, he stepped out and walked to the restrooms and thought, *Breakfast sounds good!*

Entering the restaurant, he was seated and decided on the Trucker's Special. Three eggs, ham, two pancakes, hash browns, toast and juice. Waiting for his meal he removed an envelope from his shirt pocket and reviewed the teams in the Eastern League. In the Southern Division where Akron played there were five other teams. The Bowie Baysox, Harrisburg Senators, Erie Seawolves, Altoona Curve and the Reading Phillies. The Northern Division consisted of six other teams he had never heard of.

His meal was brought to his table and as he salted his eggs he thought about Mira and his folks back home. He had driven straight through from Winter Haven to Arnold following the last day of spring training. He had arrived at his parent's house at six o'clock on the morning on March 31th. After an hour of celebrating with Rich and Monica he went to bed and slept until three in the afternoon, then he showered, picked up Mira at her grandfather's farm, and met Melanie and Drew for dinner on the first day of April. The next morning, April 2nd, he pulled out of his driveway and was on his way. Drew, who had a much longer drive, said that he was leaving for Clearwater an hour or so after dinner.

April 2nd, he thought. *Tonight, the Cards would be playing their second game of the season.* They lost 2-1 on opening day to the Rockies. It was a long season and it was just beginning. He thought about the coming season with Akron. A one hundred and forty-one game schedule that started on April 6th, just four days away. The season was to start with a four game series against the Bowie Baysox and then three games with the Trenton Thunder. According to the research he had done Trenton was last year's Eastern League Champion.

Finishing his breakfast, the sun was just starting to come up when he pulled back on 71 N. His next stop, Canal Park in Akron, Ohio. A few miles up the road he thought about how things had changed. He would always, to his dying day, be a Cardinals fan, but now he also had an interest in how Cleveland would do as well as Philadelphia, who was Drew's parent team. Cleveland, on opening day, defeated the White Sox 10-8 and the Phillies went down to Washington 11-5.

At ten thirty he pulled into the lot of Canal Park on South Main Street. In three and a half hours he was required to report to the stadium. Parking next to a long row of parked cars near the front of the lot, he grabbed his equipment bag and spikes and walked toward what looked like the main gate. He tried the gate but it was locked. An older gentlemen pushing a broom across the concrete floor stopped and looked through the gate at Harley. Noticing the bag and spikes in Harley's hands the man explained, "All ballplayers are to enter through gate #3, which is to your left around to the side." The man didn't wait for a response but just moved on with his broom.

Following the man's directions, he soon located gate #3 which was open. Entering, he saw an eight foot table next to a closed concession stand where a women and two men sat. A sign above the table indicated he was at the right place. *Player Check-In.* Approaching the table Harley laid his bag at his feet and slung his spikes over his right shoulder.

The woman smiled and simply asked, "Name?"

"Sims…Harley Sims," came the answer.

The woman removed a pen from behind her left ear and checked a computer printout. Following a few seconds, she placed a check next to his name and stated, "Yes, here you are Mr. Sims. You're a little early. You're only the second player to report so far.

If you'll go with Ben here, he'll lead you down to the locker room. Your locker number is seventeen and you'll find your uniforms there. Welcome to Canal Park."

Following Ben, who never said a word, they walked down a wide concrete walkway then made a right down a short flight of steps, then a left where there was a door that read, HOME TEAM LOCKER ROOM. Opening the door, Ben finally spoke, "There ya go, Mr. Sims. Your locker is the fifth on the right. If you have any questions don't hesitate to ask. Have a good day."

Taking a few steps into the room, he stopped and took in his new surroundings. Off to the right there was a glass enclosed room with a hand lettered sign on the door, MANAGER'S OFFICE. On the right and left side of the room there were freshly painted lockers that looked like they had been kicked on a number of occasions. Looking down at the end of the room there were two signs indicating RESTROOM and SHOWERS to the right and WEIGHT ROOM to the left. Walking slowly by the lockers, he read the names on top of each one: Franco, Lopez, Green, Pelniski and then there it was, *his locker! Sims.* On a small shelf at the top of his locker sat a new black baseball hat with a cursive stitched white *A* indicating his new team; The Aeros. In the main section of the open locker hung two new baseball uniforms. White with black pinstripes for away games and the standard white home game uniform trimmed in black. The front of both uniforms displayed the name *Aeros.* Moving the uniforms slightly to the right he admired the number on the back. Number *45!* It didn't take more than a second before his extraordinary baseball mind clicked in as he remembered that the great St. Louis Cardinal pitcher, Bob Gibson, wore number 45 for fifteen years.

Sitting on a bench in front of the lockers, he saw the name Verdon on the opposite side of the room down three lockers. Lucky Verdon would be showing up later in the day. He was looking forward to seeing someone he knew. Hearing a door slam he looked down at the end of the long room where he saw a man wrapped in a towel come around the corner from the showers. The man, actually a boy about his age, smiled and spoke when he approached. "I didn't realize anyone else had arrived yet." Plopping down next to Harley the boy ran his fingers thought his wet hair, looked at Harley's locker and then asked, "You Sims?"

Harley extended his right hand and answered, "Harley Sims. Nice to meet you."

The boy returned the handshake and sat on the bench. "Martin Klein...my friends call be Marty. This your first time in the minors?"

"Yes it is, I just left spring training down in Winter Haven a few days ago."

"I heard we were getting two new pitchers. We sure need more pitching. Our rotation has been depleted from last year. We had a pitcher move up to Triple A and another called it quits. That leaves us with two open spots in our rotation."

Harley, listening carefully, asked, "Then I can only assume you were here last year?"

"This will be my second season here in Akron. I guess you could say I'm a veteran in the minors. I was drafted right out of high school six years ago. I played Rookie Ball that first year and the next year I was moved up to Short Season. Every year it just kept getting better. After playing a year of Short Season, I moved up the ladder every year making my way through A Ball and then Advanced A until last year when I moved up to Double A and that's where I stalled out. When I was first drafted I thought I was on my way to the top. Don't get me wrong. I haven't given up, it's just that this is the first year I haven't moved to the next level. By the way, you and I are going to get to know one another quite well. I'm the starting catcher for Akron. The next two days you'll be working very closely with me as your catcher. We have to become married, as they say around here. I have to know how your fastball moves, how far your curve drops, how you think in different situations, how you communicate, what your range on the mound is, and well, quite a few other things. Our first game is in four days. You probably won't start until we're three to four games in the season, but when you look in toward the plate...you'll see me. Listen, I've got to change and hit the weight room. I'll see you later on this afternoon at a scheduled team meeting."

Sitting in a vinyl brown couch in the furnished apartment Derron had set up for him just two days ago, he dialed Mira's number and waited for her voice.

"Hello, this better be my ballplayer from Ohio calling?"

Harley smiled. "It is! I thought I'd give you a call before I step out for a bite."

"Where are you right now?"

"Sitting in my apartment. It's just five blocks down the street from the stadium. I can actually walk to home games."

"Tell me about your first day in the minors."

"I got here early and met my catcher, then I attended a team meeting and took a tour of the stadium..."

Ten minutes later the call ended. Harley checked the time: 6:15. Getting up he decided to walk up the street to a Mom and Pop café he noticed earlier. When he got back later he'd call his folks and then watch some TV and turn in around nine. It had been a long day and he wanted to be sharp for his first day on the field with the Aeros.

Harley took the mound and gazed around the stands of Canal Park. The seating capacity was just over seventy-six hundred. Despite the fact there were only about three thousand fans in the stands it was still the largest crowd Harley had ever pitched in front of. He looked around at his infielders and then to the outfield. The only player he knew on the field was the third baseman, Blake Reynolds, who he had played with down in Winter Haven. Other than a few players from spring training, he had only met his teammates seven days ago. This was an odd feeling. In Little League, pony ball, high school and even college he had spent weeks with his teammates before his first game. He had always felt a sense of security with those he played with, something he was not feeling at the moment. Besides the pressure of playing with what seemed like strangers, there was the pressure the manager had placed on him. The Aeros had lost their first three games of the season to the Baysox and the manager told him prior to the game that it was imperative that they win this fourth game against Bowie. To get swept was always embarrassing and to start the year off in that fashion would be bad for the team's morale. He had been informed that he had been sent to Double A because he had impressed someone down in Florida. The last thing the manager had said to him before he left the dugout was a cold statement, "Impress me!"

Bowie's leadoff hitter stepped to the plate. Harley took the sign from Marty, high fastball. Harley nodded, wound up and delivered his first minor league pitch. The ball sailed above Marty's glove and rolled to the backstop. Catching a new ball, Harley took a deep breath as the pitch had gotten away from him. His next pitch was called ball two as it was low. The next pitch was a called strike. His fourth pitch bounced in the dirt bringing the count to 3-1. The next pitch was a curve that caught the corner, but the ump signaled ball four and the hitter slowly jogged down to first base.

A fan off to his left yelled, "Hey Sims! We didn't bring you all the way up here from Florida to walk players!"

Another fan shouted, "Come on, Sims. Get the ball over the plate!"

The next batter set up in the box and took the first inside pitch for, "Ball one!"

There was no supportive chatter from his infielders as Harley readied himself for the next pitch. It was on the inside corner but according to the umpire nicked the hitter's right sleeve. He signaled the hitter to take his base. Harley turned and faced the outfield as the two fans continued to yell insults:

Go on back down to Florida, Sims!

It's called a strike zone, Try getting one over!

Marty walked to the mound and reassured Harley. "Don't worry about those two idiot fans. They're always here and they're never happy about much of anything. The fans here at Canal Park are pretty good, but they're just upset because we haven't won a game yet this season. So, let's look at what we've got. Men on first and second with no outs. That doesn't mean squat if they can't score. Now, I know you have good stuff. Just keep it around the plate. I know you're probably a little nervous. But, once you pitch your way out of the inning you'll feel better. Now, let's see some heat!"

The next hitter took three swings and stepped in. Harley didn't even look at the man. He was no longer standing on the mound at Canal Park in Akron, Ohio. He was standing in his backyard back in Arnold staring at the tire hanging from the old oak tree. He smiled and thought about Ozzie. A ninety-eight mile an hour fastball blasted across the pate for a called, "Strike one!"

Five minutes later after striking out the side he walked to the dugout. He had pitched his way out of not only his first inning in professional baseball, but an inning that had started out as a nightmare. Sitting on the bench, a number of players walked by and gave him a high five or complimented him:

Nice pitchin', Sims.

Ya left 'em stranded!

The top of the seventh inning came and found the Aeros with a 2-0 lead. Harley had settled in and despite giving up two hits had held the Baysox scoreless. The defiant fans had settled down as it appeared that they were on the verge of witnessing their first win of the season.

The first batter, on the first pitch bunted the ball down the third base line. The third baseman bobbled the ball and made a bad throw allowing the runner to be called safe. The next batter hit a line shot at the second baseman, who flipped the ball to the shortstop for the start of a routine double play, but the shortstop missed the bag and both runners were called safe. Bowie's clean up man stepped to the plate and Akron's manager called time while he walked to the mound. Reaching for the ball, he smiled at Harley and stated, "I'm bringing in a reliever. We can't take any chances with the leading run at the plate. Good game Sims. Now, go have a seat and relax. Let's see if we can pull this one out for you."

A combination of two different Akron relievers in the seventh, eighth and ninth innings held the Baysox to just one hit. Final score, Aeros 2, Bowie 0. The Aeros won their first game of the year and Harley notched his first game in the minors as a win.

Standing in the shower next to his catcher, Marty tossed him the soap and commented, "So how does it feel to win your first game out?"

"It feels great," said Harley. "We got off to a rough start, but once we buckled down, things panned out."

Rinsing off his head, Marty turned off the shower, "Tomorrow Trenton comes rolling in here for three games. That means you won't take the mound again until the second game with Erie. I hope you like riding on a bus because that's something you're going to be doing a lot this season."

Harley yawned and sat back in his bus seat and stared out at the driving rain beating against the window. The interior of the bus was dark with only a few lights on while players read or played cards. He checked the glowing face of his watch. Just after midnight, June 1st. For the past two months he had become accustomed to the long bus rides. He had been to Trenton, New Jersey; Binghamton, New York; Richmond, Virginia; New Britain, Connecticut; and Altoona, Erie and Reading, Pennsylvania. He enjoyed traveling at night. All he could see were the lights of passing vehicles, farms and small towns. Kicking off his shoes he laid back and closed his eyes. He wasn't the least bit tired but he knew he had to get some rest. Akron was just coming off of a three game sweep which put the Aeros at 24-27, three games below .500 ball. He was sitting currently with a win-loss record of 7-1 with an ERA of 3.25 *Not too bad,* he thought. An ERA that registered at 3.00 was considered great and 3.40 placed a pitcher in the above average category. He was right in between great and above average. The season was just over a third of the way complete. Opening a cold drink he had brought along he thought about the fact that they were heading for Reading. This was their second series of the season. The first time they had met Reading they had taken two out of three from the Aeros. The game he pitched in Reading was his only loss to date this year. It would be a few hours before they pulled into the hotel. Pulling the jacket up closer to his neck, he closed his eyes.

It was the perfect evening for baseball, mid-eighties, light breeze. Harley, as usual, went to deep center field on the grass at the edge of the warning track to go through his pre-game stretching routine. Prior to a game whether he was pitching or not, he always liked to spend time alone. Beginning with a series of Hurdler's Spreads, he slowly stretched his leg and back muscles. It was just after five thirty and the game was not scheduled until seven ten. The stands were practically empty as it was too early for fans except for a few here and there who enjoyed coming early to watch the players warm up. The flag in center field was flapping gently in the breeze, the grounds crew was watering and raking the infield, members of both teams were scattered around the field as they jogged, stretched or in some cases played catch. Tonight was the final game of the three game series with Reading. Tonight's game would determine who would walk away with the series as they had split the first two games. He hadn't pitched in either game and was not scheduled for tonight's game as well. Still, he had to suit up, and get his stretching in. After he finished with his stretching he'd do a few wind sprints followed by some light jogging. He'd finish up by throwing the ball around a little with one of the other pitchers.

He thought about how his first year in the minors seemed to be passing quickly. With fifty-three games under their belt, there were eighty-eight games left in the season. Three months from now, the season would end on September 4th, that is unless they made the playoffs and with almost ninety games to go anything could happen.

Standing, he did twenty-five jumping jacks, ten deep knee bends and touched his toes a number of times. He started to slowly jog around the edge of the outfield grass toward the left field foul pole all the while rotating his neck and shoulders. Crossing the left field foul line, he noticed a small boy standing at the chain link fence while he held a brand new baseball and a pen in his hands. As Harley approached, the boy eagerly held up the ball and pen while asking politely, "Could I please get your autograph?"

Harley hadn't signed more than five autographs since he had arrived in Akron, but when asked, he was always quick to respond. Walking to the fence, Harley smiled, "Sure…why not!"

Taking the ball, Harley asked the boy, "You play ball?"

The kid grinned widely, "Yes sir. I'll be ten years old this coming October. That means next year I'll be able to play in Little League."

Reaching for the pen, Harley inquired. "What's your name, young man?"

The boy spit on the ground and answered, "Theodore, but my friends call me peanut 'cause I'm so small. I'm gonna be a catcher."

Harley went about signing the ball; *Good luck Peanut! Your friend, Harley Sims.*

Handing the ball and the pen back to the boy, Harley remarked, "My best friend is a catcher. In my opinion it's the hardest position on a team. If you want to be a catcher you must be pretty good then!"

The boy admired what was written on his ball and then asked, "Does your friend play for Akron?"

"No, he plays for a team down in Florida."

Holding up the ball, the boy gave Harley a genuine smile and said, "Thanks!" With that the boy was off running back toward the third base stands. Harley smiled as he thought back to his boyhood days and how he had always tried to get players to autograph one of his many baseballs. To think that someone now, years later, wanted his autograph seemed amazing. Turning to run back to center field he was stopped dead in his tracks as he stared at the player leaning against the left field fence.

Drew popped a stick of gum in his mouth, tipped his hat and stepped forward. "Nothing to say to your ol' pal?"

Harley was at a loss for words but finally managed to speak, "Why are you...here? Last week when we talked you said the Threshers had a ten game road trip."

"Things change," said Drew. "I've played my last game in Clearwater." Displaying the red embossed name on the front of his uniform, *Fightin' Phils,* he explained, "Got a call yesterday from Derron informing me that I was being bumped up to Double A. Apparently, the starting catcher for Philadelphia's Triple A team got injured and will be out the rest of the season. The catcher here at Reading moves up to Triple A. They needed a backup catcher here in Reading so here I am!"

"Does Melanie or your folks know?"

"Yeah, I called them as soon as I found out. I flew into Philadelphia last evening, rented a car and drove up this morning."

"This is incredible! Both of us in Double A."

"What's more incredible is that we're both in the same league." Harley pointed toward center field. "Come on let's walk some."

Holding up his catcher's mitt, Drew asked, "You don't think this will be a problem, do you? I mean with me catching on a team that you could be pitching against."

"You catching and me pitching for different teams is not the problem, at least for tonight's game. I'm not scheduled to take the mound until two days from now when we're in Binghamton. Are you catching tonight?"

"No. They told me I might not catch until our next series which is with some team from Harrisburg. They roll in here tomorrow."

Walking over to the fence Harley picked up his glove. "The way I see this is that as long as you're catching for the Phils and

I'm pitching for the Aeros there won't be any problems. Now, when we play against one another, I'm not saying it would be a problem but it could be very interesting. I know how you hit and you know how I pitch, but at least for tonight we don't have to concern ourselves with that happening because both of us are going to be warming the bench this evening."

Leaning against the fence, Drew asked, "Does Reading and Akron play anymore this year?"

"I was just looking at our schedule for the rest of the year last night," said Harley. "If I remember correctly I think we play Reading at home in mid-August."

"Well then," added Drew. "It looks like we don't have to worry about facing one another for another two and a half months."

Harley laughed. "And that's if you stay put! They way you're going you might be in Triple A by then." Picking up a ball that was lying next to the fence, he flipped it to Drew. "How about throwing a few?"

Walking out into the outfield grass, Drew tossed the ball into the air and caught it behind his back. "Thought you'd never ask!"

Spacing themselves at the approximate length from the mound to the plate Drew threw the ball to Harley and suggested, "Why don't we try a few warm-ups and then you can give me some heat."

Catching the ball, Harley casually threw the ball back. "I almost forgot how much fun it is to throw the ball around with you."

Following nine exchanges, Drew went down into the catcher's position and slapped his glove. "Let's see one around ninety to ninety-five."

Nodding at Drew, Harley gripped the ball for a two-seamer, wound up and let loose. The ball slapped into Drew's mitt with a resounding thud that indicated speed!

Smiling back at Harley, Drew stood and held up the ball. "I've caught a lot of pitchers in spring training and then with the Threshers but I've got to tell ya. Your fastball slamming into my glove felt like an old friend. I miss being your catcher."

Two Reading players jogging by stopped and approached Drew. "Hey…new guy!"

Drew stood as the players approached. "If you're referring to me, well then I guess I am the *new guy!*"

The taller of the two players spoke up, "Whaddya think you're doin'?"

Drew gave Harley a look then answered the question. "Well, back where we come from in Missouri I believe we call it playing catch."

The tall player snapped, "I know what it is. What we're wonderin' is why you're doin' it with someone from the opposin' team?"

"I can clear that up easy," said Drew. "Let me introduce you to my best friend...Harley Sims. I guess we've been playing catch for close on to twelve years now. Is there a problem?"

The other player stepped forward and answered, "Yeah, there is. There isn't any harm in playing catch, but I think it would be better to practice with your own teammates, otherwise why don't you just hop on a plane and git yourself back down to Clearwater."

Harley walked up and joined in on the conversation. "You boys got a problem with my friend here?"

The tall player spoke up, "Look Sims, this ain't none of your business. Why don't you just mosey on over to where your Akron buddies are."

Harley looked at Drew and gestured at the two players. "I know these two fellas." Casually pointing at the tall player, he went on, "This is Bill Masey and we faced each other three times this year. Out of those three encounters I struck Bill out three times. His teammate here is Jesse Yeats. We only faced one another twice. If I recall I believe Jess struck out two times as well." Dropping the ball and glove to the ground Harley held out his hands, "Gentlemen...I drop my weapons. This is not a battlefield. This is a baseball field and we are some of the few that get paid to play this marvelous game. I see no reason why players from opposing teams cannot warm up side by side." Sticking out his right hand, Harley smiled. "Friends?"

Masey refused his hand and turned to Jesse. "C'mon let's move on. These two guys are nuts!"

Watching the two as they jogged off, Harley commented, "Ya know, Drew. Maybe you should go on back over there with your teammates. Seeing as how you are new on the team they could make things rough on you. When I first arrived in Akron, the players that had been on the team before put me through the ringer because I was one of the new guys. I had to get coffee and buy donuts and sweep up around the locker room. But, that all ended once I proved that I was a valuable part of the team. All that stuff was done in a comical sort of way, but those two guys we just talked with didn't seem very amused."

"I'm not worried about them," said Drew. "You seem to forget that I'm a second degree black belt. Those two yahoos are not going to give me any trouble. Now, let's get back to that fastball of yours."

The game started at exactly seven ten that evening and just over three hours later Reading walked away with the win 5-4 in a close contest. After the game, Harley and Drew shook hands and agreed that they would stay in touch. Walking away Drew waved at his friend and confirmed, "I'll see you mid-August in Akron!"

Walking back to the visitors' dugout Harley thought about how strange things could be at times and how it seemed like Drew was always dropping an unexpected surprise on him. Like that time long ago at a Cardinals game when Drew had dropped Aaron Buckman to the ground and then the encounter with that biker named Luke back when they were in college. Once again, Drew had intervened when unexpected. How about when Drew had entered the draft and then dropped that bomb on everyone at Harley's house just prior to the draft. And now, Drew shows up in Reading as a Double A catcher. Harley wondered, *What's next?*

June was a good month for Harley. He won four games in a row bringing his win-loss record to 11-1. He had thrown two shutouts against Binghamton and Portland and won games against Harrisburg and Trenton allowing just five runs. July turned out to be equally good. He threw five more games losing only one, his current pitching record at 16-2; best in the Eastern League. He had lowered his ERA to just below 3.00. Despite his success, the Aeros couldn't seem to get out of third place. During the July fourth weekend Mira and his folks flew into Akron for a three-game home stand. The philosophy of *anything can happen in baseball,* rang true on July 5th when Harley took the mound. In front of Mira, his parents and a packed house, he pulled off the magic once again, not only throwing a no-hitter, but hitting a home run as well for his 17th win.

It was now August 2nd and Harley found himself on a hot August evening sitting in the bleachers at a local Little League field just down from his apartment in Akron. Tomorrow he was scheduled to pitch against Erie in the first game of a three game series. Biting into one of two hot dogs he had just purchased, he watched as a young boy, probably eleven or twelve years old, threw a series of pitches to a catcher next to a chain link fence. Looking across the field and around the small ballpark he recalled his days in Little League. The catcher stood up after receiving a pitch and yelled to the pitcher, "Good pitch...give me a curve next!"

Harley's daydreaming was interrupted by the sound of his buzzing cell phone. Talking his phone out of this pocket, he answered, "Harley Sims on this end!"

A voice sounded on the other end, "Harley...it's Drew! I was looking forward to seeing you in Akron twelve days from now, but something's come up. I won't be coming to Akron with Reading."

Surprised, Harley asked, "What are you talking about? Are you all right? You haven't gone and gotten yourself injured?"

"No, nothing like that. I'm fine. It's just that I'm not playing for Reading any longer."

"I knew it!" said Harley. "There're moving you up to Triple A!"

"No, I'm not going to Triple A."

"Don't tell me they're sending you back down to Clearwater?"

"That's not it either."

Harley was confused. "Did you get traded?"

"Nope, didn't traded me."

"I'm running out of options here. What else is there?"

"I hope you're sitting down. I just got a call from Derron ten minutes ago. They're sending me up to the big club."

Harley was silent for a second then responded, "When you say *the big club* you can't be referring to Philadelphia."

"That's exactly what I'm saying. The Phillies are calling me up. I leave for Philly in the next couple of hours."

"This is unbelievable," said Harley. "How did this happen?"

"The Phillies, despite being in first place, have had a series of injuries this year. Well, turns out another catcher on the Phils has bit the dust with a torn ligament in his right hand. He's out for the rest of the year. They were going to move up a catcher from Triple A, but Derron said they wanted me. They like the way I handle the bat and also, besides the fact that I am a catcher, I can play the outfield as well. Derron feels that being the third catcher on the team that I probably won't get much playing time as a catcher but I could fill in as a utility man in the outfield or maybe even pinch hit on occasion."

"That may be," said Harley. "But the fact still remains, you're going to be member of a major league ball club...the Philadelphia Phillies! You've got your foot in the door. The Phils are in first place with just a few weeks left in the season. If they hold on, they'll probably be in the playoffs. Who knows? They might make it all the way to the World Series and you'll be a part of that. Next year, whether they get in the playoffs or not they may call you back. At the worst, they'd probably only send you down to Triple A. Either way, I think it's great!"

"Listen, I've got to run if I'm going to get to Philly. One more thing before I go. I owe all this to you. If it were not for your patience with me back when I was learning the game as a ten-year-old boy, none of this would have happened to me."

Harley spoke up, "Don't underestimate yourself Drew. You're a great ballplayer! Aside from the fact you're an above average catcher, you can hit, run and you have an arm like a rocket. I say, when you get to Philly, when and if they put you in...give 'em the what fors!"

Placing his cell on the bleachers Harley took a bite out of a hot dog and smiled at a man who sat down a few feet from him. The man smiled back and asked, "You got a boy on one of the teams?"

Gesturing with the hot dog, Harley responded, "No, sure don't."

The man moved up next to Harley and pointed down to the young man who was throwing to the catcher. That's my son down there. He's pitchin' tonight. That kid catching is his best friend. I've never seen two boys their age with such a bond."

Harley looked at the two boys and answered, "I know *exactly* what you mean mister!"

CHAPTER 38

A LOUD CLAP OF LIGHTNING CAUSED HARLEY TO SIT up in bed as he looked out his bedroom window. Heavy drops of rain beat against the glass while a roll of thunder sounded, followed by another flash of lightning. For a second his room was lit up, then he was once again engulfed in darkness. He glanced at the small alarm clock on his nightstand. The glowing red letters and numbers displayed, 3:17 - October 15.

Sitting on the side of his bed he wrapped his arms around his chest and yawned. It was way too early to be up. He thought about laying back down but then realized he was hungry. *Maybe a yogurt,* he thought. Crossing the room, he opened a dresser and grabbed a St. Louis Cardinals sweatshirt and started down the dark steps.

Stopping at the bottom of the stairs he watched while a bolt of lightning lit up the entire downstairs. Once again in total darkness, he ventured into the kitchen, crossed the cold tile floor, opened the refrigerator and reached for a yogurt when he heard a soft voice, "Good morning, Son."

Turning, with the aid of the dim light coming from the open appliance door, Harley saw his mother seated at the kitchen table. Hoisting a cup, she invited him. "Care to join me for a cuppa?"

Closing the door, Harley walked to the kitchen counter and flipped on an under counter light that flickered but then cast a warm glow above the sink. Walking to the end of the counter, he shrugged and answered, "Why not…coffee sounds good."

Grabbing a cup from the cupboard he poured the hot liquid from the glass coffee carafe, then dumped in a spoonful of sugar and sat directly across from Monica. Before he could start a conversation, Rich appeared in the doorway. "What is everyone doing up? It's not even three thirty in the morning."

Monica raised her hand and gestured to her husband. "Your son and I are just sitting here enjoying the rain. Come, join us."

Walking across the semi-dark kitchen, Rich looked toward the window and commented, "It's really coming down out there." Walking to the coffeemaker, he reached up and removed a cup from the cupboard and poured. Seated at the table, he raised the cup, "Here's to whatever you two were discussing when I walked in."

Monica smiled across the table and remarked, "Harley just sat down. I was down here enjoying the storm. Ever since I was a little girl I have always enjoyed rainstorms. I can't tell you how many times when there was a storm my mother would check on me only to find me not in my room. She always knew where I would be and that was in the kitchen with a glass of cold milk and some cookies just sitting there in the dark listening to the rain beat on the roof of our house. I haven't changed over the years." Pointing at the ceiling, she whispered, "Listen!"

Rich and Harley looked at the ceiling while Monica explained, "When I was a little girl I always thought the rain falling on our house was *my rain!* I guess I still feel that way. By the way, why are you two down here?"

Harley took a sip of coffee and answered, "The storm woke me and I decided on a yogurt."

Rich fingered the rim of his cup and explained, "I was going to the bathroom when I heard voices. So, I came down…and here I am!"

Monica stood. "Since Harley seems to be hungry how does some breakfast sound? Bacon and eggs, maybe some hot biscuits?"

Rick looked at Harley, "I'm in…how about you, Son?"

"Sure, why not. Bacon and eggs beats yogurt any time."

Opening the refrigerator Monica commented, "When is the last time the three of us sat here in the kitchen and discussed anything?"

"I think it's been quite some time," said Rich. "This kitchen has seen many a conversation over the years and I think it's safe to say most of them have been centered on baseball. I remember some of those conversations like they were just yesterday. Like that time we sat here and discussed your broken arm Harley and you were so concerned about being ready for Little League tryouts and let's not forget the talk we had about your problems with ol' Aaron Buckman years ago. We sat here in this kitchen and talked about

Ozzie's passing and we all shared tears. More recently we talked about whether you were going to sign up for the draft and a number of other things over the years, which always seem to be baseball related. I mean just look at this room. Over there above the dishwasher hangs our yearly St. Louis Cardinals calendar and then there's our framed and numbered painting of Busch Stadium not to mention our Cardinal salt and pepper shakers."

Harley jumped in and added, "And let's not forget Mom's Cardinal floor mat that leads to the mudroom and the Cardinals schedule that always hangs on the front of the fridge."

Monica smirked, "I need to take that down. It's nothing but a bad reminder of the year we had. We finished up in fourth place; eleven and a half games back. Didn't even make the playoffs." Cracking open the first of six eggs, she reached over and pulled down the Cardinals schedule. "I might as well file this with the rest of the schedules I've saved for the past thirty some years. There's always next year."

"True, very true," pointed out Rich. "The season may be over for the Cardinals but it's not quite over for us. Last night Philadelphia defeated Chicago to win the National League Pennant. The Phillies are going to the World Series. I'm still amazed that Drew is playing for the Phils. I know it's been only two and a half months since he was called up, but it's still unbelievable. Drew has been like a second son to us. When I think back to all those days when we went to Arnold Park and worked with him on his catching skills and taught him how to hit and run the bases, and now, he's in the major leagues. That's amazing when you think about it!"

Picking up a package of bacon, Monica stated, "And let's not forget the Cleveland Indians play the Tigers tonight. The Indians are up three games to one. They could close it out tonight and become the American League team that goes to the series. Think how crazy that would be. Cleveland, Harley's parent team, could be in the World Series against Drew and the Phillies. So, even though the Cards season is over we've still got some baseball to not only watch but two teams to root for."

Harley spoke up. "Hearing you say that is really strange. Here we are, all three of us in the kitchen, me with my Cardinals sweatshirt, Mom wearing one of her favorite Cardinal jerseys and

Dad with that ripped and tattered ol' Cardinal shirt he sleeps in. If someone were to walk into this room right now, it wouldn't take much to figure out that our family, every one of us, is a loyal St. Louis Cardinals fan." Gesturing toward the living room, he went on, "There isn't a room in this house that doesn't shout that we're a Cardinal family. I say we live in a House of Cards, and yet here we sit talking about The Philadelphia Phillies and the Cleveland Indians. If the Indians defeat the Tigers tonight and earn the right to move on and play Philadelphia for the World Series Title, as die-hard Cardinal fans who are we supposed to root for?"

Placing strips of bacon in a pan, Monica offered an answer, "That's an easy choice for me. If the Indians win the right to play in the World Series against the Phillies I intend on rooting for Philadelphia, because that's the team Drew plays for. Even though Harley plays in the Indians farm system, he still is not on the Cleveland Indians roster, so I'd pull for the Phils. If Detroit goes to the series...same thing. I'd go with Philadelphia."

Rich spoke up, "I think I agree with Monica on this, but depending on what happens in the next year or two, our allegiance could switch from the Phils to the Indians. If Drew remains with the Phillies and Harley eventually gets bumped up to the Indians there is the possibility that they could face each other in the World Series. If that happened I'd have to go with the Indians."

Monica agreed. "I think I would too, but thinking about rooting against Drew doesn't seem right."

Harley stood and went to the counter where he refilled his cup. "I'm hoping that tonight Cleveland defeats Detroit. I've already called Drew and congratulated him because he's going to be part of the fall classic this year."

Monica went about preparing scrambled eggs and asked, "Then I can only assume you intend on going to Philly to watch the series...to watch Drew play?"

"Of course, I'm going to Philly. Drew told me he could get tickets for not only our family but his as well. Unfortunately, his parents are not going to be able to go and you have already said that you both have to work. So, I guess it'll just be me, Mira and Melanie. Drew also informed us that whether the series goes four games or the full seven he might not even get in any of the games. He told me that out of the fifty-two games the Phillies have played since he was called up, he has not played a complete game. He has caught a total of twenty-three innings and played left field for five innings. He has had seven plate appearances, mostly as a pinch hitter, and surprisingly amassed five hits. He has thrown out three players while attempting to steal and even picked off a man on first. But, the truth is we could attend every game of the series this year and never see Drew take the field."

Placing a bowl of eggs on the table, Monica flipped the bacon. "Rich and I, as always, are planning on watching every moment and play of this year's World Series just like we always do. Aside from being avid St. Louis fans, we are also true baseball fans. And I emphasize, *true baseball fans!* I say this because in every nook, corner and cranny of this country you'll run into people who claim to be baseball fans. You can find them in every state, city and podunk town from one end of the United States to the other, but many of these people who claim to be baseball fans are indeed only a fan of the team they root for. If their team, let's say the Cardinals, are not playing in the World Series then they have no interest in watching the year end baseball event. Rich and I watch the series every year regardless of who the teams are. For me, it's like this. When pitchers and catchers report for spring training it's like a brand new puzzle that is incomplete. Before you know it the first game is played and the season just rolls along...wins, losses, rainouts, home games, away games, runs, hits, and stats galore. Then we have the all-star game and before long the playoffs and then the World Series. As the long season goes by pieces of the year's baseball season seem to fall in place. For me, the final piece of my yearly baseball puzzle snaps in place when the final out of the last game of the World Series takes place. And that, is a *true baseball fan!*"

Rich looked across the table at Harley and held up his coffee cup, remarking, "I couldn't have said it any better!"

Taking a scoop of eggs, he continued and changed the subject. "So how do you feel about your first year in the minors?"

Harley reached for the eggs and answered, "I think I did all right. I won my first game of the season and lost my last game, but overall, 17-3 turned out to be the best win-loss record in the Eastern League. I had the lowest ERA, was the best hitting pitcher and registered another no-hitter. All in all, I can't complain."

Popping some biscuits in the toaster oven Monica asked, "Aside from going to the World Series, what are your plans for the off-season?"

"Well, later on today I plan on driving over to Mizzou and checking on some fall classes. I have every intention of completing my education in the off-season over the next few years. Then, I'm planning on driving over to Mira's parents' farm. Her folks are up in Elmira on a short vacation to visit some of their old friends, so Mira has taken a few days off from school to take care of her grandparents. We were planning on going riding this afternoon, but we may have to cancel if the rain keeps up. Later this evening I'm going to help Mira prepare dinner for the four of us and then we plan on watching the game between Cleveland and Detroit. I should be back home tonight somewhere around eleven o'clock. As far as the rest of the off-season goes it's not really that long. Before you know it, it will be November and a little over four months down the road I'll be back down at Winter Haven getting ready for next year's season."

Placing the bacon and biscuits on the table, Monica winced as a nearby bolt of lightning caused the under counter light to flicker and then go off. Monica reached up and tried to switch the light back on, but they remained in darkness.

Rich walked to the counter and grabbed a candle from on top of the refrigerator. "Looks like the power may have been knocked out." Sitting the candle in the center of the table, he lit it with matches he took from the utensil drawer.

Monica buttered a biscuit as she gazed at the burning candle. "This is nice sitting here in the early morning, listening to the rain, enjoying breakfast together. The simple things in life are the best." Raising her coffee cup in a toasting fashion, she smiled, "Here's to our family and this house...a house of Cardinals...or as Harley says, 'A House of Cards!'"

The weatherman had been right on the money with his prediction of an all-day rain. It had rained during Harley's drive to Mizzou and continued later on during his trip to Mira's grandparents' farm, during their dinner and while they watched the World Series. Now it was just after eleven o'clock at night and it was still coming down. Pulling out onto Telegraph Road, Harley turned the windshield wipers on high and headed for Jeffco Blvd. He thought about the pleasant evening he had spent with Mira and her grandparents. After an enjoyable dinner, the four of them gathered in the sitting room and watched the fifth game of the World Series which Cleveland wound up winning in a close game 5-4. Turning onto Jeffco, he thought that in the morning he'd give Drew a call and start making the arrangements for Mira, Melanie and himself to fly into Philly for the first game of the series which was seven days away.

Soaked from the rain, he entered the mud room, kicked off his soggy socks and shoes, hung his jacket on a hanger and walked in the kitchen where he found Monica busy drying some dishes. "Hello, Son. How was your dinner at Mira's?"

"Turned out pretty good," answered Harley, "We watched the game and shortly after it ended I decided to venture out to my car and head on home. Where's Dad?"

"He went up to bed about ten minutes ago. I'm going to head up myself as soon as I finish up here in the kitchen. We both have to get up early tomorrow for work."

Harley headed for the stairs. "I think I'll grab a hot shower and then it's off to bed for me as well. Good night."

It was after midnight when Harley slipped beneath the covers. Just before switching off the light on the nightstand he gazed around his room. He had been sleeping in this room ever since he was three years old. On the surrounding walls, there were nineteen years of St. Louis Cardinal memorabilia: pennants, signed photographs, ticket stubs and hats. Turning off the light he turned his head sideways and looked out at the rain, thinking, *This is a House of Cards!*

"Harley...Harley, wake up...Harley!" Slowly opening his eyes, Harley heard his mother's voice and saw her face in the early morning sunlight filtering through his bedroom window. Shaking him gently, she pleaded, "Harley...please get up!"

Harley slowly sat up and looked at his alarm clock. Six ten in the morning. Staring into his mother's face he noticed she had been crying. Instantly awake, he asked, "Mom…is everything okay? Is Dad all right?"

"Your father is fine. I'm fine, but you need to come downstairs. There's something on the news that's horrible. Get dressed and come down. I'll be downstairs in the front room."

Rubbing his tired eyes, he went into the hallway bath, splashed cold water on his face and made his way down to the front room where he found Monica sitting on the couch in front of the television. Taking a seat in Rich's easy chair, Harley inquired, "Mom, what's up?"

Holding a cup of coffee in her hands she nodded at the screen and spoke softly, "Just listen, they're updating the situation right now."

Harley focused on a reporter standing near a large body of water. *"For those of you who are just now tuning in, we are sadly reporting that an AirCruise 727 flying from Detroit's Metro Airport to the Cleveland Hopkins International Airport has crashed into Lake Erie approximately three miles northwest of Kelleys Island. Flight 1517 went down around 1:15 earlier this morning. It is reported that there were fifty-two passengers including the flight crew. Rescue teams have been feverishly working at the crash site. So far forty-eight passengers have been located. Sadly, our latest update reports forty-six have perished and two, who are in serious condition, have been transported to a hospital in the greater Cleveland area. Detroit's Metro Airport's manifest indicates that the passengers not only included the entire Cleveland Indians baseball team but their coaching staff as well. The two surviving passengers are identified as a flight attendant and a member of the Indians ball club. Their names are being withheld at this time. It is with great sadness that we inform the public about this horrible crash. The Cleveland Indians, last evening, won the American League Championship and were on their way to Cleveland for a day of rest and celebration, then they were scheduled tomorrow to continue to Philadelphia where they were to face the Phillies in the World Series in seven days. Our nation and the world of baseball is greatly saddened today. Stay tuned for further updates."*

Harley and Monica sat in silence, when she finally spoke up, "While you were down at Winter Haven did you get to know any of the Cleveland players?"

"That's what I was just sitting here thinking about. I met most of the players. I didn't get to know them all that well, but in the evening if they had a game sometimes I'd hang around after my day was over. Some of the pitchers watched me on a few occasions, even gave me some tips. Now, they're gone! Practically an entire team...gone! How can you explain something like this? There they are flying along at one o'clock in the morning, just four hours after winning the American League Championship Series and just like that...they're gone! Does Dad know about this?"

"I don't think so. He left for work before I got up. Speaking of work, I have to leave for the hospital in a half hour. I'll call your father on my way to work."

"No, I'll drive over to Imperial and tell him," said Harley. "I also have to call Mira and Drew."

Getting up from the couch, Monica asked, "Are you going to be okay?"

"I'd say I'll be all right, but how do you deal with something like this? It's a lot to think about. In the future, as a major league player, I'll be flying from one end of the country to the other from time to time. It's a scary thought."

Softly, Monica added, "Don't remind me. When you were in college, and then last year in the minors, every time you had to take a bus trip I prayed that nothing would happen to you. I can't even begin to imagine how the mothers of those players that perished must feel. Some of those players no doubt had wives and children. It's just hard to understand."

Coffee in-hand, Harley backed out of their driveway and started the ten minute drive to Imperial. Once on 55 South he turned on the radio, which was always set on a local sports talk show. It didn't surprise him that the topic of morning conversation was about the recent plane crash and how devastated baseball fans everywhere were now that the Cleveland Indians team was no longer in existence. One of the show's hosts said that the remaining four passengers had been located. Two dead and surprisingly two alive...injured, but alive. That bought the total of survivors to four, three of which were ballplayers. The next topic they began to discuss fell right in line with the tragic accident.

Would the World Series be cancelled? One of the hosts stated that with just seven days until the series was to kick off that more than likely it would be cancelled. They took a couple of local call-ins who were St. Louis Cardinal fans who said that it would be a shame to cancel the series, but there didn't seem to be any other solution at the moment. The two hosts then began to talk about the fact that in the one hundred year plus history of playing the World Series that it had only been cancelled twice. In 1904, the New York Giants of the National League refused to play the Boston Americans of the American League as the Giant's felt Boston played in an inferior league and that the rules governing a year end series was a sham. Then, more recently, in 1994 the series was once again cancelled, but this time it was due to the ongoing Baseball Players Association strike. Before Harley realized it, he was pulling into the lot of his father's business. *SIMS MOTORCYCLE SALES AND REPAIRS.*

Parking next to his Dad's Cardinal red cycle, he entered through the front door and walked to the counter where one of Rich's two employees stood. Ernie waved with a friendly greeting, "Hello there, Harley." Then with a look of sadness, he asked, "I suppose you heard about the plane crash. I know you played in Cleveland's farm system this past season. I'm so sorry about the loss of the team."

Harley smiled genuinely and inquired, "Is Rich around?"

"Yeah, he's out back by the shed. We're getting ready to give this ol' place a good paint job."

Walking past the counter toward the rear garage door, Harley thanked Ernie and entered the back lot of the shop. There in the wide doorway stood his father, stacking cans of paint. Approaching, Harley spoke up, "Hey Dad!"

Rich smiled sadly at his son and then asked, "I suppose you heard all about the crash?"

"Yeah, I did. Mom and I watched it on the news earlier this morning. I drove over here to see you. I didn't know if you heard or not."

"The first thing we do in the mornings is to turn on the news. I called your mother on her way into work. She said you had seen the news." Popping open a gallon can of paint, Rich shook his head in disbelief. "It's a hard thing to deal with, especially someone like me who has a son who plays professional ball. It really makes you think. So, how are you doing with all this going on?"

"Not that well. I couldn't just hang around the house. I feel like there's something I should be doing to help all those families who lost love ones. They were ballplayers, like me. They made it all the way to the top, and at that, they were to play in this year's World Series. I really don't know what to do, say or even think."

Holding up a four inch brush, Rick smiled. "If you're up to it I sure could use another hand on this painting. We're going with Cardinal red and gray trim. I've got an old set of coveralls over there on that crate you can wear. Job doesn't pay much. All you'll get is a free lunch from the barbeque joint up the street. They told me that if I allowed them to leave a stack of menus on the counter, they'd give us free lunch today."

Harley reached for the brush. "I get to help paint this building Cardinal red *and* get a free lunch. Where do I start?"

Stirring the paint Rich nodded at the back of the shop. "You can get started right there on that cinderblock wall and make you way around to the front. Ernie will be starting on the other side of the building and I'll watch the shop."

Walking over, Harley unfolded the ol' coveralls. "Never did much painting before. This should be interesting."

At eleven o'clock Harley was summoned by Rich to wash up as lunch was on the way and would arrive in less than ten minutes. With the aid of a combination of paint thinner, soap and hot water Harley managed to remove most of the red paint from his hands. Walking into the shop he found lunch situated on a card table next to a pile of old motorcycle tires. Rich, who was piling shredded pork on a bun offered, "Dig in. We've got pulled pork sandwiches, baked beans, coleslaw and a rack of ribs."

Harley grabbed a paper plate and took a scoop of beans when Rich spoke up. "About a half hour ago they interviewed the Commissioner of Baseball about not only the plane crash but about the upcoming World Series. The commissioner said he was organizing a meeting to be held in New York at three o'clock today to discuss the matter." Biting into his sandwich, he asked, "Have you talked with Drew or Mira about the plane crash yet?"

"I tried calling them both on the way over here this morning. I couldn't get hold of either one of them so I just left a message. They both called back while I was painting. Drew is over at Citizens Bank Park where the Phillies play, along with most of his teammates. There is an ongoing prayer vigil at the stadium as fans are pouring into the ballpark to pay their respects to the Cleveland players who lost their lives in the plane crash. Drew said it was the saddest event he has ever attended. Philadelphia fans are flocking into the stadium, lighting candles and bringing flowers. He said that many of the players on the Phillies knew players from Cleveland who had perished. It's sad. Grown men, sitting in the dugout or the clubhouse, sobbing and crying. The season has come to a sad end. Rather than the jubilation that follows the World Series, baseball season has ended this year with great sadness. I guess what they say about baseball is true. For many people in America baseball is a summer tradition. We grow up with baseball and year after year it seems to have a certain kind on continuity to it. Wars couldn't stop baseball; the Depression couldn't stop baseball. Our society over the decades has changed and yet, baseball always affects our society. It had been said that if you want to know the heart and mind of America, well then, you better learn baseball. This plane crash, the loss of this team, affects us all to some extent."

At twelve noon Harley tossed his cell phone into his car and went back to his painting. He wasn't interested in talking to anyone else about the plane crash or the loss of Cleveland's team. It was too depressing.

Two hours later he laid down the brush and took a break while he sat on a pile of old crates. Looking at an ancient Harley Davidson clock in the open garage door of the back shed, he noticed the time. Two o'clock. *Wasn't the commissioner supposed to start the meeting at 3:00 EST like he had announced.* Harley wondered, *What will they discuss? Surely they'll cancel the World Series.*

CHAPTER 39

NEARLY A THOUSAND MILES AWAY FROM WHERE Harley was seated, on the eighth floor of a downtown New York high rise, baseball's commissioner, dressed in a black three-piece suit, white shirt and dark blue tie, ran his fingers through his balding hair and allowed his chain-suspended reading glasses to fall to his chest. Clearing his throat, he looked at the eight men seated in front of him and then began, "Good afternoon, gentlemen. Before we get started I want to thank each and every one of you for making the trip here to New York with little notice. I think everyone present knows everyone here so we'll dispense with any introductions." Turning, he nodded at a middle-aged woman who sat next to him. "This is my secretary, Joan, who will be taking notes as we proceed. For the record, we have with us today the owners and a management representative from three major league teams, Philadelphia, Cleveland and Detroit. We also have with us the President and Vice President of the Players Association."

Seating himself, he folded his hands neatly on the table and looked out at the group. "Let me start off by stating that in my thirty-three year career in professional baseball, that this is the hardest meeting I have ever attended or conducted."

Motioning at a set of polished oak doors, he stated, "On the other side of those doors just down the hall to the left awaits members of the media. When this meeting ends, they'll want to know what our decision is. That decision is our say so on the cancellation of this year's World Series. In light of what has transpired in regard to the loss of the American League's Championship team, the Cleveland Indians, the easiest thing for us to do would be to simply cancel the series. I cannot imagine anyone being upset with that decision when you consider what has happened. For the past few hours my office has been flooded with calls from all across the country. In short, the world of baseball wants to know what we as the decision makers are going to do. If we cancel the series, which seems obvious at this point, we can walk away from this knowing that we have done the right thing. That being said, I want to toss this out to the group. Is cancelling the series the right thing to do?"

The owner of the Philies raised his hand and responded, "What other choice do we have?"

The commissioner pursed his lips and explained, "It has been suggested to me earlier today that perhaps, seeing as how we cannot play the series that we award the series to Philadelphia. Some people feel that it is not fair to the Phillies to just simply cancel the series. So, my question for the group is this. Can we hand the trophy and the honor of World Champions to Philadelphia without the series actually being played?"

The owner of the Phillies spoke up again and emphasized, "I, for one, would not be comfortable if that were the outcome. We will not accept the title in that fashion."

The manager of the Phillies agreed, "I'm with Jim on this. I don't think the players or the fans would go along with that. If we are to be crowned World Series Champions it must be because we won the title in four, five, six or seven games. I would much rather just cancel the series than go down that road."

Cleveland's owner spoke next. "I agree with Jim and Lester. If the roles were reversed, Cleveland would not accept the series by default or forfeit or even by order of this commission. I too feel that it would be better to just go ahead and cancel the series."

"Let me throw something else on the table," said the commissioner. Looking at the end of the table where Detroit's owner and manager sat, he suggested, "What if there was a possibility that Detroit could step up and take the place as the American League team to play in the series. This takes nothing away from Cleveland. We could still play the series; National League verses the American League. Could this be the answer to our situation?"

Detroit's manager answered instantly, "I had a feeling when we were asked to attend this meeting that this very thing could be brought up. I appreciate the suggestion, but I really don't think my players would have their hearts in it. Cleveland was the out and out American League champion and therefore receives the right to play in the World Series. I suppose we could play with the attitude that it really doesn't make any difference who wins; that we're really playing to honor the Cleveland players who have lost their lives. But, even then, I don't feel it would be right. Here's why. If it is decided that we are to play Philadelphia there is a chance that we could win the series. As a team, we would not feel like we deserved the title simply because we were not supposed to be here in the first place. Cleveland was."

Detroit's owner nodded. "I agree with Terry. Our organization would be uncomfortable playing in a series that we did not earn the right to."

Philadelphia's owner added, "And if we won the series over Detroit we would not consider ourselves World Series Champions because we did not defeat the actual American League Pennant winner."

The Cleveland owner looked at both the Detroit and Philadelphia representatives and agreed, "It looks like we're back at our original idea of simply calling the series off this year."

The commissioner held up his hand, "Not just yet gentlemen. We have one other option. It's called Rule 29 and it may be the answer to our dilemma." Turning to Joan, he proceeded, "Joan is going to pass out to each of you a folder than contains a copy of Baseball's Rule 29. Is anyone here familiar with this rule?"

The President of the Players Association opened his folder and answered, "Yes, I am familiar with this rule. I was looking over baseball rules and regulations a few years back and stumbled across it. It is major league baseball's disaster plan. I think it's safe to say that most people involved in baseball are not aware of this rule. To tell you the truth I don't know if it's ever been used. But, it was designed for just the type of situation we are faced with."

The commissioner spoke up, "Larry is correct in what he says. Rule 29, if you care to follow along states, 'If a common accident, illness, or event causes the dismemberment or permanent disability of at least five players on a team from playing professional baseball or at least six players on a team, that team shall be deemed a disabled team.' This rule is rather confusing when you read what it says. To me, it's open to interpretation. For instance, if a team loses, let's say five players that means their roster would be reduced by five active players. Myself, I don't see that as being a disabled team as a team could easily call up five players from their farm system without missing a beat. But, there isn't any reason to discuss that part of the rule. We have to concern ourselves with the section that reads at least six players because what we're talking about is an entire team that needs replaced. Now, as commissioner, I have some options here. I can at my discretion postpone or cancel games and declare a period of mourning, I can also, with the co-operation of the players' association cancel a team's season or reschedule when a team can once again play. Since we are not in the middle of the season there is no reason to cancel Cleveland's schedule because when they became a disabled team, the season was essentially over except for the World Series. At this point postponing Cleveland's remaining season is out of the question so we're still back at point A, which is to cancel the series."

Detroit's manager broke in on the conversation. "I might be getting a step ahead here but I was just reading the next section of the rule where it covers a restocking draft clause. According to this the commissioner can enact a restocking draft procedure whereas all other teams must make available five players; a pitcher, a relief pitcher, a catcher, an infielder and an outfielder that can be made available to play for the disabled team. These players must be able to play immediately. From this restocking draft, the disabled team can draft, if necessary, an entire team. It also states that only one player can be chosen from each team. Is this feasible?"

"Yes," said the commissioner, "It is feasible, but is it realistic?"

The vice president of the players' association jumped in, "In writing it sounds rather simple but in all actuality, this could be complicated and I say this for two reasons. First, let's say you're a player for the Royals, Nationals, the Rex Sox, any major league team and suddenly you're notified that you've been drafted by a disabled team. We have to be careful with this type of rule because we are in fact tampering, so to speak, with someone's career. In this case, the Indians would be drafting an entire roster made up of players from practically every team. Secondly, with the time constraints we are faced with would these players have enough time to jell into a viable team?"

The President of the Players Association added, "And here's another point to consider. Since the regular season has been over for the past few weeks most off-season ballplayers have stopped practicing their routine baseball habits. Besides that, we may not even be able to contact many players this time of year. They could be up in Canada on a fishing trip or over in Europe on vacation or even someplace where they cannot be contacted. We'd only have a week to throw this new team together. Myself, I don't see this as feasible."

"Another thing," said the Phillies manager. "Don't forget the press is waiting for our decision on the World Series. If we release to them that we are going to go ahead with this restocking draft and then it doesn't work out we'll be labeled as fools. I still think canceling the series would be best."

Detroit's manager held up his folder and expressed his opinion. "I have an idea. Is there anything in the ruling that states a disabled team cannot staff their major league team from their farm system?" Not waiting for a response, the manager continued, "It would be a far site easier to create a team from Cleveland's own farm system because the players called up are already in their organization. It still may be hard to locate all of them, but still I feel this is far more feasible than drafting major league players from other teams."

The commissioner snapped his fingers. "Ya know, you might just have something there. This could turn out to be a sliver of light in the darkness of what has recently happened in baseball. Kind of like a Rocky moment if you will. An opportunity for a mostly unknown group of players to play in the World Series."

"This sounds good," said Detroit's owner, "but what type of a series would it be? Let's face it, if we go ahead with restocking Cleveland's major league team with minor leaguers the series itself may wind up very lopsided. Even if the team is composed of mostly Triple A players you're still talking about a bunch of kids playing against experienced major league players. It's obvious that they could be swept. It could be embarrassing."

"I don't think so," said the commissioner. "If we could arrange this I have no doubt that this year's World Series would be the most tragic series ever played, but at the same time one of the most interesting and uplifting to ever be played. As lopsided as it may seem, I think baseball fans would love to see it."

Philadelphia's manager spoke up, "I don't think we should look at it that way. I feel we should promote this year's series as a way to honor the players who have died and those who are hospitalized and cannot play. If this is what we decide to do, then my team, the Philadelphia Phillies would be honored to play in the series against a Cleveland farm system team. And, if this farm system team gets swept, then so be it. There have been other four game sweeps in the past, so why should this be looked at as different. I say…let's play ball!"

The commissioner looked at Cleveland's owner and asked, "Andy, do you think you can get a team together for the series?"

"How much time do I have?"

"Not much, I'm afraid. This would have to be done in the next twenty-four hours. We can't just keep putting off the media. Can you get a team together in that time frame?"

"I believe our front office staff combined with our scouts could pull this off, but we have to start making calls immediately."

"Then, it's settled," confirmed the commissioner. Looking at his watch, he announced, "By five o'clock tomorrow I need to have the names of the players here at my office. At that time, I'll call a press conference to announce what we plan on doing. When we leave this office in the next few minutes we tell the media that we are still undecided about the series. We cannot announce our intentions until we have this new team intact."

Everyone stood as the meeting was concluded. Cleveland's owner shook the commissioner's hand and stated, "I've got to call my office before I leave. I've got a lot of work to do in the next twenty-four hours."

Harley scrubbed his hands with a small brush as he tried to get the last few fragments of red paint from his skin. The clock on the shed wall read five after six. It had been a long day, but between he and Ernie they finished painting the main exterior walls of the shop. Satisfied that his hands were as clean as they were going to get, he stood and stretched. He felt sore and couldn't recall the last time he had put in a full day's work. Throwing the empty paint cans in a nearby trash container he heard his father's voice from the back door of the shop. "Harley…you've a got a phone call in the office. It's Derron…your manager. Says it's urgent."

Harley couldn't imagine why Derron would be calling and what could be urgent. Inside the cramped and cluttered office, he picked up the phone and spoke, "Derron...it's Harley, what's up?"

Derron's familiar voice was all business. "Harley, I don't have a lot of time to talk, so just listen. The commissioner had decided to put together a team to play in the World Series. The team is to be comprised of minor league players from Cleveland's farm system. Most of the players will be drawn from their Triple A team. Cleveland's front office just gave me a call. They want you to be in their pitching rotation. What I'm saying is that if you want to play in the World Series then you need to be on a plane and in Philadelphia by tonight or no later than tomorrow morning. Are you interested?"

Harley remained silent and Derron repeated, "Harley, do you understand what I'm telling you?"

"Yes, I understand, I just can't believe it! How will all this work? I have so many questions."

"Look, Harley. I don't know how all this is going to work. The World Series is in less than a week. All you need to do is show up and play baseball. I need an answer within the next hour. Maybe I should call you back."

"If you're telling me that I have an opportunity to pitch in a major league game, in this case the World Series, then count me in. What do I need to do?"

"You need to get to Philly as soon as possible. I had a gut feeling that you'd be on board with this so I took the liberty of scheduling you on a flight that leaves out of St. Louis in two hours. I've got to run. I'll see you when you touch down in Philly. You just need to show up. Everything on this end will be handled. See ya in a few hours."

Harley hung up the phone and stared at a St. Louis Cardinal calendar hanging on the wall when Rich walked in. "Everything okay? Derron didn't sound like himself."

Standing, Harley took a deep breath and grinned at his father. "You're not going to believe this, but it looks like I'm going to be playing in the World Series!"

"What on earth are you talking about, Son?"

"I have to go home and pack a bag and then I need you to run me over to the airport. I'm scheduled to fly out of here to Philadelphia in less than two hours. I'll explain what Derron told me on the way."

CHAPTER 40

HARLEY NO MORE THAN STEPPED OUT OF THE disembarking tunnel into a wide corridor at the Philadelphia International Airport when he saw Derron forcing his way through the throng of passengers and extended his hand. "How was the flight in?"

"This is only the second time I've ever flown," said Harley. "The first time wasn't that great and this time wasn't much better, but I'm here."

Guiding Harley down the corridor, Derron explained, "It's just after ten thirty. Let's get your bag and then we can grab a bite if you're hungry."

"I am hungry," said Harley. "I haven't eaten anything since lunch earlier today and that was almost eleven hours ago."

Pointing at an escalator, Derron guided Harley to the left. "Baggage pickup is down there and then to the right. Come on. We can eat right here at the airport. We've got a lot to go over."

Seated at a small crowded restaurant, Harley shoved his bag under the table and looked out the glass partition at the large number of people passing by. "I can't believe how many people are at the airport this time of night."

Derron looked at one of the menus and responded, "This is an international airport. Philadelphia is right in the center of four major cities. Boston, New York, Washington and Baltimore. A lot of people go through this place." Laying the menu down Derron looked around for a waitress and continued, "I think I'm going with a chicken salad sandwich and coffee."

Harley agreed, "That does sound good."

A frustrated waitress stopped by their table and rudely inquired, "What are ya havin'?" Writing down their order, she filled the two water glasses on the table and then grumbled, "It'll be twenty minutes or so."

Not paying any attention to the unfriendly waitress Derron got right to business. "When we leave here we'll be driving to Allentown which is about an hour up the road. You and the rest of the team will be staying at a place called Penn Manor. Cleveland has booked every room in the place. For the next six days, you'll be practicing at Coca-Cola Park, home of the Lehigh Iron Pigs, Philadelphia's Triple A team."

Harley, somewhat confused, asked, "Why didn't they send us to Cleveland to practice?"

"Because that would involve another day of travel since the first two games of the series are scheduled here in Philly. Besides that, Cleveland is in a deep sense of mourning. They've lost their baseball team. As hard as this is we're trying to keep this as upbeat as we can."

"How did Major League Baseball come to the decision to play the series? I thought when the commissioner had that meeting it was to announce the series would be cancelled."

"That's what everyone else thought. Apparently, the commissioner received quite a few calls, many from Cleveland fans requesting the series be played to honor the lives of the players lost in the plane crash. It has been decided a team would be formed from Cleveland's farm system. Most of the players are from Cleveland's Triple A club from Columbus, Ohio. Everyone on their coaching and management staff as well will be here, except for their manager who has a severe case of the flu. They decided to have Jim Langford, Akron's Double A manager, run the team. As soon as he was assigned he said he wanted you on his pitching staff."

Harley sat back and took a deep breath. "Derron, my head has been spinning ever since early this morning when I learned about the plane crash. Here it is not even twenty-four hours later and I find myself sitting here in Philadelphia, six days from playing in the World Series. Don't get me wrong. This could be a life changing experience for me, but I can't help but think this is some sort of a publicity stunt. I'm as optimistic as the next fella, maybe even more so, but can you really sit there and tell me a minor league team has a shot at even winning a single game against an experienced major league team?"

"Look, you know as well as me anything can happen in

baseball. Can this team…this minor league team defeat the Phillies in a seven game series and win the title? Probably not. Can this team win one game? It's possible, but everyone I've talked to is of the opinion we'll get swept in four. Here's the thing. This series is going to be one of the oddest series that has ever been played. I have no doubt Philadelphia will win…hands down. But that's not the point. I don't really think it makes any difference who wins or loses this series. It's a way for baseball fans everywhere to tip their hats to those who should have been here, but are not. Despite the outcome of this series, the games, however many are played will be uplifting. This team you will be playing on will be a huge underdog. Think about it? A bunch of kids, except for a few veteran Triple A ballplayers with a few years under their belt going up against a major league team. Why, you're only twenty-two years old yourself. I bet there won't be a player on this team over twenty-five. This is an opportunity for you to shine. Even if this team gets swept in four you're going to pitch in at least one game. You'll be pitching in front of millions of baseball fans across the country. This game that you're going to pitch could be the most significant game of your young life. If you somehow manage to win this game or even give a good showing you'll be punching your ticket for the future. Remember, next year Cleveland is going to have to rebuild their team and you could be part of that. Don't forget who you are Harley. You can throw a fastball consistently at ninety-eight miles per hour. That's nothing to sneeze at. You know what I think? I think when you take the mound you're going to give those boys from Philly something to think about."

"That's exactly what I plan on doing," said Harley. "I can't speak for the rest of the players on this new team, but when and if I take the mound I'm not just playing for the sake of playing the game. I'm going to try and win! I won't let up because this is a game that no one is taking seriously. This series could turn out to be nothing more than a series of all-star games. What I mean is that I never really enjoy watching the all-star game because a lot of the passion for the game is lost. The all-star game is hardly ever controversial; no one argues with the umpires, no one gets kicked out of the game, no one gets upset at a bad call, most players are not going to try and make a play that's risky. The fans know this and the game winds up being more about entertainment than a competitive game. I mean, how serious are the Phillies going to be about this series? They know they're going to win. If they get too far ahead in a game are they going to back off? This team that Cleveland is putting together already knows our chances of winning this thing borders on impossible. Will both teams just go through the motions or will they really try to win. The way I see this is, the Phillies have to win. If they lost the series it could wind up being an embarrassment to their team. I've never played a baseball game in my life where I didn't give my all in order to win."

"I wouldn't expect anything less from you," said Derron. "When you step on that field, regardless of whether it's the World Series or not, you should always play the game to the best of your abilities."

The waitress plopped down their plates of food and moved on without a word. Harley asked, "Does Drew know I'm here in Philly and that I'm playing for Cleveland?"

"Drew may not even be aware the series is going to be played, let alone realize you're here. The concept that this series will be played has not been released to the media yet. That announcement will not be made public until around five o'clock tomorrow. I'm not even sure the entire minor league team has been put together yet. I called you as soon as I was notified they were interested in having you on the team. Some of the players may not be as easy to contact as you."

"Are you saying there's a possibility the series won't be played?"

"No, I think it'll be played. Between Cleveland's entire farm system, I have no doubt they'll come up with a complete team. Between tonight and tomorrow, Cleveland minor league players will come rolling in here, whether they are from Triple, Double or even Single A ball. Tomorrow after the announcement is made and the media gets hold of the decision it'll be Katy bar the doors! I'm sure Drew will be in touch with you later on tomorrow."

Looking at his watch, Derron suggested, "Eat up. If we leave here around eleven thirty that will put us in Allentown about twelve thirty. You should be in bed by one o'clock because tomorrow is going to be a long day. You're going to be fit for uniforms and then there are papers to sign, mainly a major league contract even if it is only for seven games at the most. I'll need to be with you when you sign. After that, you'll have six days to get ready for game one of the series. It's been what…about six weeks since you've thrown some serious pitches. So, what I'm saying is that you've got about six days to get back what you had six weeks ago. The Phillies will be in top physical condition, still in their regular season mode. You have to get back in the groove and you have less than a week to do so. The next few days you need to focus."

It was one ten in the morning when Harley said good night to Derron who was staying back in Philadelphia. Sitting on the side of the bed at the Penn Manor Inn, Harley pulled back the sheets, but at the moment he was too keyed up to try and sleep. During the trip from Philadelphia to Allentown, Harley called his parents and Mira to update them on how things were going. Everyone was still amazed that he was going to be in the World Series and more than likely would get to pitch a game. Deciding that sleep, at least for now, was out of the question, he opened the door to his room and looked out at the parking lot. The pool had been closed for the season but there were a number of plastic chairs scattered around the covered swimming area. *Maybe I'll just sit outside for a while,* he thought.

Crossing the paved lot, he opened the gate and entered only to find another person who was smoking sitting in one of the plastic chairs. The individual looked up when he heard the gate unlatch, stared at Harley and then asked, "You a ballplayer?"

Harley approached the friendly young man who appeared to be a few years older than he. "Yes, I am a ballplayer, Name's Harley Sims."

The boy reached up and shook Harley's hand, introducing himself, "Samuel Beach…friends call me Sam. I'm starting catcher for the Columbus Clippers, Cleveland's Triple A club. I've heard of you. The word is you tore things up in Akron this past season."

Humbly, Harley responded, "I had an okay year." Sitting on a chair next to Sam, he probed, "I can only assume since you're from Cleveland's Triple A club that you're here to play on this last minute team they are putting together for the World Series."

Taking a final drag on his cigarette, Sam dropped the butt to the ground and smothered it with his foot. "That's right and more than likely depending on when you pitch in this series, I'll be your catcher. Last year when you pitched for Akron. Was that your first year in the minors?"

"Yep, my first year. How about you?"

"Heavens no!" blurted out Sam. "This is my eighth year. I was drafted right out of high school. After four years of working my way up I found myself in Columbus and the world of Triple A ball. I've been stuck there for the past four years. I have a wife and two beautiful daughters back in Columbus. As you are probably well aware, playing in the minor leagues, you're not going to get rich or even anywhere close to it. My wife has a good paying government job and if were not for that I don't see how we'd get by. When this opportunity came up to play in the World Series I figured this was my curtain call. If I can do well during the series then maybe next year when Cleveland rebuilds, I might get called up." Realizing he was rambling, Sam stood and yawned. "It's late. I guess I better turn in." Walking toward the gate, Sam yawned again and waved back over his shoulder. "I'll see you tomorrow Harley."

Watching Sam walk across the lot, Harley felt like he had just watched a bad movie; one of those stories that could bring a person down. It sounded like Sam was on his last leg as far as baseball was concerned. Suddenly, he felt tired. Standing, he walked to the gate and thought, *Eight years in the minor leagues. That can't happen to me...it just can't!*

Sitting in one of three offices in the clubhouse at Coca Cola Park, Harley signed the last of three documents which Derron had reviewed word for word. Pushing the papers across the table, Harley fiddled with an ink pen while two executives from Cleveland's front office scanned the documents and then placed them in a folder. The man with the folder stood, reached across the table and shook Harley's hand. "Welcome to the major leagues, Mr. Sims. One thing I want to make perfectly clear. The contract you just signed is only valid for the next few games that are played during the upcoming series. This contact in no way guarantees you a position on Cleveland's regular season roster next year. When spring training rolls around next February you'll report to Winter Haven and we'll go from there. As representatives of the

Cleveland Indian's organization we want to thank you for your participation in this year's World Series. Good luck."

The other representative shook Harley's hand and explained, "This evening we are planning on having a team meeting here at the clubhouse at seven o'clock to go over the schedule for the next few days and to also answer any questions you may have. One thing you need to do immediately is report to the locker room where you will be fitted for your uniforms. Aside from that, you're free for the day until the meeting. In the meantime, you can use any of the facilities here at the park, whether that be the weight room or the field itself. Some of the players have indicated they intend to begin a practice of their own this afternoon by organizing a pick-up game. You can join them if you'd like."

Outside the office, Derron shook Harley's hand and congratulated him, "Welcome to the major leagues for however long that may be. Listen, I've got to drive back to Philly. Will you be all right on your own?"

"Yeah...sure. I do have a favor to ask. If you'll drive me back to the motel I can get my gear then I plan on walking back down here to the park to spend the day. Like they say, I need to get back on the horse. I'm afraid when I pitched my last game in Akron I dismounted and really hadn't planned on doing any serious pitching until next spring. It's time for me to jump back in the saddle."

"All right then...let's go. I'll be back tonight to take you to dinner after the meeting. We'll be going over what they discuss with you as I will not be present during the meeting. It's a closed session for players and coaches only. Let's go get your equipment. I'll drop you back here at the stadium, then I'll head to Philly."

Walking out of a tunnel that led from the home team locker room to the field, Harley stopped and took in the stadium. It reminded him of most of the minor league stadiums he had played in the past year. Being a Triple A stadium it appeared that it could seat more than Akron's Double A stadium. Sitting on some nearby seats, he went about putting on his spikes. Glancing out across the field there were six players standing around talking down the third base line. Picking up his glove he started across the infield, stopped at the pitcher's mound, turned and faced home plate and surmised, *I thought I was finished playing ball this year...guess not!*

His thoughts were interrupted when he heard his name called out, "Hey Harley...c'mon over here!"

Turning, he saw one of the six players waving at him. Someone knew who he was, but who?

Jogging past third base and down the line he noticed it was Sam who was signaling to him. Stopping just short of the group, Harley nodded at the players when Sam made the introductions, "Boys, this is Harley Sims, the pitcher we heard of last year from Akron. Harley, these boys played with me down in Columbus this past year." Each player stepped up and shook Harley's hand and gave their name and position.

Sam reached out and tugged on the edge of Harley's sweatshirt and read the name on the front, "St. Louis Cardinals!"

Harley, making the best of things, tipped his hat to the group, smiled and remarked, "Got a matching hat too!"

Sam, who seemed to be the leader of the group pointed out at the field. "We were just planning our day. We thought we'd start out with some light jogging and some stretching, then maybe we'll have some batting practice. Most of us haven't played in three to four weeks. You in?"

Pounding his fist into his glove, Harley feeling right at home agreed, "Sure...why not!"

Just after four o'clock, a man Harley recognized walked onto the field and signaled everyone to the third base line. Once everyone was gathered into a circle Jim Langford addressed the group. "My name is Langford...Jim Langford. I have been assigned to manage this team. I think everyone expected is here except for a few who should be arriving soon. I need everyone to get cleaned up for the meeting this evening. Be back here at the clubhouse no later than six forty-five tonight. The meeting shouldn't last more than an hour or so. If you have any questions tonight will be the time to speak up. See you all later."

Everyone started to head for the tunnel, when Jim stopped Harley. "Sims! I've only got four starters on this team and that means you're going to pitch one of the first four games. I'm not sure which one just yet, but you need to be prepared to take the mound. I'm glad you're with us, Harley."

Harley walked to a table in the clubhouse and took a bottle of cold water, then seated himself in the front row. Twenty-five minor league ballplayers and a small group of team coaches waited for the meeting to get under way. At seven o'clock Jim Langford entered the room through a side door and stood behind a desk at the front of the room. Getting everyone's attention he spoke loudly. "Gentlemen, if everyone would please be seated, we'll get the meeting started."

Seconds later, with everyone in a seat, the room grew silent while the group waited for Jim to begin. Smiling at the young players, he spoke, "My name is Jim Langford. This past season and well, for the past six seasons, I've been the manager of the Akron Aeros, Cleveland's Double A ball team. I don't know most of you and likewise, many of you are not that familiar with me, so let's start off by going around the room and introducing yourself and the position you play. After that, we'll get started."

The introductions only took a few minutes and when the last player finished Jim spoke again, "Thank you. To say that a lot has happened over the past two days would be an understatement. This team has been assembled to take the place of the American League Champion Cleveland Indians, who all, but four players, perished in a horrible plane crash two days ago. It was initially thought the commissioner of baseball would cancel this year's World Series, but due to public interest in the series and the outcry that the series should be played to honor not only the players who perished, but those who have been hospitalized, the series will be played. It has been decided that a team from Cleveland's farm system would be put together to represent the American League. You, gentlemen *are that team!* You are the best players in Cleveland's minor league system. Starting tomorrow morning we will have five days to prepare ourselves to play against the Philadelphia Phillies, the National League Champions. Gentlemen, we've got our work cut out for us. Each one of you was selected because of your individual baseball talents. I am well aware that many of you haven't picked up a baseball for the past few weeks as the minor league season has ended. I know that some of you have played with each other while others have not. We must, as a team, get to know each other well over the next few days. There is already talk that we will not only lose the series but be swept in four games. Statistically, on paper, it appears that we could be swept. But, this is baseball and *anything* can happen because the talent level between the major league players that you will face and yourselves is very slim. Let me explain. You have played in the minor leagues, and they, some not that long ago, also played in the minors. The only difference or advantage they hold over us as a team is that they have played on the big stage...the major leagues! Can they catch a ground ball or an outfield fly ball any better than you? Can they run the bases any better than you? Can they hit a baseball any better than you? The answer to these questions are no, they cannot! The team who makes the least amount of mental and physical mistakes will, in most cases, win a baseball game. This is what we must concentrate on...the basics! We have pitchers on this team that can throw the ball in the high nineties. Can they throw the ball any harder than our pitchers? Is their curve ball going to break any better than ours? I could go on and on but I think you get my point. We must enter into this series with the attitude that we can win! When we take the field next week, we must be prepared. I think they'll have their hands full. Now, if there are any questions, I'll do my best to answer them."

Harley walked out the main gate of Coca-Cola Park and checked his watch. 8:05. He noticed Derron leaning up against his parked car. As he approached, Derron walked around to the driver's side and pointed up the street. "C'mon ...get in. There's a nice little steak joint two blocks up where we can relax and enjoy a good dinner."

Inside the car, Harley buckled up as Derron pulled away. Stopping at the next intersection for a red light, Derron looked in the rearview mirror as Drew, who had been hiding in the backseat, suddenly rose up and tapped Harley on his shoulder, "What's up, ol' buddy!"

Harley shook his head in amazement as he turned in the seat and remarked, "It never fails! It seems like you always have some sort of surprise up your sleeve. What are you doing in Allentown?"

Leaning between the seats Drew tapped his friend on his shoulder. "That's a question I should be asking you, but I already know the answer. I can't believe you're going to be on the team that's being put together to play the Phillies in the series. Last evening, down in Philly, we started to hear rumors about this mystery team. As players, we just sort of shook it off. To tell you the truth I was about ready to head on back home because I thought the series would be cancelled. Earlier this evening when the commissioner announced that the series would be played I was just about to give you a call and fill you in when I get this call from Derron. When he told me you were not only on this team that was being put together, but that you were in Allentown and you were having dinner tonight, I just had to tag along. This is unbelievable! Both of us...playing in the World Series! Do your parents know? How about Mira? Is she aware you're here in Allentown?"

"Yeah, I've kept everyone updated on what's going on. They're planning on coming in for at least the first game in Philadelphia."

Seated at the Allentown Steakhouse, shortly after they ordered, Harley spoke to Derron. "Could you do me a favor?"

Derron adjusted his tie and replied, "Name it!"

"Do you think Drew and I could have a few moments alone? There's something I want to discuss with him."

"Of course. I'll just step over to the bar for a drink."

Watching Derron walk off, Drew asked, "What could be so important that Derron couldn't hear? I mean he represents both of us."

"I know that, but I want to discuss something with you that's just between you and me."

Sitting back, Drew smiled. "Let's have it then!"

"Do you remember when we talked that day in Reading about how we might have to face one another later in the year?"

"Yes, I do remember that discussion."

"Well, the possibility of facing you was something I was not looking forward to. But then, we dodged that bullet because you got called up by Philadelphia. Now, I find myself a member of this last minute team Cleveland is throwing together. I've been told that I am going to pitch one game during this series. I have no idea which game that'll be, but the fact that you and I could face each other has come to the surface once again. I can't imagine facing you as a pitcher. If that should happen Drew, you have to give me your word that you won't back off. You have to promise me you'll give it your all if that moment comes." Harley hesitated, then repeated. "You have to promise me!"

Drew sat back, crossed his legs and responded, "What they say about great minds thinking alike must be true. On the drive up here from Philly this evening I was thinking the very same thing; that we could face each other at some point in the series. So, yes, I can promise you I'll play the game just the way you taught me. Play to win! As I have promised you, you must commit to me that you will not back down when and if you have to pitch to me. You have to promise me you'll view me as any other hitter; that you'll do your best to keep me from reaching base. For that moment, our friendship must be put to the side. In that moment, you will be a pitcher for the Cleveland Indians and I'll be a man at the plate for the Philadelphia Phillies. We have to agree to let the chips fall where they may, regardless of our friendship." Drew reached across the table and smiled, "Agreed?"

Harley grasped his hand and nodded, "Agreed!"

It was just after ten o'clock when Derron dropped Harley off at the Penn Manor. After stepping out, Harley leaned in the window and gave Drew a light punch on the shoulder. "I guess the next time we see each other will be on the field in Philadelphia next Thursday for the first game of the World Series."

Drew gave Harley a thumbs up and answered, "Looking forward to it!"

Harley stood in the lot and watched Derron's car pull away and disappear up the street. Walking to his room, Harley looked up at some passing clouds as they partially blocked the moon. *Tomorrow, it starts…tomorrow!*

CHAPTER 41

SAM WENT DOWN INTO THE STANDARD CATCHER'S position and pounded his mitt, while ordering Harley, "Give me three more fastballs. One down the center, then the inside and outside corners."

Harley placed his right foot against the edge of the bullpen pitcher's rubber, gripped the ball, wound up and delivered a ninety-eight mile an hour screamer down the middle of the plate. The loud clap of the ball smacking into the mitt caused Sam to jump up and fire the ball back. "Now, that's the sound of raw power! Let's have one on the inside."

Following two more fastballs, Sam stood and walked toward Harley. "Let's call it a day, grab a shower and then a steak dinner, followed by a great night's rest. Tomorrow morning it's off to Philadelphia and game one of the World Series."

Walking with Sam across the outfield grass, Harley placed his arm around his new catcher. "I'm going to respectfully decline that steak dinner. My girlfriend from back home and my parents are in town for the series. I'm having dinner with them tonight."

Hesitating before they walked down the tunnel that led from the field, Harley reached out and shook Sam's hand. "I just wanted to take a moment and thank you for the past five days and what a great help you've been getting me back in the groove. I feel like my ol' fastball is back and my stuff is working pretty good."

Sam thumped Harley on his shoulder. "Like I said all along, I think when the time comes and you take the mound against the Phillies, they're going to realize they are facing a serious pitcher!"

Harley's attention moved from the television to the knock on the door of his room. Opening the door, there stood Mira with a wide grin on her face as she remarked, "The word is there's a ballplayer in this very room who is going to be playing in the World Series."

Holding his hands out, he replied, "That's what they say!"

Mira leaned against the door jamb and placed her hand on her hip and comically ordered, "Well just don't stand there. Give a girl a hug!"

Reaching out they embraced, followed by a quick kiss when Harley asked, "Are my parents with you?"

Angling her thumb toward the lot, she answered, "They're right outside in a rental car. We have reservations at a restaurant called the Log Cabin. It's a few miles outside of town."

Hopping in the back seat of the car, Harley reached out and shook Rich's hand, while Monica commented, "I'm going to require much more than a handshake. When we get to the restaurant I expect a warm hug!"

Pulling out of the lot, Rich started the conversation. "How has the training here in Allentown been going?"

"Very well," answered Harley. "It's not exactly what I would call training, but more along the lines of getting a group of ballplayers who haven't played ball for the past few weeks back in the mix of things."

Mira, sitting next to Harley, asked, "So, are you ready?"

"Yes, I believe I am. The first couple of days I was uncomfortable with my arm speed and the way the ball was coming out of my hand, but then it all came back."

Stopping at an intersection, Rich made a left hand turn and remarked, "Folks back home in Arnold, or for that matter St. Louis, are excited about the fact that two local boys are going to be in the World Series."

Holding up the folded hometown newspaper, Monica smiled. "The Leader printed an article about you and Drew. A reporter called us and came over to the house and interviewed your father and me. I brought a copy along so you could read it. It's really quite good."

Mira poked Harley on his arm. "It would seem that you and Drew are celebrities of sorts. This is so exciting! Do you know what game you're pitching yet?"

"No, I don't. The other three pitchers on the team are all Triple A. I think it's safe to assume they're probably put me on the mound for game four. When you consider the first two games are here in Philly, then a day of travel, then game three in Cleveland it'll be five days before the Phillies get to see me."

A large sign at the side of the road indicated that they had reached their destination. Rich guided the car into the large parking lot, clapped his hands once and suggested, "Let's go on in. I'm starving."

The bus slowly pulled away from Coca-Cola Park as Harley made himself comfortable for the short trip to Philadelphia. Opening a bag of peanuts he had brought along, he read an article in the morning paper. According to the article everyone wanted this new Cleveland team to win but no one expected them to do so. It was going to be quite the series, but the outcome still loomed as a four game sweep. It was the first time in his years of playing baseball that he felt like his team didn't have a chance. The experience level the Phils possessed and the fact the Cleveland team had been thrown together at the last minute seemed like a recipe for disaster. Millions of people were going to watch the series already knowing the outcome. Sure, they didn't know what the score would be or the plays that would be made, but they did know that Cleveland would lose.

The bus rolled up next to a side entrance of Citizen's Bank Park just after twelve noon. Jim Langford stood and gazed out the window at the group who was approaching the bus. Getting everyone's attention, he announced with frustration, "There are a number of reporters waiting at the gate. They'll be full of questions. The cameras will be rolling. When we get off the bus you need to move directly into the stadium. Keep your comments short and keep moving. Let's go!"

Harley was the seventh player off the bus. He hesitated when he stepped down to the pavement, watching Jim Langford force his way thought the pressing reporters. "Excuse me, pardon me, coming through!"

Slowly walking past three different reporters, Harley gazed up at the side of the stadium when a number of microphones were shoved toward his face followed by a barrage of questions:

What's your name, son?
Where're you from?
What position do you play?

Following Jim's advice, Harley remained polite and kept his responses short:

Harley Sims.

Arnold, Missouri.

Pitcher.

Jim stood at a set of doors that led into the stadium and herded his players quickly along, "Keep movin' boys...don't lollygag! Keep the line moving!"

When everyone was in, Jim closed the door in the faces of a few reporters who trailed the last players.

A stadium representative guided the players down a long hallway, then a left and another passageway where they came to the Visitors Team Locker Room. Jim stood on a bench and got everyone's attention, "Listen up. It's now twelve thirty. Grab yourself a locker. Try and relax. We can't go on the field until two o'clock. As far as I know no one other than stadium employees are allowed into the stadium until four thirty. That means when we go on the field we'll have two and half hours of uninterrupted time. After that, it gets nuts. Fans, reporters, people trying to get autographs and photos. Try not to let any of this bother you. Welcome to the big leagues boys!"

Taking a seat next to Sam on a bench in front of a row of lockers, Harley held out his hand and spread his fingers. "Still steady as a rock!"

Sam opened a locker and kicked off his shoes. "I wish I could say the same. I may appear solid, but inside I'm shaking like a leaf and we haven't even stepped on the field yet. It's times like this I wish I was a pitcher. When the game starts this evening you're going to sit in the dugout and watch nine innings of baseball. Me? Well I'm going to be catching Gomez in front of forty thousand some fans. The microscope will be on me and the others who take the field tonight. We'll be judged, dissected, complimented, criticized and every other emotion baseball fans bring to a game. They'll all watch the game, hoping we win, but they'll be rooting for us with their parking brakes on, because they know we don't stand a chance."

Harley removed his jacket and laid it on the bench. "If I were pitching tonight I suppose I'd feel just like you, Sam, but don't forget what you told me when we first met. Playing in this series is like a curtain call. We may not win, but, we can go the distance. Look at it this way. How we get there may determine whether you and I are playing in Akron and Columbus or Cleveland next season. All we can do is give the game our best. Maybe we can't win this thing. That doesn't mean we can't act like winners, because the fact is…we are or we wouldn't be here."

Sam laughed as he took off his sweater. "Ya know somethin' Sims. You're a pretty good ol' boy!"

At two o'clock Harley and his teammates walked through a tunnel leading from the locker room to their dugout and then the field itself. Harley stood at the edge of the dugout and marveled at Citizens Bank Park. In many ways the park reminded him of Busch Stadium. Walking to the pitcher's mound he took in the field dimensions. Left field - three hundred and twenty-four feet. Center field - four hundred and one feet. Right field - three hundred and thirty feet. The left field message and scoreboard was massive. The infield as well as the outfield grass was cut to perfection. Beyond the outfield fence the field was surrounded by thousands of red seats that rose toward the azure blue sky. A grounds crew of men wearing Phillies employee jerseys stood down the third base line making plans for the day. Scattered throughout the seats there were a number of employees who were busy wiping down seats and picking up any debris that had blown into the stadium. Laying his glove next to the mound he decided to take a few laps around the outfield. Passing a man riding a small lawn tractor, the employee waved at Harley and yelled, "Welcome to Philly. Ya gonna give us a good game tonight?"

Harley waved and yelled back, "You betcha!"

By the time he reached the center field warning track, his teammates were scattered across the outfield like ants jogging and stretching.

At four thirty fans slowly started to take a seat here and there. Walking with Harley down the third base line, Sam suggested, "I say we head on over to the dugout. Didn't Jim mention a meeting at five?"

Stepping into foul territory, Harley heard his name. Looking to his left he saw Drew approaching. Grabbing Sam by his shoulder,

Harley spoke up, "Hold on Sam, there's someone I'd like you to meet."

Displaying his Phillies uniform, Drew walked up and shook Harley's hand. "Welcome to Citizens Bank Park!"

Harley made the introductions. "Drew, this is my new catcher Sam, at least for one game during the series. Sam, this is Drew. He caught me for twelve years."

Sam shook Drew's hand and stated, "Harley's told me all about you. Are you catching tonight?"

"No, I probably won't even get in the game, unless they need me to pinch hit or maybe play left field for an inning or two."

Sam tipped his hat and congratulated Drew, "I'm glad you made it to the bigs. Good luck tonight." Walking backward toward the dugout, Sam added, "I'm gonna head on in."

Watching Sam disappear in the dugout, Drew pointed at the stands down the first base line and with excitement explained, "Your folks, Mira and Melanie just got here and they're over there waiting. They want to get some photos."

Looking over at the stands, Harley saw his Mom and Dad waving. "All right," said Harley, "but it'll have to be quick. I've got a pre-game meeting to attend in a few minutes."

As they approached, Monica held out her hands, "I can't believe this! Harley *and Drew!* Both on major league teams playing in the World Series!"

Rich reached out and shook both boy's hands and added, "And we couldn't be prouder."

Melanie held up her camera. "Can we get some photographs? Maybe one of both Drew and Harley, then maybe we could get someone to take one with the boys."

After a number of photos, Harley apologized, "Look, I'd like to hang out with you but I have to be at a meeting in two minutes. I'll try to come back out before the game starts. Where are you guys sitting?"

Mira pointed at the scoreboard. "Just to the left of the message board on the second level. By the time you get back out here this place will be packed."

"Well, then I guess I might not get to see you until after the game. That might not work either because we have to drive back to Allentown tonight. I might not see you until tomorrow's game.

Look, I really have to run. Wish us luck!"

The meeting was just about to get underway when Harley walked in the locker room. Jim stood at the front of the room while each player sat in front of his locker. "What I have to say will only take a few minutes. After that, we have some drinks and finger sandwiches for anybody that's needs to eat something. When this meeting ends, it'll be around two hours until game time. That being said we have to be back out on the field for infield and outfield practice. The team we are about to face has been through the big game experience before…we haven't! Don't let any of the hype get to you. Just play baseball and you'll be fine."

By five thirty the meeting was over. Harley grabbed a water and a handful of pretzels and made his way back out to the dugout. Standing at the edge of the steps he looked around the stadium. In just the last half hour it seemed like thousands had shown up. Sitting on the edge of the steps he opened the water and watched as the infielders took their positions for some quick drills, the outfielders tossing a ball back and forth across the outfield grass. He looked at his watch. According to what he had been told at the meeting the pre-game schedule would begin at seven and then twenty-five minutes later, the game would start.

At six thirty the entire team assembled in the dugout. Harley stood at the edge and watched the spectacle of the World Series unfold before his very eyes. Crews were setting up cameras and wires were being run from the home team dugout to the pitcher's mound. The final touches were being put on the foul lines and the batter's box. There was hardly a seat that was not occupied. Vendors were circulating throughout the stadium as they sold their products. Beer, sodas, hotdogs, popcorn and on and on. A group of reporters gathered to the side of home plate, a few players here and there were being interviewed.

The next half hour passed as Harley watched the ever growing crowd and listened to the sounds of baseball. A vendor off to his left yelled, "Ice cold beer here!" Another vendor hollered, "Dogs…get your dogs!" Looking down the third base line, he saw a young boy eating cotton candy and a hot dog at the same time.

Another boy, sat with his father, his glove in his right hand as he anticipated catching a foul ball at some point during the game. The buzzing of the crowd was invaded by an announcement. *If we could have everyone's attention...please. At this time, the Commissioner of Baseball would like to make an announcement.*

Harley stood at the edge of the dugout and watched as a man in a three piece suit walked to the front of the pitcher's mound and stepped up to a microphone. The man hesitated and then began, "Welcome to this year's World Series. Before we begin we would like to take a few moments to honor those who could not be present tonight. Our friends and family members who perished a few days past. This year's American League Champion Cleveland Indians."

A young woman then walked to the microphone, unfolded a piece of paper and slowly read the names and positions of the players and managers who had died in the plane crash. Finished, she nodded at the commissioner, who went on to explain that four players had survived and had been hospitalized. The woman then announced the four surviving players and lowered the list as she introduced one of the players, Hank Flynn, who was able to make the game and that he was going to throw out the ceremonial first pitch. An usher then pushed a man in a wheelchair wearing a Cleveland Indians uniform to the pitcher's mound where he was handed the mic. Placing the mic to his lips he asked, "In honor of my teammates who could not be present tonight, could we please have a moment of silence."

Harley removed his hat along with all the other players while they waited in silence for a good thirty seconds. It seemed amazing to him that with nearly forty-seven thousand fans crowded into the stadium that it could be this quiet. Finally, the man handed the mic back to the woman who handed him a brand new baseball. A catcher for the Phillies knelt behind the plate while the woman pushed the wheelchair to the front of the mound where the injured player wound up and threw the ball which bounced a few feet away from his wheelchair. The crowd roared and the catcher ran out, picked up the ball and gave it back to the player.

As the commissioner escorted the woman and the player from the field an announcement came over the stadium P.A. System. *And now for the team introductions!* The Indians were introduced first as each player jogged out to the third base line and stood. Harley was the seventeenth player when he heard his name. *Harley Sims...pitcher.* Standing in line, listening to thousands of people cheer, he looked to the left of the scoreboard, where somewhere his folks and Mira were seated. At the moment, they were probably busting with pride.

The introductions of both teams were followed by the singing of the National Anthem and as usual the applause near the end of the song drowned out the umpire who stepped in front of home plate and yelled, "Play ball!"

The Phillies took the field while Jim spoke to his leadoff hitter. "Okay Mick...let's get us started!"

Mick stepped into the batter's box, took two swings and waited for the first pitch of the World Series. A called strike on the outside corner.

The next pitch was right down the pike. Mick swung and missed for strike two.

On the next pitch, he hit a lazy grounder the first baseman easily fielded for the first out.

The next batter struck out on an inside curve and the third batter of the inning hit a high pop up to the second baseman. Jim clapped his hands as the Cleveland players ran from the dugout. "C'mon boys...hold 'em!"

Gomez didn't wait long to deliver his first pitch as soon as the Phillies leadoff man was set. A line drive that the shortstop jumped up and stabbed. The crowd roared with delight. The next hitter on a 3-2 count hit a sharp grounder that took an odd bounce at the feet of the second baseman, allowing the man to reach first. The third batter for Philadelphia, after taking two straight balls, hit the ball to the shortstop who fielded the ball, flipped it to the second baseman, who stepped on the bag and fired the ball to first for a clean double play. The first inning ended with no score.

The second inning for Cleveland was a repeat performance as they went three up, three down, two players striking out and the last man at the plate fouling out behind the plate. In the bottom of the second the Phillies fared no better. After walking the first batter, Cleveland pulled off their second double play in two innings much to the delight of the crowd. The final out of the inning was a long fly out to center field.

In the top of the third Sam stepped to the plate and on the first pitch slammed an outside curve down the third base line into the corner. The crowd roared in approval as Sam stood on second base pumping his fist. Harley, along with the rest of the team stood at the edge of the dugout, clapping and waving their hats.

The next man attempted a bunt, was thrown out, but allowed Sam to advance over to third. Jim shouted to his next hitter, "All we need is a hit or a sacrifice fly to bring Sam in!"

After taking the first two pitches for called strikes, the batter hit a shallow fly ball to center field. Sam, poised like a cat ready to spring, took off for home plate as soon as the ball was caught. Philadelphia's center fielder rifled the ball toward the plate. The ball one-hopped into the catcher's mitt as Sam started his slide. The catcher applied the tag when Sam slammed into the catcher's body. Following a cloud of dust the umpire hesitated to make sure the catcher held the ball, then signaled, "Out!" The crowd roared in disapproval. The top half of the third ended with the next batter grounding out to second base. Shouting words of encouragement, Jim slapped each of his players on their back as they took the field. "That's okay. We gave 'em something to think about!"

The bottom of the third, Gomez, after walking the first two batters, gave up a towering right field home run, giving Philly a three run lead.

By the time the seventh inning stretch came around Philadelphia had added two more runs for a 5-0 lead. Cleveland only managed to get two more hits one of which was Sam's second double of the game.

Rich stood, stretched and asked, "I'm going down for a dog. Anybody want anything?"

"Think I'll tag along," said Mira. "I might just get a beer. Normally, I don't drink all that much, but with the way this game is going, I could use one."

Monica waved Rich's offer off. "No, I'm good. On second thought, I could use another beer."

Melanie looked down at the field and remarked, "It's a shame Drew hasn't gotten into the game yet. We already knew Harley wasn't going to play tonight. I guess this night is turning out to be a bust. We're down five runs and it's late in the game and neither

Harley nor Drew has played. Maybe tomorrow night will be better."

Mira, trying to look at the bright side added, "Cleveland still has the eighth and ninth innings yet. Maybe they'll get something going?"

With two outs in the top of the ninth, Harley watched as Sam stepped to the batter's box. Philadelphia had added two more runs in the seventh and eighth innings bringing the score to 7-0. Since the bottom half of the eighth inning droves of fans were filing out of the stadium. Part one of what everyone thought was going to be a four part series, or a sweep as baseball fans referred to it, was about to end. The Cleveland minor league team that had been assembled only managed to collect three hits and no runs. The only thing they could brag about was the fact that their infield had turned four double plays during the course of the game.

Sam took the first pitch for a called strike. The next pitch was in the same spot. He hit a line drive down the third base line just out of reach of the third baseman for his third hit of the game.

The next batter on a 2-1 count hit a deep fly ball that took the right fielder to the fence before he caught the ball. Game over! Final score: Philadelphia 7 - Cleveland 0.

Harley stood at the edge of the dugout and watched the Philadelphia players' reaction to their win. There was no jumping up and down or fist pumping. The victory celebration if one wanted to call it that was very subdued, reduced to a few high fives and the familiar butt slapping with a glove. Harley turned to walk down the tunnel when he was joined by Sam who nodded out at the field. "They don't seem to be that excited, do they?"

"Look," said Harley, "you and I and everyone else including the Phillies who watched the game knew what the outcome would be. Man for man, position by position they are the superior team, that is except for you. You went three for four tonight. I think you did excellent and I think you turned some heads. Tomorrow when we return for game number two fans will be expecting more of the same from you. You were definitely the bright spot on our roster tonight."

An hour later, following hot showers the team boarded the bus for Allentown. Harley decided to sit in the very back of the bus where he could stretch out. The bus was no more than a few minutes down the road when Harley noticed Jim making his way toward the back. Taking a seat across from Harley, Jim sipped at a cup of coffee and smiled before he spoke, "Harley, got something I want to talk over with you. I've made the decision that you're going to pitch in tomorrow's game. I was going to hold off in bringing you in until game four, but after what I saw tonight, I need to shake things up, to stop the bleeding as they say. I don't know Gomez or the other two Columbus pitchers all that well, but I do know you. I was debating whether I should tell you this tonight or wait until tomorrow. I don't like last minute changes myself so I decided to let you know about my decision tonight. How do you feel about going on the mound for game two?"

Harley sat on the edge of his seat. "I feel good. To tell you the truth I was a little concerned about waiting until after we got to Cleveland to get in. It's like being all dressed up and having nowhere to go. I felt so helpless tonight sitting there in the dugout unable to do anything to help my teammates out. Now, I feel like I'll be able to contribute. Do the other guys know about this yet?"

"No, and I don't plan on telling them about this until breakfast in the morning. I'm sure you and Sam will have a lot to talk over on the trip back down here tomorrow." Standing, Jim finished his coffee and winked at Harley. "Tomorrow will probably be the only game you pitch in this series, so when you get out there tomorrow night don't hold anything back. They won't be expecting someone like you. Maybe we can catch them off guard. Get a good night's rest."

Jim no sooner walked to the front of the bus when Harley whipped out his cell phone to call his parents and Mira. They were going to be excited beyond what he could imagine!

CHAPTER 42

HARLEY STARED UP INTO THE DARK CEILING OF HIS room at the Penn Manor, rolled over and looked at the glowing face of his watch on the nightstand. Five fifty-eight in the morning. *In an hour,* he thought, *the sun will be coming up.* Kicking back the sheets he sat on the side of the bed. Following the bus ride back from Philadelphia he had crawled in the sack just after midnight, which meant if he got up now he had only logged around six and a half hours' sleep. Getting up, he walked to the tiny bathroom and splashed cold water on his face. *I'm definitely awake now!*

Walking to the window, he pulled back the drapes and looked out at the paved lot, a nearby light casting a warm glow across the swimming pool area. Sitting in an easy chair in the corner he realized in thirteen and a half hours he would be taking the mound at Citizens Bank Park as the starting pitcher for the Cleveland Indians in game two of the World Series. Turning on a lamp next to the chair he reached down and opened his equipment bag and removed one of two brand new baseballs he always carried with him. Gripping the ball as if he were preparing to throw a two seam fastball, he thought, *Tonight is the most important game of my life. I've got to bring my A game.* Switching his grip to a four finger fastball, he reviewed his arsenal of pitches and continued to change his grip. *Split finger, slider, cutter, curve, changeup, drop, knuckle curve.*

Getting up, he paced back and forth across the small room and repeated his varied grips as he recalled what he had learned about Philadelphia's lineup. Between innings of Game 1 he had sat with Sam and asked questions about the hitters because he knew he would be facing them in a matter of days. That had changed. Now he was going to be facing these very men later that night in front of a packed house of yelling baseball fans. Flipping the ball behind his back, he decided on a long, hot shower.

Twenty minutes later, after toweling himself dry, he slipped into a fresh pair of socks and undershorts along with one of his favorite St. Louis Cardinal jerseys and plopped back down in the chair. Turning on the television, he flipped through the channels until he found what he was searching for. One of the early morning sports talk shows he liked to watch. Following a commercial break the two show hosts welcomed the viewing audience back as they resumed their previous conversation. *Back to what we were discussing before, Les. I think tonight's game two of the series will be a repeat performance of game one. These Cleveland minor league players, despite the fact that they may be the best in Cleveland's farm system, are no match for an experienced major league team like the Phillies.*

The other host adjusted his mic and spoke. *So, let me ask you this, John. Are you saying you feel Cleveland will not only lose tonight's game but get shut out again?*

I'm not saying they'll get shut out again, but that more than likely they'll lose game two. Following this evening's game both teams will have a day off to travel to Cleveland for the next three games. From what I have witnessed so far after the first game, we'll never see the third game in Cleveland. Monday night this series will be over and the Phillies will walk away with a four game sweep. It's just too lopsided. I mean, look at last night. Cleveland got four hits and no runs. You cannot win ball games on those kind of stats. The cards are stacked against these minor league kids and the sad part about it is...I think they know it! Everyone knows it!

What about their pitching? Let's face it. Last night Gomez gave up five runs on ten hits and then their relievers gave up another two runs on seven more hits. Who have they got going tonight?

They have two other Triple A pitchers, Pender and Valquez. They'll bring one of those two tonight. Aside from the fact this Cleveland team doesn't appear to be able to produce runs, they're pitching, as well, is suspect.

Harley shouted at the screen as he turned off the TV. "Hey...I'm sitting right here! There happens to be a fourth pitcher on this team!" Upset that he hadn't even been mentioned, Harley decided on a short walk around the parking lot.

Walking across the lot to the pool, he leaned on the fence and thought, *I've got to make a difference tonight. I just have to.*

Just like the previous morning the bus pulled out of Allentown at ten thirty on its way to Philadelphia. Harley and Sam sat in the back of the bus. They had a good hour and a half to discuss how they were going to handle the Phillies lineup. Taking a bite from an apple, Sam pointed out, "One of the things we'll have going for us is Philadelphia doesn't know anything about you. Jim told me he plans on announcing Pender or Valquez as our starter, then at the last minute is going to make a pitching change. That's where you come in. Jim's banking on the fact that when you take the mound Philadelphia's hitters won't know you from Adam! It'll take them at least one trip through their lineup before they can begin to figure you out. Hitters are always interested in what pitcher they'll be facing in a game and if they have faced that pitcher before or have heard about the pitcher, they'll prepare themselves mentally for what they expect. They won't have any time to prepare for you. I figure if we can keep them from scoring more than one or two runs we'll only have to run through their lineup about four times."

"I agree," said Harley. "We have to throw off their timing. We need to keep them guessing."

Pointing his half eaten apple at Harley, Sam went on, "Each time you face a player you have to change things up from the time you faced him before. If he faces you four times you have to be a different type of pitcher each time. He must not be allowed to gain an advantage from the previous time he went up against you. You have to have four different mixtures of pitches to pull this off. Let's say the first man at the plate gets a steady diet of off-speed stuff. Sliders and sinkers, cutters, mostly on the corners. The next hitter gets a combination of fastballs, change ups and curves. The next man is on the end of your knuckle curve and short stride delivery. When you face batters for the second time around if you pitched them off-speed stuff then they now get your heat, change up and some curves. I think this will get us through their lineup at least twice before they figure out what's going on. That could put us somewhere around the sixth inning. After that, you can mix things up however you want."

"This sounds good in theory," said Harley, "but will it work? These guys have been playing all year against major league pitching. Do you really think we can keep them guessing for the entire game?"

"If we use our heads, we can. You have what…nine or ten different pitches at your disposal. Most pitchers utilize the fastball, curve and changeup as their bread and butter. And, because of that very fact, the longer a pitcher remains in the game the more opportunity the hitters have to figure him out. Just about the time they expect a fastball or a curve, you give them a knuckle curve or a slider. When you mix in an occasional short stride delivery there are any number of combinations you can throw at them. What do we have to lose? If our team can get you a couple of runs and if we can keep runners off the base paths we might just be able to walk away with game two under our belts."

Harley checked his watch. Three forty-five. In fifteen minutes, as agreed, he and Sam would meet in center field to go over their game plan again while throwing the ball around. Since they had arrived at the stadium the process was much the same as game one had been. The team relaxed in the locker room and ventured out to the field at two o'clock for stretching and pre-game warm-ups. Spreading his legs, he touched his toes. In his mind, he kept running over Philadelphia's lineup and what he and Sam talked about. Standing, he raised his pitching arm above his head and turned to the right and then the left. His muscles felt good. He just had to make sure he kept moving until he stepped on the mound. Zipping up his warm-up jacket and following some high leg kicks, he sat down on the grass and took a swig of water. He knew his parents and Mira would be at the stadium around four thirty. His mother told him they would meet him at the same place they did yesterday prior to the game.

Looking across the outfield grass toward first base he saw Drew jogging in his direction. Walking up to his boyhood friend he extended his hand. "How are ya today, Harley?"

Shaking Drew's hand, Harley responded, "Doing well…and you?"

"Apparently, not as well as you. Melanie just gave me a call. She, Mira and your parents are on the way in. She told me you're pitching tonight. When she met Mira and your folks for breakfast this morning, your mom told her all about the phone conversation she had with you last night after the game. I was under the impression you were not going to take the mound until the series moved to Cleveland."

Harley smiled and answered, "Yeah, well I guess our manager changed his mind. Are you getting into the game tonight?"

"The way it stands right now, probably not. I'll probably just keep the dust off the bench again." Placing his arm around Harley, he went on, "As a player for Philadelphia I'm excited about last night's win but I'm also sorry you were on the losing end. Maybe things will go better tonight. Your parents must be excited. All those years of training, and tonight, you take the mound as a major league pitcher. If anyone deserves to pitch out there tonight…it's you. Look, I can't hang around out here. I've got to go and warm up one of our pitchers. I just thought I'd run out here and congratulate you on your appearance tonight. In a way, I hope they don't put me in. I don't want to have to face you as a hitter."

Harley reassured Drew. "We already talked about that the other night and agreed that if that happened we would both play the best for our team."

"I know, but I just don't like the thought of that happening. Gotta run!"

Watching his friend run back across the field, Harley picked up his glove and walked across the field to the area where he had met his parents the night before. Surprisingly, they were just walking down through the box seats to the fence. Joining him at the fence, Mira gave him a hug and nodded toward a group of Philadelphia players who were standing just behind first base. "Those boys don't have a clue what they're up against tonight."

Harley smiled and commented, "Thanks for the vote of confidence." Staring at Mira and her parents he had to laugh. "You guys do realize the game tonight is being played between the Cleveland Indians and the Philadelphia Phillies…right?"

Rich answered the question, "Why would we think otherwise?"

Harley shook his head in wonder, "Well it might have something to do with the way you're dressed. You and Mom standing there decked out in St. Louis Cardinal Jerseys and hats and then Mira with her New York Yankees outfit!"

Monica chimed in, "Our son may play for the Indians and his best friend may play for the Phillies but we are still dyed in the wool Cardinal fans."

"That's right," agreed Mira. "I'll never give up on my Yankees!"

Looking around, Harley asked, "Where's Melanie?"

Mira explained as she angled her thumb back up toward the main part of the stadium. "She's up at one of the gift shops purchasing a Phillies hat and jersey."

Holding up her cell phone, Monica proudly remarked, "You wouldn't believe how many calls I've gotten from Arnold last night and this morning. The newspaper article about you and Drew has really caught hold."

Rich motioned Harley off to the side and took on a look of seriousness. "All things aside...how do you feel about tonight? Are you ready...I mean...really ready?"

Harley smiled back at his Dad. "Don't worry, Dad. You and Mom have been preparing me for this very moment for a long time. My catcher Sam and I have a plan that we think will work. I don't have time to explain it right now. I have a locker room meeting at five." Giving Mira a quick kiss, he hugged Monica and shook Rich's hand. "Enjoy the game tonight. We leave for Cleveland tomorrow afternoon so I might not get to see you until the day after tomorrow. Maybe we can get together for dinner then."

Sitting in front of his locker, Harley tightened the webbing on his glove when Jim stood before the group and announced, "All right fellas. There isn't anything I can teach you in the next couple of hours before our next game. All of you have come a long way in your ball careers. You are, at this very moment, where many a ballplayer would like to be and where many may never be. Last night we got skunked! Today is a new day. I'm going to shake things up a bit this evening. Rather than Pender taking the mound, tonight we're going with Sims. We're also going to play small ball. We're going to bunt a lot. When on base we're going to steal. We're going to use the hit and run whenever we can. If a pitch is way inside, stand your ground and take one for the team...take your base. Anything close to the plate...swing at it. We must make Philadelphia react to the way we play tonight. Now, let's get out there for infield and outfield drills. Sam, Harley? You two need to remain behind. I want to talk with you both."

After the room emptied out, Sam and Harley entered a small manager's office and each took a seat. Jim propped his feet up on a desk and asked, "Have you fellas talked over about how you're going to handle this lineup tonight?"

Sam confirmed, "Yes, we have."

Five minutes later, Sam finished up with a rundown on their plan. "And if we can put a couple of runs up early, I think the different looks Harley will give them will throw them off their game."

Jim stood. "Your plan sounds good. We'll get you the runs. All you have to do is keep men from reaching second base. This should be an interesting game."

The pre-game activities were a carbon copy of game number one. A moment of silence was again honored, followed by the ceremonial first pitch by some local dignitary and then the team introductions. When Harley was announced as the starting pitcher he took his place standing on the third base line with his teammates and looked up to the area where his parents and Mira were seated. He knew they were up there, jumping up and down, shouting and yelling in support.

When the Phillies were announced and Drew jogged out to stand in line, he hesitated and tipped his hat in Harley's direction. Harley returned the favor by giving him a thumbs up.

An announcer high up in the press box talking about the pre-game activities spoke to his co-host. "Did you see that? That Scott kid tipped his hat to Cleveland's Sims and Sims sort of waved back. They must know each other."

"They do know each other," remarked the co-host. "My wife came across a newspaper article from some town outside of St. Louis. I've got the article right here. Apparently Drew Scott and Harley Sims met when they were ten years old. The Scott kid was scared to death of a baseball but this Sims kid teaches him how to play ball. Scott becomes his catcher for twelve years all the way from Little League up through college. Now, they find themselves on opposing teams in the World Series. Talk about your boyhood dreams coming true!"

The hoist asked his next question, "What do we know about this

Sims kid?"

"Just what the article says. He can throw in the high nineties consistently. Last year he played for Akron in Double A and threw a no-hitter. According to the article he threw back to back no-hitters while in college. That being said the kid must have something on the ball."

"I agree, but tonight is his first major league appearance. It'll be interesting to see how he holds up."

"We'll see. It's a known fact the Phillies can really hit. Look what they did to Gomez last night. I think this Sims kid has his work cut out for him. Welcome to the big leagues Harley Sims!"

The National Anthem was sung by some person Harley had never heard of followed by the Phillies taking the field for the start of the game. Jim stood with his lead-off hitter and reminded him. "Remember what we talked about…small ball."

Mick dug in at the plate and waited for the first pitch of game two. The Phillies pitcher took the sign from his catcher, wound up and delivered. Mick changed his stance at the last fraction of a second and dropped a perfect bunt down the third base line. The ball rolled too far down the line from the catcher, and the pitcher, not expecting a bunt hesitated. The third baseman, playing back, charged the ball but by the time he got his hands on the ball Mick crossed first base. Jim pumped his fist. "Perfect!"

The next batter stepped into the box as Mick took the sign from the third base coach. The pitcher no sooner released the ball when Mick took off for second. The ball was low and the catcher had to dig it out of the dirt. The throw was on time but bounced in front of second base, causing the ball to roll out into center field, which allowed Mick to run over to third. "Excellent," said Jim, "Man on third…no outs!"

The batter fouled off the first two pitches then hit an inside curve down the third base line. The third baseman fielded the ball, looked Mick back to third and threw a strike to first. The next batter, after running the count to 3-2 hit a long fly ball to center field, allowing Mick to tag up and score the first run of the game. The final out of the inning was a strike out. As the Indians took the field, Jim gave Harley a pat on his back. "All right, you've got the lead. Let's see what you've got!"

Harley jogged out to the mound, took a deep knee bend, then

moved the dirt in front of the rubber around with his right spike. He looked at the sea of faces behind home plate, but did not look around the stadium. He didn't want to give an impression of being overwhelmed or nervous. Surprisingly, he wasn't nervous. How many times had he stood in his backyard and envisioned a moment such as this? His first major league game. The crowd noise was subdued at the moment, thousands of fans talking with one another. Philadelphia's first batter stepped to the plate.

Wiping his forehead, Harley triggered the signal to Sam for the first series of pitches. The batter looked out at Harley and nodded slightly as if to say welcome to the big leagues! Harley gripped the ball for a slider, stared at the outside corner of the plate and delivered his first major league pitch. The ball passed over the strike zone and tailed away from the hitter for a called, *Strike one!*

His next pitch was another slider, but farther out from the plate. The batter held up. *Ball one!* Harley followed up with an identical pitch that Sam framed perfectly. *Strike two!* Harley's next pitch was a sinker that the batter swung over top of. The umpire signaled, *Strike three!* A loud cheer went up from the crowd.

The second hitter positioned himself in the box, but further back. Harley gave Sam the signal for the second series of pitches then delivered a ninety-nine mile an hour fastball on the inside corner for the first strike. His next pitch, another fastball, just missed the outside corner. The count now 1-1. The batter moved in closer to the plate and Harley brushed him back with an inside blazer that was called, *Ball two!* His next pitch was up and in for the second strike. The next pitch was right over the center of the plate, but high in the zone. The batter fouled the pitch off, but then Harley came back with a changeup. The batter was way ahead of the pitch, swung and missed for the third strike. Harley thought to himself, *Two up, two down!*

Sam received the signal for the next group of pitches. The batter stared at a knuckle curve for strike one, then on the second pitch hit a lazy grounder to the first baseman. Inning over. At the end of one inning Cleveland held a 1-0 lead.

Monica jumped up and waved her Cardinals hat and yelled, "Go get 'em, Harley!" Thumping a man on the shoulder who was wearing a Phillies hat sitting next to her, Monica informed the fan with great excitement, "Your Phillies are in for a long night! That's my son out there pitching for the Indians!"

Rich leaned over and whispered to Mira, "So far, so good!"

In the top of the second, Sam came to the plate and drew a walk. On the first pitch to the second batter, Sam got a good jump on the pitcher and easily stole second. Two pitches later, the batter laid down a bunt, which he did not beat out, but Sam was now standing on third. The next hitter hit a high fly out to right field. Sam tagged up and scored. The next batter grounded out. The score now stood at 2-0, Cleveland in the lead.

In the bottom of the second, it was three up and three down for the Phillies, Harley's variety of pitching styles striking out the first two batters and getting the third man to pop up to the shortstop.

The third inning was uneventful, both teams unable to get a man on base. Harley picked up another strike out and got the other two players to ground out. One of the press box announcers spoke to his co-host. "Is it just me, Richard, or do the Phillies seem to be confused by this kid from Missouri. Their timing seems to be off. This twenty-two year old pitcher has struck out five of the nine men he's faced. When they have hit the ball, there're routine grounders and outfield pop ups. It appears that they can't figure this kid out."

The co-host responded, "It's only the third inning. We've got six innings of baseball left. I think it will be a different story the second time through the lineup."

In the top of the fourth, after a hit batter and a stolen base, followed by a single to left field, Cleveland was unable to score leaving men on first and third. In the bottom half of the fourth, Harley had to switch gears as each man that he faced the second time around would see a different series of pitches than they did when first facing him. The inning ended with Cleveland once again unable to put a runner in scoring position. Following a single, Philadelphia was doubled up and then the last batter was called out on a foul tip that Sam snagged.

In the top of the fifth, Sam, who was not scheduled at the plate sat next to Harley and adjusted one of his chin guards. "They still haven't figured you out yet, Harley. The hitters you faced in the fourth were the first to face you for the second time. Things seem to be working like we planned. It's like they're facing you for the first time. When we get into the late innings I think you may have to go with more of your short stride pitches."

The announcers in the press box were still discussing this new Cleveland pitcher. "This Sims kid seems to have adapted well to pitching in the majors. I still quite haven't figured out what his bread and butter pitch is. Just about the time you think he'll throw a fastball he drops a cutter, changeup or curve on the Phillies. So far, he's got their number."

For the next hour and a half, the game settled into a pitcher's duel, Cleveland unable to get a single man on base. Philadelphia managed to get three more hits, but each hit came in a different inning. Through the eighth inning the score remained at 2-0, Cleveland holding on to their slim lead. With two outs in the bottom of the eighth Harley, after throwing five consecutive fastballs with a 3-2 count on Philadelphia's lead-off hitter, delivered a short-stride curve that completely fooled the hitter. He swung early and looked like a fool as he struck out, falling to his side. Getting up, he slammed his bat down into the grass and walked back to the dugout.

Rich reviewed the scorecard he had been keeping. "One more inning to go. So far, Harley has faced twenty-eight batters, struck out twelve, allowed four hits and hasn't walked anybody."

Mira added, "It sure would be nice if they could pick up an insurance run in the ninth."

The man sitting next to Monica stood and excused himself. "I've seen enough tonight. Your boy really put a whuppin' on us. Good luck in Cleveland."

Jim gathered the team together in the dugout and spoke softly, "We've played a smart game, but it's not quite over just yet. We need to get these next three outs before they get three runs. Don't do anything stupid out there. If you're involved in a play, complete it in a routine fashion. Let's not get fancy."

Harley walked to the water fountain and took a long swig. When he went back out there he was going to be facing the top of their order. Three of the four hits allowed had come from these hitters. This was the fourth time they would face him. Each one of these players had seen all of his pitches. He felt as if he didn't have any tricks left in his bag. They knew what was coming. He just had to be better than they were one more time.

That *one more time* came quicker than Harley wanted it to. A new reliever sent down the three Cleveland players that came to the plate in the top of the ninth with a total of eight pitches; a first pitch bunt attempt, a pop up to the catcher and a 3-2 strike out.

Thumping Harley on his knee with his mitt, Sam hopped up and stated. "This is it, Harley. You're about to win your first major league game. I know we're playing in Philadelphia but there are a lot of fans not only here at the stadium, but across the country who are rooting for you. Let's not let them down."

Watching Sam run to home plate Harley realized that for the first time during the game he felt nervous. *Why now,* he thought. *Why, after eight and a half innings was he suddenly nervous?* Taking a deep breath, he remembered something his father had told him many a time while growing up. *Never allow your emotions to overpower your physical ability to pitch.* Then, he recalled more words of wisdom his father had given him. *Feel the fear and do it anyways!* Pounding his glove, he stepped out of the dugout and sprinted to the mound. The fans, seeing his last inning enthusiasm started to chant, "Harley, Harley, Harley!" Monica joined in on the chant and then hugged Rich. "Listen to that! Have you ever heard a sweeter sound?"

Rather than walking around the mound or fiddling with the dirt, Harley stood on the mound in a stance that almost gave the impression that he defied the first batter to come to the plate. The chanting continued as the first man stepped to the plate. He had struck him out twice, but then in the seventh inning he had driven a base hit to right field. Sam signaled for a fastball on the outside corner. Harley agreed, wound up and let go with a ninety-five mile an hour sizzler that trimmed the outside corner. The batter held up for a called strike. Sam called for the pitch again, which Harley delivered with the same velocity. This time the batter swung and missed. *Strike two!* Sam called for the short-stride delivery, again on the outside part of the plate. Harley let loose with a two-finger, short-stride fastball. The batter was out in front of the ball, his timing off as he weakly waved the bat the ball. The umpire pumped his fist. *"Strike three...you're out!"*

Sam fired the ball back to Harley who immediately took his position on the mound and stared at the on deck circle where the next Philadelphia player stood. One of the announcers in the press box threw his pencil in the air and sat back. "Can you believe this kid! He can't wait to pitch to the next hitter. It's almost as if he's challenging them to face him. Listen to the crowd. I don't think there's a person in this park who is not pulling for him."

The next batter stepped to the plate and stared back at Harley. Out of the four hits Harley had given up, this particular batter was responsible for two. *This guy likes the fastball,* thought Harley. *I won't give him what he can hit.* Harley shook off two different signs from Sam and gave him the signal back that he was going with the knuckle curve. Gripping the ball, he stared at Sam's glove that had moved toward the outside of the plate. Winding up, Harley released the ball that started way outside but was moving in toward the plate. The batter hung back and swung at just the precise moment hitting a line drive up the middle. Harley had little time to react as he raised his glove to shield his face. The ball bounced and slapped into the webbing knocking Harley to the ground. Sitting spread eagled in front of the mound, Harley briefly looked at the runner who was already halfway down the line. Composing himself for a fraction of a second, he side-armed the ball from a sitting position to first base, the ball hitting the first baseman's glove a full step before the runner arrived. The umpire signaled by pointing his right hand at the bag. *Out!*

The announcer held his hands out in amazement and remarked in wonder. "There doesn't seem to be anything this kid cannot do! What's next?"

Rich was jumping up and down as he hugged Monica. "Can you believe that play? Do you know how many times I went over that very thing with Harley out in the backyard?"

Sam walked to the mound and held his hands out in amazement. "That was incredible. Now, let's get this last man out."

Harley stood on the mound and listened to the crowd cheering while they performed the wave as it circled the stadium. He readied himself for what he hoped was the last batter of the game. But then, he noticed something that was disturbing. Drew stood in the on deck circle. They were bringing him in as a pinch hitter. But that was only going to happen if the current man at the plate got on base. *That can't happen!* thought Harley. *I've got to get this batter out!*

The man standing at the plate had struck out two times at the hands of Harley. The man adjusted his batting gloves and stepped into the box, a stern look of determination on his face. Getting the sign from Sam, Harley let loose with an inside fastball. The batter held up for a called strike. Shaking his head in disgust the batter dug in for the next pitch. Harley placed the pitch in the same area of the plate. The batter inched toward the plate and took the ball off his elbow. The umpire signaled that the man had been hit and motioned for him to take his base. Harley silently objected, feeling the hitter made no effort to get out of the way of the pitch, but there was no sense in arguing. Apparently, Jim was okay with the call as he clapped his hands and yelled out to the mound, "Don't worry about the runner. Just get the last out!"

The man standing on first placed his hands on his hips and gave Harley a look that was anything but friendly. The thought of pitching to Drew was unnerving. Drew knew the way he thought. He knew what pitches he would throw in a situation like he was facing. Going into his stretch, he looked over at the runner who took four steps off the bag. Harley stepped off which caused the man to return to the bag. Thinking he was bothering Harley, the runner smiled and stepped off the bag again. Harley went into his stretch, wheeled and lobbed the ball to the first baseman. The man returned to the base easily, but then stepped off when Harley returned to the stretch. Drew swung his bat and waited for the pitch. Checking the runner, Harley noticed that he had ventured another step further from the bag, no doubt because of the weak throw he had made to first. The runner took another half step toward second when Harley turned and tossed another lob to the first baseman. The runner returned to the bag without even sliding. Holding his hands out ever so slightly the runner gave Harley a silent message of *Is that all you have?* Harley went into the stretch again, looked in at Sam, then checked the runner who was even farther off the bag. In a fraction of a second, Harley turned and threw a ninety-eight mile an hour bullet directly into the first baseman's mitt that was resting against the bag. The runner dove back, his hand outstretched. The ball smacked into the glove just before his hand touched the leather. The umpire, in an exaggerated move pointed directly at the runner who was laying in the dirt. "You're out!"

The announcer in the press box jumped up and placed his hands on his head. "I can't believe it! You've got to be kidding me! In all my thirty-five years of announcing major league baseball games I cannot recall a World Series game ever ending in a pick off play. What a gutsy move!"

Cleveland's dugout emptied out and the players on the field mobbed Harley on the mound. Rich, from up in the stands couldn't believe what he had just seen. "Just look at those kids! Why, you'd think they won the final game of the series!"

Monica stood and stared down at the celebrating Cleveland minor leaguers. "I've attended many ball games in my life, but this by far in is the most exciting game I've ever been to!"

A few minutes passed when the celebrating started to tail off. Harley stood and watched as the Phillies vacated the field. Then, he noticed Drew standing at the edge of the dugout. Walking across the first base line, Harley approached Drew, reached out and shook his hand. "We dodged the bullet tonight. We faced one another but I didn't have to pitch to you."

"Yep, we came close, that's for sure," said Drew. "The game you pitched tonight was amazing. You really had 'em guessing. You should have heard my teammates in the dugout. They couldn't figure you out. If you want my opinion you pretty much made us look like fools out there. I'm sure your parents are going nuts!" Drew picked up his mitt and asked, "When do you leave for Cleveland?"

"Tomorrow," said Harley. "We're scheduled to go back to Allentown tonight then tomorrow afternoon we have a flight to Cleveland."

Shaking Harley's hand, Drew turned to walk to the tunnel leading from the dugout when he stopped and remarked, "It seems these past few days we haven't had much time to talk. Give me a call after you get settled in up there in Cleveland. Maybe we can get together for dinner."

Harley smiled. "Count me in!"

Walking back across the infield grass Harley looked up at the surrounding stadium. The place had emptied out quickly, the crowd reduced to a couple of thousand lingering fans. The grounds crew was already busy repairing the infield dirt around home plate and the pitcher's mound. On Sunday the series would resume with the next three games in Cleveland. Hesitating at the dugout he turned and looked out across the field again. If the Phillies won the next three, then that was it. The World Series would be over and he had pitched what could be his first and last game here in Philadelphia.

CHAPTER 43

HARLEY SAT IN A SMALL DOWNTOWN CLEVELAND CAFÉ and looked out at the pouring rain. Sipping at a cup of coffee he looked up when a bell signaled that another customer had entered the tiny eating establishment. Drew, noticing him at the window table, removed his coat, hung it on an old-fashioned coat tree and sat across from him. "I can't recall the last time I saw it rain this hard. They thought this storm was going to bypass Cleveland but last night around midnight it shifted south and now it's supposed to rain until around two in the morning. I guess that puts the skids on game five tonight. We'll have to wait until Wednesday for our next game."

"I reckon so," said Harley. "I guess most folks feel with the Phillies being up three games to one that tonight would have been it. Series over! Let me ask you, Drew. It's been what...about twelve years now we've known each other. In all that time have you ever known me to go negative?"

"Come to think of it, you've always been on the upside of things."

"This bad weather will accomplish nothing more than put off the inevitable. We'll still lose the series; it's just going to take a day longer. The one good thing is, with this rain delay Gomez will get an extra day of rest. When it's all said and done, I don't think it'll really make any difference. You guys clobbered him in game one; knocked him out in the fifth. At least we can say we won one game, especially when everyone thought we'd get swept in four."

"You're getting a little bit ahead of yourself in assuming they'll put Gomez on the mound tomorrow night. This rain out day also gives you four day's rest, which means they could bring you in for game five."

"No, I don't think Jim would do that. Something else to consider. Let's say, he does decide with the extra day of rest that I can go in game five. Even if I should somehow pull off another win then it's back to Philadelphia for games six and seven. No matter how you look at the situation, we're going to lose. The second game of the series was Cleveland's moment in the limelight. To think that we could win again just doesn't seem logical. In game one we got shut out 7-0, then in game three we get absolutely clobbered 8-1 and this last game we lost 6-2. Game five will be nothing more than the final act to this year's World Series."

Pouring himself a cup of coffee from an urn sitting on the table, Drew looked out at the rain and commented, "Sitting here listening to you, I might have to take back what I said about you always being on the *upside!* You almost sound like you've given up."

"Look, I'd be the first person to say never give up. But, you cannot defeat the reality of what's happening here in this series. From the very moment this team was put together there was never a thought that we could possibly win this thing. This series has been a tribute to the players from Cleveland who lost their lives. I don't think there's anything wrong with that, but from the outset of the formation of this team of minor leaguers no one thought we had the remotest chance of winning. The fans, the media, even my teammates. They all knew we would come out on the losing end. I was excited about the idea of playing in the World Series and having an opportunity to pitch one game, but it's difficult to remain upbeat when everyone knows you don't have a chance. I don't like this feeling of being viewed as a loser."

"I don't think anyone who has watched the series, especially game two, would refer to you as a loser. You should have seen yourself out there on the mound. You mowed us down like nobody's business! Think about it. A twenty-two year old kid from Double A ball handles a power hitting team like the Phillies like it was nothing?"

Harley changed the topic as he picked up one of the menus and inquired. "Do you think you'll get into game five?"

"It's hard to say. If I do it won't be until late in the game. I may have had my moment of fame in game four when they let me catch the last three innings."

"And let's not forget you got a hit in the eighth and drove in a run."

Waving off the fact that he had got a hit, Drew laughed, "As far as this year is concerned I've probably seem my last playing time unless they decide to put me in tomorrow." Picking up a menu, he looked out at the rain. "I say we go ahead and order lunch then take in that war picture down the street."

Motioning at the rain running down the window, Harley agreed, "What else is there to do?"

Standing in front of the Holiday Inn, Harley turned his face to the sky. Clear blue, not a cloud to be seen. He noted the time on an ever-changing automated sign above a bank. Two ten in the afternoon. The rain had stopped, the temperature was in the mid-sixties. Perfect weather for game five. Starting up Ontario Street, Progressive Field was only three blocks away. He was scheduled to be at the park no later than three o'clock. He had plenty of time. Slinging his bag over his shoulder he started his short pre-game journey. *A sad journey,* he thought. He would suit up, stretch, throw a few pitches and then sit in the dugout and watch his team lose what was to be the final game of the series.

Passing a small grocery store he noticed three small boys sitting on an old bench while they shared one coke and a small bag of chips. Hesitating, he stared at the trio when one of the boys looked up and seeing his St. Louis Cardinals hat, asked, "Do you root for St. Louis?"

Harley smiled and answered, "Yes, I'm a big Cardinals fan."

The boy holding the bag of chips gave Harley a long look and then explained to the others. "Do you know who that is?"

Before the other two could respond, the boy went on, "That's Harley Sims! He's that pitcher who shut out the Phillies in game two!"

Harley smiled back at the boys and confirmed, "That's right! You boys watch the series so far?"

"Yep," said one of the other boys. "We been watchin' it on the television in my Mom's bedroom. We can't afford to go to the games."

The third boy asked, "Are you pitching tonight?"

"No, I'm not."

Harley was about to walk off when he stopped and looked back at the threesome. "Let me ask you boys something. Why are you sharing a coke and a bag of chips?"

The boy holding the coke handed it to one of the others and

explained, "Cause we ain't got enough money for us each to have our own."

Reaching into his wallet, Harley stated, "Well now, that's just not right!" Handing a twenty to the boy who seemed to be their leader, he suggested, "Why don't you boys go back inside the store and get yourselves each a coke and your own bag of chips. If there's anything left over maybe you could get a couple of candy bars."

The boy reached out, took the twenty and with a wide grin spoke, "Thanks!"

Starting up the street again he heard one of the boys shout out, "Go Cards!"

He wasn't even up the street fifty yards when an older man, dressed in ragged clothes walked out from between two buildings. Setting an empty wine bottle on top of a trash container, he gave Harley and odd look and then asked, "Don't suppose ya got a coupla dollars so's a fellow could eat?"

Normally, Harley would have gladly given the down and out character some money but he had just given away the last twenty he had. Smiling at the man, Harley replied honestly, "I'm sorry mister, but at the moment I'm tapped out. Just gave the last money I had to some kids back up the street."

The man, refusing to accept Harley's answer stumbled and leaned against the side of one of the buildings and mumbled, "Then, I'll just take some loose pocket change!"

Harley apologized a second time. "Like I said, old fella, I just gave all my money away." Taking a few steps up the street, Harley felt bad, but was not in a position to help the man.

From behind him he heard the man shout, "Well just go on then and leave a man to starve in the street!" The next thing Harley knew the wine bottle smashed in the street a few feet behind him. Picking up his pace, Harley thought it best to move on, and quickly!

Five minutes later he walked around the massive stadium to the player's entry gate where he was confronted by five reporters who smothered him with a series of questions:

Are you pitching today, Harley?

What do you think your chances are of going back to Philadelphia?

Are you going to pitch for Cleveland next year?

Taking Jim's advice Harley's answers were short and to the point.

No, I'm not pitching tonight.

I think our chances are good.

I'm not sure if I'll be back next season.

Inside the gate, he walked down a long hallway and entered the home team locker room. Sitting in front of his locker he laid his bag down and took a long, deep breath and thought, *What else could possibly go wrong today?* His relaxing walk from the hotel to Progressive Field had turned out to be anything but.

Changing into his sweat suit, he grabbed his spikes and glove and walked through the tunnel that led to the dugout. Sitting on the long wooden bench he laced up his spikes and looked out at the ballpark. This would be his third day in Cleveland of sitting in the dugout and watching his teammates play the game he loved so much. Getting up, he stepped out onto the grass and began to walk the inside perimeter of the ballpark before he began his actual warm-up.

By four o'clock the stadium was buzzing with activity as grounds crew members, vendors, umpires, reporters, ball players from both teams and a few scattered fans began to prepare themselves for game five of the World Series. Looking toward the visiting team dugout Harley saw Drew break away from a group of players and start in his direction. As his friend approached, Harley realized this could very well be the last game either of them would play this year.

Drew approached and looked up at the seats next to the right field fence and pointed with his catcher's mitt. "Looks like some of the fans have started to arrive."

Looking in the direction Drew indicated, he saw three men next to the fence. All three were holding large beers and the man in the middle also held a fielder's glove. From their actions and their loud voices it was easy to determine that they were already half tanked.

Drew laughed at the spectacle and suggested, "Let's toss a few."

Harley held up the ball he had with him and answered, "Maybe just some light stuff."

Drew jogged about twenty yards away, turned and pounded his mitt. "How's this distance?"

Harley threw the ball and replied, "Good!"

They hadn't even thrown the ball back and forth three times when one of the men shouted, "Hey, Sims! You pitchin' tonight?"

Harley ignored the man and threw the ball back to Drew when the man shouted again, "What...you think you're too good to talk with me?"

A second man in the group, yelled, "Why don't you practice with somebody from your own team? Cleveland not good enough for you!"

Harley continued to ignore the three men.

The first man yelled again, "Why don't you throw the ball to me. I'm from Cleveland."

Another man shouted, "Yeah, you too good for us?"

Harley caught the ball, turned and looked at the three loud men, but remained silent. Drew jogged up next to him and suggested, "Forget those idiots. They've had way too much to drink."

Harley was about to agree when the man with the glove shouted belligerently, "This ain't Double A Sims. This is the majors. The players that died in that crash wouldn't be throwing no ball around with some player from Philly! C'mon, let's see what ya've got, boy!"

Harley shouted back at the man, "You want it?"

"Yeah, I want it. I can catch anything you can throw!"

Harley nonchalantly turned to walk off but then turned a fired a ninety mile an hour fastball at the man's glove. The ball slammed into the leather, knocking the glove back to the man's chest, the force from the pitch knocking him back over the first row of seats. While in the process of falling, the man's beer spilled on the man next to him, who reacted by stumbling sideways into the third member of the group, who dropped his beer on the first man.

Drew stood in silence, amazed at what he had just witnessed, then asked, "What were you thinking? You can't throw a ball at a fan, especially one of your fastballs! You've could have killed that guy! C'mon, we better move to the other side of the field."

Just prior to five o'clock Drew and Harley parted ways. Harley reported to what had become Cleveland's pre-game meeting for the past four games. The meeting was rather quick, Jim explaining that their starting pitcher for the game was going to be Gomez but that since their backs were against the wall, all relievers and starters needed to be ready if called upon. Finishing up the meeting, he emphasized, "If the Phillies win tonight then that's it…we go home and we are done playing ball until next season. If you have paid any attention to the talk around the ballpark or the media it was thought that we'd lose this series in four straight games. As a team, we have debunked that line of thinking by winning game two of this series. We are now down three games to one. So, the question remains. After tonight's game will we head on to our individual homes or will we fly back to Philadelphia tomorrow morning for game six and a possible game seven? No one, including myself, can accurately predict what the outcome of tonight's game will produce. For this reason, I have no game plan for tonight's contest other than to simply play baseball. So, I say we have some fun tonight playing this game that we are so privileged to be a part of. Run, hit, throw, field, slide, however this game presents itself to you. Do your best tonight gentlemen. This is all I ask. Let's give the fans their money's worth this evening. Now, let's hit the field!"

Harley stood with the other Cleveland pitchers in the bullpen and removed his hat during the singing of the National Anthem. Forty-six thousand fans began to cheer and clap just prior to the song ending. The head umpire stepped in front of home plate and shouted, "Play ball!"

Gomez took the mound for the top of the first. He waited patiently for Philadelphia's lead-off hitter who walked slowly to the box and took his time preparing himself for the first pitch of the night. Finally set, he looked out at Gomez who wound up and delivered a fastball down the center of the plate. The batter swung and hit a line drive the first baseman snagged. The next batter, after taking the first pitch for a ball, swung and hit a hard grounder to the third baseman who fielded the ball cleanly and threw the runner out. The third hitter of the inning on a 2-0 count hit a long fly ball to center field.

Leaning on the low bullpen fence, Harley watched as their lead-off-man walked to the plate. Philadelphia's pitcher looked around at his infielders, then concentrated on his catcher who flashed him the sign. On the first pitch Mick hit a line drive single to right field, the crowd roaring loudly. The second man at the plate showed bunt but held up for ball one. The infield moved in a few steps in order to field what was most certainly going to be a bunt. The batter swung away, hitting a two hopper to the short stop who flipped the ball to the second baseman, who tagged the bag and completed the double play, firing the ball to first. The next batter, after running the count to 3-2, hit a long fly ball that was caught by the left fielder in foul territory.

Harley, still leaning on the fence remarked, "Six men up, six well hit balls. It seems everyone is hitting tonight."

In the top of the second Harley watched Philadelphia's next three hitters go down quickly. Two long fly outs to center field and a pop up caught by the second baseman. Philadelphia's pitcher, likewise in Cleveland's half of the inning, quickly disposed of the next three hitters, all three grounding out to the infield. The next four innings were much the same, both Cleveland and Philadelphia unable to get anything going.

Prior to the top of the seventh, Harley sat back down on the bench in the bullpen and gazed up at the scoreboard. The game was scoreless and Cleveland had the only hit. If things kept going in the direction they were it looked like this game was going to be a pitcher's duel. *An odd pitcher's duel,* he thought. Despite the fact that thirty-six men had stepped to the plate, so far there had not been one strike out. Every batter had hit the ball. The infield grounders were not finding their way through and the balls hit to the outfield were not finding the gaps.

The first batter for Philly stepped to the plate for the beginning of the inning. On the very first pitch, following a crack of the bat the predominately Cleveland fan based crowd was silenced. Getting up to see what happened, a ball suddenly cleared the bullpen fence and ricocheted off the back wall. Standing at the fence Harley watched as the Philadelphia player rounded the bases, his hands held high in celebration. Harley looked at the scoreboard. The Phillies had taken a 1-0 lead due to the solo homerun.

Out of disgust, Gomez kicked at the dirt on the rear of the mound. Jim walked from the dugout to the mound while two Cleveland relievers got up and started to throw. The conversation on the mound was quick and whatever Jim said to Gomez seemed to calm him down. He struck out the next two batters, walked the next and got the final batter to hit a ground ball which caused a force out at second to end the inning.

George Pender, one of Cleveland's starting pitchers, joined Harley at the fence. "It's getting late in the game. The later it gets in the game the more the mathematical numbers stack up against you. They've got the lead 1-0, it's the seventh inning and we've got nine outs left. We've only got one hit. We need two runs to win. Gomez has done a pretty good job of keeping the score low, but we need to make something happen…and soon!"

Harley watched as Philadelphia took the field for the bottom of the seventh. George, who was paying attention to the message being displayed to the right of the scoreboard, pointed and remarked, "Looks like they're changing things up some. They're moving the shortstop to second, the second baseman comes out and they've got a new catcher."

Harley looked up at the board and saw Drew's picture and name flash momentarily across the large screen. Harley smiled and thought, *Drew's getting another chance to play, that's good.*

Drew played flawlessly behind the plate in the seventh, framing a 3-2 count pitch for a called strike three, fielding a bunt for the second out and catching a high foul ball against the fence to retire the side.

Gomez struck out the first man in the eighth, then their next batter, who in six pitches earned a walk. Prior to the next pitch the runner took a long lead, but returned safely to the bag when Gomez threw over. The runner once again ventured off the bag. Gomez threw over to first a second time, the runner getting back in plenty of time. The third base coach flashed a sign to both the runner and the man at the plate. Harley surmised, *The hit and run is on!* He could see the scenario unfolding right before his very eyes. If he were pitching he'd keep the runner close and keep his pitches high and tight. Just as he had predicted in his mind on the next pitch the hitter slammed a ground ball between first and second. The man on first was off and running with the pitch, rounded second and slid into third ahead of the throw from right field. Men on first and third with one out. Jim, realizing the man Gomez walked was now in scoring position, walked to the mound and signaled for a reliever. The bullpen coach got off the phone and spoke to one of the relievers, "Micheals...you're in! Sims...start warmin' up!"

Micheals jogged from the bullpen to the mound where he took the ball from Jim, who gave him some quick instructions and walked back to the dugout. Walking to the corner of the bullpen Harley determined what he would do if on the mound. *Men on first and third with one out, late in the game, the opposing team ahead by one run. Be prepared to field a bunt and prevent the squeeze play. Force the hitter to hit a groundball resulting in an inning ending double play. Walk the hitter loading up the bases which would set up a force out at any base. If he struck out the hitter then his options for the next batter would be different. It was always easy when watching someone else pitch,* thought Harley. *It was always more difficult to execute a play rather than thinking about it.*

The batter, now in the box took the sign from the third base coach and awaited the pitch. Micheals no sooner let go of the ball when the runner on third started for home. *The squeeze play,* thought Harley. *I was right!* The catcher ran up the third base line, scooped up the ball, looked the runner back to third and then proceeded to throw the runner out at first. Harley smiled, *Textbook!*

Now, the next scenario presented itself. Men on second and third, two outs. Any pitcher who had half a brain knew that with two outs the obvious thing to do was get the hitter out and end the inning. At the same time, the possibility of the squeeze play was still hanging out there. The Phillies weren't wasting any time as the batter took a cut at the first pitch which he fouled off. He swung at the next pitch and hit a roller down the third base line the runner had to hop over, but the third baseman backhanded the ball and threw the runner out at first. At the end of seven and a half the score was 1-0, Philly holding on to a narrow lead. The crowd was still optimistic and had not given up on their Indians.

In the bottom of the eighth Jim gathered his team together and spoke, "All right boys, it's getting late in this game. If we want to fly back to Philadelphia for game six then we better rustle up some runs quick! They'll probably bring in Phil Christian for these last two innings. He's one of the best relievers in the game. Let's go get 'em!"

Christian made quick work of the first two batters striking them out on eight pitches. Mick stepped to the plate and ran the count to 3-2 and then drew a walk on a close call that the Philadelphia manager argued over, but relented and returned to the dugout. Sam stepped to the plate, and Harley watching from the bullpen thought, *Well Sam, if you ever wanted to punch your card to the majors right now would be a great time!"*

Almost as if by some sort of baseball magic on the first pitch Sam hit a line shot opposite field home run to right field, the ball just clearing the fence. The crowd was going crazy, Sam running so fast he had to hold up for the lead runner. When he crossed home plate he was mobbed by his teammates. Harley, who had thrown his hat into the air, was picking it up when the bullpen coach got his attention, "Sims, you're goin' in for the ninth!" Three minutes later, Harley watched as their next hitter connected with a low curve for a routine groundout. Cleveland now had the lead 2-1.

The bullpen catcher shouted, "Keep em' comin'! Ya've only got maybe two or three more minutes before ya have to report to the mound." Throwing a mid-range fastball, Harley's mind was racing. He hadn't really expected to get in the game. All he needed to do was get three outs and tomorrow they would be on their way back to Philadelphia. The pitching change was put up on the message board and upon seeing his name the crowd started to chant, "Harley, Harley, Harley!" It was obvious the fans knew who he was. They would be expecting a short version of a repeat performance of game two.

Harley's racing thoughts were interrupted by the bullpen catcher's voice, "Time to get in there, Harley!"

Opening the bullpen door he slowly jogged across the outfield grass, across the infield dirt and then stopped at the mound, all the while the packed stadium chanting his name. He knew his parents and Mira would be watching the game back home.

The first Philadelphia batter strolled up to the plate, looked over the infield and then stepped in and took three swings. Harley remembered facing this player three times in game two. He had grounded out twice and went down swinging. The player as he recalled had a pretty good eye, but was weak on the lower part of the strike zone. Winding up, Harley threw a two finger fastball right at the knees. The man held up for a called *Strike one!*

If Harley threw that pitch again the man would swing. Gripping the ball for a knuckle curve he let go. The man watched as the ball approached the outside of the plate but then started in. He started to swing but held up, swinging through the ball for *Strike two!*

Now that he was ahead 0-2 in the count he could throw some off the plate stuff and try to get the hitter to go after a bad pitch. The next pitch was a cutter that sank at the last fraction of a second. The batter swung and hit a lazy foul ball down the line. Harley gripped the new ball, wound up and delivered his changeup. The hitter looked foolish when he waved the bat at the ball for the first out. *That's one,* thought Harley.

Harley waited for the next man in their lineup, another player he had faced three times back in Philadelphia. Using a combination of two fastballs and a slider he short-stepped the batter to hit a ground ball right at him. He fielded the ball easily and tossed the ball to first for the second out. *That's two!*

The next man to the plate worked the count to 3-2 and took a pitch that could have gone either way for ball four. A man on first with two outs.

The man who had been in the on-deck circle, hit the end of the bat on the ground loosening the bat weight. Standing at the edge of the box, he adjusted his batting gloves and hat. Harley's attention had been diverted from this player to the one who now stepped in the on-deck circle. *Drew!*

He didn't enjoy the thought of pitching to Drew. On the other hand if he simply got the man at the plate out, then Drew would be of no concern. The game would be over. Drew didn't look in his direction while he went about tightening the strap on his batting glove. Bending down, he tied his right shoe then the left.

The crowd continued to chant Harley's name and everyone was on their feet. Just one more out and there would be a game six in Philadelphia. Turning, he faced center field and took three long deep breaths to relax himself. Time was called and Sam jogged out to the mound. "I know you're concerned about pitching to Drew, but when you get this guy at the plate out, then that's it...it's over! Concentrate on the batter in the box. I say we get this guy out, end the game, go out for a big fat steak tonight, then tomorrow we're off to Philly. One other thing. You've never faced this batter before. So, we don't know anything about him. Let's try some heat and see how he reacts."

When Sam returned to the back of the box the hitter stepped in and smiled down at Sam and remarked, "The one thing I hate about baseball is being the last potential out."

Harley stepped on the rubber and looked in for the position sign. Sam indicated fastball on the outside part of the plate. The batter swung, the fat part of the bat connected with a loud smack. The ball bounced right in front of first base. The first baseman tried to backhand the ball but it hit off the heel of his glove, high into the air and into foul territory. The umpire called the ball fair and the go ahead run stood on first base. Harley caught the new ball from the umpire and watched as the moment he dreaded began to take shape. Drew walked to the box, dug in and swung the bat once. Harley didn't go into his windup so Drew stepped out and looked down at his third base coach. The last time he faced Drew, he hadn't thrown him a single pitch. He had concentrated on the runner on first who was showing steal. He had picked him off and ended the game. He casually looked over at the runner who was staying close to the bag. He took a conservative lead, but not enough to get a good jump. The man appeared to have no intention of stealing. Harley looked in at Drew, who at the moment wore a look of passiveness. *A great poker face,* thought Harley.

Sam flashed the sign, fastball, a bit farther out than the last pitch. Harley checked the runner then delivered the pitch. Drew watched the ball from the moment it left Harley's hand but held up swinging. The umpire signaled, *Ball one!*

Sam fired the ball back, crouched down and gave the sign, Fastball, outside corner, but closer to the plate. Drew held up again. *Ball two!*

Harley twirled the ball in his glove and thought about how Drew knew him well, better than anyone else. He knew what pitch Harley would throw in every possible situation. The only chance he had of taking Drew out was to think differently than he normally would. Normally his next pitch selection would be fast, up and in. Drew would be expecting that pitch. Instead Harley delivered the third outside corner fastball in a row. Drew swung late, realizing that if he didn't it would be a called strike. He fouled the ball down the first base line. *Strike one!* Harley came back inside with the next pitch which Drew backed away from but the ball hit the bottom of the bat. *Foul ball. Strike two!* The next five pitches; a cutter, fastball up, changeup, short-stride sinker and inside curve were all fouled off as Drew protected the plate. It was Harley's power pitching against Drew's incredible eye and ability to stay at the plate and make contact. With each foul ball the crowd got louder and louder.

With the count 2-2 Harley could afford to waste another pitch. Drew would be expecting something off the plate. If it was even remotely close he'd swing. Harley decided he'd go against his better judgment and try to throw the heat right by him. He was confident the fastball in the zone would fool Drew. Winding up, he let loose with a ninety-nine mile per hour heater than was low, at the knees. Drew swung and hit the ball sharply to the right of the shortstop who dove as the ball sailed a foot above his glove. The outfielder started in but then realized the ball was rising. Correcting himself he put on the brakes and started to sprint toward the warning track. The ball, on a straight upward trajectory, tipped the top of the player's glove and continued on clearing the fence by a foot. A moan settled in over the Cleveland crowd. The lead runner, watching the ball go over the fence was jumping up and down as he pumped his fist. Harley shook his head in admiration at how well Drew had fared at the plate. He watched his best friend as he rounded second base. There was no celebrating about his mood, he was all business. As he touched third he looked over at Harley and shot him a sad look. Harley stood and watched as Drew's teammates mobbed him when he crossed the plate. Jim walked to the mound and asked, "Don't worry about it! He was a tough out. Do you want to stay in and get this last man or would you prefer to come out?"

"No, I want to stay in. If I come out now, I won't be able to forget that last pitch. I need to get this last out."

Harley didn't waste any time, throwing two fastballs and finishing the batter off with his changeup to end the inning. Back in the dugout Harley looked up at the score board. Philadelphia 4 - Cleveland 2.

Despite the enthusiasm the Cleveland fans displayed in the bottom of the ninth, it was three up and three down. The World

Series was over and Philadelphia walked away with the title, four games to one. Harley sat in the dugout and watched as the Philadelphia players gathered together on the field, celebrating their win.

Ten minutes passed when Harley found himself alone in the dugout, most of the Philadelphia players as well vacating the field. Getting up to walk down the tunnel Harley saw Drew standing on the mound. Drew held his hands out to his side indicating he was sorry. Harley got up and stepped out of the dugout and walked toward the mound. Smiling, he nodded toward the outfield fence. "Boy, you really clocked that one!"

"I hated having to face you, Harley!"

"Not any more than I hated pitching to you." Harley reached for Drew's hand and explained, "But things worked out the way we planned and I'm good with that."

Shaking Harley's hand, Drew inquired, "The way we planned...I don't understand."

"We agreed if we faced each other we would play the game. You would try to hit the ball and I would try to prevent you from doing so. You never backed off. After the count was 2-2 no matter what I threw, you kept getting a piece of it. I finally decided to go low on the plate with the fastball. That was a tough pitch to hit but you nailed it! I'm not upset because we lost the game or even the series. That was a given from the very get-go. I couldn't have been prouder of you while I watched you round the bases. I thought back to when we first met when we were both ten. You were this nerdy kid who collected stamps, played the piano and practiced karate. A kid that was scared to death of a baseball. You've come a long way, Drew. The Phillies would be foolish not to bring you back next year."

"These past few days I've done a lot of thinking myself. All those days in your backyard or when we went to Arnold Park and practiced, who would have thought that we'd be standing here in a major league ball park, after participating in the World Series. Thinking back to those days we've both come a long way." Reaching out, Drew offered his hand again. "Thanks, Harley. You're the best friend anyone could ever have."

Shaking Drew's hand, Harley asked, "When are you heading home?"

"If it was up to me I'd just as soon start back right now, but I'm required to fly back to Philly with the team. I guess they've got some sort of celebration lined up tomorrow for the fans. It'll probably be a couple of days before I get back. How about you?"

"As soon as I get showered I'm renting a car and then I'll start the long drive back to Missouri. I'm kind of anxious to get home."

With that, Drew turned and started to jog across the infield grass as he waved and shouted, "Let's get together when we get back?"

Waving at Drew, Harley started to walk from the mound when he noticed a grounds crew member with a rake walking toward the mound. Stopping momentarily, Harley removed his hat and gestured back at the mound. "Take good care of that spot. I'll be back next year."

CHAPTER 44

MONICA TURNED OFF THE LAMP, SAT BACK ON THE couch and looked at the dim light coming from a Budweiser sign in the kitchen. Raising a bottle of beer to her lips, she remarked, "It's nice sitting here in the dark and just relaxing." Gesturing at the clock on the fireplace mantle, she smiled. "Four days from now is opening day for the Cardinals. How many years have we been going down to the stadium to celebrate the first day of baseball here in St. Louis?"

Seated on the other side of the room in his easy chair, Rich raised his bottle of brew and calculated, "Well let's see. Harley is twenty two. We've been married twenty-four years, so I guess it's close to a quarter of a century that you and I have attended opening day together. Last year was not what you would call a great year for the Cardinals, and despite the fact they didn't make the playoffs we still experienced a great year. Both Harley and Drew getting picked up in the draft, then going off to spring training which resulted in both going to Double A, and later in the season Drew gets bumped up to the Phillies."

Monica sat her beer on a coffee table and threw a quilted afghan over her shoulders and held up her right hand to make a point. "I have thought about that often. It's so strange the way things work out. Ever since Harley has been three years old he's talked about being not only a major league pitcher, but being a pitcher for the Cardinals. That has been his ultimate goal from the very beginning and even though he's going to be pitching for the Indians this season, he is still determined in the future to pitch for the Cards. All the years we've known Drew, whenever the subject of playing in the major leagues came up he was always so nonchalant about the possibility of his ability to play in the majors. How many times when that topic came up did he mention that it wouldn't bother him if he didn't get to play in the majors? It was almost as if he could take it or leave it. Harley, never for one moment in his young life doubted that *he* would make it to the majors and yet Drew wound up playing for a major league team before Harley."

"Correct me if I'm wrong," said Rich, "but it almost sounds like you're jealous!"

"I'm not the least bit jealous," pointed out Monica. "Drew has been like a second son to us. We never showed any favoritism toward Harley while they were practicing or playing together. Those two young men have a bond that I never had with a friend when growing up. They shared a common goal of being major league ballplayers and even though Harley was more vocal about his ultimate goal, Drew just kept plugging along as if he were a shadow of Harley. I'm very proud of both of them. A tighter bond of friendship you'd be hard to find."

Rich pointed his beer bottle at Monica. "Getting back to what I was saying about last year. Everything wasn't peaches and cream. I'll never forget the moment when I heard about the Cleveland Indians plane going down. What a blow that was to the world of baseball. And, like you said a few moments ago…it is strange how things work out. Who would have thought that the Commissioner of Baseball would sanction a team of minor league ballplayers to take the place of the American League Champion Cleveland Indians to play in the World Series *and* that our own son would be on that team? If I don't take anything else to my grave with me I'll never forget every moment of game two of that series. Harley was really on. There have been many moments since I watched that game that I have thought about all the time Harley spent out back in the yard throwing at that old tire in rain, snow, sleet, hail, hot or cold. It never made a difference to him. He has always strived to become better."

Monica pulled the afghan closer to her body. "Last year at this time, we sat in this room and we talked about spring training. Harley and Drew made the cut. Harley was headed for Double A ball in Akron and Drew with Clearwater. Here it is over a year down the road and here we sit once again talking about this season's spring training. Drew has signed with Philadelphia once again as their backup catcher and Harley is on Cleveland's starting rotation. It seems so odd sitting here in our home that is, to say the least, crammed with St. Louis Cardinal paraphernalia." Pointing at the afghan and then around the room she went on, "This Cardinal afghan, those Cardinal coasters on the coffee table, the Cardinals player bobble heads on the mantle, the T-shirt I'm wearing. I could go on and on talking about every room in this house. This is a House of Cards and we are true blue, or I guess I should say red, St. Louis Cardinals fans and yet here we are talking about the Philadelphia Phillies and the Cleveland Indians! What are we going to do when the Phillies roll into town to play the Cardinals? Like I said, Drew is like a second son to me, but I don't think I could root against the Cards."

"This would be a problem for me also," said Rich. "But as far as Harley is concerned this is something we don't need to be concerned over. Drew and Harley, who will be playing in different leagues, will never face each other this coming year unless they meet in the World Series again. In short, even though my son may be playing for another major league team, I don't think I'd ever be able to go against the Cards."

"Speaking of the Cards, who have they got going opening day?"

"I'm pretty sure they're a go with Wainwright, but I could be wrong."

Peeling the label off her beer bottle with her thumb, Monica pondered, "I wonder if winning opening day makes any difference in a complete season."

Rich verified, "Every game is important to the outcome of the season. Now if you're asking me if winning opening day specifically makes a difference I don't know how to answer that. Baseball is very complex and if I had the secret to creating a winning team every year, I mean a team that could go all the way, year after year, why there would not be a team in existence that would not pay me a fortune for that formula."

"I agree," said Monica, "but then again there is no secret formula, because there are too many unforeseen obstacles that can get in the way in having a winning season, let alone taking the series. Player injuries, player slumps, trades that go belly up, free agency, personal problems players may have, even the weather at times. And all these things can and often do effect the outcome of the season. There is no secret…it's baseball. It's a game. Look the definition up in a dictionary. 'A game played with a bat and a ball between two teams.' Once again, there is no secret to winning this game. Prior to a game any number of people can predict the outcome, but then the first pitch is thrown and it's off to the races. Any number of situations or plays can crop up with any number of results. It's like a nine scene play that the players have rehearsed countless times but as each scene unfolds the story changes. The plot is the same. Someone has to win and someone has to lose, but who? There are heroes each and every game and just because you're a hero one game does not mean you'll repeat with a great performance the next time. This is the game, that especially here in America we have come to love. And here in St. Louis for many a fan it's a way of life..."

Monica's rundown on her personal version of St. Louis baseball was interrupted by Harley's voice as he entered through the back door and walked into the semi-dark kitchen, "Anybody home?"

From the darkness of the front room came the answer in the sound of his mother's voice, "We're in the front room, Son. Come, join us."

Carrying a cardboard box, Harley made his way across the living room to the front room where he placed the box on an old hassock and plopped down in a rocking chair. "Why is everyone sitting here in the dark?"

Rich answered as he held up his beer. "Someday when you're old and married you'll understand. Sometimes it's just nice to sit in the dark, drink a beer and talk with your wife."

"So that's what I have to look forward to in the future. What's the topic this evening?"

Monica took a drink. "Baseball...what else!"

"Pardon me," said Harley. "I should have known. If any other subject was discussed in this house the paint would probably peel off the walls."

Monica smiled at her son. "And you, my dear Son, have either been the subject or have brought up the subject of baseball more times that I could ever possibly count." Leaning forward, she lowered her voice, more for effect than any other reason and asked, "Did you pop the question tonight?"

Harley, not really desiring to discuss that particular situation with his parents, but realizing that he could not sidestep the answer, responded, "Yes...yes I did. I finally got up the nerve. As you well know I had plans on asking her last Christmas but I froze up. I mean I sat right there next to her with my hand on the ring box in my pocket and I just couldn't get the words out. I remember what you told me later that night when I told you how I had chickened out. You told me I'd know when the right moment came and I'd do just fine. Well, tonight was the right moment. After dinner, we went out onto her grandparents' front porch and sat on their porch swing. Mira was talking a swig of iced tea when I whipped out the ring, went to my knee and asked her. She nearly spit out her tea. I immediately tried to apologize, but before I knew it she kissed me and gave me a hug and simply said, *Yes!*" Looking at Rich, Harley tried to explain, "It was the hardest thing I've ever had to do in my life!"

Holding his beer up high, Rich announced, "Congratulations, Son! You've just made a commitment to spend a fortune because you're in love with a woman. There's going to be house payments, insurance, all the furniture you will have to buy, water, gas and electric bills and on and on and then when the children come it's a whole new ballgame with a new series of unending expenses!"

Monica got up, walked over and hugged Harley. "Congratulations. It really isn't all that bad. As long as you have one another you can get through anything." Returning to the couch she asked, "So, when is the date, where do you guys plan to live, do you need help planning the big day?"

Harley laughed. "We haven't discussed any of that stuff. The only thing we did agree on was that we'd wait for at least a year. After I get to Cleveland I'll probably get an apartment up there somewhere. Mira is going to continue to stay with her aunt and uncle and work in Versailles. She has always said that with her love of horses she might want to live in that area after we get hitched. I'm okay with that for now. We're just going to take it slow and save as much money as we can."

Rich asked, "Does Drew know about this yet?"

"No, he doesn't. He flew out yesterday to report to Philly. I'll have to give him a call. With our upcoming league schedules being so different, I'm not sure if we'll even see each other until the All-Star break. I know he'll be excited for us."

Monica, for some reason finally took note of the cardboard box and asked, "What's the box for?"

Harley sat forward on the rocker and touched the edge of the box and answered, "It's a surprise...for our family. It's from Mira.

After she accepted my proposal she told me to follow her out to their walk-in pantry and there on the floor was this box. Inside there was a surprise just like she said, so I brought it home and, *here it is!"*

Reaching in the box Harley extracted what appeared to be a small ball of black fuzzy fur. Approaching Monica, he handed the furry object to her and as she took it in her hands she realized what it was. *"A puppy...Mira gave us a puppy?"*

Kneeling next to Monica Harley explained, "It's not just any ol' puppy. Take a close look."

Monica reached up and switched on the lamp and then in amazement exclaimed, "It's an Ozzie! Don't tell me this is a black Lab? This little fella looks just like Ozzie when we first brought him home."

Harley confirmed, "It is a black lab. He's a male and he's about six weeks old according to Mira."

Rich, now at Harley's side, asked, "Where did she get this little guy?"

Returning to the rocker, Harley answered, "Mira and her folks were in the process of delivering an old sewing machine her grandmother had no more use for to some people they go to church with who live out in Hillsboro. When they get out there, they stumble across this box with two puppies inside. When the woman answered the door, Mira asked where the pups came from and was told they were left on their porch. Originally there was six, but they had given four away to neighbors. Out of the two left only one was not spoken for. Mira asked which one and the woman reached in and withdrew that guy right there that you're holding, Mom. The woman said she figured he was the runt of the litter. Monica said she couldn't leave him behind and immediately thought of us. About how we lost Ozzie. It seemed like the perfect match to her. We needed a new dog and that little ball of black fur needed a home, so now we have another mouth to feed. I thought if it was all right with you guys we could call him Ozzie. Not that any dog could ever replace ol' Ozzie. This is just a new Ozzie! I mean you guys have always said that this is a House of Cards. Since Ozzie's been gone there's been something missing in this house. If this is really going to be a Cardinals house then I say we need an Ozzie running around here."

Monica held the pup to her cheek as tears ran down her face. "Rich, we just have to keep him. He looks exactly like Ozzie when we first got him. Do you remember?"

Rich laughed, "Just when we thought we had this house all to ourselves, up pops a new pup! This new Ozzie has a new home."

Rocking gently in the chair, Harley suggested, "With me leaving for Cleveland in the morning you and Dad are going to have to take care of him until I get back which might not be for some time."

Stroking the pup's soft fur, Monica assured him, "Don't you worry about a thing. Ozzie will be well looked after. Did Mira say if he had any shots yet?"

"She did say that he had all the shots needed for his age but that we might want to get him to the Vet for a good going over."

"That'll be the first thing on my agenda tomorrow after you leave."

Harley, satisfied with the way his family had accepted the new dog, stood and stretched. "I think I'm going to head on up and hit the hay. It's been a long day. I need to get some rest. I've got a long drive ahead of me tomorrow."

Monica got up and placed Ozzie back in the box. "Why don't you take Ozzie up with you tonight? I think he'd like that."

Picking up the box, Harley agreed. "All right. Who knows? Maybe he'll wind up sleeping in my bed like ol' Ozzie used to. Good night, I'll see you in the morning for breakfast."

Placing the cardboard box on its side between his two pillows Harley arranged Ozzie so that he was comfortable. The small black bundle of fur curled up in the corner of the box and went to sleep instantly. Harley brushed his teeth, slipped into a pair of old cutoff jeans and a tattered Cardinal jersey and slipped beneath the sheets after switching off the light. He checked on the pup who was still sleeping peacefully. Laying back he stared up into the ceiling as a clap of thunder sounded nearby, followed by lightning that temporarily lit up his room. The pup whimpered and crawled from the box and curled up next to his head by the pillow just like ol' Ozzie used to do. Harley smiled to himself as another streak of lightning lit up his room displaying a museum of Cardinal items. Pennants, autographed photos and other assorted baseball stuff he had collected over the years and shelves lined with his baseball trophies. He placed his hands behind his head and looked out the window at the familiar sound of the big oak tree limbs beating at the side of their house as they often did during an upcoming storm. It was at that moment that he realized how blessed he was. Ozzie was once again in his life, he had a great set of parents, Mira had agreed to marry him, he had reached his goal of becoming a major league pitcher and for the moment, surrounded by everything that was in his room that seemed to represent his life, he felt like he was ten years old again. Turning sideways he spoke gently to the sleeping pup. "I've only got one more thing to accomplish and that's to pitch for the Cards. Maybe in three years, just maybe, when I'm a free agent, then I can snap the last piece of the puzzle in place." Stroking the pup gently on his head, Harley whispered, "Tell ya what. In the morning before breakfast maybe you and I will go out to the backyard and throw a few pitches at the tire!"

ABOUT THE AUTHOR

GARY YEAGLE has written eight previous novels and one work of non-fiction, *Little Big Men – The Road to Williamsport*, published in 2005. He lives in Arnold, Missouri.